The Lord of Necrönd

Jane Welch was born at Foremarke, a hamlet in the very centre of rural England, exactly where more than a thousand years ago the Viking Great Army camped for the winter, their forces led by three of Ragnar Lothbrok's sons, including Ivar the Boneless.

Jane spent much of her childhood in a remote coastal wilderness in the Scottish Highlands. With no electricity, TV, and before internet, Jane immersed herself in reading the world's best fantasy novels and scribbling her first short stories on any paper she could find. School and work competed with her writing and it was not until taking a part time job teaching skiing in the Pyrenean mountains that she finally had the space and time to write. Surrounded by the magic of those ancient mountains, she embarked on the first of the nine books that make up the Runes of War Saga.

Jane has continued her travels and research and is now working on a new series, inspired by the beauty of the Mediterranean Sea and its remote islands. In particular, her imagination was caught by a climb to a lighthouse, ruined since antiquity, standing sentinel above twin harbours.

Jane lives and writes in beautiful Devon on the south-west coast of England with her family and noble dog, Odin.

Also by Jane Welch

The Runes of War Saga

The Runes of War Saga

PART TWO:
The Book of Önd
Vol 6. The Lord of Necrönd

JANE WELCH

HARPER
Voyager

Harper*Voyager*
An imprint of
HarperCollins*Publishers* Ltd
1 London Bridge Street,
London SE1 9GF
www.harpercollins.co.uk

HarperCollins*Publishers*
Macken House, 39/40 Mayor Street Upper,
Dublin 1, D01 C9W8, Ireland

This paperback edition 2024
1

First published in Great Britain by Earthlight,
an imprint of Simon & Schuster Ltd 2000

A catalogue record for this book is available from the British Library

ISBN: 978-0-00-860905-4

Typeset in Goudy by Palimpsest Book Production Ltd, Falkirk, Stirlingshire

Printed and bound in the UK using 100% renewable
electricity by CPI Group (UK) Ltd

MIX
Paper | Supporting
responsible forestry
FSC™ C007454

This book contains FSC™ certified paper and other controlled sources
to ensure responsible forest management.

For more information visit: www.harpercollins.co.uk/green

For Richard, my love.

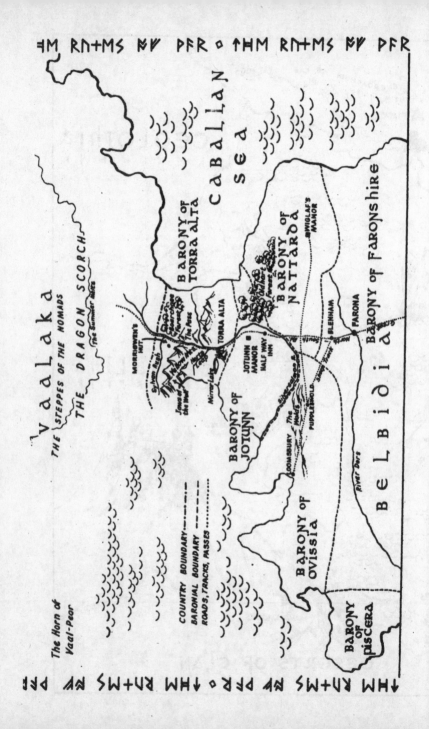

PROLOGUE

"A bargain, you say?" Tartarsus stared thoughtfully out of the high turret window overlooking the forests of Rye Errish. "There are no bargains for the dead. You are here in the Otherworld and will be tortured until you move on freely to the forgetfulness of Annwyn, whence all are reborn."

"You will bargain with me! They must suffer as I have suffered! Until they are in utter misery, I shall withstand any pain that you inflict. I will never let go of my last life until I have laughed at their pain and despair." The prisoner strained at the bonds that tied him to the chair.

"Then your torture will continue." Tartarsus turned, the sunshine slanting in from the window flashing brightly in his yellow eyes.

Bending, he retrieved a bridle of steel bands, screws and buckles from where he had discarded it after ripping it from the wolfman's hairy muzzle so that he might talk. Attached to the metal circlet of the head-brace were two plates of steel designed to be strapped over a man's eyes. Through the centre of each plate wound a thick screw and these screws were coated with brown blood and gelatinous tissue that had clumped and dried into dark lumps.

Tartarsus continued, "Saille has healed your eyes but I

can have them put out again – and again. That is the ingenious thing about torture here in Rye Errish. You can suffer to the third degree, time and time again." He laughed at the cleverness of it.

The creature that once had been man but now was almost half wolf nodded, his movements limp from pain, his head lolling against the thick armchair. "Stop my torture and I shall bring you rubies. I shall fill this tower of yours with sunburst rubies, Tartarsus, such as these."

The wolfman awkwardly reached into his breast pocket and, with short, unnaturally curving fingers now tufty with fur, dragged out a radiant red ruby and, holding it up, revealed its glowing heart of brilliant yellow.

The newly appointed chief verderer snapped his head away from the window to fix on the ruby, the glow in his eyes pulsating with the thrill of beholding the gem. Barely breathing, he swept across the floor of the hunting tower, which had once belonged to Talorcan before his fall from grace, to stand over the wolfman.

Tartarsus snatched the ruby, his glinting eyes bulging with delight as he drooled at the brilliant gem. "A snatch of the sun in its heart, a rare magic to enhance my own." He threw back his head and a piercing note rang from his mouth until the pitcher of wine on the low table beside the wolfman shattered into a thousand pieces. He laughed delightedly and, with one strong sinewy hand, grasped and lifted the wolfman from the chair. "Give them to me! Do as you say and fill my tower with rubies."

The wolfman swallowed hard, trying not to show any emotion; already his battle was won. "If you want rubies, you must give me this upper tower room of yours, with freedom to come and go as I wish. Rubies cannot be accomplished overnight; there are many wheels to set in motion," he said as silkily as he could, though he could not disguise the growl in his lupine throat.

The verderer nodded, "It can be arranged – though secretly of course. The High Circle would never allow it and they must never find out until my power is great enough. Those fools have ruled Rye Errish from before the first troublesome man crawled out of his caves – and they have ruled it badly. Just because the ealdormen have their fine wings, they think they are so superior to the verderers. Ha! Talorcan was right. They are not fit to rule. I shall have the power. He loved beautiful women but who wants women when I can have rubies?" He licked the gem in his hand. "You may have my rooms."

"And the head-brace? No more torture?"

Tartarsus dropped the wolfman and nodded. "So long as you bring me rubies. You have a way to achieve this?" he asked, sliding his tongue avariciously over his lips.

The wolfman laughed and held out a ring on his finger. The verderer stared closely at it and saw that there were three hairs woven about the ring. He frowned at it. "That is but a ring. I see no magic in it."

The wolfman gave him a twisted grin. "Indeed, the ring is nothing but the hairs are much. They are taken from one who still roams the world of the living, one who holds a great artefact of power that directs the channels of magic bridging the worlds. Through these thin tendrils, I invade his dreams and so tease him into my service. An unreliable method, I agree, but I have planned for that. The last time I broke across the divide between worlds, I did not pursue him or his precious power. For I have found another: an artefact that the priestesses discarded when they fled from the King's Inquisitors. Every man, whose breath of life is caught within it, will give me the strength to cross the chasm."

Tartarsus shrugged. "Fill this tower with rubies," he warned, "or I shall feed you to the Commoners, and all your worthless pursuits and vendettas, along with your puny soul, will be lost to oblivion."

The wolfman bowed. "I shall not fail." Jerkily, he threw back his head and, holding the ring aloft, wailed out a lonesome howl of the wolf, its echoes rippling through the channels of magic to disturb the peace of the world. "Tartarsus, wait! There is one last thing."

"More? You demand more?" the chief verderer said with haughty disdain.

"Indeed more. You want the rubies, don't you? The High Circle punished Talorcan cruelly and they will do the same to you if you cannot match their power." The wolfman turned his head on one side and gave him a sly and hideous grin. "My soul is starved of pleasure. Let me view the torture halls of Abalone. Already there is one there whose suffering I must witness and relish."

Tartarsus nodded warily. "If you wish to enter the chambers you must submit to torture lest the High Circle suspect I have struck a bargain with you. Is it worth it to witness one soul's agony, if you are then to suffer equally yourself?"

"Oh, yes, it is! A thousand times! I must see their pain!" the wolfman said wildly.

"Then come! It is of no consequence to me!"

Tartarsus handed him over to one of his minions with detailed instructions as to how he should be tortured in the chambers deep beneath the castle of Abalone.

The wolfman was led across the grease-smeared floor of the smoke-filled cavern, weaving his way between the writhing bodies until he reached the wretched soul he was seeking. Here he was permitted to halt while, gleefully, he inhaled the aroma of burning flesh and spilt blood.

"Morrigwen, old woman," he called softly, gloating over her pain.

The woman's eyes slowly opened and stared up at him with faint recognition.

"Know that I pleasure in your pain and that I strive to bring your loved ones to join you," he snarled, before the verderer dragged him to an iron chair.

Nearby, sizzling pokers were buried in the glowing embers of the fire in readiness to be stabbed in his eyes. But, as instructed, the verderer waited, allowing the wolfman time to witness the old Crone's torture.

A green-jacketed verderer, sweating in the heat from the fires, stood astride her wasted body and looked on her without emotion. "Old woman, your time is done. Move on! Let go! Bliss awaits you. New life awaits you."

A halo of red rimmed her vision. She looked up numbly at the hazy figure standing over her and fought to find that essential part of herself that was separate from her body. She had to separate herself from the pain, the unbearable pain. Yet she must bear it! She had to return. They were too young, too innocent, too foolish to cope without her.

Screams were beyond her now. She did not know how long she had screamed. Was it days? Was it weeks? Was it months? All was a raw nexus of pain.

She stared coldly into those yellow eyes of her torturer. "You miserable fool!" The words bubbled from her bloodied mouth. "I must see the High Circle. I must speak with Nuin. She, at least, must understand that a new Maiden must be found. The ways of—" Her head jerked sideways, her words shredded into a scream of anguish as the verderer prodded her body, searching for an area as yet undamaged. The point of a skewer, such as might be used to pin a roll of meat ready for roasting, pricked the flesh of her outer ear.

"Woman, join the march of souls through the forest."

"Never!" she screeched. There was no need to reply but it gave her courage. She needed courage. Already they had cut out her kidney and forcibly stuffed it into the mouth of the man opposite and she knew the savagery of the pain they could inflict. The fear never left her. The fear never left any of the miserable souls trapped down in the dungeons of the Otherworld.

Her head was held steady by a brace and all she could do was gasp and tremble. A mallet tapped against the butt of the skewer until the point touched the drum of her inner ear. The pain was so sharp, she sucked in her scream that rang silently within her head as the blinding flash of pain jolted her brain. They knew well what would cause the most suffering. Convulsions racked her body.

But she would hold out. Brid needed her. The helpless little child that she had taught so well, the girl who hid all her insecurities in a blanket of competence, who had worked so hard to reach that higher plane required of a high priestess, needed her desperately. She would not fail Brid.

Pain tore at her brain.

"Give in; let go and all will be peace. Love awaits you; bliss awaits you."

"Never!"

The skewer twisted. Pain raked through her entire body until, at last, the mercy of blackness drowned her mind. Though the verderers knew how to induce maximum pain whilst still keeping their charges conscious, Morrigwen's mind-control was too strong for them. In her one hundred and fifteen years on earth, she had learnt to find that state of trance, that inner world beyond the flesh where her body could be separated from her inner soul. She retreated there now.

Much of the pain she had borne in such a manner and knew that those about her survived their tortures in similar ways, reaching for that inner strength that so bemused the verderers and was the reason why they would never fully dominate the human spirit.

She swam in blackness, a ribbon of light swirling and dancing in the void. All was thought, detached and abstract. There were more important things to her than being a part of the cycle. The full weight of consciousness that slid eternally round from life, death and rebirth was beyond all else more important than her own part in it – and those fools had found a way to distort the flow of life. So young, so earnest, so determined to do such good and win such acclaim. That was the thing, she mused, retreating deeper into that intensity of thought that found only inner consciousness and that sweet release from pain.

The Great Mother had been so right, she considered, to see that it was three women who represented her, spoke for Her on Earth. Men sought too much for glory. They were dangerous. The proof was all about her in the dungeons of Abalone. So few women yet so many men went against the circle of life. She knew it was not that the women were unable to bear the pain. Indeed not. Bearing pain was not a physical strength but a state of mind.

The skewer was withdrawn and colour flooded back to her mind. The yellow-eyed verderer's attention had been snatched away. A sudden hush overlaid the fug of the chamber; even the wailing screams of defeated souls trailed off. A soul had entered; a new soul, someone of great importance.

Tartarsus swung down from the viewing gallery and stared. The leaping, spitting fires sank down, cringing back into the bed of embers like raging tigers calmed by their trainer's presence as the soul drew close. Though small and sprightly, he bore an air of intense presence.

"Talorcan!" Tartarsus greeted him with mock warmth.

CHAPTER ONE

Caspar wrapped his arms around May, pulling her head down against his chest and hunching his shoulders protectively over her. The walls shook. Chips of masonry fell from the arches overhead, glancing off his bowed back.

"Get us out of here," the girl begged.

"I shall, don't worry," Caspar said bravely though he had no idea how they were going to escape from where they were trapped in the secret halls deep beneath the ancient palace of Castaguard.

The ground beneath his feet trembled and Runa, a white wolfling, yelped as plaster flaked from the vaulted ceiling and crashed onto her back. She pressed close to May's side as choking dust billowed up from the floor.

Caspar blinked, trying to see the others through the cloud of dust and prayed they were still safely tucked beneath the spread arms of the great stonewight.

"Perren!" he shouted, trying to make out the hulking form of the stonelike creature who had twice the girth of a man and a grey rindy skin the colour of granite.

"Spar!" Perren's rumbling cry came back, followed by excited yips from Caspar's thickset terrier, Trog and a wild shriek from his horse, which echoed loudly in the vaulted halls.

The youth heaved a sigh of relief. The dust was settling and he could see the others now. Ursula, Reyna, Elergian and Fern were all crouched at Perren's feet. "We've got to get out of here before we're all crushed!" Caspar shouted.

How was he, a Belbidian, a stranger in this wet land of Ceolothia, going to find escape from this warren of a city? Silently and without venom, he cursed May for setting in motion the events that had caused him to abandon his command at Torra Alta to cross Vaalaka and half Ceolothia to rescue her. Now they were trapped in the depths of the palace, hiding from the slave master, and all his outraged men, who sought them in the city above.

The ground shook again. A block of masonry, dislodged from an arch above, landed inches from Fern. The trembling woodwose that looked most like a spindly pot-bellied dwarf, flung his arms about the slave-girl. Her naked limbs grey with dust, Ursula stood calmly though she her eyes were wide with fear.

"Which way?" Caspar asked them all urgently, fearfully wondering what caused the ground to shake.

"Not down!" The stonewight sounded unnerved. Caspar couldn't believe it. Perren had never shown fear, not even in the face of the abyss worm. "They're coming!" Perren's grey skin turned chalky, his huge round head held stiffly erect.

"Who's coming?" Caspar demanded, spreading his arms protectively over May and wincing as a stone cracked him on the crown of his head, flooding his senses with dull sickening pain.

Head ducked down, the salve-girl, Ursula, ran across the hall to him. "You're bleeding, master." She tugged at Caspar's outstretched arm and the youth caught the intense look that passed between her and May, declaring, if not animosity, then at least deep suspicion.

Caspar ignored the two young women and turned

instead to Reyna and her elderly mage, Elergian. Surely, with all their ancient knowledge of Castaguard, they would know of an escape route. Huddled together beneath Perren, Reyna was fretting over her unborn child while Elergian did his best to shelter her. Though Reyna was well into her middle years, she was pregnant and claimed to be carrying a son who was the rightful heir to all the extensive and rich lands of Ceolothia. She looked faint and frail in the embrace of her mage.

Elergian looked about him in dismay at the rubble and falling dust. "The only way for the horse is back out the way we came in, and then out of the city along the canal paths. Mamluc and maybe many other slave masters by now will be searching for us but one on the horse might be swift enough to escape him. The rest must pass through the servants' halls and from there up through the palace. You can reach them from here through the wine cellars and then work our way." He nodded at an arched door to the right of a cavernous fireplace.

Caspar nodded. "And you?"

Elergian nodded to a door at the rear of the chamber. "It's best if we split up. We'll be less noticeable in small groups. Reyna and I will head through the tunnels into the mines of Kalanazir where we would least be expected to go. We have knowledge of secret ways and halls within the mines and from there we shall gather followers to our own cause."

Caspar hastily appraised his options and then spoke decisively. "Fern, you must take Cracker. Obviously, I must stay with May and so you will have to ride the horse out of here."

Even with the fearful urgency of the situation, it grieved him to abandon Firecracker to Fern. The magnificent Oriaxian purebred was fully recovered from the poisons that would have claimed its life if it hadn't been for Reyna's healing potions of trinoxia, and Caspar could only pray that Fern was capable of controlling the snorting, stamping stallion. Still, the woodwose was devoted to the horse and he had no option.

Being part creature, Fern had a deep understanding of animals. In his last life he had been a deer but, on the point of death, had wished to return in his next life as a man. Such a wish, at the moment of death, governed what physical form souls would take upon reincarnation and, when Caspar had first met him, the woodwose was still in the early, painful stages of metamorphosis. Since Fern had never fully completed the change in the Otherworld, he had arrived back in the world of the living still in a state of flux but was now more man than beast.

The woodwose twitched his nose at Caspar and looked as if he were about to object but then said, "Do I take the saddle bags with the grain in?"

"Yes, anything!" Caspar shouted in exasperation. "Just get going. I'll meet you beyond the eastern walls of the city. Good luck!" He turned to the others. "The fewer of us that work our way through the palace the better; we'll be less conspicuous like that. Ursula, you must stay with Reyna. Your looks and dress cut you too much apart from the Ceolothians and there will be much you can do to help her."

"But, Master—" Ursula objected.

Caspar raised his hand to silence her. "Do as I say. We haven't got time to argue." He spoke harshly but he had an onerous task to fulfil and couldn't allow anyone to jeopardise his mission. He must be rid of Necrönd and hide it for all time beyond the reach of man. The fewer people with him at the end the better.

The ground trembled again and Reyna moaned fearfully, cupping her hands around her hugely swollen belly. Elergian sprang into action and swept aside vast curtains of dust-choked cobwebs that draped the ancient halls to reach the door that he said led to the wine cellars. With a grunt of effort, he heaved it open and gestured Caspar through.

"Go, Spar. Hurry!" he urged. "Get out of here now. You bring danger to my Reyna. Go!" There was sympathy in the mage's voice but an urgency that made it certain he would turn against anyone who threatened Reyna's well-being.

Caspar hesitated. Ursula was still begging him to take her with him and, for a moment he couldn't think clearly. Perren's great fist clamped him about the wrist and snatched him forward. "Fool, human, move!"

Caspar had no time to make his farewells. He hoped that Reyna might understand that he wished her well. He hoped the child she carried within her would be born alive and that, even at her advanced age, she might survive the ordeal of labour. It would do no harm, he thought, for the King of Ceolothia to be removed and replaced by the ancient line whose right to the wealthy kingdom had been stolen away so long ago. He prayed she was strong enough to survive this thirteenth pregnancy and so break the curse that kept her and her daughters in exile. Her mind was strong, of that there was no doubt but, though she constantly drank her restorative potion of trinoxia, her body was that of an ageing woman.

"Get out of here," Reyna urged as he gave her one last backward glance. "You're drawing them to us. Get away fast! Don't worry about us. My time is now; I shall rouse the slaves of Kalanazir and unite them under my cause."

Holding a spitting torch, Perren squeezed through the

door first. With May's wrist locked in his fist, and Runa and Trog at his heels, Caspar burst after him. He was glad that, at least, he was taking Necrönd, locked in his silver casket about his neck, away from Reyna, Elergian and Ursula. Now he would no longer endanger them. Apart from Perren, who had vowed to help him in his quest, he meant only to take May with him.

He would flee east and, when he was beyond the reach of man, he would be rid of that dreadful artefact of power so that never again could the souls of those dead beasts banished to the Otherworld be summoned to walk the Earth. He longed to be rid of their daily pecking at the quiet of his mind, longed to silence their shrieks and roars that flooded across the chasm between the worlds, breaking through the barrier between life and death.

He ran hard, tugging May up winding staircases. She breathed heavily, her hand hot in his and her light feet slapping on the hard stone. Shortly, he realized that a further set of footsteps sounded behind him and he glanced back to see Ursula, hot on his heels.

"Go back," he ordered, stopping to face her and giving May a moment to catch her breath. Ursula on the other hand was only very slightly out of breath. She stared at him defiantly, her dark eyes appearing even blacker in the gloom. Caspar studied her black hair; the way it was cropped short at her firm jaw, the animal skins that barely covered her lean and tanned limbs and the three enigmatic tattoos high on the smooth flesh of her left arm. Her eyes spoke of a harsh life but at least he had rescued her from Mamluc. "I told you to stay with Reyna."

"But tell me! Where will you go?" She clutched at him possessively.

He prized her fingers off him. "East to the great ocean you told me about. I must cross the seas."

"But you will never return," she said in dismay. "Remember, I spent my childhood on the east coast of Oriaxia lapped by the great uncharted ocean of Tethys. No ship that sailed east ever returned. There is no way back. The winds blow ever westward over the Tethys. Don't abandon me."

"Go back to Reyna; there is a life for you there!" he ordered again.

She smiled and shook her head. "Master, I cannot leave you," she defied him.

Caspar had no time to argue. The halls were dark and their footsteps on the stone steps slapped and slipped on the slimy walls. The foundations of the palace were clearly not as strong as they might have been and groundwater leaking from the canals was working its way between the masonry and trickling out onto the floors.

"The Great Mother will reclaim all," Perren said with certainty, striding towards an aged door. "Whatever you creatures of the surface do to her, she will take back what is hers. The tears from the skies are washing her bones back into her body!"

The huge square being, no taller than a man but twice as wide, dipped slightly at the waist and shouldered his weight against the door, the sodden timbers tearing easily away from the rusted bolts and hinges. He punched aside the door with his closed fist and, in the light of the flickering torch, they saw before them a low-ceilinged room filled with vast barrels. Beyond that, through an arched opening, Caspar saw the unmistakable brightness of daylight spilling down a flight of ascending steps.

Caspar was about to sprint for the steps at the far side but leapt back, pressing May behind him. The floor before him bulged, slits in the flagstones cracking open. Runa, the white wolfling gave out a low and blood-curdling snarl, while Trog bristled and growled from behind Caspar's legs.

Panting heavily, the others stood at the youth's shoulder, all staring in horror.

Caspar knew now that he had made all the wrong decisions. So long as he was guardian of Necrönd, he was a danger to them all, a danger to May whom he loved deeply. He must go on alone.

"Trog stay! Guard May! Get back to Reyna, all of you," he yelled and ran. The ground moved beneath his feet but he kept running, Ursula's cries of protest loud in his ears.

"No, Master, no!"

One of the great wine barrels burst up into the air and crashed down onto the heaving floor. It split open, filling the air with a yeasty aroma and sending a pink wash rippling across the floor. Something moved fast through the periphery of Caspar's vision but he focused on one thing alone – the steps at the far end of the low hall. His footing gave and he stumbled onto one hand. For a second, he looked down into a widening fissure in the floor. An eye glistened in the dark beneath him and a hooked paw snatched up at him. He didn't know what it was but he wasn't prepared to wait and find out.

Falling to his knees, then scrambling up and leaping, he raced on, the horrendous sound of splintering rock hammering around him. The screams of the others pierced the roar around him.

"Master, no! Come back!" Ursula shrieked.

"Don't leave me – not now!" May's forlorn cry made him cast back over his shoulder and he stumbled as he twisted to look back. To his amazement, Trog had actually obeyed his commands and stood at her side, a ball of furious muscle bellowing and snarling at the creatures below the floor. He was not surprised that Runa, who had always been devoted to May, stood on her other side, her thin body taut, ready to spring at anything that attacked.

The creatures that Perren had appeared so frightened of were not vast by any means but only half the height of a human, hairy and stooped with vast eyes, giving them a curiously babyish look. A few were turned on him and the rest faced the stonewight who pressed the two women behind him.

Caspar punched up his fist, a flash of silver in his hand. "This is what you seek!" he cried knowing that Necrönd would draw these creatures to him. Gnomes they were, he decided, still having no notion as to why Perren feared these small, fur-clad cave-dwellers.

Like moths to a light, they swarmed to him, their large eyes flashing greenly. He stared for a split moment, wondering how such small, silly-looking creatures had managed to erupt through a stone floor, before turning to run. Their footfalls came, pattering and scratching up the stone steps behind him like rats. They sought him; they wanted him for the Druid's Egg that was known by its ancient name of Necrönd.

Ever since the First Druid captured the breath of life of the ancient and savage beasts of legend within the Egg, so banishing them to the Otherworld, the less dangerous beasts had, for a time, freely roamed the Earth. But as man grew in strength and cunning, they retreated to Earth's darker realms where they lurked, half forgotten, licking their wounds and cursing mankind. Now they stalked Caspar, longing for the power that had swept them aside for the swelling civilizations of man.

The steps split before him and Caspar had no thought as to which way to turn. After hesitating too long, he decided that the steps leading to the right were narrower and so would lead to quieter rooms. Instinctively, he chose those.

But the gnomes, like rats escaping a flooding sewer, were soon at his heels. A door! He saw a door. He fumbled at the looped handle, kicking out at the first of the creatures that grappled for him. Their spindly bodies folded under his blows to be trampled beneath the rush of the others following. The hasp was rusted up. He rattled it violently, struggling to stay on his feet.

Should he wield Necrönd and summon a beast that might protect him? In desperation, his mind leapt eagerly at the thought but a core of inner reserve warned him not to do so. He was tired and, with so much chaos about him, there was no knowing how much control he might have. In an hour of need, he had summoned hooded wolves to drive back the invading Vaalakans from his father's castle, and, three years on, those same wolves had multiplied into a plague. He knew he must never wield Necrönd again.

The door gave and he fell through onto more steps that spiralled upwards. He slammed the door on the arms of several gnomes and turned to attack the stairs, leaping up them, his muscles screaming with the effort, his legs like lead. His breath rasped in his pounding ribcage and his head swam giddily.

Soon, a gnome caught him up and clung to his leg. He turned, grabbed it and hurled it at the others behind. They toppled back down the stairs, landing in a twisted knot of flailing limbs from which they would take some while to right themselves. Caspar laboured, struggling to lift his legs high enough for each step.

This wasn't right. Something was weighing him down. He had the curious notion that it was the Egg itself, loath to let him escape.

The rough stone walls became fine brickwork and then plaster painted a chalky white. One gnome caught him and clamped itself about his calf. He stamped his other boot down on its head and staggered on. Over his rasping breaths, he could hear women screaming. An open doorway in the stairs led him to a corridor and he chose the first door, managing to squeeze through and hurl back a half dozen of the little beasts so that he could close and bolt the door behind him. He was left with no more than three of the wretched creatures clinging to him.

They had apparently no language but screamed with a thin breathy note whilst flinging themselves up and clawing at his neck. He scrabbled frantically to rid himself of them. One bit him, long teeth hooking deep into his flesh. With another still wrapped about his hand, he hauled the third off his neck and was revolted to feel its flesh tear in his grip. The first then sprang for his throat, teeth raking through his skin.

With one slash of his knife, he cut through its body. The legs and hips fell away but the top half still clung to him as watery blood and foul-smelling entrails fell from its stomach. It was a full minute before he managed to unclamp the teeth, needle-sharp like those of the wolfling, from his neck. Fortunately, the teeth had pierced skin and tendon only, missing any major blood vessels.

The door held and Caspar sighed with relief, pondering his next move. He found himself in a long gallery and guessed he was right in the heart of the palace. The palace servants were unlikely to pay him any heed with all the commotion that he could hear outside. It sounded like a stampede raged through the city.

He tiptoed out into a sumptuous hall, the panelled walls clad with tapestries and the floor soft beneath his feet. He looked down in surprise. Woven carpets! He had heard that some of the grander palaces in the countries surrounding the Caballan Sea had woollen carpets on their floors though he wondered at the practicality of it. Straw and reed matting had always served them well in the halls of Torra Alta.

Voices came from the door of an antechamber. Keeping himself hidden behind the door, he glanced in. Servants in long robes stood with their backs to him, their faces pressed against a glazed window. The women amongst the number were chanting distractedly. Caspar was not quick in the Ceolothian tongue but he understood that they prayed to their god of the New Faith for protection against what they thought to be an earthquake.

Calmly, so as not to draw attention to himself, he crossed to the tall windows at the far end of the gallery and looked out. He was surprised at how high he had climbed. Below him, the city of Castaguard shrank away, dipping into the gloomy hollow around the base of the black tower.

Hot as he was from his exertion, a chill spread through him at what he saw. He was certain he had not summoned such creatures from the Otherworld and yet could not explain how there came to be a vast sea of wraithlike creatures marching out of the ground at the foot of the tower. So that was why the earth trembled and why Perren had been afraid. How could he possibly have thought him fearful of the gnomes?

Hazy apparitions of monstrous beasts – two-headed lions, a lequus, sabre-toothed wolves and what Caspar thought to be huge hobgoblins, naked and sinewy – poured out from the black tower. The guards and slave masters were marshalling them into ordered lines. Caspar was afraid now too. Someone, something other than himself, was controlling them. But how?

He cradled the casket containing Necrönd protectively against his breast, watching with horror and disbelief as the monstrous phantoms marched into the market square and joined the men, already marshalled into ranks around the edge of the square. The slaves swayed fearfully but were too disciplined or frightened of their commanding officers to flee. As he watched, a sickening pain began to throb in his head.

Trying to think clearly through the pain that spread down from the crown of his head and cramped his brain, he stared down at the massing army. Raised to be lord of a frontier castle, he instinctively knew these men that were marshalled into lines were being mustered for war. Judging by their chains, some were from the slave pits; others looked like townsfolk; and those bearing farm tools, billhooks and pitchforks were no doubt from the surrounding countryside.

The Ceolothians gathered an army! From his thorough schooling in history, Caspar knew that Ceolothia had been at war many times in the last thousand years, mostly with Lonis and Salise but in minor disputes only. However, she had fought three major wars, the last admittedly over four hundred years ago, but all three had been with Belbidia. Caspar knew the history particularly well because his own forefathers had been instrumental in fighting back the aggressors. If the Ceolothians were again mustering to attack his homeland, he must do something.

They would march, as all other Ceolothian armies had done before, through Vaalaka and then turn south to attack his father's castle of Torra Alta at the northernmost border of Belbidia. But this time, he could stop them long before any Belbidian blood was shed. A stab of guilt harried his soul. His father had left him in charge of the castle; Torra Alta and its young garrison were his responsibility and, though it was for a higher cause, he had still abandoned them. He must do something. After all he had the power; he held Necrönd. What would it take? He had commanded dragons before; what could be harder? His hand moved to his chest.

But no! He had sworn to his mother that he would not again wield Necrönd. He could not break such a solemn oath; not one made to a high priestess. It had meant so much to her and he could not disobey. Keridwen's reasons were sound; she and the other two high priestesses, Brid and Morrigwen, had lectured and scolded him at length. It seemed certain that all their troubles had been caused by Necrönd; the more he had used it, the more their woes had been compounded. He stared glumly down at the monstrous throng. There was even a unicorn amongst the ghostly number.

His heartbeat boomed in his throat; the forms of the ghostly beasts were becoming firmer in outline until they were solid blocks of colour, the beasts fully formed in this world and no longer phantoms. Yet he had not summoned them. He hoped that his mother and the very beautiful Brid, who held the office of the Maiden, and even Morrigwen, if her soul could see him now, would believe in his innocence in this.

Someone was shouting at him. Evidently, he was not so inconspicuous as he had thought; a manservant had spied him and recognized him as an intruder. The man began yelling more insistently though Caspar was not familiar enough with the Ceolothian words to translate them when they were shouted in vehement outrage. He ran. Skidding to a halt at the end of the galleried hall, he found a low arch that led to a corridor and that to a huge staircase cut around the outside of a central well. Surely this was a way out. With the agility of youth and the sure-footed speed of a Torra Altan born to the mountain heights, he hurtled down them.

He couldn't think straight. His head hurt and Necrönd felt strange in his hand. It radiated a warm wet pulse, as if he grasped a living heart. Feeling faintly sick, he dabbed at the crown of his head and felt the moistness of unhealed skin. He must run, get out of the palace, join the milling mob about the panicked city, where there was already so much disorder that he would never be noticed.

The huge staircase led to a ballroom and he ran for the narrow service stairs at the back of the hall. He spun down them, his hand hot from rubbing against the stone of the central newel that supported the stair.

At last, he was out into fresh air. Racing along what he thought to be a likely alleyway, he soon found himself on the edge of the central market square, where he least wanted to be. But, though there were many soldiers, there was also enough of a mob to conceal him and at least he would be able to follow the main east street out of the city without becoming lost. Here, he was anonymous; all eyes were turned towards the yawning portcullis of the black tower. A great rumbling, like the sound of a distant stampede groaned from the dark mouth. He halted and stared in horror.

Guards charged forward, pikes at the ready, to meet whatever was about to burst out from the gateway to the infamous mines. Great black war-horses, snorting and chafing at their bits, bore armoured knights that lined the road out from the tower. The ground shook and the air trembled with a deep rumbling roar.

The mouth of the black tower was suddenly filled with emerging grey faces. They stumbled and blinked in the sudden light. Emaciated men and women staggered into the square, some with their hands outstretched pleading for mercy, others glancing back into the dark mouth of the tower in terror. The guards outside the tower showed no mercy but levelled their crossbows at the stampede of slaves and, forming two lines channelled them into the centre of the square. Most of the terrified slaves ran as they were directed though others, in maddened terror, fought to break through the ranks of guards. Caspar saw several shot through with crossbow bolts and many trampled to a pulp by the great horses.

He knew he should run but he could not yet pull himself away from the sight as three-headed bears and lion-faced dogs sprang out from the foot of the tower.

The guards shouted in both Belbidian, the most widely understood language of the Caballan, as well as Ceolothian so that all might obey them. With angry words and sharp pikes, they organized the slaves pouring from the mines into ranks alongside those already gathered.

A guard thundered, "Stand! They are ordered not to hurt you. Like you, they now form Prince Tudwal's army."

Tudwal's army! The words jolted Caspar's thoughts. But that was good. If Tudwal raised an army then he and Cymbeline must have been rescued. All must be well; his father must have returned from Farona and organised a search party for the prince and princess.

No doubt Prince Tudwal mustered the army to rout out the outlaws who had ambushed him and his sister, Princess Cymbeline, and slaughtered the major part of her escort. Princess Cymbeline had been on her way to marry King Rewik of Belbidia and the Ceolothians had blamed the Belbidian escort for the loss of the precious princess. King Dagonet threatened Rewik with war if his precious daughter was not quickly returned in good health. But his thoughts strayed quickly from the politics as more and more beasts, mainly rangy hobgoblins now, emerged from the black tower that was the entrance to the long tunnels that led to the mines of Kalanazir.

He trembled at the sight of the monstrous beasts, fearful as to how they came to be in this world. May had been in possession of the Egg for a dangerously long time but it was still difficult to believe that she could have unwittingly summoned so many beasts. Should he now wield Necrönd to send them all back to their exile in the Otherworld?

The thought of May brought him out of the dark confusion that swirled around the Egg. Every day that passed, the thing becoming more alive, less of an inert artefact but something with life and power of its own. He must get it away from all these people, away from everyone. He must cross the sea and find a vast wilderness. He turned and ran, pushing his way through the crowd.

"There! You! Hey, you!" came a sharp yell, the voice horribly familiar.

Caspar instinctively knew the cry was aimed at him. He glanced over his shoulder and ducked. Mamluc! Mamluc, the slave trader! Amongst all these people he had to be seen by Mamluc! Head stooped and shoulders hunched, he dodged amongst the crowd and ran for the eastern exit to the square only to find himself in a maze of streets. No one road led straight and, again and again, he was confronted by canals blocking his path or roads ending in a congestion of huts and crumbling houses. Middens steamed in the streets. Dogs growled, their coats straggly from mange, patches of scaling bare skin showing through the matted fur. Soon he was completely lost amongst dark alleyways twisting between the backs of tall windowless buildings.

As he stood staring helplessly around him, a boy trotted

up to him, his face as muddy as his clothes, red toes breaking through the rags that bandaged his feet.

"The way out! How do I get to the east gate?" Caspar fetched in his pocket for a coin. Without even looking at it, he tossed the urchin a gold piece.

The boy's mouth dropped and his eyes brightened. "You're in big trouble, mister." He looked gleefully at the glinting coin. "Follow me!" The boy, who could have been no more than ten, had the eyes of an old man. "This way," he said, leading him over a broken gate at the back of a tall derelict building and through into a dark alleyway beyond. Caspar could hear the strike of galloping hooves on cobbles and raced alongside the boy. He hoped it was not Mamluc on his trail.

"Already this week, I've got four men away from the slave-masters. This is a good way," the boy reassured him breathlessly as they ran on. "Here we are!" The alley spat them out onto a broad sweep of open lawn that footed the great black walls, skirting the city. Caspar stopped short. Looking from across the hundred yards of open grass, he saw no way to scale those black walls.

"The canal." The boy pointed to his left. "It slips under the wall. You'll have to get wet. The bridge in the wall is low and the water high at the minute but it's the best way out of here and as close to the east gate as I can get you."

Caspar smiled his thanks and scurried along the edge of the ramshackle houses towards the stone-walled canal. The water stank. A deep murky brown, it was littered with debris. He looked ahead along its length to where it slunk beneath the great black walls. No light emerged. The walls must be thirty foot thick at least and he hoped the water was low enough to allow him room to breathe. He dropped down the banks of the canal, thankful to find a ledge that he could work his way along rather than immediately plunging into the water.

He was nearly at the walls when he heard shouts and the sound of the boy's voice yelling in Ceolothian. He didn't need to translate to know that his little helper had turned traitor and sent his pursuers after him. Caspar rued his innocence. When was he going to learn not to trust people?

He fled on until he reached the arching stones that bridged the canal and supported the great wall above. There was no more than a six-inch gap between the surface of the water and the underside of the bridge. He shuddered. He was not a great swimmer.

An arrow sloshed into the water and another thudded at his feet. He gave it no more thought but ripped off his bearskin, holding the hem and neck together, reasoning to use it as a balloon to trap air and so help him float. He plunged in, swimming for the middle point of the canal where the airspace was greatest.

As he paddled, his body rose and fell, his head grazing on the water-worn stones beneath the wall. But the bearskin worked and he hoped that, so long as he was only in the water a short time, it would not become waterlogged. He was thankful that at least he hadn't dragged May out this way and prayed that Perren had led her safely back to Reyna and found another way out.

Shouts rang out from behind. Hooves pounded turf. Then came a splash as someone plunged into the water behind him. Caspar redoubled his efforts, gasping in air and kicking furiously. Something snagged his ankle. He kicked back and connected with flesh. The hands scrambled for him but evidently were not quick enough to catch him. Then he heard the bark of a dog ahead. His heart sank: they were waiting for him on the far side of the walls.

Men shouted. Mixed in with the excited yells and the angry barks of a dog were the painfully shrill howls of some animal that Caspar did not recognize by its cry.

Cursing the wretched boy for betraying him, he swam on, preferring to face the danger ahead rather than struggle in the water with his pursuer; he doubted his chances in the water.

Daylight washed down on him and he didn't even need to go to the effort of pulling himself up out of the canal. Someone hooked his belt with a billhook and hauled him out, the weight of his bearskin dragging at his arms. He was rolled over onto the ground and looked up at the long, feathered legs of a great war-horse. Caspar knew the breeding well; such clean lines, the deep chest: it was a foal out of Demon Black, one of his father's best stock stallions and, no doubt, exported several years ago. Such fine horses raised and bred on the beautiful soil of Torra Alta brought to this dark land, it was tragic!

Caspar's gaze slid upwards. Long feet dressed in thong sandals dangled from golden-coloured calves. A lion's tail, discoloured and losing its hair, swung down alongside. Caspar looked up at Mamluc whose squinted eyes, one black, one pale green, only half looked back at him.

Behind the slave master stood a squat furry animal with human hands. Its eyes glinted red just like the eyes he had seen looking up from the bulging, broken floor beneath the palace.

Mamluc's mouth twisted into a delighted sneer before growling at the eight men about him, "Don't let him get away! Keep him with the girl."

Caspar's heart sank. He knew who the girl must be. Soon, three more of the furry creatures lumbered into view, May held fast in the grip of the largest. Caspar had no name for these beasts. He focused intently on the one holding his beloved. It looked vaguely human only more coarsely built, the limbs tremendously thick, the skull heavy and with a short forehead. It had peaceful eyes but they drooped with deep sadness.

Caspar watched how its eyes flitted warily. There was no doubt that it hated man and he instinctively knew that it was one of those creatures of the dark dank corners of the forgotten earth controlled by Necrönd but not banished to the Otherworld. This time, he didn't hesitate to use the Egg. Concealing his hand in his shirt, he reached into the silver casket at his chest that held Necrönd. "Go!" he shouted.

The creature looked at him blankly and shook its head, its grip tightening on May.

"Drop her," Caspar demanded again, now panicked. He had lost control of the Egg just when he needed its powers to rescue May.

"Let her go." Caspar turned to Mamluc, his voice full of reason. "You can have no need of her. Let her go and take me instead."

"We already have you," Mamluc laughed. "Now get to your feet. He wants you alive."

Caspar felt sick and giddy. He slung his sodden bearskin cloak over his back and wondered whether he shouldn't just try and fight his way out of here. He knew he would never escape but perhaps he could cause enough of a diversion to help May.

A dog barked again. Caspar had forgotten that he had already heard that bark but he concentrated on it now. The same animal gave out a deep growl followed by a high-pitched yelp, sounding completely ridiculous coming from the same throat. It had to be Trog!

He moved; one hand reached for his belt, the other for his boot where he kept an additional hunting knife.

Knowing that he could not get a true aim at Mamluc swaddled as he was in his lionskin – and Caspar was no great expert with a throwing knife – he aimed for the larger target of the horse. The blade stabbed into its chest and the animal reared. Toppling backwards, it crashed down on its cursing rider and one of the guards midst screams of pain.

Trog's salivating growls added to the raucous chaos. Though short and squat, the animal had a terrifying growl and overlarge jaws for his size. He was lazy and cheeky but immensely strong and loyal; the sight of May in danger turned him into a savage fiend. Mamluc's men shrank back but there were still six of them on their feet and Caspar saw no way that he was going to fight his way out of this.

The guards surrounded Mamluc, who was still pinned under the horse. Bent on pulling the screaming slave master out from beneath his great black destrier, they seemed lost without his clear orders. Caspar seized his opportunity. Darting forward, he plunged his short knife into the arm of the furry, manlike creature holding May and dragged her from its grasp. Holding his knife up in front of him, warning all to keep their distance, he stepped slowly back and then ran, dragging May behind him.

Hooves, fast and light, galloped towards him.

Desperately, Caspar looked for somewhere to hide. Though injured, the furry man was already after them, a trail of blood darkening the ground behind it. Grunting and coughing with the effort, it was slowly gaining on them since May was not fast, her skirts flapping around her legs and her breath coming in panicked grasps. The men were shouting in disorganised alarm and Caspar heard the first sounds of their pursuit as they ran for their snorting horses. He had seconds only to think of a plan but he suddenly didn't have to.

Firecracker! Caspar rejoiced at the sight. His fiery red stallion was galloping towards them, Fern running alongside rather than riding the horse. Caspar would never have imagined that the woodwose would come to his rescue and certainly hadn't credited him with such bravery.

"Fern!" he cheered him. "You made it!"

Firecracker skidded to a halt before them, Fern swinging on the end of the reins. Caspar flung May up onto the horse's back.

"Get her out of here!" the heir to Torra Alta yelled at the woodwose.

Fern obeyed though May shrieked in protest, "No, I can't leave you, Spar. No! Not after everything that's happened."

Her words were whisked away and the youth spun on his heels to face the furry human. "Stand back! I am your master; obey me!"

The creature showed no recognition of his authority but rammed into him, bowling him over. It was like being hit by a galloping horse, and the air was knocked out of him. He lay flat, face down in the mud, and shook his head to gather his senses. The furry man growled and snarled, blood from his wound trickling down onto the youth. Before he could draw his breath, the creature had him by the neck in one fist, his other raised to strike, but he hesitated. The creature looked puzzled, uncertain as to how to kill a human being.

Mamluc was out from beneath his horse and hobbling towards them, yelling at his men, "Get him!"

Then something grabbed both the beastly man and Caspar from behind, rolling them over. The furry man squealed and instantly released Caspar, who found himself held fast in an even fiercer fist. A strange deep cracking noise, halfway between a growl and splintering rock, sounded loudly in his ears.

"Perren!" He grinned gratefully.

The stonewight shoved him aside and, with one punch to the temple, flattened the furry man before scooping Caspar up under one arm.

The guards thundered towards them but they were diverted by a howl of attack from another quarter. Thin men with grey-white skins and wielding shovels, charged in attack. Judging by their pallor, it was clear they were slaves from the mines and Caspar concluded that Reyna's uprising was already underway and gathering force.

Their clothes in rags, black crosses marked their lower arms. Amongst their number, Caspar spied Ursula who wielded a club and, with relish unnatural in a woman, thumped it down on the back of one of the guards. Though the blow was vicious, she clearly lacked the skill of a trained soldier and the guard was able to twist away from the main force of her blow. Caspar was greatly relieved when a male slave dragged her back before she could be hurt. Her eyes reached out to him across the distance, wishing him well, and he raised his hand in farewell.

With long smooth strides, Perren raced after Firecracker, Caspar thumping against his stone-hard side. Fortunately, Fern had halted the horse just a couple of miles outside the city and so it wasn't long before they caught up. Castaguard was set in a shallow bowl in undulating land-scape just south of the mountains of Kalanazir. In the grey flatlands bottoming the bowl, water lazed in silver pools reflecting the grey clouds that darkened the rainy lands of Ceolothia. There was no shelter. Instinct drew

Caspar towards the hills and he yelled at Perren and Fern to turn north.

As they ran, May whimpered softly, her head buried into Firecracker's mane, and Caspar remembered how she so hated riding the stallion who would buck, rear or shy without warning. He himself loved the Oriaxian purebred, believing it to be the finest of its breed, and enjoyed its feisty nature; but, unlike Brid the Maiden, May was no horsewoman.

Eventually, they reached the leafy willows that marked a river tumbling from the mountains and drew to a halt. There was no sign of anyone on their trail and, breathlessly, they stopped to look back at the city.

"May, are you harmed?" Caspar asked anxiously.

Perren released him and he jumped down onto the pads of soft mossy plants growing at the edge of the brimming river. Water oozed up over his boots as he ran to help the slender, chestnut-haired girl down from his horse.

She fell heavily into his arms. Though light, her fear had made her clumsy. Sobbing, she clung on tight to him and Caspar wondered, not for the first time, where she had found the courage needed to steal Necrönd and find her way alone all the way to Ceolothia. It was extraordinary.

"That creature," Caspar began to explain. "That hairy man . . ."

"That troll," Perren supplied for him.

"He wasn't a troll. I've seen trolls in Vaalaka," Caspar objected. "Creatures nearer the size of an ox with leathery skin and no more than hog's bristles for hair."

Perren looked at him patiently. "A Ceolothian troll."

"Anyway, we've lost Mamluc," Caspar said with relief as they looked back over the plain.

Perren shrugged. "For now, but we are easy enough to

follow. We must move." He paused, looking down at the trickling water that bubbled over May and Caspar's feet and tickled his toes, and then looked up at the couple for a long while and gave May a curious look. "A girl," he said at last.

Caspar laughed. "What do you mean, a girl? Of course, she's a girl."

Perren laughed. "It must be strange to be a human being; you have so many secrets from one another."

"Secrets?" Caspar did not like the way Perren looked at May and suddenly knew he was going to like even less what the stonewight had to say.

"She's carrying a girl," Perren proclaimed.

May's eyes widened. She looked shocked, elated and, as she glanced at Caspar, almost fearful.

"You didn't tell me!" he said slowly and coldly, wounded to the core.

"It didn't seem like the right time," she admitted. "I . . . I," she stammered.

Caspar knew that she was pleading for his love. He swallowed his storming emotions that were too shocked to even know what he felt. Coldly, he told himself that the other man was dead – dead at his own hand. That at least should make it bearable. Who was he to judge May after all the horrors she had been through? Stiffly, he forced himself to hold out his hand and took hers though he would not pull her close.

"I'm sorry. I was thinking of you," she said lamely.

"Of me!" Caspar's blood boiled and flushed to his face, his composure gone in an instant. He shoved her away and snatched up his hand to hide his expression, nudging at his crooked nose. Hal had broken it all those years ago and it reminded him that this sort of thing would never happen to his young uncle; it was the kind of thing that

Hal might do to someone else. "How could you, May?" he asked bitterly.

"I was trying to protect you from Necrönd." She was crying now, her eyes pleading. "I thought that if I gave myself to Amaryllis . . ."

"Talorcan!" Caspar snapped. "His real name was Talorcan."

"Talorcan then," she said quietly, sniffing intermittently but regaining some of her self-control. "I thought that, if I did, I would never be able to succumb to my longing to go back to you and so I would avoid endangering you. I reasoned that if I came home after hiding the Egg, you might force me to tell you where I had hidden it and so I had to be certain that I could never go home."

Caspar did not see the logic in it. All he knew was that he had slain Talorcan in error, believing him to be the one that had stolen Necrönd. All he had been able to do to make amends, as the verderer lay gasping his lasts breaths, was to grant him his dying wish. That wish had been to look after May. And now he knew why. A black pit of jealous hurt bored deep into Caspar's stomach. He couldn't look at her. He had heard her declare her love to Talorcan and, though that had hurt, it was not so painful as this. His child! She carried Talorcan's child! He loved May with all his heart and she had done this to him!

His first love, Brid, had wounded him by never returning his love; instead, she only had eyes for Hal. He had finally accepted that and, in so doing, discovered his love for May, who had remained devoted to him throughout. He had waited too long to tell her of his love and now, when he had the chance, he had to discover that she had already given herself to someone else.

They could not look at each other.

Perren coughed uncomfortably. "I see that perhaps I shouldn't have said anything."

"I would have found out," Caspar snapped angrily. "Eventually! It's the kind of thing you can't hide for long. Though you could have had the decency to admit it yourself." He glared bitterly at May.

"I don't know I am pregnant except on the say so of this talking rock. How do you presume to know?" she demanded, her eyes stabbing at Perren.

"I might only be a very young stonewight but we sense things in the water." He looked down at his feet. "It is a gift from the Great Mother; we share the thoughts of all things that are joined by Her waters."

"Truly!" May exclaimed. Her expression changed. Somehow, she appeared to draw into herself while her hands protectively cupped her flat belly. The orphaned daughter of a woodcutter turned haughtily on the Baron's son. "And you have no claim at all to be angry with me."

The wolfling ran to her side, growling at Caspar – something she had never done before.

"Hush, Runa," he said with restraint. "I will never hurt her."

"Indeed!" May replied with flat emotion. "It would have been better that you stabbed me with your sword than cut me with this scornful rejection. You behave as if you are so innocent. Ha! The high and mighty Caspar who all praise as the best of souls! They wouldn't believe this of you at home, you know. They would not believe that you could treat me so ill. They would believe you were a bigger man inside than this spoilt, jealous child. Talorcan gave all for me, faced oblivion for me, and I had the power to give him a soul."

Caspar's conscience was piqued. She was right. At home they would expect him to be magnanimous but he was still human. "I didn't expect such treachery," he growled at her, the hurtful words springing from his wounded soul.

Her eyes grew slitted and she glared venomously at him. "*You* accuse *me* of treachery! You who has shunned me all these years whilst drooling after Brid. You expected me to save myself for you after that?"

"It's not the same."

"All those years you said you loved Brid!" she shouted at him.

"Yes, but I didn't lie with her."

"Only because she didn't invite you to."

This was undeniably true. Caspar opened his mouth to shout his retort back but could think of none.

She smiled in triumph. "You see!"

"But I'm a man. It's different."

"Is it?" she asked scornfully, her eyes no longer begging for his forgiveness. She turned her back on him and Caspar suffered not only the gouging pain of his jealousy but also the hollow ache of rejection. He wanted to forgive her, wanted to hold her close and say that it didn't matter. But it did!

CHAPTER TWO

Ceolothia was many weeks behind them now and it was getting late as they crossed through an unguarded pass from Salise into Oriaxia. The twilight landscape of rocky hills parched by a drying wind became patterns of dark valleys and crimson peaks as the sun set.

Caspar's flesh tingled as they moved into the dark; everywhere he sensed strange stirrings. The feelings in themselves where not new to him. Whenever he had previously held the Egg in his possession, he had been plagued with an uneasy sense of monstrous spirits around him but ever since he had retrieved Necrönd from May, those feelings had intensified.

During their journey, he had managed several times to track ahead on his horse and, while away from his companions' prying eyes, he had closely examined the marble shell with its fine blue veins. He had been horrified to discover the black jagged line that now marred it. How May had let such harm come to the Egg, he couldn't imagine and could only presume that it was this defect that had distorted its magic. He rubbed thoughtfully at his head that still ached.

A shudder chilled his spine. He sensed the deepening hatred of the unseen spirits about him. Drawing his cloak tight about him, he glanced tentatively towards May in hope of drawing some comfort from her. She was so beautiful, her long curling chestnut hair coiling and bouncing to the rhythm of Perren's stride. Gripes of jealousy sucked the blood from Caspar's head; he felt weak with sickness. Overwhelmed with loneliness, he looked away.

May was close beside him but he felt more lonely now than he had when they were parted. As though the weeks wore on, there was no thaw between them and they barely spoke until, one morning, May awoke, complaining of feeling unutterable sick.

"And you're asking for my sympathy?" Caspar asked brusquely, unable to conceal his displeasure at her symptoms.

"I wouldn't dream of it," she retorted huskily. She never lost any trace of her woodland accent that was soft and pretty like Brid's.

Though she turned green as Perren hoisted her onto his shoulders, ready for the day's march, Caspar refused to feel sorry for her. Of course, she felt sick; she was pregnant with Talorcan's child.

With May high on his broad shoulders, Perren hummed through the uncomfortable silence. Caspar rode off ahead, trying to appear unconcerned though, truthfully, he felt betrayed even by Runa. The white wolfling, with strange holly-green eyes, no longer trotted at his heels but kept close by Perren, constantly looking up to May.

The stonewight had grown lean since leaving the safety of his nursery caverns deep in the eastern ranges of the Yellow Mountains. His life there provided little cause for movement but, since leaving, he had found great pleasure in their constant journeying, and was so tireless and encouraging that they made good time. Caspar did not have to check his feisty stallion's stride so much now as he rode indignantly before the others with Trog strapped to the back of his saddle. The blunt-nosed, aggressive-looking terrier tired quickly and could not keep up on foot.

Caspar fancied that Trog was also put out by Runa's shift in affections towards May. Runa had been inseparable from the dog but the moment they had found May, the wolfling had not left her side.

Caspar continually glanced back to check that Runa was well; the wolf meant a great deal to him. Before her death, Morrigwen, the ancient Crone, had told Caspar that Runa would lead them to the new Maiden and so enable the Trinity of high priestess to continue. But Morrigwen had died before a new Maiden could be found and the power of the Trinity was lost. The new Maiden had to be an orphaned girl, since it was decreed that only a child without living parents might take up the holy office. But Runa had led them only to May who, though an orphan, could certainly never take on the office of the Maiden. He twisted to look at her and scowled at her growing belly.

He had to admit defeat. He had failed Morrigwen and must now look after his own concern: Necrönd. Somehow, he must find a place of safekeeping so that none could ever again summon the dreadful powers that it commanded.

He shrugged his thoughts away and looked out across the landscape. They had worked their way through the wooded areas of Lonis, where they had stocked up on grain and the sweet pancakes that Fern adored, and on through the northern tip of Salise without mishap. Now, ahead, lay Oriaxia; the land of the east; the land of the sun. It was hot.

May looked tired and sat listlessly atop the stonewight's shoulders. Though she did not again complain of her sickness, she moaned softly to herself, and Perren periodically reached up to pat her hand sympathetically.

"I had no idea of the hardships of bearing young," he rumbled.

"Tell me another story," May pleaded. "It helps keep my mind off things."

"Indeed!" Perren was delighted and began a tale of rabbits that worked their way right down to the deep chasms below the Yellow Mountains. "As my great, great, great-grandfather, Lias, son of Colossus, son of Rollright, and father of Bollon, father of Heel, father of Tecton, father of Ham, father of Perren – that's me – would say, all rabbits, even now, can thump their feet and murmur the ancient call of the stonewights to rouse us from our sleep. A rabbit has so silent a voice that it is not normally heard but our ancient name is loud to us however softly spoken. Virlithos," he murmured.

Caspar almost believed he felt a tremble ripple through the stony plain.

There was no apparent story in the stonewight's lengthy tale but they all saw how Perren delighted in speaking of the one hundred rabbits. He described in infinite detail the colour, size and number of whiskers of each of the creatures involved. Caspar wondered at the stonewight's memory – or imagination.

But he was also heartily tired of such tales and infuriated that May should look so intent on the stonewight's story. Perren doted on her. The jealous youth was not comfortable with the way she deliberately aimed to please the stonewight, who now had a broad grin on his huge round face, his whiskery eyebrows even tuftier than before. Yet she so persistently ignored his own presence.

Despite the heat, they maintained an impressive pace, as they travelled east. The further they went, the hotter it became. Soon they reached a sandy plain cupped by hills and dotted with outcrops of rock. Blue-green grasses grew in tufts and runs of gravel provided them with an easy footing and they were able to avoid the occasional areas where the vegetation was completely stripped from the pale sand. From a distance, the hollows looked as though they were coated with frost but, close up, Caspar saw they were salt beds, cracked and hard underfoot. Around the huge lone rocks that stood like pieces on a chessboard, were strewn fossils of lobsters, sea snails and other sea life.

"Shouldn't we go round by the hills?" May asked, pointing to the purple shapes far to the north and south.

Caspar nodded due east straight across the desert at the brown hills that were very much closer. "It'll take us forever to go around and we'll cross this in a matter of hours."

To his satisfaction, no one argued with him and so they continued into the desert. With no shelter, Caspar was eager to cross the plain as quickly as possible before the heat of the day blazed down. His hot-blooded stallion showed every sign of having more stamina than even the young wolf and they never slowed from a steady canter. Unburdened, Fern was also quick and light on his horny bare feet and Perren's strides were deceptively long and steady.

But as the morning wore on towards noon, the stone-wight was beginning to slow. "It's hot!" he panted. "I need water!"

About them, the sparse grassland was crisp and brown though evidently nutritious enough to support the herds of antelope. Other animals grazed the savannah and Caspar at last saw in the distance what he was hoping to avoid – a lion.

He glanced anxiously at May. He had was familiar with mountain lions and the sleek tufted-eared lynxes of his homeland but he knew from his childhood studies that the lions of the Oriaxian grasslands were twice the size, the males proudly bearing vast manes. His instinct was immediately to protect May and, for a split second, he forgot his jealousy and reined in to stay level with her and Perren but she looked away disdainfully. He pouted and kicked Firecracker forward a pace. What had he been thinking? May did not need him. Perren would protect her. It was Fern he needed to be concerned about.

Something moved behind them. He had not been certain at first – after all many creatures lived in this wide hot land, creatures like rhinoceros and buffalo that he had only ever heard about from Morrigwen – but now he was sure something was there.

He reined in and, with his bow strung and ready, kept vigil at the rear of their party. He was about to ask the stonewight if he sensed a presence stalking them, when Perren stumbled but recovered himself. It was remarkable in that the stonewight's broad flat feet had previously moulded to the sandy ground as he strode foot-sure across the arid landscape.

"Perren?" he asked. "Can you sense anything different?"

"Yes, I can!" the stonewight snapped with uncharacteristic irritability. "It's too hot!"

Caspar turned to Fern instead. It occurred to him that the wolfman had been so close on May's trail before that it seemed unlikely that he would just give up on his efforts to steal the Egg now. "Fern, have you smelt *him* – you know, the wolfman – on the wind at all?"

Fern shook his head. "I thought Talorcan's magic banished him back to the Otherworld."

Caspar itched his scalp. It was distasteful to talk of Talorcan but he could see that he must. "I don't think so. Talorcan was still afraid for May; he begged me to protect her. He had kept her safe from the wolfman's dark spirit all through her flight from Torra Alta and, on his death, he was still afraid for her."

Guiltily, Caspar realized how utterly he had failed May. It was his own weakness, his own inability to resist the lure of Necrönd that had forced her into stealing it in the first place and so laying herself open to such terrible dangers. If he had been stronger, she would be safe in Torra Alta now.

"Someone is on our trail," Caspar insisted, "and if you can't smell wolf, it must be one of his minions."

"I smell lion," Fern replied emphatically and nodded towards the tall grasses that shifted and rippled though there was no wind to stir it.

Any number of beasts could be lurking in the arid grassland and Caspar almost yearned for the open desert he could see ahead, which they must cross before they reached the hills. Beyond that they would find the sea. He had not given much thought to what they would do once they reached the Ocean of Tethys but presumed that they would find a coastal village where they could purchase a vessel to take them beyond these shores.

A yell of alarm snapped Caspar's head round. He couldn't see May! What had happened? Normally she was distinct, sitting tall on Perren's shoulders, but she and the stonewight had vanished. Caspar galloped back, dust flying off Firecracker's hooves. Perren was nowhere to be seen. Suddenly the ground shifted beneath him and the stonewight's grey shape emerged from the earth. He rolled over and apologetically lifted up May.

"Are you hurt?" the stonewight asked in alarm.

She looked startled and her hand tentatively prodded her belly that was now softly rounded. "I don't think so."

One tiny part of Caspar's mind had wished that the

fall might have caused her to lose the child and he was horrified that he could have allowed himself to feel such a thing. Runa anxiously snuffled at May's side as the girl gingerly rose to her feet, pulling the crisp grasses from her hair.

Perren sat back in exhaustion. "Is it far to the next waterhole? I never imagined that the sun could be so hot. Ceolothia was wonderful, all that beautiful dampness, but here it's so dry. I must have water," he told Caspar, pointing at the gourd about his neck. "I must have it. I am crumbling. The sun is too hot; I will last only moments more."

Caspar gripped the gourd and rattled it. It was about half full and he looked ahead to the hills where, surely, they would find water. The hills were no more than a few miles off now but their progress had become painfully slow. He had another gourd hidden in his saddlebag still so he handed the half-empty one to Perren.

"Here, drink it but it's the last we have," he lied in the hope that the stonewight might ration himself.

He slipped down from his saddle to help Perren to his feet but discovered the rocklike being was impossibly heavy. All he could do to help was to lift May onto the back of Firecracker. An hour later, Caspar was ruing his decision to cross the desert rather than listen to May. The sun was high, the glare bouncing up from the hot sand stung his eyes and his lips were beginning to chap. Perren had guzzled every drop from the gourd given him and they had not found another watering hole. The crisp grassland had given over to rock and sand. Stoically they plodded on across a flat dry plain, which was broken only by isolated boulders, yearning for the cool of the low hills.

The heat hammered down on Caspar's stooped head.

All he could think about was the need for water and he fixed his eyes on the hills that were now no more than a league ahead though they seemed impossibly far off; even Cracker was slowing in the heat that pounded down. The air scorched Caspar's lungs. His eyes hurt from squinting against the glare and his tongue felt thick in his mouth. Exhaustion dragged at his muscles. The sand was so dry and light that it gave way with each footfall and he was forever stumbling.

After a long period of silence, Perren was again grumbling that he wouldn't make it. "Water, Spar. I've got to have water."

Up until now Caspar had forgotten how the old stone-wights at the roots of Old Man Mountain had warned Perren against the heat of the sun.

The going was soft and slightly uphill, the sand slipping beneath each footfall reducing their progress to a stagger. Caspar, too, craved water and thought only of the gourd in his saddle pack that he knew he must save. Between them it would be barely enough and he had to think hard how best to use it, knowing full well that it was still going to be some hours before they had crossed the plain. Even if they gave all the water to Perren, Caspar doubted he would make it, judging by the rate at which he was deteriorating. And what then of the others? There was water ahead in those hills, he knew it; he could make out dark shadows which he hoped were swathes of trees.

If one of them went on alone with Firecracker, giving the horse the last of the water, they could make it back with enough water for everyone. If they rested, Fern and May and, he prayed, Trog and Runa would survive but he had grave doubts about Perren. If they stayed Perren would take all the water and then they would all die. He didn't want to leave May but he could think of no other way. She would never manage Firecracker, and Fern was not predictable enough to be entrusted with the task.

The heat fuddled his brain. He could not make a decision. He knew that he must but he could not. Though he was born to be a leader of men, he knew he didn't have it in him. He wondered what Hal would do; Hal would make the right decision. He pondered but couldn't decide on what that might be. Finding his mind wandering uncontrollably, he called a halt.

"I do not know what to do," he admitted and told them his dilemma.

"You mean you have water, more water on you?" Perren asked savagely, closing in on Caspar. "I must have it. I cannot die out here under the sun. I am too young. You must give it to me." He shoved Caspar aside, snatched at Firecracker's bridle and started shouting, "Where is it? Give it to me!"

The stonewight dragged May from the saddle, letting her thump heavily to the ground, and clumsily fumbled with the straps to the packs. A squeal from Trog followed by the sound of grinding stone halted the stonewight a moment as the snake-catcher grabbed hold of his solid grey fingers. Without any hesitation, the wolfling launched herself at Perren's calves.

Caspar felt futile. The one way they would not survive was if Perren drank the water. It was not enough to see the stonewight through the heat to the hills. He was crumbling fast but still managed to lurch at Firecracker. Caspar was quick and wheeled the horse away but he knew he was no match for the stonewight, who was bellowing at him for the water. He had no time. If he were to prevent Perren from drinking all the water now, he would have to flee right away even though May was still on her knees in the sand. His decision made for him, he leapt into the saddle and, turning Firecracker for the hills, pressed him to a brief gallop to break away from Perren before slowing to an energy-conserving jog.

"No!" May's voice rang out across the desert. "No, don't leave me! Spar, you can't. The baby! I must have water. I'll die and my baby will die. You cannot do this."

Caspar yelled back. "Rest! Keep still! I shall be back with water!"

After that he would not look round; he had to keep going though Firecracker's head was low between his knees. The horse staggered and stumbled once or twice but still kept moving. Caspar soothed the stallion's sweat-soaked neck, fearing that he would not make it. But he had to keep the horse alive and so halted every ten minutes to give him sips of water and wherever possible crept under the shade of one of those strange, lone rocks that were scattered through the desert floor.

The first few miles had passed quickly but now, with just the last mile ahead, the sun overhead hammered down and even Firecracker was reduced to an exhausted stagger. The thirst drove Caspar to madness, the shimmering air rising off the desert plain disorienting him, yet he would not drink. He needed to save every drop for the horse.

Dizzily, he thought that it would take so little to wield Necrönd. He had summoned dragons before. One right now could scoop him up, return for the others and, in minutes, have them to water. It was so easy, too easy. He gritted his teeth. He had promised his mother he would not tamper with Necrönd but wondered whether she would really wish to hold him to his promise even if that meant death. He doubted it very much.

Then perhaps he *should* use the power of the Egg? As the thought took hold, a cold shudder ran through him and he felt the immediate presence of dark shadows close by. His head began to throb. They were close, watching, waiting for their chance of freedom. The sound of panting behind him made him snap his head round. He relaxed; it was only Fern, who had somehow managed to keep up with him. If the woodwose could keep on, then so could he.

His mother was right; he must not use Necrönd. The panting had only been Fern but he could still sense the heavy presence of the savage beasts of legend close by. Blood trickled from his head and he wiped his crown, knowing that, yet again, the wound had opened up. He looked at his fingers. There were traces of pus. Horrified, he struggled to banish all thought of the Egg. If he was not concentrating on a task, the notion constantly formed in his mind that a hand was reaching in through the top of his head and snagging at his brain with broken nails.

Both Fern and Firecracker sniffed the air and quickened their pace. Water! Caspar could almost smell it. The horse's ears pricked forward and he whickered excitedly. Soon they reached darker soil. Firecracker scraped with his hoof and snuffled the ground. There was surely water nearby. With huge relief, Caspar drank the last from the gourd and dropped from Firecracker's back. A row of dark green lime trees grew up the mountainside, following a crack in the rock.

He stumbled to its foot and unhooked the empty gourds from Firecracker's saddle. They lightly thumped against one another on his back as he scrambled through the ferny cover to find a clear trickle running over a slimy green rock and dropping into a shaded pool. Water, precious water! It was a commodity that they were not short of in Torra Alta and he had never been so acutely aware of the need for it. He drank, his tight, rough throat relaxing with each gulp. He still felt light-headed with dehydration and, guiltily, he lay back to gather his strength. While he relaxed, the others were dying. He must get back – and quickly.

But Firecracker was still drinking and he knew he must have patience. The animal must have his fill since he had to make that sandy journey twice more. The youth waited, watching as at last the horse snorted and blew at the water, tossing his head and allowing much of it to slosh out the sides of his mouth. He allowed him one more minute and then decided it was time to go.

He mounted Firecracker, who was reluctant to turn back, flaring his nostrils and sniffing the scorched air rising off the sandy plain. He danced on his pale hooves, tossed his head and, holding his tail high, shrieked his challenge at the desert.

"We shan't be long," Caspar told Fern, who seemed quite happy to sit by the pool, watching the water flow over his coarse black toes.

With a loose rein, Caspar encouraged his horse to a low canter, a natural pace for the animal. The distance was not far but the wind was picking up and a haze of sand filled the atmosphere. Caspar halted to wrap his shirt around Firecracker's nostrils to protect the horse.

The red roan was growing uneasy, snorting and chafing at his bit, his fear infecting Caspar. Firecracker was an Oriaxian purebred and, the desert environment was undoubtedly a part of his subconscious memory. Finally, the stallion stopped in his tracks and reared up, squealing savagely, fighting Caspar's control on the reins. Alarmed, the youth had no notion of what distressed the horse until, looking up he saw on the skyline a dark line. It was growing notably larger and darker in the short time that he stared at it. Darkness rolled towards them across the plain.

Caspar had never known his stallion to be frightened before, not even with hooded wolves at his heels, but now he trembled and backed up, half rearing and fighting with the bit in his mouth.

"It's only dust," Caspar tried to sound reassuring though the animal's terror was beginning to infect him.

The dust clouds rose like vast monsters high into the sky. He had no experience of desert storms, only of snow-storms where the snow clawed away skin and the cold stabbed into the lungs. He had no idea what it was to breathe sand-choked air but, since the horse had an instinctive fear of the wind-tossed dust, he knew it must be perilous.

May! Whatever she had done, he knew that he loved her. He had to get to her. Not far ahead, buzzards circled with difficulty in the swirling brown sky close to the point where he had left them.

Firecracker bucked as the youth kicked his heels into his sides but the stallion refused to go on. He whipped the reins back and forth across the horse's neck but still Firecracker would not move. In desperation, he drew his dagger to prick Firecracker's side and shrieked out the Torra Altan battle cry that they used whilst training their war-horses. At last, the stallion laid back his ears and burst into a flat gallop. The sand whipped into Caspar's face and he screwed his eyes up against the pain.

A dark shadow loomed to the left and Firecracker veered towards it. Caspar tugged on the right rein to hold him straight as he saw it was only a huge split rock, the sand dividing and swirling around it. Undoubtedly, the horse was instinctively drawn to it for shelter but Caspar had to rescue May first.

He could barely see. The sky was darkening, the blazing gold sun a sullen red as the dust clouds billowed higher into the sky. But there they were! His heart rejoiced. Then panic drove him to beat Firecracker to a wild pace. Now that he was close, he could see something was wrong.

May could no longer speak. Thirst raged in her mouth and she could only pray that Caspar would be quick. She didn't doubt him for a moment. Whether he forgave her or not for lying with Talorcan, whether he loved her or not, it made no difference; he would do all in his powers to return. He was a Torra Altan lord born to responsibility and he would never forsake one of his people.

She stared eastward along the line of his tracks, which the wind was beginning to cover, to the brown line of hills where she hoped he would find water. Her tongue was thick in her throat and her head swam dizzily.

They would not last much longer; she knew it but struggled to keep defeat from her mind. She knew that those who gave up hope died the quickest and so she must keep alert. Her eyes began to sting in the raw heat and she dropped her gaze to her sore swollen feet and turned to look back at the cruel desert.

That was strange! She had not remembered that dark line of hills on the horizon before. She frowned and glared. The line seemed to be thickening, rising up out of the plain. It was too peculiar; surely the heat had touched her mind. She looked around to see how the animals fared. Trog lay flat out on his side, his great chest heaving in and out like bellows, his thick tongue hanging out. Runa still sat upright, though her head lolled and her once bright green eyes were beginning to dull. Still, the animal watched her with devotion.

"Runa, dear Runa, you've been such a friend," May mumbled.

However, it was for Perren that she feared the most.

She had grown fond of the strange creature who appeared to be sculpted out of solid rock. He had been so strong and carried her all that way but now he was slumped to the ground, his coarse skin whitening before her eyes, sloughing off in chalky lumps. And there was nothing she could do about it. She crawled to his side.

"I'm dying," he groaned. "Dying!" His grey sunken eyes looked from her and fixed on Trog. Slowly the stonewight drew himself up.

She was too exhausted to think clearly and watched him as if he were part of a dream. A sudden, intense look narrowed his eyes. She had liked him so much, loved his slow easy nature, his delight at simple stories and his constant craving for detail. It was charming, childlike and yet he had been so strong. But now, near death, she realized that she did not know him, and that was she was afraid of him.

Too disbelieving to react, she watched as the creature's arm snapped forward to grab at Trog.

Runa was quick and, with a snarl, lunged at Perren, scraping the stonewight's skin, the rasping noise loud in the desert. Trog was instantly alert and struggled free, evidently not quite so near death as he had appeared.

Perren looked at the two animals and then slowly his eyes rose to meet May's. She knew at once his intent and began to run. Near collapse, her breath squeezing through her swollen throat, she could only stagger. The thought of the child within her drove out the cankerous sense of complacency induced by the giddiness of exhaustion. Dragging herself forward, she slipped and stumbled to her knees, only to force herself up again.

Her one last straw of hope was that the stonewight was even less able to adapt to desert conditions than a human and that, just perhaps, this sudden burst of activity would bring him to the point of collapse faster than it did her. She kept her footing until faced with a dune and, as she began to crawl up the loose sides, she became quickly exhausted. A great hand gripped her ankle and pulled her back. She twisted round and she looked into his mad eyes that had become tight and beady, his eyelids grating over them as he blinked.

"No!" She kicked out as his huge fist snatched her wrist and yanked her towards him.

His mouth closed around her arm, his jaw clamping her in its terrifying grip. May screamed, fighting to tear herself free. Then something white flashed into her vision and Runa flung herself into Perren's face, her curving fangs raking over his cheeks: Though the wolf could not cut deeply into the stonewight's rocky hide, the attack was enough to knock the exhausted stonewight off balance and for May to stumble free.

Clutching her arm across her body, she ran, stumbled and ran, the savage noise of Trog and Runa growling at Perren thick in her ears. Her arm throbbed with pain. She didn't think it was broken. Though she was quite certain that Perren would have been able to rip her arm straight off, he had held back since his intention had been to break the skin so that he might suck out her blood and drink from her body as if she were no more than a chalice. If it hadn't been for Runa, she would have been dead in seconds.

Disorientated with heat, she barely cared any more if, personally, she lived or died but she did care about her baby. The thought that this stonewight might kill her child was too much and so she kept running. She staggered on but after only a few more paces collapsed, unable to force herself further.

Runa was still at Perren's face and she wondered at the

wolf's courage and loyalty. She raised her head to see if Perren was after her yet. Instead, she saw that the thin dark line on the horizon had swelled into a billowing black mass that was rapidly sweeping towards them.

Gasping, she tried to crawl. Her head swam and it took every ounce of concentration to make her arm reach out painfully for the next stretch of hot sand before her. Was she dreaming? A ghostly image danced in the billowing sand downwind of the storm. She blinked, her eyelids feeling like grit. She could see a horse, its legs disjointed and wobbly in the heat haze.

"Spar!" she gasped.

In seconds, Caspar was alongside May. Great streaks of blood striped her arm, which she held cradled against her body. He could barely think for the noise of the dog and wolf a little way beyond her prone figure. Side by side, they were snarling savagely at Perren, who was on his knees, his skin cracked and flaking in the wind.

"Water!" he gasped at the sight of Caspar and crawled towards him. "Water!"

Tossing several heavy gourds at Perren, Caspar leapt from his horse to help May. He held out another gourd to her and dragged a sheet of canvas from his pack and emptied a third into it for the animals.

"He tried . . ." May could barely speak between gulps of water. She kept on drinking long steady draughts while her big wide hazel eyes gaped in horror at Perren.

"Hurry! The storm," Caspar urged impatiently, struggling to hold his stallion, who shrieked and tossed his head at the black wall of cloud racing towards them. The stonewight sat back and grinned stupidly at the gourds about him.

May clutched at Caspar. "He— he—"

Caspar ignored her. "We've no time. The storm!" He threw May up onto Firecracker's back.

They would not make the safety of the mountains but they might make that split rock he had seen earlier, which might at least offer some shelter. "Tell me later," he told her, calling the animals and spurring Firecracker to race before the wind.

He galloped hard that short mile back to the rocks, May's long hair blowing forward, flapping into his face. Runa kept alongside, a growl worrying in her throat. The air had grown cold and he coughed as the sand whipped up around them, dragging at their clothing and clawing at their skin, scratching and beating them mercilessly. But worse was the way it stuffed itself into their nostrils.

They reached the rock, that was as broad as it was tall, its leeward face split by a fault. Close up, it was much larger than he had imagined. Trails of sand swept up into sculptured ridges around the edge of the rock but at least it protected them from the breath-stealing wind.

Caspar could not believe his luck as he stared at the fault. It was wide and black and led deep into the rock. Hastily, he dismounted and dragged May forward to explore the rift that led down into the dark. They had found a sheltered cave; for once fate had been with him. Firecracker snorted and pawed the ground but didn't take too much persuasion to be led into the dark recess.

The cave was lit by the ghostly light reflecting off the desert but it grew darker in seconds.

"Trog, please make it," Caspar prayed.

He drew the others deep into the cave and looked around him for a place to set May down. At the back of the cave the rock floor was only lightly dusted with drifts of sand whereas they had waded through fluted and corniced waves of desert around the entrance and Caspar judged that no previous desert storm had blown grit so deep into the cave. He relaxed a little. They would be safe here.

Hastily, he bound May's arm while continually casting back at the muddiness of the outside world, praying for Trog to come staggering in. He knew the animal had only seconds in which to reach them but those moments felt like an eternity and he watched the cave mouth until, out of the blackness, he came, coughing fitfully, his white coat grey with the dust. Caspar dragged him to the back of the cave and wiped the sand from his nose.

May was still trembling violently and Caspar, forgetting their quarrel, wrapped her tightly in her arms.

She began to sob. "He tried to eat me, tried to suck out my blood."

"What! Perren?" Caspar was aghast. "Never! I don't believe it. Can you move your arm?"

She nodded. "He never quite got a firm grip of me. Spar, he went on and on that he would die without water, that he would crumble away and that he was too young to die. He tried to catch Trog and Runa too but they were too quick for him."

Caspar coaxed her to drink, which at least calmed her a little, and soon they fell silent, transfixed by the fearsome roar outside. He could not believe the power of the wind and rose to steady Firecracker, whom he feared would crack his head on the ceiling as he reared and snorted, shrieking out his defiance at the storm.

At last, the horse became still. Staring at the moving blackness that whipped across the mouth of the cave, Caspar's thoughts turned to Perren, who was still out there. He should have remembered, of course. Since Perren was always chewing roots and twigs, which he ate in preference to meat, he had come to think of him as a peaceful herbivore, but now he remembered the stonewights' cavern under the roots of Old Man Mountain. The cave-water had been littered with the half-eaten carcasses of those animals who had had no story to tell the stonewights. He looked longingly at May but, the thought of her lying with Talorcan crept back into his mind and, to his shame, he could no longer bring himself to comfort her.

He sat and glared into the storm, withdrawing into his dark, lonely thoughts until his body was cramped with lack of movement. He was not sure whether it was day or night. The raging storm without had been a swirling mass of cloud for hours and his ears rang with the booming noise that roared on and on, drinking up his thought, churning his emotions. It was dark but a flickering light radiated from May, who had found a ceremonial candle in her pack. The small light was at least cheering.

Stiffly, he forced his limbs to move and found himself surprisingly cold. There was no firewood or brush to light and he was beginning to shiver. Furtively, he glanced at May, who was huddled with Trog and Runa for warmth, and a part of him yearned to curl up next to her.

He longed to hold and kiss her, but honour forbade. She was pregnant by someone else! Perhaps if he hadn't allowed his jealousy of Hal to grow for all those years, resenting him for winning Brid when he had loved the priestess so much, perhaps then he would have been better able to cope with his jealousy now. He despised himself for his small-mindedness but the tight knot of envy in his stomach twisted a little tighter as the image of May wrapped in Talorcan's embrace flashed into his mind.

Of course, he knew that he loved her but now he also hated her for causing him such pain. To make matters worse, another thought swelled in his head; she had stolen Necrönd from him. Suspicion, like a cancer, had invaded his body, swelling in the fertile swill of his jealousy. When he and Brid had been inadvertently dragged into the Otherworld to be confronted by Talorcan, the chief verderer had used Brid in the hope of getting his hands on Necrönd. Perhaps the verderer had been using May in the same way. Perhaps she, too, had come under Talorcan's spell. Perhaps she had stolen the Egg and taken it at his direction? Had her story of stealing Necrönd to protect him, been all lies?

He shook himself. No, that was ridiculous. Whatever May had done to him, she was still May; she was always earnest and devout and would do nothing against the wishes of the Great Mother.

Her silhouette turned towards him and, evidently, she saw he was studying her. He thought to look away but decided to hide his feelings in order to avoid embarrassment. With cold politeness, he inquired after her arm.

"I trust you are rested and your arm comfortable. Is there anything you need? I was wondering whether you wanted—"

She shook he head. "No thank you, Master Spar, I am quite able to look after myself."

He turned away and, after feeling his way towards the warmth of Firecracker and bidding him to lie down, he pressed himself against the horse's flanks. Finally, he slid into a deep sleep drenched in fearful dreams where trolls and hooded wolves burst out from his brain. Night after night, he had suffered the same vile dreams and he always awoke feeling sick, the crown of his head throbbing.

He had been woken by silence. May's candle had burnt out and it was dark with no sign of dawn but he had the sense that soon it would be coming. Stars cast the faintest of light onto the pale sands outside but, within the cave, it was black and he could see nothing, not even his fingers, which gave him the peculiar sense that he was somehow disembodied. At least the sounds of the animals and May's steady sleeping breaths gave a sense of reality.

His ears strained. There was another noise too. He hadn't been sure at first but now he could hear the soft rhythmic thump of padding footsteps. At first, he rejoiced that the stonewight had safely weathered the storm but soon his heart thumped in his throat as he heard Perren's croaking voice mutter, "Water! The varmints must have water."

The footfalls faltered and Caspar guessed that Perren was still weak. The drying blast of sand would have further dehydrated him. Caspar feared the great stonewight would trap them in the cave and, though he had water to give him, he considered that this stricken Perren was too dangerous to be near. They must move now. He tiptoed back to May and rocked her shoulder.

"It's Perren! I can hear him out there in the night," he hissed.

She responded with instant alertness and gathered herself up while he flung his saddle over Firecracker. He lifted the girl up so she could struggle onto the horse's back and noted how she stifled her winces at the movement.

"Are you all right?" he asked sympathetically, again forgetting his anger with her.

"Just the sickness," she stoically whispered back.

They crept out of the cave, Firecracker's footfall muffled by the deep sand, and looked anxiously around. "There's no sign of him," May blurted.

Caspar waved at her to be quiet. "He's difficult to see

even in daylight if he lies close to the earth. But he will be disorientated without water. It's his medium and he senses much of his surroundings through it. Out here in the desert that has not seen water in years, he will be lost. If we move quickly . . ."

Refreshed from his sleep and feeling so much better for the water that he did not notice his hunger, Caspar led Firecracker, trotting alongside as they beat a path towards the hills that now seemed surprisingly close.

"He's coming," May said. "I know he is."

Runa kept close alongside, hackles up, sniffing nervously around, but Trog was lagging, unable to make the pace. The wind still blew, whisking a haze of sand over the ground. Caspar's hands were sore from where the sharp grit continually rubbed at his skin. Apart from the abrasive quality of the sand, it was like riding through low-lying mist. One minute everything below his waist was obscured, then the swirling sand welled up to cover their faces before subsiding again so that they glimpsed the rippled sand at their feet.

Soft drifts made the going difficult and Caspar laboured hard. The wind abated for a moment and he called a halt to put Runa and Trog up on the saddle behind May so that he could keep them above the level of the choking sand. Trog was hugely heavy and hung limply in his hands so it was only with May's help that he was able to lift him. Runa, though taller, was lank and spare and easier to lift, but she was still very unhappy about being slung over the saddle. She squirmed uncooperatively, nipped at his hand and leapt down, her hackles raised, growling at the sand ahead.

Caspar leapt back. The ground at his feet bulged. Sand cascaded from a rising bulk. Caspar knew at once that Perren had somehow caught up and overtaken them. He was barely recognizable. His round face was drawn, his eyes drooping and his great arms withered. He moved forward unsteadily.

"Water!" his face cracked as he spoke and more grey-white flesh sloughed off.

"Perren, my friend, we have water!" Caspar plucked the gourd from Firecracker's saddle and tossed it at the stone-wight. "Perren, it's me, Spar. We're nearly there and there's all the water you could want just half a mile ahead."

Perren drank the first gourd that held a quart in one draught. "Water!" he gasped.

Caspar threw him the next two gourds and then the last, hoping that would be enough to bring the stonewight to his senses but Perren still staggered forward, his arms waving before him as if he were blind. Firecracker snorted.

"Water!" Perren cried. Lunging, he caught the horse's bridle.

Firecracker reared and lashed out. May screamed and flung her arms around the horse's neck. Then she was caught in the stonewight's fist. Caspar hammered at the huge creature until his skin was bruised and split but he could not stop Perren hauling May off the horse and closing his mouth around her leg. She suddenly went limp and flopped back and forth like a stillborn lamb in the jaws of a scavenging wolf.

Caspar's instincts were to reach for his bow. Perhaps a shot through the eye would bring Perren down but he hesitated; it was too dangerous; he could so easily hit May instead. Maybe Firecracker could knock him down.

While Caspar was still frozen by indecision, Runa launched herself at the stonewight who swatted her aside with one flick of his free arm, sending her bowling along the sand like brushwood tossed in the wind. When at last she rolled to a halt, she staggered upright and launched her attack again. Trog, in the meanwhile, burst forward and caught hold of Perren's arm. The dog hung there by his jaws, snarling savagely, but apparently having no effect on the stonewight, who now had May in both hands and was poised to bite her as if she were a chicken leg.

"Perren, no! Let her go! It's us! It's Spar. You mustn't hurt her. Perren, Perren!"

But clearly Perren, if the same being still existed within that cracking shell, could not hear him. Caspar's only thought was for May. Before he knew what he was doing, his fingers had flicked open the casket at his neck and his hand was on the Egg. He didn't know what manner of beast to summon, made no rational decision, but just pleaded for help.

At that moment, Perren flung May aside and grabbed Caspar about the neck. "Water!" he roared. "Bring me water!"

He was knocked over by the force. A blackness swarmed up out of his mind and punched into him. A bulbous head with a huge lipless jaw snapped open and Caspar looked in it and saw only the sea, heard its roar and smelt the stench of rotting seaweed.

Suddenly he was submerged in deep water. He was no longer the Egg's master but had been sucked into its magic to become one of the creatures banished to the Otherworld. He tossed in the water, struggling for the surface yet certain, as his lungs burst for air, that he would drown. He swam up and up but there was still no sign of the surface. Quickly, he was dizzy and faint and knew that he should be drowned already but his body still had life; it seemed that, though he could not breathe, he would not drown either.

Huge squid and octopus stirred in the water about him. The creatures fought and wrestled amongst themselves, ignoring him as too insignificant to be of interest. He swam upwards into the paler waters above, looking for the brilliance of the sun above the water and instead saw a blue-white light that, at first, he thought must be the moon.

A madness overtook him. All that mattered was to reach the moon, the light of the life above him, the beacon that would take him home. He was lost. He didn't know where but he was drowned in the spirit world and was there forever if he could not reach the light. He swam upwards alongside vast beasts, a kraken's great tail whipping the water. Over his head, the surface of the water boiled but he could not reach the light. If only he could put his hand into the beam, he was sure he would be drawn back into life. He struggled to gather his thoughts and senses. It was so horribly cold in the water and that, at last, had a sobering effect on him. He felt for the casket at his neck as more lucid thought returned.

The Egg! He could use it to save himself. He didn't know where he was but surely the Egg would save him. But where was it? The casket was no longer around his neck. Perren! Perren must have snatched it from him and, of course, Perren had summoned water. Somehow the command must have gone awry and, when Perren opened up a magical channel to the waters of the Otherworld, Caspar had been sucked through it and plunged into the deep.

He was in the sea; in the freezing sea, his starved lungs screaming for air. A thrashing concentration of monsters was thick in the water. The Egg had got him here, wherever here was, and so, surely, the Egg could get him back. But would Perren ever summon him?

All he could do was keep swimming, desperate to reach the light. Something buffeted him from behind.

It pushed him upwards before its bulbous head and Caspar found himself amongst clinging tentacles. A black octopus gripped him, spun him round and then rejected him, pushing him back down.

He gripped onto its tentacles, aware that the octopus had the same intense, overriding desires as himself. Perhaps it would have the power and stamina to reach the surface.

The water became a boiling foam as he was dragged through it, the pain in his lungs ever increasing, the numbing cold ever more intense. But he knew there would never be any release, any lessening of his agony, ever, if he could not reach the light.

Then he was in the air, gasping for breath. But the air was thin and icy. Stabbing cruelly into his lungs, it did not feed him with the warmth of life as he had expected.

Instinctively, his eyes turned towards the moon that was larger and more brilliant than he had ever seen before. It was larger, even, than the swollen moon seen through the thin atmosphere of his home mountains on a crystal-sharp night.

But it was not the moon!

Clearly, he could see the creamy white surface marbled with veins of blue and now slashed by an angry black scorch. A vortex of clouds stormed about the flaw.

He was looking at Necrönd that was as big as the moon.

CHAPTER THREE

Hal drew his sword, the motion near silent as the cold white steel brushed against the oiled fleece that lined his scabbard. The blade was long and weighty but his upper body had grown to accommodate it and he knew he cut a handsome figure; a broad strong man just entering his prime.

A sudden flash of light had broken through the trees to his right, and though it was probably just sunlight dancing on a forest pool, it was his duty to be alert. For no accountable reason, his imagination told him that the flash of light had been from the metal of a knight. Experience warned him that the thick bramble-strangled forests of western Ceolothia were an ideal place for armed men to lay in ambush, ready to prey on passing travellers.

He tightened his rein on Secret and smoothed her glossy, liver-chestnut coat, urging her on along the muddied track that wound through Trows Forest. She was edgy, a behaviour quite unnatural in the normally steady beast, and this did nothing to expel his own sense of unease.

For some while, though he stared hard into the patchy shadows of the forest, he saw nothing more to make himself suspicious of an attack. Chiding himself for allowing his imagination to get the better of him, he sheathed his sword. Perhaps, when they finally escaped this gloomy, dank world beneath the trees and reached the open terrain of the Goat Country, he would feel less ill at ease. They had travelled far and the edge of the forest couldn't be too distant now.

The sound of cantering hooves behind him made Hal twist round in the saddle. He relaxed; it was only the irrepressible lad, Pip, moving up from the rear of the party, where he had no doubt been trying to impress Prince Renaud and Lord Hardwin. As the boy drew level with the Princess, he nodded politely at her, no doubt asking after her health and whether he could be of any use to her. Hal shook his head in wonder at Pip's nerve. The cheek of it, just riding up to a princess like that! Then he grinned in mild amusement and a little admiration for the way the low-born lad laughed in the face of protocol.

Princess Cymbeline curtly waved the boy away and returned to staring down miserably at her hands that were twisted through the sodden mane of her mount. Hal could only presume that she was still fretting for her brother's safety. Though Hal had succeeded in rescuing the Princess from Tupwell, eldest son of the Belbidian Baron of Ovissia, he had failed her brother. Tudwal had last been being dragged off by the treacherous Ovissian.

Hal was still gazing pensively at Cymbeline when Pip drew level with him, his horse bumping flanks with Secret. Brushing back the wet fringe of his peppercorn hair from his face, he looked at Hal with bright eyes.

"Is there something wrong?" he asked over-eagerly, nodding at Hal's hand that was still on the hilt of the sheathed runesword. The young woodcutter's son was evidently longing for the chance for daring deeds and to prove his courage to the royalty in the party.

"No, nothing," Hal assured him. "And don't look so disappointed. I know you are longing to champion

Princess Cymbeline or rescue Prince Renaud so that they might be forever indebted to you." A grin sprang to Hal's face. It was his own dream to be someone, to make a difference to all Belbidia, to influence the course of his nation and so be sung a hero. He appreciated the boy's ambitions.

"I just thought you might need my help," Pip said disappointedly.

"Well, I don't," Hal rebuffed him more harshly than he had meant to. "Your help! Don't you think I'd call on Abelard or Ceowulf first, if there were any threat?" He nodded over his shoulder at the plainly clad archer and the big Caldean knight who looked most impressive with lance, sword and red and white chequered surcoat. Hal was glad to see that the two hardened fighting men flanked Brid's horse. He could wish for no better protection for his betrothed. He flashed her a handsome grin and she smiled back.

A blink of light in the periphery of his vision caught his attention and wiped away his smile. With slitted eyes, he stared into the forest umbra, again convinced that he had seen the glint of metal. Blood throbbed through his veins, instinct warning him of danger though reason told him that it was absurd that a knight could track them so closely through the thick undergrowth beside the track without being heard. He looked at Pip, wondering if the boy had also seen anything untoward.

Clearly, he had. Frowning, he scanned the forest shadows and then his dark eyes slowly blackened with fear. "What do we do?" he squeaked, his face white.

Hal was surprised by the lad's reaction. Pip was bold to the point of recklessness and he had never seen him so troubled. "First, we'll close ranks and find out what the others have seen," he said calmly, halting and waiting for Ceowulf and Abelard to draw level.

Abelard shook his head. "I say we head right for high ground and take a stand to defend ourselves."

"What? Against that many?" Pip asked, aghast.

"I see only one," Ceowulf said, bemused. "Since it hasn't attacked yet, I think we should keep our heads down."

"Just what exactly are you talking about?" Brid demanded archly, though Hal noted an uncharacteristic hint of doubt in the way her bright green eyes warily blinked at the men and then back into the forest.

As Prince Renaud and Lord Hardwin were beginning to tremble and urged their horses forward to press up close behind him and Ceowulf, he bit his upper lip apprehensively. They couldn't allow themselves to make any more mistakes; they had to get Princess Cymbeline safely to her betrothed, King Rewik, or her father would wage war on Belbidia.

Ceowulf had his javelin raised at the ready, though he looked steadfastly ahead. "You must remember not to look directly at it," he warned.

Everyone at once asked what he meant, confusion compounding their fear.

"It?" Pip queried. "Them, surely. And why shouldn't we look at Vaalakans?" he demanded.

"They ain't Vaalakans, lad," Abelard contradicted him. "There's a yard of difference 'twixt a Vaalakan and a Ceolothian."

"I would recognize Vaalakans anywhere," Pip contradicted huskily. "They killed my mother."

"Look at the helmets and those nose-guards. Distinctly Ceolothian. I'm telling y', lad, I'd recognize one of those demons anywhere. It were one of them that took my life," the man said emphatically and ground his teeth, the pulse in his temple throbbing as he remembered.

Hal wondered what it was like to experience death.

Abelard, though he looked to be in his late thirties, was from an era long past, a man lauded in ballads, a man that gave his life to save others. Even in death, he had run against nature, and returned through the channels of magic that linked this world and the Otherworld to aid his countrymen.

"There's no men," Ceowulf muttered. "But—"

"There is. I'm with Pip there," Abelard interrupted. "Only they're Ceolothians not Vaalakan warriors."

Hal did not understand. He had seen nothing more than a flash of silver and yet his heart had told him that it was a single knight on a horse clad in a full bard of armour and bearing mace, cudgel, sword and knives. Self-consciously, he plucked at his worn leather gambeson and looked at Brid.

"There's nothing there," Brid said flatly. "Just pull yourselves together."

"But we're lost!" Prince Renaud unexpectedly blurted and then started to moan in misery. "We've been going round and round in circles for hours."

Brid shook her head. "No, the sun's always been to our left," she calmly assured him.

"If that is so, how is it I can see my own mark there on the tree ahead?"

"Where? What mark?" Hal demanded incredulously.

Renaud nodded at a clump of fungus sprouting around the base of a pine. "There. That fresh cut in the bark!"

"But—" Hal started to contradict him but the prince would not be reasoned with.

"We're lost," he wailed. "I told you we're lost."

"There's no mark on that tree! And we're not lost," Brid said with a touch of frustration to her voice.

"I know what I saw, and . . ." Hal let the words die.

"Don't you understand? You're seeing your fears. Prince

Renaud's petrified of being lost. Ceowulf thinks that wyverns are the most dangerous thing alive, naturally Abelard cringes at the sight of a Ceolothian, especially one with a bow and—"

"I'm not—" Hal swallowed his words mid-sentence.

He was about to proclaim that he wasn't afraid of a lone knight. Then he realized how foolish he would look. The others were all frightened by things that had nearly devoured them – though Renaud's fears were perhaps related to a past childhood experience. Perhaps an older friend had once abandoned him for a joke that went too far, who knows? But to be afraid of a lone knight was a humiliation. How could he? He felt his cheeks burn, grateful only that his dark colouring would hide any flush.

"But, Brid, I saw something out there," he said with perfect control, as if he were only interested in the problem as an academic debate. "How do you know there's nothing? Are you trying to tell me you're afraid of nothing and that's why you see nothing while the rest of us imagine we see some dreadful terror?"

"Of course not. I saw . . ." she started but, like Hal, she stopped before saying what she had seen. "It doesn't matter but I know it's not possible."

"The wizards," Ceowulf surmised. "It's all illusion created by the same wizard-wraiths we came up against in the black castle where Tupwell held Cymbeline prisoner. Tupwell must have sent them after us to recapture the Princess."

Brid nodded.

"Then we have nothing to fear," the big Caldean knight said in relief. "If it's only their tricks, we just have to ignore the strange things around us."

"The mind is a strong weapon." Brid would not dismiss

the power of the wizards so lightly. "Come, we're all tired. We've been travelling for days, our hands and backs are covered with tears from these wretched, over-sized Ceolothian brambles. We should rest. It's too easy to get confused when you're tired."

They hurried on until they came to a broad glade where the leafy branches of the trees at the fringes drooped, heavy with rain. As Brid suggested, they made camp; though it took a lot of persuading on Ceowulf's part to get Hardwin to dismount. Finally, the second son of the Baron of Piscera forced himself to alight and, with a drawn mouth, was curiously picking his way so very carefully thorough the rough grass, looking anxiously at the ground at his feet and cringing at each step.

Hal looked up smartly. Someone was calling his name. The voice he knew as well as his own. Spar! But how could he be here? He had presumed that Caspar was held prisoner by of the Ovissians that had been given command of Torra Alta. He growled at this atrocity. King Rewik had accused Hal's brother, Baron Branwolf, of Cymbeline's abduction and so, after imprisoning him, had confiscated his lands and handed them to Baron Godafrid of Ovissia – not knowing, of course, that it was Baron Godafrid's son who had mastermind the treasonous abduction.

Had Caspar somehow escaped and tracked them here? He blinked. The light was bright and he could barely see for the dazzle. He tried to busy himself with his horse and reminded himself of Brid's theory about the wizards; but then Spar's voice called out again.

"Hal! You can't ignore me."

The knight before him was magnificently clad from head to toe in a gleaming armour, and he only knew it was Caspar by the voice and the horse beneath him. Though draped in a white caparison, he knew it was

Firecracker. Any other war-horse would have stood four square, solid hindquarters slightly crouched, ready to spring forward in attack. But this lean-legged beast was dancing and jittering enough to unsteady the best of horsemen save Caspar, who had that light fluidity of movement that gave him such ease astride a horse. Only three years his younger, his nephew was still small though nearly of age but he had toughened up of late and was remarkably strong for his size.

Hal squinted at the dazzling knight before him, who, surprisingly, bore a lance, sword, mace and throwing knives rather than Caspar's usual weapon of a bow. Held back by taut reins, the horse danced on the spot, ready to charge.

"You knew I would come one day," the knight spoke. "I had to come for her sooner or later and no one will know out here what has happened."

"I'm not afraid of you," Hal shouted.

Brid touched his arm. "There's nothing there."

Hal noted, however, that she was looking straight at the shining knight.

"I'll fight you on whatever terms," the knight challenged.

Hal turned angrily on Brid. "You can see him! You still want him!"

"I never wanted him."

"First Talorcan, then Spar. Is it to be like this forever?" he asked cruelly.

"It's just a trick," she retorted indignantly.

"Yes, it's a trick, but you can see him too, whereas the others see their own fears." Hal's mind raced. "That means you fear Spar in some way. You're fearful, perhaps, that you made a mistake by not choosing him and taking me instead though he was so devoted to you?"

"But he's so young and innocent, Hal. It was more worship than love."

"Yes, but he's growing up. And you always shared so many views."

"But he's like a little brother," Brid protested though Hal thought she sounded insincere. "Just like he is to you."

Ceowulf coughed. His eyes were hard down to the ground and he deliberately avoided looking up at Caspar, who still stood, declaring his challenge. "We must not fight. It's the wizards' trickery and we simply need to undo their magic. None of this is real. You must have faith that it is only their tricks playing with your mind."

"If you can say that, why won't you look up?" Hal demanded.

"The wyvern," Ceowulf choked. "I know it's not real but their eyes induce such fear, such terror, that even if I just imagine it, I may be struck down with fright."

Brid tugged at her plait and stroked her palm with the feathery ends of her hair. "Fear kills. These things might be imaginary but they have induced real fears."

Hal looked at her bitterly. "You love me, Brid. I know that beyond all doubt, but I also know that you wish I were like Spar. Why him? Why him? Anyone else I could bare but not Spar. Why do you make me fight Spar for you? I have no wish to harm him." Hal wouldn't say what also worried him. He had always bettered Spar but what if he the youth grew up and bettered him? Think of the shame being beaten by Caspar, who was, as Brid had said, just like a little brother to him. Put Spar in a coat of armour and he might be the superior knight. Of course, Spar was small but he was skilful.

"Hal!" Ceowulf snapped, still looking down at the ground. "Stop it! Whatever it is you're brooding about now, just stop it."

"Well, you stop it. Face your fears." Hal pointed at the image of Spar that Ceowulf believed to be a wyvern.

The Caldean knight shrugged his broad shoulders. "I can't risk it. I told you, if there's just the tiniest bit of me that believes it might be real, I could be struck down by the terror in its eyes."

"Yes, well, I've just learnt that my fears are true." Hal glowered at Brid. "She wishes she didn't love me. She loves me and yet she despises me. She thinks I'm not enough of a man."

"Stop it!" Abelard's face was drawn and white and he, too, glared at the same spot in the forest, his hand shielding his breast, which four hundred years ago had been pierced by an arrow that had ended his life. "We're certainly lost if the wizards paralyse us like this with our own fears." He looked tired and suddenly horribly old, his hands shaking.

"What is it?" Brid asked softly.

"I'm four hundred and thirty-two years old and I feel it!"

Hal stared from Abelard to Ceowulf and back again, swallowing his own fears as he studied his companions.

Pip was pacing up and down, twanging his bowstring as if trying to make a decision. Hardwin was vomiting on the floor, his entire body shaking. But Cymbeline . . . ? He couldn't guess at her fears. She looked white and withdrawn, twisting a lock of her hair round and round in her finger. It suddenly struck Hal that she looked guilty and was fearing discovery. Like a young child that had broken something and was trembling in anticipation of an adult's wrath, he mused. No, no not that. Not wrath. There would be more a look of defiance in her face if she were braced for a scolding. No, she feared their disappointment.

And Renaud. He looked around for the prince. Renaud was gone!

"The fool!" he exclaimed though in a hushed voice. "We've been such idiots worrying about mirages that we've let him go. We can't lose him. Without Renaud, we may never convince the King of Branwolf's innocence."

"Where's he got to?" Abelard muttered. "He couldn't go too far. Not the prince. Not alone."

"He's got lost," Pip said simply. "He was terrified that he'd get lost and that's what he's gone and done."

"Then we'll search for him," Ceowulf said. "Instantly!"

"You won't find him," Brid said slowly as if still thinking through the events and gradually reaching some conclusion. "We must tackle the wizards directly. Renaud could be right by us but we won't see him because we believe him to be lost."

"This is absurd," Abelard grunted, sitting and rubbing his knees that evidently were beginning to pain him again.

"I know where he is," Hal said quietly. "It's obvious, isn't it?" He looked towards what he saw as the embodiment of his nephew, who still sat astride his horse, sword in hand, ready to fight. "He's there. He's behind all our fears. To find Renaud, we must face them."

He looked at his companions. He understood all their fears well except for Cymbeline's, which he could not guess at. They had to find Renaud and he wondered if, perhaps, she could see him.

Edging towards her, he took her arm and she looked up at him with frightened eyes. "You won't tell, will you? You won't tell him, not father. You mustn't tell him. What'll he do? What'll he do?"

"Cymbeline, no. Your fears are not real; it's the wizards playing tricks with your mind."

"It's all gone wrong," she ranted. "They've taken Tudwal. It's all your fault and what will happen when father finds out? What will I do?" She was wringing her hands in severe distress. "You're going to tell him! It's all your fault! You've done this to us! Ruined everything!"

Pushing the princess behind him and glowering at the shining knight, who bellowed out his challenge, Hal gritted his teeth. Why was he so afraid when it was only Spar?

Abelard was still rubbing at his knees, his face tight with anxious strain. "I can't do it. I know there's nothing there but I can see those Ceolothian archers and I can't make them go away."

"I shall go," Brid said firmly. "It's nothing. It's only Spar."

As she stepped determinedly forward, Abelard grabbed her and pulled her back. "They'll kill y', my lady. Y' can't walk there."

"They're not real."

"They look real," Abelard insisted. "I'd risk anything but y', my lady. I'll not let y' go, not y', Brid, not the Maiden."

Hal agreed. "I shall go," he said firmly and in seconds was mounted. Squeezing his calves into the mare's flank, he urged Secret towards the knight in a slow, unthreatening gait. Surely, he could reason Caspar away. Surely that was possible.

"Spar," he said warmly as he drew alongside, "I have no wish to fight you."

"Of course not," Caspar replied. "You have no wish to fail."

"That's not what I meant," Hal protested.

"You're frightened that you'll be beaten by your little nephew."

"I most certainly am not!" he retorted.

"Well, prepare yourself. You've got her and I want her."

"Spar, I love you like a brother."

"Stand aside for me then," Caspar's voice echoed from

within his visored helmet. "You know I would bring her happiness, whereas you . . ."

"When my soul was able to reach out to hers trapped in the Otherworld, she and I proved our love," Hal proclaimed though his heart misgave him. He knew he loved Brid but was covetous of her love. Right from the beginning, Caspar had wanted her and he had always been suspicious that Brid returned that love. The youth did indeed look fine. Perhaps that was why Brid would never come to his bed, not because of her religious office as the Maiden but, in truth, because she was waiting for Caspar, saving herself for him.

"If you truly love her, you would stand aside. You know I offer her more. Has she not always been happiest in my company?" Caspar argued.

This Hal could not deny. His nephew might not excite Brid's passion but she was more at ease with Spar. Wasn't that truly what mattered? Love was a wayward and reckless emotion that had little to do with happiness. Spar's gentler, devoted ways offered her happiness.

"To the death!" Caspar bellowed, his voice filled with the ferocity of his passion. He turned his horse to prepare his charge and Hal wheeled Secret.

Brid's face twisted with concern.

"I shall be fine," he promised her.

Her eyes pierced his. "Of course, you'll be fine," she snapped. "You'd beat Spar on any field of combat; Secret won't let you down nor the runesword entrusted to you by Morrigwen. No, it's Spar I fear for."

"Ha!" Hal snorted, raised to anger by her words.

He reached the edge of the glade and turned to charge. Secret was heavy and had great power, a horse bred to carry the weight of an armoured knight. Hal wore only light leather leggings, a metalled tunic with studs across his breast and a pair of chain-mail gauntlets to protect his hands. But Secret, though obedient and strong, was slow into action. Lance lowered, Caspar charged at a hectic rate, almost too fast for Hal to think. The speed was confusing, frightening even.

Hal checked the grip on his sword and, for the first time, felt no strength from it. He could not use the mighty runesword against his friend; the power of the Great Mother would not allow it. And though he knew Caspar's image was only illusory, he couldn't fully convince himself of the fact.

Secret slowed in response to his lack of command. He gritted his teeth. He had to do this. Spurring her on, he shouted out the battle cry of his household, "Torra Alta! Torra Alta!"

The lance punched into his ribs and, though he twisted away from the blow, the pain was acute. Doubling up from the impact, he knew, for certain, the pain was real. Clutching his side, he wheeled Secret, turning her sharply to strike before Caspar could ready his lance again.

But the young knight dropped his lance and swung his barbed mace at the point of Hal's shoulder before his own strike could touch his opponent. The pain excruciating, Hal gulped back on his yell and swung his horse away in wise retreat and thundered back to the others.

"Your helm, breastplate and shield, I must have them," he told Ceowulf as he dismounted.

The Caldean didn't hesitate and hastened to free them from his pack while Brid tended Hal's wounds. That she knew where his injuries were made him all the more certain that this image of Caspar was in some way real.

He clenched his fist as Brid strapped his shoulder. The injuries, though painful, would not stop him from fighting – not today at any rate. Tomorrow the muscles would cramp up round the trauma and he would probably be unable to raise his sword-arm but today he would be able to fight.

Finally, he was prepared and struggled back into the saddle. Glaring out through the slit of his visor, he perceived Caspar as somehow smaller, horse and knight entirely visible within the narrow frame of his vision. He pressed Secret forward. Remarkably, she felt better balanced with the extra weight on her back.

Caspar charged. This time the lance skidded harmlessly across Hal's breastplate and, as his opponent galloped by, Hal swung his sword in a mighty arc. Twisting it in his grip, he struck the flat of the blade against the back of Caspar's neck and the weight of the blow was enough to send the youth bowling forward over his horse's ears and rolling to the ground. He landed awkwardly but was still moving.

Hal was acutely aware of Brid's gasp – her fear for Caspar not him. Halting Secret, he dismounted, the steel of the ill-fitting breastplate jarring his movements.

"Nephew, I come to fight you on equal terms. Man to man. Here, now, in front of Brid."

The fallen knight rolled over and leapt to his feet. Without a word, he charged, screaming out the Torra Altan battle cry that was the war-song Hal knew as his own. Hearing his own cry used against him, he faltered and stepped back. Caspar came on, flinging aside his helmet in a show of bravado and contempt.

"You would take everything from me, Hal, my birthright, my woman. Perhaps once I would have stood by and let you do it but not anymore." His sword crashed against Hal's helm, knocking him to his knees.

"Get up and fight," a voice rang in his ear. "Destroy him; he's only an image."

At last, Hal raised himself and his sword and slashed it against Caspar. The metal of his armour split and Hal saw the gory wound but Caspar just kept coming. Hal dropped his sword, braced himself and then wrestled the youth as he slammed into him. Hal was still the better fighter and wholly believed that he could wrestle his nephew any day. But Caspar would not give in and began lashing out with his fists. Hal hit him and then hit him again, harder and harder. His nephew should have been unconscious at the first blow but kept on fighting.

"Just stop!" Hal yelled. "Stop!" Tears were streaming down his cheeks as, again and again, he punched his mail covered fists into the youth's exposed face, smashing the flesh and bone into a featureless pulp; but Caspar would not yield and fought on.

"Stop it! Stop it," Brid cried. "Stop it, Hal! What if this has some effect on the real Spar? What if this image of him draws life from him through the Egg?"Consumed with guilt and confusion, Hal staggered back from Caspar's body only to glance back and see the broken body move, the fingers stretching for the hilt of the runesword. Hal was too slow. Caspar had it. Not even Ceowulf's helm and breastplate gave him any confidence now. He retreated.

"Now what, Brid?" he asked coldly. "You would put Spar before me?"

"You were going to kill him," Brid accused.

"I thought that was what I was meant to do," Hal said edging away, thankful that Caspar did not pursue him. "You said destroy the image. But the more I fought it, the more real it seemed."

"You were killing him!" Brid accused again.

"Look out!" Ceowulf yelled.

His javelin was poised in readiness. Clearly the yelling and fighting had consumed his mind. He hurled his weapon straight at Caspar and the image gave out a horrible shriek like the cry of an eagle, loud, piercing, terrifying and yet full of loss. Then came a thunderous crash as something hugely heavy thumped to the ground and Hal even felt the ground shake.

Caspar was gone and, in his place, a huge scaly monster lay writhing on the ground.

"That's real!" Brid exclaimed with aghast certainty.

Hardwin was shrieking fitfully but Pip had stopped his pacing and, together with Hal, Ceowulf and Abelard, approached the dying beast.

"You have to hit it just in the right spot," Ceowulf explained, examining the bloated beast.

"I thought wyverns had leathery skin and weren't scaly like dragons," Hal said a little dizzily, gasping for breath and stooping and picking up his sword from where it lay discarded amongst the grass.

"There are as many types of dragon and wyvern as there are cats and dogs," the knight said, prodding the beast with his lance and then closing in with his knife.

"It's not dead," Pip breathed in Hal's ear.

"What do you mean, it's not dead? Ceowulf's just pierced its throat."

"Look!" Pip pointed at its belly.

All but Hal leapt back in horror. He stood alone, brandishing his great runesword. For the moment all they could do was stand and stare as the pulse in its silvery belly become a throb and then a huge beating, kicking motion before slowly the skin began to split. First came a trickle of watery red liquid and then the belly erupted and a grey blue twist of gut slithered out. Then came a hand – a man's hand with several rings, one set with two vast red rubies with radiant yellow hearts.

The flesh was grey and partially digested by the wyvern's

acids. Then came an arm and shoulder, clad in a heavy, thickly studded, leather gambeson. Hal gasped. He had at once recognized the emblem of the royal house of Ceolothia. Forgetting the wyvern, he ran forward to heave at the body.

Cymbeline screamed. Then moaned, "Tudwal" before staggering to her knees and fainting.

No one caught Cymbeline as she thumped to the ground but all stared as Hal dragged at the steaming, slime-covered, stinking body. With a final heave, it slithered out and settled face down upon the grass. Panting from his efforts, Hal took a moment to catch his breath before rolling the body over. But it wasn't Tudwal!

He had immediately presumed that the wizards had got to the young prince who had fled their black island by ship, but it wasn't him. While Hal wiped clean his gauntlets on the grass, the others gathered round and stared at the blue-grey face that was slightly twisted and misshapen. One arm was bent back at the elbow, evidently dislocated when the poor man had been swallowed whole by the wyvern. Protruding from his chest was the ornate handle of a knife.

"Who is he?" Pip asked.

"Prince Turquin, heir to all Ceolothia and its riches," Ceowulf said calmly.

Hal was still too flabbergasted to speak. He reached forward to the body and took hold of what everyone was staring at: the gleaming dagger embedded in the prince's chest. He pulled it out and a congealed blob of dark purple blood came with it. The body had evidently been dead a little while.

"Poor Turquin," Brid breathed. "This is not going to help us in King Dagonet's eyes. It's as if someone wants to do away with the entire Ceolothian royal family. Tudwal kidnapped, Cymbeline kidnapped though thankfully rescued, and now poor Turquin murdered. It would leave him only the simpleton, Tullis."

"What do we do?" Abelard asked practically, moving forward to examine the blade. It was short and of white steel, the hilt encrusted with small sunburst rubies and a crest etched into the metal.

"What do you mean, do?" Hal asked, his pulse still throbbing in his throat.

"I mean after we find Renaud."

"Why? Get home as fast as possible, of course. Assuming . . ." Hal looked around anxiously.

"The wizards?" Ceowulf concluded for him.

He nodded. "Yes, the wizards."

"But what about Turquin?" Abelard went on.

"We shall have to bury him and take home his rings as evidence," Brid said decisively. "I know it looks bad. We, whom Dagonet blames for all his woes, we come home bearing the ill news of his heir's death. He will not be best pleased with us," she pointed out. "But at least we have Cymbeline to corroborate the events."

The princess was moaning on the ground, head curled up into her chest, clutching fistfuls of hair and yanking at them in her distress. Brid, who looked so small beside the strong, elegant woman, put her arms round her and hugged her tight. Hal assumed that Cymbeline would push Brid away but instead she curled up like a small child against the priestess, who drew her close to her bosom and rocked her back and forth.

The Princess was wailing in incoherent Ceolothian and it was some minutes before her body stiffened, her grief turning to rage. She clawed her way out of Brid's embrace and, on hands and knees, sobbed her way towards the twisted body. She slumped onto its slimy chest, shrieking, then she sat up and pulled its crooked head round to face her. Hal was confused by the sudden change in her expression.

She sucked in a deep breath and then in a whisper breathed, "Turquin!" She flashed a look back at the rest of them. "But it's Turquin. You said it was Tudwal."

Hal was certain they had not. Quiet tears now ran down Cymbeline's cheeks. There was grief there certainly but none of that gut-tearing distress that they had witnessed earlier. She sat back and pulled at his arm to straighten it but the joint was clearly out of its socket and it sprang back. She whimpered and shrank from the body in alarm.

Hal pulled her away, trying to hide his grimaces as he touched on the slime coating her dress. "I'm sorry, we shouldn't have let you see that."

"How did it happen?" she stammered after a moment, looking in bewilderment at the dead wyvern and her brother's broken body.

Hal shrugged. "Who is to say except the owner of this knife?"

Cymbeline's face paled and her lip trembled. "Murder!" The word slipped unbidden through her lips and Hal saw her horror at the thought.

Carefully, he inspected the knife, noting the insignia of a ram locked horns with a goat stamped into the pommel, before wrapping the blade in cloth and placing it deep inside his pack. He had no doubt that King Dagonet would want to see the blade.

"Let's get him buried. Then we'd better start looking for Renaud," Brid said quietly.

Cymbeline watched silently as they placed her brother in a shallow grave. She then began pacing, her tears already dried but her grief evident. She clutched at her hand that would not stop trembling while the rest deliberated on what was to be done.

"They are certainly playing with us," Brid concluded. "First, they terrify each of us with our worst fears and, just as we learn to conquer those fears, they present us with a real danger that undermines our confidence to judge real from imaginary."

Pip was staring wide-eyed into the forest again, his hand creeping to his sword.

Hal steadied his arm. "There's nothing there," he said but as he touched Pip, he, too, saw the three Vaalakan warriors with their axes swinging above their heads and screeching vile obscenities. He took his hand off Pip and the Vaalakans vanished; he touched him again and they returned.

"I see them," Hal said. "But you need not fear them."

"I don't fear them," Pip retorted over-ardently, the muscles in his cheeks clenching.

"I'll show them, Pip," Hal said kindly. Raising his sword at them he shouted, "Go away!" Gradually they faded though Hal was amazed at how simple it was to be rid of them.

Brid laughed. "Have they gone, Pip?"

"Oh yes! The minute Hal raised his sword they were gone."

She grinned at Hal. "The image went because Pip's fear went. And that went the moment your threatened them because he is certain of your power to vanquish them."

"We must hold hands," Hal suggested, "so that we can all see each others' fears. That way, we can rely on the others to conquer them for us."

"Or perhaps add to them," Brid warned. "Not many people would be undaunted at the sight of Vaalakan warriors."

"Still, it's worth a try. Renaud must be beyond our

fears, hidden behind the illusions, and we must reach him," Hal continued.

They formed a line though Hardwin held back.

"Come on, " Abelard urged, stretching out his callused hand.

"I— I can't," he gibbered. "I can't move. The rats . . ."

Hal swallowed hard. He was not particularly fond of rats but he was confident that Brid would never be irrationally afraid of an animal. As Abelard took hold of one of Hardwin's arms and Hal the other, a rat appeared and ran over Hal's foot. He felt it and shuddered.

"What if the rat's real?" he asked. "We couldn't see the wyvern for our own fears blocking the way but Ceowulf saw it. Does that mean he's frightened of nothing?"

"I shouldn't think so," Brid argued. "I can only guess that the wizards hoped to confuse us all with the sudden arrival of a real threat."

Hal gaped at her. She was talking quite casually while rats swarmed in great waves about her ankles.

"Are the rats real?" Hal asked again and their number suddenly doubled.

"No, of course not," Brid laughed. "It's just an image of three rats repeated over and over. You'll see if you look hard enough. There's a big rat with a pale tail, a black-faced rat and a thin long one."

Hal saw she was right and just as he realized it, the rats vanished and the stirring ground was still again.

Hardwin's clutch became rigid in Hal's grip and then the Pisceran laughed. "They've gone! It worked."

"But this still won't help us reach Renaud," Brid admitted as they retreated to think after their experiment. "Between all of us we must have an inexhaustible supply of fears. The wizards could keep us busy with them for an eternity and we would never reach Renaud."

"I hadn't thought of that," Hal mused.

"Surely, we're all afraid of being lost. It's only natural," Abelard said.

Brid nodded. "Yes, but not irrationally so. I've never been unable to find my way home."

"But y' can imagine the horror of being lost?" Abelard asked.

All nodded at this.

"Well, if Renaud is lost, perhaps the best way to find him is to get lost too," the archer suggested.

"It sounds dangerous," Brid warned.

"It does indeed! Too dangerous!" Ceowulf advised against the plan.

"But we've got to find him." Abelard was still enthusiastic about his idea. "If we stay together, we have every chance of defeating the wizards."

"Absolutely!" Hal exclaimed. "I'm not going to be beaten by three ghosts, even if they are the ghosts of wizards. My mind is stronger than theirs."

"Perhaps, but I don't think we should all go," Brid said quietly. "Not Hardwin and not Cymbeline."

"You think I'm too weak-minded?" Hardwin asked.

"I'm sorry; we've no time now for niceties," Brid apologized with kindness, "but, yes, I think you are."

"Oh!" he said but more with relief than affront.

"Nor you, Abelard," Brid continued.

"Me!"

"Yes! I know it sounds rough. You have withstood so much through so many years but you have seen too many terrible things. You know better than any of all the horrors there are in this universe. Besides someone has to stay behind to look after Hardwin and Cymbeline and we can't very well leave Pip to do that."

"No, we can't, can we?" Hal agreed.

"Well, I agree with that," Abelard conceded. "And y're right. Youth has very little fear. They know too little to be fearful and have too few responsibilities."

Pip sniffed but said nothing, evidently concerned that if he objected, he might sentence himself to the ignominy of being left behind.

Hal, Brid, Ceowulf and Pip gripped hands.

Before Hal there suddenly stood an army of Vaalakans led by Caspar and a line of bishops of the New Faith bearing flaming torches. Purposefully, the four companions advanced.

"They're not real," Pip said brightly though clearly focusing on the Vaalakans. "Like the rats, they're just the same three men whose image is repeated over and over again. And so are the bishops." Gradually the ranks of men faded. "But there's only one Master Spar," Pip pointed out though without fear. "Does that mean he is real?" he asked.

"He's not real," Brid said firmly, though she couldn't quite disguise the tremble in her voice.

"You're afraid of Spar!" Hal said in accusation.

"So are you," Brid confirmed his self-doubts.

"That's absurd, why would either of you be . . . ?" Ceowulf's voice trailed off. "Of course! He holds Necrönd. Spar, is in truth the most dangerous being alive."

Pip snorted. "That's quite ridiculous. He would never do anything to harm any of you."

"Not deliberately. Of course not. But unwittingly . . ." Brid said.

"It's not real," Pip insisted.

"How do you know?" Hal demanded. "He might have escaped from the Ovissians and fallen foul of the wizards, who are now manipulating him and, through the Egg, doing all manner of harm. It's at least plausible."

"If you think that you don't know Master Spar though he's your own kin," Pip said indignantly. "He would never turn against any one of us. He has no cause."

"Doesn't he though?" Hal said, still believing that Caspar was capable of anything to finally win Brid's love.

"I'll prove he's not real," Pip insisted and marched straight up to the point of the lance that was lowered at him and touched it flippantly. The image of Caspar remained. Pip frowned and then went up to the horse and hit it hard across the nose. It didn't stir. Hal laughed and the image vanished. The horse certainly wasn't Firecracker. Cracker would have struck out with tooth and hooves under such treatment.

Hal ran forward to stand by Pip, who was staring into the forest beyond. There was no sign of anyone or anything other than tangled vegetation knitted into deep mats beneath the rustling canopy of the trees.

"Renaud!" Pip called out loud.

"Hush!" Brid warned. "Now let's do as Abelard suggested and imagine ourselves lost." She released Hal's hand and smiled. "I could never be lost with you."

Hal closed his eyes, trying to think of a time when he had been lost. He couldn't think of one and opened his eyes again to see the others still standing there, looking around them. He closed them again and remembered his mother, Lady Elizabetta, pacing around the walls of Torra Alta soon after his father, Baron Brungard, had died. Elizabetta had been arguing with Branwolf. After that he had gone with his mother to Farona to a large mansion at the edge of the city. He hadn't been physically lost – he knew his way around – but he had felt alone without Spar.

New faces had examined him and constantly told him he misbehaved or did not dress correctly or had improper manners. He found the Faronans fastidious in their ways, their manners prissy. In Torra Alta, a feast was a feast where you ate well. In Farona, one was supposed to pick and choose, savour titbits and dainties and feel starved. In Farona, a feast meant pretence at a poor appetite in case you stretched your doublet or spilt wine on your tunic. He had been laughed at and made to feel uncomfortable for enjoying his food.

All that summer he had suffered until finally his mother, who loved him dearly though was never good at openly expressing her emotions, agreed to return to Torra Alta. That homecoming had been one of the happiest moments in Hal's life. Oh, the relief to be with Spar again, charging around on their shaggy ponies rather than practising the latest courtly bow or wearing a handkerchief in the correct manner.

To be in the Faronan court was to be lost. The fear that he could return to such an uncomfortable situation overwhelmed him. He opened his eyes and could no longer see the others. Suddenly, he was outside the buttressed curtain walls of a castle, the battlements of a blocky keep just visible beyond. He could hear the cries of battle within and the thunder of jousting horses.

He marched stiffly across the drawbridge, aware of his travel-worn clothes, the hem of his bearskin muddied where it had dragged in the ground, and entered a bustling square where he was jostled and shoved. Men clad in armour brushed him aside as they strode with confidence towards their great mounts. Though tall, his dark looks striking, few took any note of him beyond the briefest sneering glance. He felt acutely self-conscious.

Feeling foolish, he realized he had no money, had no idea where he was and was suddenly famished. He looked around at the bustle of a castle, which rang with the constant clank of metal and the grunts of sparring men and grinned to himself. Knowing that soldiers were invariably keen to make a wager, he knew a sure way to make money. He could beat any of these men.

"Come!" he cried in his best Ceolothian. "Who will take me on? I have three fine hunting knives of the best steel, tempered in Ophidian fires, that say I can better any one of you knights in swordplay."

"A mad man!" someone laughed.

Meaning to impress them, Hal drew his sword but then looked at it in horror. It was not the bright runesword carved with chilling runes, not the great broad blade of white steel with its core so hard and its edge so sharp that it would shatter metal. He was holding his old sword that was now a little rusty with neglect and felt light and flimsy in his grip.

"You won't so much as scratch a breastplate with that needle," they mocked him.

"Use it with some thread to mend your hauberk, instead," they laughed.

Hal barely heard them as he gapped at his sword. He felt intensely vulnerable without the runesword. All this time it was the sword that had given him courage, given him the real skill to fight his enemies; and now he was without it. He shook himself. This was all but a nightmare conjured by the wizards. None of this was real. But, still, he could not rid himself of the images and soon realized he was trapped in this unreal world.

Then, through the busy crowd, he glimpsed her.

"Brid!" he shouted "Brid!" His fears were growing. She did not turn but walked away at the side of a tall knight in black armour. Enraged, Hal fought his way through the crowd and barged in front of the man. "Unhand my woman!"

The knight laughed. "You'll have to fight me for her."

"Gladly!" Hal bellowed but the knight merely laughed the more before kicking him full in the groin and sending him sprawling into the dirt.

But this wasn't real, he groaned to himself. He mustn't let himself be fooled.

Brid was looking at him with begging eyes. "Hal, save me! Don't let them take me like this."

Hal screwed up his eyes, trying to think what he must do. He had to break the spell; they had to find Renaud.

"Renaud!" he called, long and loud. "Renaud!"

The crowd drew away from him as he shouted louder and louder until, presently, a dozen foot-soldiers, directed by a knight on a huge, dappled grey, surrounded him. They stripped him of his rusty sword and all his knives and dragged him through the streets to a small green where a dozen stocks warned him of what was to come.

They shoved him onto his knees, bruising his throat as they forced his neck down onto the plank. Held by his hair, he could not escape as they clapped the bar down over his wrists and neck. Someone pissed over his head. One or two children laughed and then he was alone. He yelled in rage until his throat was sore before, at last, he fell silent and considered his situation.

He didn't know if any of this were real, if the Brid he had seen were the real Brid or the Brid of his imagination, but certainly the exquisite pain was cramping his arms and neck was far too genuine. He must relax and keep calm. Struggling would only make it worse. He closed his eyes and imagined he was lying in bed but to no avail; castle life continued around him, few paying him more than a cursory glance and it seemed an age before night-fall. Even then no one came to free him.

It was a long cold night and he kept his eyes screwed

up tight, trying to blot out the sleeping world around him. He was lost, deeply lost in an all too real world of the imagination. Morning came, along with the local children, who laughed in delight and picked up handfuls of mud from which they carefully fashioned mud-castles on his pinned shoulders.

He wanted to scream but instead sang ballads within his head to try and blot the discomfort from his mind. Then he stiffened and stared. Another man was being dragged to the stocks opposite.

"Renaud! Renaud!" he shouted. At least he had found him.

The prince looked across at him, his eyes wild with fear. "Hal, get me out of here," he begged.

"Just keep calm," Hal advised. "They'll let us out shortly and then we'll just walk out of this castle and back into the forest."

Renaud whimpered and whined, which made the discomfort all the harder to bear, and it was late morning before anyone brought them food. Hal rejoiced. He thought this was it, that they were freed, but he was roped while he ate and drank and allowed just a minute to squat in the gutter before he was hauled back to the stocks.

He twisted his neck up and swore. Someone else was being jammed into the neighbouring stocks.

"Master Hal!" Pip greeted him with remarkable good humour. "You've found Prince Renaud! Can we will ourselves out of here now?"

Hal tried. He tried all the rest of that day until Pip's humour was gone and Renaud was sobbing. Then Ceowulf appeared. It took four men to ram him onto his knees and force him down until the stocks were closed about his neck and wrists.

"This isn't real," Ceowulf kept telling himself as the

children tied ribbons in his hair and an old woman sloshed a bucket of water into his face. When they eventually tired of their sport, the knight twisted his head and growled at Hal. "This was a bad idea."

"Where's Brid?" Hal demanded, no longer caring about his own discomfort. "We're all here stuck in these unreal stocks except for Brid."

"I think they're real," Pip said quietly.

"Don't be daft. The castle's not real," Hal retorted.

"What castle?" Ceowulf demanded. "I can see only a farmhouse."

"No, a town, the houses all timber and painted red and white." Pip looked about him.

"But we can all see and feel the stocks, can't we?" Hal asked.

They all grunted and nodded in agreement and Hal's heart raced.

"I told you it's real," Pip moaned. "We were just tricked into coming here."

Hal was deeply concerned. "But where's Brid?"

Ceowulf had no answer but nodded at the centre of the green. "Brid isn't here but they are! And they're real, aren't they?"

Hal followed his gaze and blinked. Suddenly there appeared midst a circle of lean naked goblins, three wizards hunched over a cauldron.

The castle was gone, the crowds were gone but the wizards remained.

CHAPTER FOUR

A scream of despair exploded from Caspar's throat as he thrashed in the tossing waves of the sea.

"Perren, no!" he yelled though he knew his voice could not carry back across the divide between life and death. "Leave her be!"

The thought of what harm the maddened stonewight might inflict on May drove Caspar to the point of frenzy but there was still nothing he could do. Perren's mad touch and plea for water had surely caused this distortion in Necrönd's magic and plunged him into the depths of a sea in the Otherworld. And what of May? He feared that Perren may have sucked the blood out of her and she was lying in the desert, a ragged hulk of skin and bones for the buzzards to squabble over.

He kicked and thrashed on the surface of the water, desperate to get back to life though he could see he was trapped. Already, he was aware of the sense of eternity around him. In hope, he strained up to see over the tossing waves, his lungs still screaming with the pain of the deathly cold air that fed them.

The sea surged and swelled, pushing him up until he glimpsed distant land. But that was not his route to salvation. For as far as he could see in all directions, sea-beasts thrashed in their thousands on the surface, leaping and crying for Necrönd, wailing to get home. But like him, they remained here in the soup of banished life.

He tried to keep calm and think. There must be something he could do to help himself. Firstly, he wondered how he had been in the desert and yet, here in this parallel world of spirit, he was in the sea. Then he remembered struggling through the desert and trudging over crisp beds of cracked salt and lumps of stone, which carried patterns of sea fish imprinted in them. He had never seen so many fossils before and surmised that the desert had once been seabed. None of that helped and he was certain that, unless someone or something sought him out with the Egg and drew him out of this thrashing brew of life, he was stuck here forever.

The thought sapped his strength and he sank back into the cold, lifeless water, coiling down through the desperate, thrashing animals, down and down into the depths until he bumped against the bottom. Here, forever! Hopelessness consumed him. Gone was life; gone was everything that mattered: this was his entire existence. There was no point in trying anymore.

He lay there, fearful and terrified, his mind crazed by the impossible notion of forever. The awareness grew and the grey cloud of empty despair overwhelmed him until he thought his head would explode.

The loneliness was everything; here he was outside the unity of the cycle of life. Other animals, giant squid, great whales, a unicorned shark, lay with him, their misery as plain as his own. At least, when he had been on the surface, struggling to get home, he had possessed the will to fight; that had been so much better than this void of emotion. At least, on the surface, there was hope. Hope was everything.

If he were nearer the Egg than any other creature, he

stood a chance; if May, perchance, picked up the Egg, she might open the gateway home to him. He lifted his head and stretched a hand upwards, ready to fight on.

But if May were eaten by the monster Perren had become, who then could release him? His hand sunk down and his head drooped. But there was always hope. If he kept on struggling, maybe not this day nor tomorrow nor this year but maybe in a thousand years from now someone would put their hand on the Egg and draw him out. They might rescue him so long as he was closest. He must swim and never lose hope because, surely, to be rescued in a thousand years' time was better than remaining lost forever. Forever was beyond thousands upon thousands upon millions of years; something unimaginable. Someone would have to find him. He wasn't meant to be here.

Outrage against the injustice of it fired his will and he began to kick upwards. Hope was rekindled. What if he shouted?

"May!" His yell exploded into a foam of bubbles. "May, find me!"

But she might be dead. And why should she look for him when he had spurned her? Even here in the depths of the Otherworld, the pain of his jealousy bit deep into his heart. But if May couldn't help him, who then? All that was left were Perren and the animals. It was ridiculous that any of them might understand what had happened and yet some part of him cried out for his horse. Firecracker had never let him down. Cracker was the only thing that he truly owned and perhaps that bond might be strong enough to reach across the divide. And even if all the others were dead, he was certain that Firecracker had the strength to survive.

"Cracker!" he yelled. "Cracker, hear me! Help me!"

He stretched up for the light, grasping the spray-filled air, only to be knocked back down again by a vast tail thrashing on the surface. But this time he was not so easily defeated. He had faith in his horse. Firecracker, of all of them, must hear him. He had always had the understanding that animals were far more aware of the Egg than humans. Kicking hard, he swam close to the huge bulk of a horned whale and scrambled over it, too small to be felt through its smooth, tough skin, and climbed into the air. The waves washed around his thighs and the air was cold but at least he achieved something.

From the back of the whale, he stretched up higher than the others and called to his horse, "Cracker! Cracker! I'm here. Find me!"

On and on he called, aware that his hope was crazy, that Firecracker would never comprehend the situation even if he could hear him. It was madness but his horse was his last hope, and he must cling to that otherwise there was nothing.

Looking up, he stared at the vast globe of Necrönd. Suddenly, a burst of light flashed out from its surface. Like sheet lightning, it illuminated the sky and snagged through the clouds before striking the distant shore.

"No! No!" Caspar wailed at the huge orb above. He had hoped the burst of light was reaching out for him. "I'm here! Cracker!"

His heart stopped as he watched a ghostly stream of white vapour rush overhead and curve up towards the Egg. In its wake trailed a dark storm that formed a spearhead and slipped through the jagged black crack that marred the orb's creamy, veined surface. His head throbbed with pain and he sank back down in despair.

*

May screamed. All had been blank; sight, sound and touch gone from her senses. Now everything came back in a rush. She was awake and spluttering. Water!

There was water everywhere, falling out of the sky as if a giant bucket was being emptied onto her. The stone-wight flung her aside and began guzzling it, running his hands through it and drinking madly until his stomach bulged. He retched, spuming out a greyish liquid, before immediately beginning to drink again. May spluttered and choked and crawled aside, her leg cramped solid with pain.

The bone was whole. It would bare her weight though her muscles screamed in agony if she tried to bend it. She knew from helping Morrigwen nurse the youths in Torra Alta after sparring practice that the soft tissue damage of a deep bruise could be more painful than many types of break.

She looked for the animals. Runa was tugging at her to get up though Trog had fled from the unnatural cascade of water pouring from the sky. For all she knew, a hole in the heavens had opened up. The water that ran down her face was salty. She shook herself, thinking all the time that she must get herself to safety for the sake of her unborn child; Talorcan's child. Though she had lost Caspar's love because of it, her unborn child meant everything to her.

She pushed herself up, Runa whimpering at her feet and nuzzling at her thigh. Plucking at the animal's ear, she stared in disbelief at a shallow pool, the water's edge lapping at her feet.

She looked around her. Spar! She couldn't see him anywhere.

She might be furious with him for his treatment of her, but that didn't mean she didn't care. Of course, he had never treated her right, saying one minute that he was devoted to her and the next minute drooling after Brid. She could not believe that he was so callous with her emotions simply because he was a baron's son and she, effectively, a servant. True, the Baron was her guardian but, for all that, she and Pip were still the orphans of a woodcutter – and woodcutters, she knew, had a very low status amongst a castle of archers and horse trainers; they rated somewhere close to shepherds. But it was not because of her status that he treated her with so little respect. It was simply that he was young, artless in love and confused about his emotions.

She would have understood if it had been Hal. Hal was driven by sheer red-blooded lust, something he took no pains to control. Lust was more blatant, more understandable, and for that more honest and so more forgivable. Caspar was motivated by a deeper, more spiritual love.

"Spar!" she shouted again. "Spar, where are you?"

She loved him and always would love him. She had waited so long for him and then, at the last, just before he was about to prove his love for her, she had ruined all by lying with Talorcan.

"Spar!" She called again and plunged into the pool. The wolfling howled in dismay, charging in after her. May found herself sinking to her knees in the sand but she still struggled to get to Caspar, who lay face down in the brackish water.

"Spar, wake up! Get up!" she yelled in dismay, rolling him onto his back.

He didn't move.

"Perren, help me!" she cried, finding her injured leg made it impossible for her to pull Caspar clear. Trog succumbed to her cries for help and dashed forward to tug at Caspar's collar, managing to move him a little way. But it wasn't enough.

"Perren, help!" May shouted, hoping that the stonewight had regathered his senses. But he looked at her like a drunken man, his eyes rolling. Only then did she notice that he held Necrönd. The fool was summoning water out of the Otherworld. What madness! "Perren, we need your help!"

Clutching, Caspar she put her head to his chest. He wasn't breathing! His skin was the colour of chalk and his eyes, unseeing, unblinking, stared up into the brilliant sky.

"Spar!" she cried.

He couldn't have drowned that quickly. Something else, surely, had happened to him. Perhaps Firecracker had caught him with his hoof as he galloped away or, more likely, Perren had clubbed him with that great fist when he had struggled for Necrönd. But whatever it was, Caspar needed help and she must act.

She screamed frantically at Perren to help but clearly the salt water was doing nothing to restore his faculties. He sat tossing the Egg up and down in the air, giggling like a child, while repeating the word, "Water!!" over and over as if he had discovered the key to life itself.

At last, it struck May that Perren was holding the Egg and clumsily wielding its power. Perhaps the magic he manipulated had harmed Caspar. "Where is he? What have you done with him?" she demanded.

"Done with him, little storyteller?" Perren giggled. "Why nothing! He is safe, quite safe forever in the Egg. He fell in. He was about to summon beasts, all manner of beast, to drive me away when all I wanted was water."

"Give him back to me," May begged, not fully understanding what had happened.

"I haven't got him. He's in the water."

"This is madness!" May screamed. "What have you done to him?"

"He's in the water, in the seas of the Otherworld, living like a fish, stranded there until someone can summon him back."

"I don't understand!" May cried.

"I don't understand, I don't understand," Perren mocked her. "You're too stupid. He's in the Otherworld at the bottom of the ocean. I can feel his presence in the water."

"Get him out!" May screamed wildly, wading out into the pool.

"I can't! I don't know how," Perren laughed and sat down in the water, splashing like a rebellious child that had been specifically forbidden from splashing.

"Give me the Egg!" she commanded.

Perren shook his head. "Oh no! You cannot have it. You will stop the water. I need it. You were all prepared to let me die in the desert."

"You were prepared to drink my blood," May pointed out in retaliation. "Perren, please! Save Spar! Give me the Egg so that I can find him."

"Nope!" The stonewight's stupid grin remained fixed and, like a stubborn child knowing that he had his parents in his power, he clutched Necrönd possessively to his chest.

May knew at once that the stonewight needed delicate handling. Knowing that, while they both stood in the water, he could read her mind, she forced a cloud of empty thought into her head and retreated from the pool. With relief, she decided that he had been too preoccupied with the joy of splashing to trouble himself with what was in her mind.

Once she stood in the dry sand, she said with artfully, "Tell me what stories you feel in the water. Tell me the stories, Perren."

His eyes widened. "There are so many – so much

suffering and hatred. The story of the unicorn hunted for the prize of its horn and the glossiness of its white coat and simply because it competed with the sheep for grazing."

"Let me see!" May cried excitedly, her eyes bright. "I cannot feel the stories in the water like you can but maybe I could see them through the Egg."

Perren's eyes glinted back enthusiastically. "Maybe. A story is far better shared. You were always so good at listening to my stories." He gave her a guileless grin and unexpectedly tossed Necrönd to her.

She caught it lightly in her left hand, closing her mind against the sudden rush of thoughts, remembering instantly the cold dread she had felt before on touching Necrönd. Perren, it seemed, had been so focused on the water alone that he had not summoned any dangerous beast into the world.

Hastily, to avoid touching it with bare flesh, she rolled the Egg into the bandaged crook of her right arm. Whilst fleeing Torra Alta, she had managed to muster the presence of mind to summon a powerful male unicorn and she prayed she could still find the same self-control to guide her thoughts now. She must not think of wolves, she told herself, fighting away the image of thousands of wolves pouring out of the Otherworld. Or worse the dreaded wolfman who had stalked her all the way to Ceolothia!

"Do you see them?" Perren demanded

"Oh yes!" she exclaimed enthusiastically, her heart racing as she noted that the great stony creature was slowly sinking up to his calves in the waterlogged sand. She prayed he would have trouble extracting himself.

"What do you see?" he asked eagerly.

May tried not to think as the picture of fanged hooded wolves swam through her mind. "Er . . . I see unicorns," she lied, noting that the fall of water from the sky had now almost abated. Perren was already thigh deep in the sand and, deciding that now she could risk re-entering the pool, she splashed towards Caspar lying at the edge of the briny waters.

Perren wailed furiously, grunting in his efforts to wade towards her, but the more he struggled, the deeper he sank.

She flung herself down beside Caspar, all images of the wolves gone from her mind; she thought only of him. For once, focus was easy and she didn't stop to question her competence to touch the Egg and summon him back from the Otherworld.

But then she snatched her hand away. Something had changed within the Egg. It was behaving differently from the last time she had touched it. Her thoughts had been instantly sucked towards a thrashing swirl of life and she retreated fearfully, hastily stuffing the Egg into its silver casket around Caspar's neck and snapping the lock shut. She clutched her hand to her pounding chest and tried to calm herself.

Evidently Perren had opened up a great rent in the channels of magic and Caspar had fallen through; she must not do the same. She glanced anxiously at the stonewight, who was bellowing with rage but had not yet managed to move. Somewhat calmed, she turned her attention to Caspar whose face was a ghostly white. She must at least get his body out of the sun until she could figure out how to call his spirit back from the Otherworld.

She couldn't do it. They were so close now to the hills and the dark shadows at their base but she was weak with exhaustion, her right arm virtually useless and her leg screaming with pain. Firecracker! She needed Firecracker but where was he? No doubt he had fled from the madness to the rocky bluff and into the shaded hills in search of water and food. All she could do was drag Caspar inch by inch, leaving a deep furrow in the powdery sand behind them.

"Treacherous woman! You've stolen the water," Perren shrieked after her.

May feared that the stonewight would soon struggle free and so she heaved at Caspar's inert body with all her strength. But she was small and light and her grip was failing. The only positive thing was that the movement helped clear the stiffness in her leg and it flexed more easily now.

Perren thrashed at the water and bellowed like an enraged bull but he only sank deeper. Trembling with exhaustion, May decided she must try the Egg again. Pushing back her hair, which had rapidly dried into salt-caked spikes, she knelt down over the casket.

She flicked open the casket and, filling her mind with the image of Caspar, which was easy to do since his quiet face stared up at her, she tentatively put one finger on the white marbled surface of the Egg. She leapt back in horror as a snout snatched up at her and, before the image vanished, a sharp curving fang snagged her thumb and a trickle of blood ran down over her palm. Trembling fearfully, she didn't know what she must do.

Wrapping her hand in a strip of cloth torn from her ragged dress, she forced herself to flex the fingers of her damaged arm. Her pain made her feel sick and at last the tears of self-pity began to roll down her cheeks. She rocked back and forth on her knees, still stooping over Caspar. Was she never going to get him back?

Trog's wet nose nudged at her elbow and she looked at him forlornly, her eyes stinging in the heat. The wolf stood by her, casting its shadow over her and whimpering at her to move.

"Go on! Save yourselves. Get out of here," May croaked at them.

She wondered that she should go herself for the sake of the unborn child but she could not. She could not leave Caspar trapped for eternity in the Otherworld and nor could she leave his body to crisp and blister in the heat of the sun.

The dog nudged her more insistently.

"What is it?" she demanded and then felt the soft sand quiver beneath her knees. She looked up. "Fern!" She had forgotten all about the funny little man because she hadn't thought him capable of helping her but, now, here he was, leading Firecracker.

"Fern," she croaked in excited relief. "Fern! Oh Fern, help, please help me!"

He came running, the horse trotting alongside.

May thought she had never been so pleased to see anyone in all her life. "We've got to get him up onto Cracker."

"What's happened?" Fern asked. "I waited just as Master Spar told me. Waited and waited! Then black demons swallowed the desert and then a fountain gushed from a clear sky and now Master Spar!" He sniffed at him cautiously. "He's dead!"

"He's not dead," May insisted. "I can feel his pulse."

Fern frowned and put his tufty-haired head against Caspar's chest and then sniffed at his breath but he shook his head. "Something to do with the nerves. I've seen many an animal twitch for some while after death. He's dead. He's not breathing and he smells dead; the truth is always in the scent." He sighed regretfully. "That is a great sadness."

"He's not dead!" Though her mouth was dry and she kept casting back over her shoulder for signs of Perren wading out of the quicksand, May tried to explain as briefly as possible about slipping through the channels of magic. How could she make this creature understand that Caspar's spirit had somehow fallen into the Egg? She had little hope that such a simple fellow would understand. "He's alive, believe me. Now just help!"

He looked indignant at her over-impatient tone. "I understand better than you, dear girl." Fern sniffed. "You forget. I have been there and returned through the channels of magic. We used the Pipe. There is more to this than you can imagine. These things are tricky, I know. We needed Brid to use it properly for us but she's not here now. We must find someone else. Come on! What are we waiting for? Where's Perren? We need him to lift Master Spar onto Firecracker."

"He's stuck in the sand," May began to explain, tucking her bruised arm inside her shirt to support it. "He's dangerous; driven mad by dehydration."

Fern shrugged. "Never did trust the fellow. Ate meat, you know." He looked down at Caspar, his head tilted sympathetically to one side. "He was the only soul on Earth that I cared about, you know," he said in confidence. "We'll just have to lift him up ourselves."

May couldn't see how. Eventually, they rolled Caspar onto his bearskin, which they tied to a length of rope and strapped that to Firecracker's saddle so that they might drag the body. Soon they were at the base of the hills and in the cool shade.

May looked back and saw that Perren had all but disappeared into the sand. She blotted from her mind the thought of his inevitable death. He had been so childishly content in the water but that would soon evaporate and, stuck fast, he would crumble little by little until he was indistinguishable from the sand.

She felt no sympathy for him. He had attacked her and sent Caspar to the Otherworld. She gave him no more thought as she concentrated on finding a smooth way for Firecracker to drag his master into the mountains, though she knew that, whatever she did, Caspar's body would be heavily bruised by the journey. At last, they reached the spring where Caspar had left Fern.

Water! Trees! Cool shade! The relief overwhelmed her and for a moment she just stood in the trickling stream, watching the clear water bubble around her cracked boots and smiling as it seeped in through the holes. She then ripped off a strip of cotton from her shirt, dipped it in the pool and trickled water into Caspar's mouth. It had no effect. She tried cupping the water with her hands and pouring it over him but still he did not react.

"Once we're rested, we must continue to head east and pray we find help," May told Fern. But who could help them?

After a short sleep, she was stronger and soon worked out that, if they tied Caspar's wrists together and dragged the rope over the saddle, she could pull on it while Fern helped ease Caspar's body over the horse's back.

"Trog!" she commanded, once they had manoeuvred Firecracker into position ready to haul up Caspar's body. "You can help." She dangled the rope in front of the dog's mouth. "Pull!"

He gripped the rope in his teeth and shook it furiously as if he were killing a snake.

"No, Trog. No!" Her irritation with the dog lent her strength and she heaved and tugged. Finally, the dog seemed to understand what she wanted and pulled hard with her until Caspar's body was draped over Firecracker's back. The horse snorted but seemed to understand that his master was hurt and stood still throughout the awkward manoeuvre.

Fearing that the casket would slip from Caspar's neck, May carefully placed it into one of Firecracker's saddlebags. After about a mile, she realized her mistake. Something was following them. Glistening white shapes marched along the edge of the flat valley. Weaving in and out of the silver birch trees that grew well in the shallow soil. The ghostly shapes appeared like dots of moving light. Squinting, she wondered if the desert sun had damaged her eyes, but when they drew closer, she saw the long lean legs of horses and fine horns sprouting from proud heads. Unicorns! But their horns were only half the length of the unicorn she had summoned to carry her across Ceolothia and their necks were less muscly, lacking the arching crest of the stallion. So, this was a herd of female unicorns.

It must be Firecracker summoning them. Firecracker was in possession of the Egg and his thoughts were summoning a most beautiful herd of ladies for himself. In other circumstances May might have found it amusing but now everything was far too serious. She moved to retrieve the Egg only to find that Firecracker would not let her near his flank. He lashed out, though his hoof only snagged in her skirt and did not connect with flesh.

Fearing for her baby, she leapt back. She could not risk injury.

The stallion snorted and whickered, tossing his head excitedly, and May feared that Caspar's inert body might slip from the saddle onto the dusty rocks. Worse, the herd of unicorns was drawing closer. She was amazed at Firecracker's skill at summoning them, remembering how hard it had been for her to focus on a specific beast. He had done it immediately, his strength of focusing so strong. Presumably, the lack of imagination helped, May decided. But what was she to do now?

She felt so unutterably alone and helpless yet the responsibility of protecting Necrönd, rescuing Caspar and keeping herself well for her baby's sake was all on her shoulders. Caspar was helpless and all she had for comfort were Trog, Runa and Fern – who was little more than an animal. She must take control. It seemed so ridiculous that, out here in the wilderness of Oriaxia, with a horse, a dog, a wolf and a woodwose for company, that her actions, her ability to cope with their predicament would have repercussions on the rest of the world. If only she could just crawl into a cave and stay there forever.

She reined in her self-pity. Something was wrong, or rather more wrong than it had been before. Firecracker's ears were laid flat and he kicked out at the thin air behind him. The unicorns pressed close and May was acutely aware of their hot steamy breath and their whinnies of fear. Something else was out there, lurking waiting. A predator! Instinct told her at once that *he* was back on her trail, stalking them; the wolfman, as Caspar had called him.

Her fears grew as Fern climbed onto a boulder and stood, neck upstretched, his nose twitching.

"Cracker is summoning beasts," May said with as much casualness as she could muster. She did not want to alarm Fern and frighten him into running off since she was painfully aware that she relied on him to control the horse. "Fern, you must get the Egg from Cracker. I can't get near him."

"I can't touch it!" Fern squealed. "I can't! It sucked Master Spar in. What will it do to me?" The woodwose's nose twitched rapidly. "And *he* is here. If I touch it, he might suddenly notice me and grab me. I can't risk it."

May had to do something. She was no horsewoman

but surely Firecracker was like any other creature. A bribe might do it. She still had one of those curious pancakes that they had brought in Lonis. They were horribly sweet in her opinion but Fern craved them so perhaps Firecracker would be tempted by them. Her notion was right. As she dipped into her pack, the horse snuffled at the back of her hand and then, in his normal belligerent manner, thumped his muzzle at her in his impatience.

It was a mistake; the unicorns scattered as the horse's thoughts were diverted from them. She could hear the echo of their cries; she could smell their fear. They were running and she knew at once they were running from wolves that had crossed the divide, as Firecracker's concentration was broken. She stuffed the cakes up against Firecracker's muzzle. "Fern, quick, snatch the saddle-bag!"

"No, you!" He was eyeing the pancake in her outstretched hand.

The sound of thundering hooves rang through the hills only now they were growing louder, closer. May shrank back in as they suddenly thundered into view. Within moments, fully formed unicorns were pressing close, their breath hot and steamy, marching like a flanking escort alongside, controlled by the hot-blooded stallion.

Then shrieking, one stumbled to its knees, its great horn twisting and stabbing at a liquid shadow. The other unicorns did not scatter as before but, slaves to the stallion, they were compelled to stand their ground. May trembled, terrified as she stared into thin air, waiting for some monster to attack.

Who would save her now? Amaryllis was gone . . . Yet there was some part of her, some small illogical part that told her he was near. She put her hand on her belly that was now swollen and taut. Perhaps it wasn't him but the life of his child that she sensed. She shrugged. If only Caspar had been so impassioned by her.

Fern finally managed to whisk the saddlebag from the horse's back and let it slump to the ground.

"Careful!" May exclaimed.

The unicorns all turned as one, horns lowered, as the Egg lay on the ground, unclaimed. There was a moment's pause as May looked to them and then back at the Egg before the unicorns made a mass stampede to claim it. It was only at her feet but she was so horrified at the speed at which they moved that it took her a further moment to reach out and grab the bag. They still charged, a tightening circle of frosted lances aimed at her.

"Go!" she yelled.

The sudden silence was chilling even in the noon heat. She blinked. Amongst the light hoofprints and swirling dust something glinted. She stepped towards it and delightedly snatched up a single horn. It was marvellously beautiful like a glittering icicle.

Firecracker stood sniffing the air, looking around him in disappointed bewilderment. May breathed a long sigh and, tucking the horn into her belt, hurriedly slipped the Egg back into the casket chained around Caspar's neck.

But her relief was short-lived. The unicorns had vanished but gone also was their protection. Within the silver birches shadows moved. Her mind raced. Clearly it was too dangerous to wield the Egg but there must be something she could do. She toyed with the unicorn's horn, surely a thing of great power. She pondered. The unicorn was a creature of the Great Mother, its horn the symbol of its power. Perhaps she could use it to summon help.

Remembering Caspar's tale of how Brid had once summoned the Mother's help using the bone from a horse's jaw and striking it into the earth, she thought she might do the same with the horn. But wait! That had not been all. It had to be at a place of great power, at a place where the magic of the Mother flowed up to the surface.

May knew she had to find such a place but how? Brid had explained how she sensed these things instinctively but May had no such gift. Then a new-found confidence grew within her. Everyone knew that a pregnant woman had heightened levels of awareness. Of course, she was mystically at her strongest now. She felt exhausted and sick but her psychic powers were surely enhanced.

With a fresh eye, she surveyed the surrounding country. There was little to see from down here in the valley and so she urged them to the head the pass before them.

Instantly she saw it; a place of great power, a place where Önd was concentrated, a place of magic. To her left rose three wind-sharpened peaks; to her right was a blocky plateau but, in the distance, framed by the dramatic mountains, lay a conical hill. It was nothing like so striking as the surrounding landscape but on its summit was a single tree, an oak, and she knew that a single tree drew the Mother's power up through its roots.

"Hurry, Fern! We must get there before dark, before the wolves are at their full strength. Hurry!"

She could not run; she was too pained and too tired; but Fern appeared to understand her problem and helped as best he could, tugging her along. Runa kept close to her heels and, just as the sun began to dip towards the horizon, they reached the bottom of the conical hill. It was not high, merely distinctive, but May doubted she had the strength to make the summit before dusk.

She could hear them now and feared that, as night took hold on the world, the shadows would draw strength and solidify into fearful beasts. Her breath coming in short bursts, she clutched at a sharp pain in her side. She told herself it was only a stitch but any pain in her abdomen now made her fear for her child.

"Fern, take the horn and plunge it into the ground by the roots of the tree up there. It will surely summon help for us. Otherwise . . ."

She didn't need to say more. Without Amaryllis, Caspar or Perren they could not possibly survive if hooded wolves attacked them. Fern ran ahead, effortlessly skipping up the hill, a black figure now in the lengthening shadows, while May was left to do her best to control Firecracker who tugged and heaved on the rein.

She was looking at the horse, trying to soothe him, when Fern struck the ground with the unicorn's horn but she knew the instant he had achieved his task. The baby within her kicked and she felt a shiver run through her body. The sun was setting directly behind the hill and, though she could not see the great globe itself, the rays fanned out, breaking through smoky clouds. Silhouetted by this red halo was the black of the oak and Fern's strange figure holding his arms aloft in triumph. She had not realized it until now but Fern was also magical in his own right, a creature returned from death, a woodwose. Was he not specially blessed?

May was disappointed. Nothing happened though she could see that Fern stood there, waiting. Her breathing laboured and raw in her throat, she allowed Firecracker to drag her to the top of the hill. Once there, she could do little else other than sit and breathe, massaging her thighs and tentatively probing her bruised arm until she was recovered.

"Great Mother, answer our prayer," she called out loud. Then, as the last sliver of a burnt red sun was swallowed into the west and a mauve twilight washed over the land, she plucked up the horn and, again, struck it into the earth. The baby kicked and a long low moan wailed out from the blackness of mountains to the north-east behind them.

CHAPTER FIVE

A dark shadow swept across the sky. It clasped the moon-like form of Necrönd that was bright and vast in the sky of the Otherworld. The Egg began to throb. Caspar stared at the giant shadow and wondered that it wasn't the form of a hand that moved to touch the Egg. He prayed that, back on earth, someone was reaching out to grasp Necrönd and call him home.

Shouting wildly, he clawed up out of the water and stretched up in vain for the vast globe above his head that dominated this world.

Necrönd pulsed, the sound of each beat roaring in Caspar's ears, the intensity growing until a shaft of blue-white light burst out from the globe. The water hissed where the light touched the surface, billowing clouds of vapour rising and twisting into a coil of cloud. Little spikes of water began to form and stretch up from the surface of the sea, swelling into spiralling pillars. The spikes twisted into one spire and the tower of twisting water grew up and up until it kissed the pale silver sphere above. The creatures around him surged towards it, the water boiling as the animals leapt for the roaring tower of water. Caspar stared in wonder – in hope.

The narrow base of the enormous, twisting spire skimmed over the surface, sucking up water and the smaller creatures, sea snakes, octopuses with sharks' heads and silver narwhals. Caspar wasted no time. This was, perhaps, his only chance.

With all his strength he swam, desperation lending power to his unpractised strokes. He had to get to it! He struggled furiously. But no! His heart sank; it was twisting away. Then it turned back and came racing towards him.

With one last burst of effort, he kicked upwards, hoping to be sucked into the fountain of water. For a second, the force of it tore the breath from his lungs and he hurtled upwards, churned in its terrible power; but then he was falling. He hit the water and plunged deep into the dark of the sea, plummeting away from Necrönd. Furiously, he swam to the surface but the moment was lost. The tower of water was gone, sucked back into the Egg. The giant shadow clasping Necrönd was fading away as if whoever sought him had already given up on him.

He screamed, "No, no! I'm down here! Try again! Try again! You must find me. You must help me. Help!" he yelled on and on until his voice was hoarse and he sagged down in the water in despair.

He realized now that, whoever held the Egg, had no notion of how to wield it. At last, he fully understood why it was so dangerous to tamper with Necrönd and why the wolfman had not taken it from May; the wolfman had known the danger. Now Caspar saw why Keridwen had been afraid for his soul. He had thought that she feared he would be corrupted by its power but that was not the real danger. No, the simple risk of the magic working in reverse, taking life to the Otherworld rather than summoning it back, was the true terror of being its guardian.

Around him the water was calm, the creatures who shared his exile caught in the same quiet anticipation, waiting, hoping for the shaft of light to burst out from the Egg again. Minutes stretched into hours but his hope lived on and then swelled; the light from Necrönd was brightening by fractions. Whoever held it now was working it in a less haphazard manner; someone with great skill and power, he guessed as a beam of light fell from the Egg to the water. At first, he thought they were searching for him but, as the pool of light remained still on the water, it struck him that they were using the beam more as a beacon to guide him home.

But he was not the only creature that saw light as a pathway home. The mass of life was swimming towards it until their crowded bodies, like writhing giant tadpoles in a rapidly evaporating pool, were so closely packed that not even an elver could have wriggled between them.

Caspar redoubled his efforts. A wall of grey-blue skin blocked his path. Guessing it was a whale, he drew his knife, which he used like an ice-pick to help him claw his way up its barnacled flesh to climb over its back. Leaping down the far side, he plunged back into the squirming mass of tentacles and fins, uncaring as to what he must do to get to that light; it was the way home. He fought his way over them, no longer needing to swim for the sheer mass of bodies beneath him.

He crawled and jumped and ran until there was just the one soft head of an octopus between him and the light. It squirmed beneath him but his momentum carried him forward. Stretching out the fingers of one hand, he reached into the light. The world about him swirled with muddled colour, the creatures rushing with him, spiralling giddily upwards.

He tried to narrow his body to be thin like an arrow and so streamline his flight through the channels of magic but it made no difference. The monstrous beasts overwhelmed him, slapping him down, slowing his progress until it was too late and suddenly the beam was gone.

"No! No!" he yelled. "Please! Don't leave me here!"

To May's fearful ears, the long low cry moaning out from the mountains was like the wail of wolves.

In panic, she dropped to the ground, cradling her belly. Her legs weak with fear, she looked about her into the twilight but could see nowhere to hide. The wailing grew louder and nearer but she calmed herself, realizing that it could not be wolves that approached. She saw points of light swinging to a steady rhythm and the hollow song, which she had thought was the cry of wolves, was, she now realised, the sound of singing. Soft and melodious, it wafted clearly to her ears now. The words were in a foreign tongue, which she recognised from her time in the mines of Kalanazir as Oriaxian.

Trog growled and Runa pressed close to her thighs. Quickly, the lone conical hill on which they stood was surrounded and the soft lullaby turned to an aggressive chant. The horse pawed the ground, threateningly. May cursed. Fearing for Caspar still slumped over the horse's back, she took a firm grip on Firecracker's bridle, though she knew there was little she could do if he did decide to charge the oncoming men. He was a war-horse of the most aggressive nature and he scented battle.

"Steady, Cracker!" she exclaimed in her panic. "Fern, Fern, I can't hold him!" she cried. "He's tearing my arm out."

The woodwose was instantly beside her. Rather than trying to hold the horse, he worked his clumsy fingers to unbuckle the girth so that the saddle packs and Caspar's limp body thumped to the ground. Caspar landed heavily beside a low flat rock but May did not rush to his side but retreated back against the coarse bowl of the lone oak as the ring of swinging lanterns advanced. The air trembled with the rattle of sticks and the beat of a battle drum. The light thrown out by the lanterns did not illuminate the Oriaxian faces but threaded through the eye and mouth holes of masks.

Snorting, Firecracker pawed the ground, head lowered like an enraged bull. May drew courage from the horse and inched forward from the tree. Reaching for her dagger, she stood over Caspar's body. It was almost ludicrous to her but some ancient instinct bred from her frontier forefathers must have made her want to stand and fight. She was a Torra Altan with the high ground to defend.

Dressed in robes of white like religious warriors, the Oriaxians came on until they were but twenty paces from the oak, beating their sticks over their heads. Firecracker bellowed and stood up on his hind legs, his forelegs raking the air. The circle of lanterns halted and the united chants broke up until only one voice was left singing and that, too, soon died away. An awed murmur filled the space. Firecracker screamed again and several of them flung themselves to the ground.

"Fern," May hissed, "see if you can't calm the horse. I think . . ." she began but let her words remain unfinished as she dwelled on her thoughts.

They were in Oriaxia and Firecracker was an Oriaxian purebred, a prized breed, and he was a particularly fine example. Was it possible that they saw him as some kind of horse god? Morrigwen had told her that there were many people who worshipped horses.

Fern was swung round by Firecracker and dangled feebly on the end of the reins until the woodwose was able to get his hand to the horse's muzzle. Although he and Firecracker possessed very different natures, they had a basic understanding of one another's needs and Fern's touch seemed to calm the raging stallion.

Once the red-coated purebred was still, a mutter swelled from the surrounding crowd that drew close, all aggression swept away by a tide of wonder and curiosity.

"We mean no harm. We just need help," May stammered as they gathered around, bowing at Firecracker and chattering excitedly.

Relieved that they no longer appeared hostile, she was deeply disconcerted that she could not see their faces. How could she have possibly hoped to find help here? These peoples were Oriaxian and she could barely understand one word. Hands lifted her aloft and, with much cheering and shouting, garlands were thrown over Fern.

Dancing around, trotting and snorting like horses, they cheered her and the woodwose and all she could do was grin in embarrassment. Firecracker was central to their attention and they bowed at his feet, making ridiculous neighing noises at him. But her trepidation soon returned when they investigated Caspar's body and laid him out on the slab of stone beneath the tree. Only when they stepped back did she note that the flat rock was reminiscent of an altar.

"No!" May squealed. "Leave him be! He is not a sacrifice!" She ran over to Caspar and put her arms protectively around him. "No!"

The masked Oriaxians stood back in bewilderment, muttering rapidly in their indecipherable dialect and obviously in some confusion.

"No!" May repeated as they advanced, batons raised.

They stood in a tight circle around her and, in the concentrated light of the lanterns, she could see that the ends of their batons were capped with horse's hooves. The two closest to Caspar smacked their clubs down hard on the stone table. She flinched but kept herself pressed protectively over him, fearing that they wished to beat his body to a pulp in honour of the horse god.

She was flung aside and gaped in alarm at the strangers. Runa and Trog leapt to her defence, growling savagely. One man was caught between the two animals that lacerated his arm but they were dragged off and restrained by half a dozen enraged men. The Oriaxians turned their attention back to Caspar.

May screamed in dismay as they began to strip off his clothing, ripping away his shirt. Then they suddenly paused in their action, hovering over him, their excited, bloodthirsty cries ebbing to curious murmurs. Stepping slowly back, they pointed warily at the silver casket, until one, braver than the rest, lunged forward and snatched it open.

As if seeing the world through a misted glass, May watched in dismay as the Oriaxian held up the Egg and shrieked in triumph. A flash of light sparked up from the root of the tree and then a crack of lightning split the sky, the following boom of thunder sending all sprawling to cringe on the ground. A horrible shrieking cry came from above their heads and all looked up into the blackness. Out of the mauve night sky, billowing shapes were massing like brooding thunderheads.

Then they were falling!

May spread herself over Caspar's body and prayed that thick spread of the huge oak above would protect them. The earth shook as something enormously heavy crashed to the ground. She buried her head into the ground and flinched as many more vast objects thudded down, the air thick with unworldly shrieks and screams. Peeking out between her fingers, she was wide-eyed at the sight.

Huge fish and other slimy creatures of the deep

writhed all about, flapping fins and tentacles thrashing the ground. She curled into a tight ball as one crashed through the oak's branches and landed only inches from her, its great tail swatting a half dozen of the Oriaxians and crushing others against the solid flank of another squirming creature.

Something coiled around May's leg and began dragging her towards its mouth that was like a pair of crab-like pincers set in the middle of its body. She squealed and clawed at the ground, trying to wrench herself free from its giant clasp that was crushing the breath from her lungs. Then the creature began to weaken and the tentacles fell limply away. All around her the flapping, stranded animals from the sea were dying, yet more were falling from the sky. Dragging Caspar with her, she pushed herself up close to the thick bole of the tree to protect herself from the bodies that fell like boulders from the sky, many splitting open on impact, rivers of blood and snakes of gut spewing over the ground.

Dodging left and right, she ran, keeping low alongside the fallen bodies that lay groaning and gasping until she reached the spot where she had last seen the Egg. The man who held Necrönd lay crushed beneath the cracked shell of a huge crab, the hand of his outstretched arm still grasping the Egg. Without pausing for thought, she grabbed Necrönd.

"Away! Be gone!" she commanded.

The black thunderclouds instantly vanished and the dying creatures faded before her eyes until they were all gone. Tears flooding from her eyes, she threw herself down alongside Caspar and thrust the Egg back into the silver casket before wiping her hands on her ragged skirts as if trying to rid herself of its contaminating touch. Lying back on the grass, she breathed heavily and, through the broken branches, stared up at the bright stars. The pain in her hand returned with a rush and, clasping it to her, she bit on her lip.

Presently, she became aware of an uncanny silence hanging over the place and sat up to see that those men in white robes who had not been crushed had abandoned their lanterns and fled. One or two lamps were toppled and had spilt their oil, igniting a small patch of dry grass.

She lay still, breathing heavily, wondering in the silence what she should do. Then she was aware of Fern chattering in alarm at a white shape standing over her.

"Impressiveness! A Belbidian, I thinks, and so long from home. Remarked to be! Remarked happenings! A woman, too, and such powers unguided. You have speech, Belbidian?"

"I— I—" May stuttered, not sure that she had. A light shone into her face so she could not fully make out the features of the old man standing over her. All that was clear was his conical hat with its broad rim that blotted out a circle of stars in the sky, and a long beard that tickled her face.

He spoke. "Wizardess, why come you to our worshipping place? Why bring you this sacrifice? Why call you monsters out of the sky?"

"I didn't. I don't know what's happening. I need help. Please, please you must help me," she begged.

The man laughed. "The warriors ran. They were thinking you a demon sorceress. You knew the point of power. You have with you . . . I do not know the word." He pointed at the unicorn's horn in her belt.

"A unicorn's horn," she supplied.

"A unicorn's horn. You have ball of magic, horn of magic and horse tamer." He nodded his head at Fern. "Much power! And a woman with child is at very heights

117

of her powers." He stared at her bulging belly. "Yet you show no ability to control it. Ha!" He snorted.

"I need help!" May felt her voice beginning to crack. She knew she should trust no one but she was desperate. "I am not a sorceress," she stated but nodded at Caspar and wondered how simply to explain. "It is he and . . . well, his spell went awry. He is guardian of a power but it is not to be relied on."

"All magics can work against the mage. All delvers into the darkness world of magic must take armour up against it. Come, help me with sorcerer." He indicated Caspar's body.

May decided she had no option but to trust him. Between them they struggled to lift him onto Firecracker's back, while Fern held the horse. The exertion taxed May's pregnant body and she put her hand to her belly, soothing it while she drew breath.

"Problems are all about you when seeking to steal power from the gods. You must always be offering to give back more than the taking. You sought power from this bauble but are giving nothing of yourself."

"I have nothing."

"You have a horse and a magical horn. That is enough."

It was at the darkest point of the night after the moon had set, when the man led them to his simple dwelling set at the edge of a small village. Globelike flowers set on tall stems were silhouetted against the light flooding out from the cottage and the air was thick with the scent of onions, thyme and sage. When he reached the door, he muttered irritably to himself. His porch was thick with moths and crane fly that had swarmed towards the light and, in his haste to join the throng on the hill, he had left his door open. The hall within was choked with insects.

The instinctive fear of plague shuddered through May's body.

"You'd be thinking that my woman would have made things shut," he grumbled.

After helping to lift Caspar from Firecracker's back, the man snatched up a broom and scrubbed the walls, crushing insects and sweeping them away. "There's a barn and much hay and water short behind the home," he said nodding dismissively at Fern. "Be sure the proud horse is comfortable. He has great magics."

"Solace!" he called within and after a short while a young girl, her hair in plaits and wearing nothing but an overly large night-shirt, scurried out from one of the back rooms. He spoke to her in Oriaxian and soon she had cushions laid out on the floor by the fire and the old man gently laid Caspar's body down onto them. An old woman shuffled in from the back, took one look at the commotion and set a kettle over the fire. She sat on a low rocking chair, waiting for it to boil but, within seconds, she was asleep.

Runa was tentatively eyeing the fire but Trog was already snuffling at the table. He climbed up onto a stool to steal a discarded crust of bread and a bone from the uncleared table. In moments, he had knocked over a carafe of wine but May had no thought to trouble herself with his behaviour. She knelt anxiously beside Caspar and cupped his hand in hers.

"He's dead!" the old man pronounced.

"I said he was dead." Fern came trotting in from the barn. He sniffed at Caspar and wrinkled his nose. "The smell of the Otherworld is all about him."

May put her head to Caspar's chest and, despite the thump of her own racing pulse in her ears, she could hear the faint but reassuring boom of his heart. "He lives. His heart is beating," she insisted.

"That is not near the same as being alive." The strange

119

man rolled up his long floppy sleeves and, for the first time, May saw that he had a withered arm.

The man instantly caught her glance and flashed her a look of resentment. "Go on, stare!" he challenged, holding out the arm for her inspection. "You think you are such perfection and so mock me."

"I do not mock," May apologized. "I merely noted."

"You are not afraid then?"

"No, of course not," she said with kindness.

"Nor pity me?"

"Not so long as you are not in pain."

He smiled and flapped his whip-thin arm in the air. "No, no pain." He seemed pleased with her answer. "Come, we must be undoing the spell. Tell how all happened."

May explained as much as she could and, eventually, the bearded old man shuffled over to the open silver casket that May had place upon the table.

"You say he fell into this bauble?"

The mysterious old man put on a pair of thick fire gloves and took a pair of tongues from beside the hearth before carefully manoeuvring the Egg out of the casket and onto the table, placing it midst the dirty plates. It rolled and wedged itself up against a piece of bread. The man stooped over it and stared long and hard.

"I cannot see him," he said, drawing a lantern closer and returning to examine the Egg.

He looked at it all night and, to May's shame, she fell asleep, resting against the old woman's rocking chair. She was awoken some time after dawn by the woman coughing. She snapped her head up to see the old man shaking the woman's shoulder to rouse her.

May immediately turned to Caspar and gasped in horror. His face was splattered with blood. "What have you done to him?" she shrieked.

"It is the blood of the horse. I hoped for invoking the powers of the great horse in the sky."

"You've killed Firecracker!" May gasped and staggered to her feet.

The man shook his head. "No, I have leaked its blood but a little. A full sacrifice might yet be necessity."

The old man waved his arm at her as if she were hysterical and turned his attention to his wife who still slouched in the rocking-chair. "Sidra." He stooped to kiss her but she pushed him away in favour of the young girl who crawled into the woman's lap and hugged her. The old couple argued for some while in their own tongue and then Sidra set the child aside and hobbled over to May. Cupping May's chin and lifting her face, she looked into May's eyes.

"My foolish husband, who has able to speak with me only on concerns of our grandchild since Solace's parents are gone, wakes me in midst of the night for help in waking a dead man. Well! I'd best be dressed before I make sense at all of this."

She shuffled away and returned shortly, looking stronger and taller than before. A huge smile beamed from May's face. "You will help me!"

The woman's robe was emerald green and laid over it was a black cloak marked with white runic symbols. The broach pinning it had a thick circular rim and its centre divided into three segments in the design of the rune of the Mother. May put her forefinger and thumb together and held her hands up over her head, greeting her with the sign of the Mother. The woman beamed back.

May fell down and kissed her hand. "He was going to kill Cracker but you will help us; you are of the Great Mother." She indicated the broach.

The woman smiled. "I shall oust your man. He is in

an egg, which is a thing of femaleness." She scooped her hands around it and frowned. "A device most curious. Do you divine with it? Does it show the future?"

May shrugged but the woman seemed too intent on the Egg to be interested in her opinions. She was reaching for a knife. "You say he is inside. We must be cutting it open and letting out his breath of life."

"No, no!" May said hurriedly. "Terrible things, like the monstrous sea creatures that fell out of the sky, and dragons and beasts will burst out too. It would be the end of mankind. We would all be killed. The Egg must never be broken."

"How would you suggest to call his breath then?" Sidra turned to May.

She shrugged. "I would hold the Egg in my hands and summon his image to my mind but that's also too dangerous. I fear the power is awry and, rather than summoning him, I might be sucked in myself."

"You wish for summoning him but without touching the Egg with the bareness of your skin?" She reached for a feather – the tail feather off an eagle, May judged by its size and colour – and cut the tip at an acute angle to form a quill. "What is his name?"

"Spar," May said softly. "Lord Caspar, son of Baron Branwolf of Torra Alta," she added.

"That is too long," the old woman said. "We shall be calling him Spar. You, girl, be looking into his eyes and call him in the moment I am writing his name on the Egg. But you have payments to make; one to me and one to the Great Mother."

May nodded and bared her arm. "I have nothing of my own to offer other than my blood or the unicorn's horn. Take what you will."

"The baby!" The woman exclaimed and, in that instant,

she seemed tall and terrible, her soft mouth beak-like and her expression vulturish. "I have expelled from my body many sons but never a daughter for passing on my arts to. You shall be giving me the child."

May thought she would faint. The thought of losing her child was so terrible that she curled up around her stomach.

Runa and Trog sensed her dismay and both stood beside her, hackles up and teeth bared, the sound from their snarling throats chilling. Snatching up the unicorn's horn and holding it before her as a weapon, May inched back towards the door and was relieved to hear Firecracker's snorts and squeals. Fern must have realized their danger and released the stallion from the barn. She turned and was through the door in seconds only to be confronted by the ring of masked faces from the night before.

Someone slammed the door on Trog and Runa behind her, keeping them from her side.

She began to sob in panic. "Oh, Great Mother, help me. What have I done?" she cried, thinking that these terrible things happening about her were all due to her own idiotic foolishness.

"I can take it from your belly and still keep you both alive," Sidra promised, advancing.

Runa howled like a demon in despair and was scrabbling at the door behind her while May screamed and ran, only to be caught by the men of the horse cult and tossed back and forth. Four of them grabbed a limb each and pinned her down while the old woman approached, a sickle glinting in her hand.

A rumbling roar burst out from soil beneath her and the ground erupted. A huge figure of stone broke out, uprooted a small tree with one hand and used it to swipe at the Oriaxians who fled in terror.

"Perren!" May yelled in overwhelming relief. She had thought him dead, sucked deep into the quicksand, but he seemed fully recovered.

Growling in some deep terrifying language, the stonewight ran into the house, scooped up Caspar and threw him over his shoulder. Runa and Trog burst out and stood stiff with bristles either side of May.

"The Egg!" she exclaimed. "We can't leave it."

"I have it," Perren assured her, stuffing it into Caspar's silver casket and licking his fingers as if its touch had scalded him. "Now, quick!"

Firecracker had already bolted into the rolling hills, dust flinging up from his hooves. May snatched Fern's hand and, pulling him up from where he lay cringing on the ground, urged him to follow as Perren swept her from her feet.

"I thought you were dead," May gasped when at last he slowed, the conical hill with the single oak some way behind. Gently, he lowered her to the ground so that she might walk a little while they looked for a suitable place to stop.

The stonewight was so much thinner, his face drawn and craggy and his once grey eyes were now a dusty brown colour with no shine to them. He smiled with the aged smile of one that no longer found humour in life.

"May, I'm sorry. I don't know if you can ever forgive me. The sun! The old ones warned that the sun would harm me and it did. It drove me mad. Your arm! I didn't know what I was doing. Can you ever forgive me?"

"You didn't hurt me nearly so badly as you might have done," she said, forgetting her grudge against him. "Besides, I know how to get Master Spar out now and you found us, Perren, and saved me." She looked at him thoughtfully. "Though how did you find us?"

"You were clever, May." He nodded back at the hill. "You sought a place of great power and plunged that horn into it, sending ripples of magic through the earth. I had no trouble, none at all, finding you. But nor will the wolfman." He looked remorsefully at Caspar. "But what have I done to him? It's all my fault. What do we do?"

"I was trying to tell you. It's so easy! The old woman showed me. As soon as it's safe to stop, we'll get him free," she gasped, limping on, finding it awkward to move now that they baby was very much larger. It was only minutes before she accepted Perren's offer to ride on his shoulders again.

The dog and the wolfling kept close to their heels while they climbed a slope thick with hazel and rowan trees and reached a bare ridge. From the top, they looked down a grassland plain that stretched out for miles. In the far distance they could make out the hazy line of the sea. Here they stopped. Perren chose a boulder and gently lifted Caspar from Firecracker's back and laid him down on it.

While Fern and Perren built a fire to keep Caspar warm, May took a stick from one of the rowan trees, which grew in profusion just below the exposed ridge, and whittled its end to make a quill of sorts. Feeling queasy, she drew back her shirt and pulled the skin taut.

The wind was hard and she fancied that she heard the echo of Morrigwen's voice chiding her for her squeamishness. "We are as the Great Mother made us and should not feel ill at the sight of flesh, blood and bone." She sucked in a deep breath to drive away the sickness.

Gritting her teeth, she slid the small blade taken from Caspar's boot across her forearm. It was a sharp pain but not so sharp that it made her jerk the blade away before the cut was made. After opening the casket and very carefully dipping the rowan twig into the beads of blood, she used the bright liquid to trace out the runic letters of Caspar's name onto the Egg. Expectantly, she peered at the creamy marbled surface of the shell.

Languishing at the bottom of an ocean, his brain cramped by the cold and the terror of loneliness, Caspar thought himself to be dreaming. A coil of light was falling through the layers of water like a feather falling through still air. It was coming for him. He stared as the spiral of light settled onto the ocean bed just before him and then swelled to encompass him.

A sense of peace overwhelmed him as the light embraced him and drew him up through the water to the surface. Above, the light of the Egg was bright but tinged with crimson. The air was magically beautiful about him, the strange light split by the droplets and refracted into bows of gold, silver and scarlet. Cupping the water in his hand, he delightedly watched as the light from Necrönd fell on him. The water began to warm and solidify in the light, hardening, not into ice, but more into something like glassy resin. It was a glorious colour, white and glistening.

Cupping the watery resin in his hands, it absorbed his thought for only the briefest moment before he stared into the glorious light that drew him upwards. Bewildered, he looked up at the moonlike sphere in the sky that dripped blood.

Gloriously warm air flooded his starved lungs, the breath of life.

"Is that it?" Perren asked, pressing close to May. "Just runes?"

May edged away from him. "The writing of the Gods will reach across the dimensions. It's so simple once you know how." With her heart in her mouth, she peered harder at the Egg. "But it isn't working!"

Perren laughed. "He won't pop out of the Egg. You need to look at Spar."

She moved her focus to the still body on the stone. He looked rigid with pain or effort; his fists that had been limp were now tightly clasped, the fingers hooked together, but there was still no breath. He had only a pulse. It was so strange, so unnatural.

"Look; he's holding something," May said softly, hardly daring to believe what was happening.

A soft glow broke out from between his fingers. The sight distracted her from his face and so she almost leapt in fright when Caspar's body jerked.

"Spar!" she cried, wiping her arm across her eyes to clear her tears.

He gasped in breath and doubled up coughing before huge quantities of water vomited from his mouth. For over a minute, the water kept pouring out and then he coughed and coughed, his grey face turning crimson and then puce. At last, after that came breath, raw and painful but continuous. His eyes opened wide, staring fearfully about him but it was only a few seconds before he began to gasp and choke, his face turning blue.

"No! No!" May cried, gripping his shoulders and shaking him vigorously.

His mouth gaped like a landed fish, and he doubled up, rolled onto his knees and finally spat out a sliver of what looked like seaweed.

"May!" he spluttered and weakly reached out a hand. She caught it and both looked down in surprise as something fell from his hands and rolled to the ground.

"The moon!" he said. "A sliver of the moon caught in the channels of magic."

It was so beautiful, a white crystalline sphere, with swirling clouds deep within it.

"A moonstone, like the one that showed you where your mother was, the one the dragon had," she gasped, stooping to pick it up and pressing it back into Caspar's trembling hands. She had had quite enough of magic.

He nodded weakly while Trog and Runa pressed close, wagging their tails excitedly at all the human rejoicing, though Fern had skipped away to look for Firecracker and Perren tactfully withdrew. May gave them no thought. Right now, she didn't care about anything except that Caspar held her in his arms and was looking tenderly into her face.

"May, I thought I had lost you forever."

She choked back tears of grief for the years lost, for the suffering she had endured waiting for this moment. Burying her face into his chest, she wept tears of joy.

Overwhelmed by relief, Caspar clung tightly to May. The loneliness still haunted him and he daren't close his eyes for the fear that the cold suffocating emptiness of oblivion might return. The presence of her warm body meant everything to him. He was alive!

"Keep talking to me, May," he begged. "Don't ever leave me! Ever! Please just keep talking," he murmured, his voice weak with exhaustion.

May cradled his head and rocked him back and forth, her eyes blinking away the tears. "At last, my Lord, I have you," she murmured, soothing his head, her hands warm on his neck and chest. She kissed his forehead. "You are safe, Spar. I love you!"

"And I you," he said, though drowsily. Now that he was safe, exhaustion was rapidly claiming his senses.

"You must sleep," she said with motherly concern.

"I cannot. I never want to sleep again. I want to treasure every moment with you. I want . . ." His voice trailed away.

Perren was looking at him and Caspar shuddered, now totally aware of the stonewight's treachery. The stonewight was gazing at him as if he knew exactly what he was thinking. He had that mysterious knowing look on his coarse grey face that Caspar had only seen when they had both stood in a water that acted as a medium between their minds – yet there was no water now.

"I'm sorry," Perren stammered. "The old ones warned me about the effects of the sun but I did not heed it. The madness swept through me; I had no control."

"You sent me to oblivion and tried to eat May," Caspar accused.

Perren hung his head. "I know," he murmured and would not speak more.

For the first time since Caspar had met him, Perren was silent and just sat there, staring at the earth. The stonewight looked aged and tired, his chest heaved and his skin was dappled with cracks and fissures

"Leave him be; he has already made amends," May said, soothing Caspar's brow.

Perren was still looking at the earth when Fern returned with Firecracker. Caspar was amazed to find that he had fallen asleep beneath May's gentle touch. The sound of his horse's footfall on the rock had snapped him out of his dream where he was lolling on the ocean waves, some huge monster beneath rising rapidly from the depths, its jaws wide as it sped towards him. The monster had turned into the wolfman and he awoke with stabbing pains radiating out from the sore spot on the crown of his head.

Perren struggled up in alarm. "Where?" he demanded of Fern as if the woodwose had warned him of something.

"Quick! Quick! They are coming from the north. We must get to the sea."

"How many?" Perren asked.

"Too many. Every one of them fully formed. The unicorns are with them now too. All driven as if by one force."

Caspar didn't need to ask more; he knew Fern spoke of wolves. Rubbing at the sore spot on his scalp, he asked, "The wolfman?"

Fern nodded. "And there were more men about him, shadows of men. Warriors! Master Spar, wield Necrönd! Send them back!" he shouted. "Quick! Quick! They are coming fast."

Caspar did not need to remember the words of his mother to know that he must not. He had seen oblivion and would never seek to touch Necrönd again. He knew now that they must be rid of it for good, take it to the ends of the earth and as far from their loved ones as possible. He only hoped that, as many philosophers claimed, the world was flat and that he would be able to take it to the edge of the world and throw it off.

"Get to the sea," Perren urged him. "They won't easily be able to cross the sea."

The stress of the situation restored Caspar's strength. He had slept long and fear filled him with an urgent strength. He threw May up into the saddle, who clutched at her belly in alarm and clung on to the horse with white-knuckled fingers.

"Perren, you carry Trog," he instructed, knowing that the dog wouldn't be able to keep up otherwise.

With Trog hanging over the stonewight's shoulders, they began to run, crashing through the steeply wooded slopes and out onto the plain. Caspar knew he could urge Firecracker on faster but he feared for May behind him. Her tight grip around his waist made him feel strong and proud as her protector. He loved her more now than ever before.

"This won't hurt the baby?" May shouted, her words indistinct as they were snatched by the wind.

Caspar gave it little thought. All he did know was that her baby was not his priority. May mattered far more and he had Necrönd to care for. "Lots of women ride when they are pregnant," he reassured her.

The grey haze of the sea that had been nothing but a thin line before was now a vast expanse of greenish blue beyond the plain. Runa was running so close to the horse that, at times, he was fearful they would trip on her and when Perren stumbled, Caspar slowed to check that he was all right.

"Keep going!" Perren shouted, his panted breaths rasping loudly. "Head a little to the south."

Caspar had never before known the stonewight to be out of breath and he guessed that he had not yet fully recovered from the effects of the dehydration and reminded himself to be wary of the stonewight. "Why south?"

"Trust me!" Perren waved him on, still clinging to Trog. "You'll need a boat and there's a port just a little to the south along the coast."

"How do you know?" Caspar shouted suspiciously though he had no option but to follow Perren's instructions. There was no time to lose. He swerved to the right and galloped on. Behind him he could hear that fearful ululating sound that was more chilling than any bestial cry or supernatural howl. It was the sound of men on the hunt, the howl of their bloodlust.

Fern leapt ahead, more terror-stricken than ever before. The going was firm, the grass crisp in the Oriaxian heat and it was becoming sandier as they approached the sea.

Sweat foamed over Firecracker's shoulders and the reins became slippery from Caspar's own sweat.

The ground dipped and, for a while, they lost sight of the sea but, when it came into view again it was start-lingly close, a sparkling blue flecked with patches of brownish green over the deeper water. The coastline was pitted with coves, shingle beaches and crumbling cliffs that had sloughed great boulders into the stirring sea.

Spurring Firecracker to a last burst of speed, they left Perren behind. He could see a walled port and ships, enormous vessels like great wooden fortresses rising out of the harbour waves.

Abruptly, he hauled Firecracker to a halt, May's body thumping heavily into his back. The bellowing yammer of camels within the port competed with the knell from a great bell. Black shapes were streaking out from the city gates towards them.

"Oh no!" May gasped. "They've got ahead of us. We're trapped!"

For a split second, Caspar stared at the shapes that raced towards them, quickly discernible as wolves. While thinking that the wolves must have skirted round and out-paced them, he looked for some way to turn. Already, he could hear the cry of men flooding out from the plain behind them. Praying that the others would make it, he veered south away from the port and the wolves. Then he galloped flat out straight for the coast, hoping to find that the gentle slope beneath him would dip towards the shore.

Instead, he was faced with a low crumbling cliff and jagged boulders below. Beyond the rocks, a row of masted fishing boats was pulled up onto a shingle beach. Knowing that he might mange to drop down the cliff-face but that it would be slow-going with May and impossible for

Firecracker, he was forced to continue further along the top of the cliff. Desperately, he sought another way down, hoping to get back to those fishing boats.

Forced to a heart-bursting pace by the wolves behind them, they galloped before the line of ghostly men mounted on unicorns that poured out from plain. Caspar's only hope of survival came when the unicorns slowed and the men dismounted. He snatched a glance. Clearly, they were warriors unused to mounted combat and wished to meet them on foot, relying on the wolves to trap them. The wraiths moved awkwardly, limping or dragging arms or legs, gliding closer through the silvery grasses. He saw tall, big men, scantily clad in skins and furs, their boots laced up round their calves. Wielding axes and crossbows, they wore blond war plaits that dangled to their shoulders.

Vaalakans! There was no mistaking them. Caspar gritted his teeth in the face of the rushing wind as he whipped his horse on. Somehow, they had slipped back across the divide between worlds, perhaps riding the winds of magic opened up by Necrönd, he did not know. What was certain was that the maimed and mutilated warriors that bore the scars of their death had died at his command. They must hate him with every drop of their souls.

The men advanced with unnatural speed, the wolves swerving to blend with their ranks. He jabbed his heels into Firecracker's sides and, with enormous relief saw that the ground dipped towards a sandy cove, the tide far out, striped from a long reach of beach. Perhaps he could reach the beach and gallop around the short headland, back to those boats. He prayed that Perren and the others had managed to clamber down the ragged cliff-line; they would be safe if they reached the sea.

From the ranks of the men at his heels came a snarl that chilled Caspar's blood.

"Get him!" it roared, in a deep growl, neither lupine nor human.

Caspar's head suddenly stung and he felt faint with the pain. He was aware that May's grip about his waist was holding him up.

She was shouting in his ear, "Hold on, Spar! Hold on!"

He felt giddy. Firecracker galloped beneath him, careering down the slope to the beach, the movement strangely remote. He was drunk with the throbbing pain to his head that filled him with the overwhelming desire to throw himself from the saddle and smash his head against the rocks heading the beach just to be free of it. The sea! He needed to get to the sea.

"Spar!" May squealed. "Do something! Vaalakans, Spar!"

Without waiting for Caspar's command, Firecracker clattered across a narrow strip of leg-twisting shingle, slowing only fractionally, before reaching the sand. With ears laid back, the noble beast galloped across tufted sand-dunes. The pain in Caspar's head was so intense that, at first, he could barely see, but then, as he felt the dampness of the sea air on him and they reached the rippled plain of a flat beach, he made out the outline of a sailing boat in the shallow waters. It was making straight for the beach.

He could hear barking and knew that Trog was aboard. The wolves must have ignored the others in favour of trapping him and May, allowing Perren the chance to descend the crumbling cliff and cross to the fishing boats. Wasting no time, the stonewight must have set sail to cut around the headland to rescue him.

Encouraged, he pressed his heels to Firecracker's side, the hope of salvation dulling his pain. They had to make the boat!

Ghostly Vaalakans mounted on living trolls pounded

the ground at their heels and the air was thick with crossbow bolts that thumped into the sand, burying deep into the soft ground. Firecracker stumbled and tripped, the very soft sand providing little footing; they lost ground. The horse swerved violently as a quarrel sliced across the skin of his flank, tearing out a strip of hide but, a true war-horse, he kept going. They made better time as they reached firmer, wetter sand that had been beaten to rows upon rows of ripples by the retreating tide.

May squealed as a quarrel whisked past her ear and, though the lapping waves were only just ahead now, Caspar's hopes plummeted. The wolves had swerved away to come in from the side, aiming to cut him off from the boat.

"Great Mother, help us!" he cried, looking to the boat, its keel preventing it from coming in closer and they still had another twenty paces to make.

Chest deep in water, Perren was splashing towards them, brandishing an oar in one arm and yelling savagely at the wolves on Caspar's flank. The youth's only thought was to get May to safety and he charged past the stone-wight, plunging through the waves to the boat.

It was bobbing in shallow waters, an anchor rope thrown overboard. Caspar swung May forward and flung her onto the deck while Fern and Runa scrambled in after her. Fern and May struggled to lower a broad plank to help Firecracker on board. Caspar leaped into the water to lead his horse up and was ducked under three times before he succeeded. Bruised and exhausted, he looked back for Perren.

The wolves and the Vaalakans stood on the beach, fearful of the water, but the trolls had waded in to attack Perren, who beat at them with the oar. One troll fell and the one following tripped over the fallen carcass, giving

Perren time to smash the skull of a third but still more advanced. Caspar winced as the crossbow bolt thudded into the boat's side, splintering wood. Perren charged at the next troll who nearly got a hand to the boat.

"Pull the anchor up," he cried.

"Hurry, get on board," May urged from where she sat clinging to the wooden thwart at the stern. Runa pressed close up against her and Trog lay flat at her feet. "Perren, hurry!"

The stonewight shoved the troll backwards and began to wade to the boat.

"Spar, I'll get you!" a tall dark shadow shrieked from the shore.

Perren faltered and looked urgently to Caspar. "See that you hide Necrönd well." He then turned back for the shore.

Caspar stood up and shrieked. "No, no! Perren, we can all make it."

The stonewight was splashing wildly towards the dark shape of the wolfman while trolls moved in from either side. Terrible shrieks rang out across the bay and many died, their throats ripped out by the great power of the stonewight.

The anchor clattered onto the decking. Wielding an oar, Caspar pushed off from the sand and they struggled to turn the boat. Then suddenly the wind caught them and they were away as the water around bubbled with quarrels. One or two landed in the canvas rolls behind May who was crouched beneath the deck.

"Perren, hurry!" Caspar shouted, turning the boat into the wind to keep it still in the deeper water out of range from the crossbows. But the stonewight made no attempts to turn back as more trolls surrounded him. Then they had him by a leg and were dragging him back to the beach and their ghostly masters. Wraiths wielding great Vaalakan axes surrounded him.

"No, no, Perren!" May screamed. He was suddenly no longer visible beneath squabbling mass of roach-backed trolls and axemen. One cracked a whip, forcing the reluctant trolls to leave their prey.

"He's still moving," May moaned.

A great grey arm flailed as the Vaalakans formed a circle around him, raising their axes in turn and hammering them down time and time again. A roar as if it had come out of the earth itself shook the rocks around and echoed back and forth within the cove.

Caspar stood in silent salute to the bravery of the stonewight, the boat rocking beneath his feet.

CHAPTER SIX

Night after night, Hal awoke sweating from the same nightmare. He shook his head, trying to dispel the sickening emotions from his mind, but he was still confused and irrationally fearful. His body was unbearably cramped. Unable to move a single muscle, he felt as if he were locked in a coffin though his eyes told him he was pinned into stocks.

A swirling, smoky blackness surrounded the airy green though his nostrils were stuffed with the scent of leaf-mould. Giddily, he stretched up his head to see that the wizards were still hunched over their cauldron, casting their mind-twisting spells over him. Green smoke drifting through their insubstantial bodies, they flung their hands up, snatching at the emptiness and drawing it into them as if trying to catch his thoughts on the air.

His thoughts! The outrage of it! They were stealing his thoughts and using them against him. He could not plot his way out of here without the wizards knowing his plans. And where was Brid? He was terrified for her.

Time wore on and he could only stare bitterly at the wizards. Aching in agony, he pondered over what exactly they were doing. Slowly, a small image materialised above them, borne on the vapour that rose from the pot. The hazy outline of a figure standing on a rocking deck, hands raised in salute, began to form and the wizards rose to march withershins around it, chanting. Hal had the sense of something huge and black crouched just beyond them, salivating impatiently.

Time passed; he didn't know how much time as it had become twisted and stretched in the torture of his dreams. Night after night, the wizards conjured the same image and each time Hal instantly knew it was Caspar. Now he looked on as the hazy outline of his nephew lay in the bottom of a rocking boat. From time to time, Caspar rubbed at the crown of his head, obviously in some irritation. Then the apparition looked up uncertainly, squinting at the wizards, clearly not seeing them yet somehow aware of something sinister. He looked anxiously about him as the chanting wizards circled his fetch, the purple smoke from their cauldron wafting over him. Then, as he lay back down to sleep, the black shadow slunk forward between the wizards. But Hal could see nothing more as the smoke around Caspar thickened and the shadow slipped into it.

"Spar!" Hal called but there was no reply.

He gritted his teeth on his despair, knowing that his own nightly nightmare would soon begin. The black mist at the edge of the green was gone and with it the stocks. He stood upon the rutted turf of a jousting field. Shaking with anger, he watched helplessly as three knights dragged Brid across the field and tied her to a stake. Every night he listened to Brid scream for him to save her. At this point in his dream, his old sword appeared in his hands and he fought like a raging bear to protect her, thrusting and slashing at the covetous knights that came for his beautiful woman.

Persistently, a black knight thundered across the arena to claim Brid.

"I will have her! I will have her before she burns," he

taunted. "She is overly small but taking her maidenhood before she dies will be a satisfying interlude before supper."

"Foul words from a worthless being who is not fit even to kiss the sole of her boot, and even for that I would take your life!" Hal challenged.

The knight charged, steel lance aimed at Hal's throat. He stood firm. The lance grazed his shoulder and spun him round but he was able to find his balance and take a backward swipe at his opponent. Still, it was useless. The knight wheeled his charger and bore down on him, a thundering ton of muscle and metal powering the point of his lance at Hal's breast.

Flinging himself to the ground to dodge the point, he rolled and slashed at the horse's feathered legs as they pounded by. He felt the jolt as the sword's edge bit; the ground shake as the horse crashed and rolled, crushing his rider.

Hal staggered to his feet. Raising his sword above his head with two hands as if wielding a splitting axe to chop logs, he smote at the man's neck. It split the armour and gouged into the flesh and bone, a jet of purplish blood squirting upwards.

Stumbling back, Hal stared in horror. He had killed men before, the distressful, messy business barely troubling at the time for the rush of bloodlust pumped into his body by the need to survive. But this was revolting. The blood began to foam and darken to a muddy green. The knight was shrivelling within his armour and began to stir and shriek, the neck not fully severed still waggling like segments of worm that do not die. Hal smote again to put the man out of his misery and then twisted the body over to see that it was no longer a knight but a ribby, long-limbed goblin.

The black horse, too, was now three writhing goblins.

Night after night the same creatures attacked him; he soon learned that killing the sturdy black horse was the fastest method of vanquishing his opponent. Every time, the beautiful horse and the powerful knight turned into shrieking, half-starved goblins whose bodies were dragged away by others of their kind. And every time the image of Brid would simply vanish.

Then one night he was faced with the same black knight but the horse was different; he was riding Hal's liver-chestnut mare, Secret. Hal had never been sentimental over any horse but Secret was special; impeccably trained, strong and fearless. It would be terrible to kill her.

But it's not her, he told himself.

Tied to the stake, Brid was shrieking for his help. "Get me home to Keridwen," she cried. "All will be lost if we don't get home with Cymbeline."

He didn't know if it was an image of Brid imposed over some revolting goblin or whether he saw the real woman; it was driving him to madness.

The black knight charged, Secret's smooth heavy legs pounding the ground, bearing the knight with huge and terrifying speed. Hal held up his sword. Secret's ears were pricked and her eyes, those good kind eyes, were trusting.

But it's not the real Secret, he reassured himself again, drawing back his sword, ready to strike at her breast. He had left Secret with Abelard. Standing square, he braced himself. Leaping aside to avoid the flailing hooves, he swung the sword. The horse careered past him, his blade biting deep through chest and foreleg. Blood burst from the wound, splattering the ground. The near-severed limb folded back and she crashed to the ground, crushing the knight beneath her.

Blood foaming around the gash to her breast, Secret squealed and kicked, her foreleg flailing where it had broken in three places. She rolled upright, half staggered up and then fell against Hal, her body solid and hot. He leapt back just in time to avoid being crushed and watched in distress as she crashed to the ground. Twice, she tried to get up before collapsing, her sides heaving, her eyes wild and frightened.

She did not shrivel up into nasty green goblins.

"Oh no! Oh Mother, what have I done?" he said softly, watching as only the goblin that had enacted the part of the knight was dragged away. The horse remained a horse, slowly dying and in agony.

The wizards shrieked in delight. "You see, Hal, you never quite know when it's real or not. It all looks exactly the same."

Hal was barely listening. His vision blurred by pricking tears that he would not surrender to, he stood over the horse and raised his sword, ready to end her suffering. But, before he could bring the blade down, the long-limbed goblins snatched him and dragged him back to what he believed to be the stocks.

All that day, he watched his horse slowly dying, waiting for her agony to cease. He closed his eyes, squeezing back tears, wondering how long this agony would last and dreading the next night when he would have to fight again, not knowing if it this time it would be the real Brid lashed to the stake or not.

At last Secret died and Hal prayed that, now, she would shrink and twist into one of those nasty little green creatures but she did not; she remained the big faithful destrier he had learnt to cherish so much. He wanted to beat his fists in anguish but he was locked in the stocks, unable to move.

Evening fell and with it came his inevitable nightmare. The image of Caspar faded from his mind and he found himself back in the jousting field. The trial began again only this time he knew by the red and white chequered surcoat that the knight facing him was Ceowulf. His heart leapt into his mouth and stuck in his palate. He had killed the real Secret; was this the real Ceowulf? And the girl tied to the stake? He glanced at the beautiful creature, taking in the long brown hair glinting with flecks of copper and the defiant thrust of her delicately rounded chin. Was that Brid? Would he be killing the real Ceowulf in defence of a goblin that he was tricked into seeing as Brid?

The girl caught his gaze and cried, "Hal, I love you."

Every time she had cried out to him, she had not always used the same words but the meaning had been the same. "Save me. Get me out of here; we must get home. We have to succeed; we must get home to save Keridwen." It was so typical of Brid not to be afraid for herself but for others. Now, however, her cry was different and Hal faltered.

"Don't touch him, Hal. You can't risk it. It's Ceowulf maddened by this torture. He sees you as a goblin; his mind is fooled. You must stand aside. He'll fight you to the death. Stand aside."

Hal could not. He still had to defend the image of Brid in case it was really her. All he could do was yell, "Ceowulf! It's me, Hal!"

"You cannot reason with him! His ears will be deceived just as easily as his eyes," the girl on the stake warned.

At the far end of the field the knight had turned his black steed and was thundering towards him. Hal had to make a decision. Was it the real Ceowulf; was it the real Brid; were they both real? He didn't even know whether he could better Ceowulf in a straight fight and somehow doubted it. Yet he couldn't risk Brid.

In desperation, he raised his arms, imploring for help. "Great Mother, give me strength. Tell me what I must do."

No answer came to him, only the sound of the wizards hooting with pleasure at his distress. Hal gritted his teeth. He had no choice. He had to fight Ceowulf who was his dearest friend, because he could take no risks with Brid.

At the last second, he swung up his sword to do battle and speared the horse between its forelegs. His sword glanced off the breastplate before piercing flesh. He was lifted off his feet and carried backwards several paces before the animal stumbled and crashed to the ground. The rider rolled clear. Hal stepped back in horror and guilt as he beheld the war-horse.

Instead of shrivelling and twisting into the form of one of those green-skinned goblins, the creature remained as it had fallen. This really was Ceowulf's sleek black stallion, Sorcerer whom he had slaughtered. No slimy goblin squirmed on the ground, its purplish blood oozing out over the soil. No, it was a bright red pool of blood that swelled around the horse. He had just a few seconds to stare at it, taking in the horror, before the knight was on his feet.

"Fiendish goblin, get away from her! Get away from Brid!" the knight in the red and white surcoat bellowed.

If this knight really was Ceowulf, then Ceowulf saw him as an enemy goblin and he had no doubt that the big knight would give his all to save Brid. Hal had the barest moment to raise his sword and brace himself before the power of the man's blow stunned him. He had never fought Ceowulf in earnest. Of course, he had sparred with the knight, always aware that the mercenary held back. Now Hal would find out the truth of it.

Anticipating that Ceowulf would reach for his sword, he was shocked when he tossed it into his left hand and snatched up his mace, swinging the ball up and back, ready to hammer down on Hal's head.

Hal ducked, raising his sword to block the blow too late, the chain lashing around the blade, accelerating the ball into his left shoulder and ripping the sword from his grip. Sickened by the pain, he dropped to his knees, cradling his arm.

He knew the next blow would finish him. The crushing, shattering pain was too real. Though he guessed that all this was illusory, there was little doubt in his mind that if he imagined himself to be dying, he would die. Ceowulf stood over him with both hands on his sword, ready to slash down and cleave him in two.

A moment's hesitation flickered through the knight's eyes before he bore down. Hal feinted a roll to the right and then, knowing the move would never be anticipated, he rolled hard left, crushing his broken arm beneath him, the pain blackening his vision. Ceowulf's sword gashed the ground, scoring deep into the earth only an inch from Hal's ear. Hal rolled hard again and flung out to reach his sword. He was about to lash back and cut through the knight's hamstring, when he too hesitated.

It was Ceowulf, the real Ceowulf. He had seen that split second of hesitancy in the knight's eyes, that hesitancy which so experienced a mercenary as Ceowulf would never show against an enemy. A goblin would have continued to attack with frenzy but, in this knight's mind there had been doubt about moving in for the kill.

Hal wondered how he could rightly reveal himself and cut through the illusory magic that, no doubt, shrouded his own form and made Ceowulf see him as an enemy.

"Ceowulf, stop! It's me, Hal!" he shouted, backing away beyond the knight's reach.

Brid wailed in distress. "Be careful, Hal. He won't necessarily hear your words aright."

Evidently Ceowulf did not. He burst forward, kicked Hal hard in the ribs and slashed with his sword, slicing deep into the muscle of his remaining good arm. Hal dropped his sword and watched helplessly as the big knight stood over him.

Trembling with pain, both arms useless, Hal begged, "Great Mother, show him who I am!" His eyes looked with pleading at the knight. "For pity's sake, you bastard, Ceowulf, look what you've done to me!"

The knight stood back. "Hal? Hal, is that you? I can't tell. I don't know. I see a richly armoured knight with throwing knives at his belt and a scimitar who attacks and attacks however much I beat him back. Hal, is it you?"

"Yes, it's me! Ceowulf, it's me."

The knight responded by making a crunching blow with his armoured boot into Hal's ribcage. He heard the snap, snap of bone and groaned. He hadn't moved but clearly Ceowulf thought he had reached for his sword or a knife.

He closed his eyes and prayed. "Great Mother . . ." he began then decided that he didn't truly know the Great Mother whereas he did know Brid. "Brid," he cried, "why have you forsaken me? Brid, why? You must surely be strong enough to break this illusion."

But she wasn't; the Trinity was broken.

Ceowulf was raising his sword to strike but, again the knight hesitated. "Hal, for pity's sake, is that you?"

Hal's courage wilted. He would have given anything to be clad in armour to protect him from Ceowulf's sword. He knew now, too, that he had always underestimated his friend's skill and the savagery and strength with which he applied it. Caspar, he thought, would make a runic sign to break the enchantment but he was too late and could no longer move his hands to write.

"Mother, Great Mother, make him hear me!" he shouted as the knight used his mace again to crush Hal's shattered shoulder. The pain blackened his vision and ran through all his body. He arched his back away from it.

Why wouldn't Ceowulf hear the name of the Great Mother? Why? In his agony the answer came to him. Because Ceowulf was a disillusioned man, a cynic and the warrior in him would never allow him full faith. He had often said that he had seen too much bloody slaughter to believe in gods. But if he would not hear the comfort of the Great Mother's name then what? The name of his own mother, of course. Oh, in pity's name, what was it? Hal struggled to find his strength of mind.

"Alicia!" he yelled. Of course, that was it. "Alicia!"

Ceowulf stepped back. "Oh Hal, oh by the sweet earth!"

The knight dropped his sword and mace and leant down by his friend's head, his hands hovering uncertainly over Hal's wounds before he shook himself and ripped off his shirt, tearing it into strips for bandages.

"Oh Mother! The knight I fought had plated armour; I heard the resounding clang as my sword skimmed off it. I thought only to stun. Oh Hal, oh Mother, what have I done to you?" he whispered, ripping the fine cloth of his surcoat into lengths to bind and stem the flow of blood from Hal's wound.

Hal thought he would vomit with the pain.

"Hal, are you alive?"

"Ugh!" the Torra Altan grunted in acknowledgement but wished he were not.

His right arm was not too bad, the gash in his muscle long rather than deep and nothing that some stitches wouldn't heal in time. The left shoulder and upper arm, however, were a different matter. Ceowulf did his best to splint the pulpy mess and clean the jagged flesh broken by splinters of bone that poked up from beneath.

"It needs Brid to mend it," he said heavily, glancing towards the stake though the image of Brid was gone.

Hal squeezed his eyes tight against the pain. "Brid, where are you? I crossed worlds for you; find me now." He blinked up at Ceowulf. "Where is she?"

"Hush, Hal, keep calm. We don't know where she is and, if we don't find her soon, I'll have to cut this arm off or you'll die."

"Don't you touch me!" Hal hissed back, shaking with the pain.

CHAPTER SEVEN

May traced the arc of green bruising on her lower arm where the stonewight's great teeth had left their imprint. Her lip trembled as she thought that those bruises were the last testament to Perren's life and all they had to remember him by. Stinging tears glazed her eyes.

"I can't believe he's gone." She sniffed and finally broke down into sobs. "He could have made it. Why didn't he try? Oh Perren!"

Fern nodded his head, his jaw working vigorously over something in his mouth. Caspar noted the soggy bag of food in his hand and snatched it off him.

"How could you eat at a time like this? Perren is dead. He gave his life for us; you could at least show him some respect."

Fern shrugged. "I wept for him yesterday. I never did much like the fellow but I couldn't help myself for one so young. He was already dead."

"What do you mean?" Caspar checked the croak in his voice and wondered how he could raise some worthy memorial to the stonewight.

"You didn't notice? He knew our thoughts even when there was no water linking us."

Caspar stared blankly at the woodwose.

Fern snorted impatiently. "He felt our thoughts through the bones of the Great Mother. He knew his time was near as he grew closer to Her. Don't you remember? He told us that stonewights gain this privilege when death calls them. Apparently, the desert was too much and, though he regained his senses, his body had crumbled away from within."

Caspar swallowed, remembering how Perren had flagged and stumbled but aided them right to the very last.

"Anyway, I don't feel guilty; he gave his life for Necrönd not for me," Fern added.

Caspar ignored the woodwose. "We must see that we do not fail him. We must get Necrönd far from these shores and to a place of safety." He leant over the rail and called out over the waves, "Do not fear, Perren, we shall see your story is told. The world will know of your courage. We must see that we write the ending to his tale."

May sobbed. "A noble and mighty being, he died at the hands of a Vaalakan axe – just as my mother did. We shall see the task is done, Perren," she spoke the words softly with grim conviction. Caspar guessed the promise was as much for her mother as the great stonewight.

He nodded and looked through his stinging tears at the green of the sea. The offshore winds sweeping the heat off the desert out over the cool waters creating a swirling haze. The breeze was brisk and he had to work hard to stop the boat being driven out to sea, east with the wind. It was where he wanted to go but not without provisions. He looked out for a small fishing village where he could put in for supplies.

They would need to carry as much water and food as possible. He looked at Firecracker and Fern, thought on their voracious appetites and his mind was resolved as to what must be done with them.

"Look! Breakwaters!" May pointed enthusiastically. "And

what's that on the shore? We must be nearing a village at last."

"Crates of sorts," Caspar said, squinting at the shoreline and remembering Ursula's tale of being fostered by the oystermen of Oriaxia's eastern coast. "I think these shallow waters must be oyster beds," he said with relief. The last few hours had been hard work, battling to keep the boat on course, and he was relived at the thought of putting to shore. He didn't know how much more he could take of Fern's grumbling about his lack of seamanship.

"Elergian didn't have this trouble," the woodwose pointed out as, again, they hit the waves sideways on and spray washed over them, drenching all to the skin. The sun was warm and dried them quickly but the salt lingered and made their skin itchy and sore.

They rounded a headland to see lobster boats working up and down the coast. Tucked behind a rocky promontory, a brightly coloured village came into view. The low houses were widely spaced and painted in lime green with yellow doors and windows. It could have been the village Ursula had come from for all Caspar knew. He smiled at the memory of her and prayed that she was safe with Reyna. The slave girl had suffered too much for one lifetime.

He steered for a barnacle-covered stone jetty and tried to let the wind out from the sails as Elergian had showed him. But he was not a master of seamanship and braced himself as the boat ground against the rough slipway and jolted to a sudden halt.

May glanced at him critically.

"I'm doing my best!" he protested.

"The baby," she insisted. "We have to think of the baby."

The wolf and Trog leapt ashore while Firecracker stumbled onto the plank and lashed out at a pallet of oysters.

Hurriedly, Caspar steered his horse away from the water-side and stopped at the head of the quay by a number of stalls and an inn.

Approaching a young man who was sorting oysters into various baskets, he cleared his throat. "Water and food?" he said slowly and distinctly. "We need water and food."

A quizzical frown on his brow, the man looked at him, watching his mouth intently. Then he muttered something in Oriaxian, put the oyster in his hand down and turned to go.

"No, don't go. We need supplies," Caspar said insistently, hurrying after the man.

May caught Caspar's arm. "He means for us to wait."

"How do you know?"

She shrugged. "Just the way he said it."

Caspar waited, feeling foolish as a crowd gathered around him, pointing and talking. "Hello!" he said brightly, trying to communicate. "A beautiful village you have."

No one made any attempt to reply and it was some while before the oysterman reappeared with an elderly man strewn with shells and coral necklaces. He chattered away to them, sounding to Caspar mostly like a sheep bleating. Not understanding a single word, he drew out his purse and chinked it. "We wish to buy food and drink," he repeated very slowly though the men still looked blankly at each other.

"Mercy, Mother!" May despaired, pushing Caspar out of the way and glaring at him as if he were an idiot. Most engagingly, she mimed out the act of eating and drinking. The men laughed in understanding and nodded vigorously, pointing towards the inn with its doors open wide, the sound of singing coming from within. May shook her head, re-enacted her mime and then pointed at the boat.

At last, the message that they needed supplies got

through and Caspar's purse was examined to see what payment they were offering. The villagers pushed it away in disappointment.

"It seems King Rewik's likeness on a coin has little value in Oriaxia," Caspar said to May as he sought through their belongings for items to barter with. To Caspar's relief, the oystermen were very enthusiastic about the unicorn's horn and shortly barrels of fresh water were being rolled down the quay and pallets of dried breads, salted fish and dates were being carried after them to the boat.

Once they were loaded, Fern looked from Caspar to the large dusty sack that was still slumped on the slipway and examined the contents. "What about the grain? Why isn't it loaded?" he asked.

Caspar shook his head. "Because you and Firecracker will need it. And this." He handed Fern a fistful of coins.

"But . . ." Fern looked at him stupidly.

"I can't take you," Caspar said bluntly. "It's not fair on Cracker to take him and I need you to look after him. You must take him home. Hal will be glad of him."

"Hal doesn't like me."

"Of course, he likes you, Fern. Anyway, you'll be taking a message to him. You must tell him I won't return. Once we lose sight of these shores, the winds will sweep us away across the ocean and, as Ursula said, we cannot return. Torra Alta will eventually be his."

Fern contemplated this for a moment and then repeated, "Hal doesn't like me."

Caspar sighed in frustration. "Firstly, Fern, the boat's not big enough for a horse for anything more than a short length of time and, secondly, you and Cracker eat too much. We simply can't carry enough supplies. Who knows how many days we'll be at sea?" His voice was harsh and he tried not to look at his horse. He couldn't bear the thought of leaving Firecracker behind but he knew that he must.

"Did you put a notch in the wood this morning or not?" May asked somewhat belligerently.

Caspar didn't reply.

"Well, did you?"

"I'm thinking," he said, adjusting the canvas he had tied between the mast and gunwale to provide some shelter from the glaring sun. The westerly wind had stayed true and filled the sail, sweeping his thick auburn hair forward over his face.

"Well?"

"I can't remember." His mind was blurry and confused. Twice now he had swooned and collapsed onto the sun-baked deck, the pain in his head suddenly unbearable. He looked at the line of notches. "Forty-two days!"

"Or forty-three!" May said pointedly.

"Or forty-three," Caspar conceded. The water supplies were low but thankfully there was still plenty of food since the inactivity had dulled all their appetites bar Trog's. The dog sat by the barrels that had the rather nasty smelling fish in it and whined continually, the sound driving Caspar and May to distraction. "There must be land soon," he reasoned. "Somehow, against these winds, Ursula came from the east." He did not add though that he had no way of knowing whether Ursula's story of her homeland was true.

With more time on his hands than he had ever had before in his life, Caspar sat back against the gunwale, fingering over the chip of bone carved with the rune of the wolf that Morrigwen had given him. He looked at the smooth chip of bone and then at Runa who lay at May's feet, snuffling at her toes. Caspar wondered at the link between the rune and the white wolf and tried to piece together the relevant events of the past year since the trapper came to the castle with the body of a mother wolf.

Morrigwen had declared that the wolf's cubs must be found and that one of them would lead them to the new Maiden. Runa was the only one they had recovered. But Morrigwen was dead and her prophecy had not been fulfilled. Runa had led them nowhere.

At first, he had rejoiced when she had found Nimue, the sick child they had brought back from the Otherworld, and then Lana, the poor orphan who had been tricked into joining Ovissian gangs that were hunting down and stealing Torra Altan bears. But in the end Runa had only led them to May, who was most certainly not the maiden-to-be. He tried not to dwell on that thought but couldn't overlook the hugeness of her belly. The sickness of her early pregnancy was long passed as they had travelled through Lonis and Salise, but not so her shortness of temper. Still Caspar had to admit that she looked more beautiful now than ever before. He smiled at her, glad, despite everything, that they were together.

"The wind is still at our back and the lodestone holds true. We'll sight land soon, I'm sure of it," he said positively.

"Hmm," she said doubtfully, whilst recounting the notches on the mast. "Come and sit by me," Caspar coaxed.

May nudged Trog aside and picked her way across the boat. Silhouetted against a glaring sky, she looked down at him critically. "How's your head? Have you bathed it? The saltwater will cleanse it, you know."

"It's a little better," he lied. For the first couple of weeks at sea his scalp had barely troubled him but lately it had begun to itch. The discomfort kept him awake but he did not mind for he dreaded the night and the silence as the wind eased with the coming of darkness. It was eerily quiet out in the middle of the uncharted Tethys Ocean at the dead of night and it was then that his nightmares returned.

Even during the day now, when lying in the sweltering heat beneath the canvas, bouts of giddiness overwhelmed him, a pain cramping his brain. For a moment, he thought he saw three wizened old men hunched over a cauldron but he blinked and the image was gone from his mind.

May stooped over him and grunted her disapproval. "You've got to stop scratching at it," she chided him, dabbing the crown of his head with a cloth dipped into a bucket of sea water. "Do I have to look after you as well as myself?" She finished bathing the wound and slumped down, wriggling into his arms where she stayed, staring at the mountain of her belly until evening, barely speaking except to complain of feeling tired. Towards dusk, she stood to look east, waiting as she had every night for the moon to rise.

"There She is!" May breathed as the fingers of silvery light rippled across the waves towards them. "There is nothing more beautiful. It's only when Her soft light touches me that this aching tiredness leaves me."

Indeed, Caspar thought. Bathed in moonlight, she seemed to glow from within as the dancing white lights raced across the sea to touch her.

"It's like she's stretching out to guide our boat," he remarked. "I have often heard of a guiding star so why not the moon."

May laughed at the idea. "I think the current is taking us. Not the wind so much, which has often died away, but the current is strong and it's as if the waters of the Great Mother are rushing us this way."

"I hope so," Caspar sighed. "We'll run out of drinking water soon. We must restrict our intake."

"I can't," May said flatly.

Caspar nodded. "I know. The child!"

She lay down beside him again and he cradled her tightly in his arms, thankful for her close comfort while he slept. He dreaded his nightmares, dreaded the stench that would invade his dreams where shadows stalked him, that soft padding of unseen beasts always directly behind him however fast he ran. He tried to concentrate on the tick-ticking of the sheets against the mast but, as he fell into a deeper sleep, the sound was replaced by the sound of someone knocking at his head, hammering as if to split the skull, trying to get within his mind.

May shifted in her sleep and he awoke with a start. His neck prickled and he was sweating. He looked around at the flat silvery-black plain of the still ocean, certain that he had heard the howl of a wolf born on the wind. Runa sat upright, the hairs of her thick coat stiff along the length of her spine. Her upper lip trembled with a low growl. Caspar looked all about the boat. Though he could see nothing, he couldn't shake the feeling that the wolfman was close by, watching him.

He dared not sleep and stared behind them, once fancying that he glimpsed the tip of a mast lit by a bobbing lantern. Eyes aching with the strain, he watched for albatrosses and gulls that floated on the breeze. May had explained Talorcan's belief that an evil spirit could not touch salt-water, but if it passed into a bird, it would be able to fly across the sea. But the very few birds that he saw, as black specks against the starry sky, behaved in an entirely natural manner.

At last, the great ball of the sun crept up over the green-blue waters to warm him. While May groaned and lay flat on the deck – she was very much at her worst in the early morning – he shielded his eyes with his hand, staring east, an uncanny feeling pricking at his skin. The air smelt different somehow and, after a while, he decided that there was a paler hue to the sea. A black cormorant dived into the water just two hundred yards from them and Caspar stared hard east, eyes screwed tight, trying to pierce the glare.

Visibility was lessening. Drifts of haze tickled the waves and beyond that a thick bank of cloud smothered the horizon.

"It's either land . . ." May began.

Caspar, May and the two animals stood and watched with bated breath as they slid into the mist that clamped around them. Soon, they could see no more than a few yards of water in any direction, the sun no more than a white spherical ghost above them. "Or the edge of the world," Caspar finished.

Slowly the pale sun grew higher and warmer until it chased away the mist. They gasped. Land was suddenly all about them, large and green and close. Caspar and May cheered and hugged each other, their voices echoing back at them from the steep lines of the shore to either side. Trog nipped Runa's ear in the excitement but the wolf remained serene and nuzzled warmly up against May's thigh.

Somehow, on reaching this unknown continent beyond the Tethys Ocean, Caspar had expected to see something entirely more dramatic, like huge volcanoes spuming magma into the sea or giant forests above golden cliffs. But this coastline looked much like the coast of Piscera in southern Belbidian. Thousands of small islands dotted the sea around them and the coast ahead was creased by a wide estuary whose finger of water worked its way far inland. And it was into this water that they sailed.

A large silence overshadowed the estuary. Caspar drew in lungfuls of air, relived that there was no sign of civilization. Forested mountains rose steeply out, either side of the boat, their reflections vivid in the tranquil water. The quiet was broken only by the sound of the boat's hull swishing through the water, slicing through the peace of a landscape where life continued day in day out, pulsing to a natural rhythm undisturbed by man. White-crested eagles circled a valley someway to the north, huge birds effortlessly mastering the currents of the sky, and, close by, a ripple formed where the silver back of a large fish broke the surface.

"Land," May gasped.

"We made it!" Caspar hugged her, lifting her off her feet in his excitement.

"Careful!" she chided though she didn't stop grinning.

They celebrated by consuming several huge tankards of water, drinking to the point of feeling sick. Trog stood up in the bows and barked at his reflection while Runa, now a tall lean beast, her holly-green eyes brightening in the clear daylight, threw back her head and howled. The cry rose above the dog's noise and echoed back and forth in the mountain-bound estuary, the lonesome howl dying slowly. Its last notes were answered by a hollow roar. May and Caspar slowly lowered their cups.

"What was that?" May asked in a tight whisper.

Caspar smiled. "Troll, wyvern, mountain lion, unknown beast from an unknown territory," he joked in his euphoria.

"It's not funny," May snapped. "We're alone out here."

"It was just a bear," he said calmly, sorry that he had upset her. "They won't worry us out here on the water."

"Bears can swim," she retorted.

"They won't trouble themselves with us," Caspar

repeated. "Besides, no bear is a match for a Torra Altan archer." He rummaged amongst his bundled belongings for his bow. "Look, if it makes you feel any better, I'll string it for you. There's none handier in all the Caballan than a Torra Altan archer," he said jovially.

She sniffed. "We're not in the Caballan now."

They sailed up the narrow, overshadowed channel, the bellows from bears becoming more frequent as the finger of sea cut between mountains whose sides were thickly wooded.

Caspar cleared his throat pensively. The bear population did, indeed, seem large. He should have expected it, of course, since Ursula came from this land and had such a strange affinity for bears, but he couldn't explain why he felt so unduly perturbed by them. The Torra Altan brown bear was notoriously fierce yet it had never concerned him. Trog's ears were laid flat against his skull and he growled low in his throat.

"What's the matter?" May asked Caspar.

"Oh nothing," he said brightly, wiping away his frown.

"Do you fear they are of Necrönd?" she asked.

He hurriedly shook his head that ached a little.

May looked at him sideways. "You're feverish. Do you feel ill?"

"It's nothing," he snapped, not meaning to be short with her but he suddenly felt faint.

"You're having another one of your spells," she told him firmly

"No, I'm all right," he insisted, struggling to keep his head clear. "Just hold the rudder a moment." Fearing that he would be sick, he stuffed the bar of wood into her hand and struggled for the edge of the boat. But in his haste, he slipped on the deck and banged his head against the rail.

His vision swam dizzily into black. Out of the darkness

leapt the snout of a dragon. A plume of red flame gushed into his face, singeing his eyebrows. May screamed, bringing him to his senses.

"Spar, Spar, your eyes!"

For a second or two, he hung limply over the side, blood trickling from the crown of his head and round down onto his cheeks. His eyes stung.

"Your eyes are bleeding!" May exclaimed.

"No, no they're not!" he snapped angrily, too much in pain to be civil. "It's just my head."

"It's him, isn't it?" May said coldly, her arm placed protectively around Caspar's shoulders. "It's the wolfman and, without Amaryllis, we don't stand a chance. He's followed us even here."

"We can manage without Talorcan," Caspar growled proudly. "And somehow we will find some way to be rid of Necrönd."

"We cannot can we?" May said softly. "Not if he is right on our tail."

Caspar heartily wished that he could just hand the Egg over to some unsuspecting soul; *anyone* to take away his burden. "It's Necrönd drawing him to us," he murmured out loud. "When you had it, these mysterious things didn't happen to me, but now I have it again, I am plagued by them. If we can just be rid of Necrönd, we shall be rid of him."

At last, the steep-sided estuary narrowed to a point where they could go no further by boat: the brackish waters were headed by a waterfall tumbling two hundred feet to the sea. Pale shingle lined a shore to the left of the waterfall and Caspar chose that spot to land. They wrapped up what food was left and prepared to set out on foot to make the climb.

"I should carry you across the beach," he told May.

"Very chivalrous, I'm sure, but why?" she asked.

"It's like carrying you across the threshold into our new life." He kissed her cheek. "You're so beautiful, May."

"You might soon *have* to carry me," she laughed. "It's getting so I can barely walk."

Grunting, Caspar lifted her across the stony beach and placed her down at the foot of the cliffs before looking back at the boat. "Well, we won't be needing you again," he said to it. "There's no returning against those winds." He turned back to see Runa and the dog snuffling excitedly at the damp soil. May was gazing along the line of the shore and up at the white streak of tumbling water.

"What about the bears?" she asked.

"Bears won't deliberately attack. You mustn't surprise them, that's all. It's only if they feel threatened that they attack."

They made their way along the beach to the foot of the falls where the roar of crashing water was deafening. Caspar looked up, searching for the easiest climb. Dense forest, grown lush on the constant spray from the tumbling water, flanked the cascade and he hoped the roots would help their footing on the slippery, stepped rocks.

It took them half a morning's hard climb to make the top. Caspar's ears rang with the roar of rushing water but he was at least thankfully that the damp air washed away most of the encrusted salt from their exposed skin. A meandering river arched over the top of the falls and, once they had made their way just a little further inland, they were soon free from the constant roar and were able to rest and talk. While May lay flat on her back, catching her breath, Trog and Runa ran friskily round and round in circles, snapping at each other's tails. Strange birdsong filled the air.

"Is he up there watching us?" May stared at the sky,

evidently still worrying about the wolfman. "Is he up with there with the eagles?"

"They're not eagles," Caspar contradicted. "They're vultures." His vision was blurred and his head thumped but he could still tell the difference. He struggled to find clear thought; Necrönd must be drawing the wolfman to them. They must be rid of the Egg as fast as possible. "Why didn't I just drop the Egg into the great ocean?"

"Because the ocean is full of life. Any number of sea monsters might find it. We've discussed that all before," May told him with a touch of irritation.

Caspar nodded and helped May up so that they could trudge on along the banks of the river, watching the flickering water race by, shredding the reflections of the vast fir trees that overshadowed it. During the weeks afloat, he had longed to see land but even now he could see no more than a few hundred yards along the river for the army of trees about him.

After four days on foot and with seemingly no end to the trees, Caspar was regretting his decision to leave Firecracker behind. May's gait had become somewhat of a waddle and their progress was lamentably slow. There had to be horses, he thought. There were deer so surely there would be horses. In fact, there were countless deer. They had feasted well on venison and the supply had been so plentiful that they had simply cooked what they needed and discarded the remains rather than carrying heavy quantities of meat against the eventuality of running out of food.

After the next meal, Caspar licked his fingers and wiped them on his breeches. "It's a good thing Fern's not with us." He said before setting off again on their long march.

"What? Oh," May said dismissively, her brow puckered.

"I know there's something following us, Spar. Runa's hackles are up."

Indeed, both animals continually cast over their shoulders for much of the day and though Caspar could see nothing, it made him very uncomfortable. As evening drew in, he said cheerily to boost their morale, "I'll build a great big fire and we'll feast well. That'll keep the beasties away from us."

Forcing a smile onto her worried face, May nodded and protectively hugged the hump of her stomach, her eyes flitting into the shadows about them. While Caspar coaxed a flame from his gathered wood, May spent her time scratching runes into the dark earth around them.

"Runes of protection," Caspar said, stepping back from the crackling wood and examining them.

"Runes of protection," May confirmed solemnly.

When the meal was over, they sat by the fire and huddled close, listening to the sound of Trog splintering bones in his powerful jaws. Runa paced back and forth, sidling up to May and nuzzling her cheek or nipping her ear on each pass.

"I love you too," May said, ruffling the fur at the wolf's neck.

Caspar smiled at the pair, wondering at the strength of the bond that had developed between Runa and May. They trudged on through the rest day and at last came to the edge of the forest, which he was heartily glad to leave behind. Before them stretched a landscape that he had never imagined. Ranks of needle-thin peaks that he could only compare to the stalagmites of the caves below Torra Alta, projected out of a grassy plain dotted with willow trees. The trees were taller and thinner than those of the Caballan, their feet in the black sheets of water. Trog sniffed the air and stretched his nose forward in that way peculiar only to the Ophidian snake-catcher before dashing madly back and forth in front of them.

Caspar looked from the dog to the black water and shuddered. "Oh no! Not snakes!"

While Runa looked on with disdain, Trog leapt up into the air and bounced back and forth for half a minute before Caspar could calm him.

May went white. "Snakes?" she repeated in question.

Caspar nodded at Trog. "He can smell them. He only ever quivers like that when he can smell snakes."

The young woman pressed close to him. "Spar, you will look after me, won't you?"

"With my life," he replied seriously and then grinned at her. "But it shouldn't come to that just yet. Not if we go that way." He pointed to the dark, blue-grey needles of stone joined by threads of land that wound in paths between the sheets of water. "The flood's patchy there and we should find a way."

May was now large, her stomach swollen with child, and she was quickly breathless. When Caspar had made his decision to cross the sea and find an empty land, he hadn't thought of how May would grow over the last month or so and he cursed his lack of forethought. They needed help.

"May, we have a task to achieve, something you started and I must finish."

She was nodding at him. "I know."

"We must find a place of safekeeping for Necrönd – and soon – before *he* catches up with us."

"But where? How?"

Caspar grunted in dissatisfaction at their situation. "There must be a way. Brid would know what to do."

"Even here you haven't forgotten her," May despaired. "I thought that your love of her would fade, that we could build a life together and start again. But it seems that was too much to hope for."

"It's a burden we shall both have to bear," Caspar retorted. "I cannot forget Talorcan." He nodded at her belly. "The fruits of his doings stare me in the face every day yet you expect me never to mention Brid."

They trudged slowly on in silence, Caspar absorbed in thought, his mind circling like a hawk, waiting to glimpse an idea and stoop on it. The ground was wet under foot, spongy mosses sucking at their heels.

"Spar, I can't keep up," May called from some distance behind.

He had been walking slowly but was amazed at how quickly May now tired. He turned back for her.

"Spar, the baby will come before too long; we must find somewhere safe, somewhere away from snakes and the beasts of the forest," she said worriedly.

Caspar grunted in agreement but he wasn't really listening. Night was drawing in and they had a patch of calf-high water to wade through before they reached the higher ground footing one of the spikes of rock. He thrashed the water with a stick, hoping to frighten away any snakes that might be wriggling in these pools before wading in. He, too, wanted to find somewhere safe; he was tired and there was a mist rising.

While Trog was obsessed with sniffing the water with snakes, Runa was, for once, more playful and kept snatching at the stick as if it were a toy. He gently chided her and ruffled the long fur at the back of her neck. She snuffled his thigh and for the first time licked his hand. He had never forgotten that she was a wild animal and was deeply touched that, at last, he had won her trust.

"One last bit of wading and then we'll be on higher ground and out of this damn fog," he said encouragingly.

"What fog?" May replied in surprise. "The evening's clear and crisp."

Caspar squinted at the dark needles of rock that, earlier, before the sun dipped, had stood out like black-cowled monks in a field of snow but now they were only indistinct shadows. "I must sleep," he groaned, exhausted by the burden of his responsibility.

"We could still go a little further tonight," May urged. "Every step takes us nearer to our deliverance."

"No, not tonight." Caspar stumbled.

"What's wrong?" May was alarmed.

"I don't know." Suddenly the air seemed oppressive and he was having difficulty breathing as if someone else were sucking up his breath. He splashed hurriedly through the shallows but, on reaching firmer footing, slumped giddily to the ground, the damp earth cool against his cheek. He lay there, blinking, trying to clear his vision but the pain returned, stabbing deep into his mind.

From somewhere distant, he heard a scream. When he decided that he could smell singeing hair and fat and could hear more agonized shrieks and the groaning cogs of a rack, the ropes creaking, he feared he was losing his mind. More screams filled his head and he coughed and spluttered, choking on acrid smoke. He had smelt that smoke before in the dungeons of Abalone. Was he somehow on the brink between worlds? Surely, he heard the torment of tortured souls. Lost in a universe of pain, Caspar could no longer distinguish reality from the fears that tortured his mind.

"I knew you would be strong, Spar," a voice growled within his head and Caspar saw the creature, half man half wolf, clawing at his scalp. "I need your strength. It feeds me!"

The pain! Caspar's thoughts were shredded by it and he felt it would never stop. And then a pinpoint of light pierced the red savagery of his world and with it brought a cooling song. The pain lessened to a throbbing ache, freeing part of his mind to think. Around him was an unbearable noise; the sound of pigs being slaughtered, he thought at first. Then, as the soothing light grew in his head, he recognized the sound as his own screaming.

Hunched up over his knees and elbows, his wail was shrieking into the ground. Someone had their arm around his shoulder and he was horribly aware of the deep heavy breathing of a large animal, and the heavy pad of their feet that was continually circling him. He judged it to be the size of a mountain lion.

"Oh Spar! Oh Spar! What have I done?" May wailed.

"May, no!" Caspar rolled over onto his side, still too weak to stand. She was clutching the Egg!

"You were screaming! Screaming for ages and ages. I thought you were dying. I thought you were going to leave me out here in this empty world all alone. Then you begged me to use the Egg, saying they had gripped your mind. You begged me!"

"Oh May, what have you done?" Caspar groaned in despair, his eyes instinctively drawn to the dark about them where shapes were gathering beyond the spires of rock. Pushing her behind him, he took up his bow and, without looking, notched an arrow to the string. Trog and Runa drew close, their warm bodies pressing against them.

Trog alternately whined and growled and began making over-excited yipping noises in his throat while the hairs on his spine bristled. Runa stood stiff and silent, muscles jerking ready for attack. Their tension infected Caspar and he took steady breaths to calm himself. What if the Trog and Runa could smell the wolfman; what if he were flesh and blood?

The attack when it came was so swift out of the black that Caspar never saw it. Something moving at great speed punched him in the chest and knocked him to the ground. Only then did he hear the snarling growls. Blurrily, he pushed himself up and then came to his senses with a start. May was screaming! He spun round, looking for her. She was running, the great shape of a black wolf snapping at her heels. Then it pounced and together they rolled into the shallow water.

Caspar sprinted after them, screaming like a demon, "Get off her! Let go!" he yelled.

Trog, whose stocky but powerful legs propelled him faster than even Runa over that short distance, got to them first. The terrier sprang at the back of the black wolf's neck.

Caspar dived into the fray with his knife drawn. He felt coarse thick hair and stabbed. His blade pierced soft tissue and then ground against bone. The black wolf screamed and twisted its neck round to snap at him with its jaws. He stabbed again but a second wolf gripped his calf, and was dragging him back, away from May. He raked and slashed and drove the knife through the animal's eye into its brain.

He was on his feet, but he couldn't see May for the tangle of writhing dog and wolves. Then he glimpsed her feeble arm clawing at the neck of the black shadowy wolf. She was pinned beneath its bulk. The creature drew back its head, great jaws gaping wide.

Runa sprang up and thrust herself beneath the black wolf, her jaws snapping at the wide mouth of the black beast. Their heads locked together, Runa disappeared underneath the shaggy black bulk and, the horrible sound of splintering bone reached Caspar's ears.

Trog was on top, gripping the back of the black wolf's

neck and Caspar thrust his blade deep into the beast's flank again and again until finally the great black wolf fell silently to the ground.

"May!" Caspar shouted. "May, where are you?"

Trog was whimpering but otherwise a cold silence hung over the scene. Finally, May's sobs broke the chilling quiet and, in the darkness, he saw that she lay the cradling the wolfling.

"Oh Runa!" she wailed.

Caspar took a torch from his fire and held it high to cast light on the tragedy. The great black wolf lay dead. He kicked it to check it was fully dead but was alarmed at its lightness. Holding the torch closer, he saw that it was no more than a hide and skull with no flesh or substance within. He left it and turned his sorry gaze back to May and Runa, instinctively knowing there was nothing he could do. Sobbing, May lay over the wolfling whose chest, neck and head were a glistening crimson.

"She's still breathing," May managed to say between sobs.

"Then there's hope," Caspar said to be kind as he knelt beside her, his hands trembling and gulping back his emotions, but he knew by the misshapen crushed skull that there was not. He looked from Runa to May and saw that she was protectively cradling her left hand in her right. "You're hurt."

Intent only on comforting Runa, May didn't bother to answer and just shoved him away when he tried to look at her hand. Unable to do anything else, he choked on his grief and looked to his own wounds that thankfully were not deep since he had been saved by the good leather of his boots.

By morning, they had done all they could to make the

wolfling comfortable. May was quiet and obviously in pain, her face drawn and concerned, anxious for the baby. Now she cradled Runa's head in her lap. They had washed the wounds around her face and neck, and she wagged her tail and whimpered appreciatively; but she would not eat or drink.

"She saved me," May murmured. "He was going for my throat and Runa savèd gave herself for me." She soothed her head and the wolfling seemed calm and content in her lap. "I think there's too much bleeding within her head. I would give her melilot but she won't drink and there's nothing more I can do."

"She's going to die," Caspar said gently and knelt down beside Runa, stroking her smooth, warm back as she lay nestled against May's swollen belly. There was an air of peace about the place though the sadness consumed them.

"I'm sorry, Runa," Caspar repeated over and over. Morrigwen had charged him with looking after the wolfling so that she might find the new Maiden. She had died with that one request on her lips but he had taken up a quest of his own. "I'm so sorry."

He glanced anxiously at May, who was still making light of her wounded hand, but at last he coaxed her into letting him look at it. He was expecting to see great furrowed marks from the huge canine eye-teeth and was shocked at the sight of little crescent-shaped indentations that were surely the imprint from a human mouth. He stared at the mark in horror and dropped her hand alarm.

"He had no eyes," May said calmly.

Caspar said no more as they watched over Runa all that day and into the night. The moon was full. It rose above two distinctive peaks and its white incandescence cast deep shadows, the sentry of rocks standing taller in its magical light. Runa raised her head, searching for the touch of a moonbeam. When it caressed her, she let out a soft moan then slowly her head sank down to rest against May's belly.

Caspar wept as he had not wept for Morrigwen or Perren. He wept for the honesty in the wolf's soul, for her courage and selflessness and wept, too, that he had failed her.

May did not cry. Silently, she stared up at the moon all that night, as if drinking in its magic. Caspar could not persuade her to relinquish Runa's body and she kept it cradled on her lap until morning. The sun shone down on Trog sitting with his head on one side, looking confused. Gently, he prodded Runa with his nose and, when there was no response, tried to lift her head as if to wake her. But when her broken head flopped straight back down again, he whimpered and ran round in frenzied circles as if trying to flee from his pent-up emotions that he did not understand.

"May, we must leave her," Caspar said as the pink light of dawn gave colour to the flooded landscape.

The young woman nodded. For the moment they had a sense of peace in their sadness. Runa had driven the wolfman away and they no longer felt hunted.

"If it weren't for her, I would be dead," she kept saying.

Caspar carried Runa in his arms, her body surprisingly heavy. Her head hung down, a blue tongue lolling to the rhythm of his stride. They chose a crag jutting out from a tall spire of rock and heaved Runa's body up to it. It was a prominent place, the sort of place where a wolf might choose to lie in the sun or squat on its haunches and throw back its head to howl at the moon.

They placed stones over her body, though Trog yipped indignantly at them for this. Every time Caspar attempted to lay a stone on her, the Ophidian snake-catcher pushed it off with his nose and growled in warning at Caspar's hand. Eventually Caspar caught him, put a rope through his collar and tied him up to a tree until he had finished building the small cairn to cover Runa's body.

All the while, Trog howled and gnawed at the rope. Caspar was about to free him when Trog snapped the cord and sprinted to the foot of the cairn, where he dug frenziedly. Before Caspar could get to him, Trog had exhumed one of Runa's paws and was trying to drag her out.

"Trog, no! Leave her!" Caspar pleaded. "She's dead, Trog. There's nothing more you can do. Trog, leave her!"

The terrier snapped at Caspar's outstretched hand, something he had never done before, and went back to the urgent business of trying to rescue Runa. May was in tears and sat down and flung her arms around the dog. "Trog, Trog, she's gone; she's dead."

The dog did not understand and, in the end, Caspar was again forced to leash the dog and drag him, howling, away. They trudged on eastward into the landscape, Caspar dragging the dog after him.

CHAPTER EIGHT

The red, orange and blue flames teased at the base of the piled faggots. Smoke coiled and twisted around Brid's feet before wafting upwards and creeping into her mouth. She strained and twisted to break free from her bonds, her muscles taught like cord as she stretched her neck up and away from the choking fumes. Eyes stinging, she stared in horror at the flames, trying to convince herself that they were only imaginary.

Heat tickled her toes, the skin beginning to itch and prickle. Soon it would singe and she would struggle to free herself from the bonds. This was how she had watched her mother die. She had witnessed her agony as her bubbling flesh became crisp until the skin charred and peeled away from the bones that were soon thin, blackened sticks that crumbled away.

The horror of the memory overwhelmed her and, in mad panic, she screamed for help. "Hal! Hal! Help me!"

"Brid!" he answered her.

"Hal! Hal!" she shrieked.

"Brid, I'll save you," he shouted and she saw him through the haze of smoke, galloping towards her; but it was no good. Every night he was attacked by fiendish hobgoblins who hacked through his gleaming armour that was all polish and no metal. They cut him to shreds. It was the most horrible thing she could imagine.

Swooning from the fumes and the pain, she awoke finding herself back in a cold, dark cell unable to move. But at least she could think. How could she be so weak-minded as to allow the wizards to manipulate her imagination? She was Brid the Maiden, One of the Three, and yet she let them beat her. A persistent voice within her taunted, "But Morrigwen is dead. Your powers are weak. You are but a woman, no longer One of the Three. The Trinity is broken."

It was true. She had no more power than May. The horror of it! Brid realized her arrogance and faced the truth. All these years, though she knew it wrong to think it, she had assumed that it was some strength within her soul that had given her power rather than a gift invested in her by the Great Mother. To prove it, the wizards had trapped her as easily as they had trapped Hal with an image grown of her own fearful imagination.

But of course! Why hadn't she thought of it before? If her imagination worked against her, it must also work for her. What if she imagined Ceowulf riding to her rescue in place of Hal? Ceowulf was a great knight; he might beat the hobgoblins. Moreover, she was not in love with him and that might ease the terror in her mind and so lessen the intensity of the dream.

"Mother, give me strength of mind," she prayed as her nightmare began again. The flames licked at her feet and, as the image of Hal formed in her mind, she struggled to blot it out and impose Ceowulf's strong face over the features of the handsome Torra Altan.

"Ceowulf!" she shouted and to her great satisfaction saw him beyond the leaping flames. She believed he would rescue her and so break the spell on her mind but then she smelt wyvern as if his nightmare was now invading and intensifying hers. The beast plunged through the flames, its huge beak wide, the tongue whipping at her, its claws raking open her chest. Pain overwhelmed her.

She awoke back in the same dank cell, unable to see or hear anything. Her mind raced. She had altered the dream. Though the conclusion was no better and she was still trapped in a cycle of torment, she had at last exerted her will on the outcome. But she had been just as afraid of the wyvern as Ceowulf had been and so she could not dispel the terror from his mind to destroy the illusion. She had to join with one of the others in a dream where she would have no fear.

As on all other nights, her dream started abruptly and, in a blink of an eye, she found herself tied to the stake, the wood crackling at her feet. Before, she had shouted for Hal, though that had never helped her, and last night she had shouted for Ceowulf only to be attacked by a wyvern. Refusing to accept defeat, she considered her options. It had to be Pip or Abelard.

Abelard was the obvious one to summon into her mind but something stopped her. Abelard had seen so many atrocities; Abelard knew the true pain of death and would fear the cruel loneliness that followed. She didn't want to enter his nightmare. Pip was young and relatively innocent and quite reckless, which meant he feared very little. She couldn't imagine anything in his thoughts that would strike terror in hers.

Her mind was resolved. "Pip, I need you. Where are you?"

Instantly the smoke was gone and the leaping tongues of fire reduced to a single, flickering flame. At once she knew she had left her own dream and braced herself to enter Pip's and face his fears. She blinked, waiting for her eyes to adjust to the gloom. She imagined she would find herself in the midst of battle, a Vaalakan axe hovering to severe her head, but she was wrong. She was in her own room in bed. Bewildered, she wondered why on earth Pip should be frightened here.

She was about to get out of bed and approach him when she saw she was quite naked beneath the cool, fine linen of the bedding. Pulling the sheet up around her, she examined the chamber. Embers smouldered in the grate. The candles that were normally arranged neatly on the table were heaped in one corner as if someone had intended to clear away all sign of her office as a high priestess.

Sitting up, she let the sheet slide down her body, stopping momentarily where it arrested on the point of her breasts before sliding further to her navel.

"Pip," she heard herself murmur softly.

He was standing before her, wearing nothing but his leather breeches. Though tall for his fourteen years, he had none of the breadth of chest of a man yet he posed himself like a man and stepped boldly forward. Puzzled, she frowned, still wondering why he could possibly be frightened by her. He moved and put a hand on the sheets. Feeling in no way threatened by the boy, she did not even snatch them back to cover herself but found that, in Pip's dream, she lay there quite naked, looked at him and laughed.

His face fell into one of horrified embarrassment and then driven desperation. Flinging himself down on her, his hands grappling for her breasts, he smothered her face in wet kisses. She twisted back and forth to be rid of him. Horrified by his strength and the warm wetness of his kisses, she struggled for breath. A small woman pinned beneath him, she could not fight the hefty youth off.

"Hal!" she screamed. "Hal!"

Instantly, he stood in the doorway, dressed in his usual leather breeches and a plain wool shirt, his black boots gleaming like his black hair. In two strides, he covered the bare floorboards to her bedside and, with one hand, wrenched Pip off her, spinning him round and hurling him against the foot of the far wall. His hand momentarily hooked over the hilt of his knife at his belt but he appeared to reconsider his actions and raised his fists instead.

Brid saw the look of utter terror on Pip's face.

"Hal, no!" he begged. "This is all a mistake. She was calling to me. I couldn't stop myself. Please believe me, Hal, I would never do this to you."

Hal dragged the boy up by the throat, pressing his head back against the stone of the wall. Then he hit him once, hard in the jaw and let him slip back to the floor. Blood dribbled from the corner of Pip's mouth. The boy coughed and choked and tried to speak but instead spat out four teeth.

For one moment of cold silence, Hal glared him in the eye before a bestial bellow of rage welled up from his gut and he lost control. Dropping Pip to the floor, he grabbed his hair and smashed his face time and time again onto the thick boards of the floor. When he eventually let go and sat back, Pip's face was a mass of red pulp, the skin split, the nose nothing but torn gristle.

Pip's nightmare evaporated and Brid was back in the silent black cell, wondering again that they were trapped here forever and could find no way out. She tried to tell herself that the emptiness around her was imaginary; the reality was that she was trapped by the three wizards, chanting their spells, but she had no sense of them even. If she were stronger, still possessed the mystical powers of the Trinity, she might escape her body; but she was nothing but a peasant girl. She needed to believe that she was still in the glade in Trows Forest but, instead, she believed her eyes.

But if she couldn't persuade herself of her delusion, she must still persuade one of the others in order to break the mind-binding spell. Once the veil of magic was ripped aside from one, it might free them all. But how? Perhaps she was simply approaching things in the wrong way.

Taking a deep breath to steady her nerves and gather her thoughts, she waited calmly until the inevitable dream began again.

In a dulcet voice, she summoned him. "Pip. Oh, Pip."

Quite naked, she was back in her room at Torra Alta, lying in her carved wooden bed. She smiled to herself, happy with her plan and her ability to influence events. It was all so easy! Why hadn't she thought of it before? Reaching for her gown, she modestly covered herself to avoid appearing provocative towards the young lad. If she was uninviting, Pip would never be so bold as to approach her.

But she was wrong. Her struggling against his eager hands incited him to a frenzy. She clenched her teeth on her shouts for help, refusing to call for Hal. Somehow, she must manipulate events to change the pattern of Pip's dream. But she could not stop the boy's bellows of frustration and the noise soon brought her beloved. Again, Hal brutally beat Pip to a pulp.

Brid despaired. Whatever she did, she was unable to stop Hal attacking Pip. Her next ploy was to let this dream play out its usual course right up until the end when Pip's gory body lay slumped against the wall. Then she ran to him and cradled his broken head.

"Pip, you're alive. It's only a dream." She shook his limp body. "Pip, this isn't real."

Nothing changed and she was back in the miserable loneliness of the black cell, wondering how she was ever going to stop this nightmare. She had tried everything, hadn't she? She sat quietly, trying to empty her mind of fear and self-doubts so that she might reach the intensity of concentration needed to gain lucid thought.

There was just one last thing! Again, she called to Pip, focusing her mind to reach his.

"I'm here," he said warmly, lovingly.

Brid was very fond of the boy, admired his courage and was not so annoyed by his wild ways as perhaps she should have been but not in a thousand moons would she have considered taking him as her lover, not even if he had as much experience and charm as Ceowulf. She loved Hal and that was that.

As before, she was in her own bed, quite naked. This time, she took no thought to her clothing but looked around for a weapon. Her eyes glanced over the heaps of artefacts that Pip had swept away and discarded from the scene; cloaks, books, hares' feet, eagles' wings, vials, all jumbled together amongst the cobwebs. She looked past them and over the candles, her eyes resting momentarily on the candleholders but dismissing them from her mind, seeking a glint of gold.

There it was! Leaping from the bed, she dug amongst her possessions and extracted the sacrificial sickle. She gritted her teeth. Pip was there in the stone arch of the doorway, as before. His expression confused, he frowned at her and looked back at the bed, as if wondering why she wasn't there. Still, he seemed little deterred and strode forward, ripping off his shirt and flinging it down into the dust.

With her sickle ready behind her back, she fixed on

him and snarled, "Stay back from me." Her voice was hard and determined. "Pip, it isn't real. It's all a dream," she tried to warn him.

He reached out a hand to touch her breast and, rather than lashing out with her weapon, she spun round to face the arch doorway, waiting to see Hal.

There he was! Wild with rage, he burst forward. She responded likewise. With flailing arms and shrieking savagely, she leapt at him, hand raised to strike with the sickle.

"Brid!" he screamed in dismay as she lashed at him.

She raked at him with the sickle, shredding flesh. He raised his arms to protect his face and she slashed at them, feeling the razor edge slice neatly through the skin and snag on bone beneath.

"Brid! But Brid, I love you!" Hal shrieked. "No!" Hal was shouting as he fell to the ground.

Someone was trying to drag Brid off, while she ranted and thrashed, tears streaming down her face. Though she saw she had inflicted such horrible wounds on Hal, she told herself that though it felt real, it was all illusion; at this moment, Hal was surely suffering in an entirely different dream of his own.

"Brid, what are you doing? Stop it!" Pip was yelling, his strong hands pulling her off. "Brid, this is madness. Stop it!"

She swung round at him, sickle raised, but he didn't flinch; the fear in his eyes was gone. He wasn't going to die any more. Looking down at Hal's broken body, he said weakly, "He didn't attack me. I'm still whole!" he laughed stupidly, looking at his thick hands then looked up brightly at Brid. Suddenly blushing at her naked body, he held up her gown and pressed it to her. He laughed delightedly and stepped slowly around, looking about.

"It's gone. The rooms are gone. The stocks are gone. Look! Trees!"

Brid knew she had won. She had swept aside the clouds of illusion from Pip's eyes and the wizards were no longer her masters; she had beaten them. She had succeeded without need for magic; she had succeeded without the power of the Trinity. Her strength of mind alone had broken the spell.

She laughed in triumph. Slowly, the room around her began to melt into oaks and a huge split willow, one bough cracked away from the crown of the trunk and resting on the ground. She could smell bracken and hear the rustle of leaves teased by the wind. There was a dampness to the air as if it had recently rained.

But she could not move her body. Her legs were utterly locked and only her head and fingers moved freely. Immediately it struck her that she was half buried in the earth. So, this had been her cell! She wriggled her fingers, the nails caked in mud where she had evidently clawed her way up from her shallow grave while she slept. Wriggling and squirming, she worked one arm free from the loose soil and wiped her mouth and nose that were stuffed with grit. Then she clawed around her neck until her shoulders were free.

She could smell smoke. Blinking, she swivelled her eyes to see about her as she successfully extracted her legs from the ground. The wizards were nowhere to be seen though their cauldron remained, belching out a dark green smoke that filled the glade. Sadly, she could also see the half-rotted carcasses of two great horses and knew by the detailing of their harness that they were Secret and Sorcerer. Her heart sank. Abelard had been looking after them and that meant that he and probably Cymbeline had also been overcome by the wizards.

Warily, she sniffed the acrid smoke. Dragon smoke, that was what it was! Intoxicating dragon smoke had surely made them vulnerable to the wizards' mind-bending tricks. So that was why the wizards had so easily conquered her mind.

She wondered where the wizards were. Presuming that it must take enormous concentration and effort for them to sustain their spell over so many people for so long, she guessed that they were only present when they inflicted those terrifying nightmares on them. During those long periods of empty thought when she had believed she was in a cell, the wizards must have retreated to recuperate, leaving them drugged by the smoke and buried.

A grunt behind her made her twist violently round. Pip was there beside her, tentatively pressing at his nose and cheeks as if feeling for damage. He seemed puzzled but heartily comforted to find his face unharmed and looked at her in great relief before blushing in acute embarrassment. He opened his mouth to speak but Brid covered her lips with her finger.

"Lie back down! Cover yourself with leaves," she warned. A prickling at the back of her neck had alerted her to something. She must still have some of her old powers, she reasoned, sensing ripples in the air like the bow-wave pushed before a blunt-nosed ship; there was something travelling towards them through the channels of magic. The wizards were returning.

She slumped back down, trying to still her breathing, the scent of leaf-mould strangely comforting. She was amazed to see that the ghostly forms of the wizards did not check on their victims but immediately huddled around the cauldron. Soon they were breathing in its vapours and chanting in a strange language. The sound was faintly musical yet without beauty as if the notes were part of some mathematical sequence.

She wondered whether she should just leap up and run before they realized she was awake but she could not leave without her friends. Lying still, she braced herself for their magic. Intense thought spiked into her mind, instilling in her head images of blazing faggots which she tried to blot out by thinking of all Morrigwen's favourite herbal remedies. At last, their images faded, and the wizards were gone, only the smoke billowing from the cauldron indicated that they had been there at all.

Earth still clinging to every inch of their bodies, they searched the leafy ground at their feet but could see no tell-tale signs of disturbed earth for the layers of crisp golden-brown oak and beech leaves. The hazy smoke was thickening and drifted this way and that, covering their feet, and made it impossible to see the ground clearly. When Brid dropped to her knees to search for signs of the others, she quickly became faint and confused.

Nevertheless, she had to crouch to sweep aside the leaves with her arms as she searched. Finding herself crawling round in circles, she realized in dismay that the smoke was overwhelming her again. She was surprised to find some leaves strangely blackened but could not attach any significance to it. They had been searching for nearly an hour; the wizards would surely return soon and they had found nothing. Brid stood and staggered to the edge of the glade, away from the smoke where she instantly began to feel better. They needed help. But what help was there to be had here in Trows Forest?

"Kobolds! That's it, Pip," she murmured. "They'll help us."

"But how?" he protested, looking doubtful. "Stupidest creatures ever. And, besides, we've seen none."

She shrugged. "There must be thousands of them about in such a remote forest but they will be very wary of showing themselves. If we use the same tree-runes that they use to communicate with, and write, 'help' on a dozen trees hereabout they might come out of hiding."

With nimble fingers, Brid used her knife to nick the bark of several beech trees nearby. Their smooth bark was easier to score than that of the gnarled oaks or the great willow. She stepped back to admire her handiwork before returning to the frantic task of trying to uncover the others, her mind churning over her lack of *sight*. How could she have just stumbled straight into the wizards' trap? Why hadn't she known it was dragon's smoke? She felt sure she would have known before Morrigwen had died but now she was losing confidence in her judgement. She wondered whether Hal would still be interested in her when he saw she had no powers, when she was no more than any other ordinary woodswoman.

Under those circumstances, she could see how he would find Cymbeline so much more attractive than herself. The thought pained her. She loved him, though she didn't even know why. He had obvious attributes of course, being strong and darkly handsome. His wit and natural manner also made him popular with the ranks, though he never lost his dignity, always seeing to it that he wasn't so familiar that he lost their respect.

But why had she fallen for him in particular? There were other men that were just as fine, Ceowulf for instance. She envied Cybillia's love for Ceowulf. The knight was steady, undemanding, cynically amusing and rarely wrong-footed. And then there was Spar, so tender and concerned. Spar she understood. But she did not love him. Everyone assumed that she loved him but she had always known she was too strong for him. She couldn't love someone whom she could manipulate. But now! Now when her powers had deserted her, when she was nothing but her real self, perhaps now it might be different? She swallowed hard and shuddered at how her thoughts had wandered from Hal. Her self-doubt grew.

With the Trinity broken, she was no one, had no special power. But she still had her knowledge. She could still cast runespells; she still understood the powers of the trees and the healing properties of the herbs; but gone was the intuitive incisiveness, gone was the *sight* that elevated her above the common people, gone was the spirit of the Great Mother within her.

Cold with cramp from kneeling over and sweeping aside leaves, she squinted out into the dark of the forest, her head spinning uncomfortably. Now she had even failed in the simple task of summoning kobolds.

"Here! Help! Quick!" Pip urged.

Brid ran to him as he dragged out a jewelled, hand the symbol of a fish carved into a heavy ring. "Hardwin!" she said in disappointment as she helped Pip drag him clear. Brid turned him over and stared into his frozen face that spoke of a catatonic mind behind. She flung herself back to the forest floor, frantically searching around the spot where they had found Hardwin in hope that Hal was close.

A boot! Her hand skimmed over the toe of a black boot. She scrambled at it and began dragging at the leg that appeared before stiffening in alarm. A hunting horn wailed out through the forest.

Pip grabbed her shoulder and tugged her back. "Quick! Hide in the undergrowth."

Brid pushed him away and pulled ever more frantically at the boot, but her efforts lessened as she cleared the mud away from a long thin leg clad in heavy wool cloth. It wasn't Hal.

But she had delayed too long. The yelp of hounds baying to the hunt filled the forest, the scent of fear heady in the atmosphere. With grunts of effort, a trembling hind staggered across the glade. Dogs swarmed after it, the ringing noise of their pursuit deafening as they howled and whooped. Still clinging to the leg she had recognized as belonging to Renaud, Brid froze as the hounds forsook their prey and bunched around her, the air thick with their steaming breath.

One came closer and put its mouth to the hem of her tunic, growling and starting to tug. At that moment, huntsmen broke through the tress. High in their saddles, hot on the trail of the dogs, they shouted and yelled at their unexpected find, hauling their steaming horses to a halt. A great chestnut mare sat back on its haunches. The richly dressed man on its back, breathing hard from the ride, dipped forward against the mane and gaped in amazement. He fixed on Brid then Pip and back at Brid again, his gaze curious and intense as he noted her fine figure beneath her earth-caked hunting leathers and her hand on the boot of a half-buried man. Hardwin was now writhing on the floor and squealing as if possessed by demons.

Think! Brid told herself, think and say something – something plausible. But she could think of nothing to say as the huntsman dismounted and cracked his whip, calling the dogs to heel. Dressed in a studded leather jerkin, his arms bare, he was dark for a Ceolothian and less brutish in build.

An older heavier man, thick about the face, his horse

sweating hard from carrying his weight, crashed out of the trees. He looked down at Pip and Brid, his eyes widening in revulsion and accused in Ceolothian, "Demons! Grave robbers!"

CHAPTER NINE

Caspar and May gazed at a beautiful, soft landscape rich with life that stretched away to distant cloud-topped mountains. Rising up through the green mat of close-cropped grass at their feet, wild flowers flourished in abundance. The blooms formed great coloured mounds and swathes of blue and ribbons of yellow, the flowers dancing in the light breeze.

May picked a few flowers at random and examined them with interest. "I don't know the half of them," she admitted. It was the first time she had spoken of anything but Runa since the wolfling's death and her voice was strained. "That looks like giant speedwell." She pointed to a large five-petalled flower that was a deep blue and not dissimilar from the colour of Caspar's eyes.

He nodded distractedly, searching the golden plain for signs of life.

May seemed to read his thoughts. "Where are the cows? This is like a giant Belbidian meadow and it looks like it should be filled with cows," she said listlessly, her face drawn and tight.

Caspar slipped his hand into hers and squeezed. "I don't know. But look at this place; it's so tranquil."

She pushed him away irritably and he withdrew for a while, thinking that she must blame him for Runa's death. She walked more and more slowly and eventually gave in to his offer to pull her gently along. All the while he watched warily about them and once thought he saw oxen grazing but it was far in the distance. He did, however, see a dry-stone wall, cutting a harsh line through the rich habitat.

"I'm so tired. I've got to stop," May moaned.

"We can't stop here," Caspar said. "We must be near people." He nodded at the line of the wall someway to their left.

"People? Where?" she asked with a little too much enthusiasm.

Caspar shrugged. "I don't know but someone built that wall and we don't want to meet anyone."

"No, I suppose not," May said doubtfully, stopping for breath. "No, I . . ." Her voice trailed away.

Hours later, their legs soaked up to their thighs from the taller stems of the wild flowers, they found the ground was rising. Caspar halted, waiting for Trog who still moped and whined, constantly trotting back and barking as if calling to Runa to follow. Caspar's throat tightened at the thought and he distracted himself by gazing at the landscape.

To the south, the brilliant golden lawn deepened to a darker heath and slate mountains grew out of the haze that lazed on the horizon. They toiled on through undulating terrain until the ground before them began to drop away to a heavily wooded land unmarked by tracks where five rivers coiled back and forth, winding through the darker places. To the east and north the forest stretched to the horizon, and to the south a volcano puffed a trill of black smoke that rose into strange shapes and trapped the sun to become a crimson bank like a far-off land floating in the sky.

Caspar halted on a sudden strip of bare earth. May

stepped back in fright and Trog sniffed suspiciously at the ground. Caspar looked down at his feet to see a line of symbols carved into the soil. Though he had no notion of their meaning there was something familiar about them, which made him feel uneasy. He concentrated, trying to remember where he had seen them before.

"Ursula!" he exclaimed in relief. "Of course!"

"What are you talking about?"

"That's where I've seen those symbols before. On Ursula's arm."

"What do they mean?"

"I don't know, I never asked her. I thought they were some slaver's mark," he explained.

"Slavers!" May looked horrified and stared anxiously at the forest below.

"No, no. Obviously I was wrong. The marks must have been from her life here before she was cast away across the Tethys Ocean."

"Oh! But still they must mean something very important," she pointed out, taking his hand and stepping over the line of runes that stretched as far as they could see in either direction along the ridge. A tremble ran through Caspar's body and he chided himself for allowing his imagination to disconcert him. He had expected some strange feeling and, no doubt, that was why he had felt something. Unconsciously, he reached in his pocket and fingered the chip of bone marked with the symbol of the wolf as if somehow it had spoken to him.

With one hand supporting May, he helped her pick her way down the escarpment and into the forest. The woodlands were not dense, the trees wide-spaced with enough room to spread their branches fully so that each was a fine majestic specimen. Caspar admired the conifers, the dark-leafed oaks and tall whispering poplars. A carpet of grass and wild flowers lay beneath them and the ground moved with the shadows of grazing deer.

"We must find somewhere soon," she murmured, looking restless and disturbed, her pace slowing.

Caspar nodded. Necrönd would surely be safe here. "Perhaps that line of runes marks the boundary of civilization between the meadow and the forest. This place is so big."

May nodded distractedly and Caspar wondered what was wrong with her – but only briefly. A deep grunting roar wended through the forest. May gripped Caspar's hand.

"It's only a bear but we'd best keep moving," he urged, pausing only to take up his bow.

For four days their tired feet beat a path through the soft grass beneath the shady trees. At night Caspar kept the fire bright and, with Trog at his side, dozed only lightly until it was light enough to move on. Barely speaking, they were constantly alert for the grunts and snuffles and the occasional growl that disturbed the quiet around them.

"Are they following us?" May whispered.

Caspar shook his head. "No, I don't think so," he said lightly but he found the situation strange; they had to be far easier prey than the deer."

"Perhaps they don't like the scent of man."

Occasionally, the entire forest was silenced by an horrendous growl followed by the squeal of a dying animal. Moving on, they heard more snarls from the great grunting creatures to left and right, followed by the yelps and screams of the animals they slew, but not once did they catch a glimpse of the bears. Caspar had never before known bears be so active but refrained from mentioning this to May. At last, the forest thinned and ahead stretched a barren plain footing blue mountains whose bare slopes were crowned by a saw-toothed ridge. A muddy river cut along the valley bottom, silent and calm, its great power revealed only in the huge logs that were tossed in the racing current.

The great river forced them north to a gorge where it spilt from the blue mountains. Caspar looked up at the stony peaks.

"This must be it. Surely, no one has trod these paths in a thousand years. We must be able to bury Necrönd and live out the rest of our days here. We could bear children and form our own sect of Keepers to guard the Egg," he said excitedly, gazing up at the mountains. He could see no signs of life, no great birds hanging in the sky, no footprint in the broken ground.

May pointed to a peak. "That one!" she declared.

Caspar shook his head. "Why not that double-headed one or the one like a horn or the one with a sheer black face? The ridge of that saw-toothed crag is no different to any other saw-toothed crag. Dramatic in its own right but not remarkable in this landscape."

"Precisely," May said wearily. "People are naturally drawn to dramatic peaks just because they do stand out so. Let's go for the ordinary and, moreover, let's stick to the valleys. Let's find a cave in the foot."

"The peaks are more inaccessible," Caspar argued.

"Absolutely!" May agreed, waddling after him as fast as she could; though Caspar felt her words were motivated more by tiredness than prudence.

There was at last a bounce in their step as they saw that their task would soon be done. Soon they could unburden themselves of Necrönd.

"Just so long as we never go home there's no reason

that we should ever speak of it again. And so long as we never speak of it, the knowledge of its location will die with us," Caspar said, offering a hand to May to help her along.

They neared the foot of their chosen ridge, when both halted in disappointment.

"Oh," was all May said but Caspar could think of nothing to say for a long minute and chewed at his tongue in thoughtful disappointment.

May stooped to the ground. "It's recent too; the ash is still hot."

"Perhaps it's just the fire of one man, a lone traveller passing through. A single traveller is little threat. He might never return. This is still the most lonely spot we have come across," Caspar argued, refusing to be put off.

They continued with their plan, agreeing that if they still saw no signs of life, this was a far better place than any other they had yet found. Then they halted again and Caspar closed his eyes in horror; a severed hand lay in the dirt. They skirted around it and after a hundred yards found a leg. The thigh was part chewed, the bare bone sticking from the muscle cracked and split as if crushed by some great jaw.

Whilst anxiously wondering what beast had savaged the man, they again heard the same deep growl that had chilled their blood in the forest.

"If that is all that remains of whoever lit that fire, we need fear them no more. And if the beast has already eaten it will be unlikely to trouble us. But we must keep going." Caspar said, trying hard to make light of the gruesome discovery. "Don't worry; we'll find the right hiding place soon. Come on." He took her hand and tugged her forward.

May resisted. "I can't go any further."

"But we must." Caspar looked at her face. She was white and sweating slightly, her eyes wide and distracted. "And this is not a good place to rest," he told her, dragging her by her arm.

"I don't have much choice," she said faintly, stumbling awkwardly and leaning heavily against him. "The baby . . ."

"Oh! Oh no! Oh Mother, no, not now!" Caspar had tried to put all thought of it from his mind. He had lain each night with May in his arms and subconsciously avoided touching her stretched belly, making great efforts for the sake of their future happiness to forget about the child that wasn't his. But he could forget no more.

"Spar, it is now whether you like it or not."

"But we must find a safer place," he said looking around doubtfully at the landscape. "A cave perhaps."

They stumbled on, May curiously keen to keep moving and only stopping every half an hour or so to moan softly. Caspar looked anxiously around, aware that they were being watched. Something way up on the saw-toothed ridge moved, darting between one boulder and the next. Later, he was aware of another shifting shape lower down and, this time, glimpsed the dark brown form of a large bear. But he kept his observations to himself, not wanting to alarm May further.

She was breathing heavily now and had become quiet and withdrawn. At last, he saw a cave, in fact several, cut into the blue cliffs and approached by a scree slope. Even as they approached, he noticed the bent handle of a cooking pot and later a wooden cup discarded on the ground. He hoped the cave wasn't still inhabited.

Pushing May up from behind, he was still aware of the bears above and now a further one across the far side of the valley. He was only grateful that they had not yet attacked. But there was something about their behaviour that was odd. They weren't behaving like the lone bears of his homeland but more like a pack of wolves herding their prey. He needed to get May into the cave so that he could build a fire and stand guard while she took care of herself.

He shoved her harder from behind, whilst himself slipping on the loose shale, and at last pushed her into the cave. There was enough scrub and dry wood at the lower reaches of the valley for him to collect firewood without having to stray too far from her and he marked the bears, wondering curiously why they sat and waited without coming closer.

He felt strangely calm. His woman needed him and he could defend her; that was what he was born and bred to do; to stand and fight. The emotion came naturally to him and, though his blood raced with excitement, he was not afraid.

May stood sweating at the cave entrance, her face tight with pain. But finding that he couldn't persuade her to lie down as he thought she must, he set about lighting the fire and soon the wood was blazing. May paced slowly around the cave that showed some signs of past use though nothing indicated that it was presently inhabited. There was a dark black circle near the mouth of the cave where someone else had evidently built a fire but no signs of discarded food or bedding and the cave smelt fresh.

He wondered if there was anything he could do to help but assumed May knew what to do since she must have helped his mother and Brid deliver many babies over the years. Anyhow, he reassured himself, women had been having babies since the beginning of time; there couldn't be that much to it. He wondered why they made such a noise about it. No one had ever given him an explanation; it wasn't the sort of thing that the men talked about.

He twanged his bowstring and kept a keen watch on the bears, uncomfortably aware of the constant, soft tread of May's footfall and the gently rasp of her hand against stone as she ran her fingers over the inner walls of the cave.

He sat and waited anxiously. The bears came no closer, undoubtedly kept at bay by the fire and his presence, while May, who had been so tired of late, kept up her endless pacing. She was beginning to mutter to herself, "I had no idea. I should have been more sympathetic."

She had disrobed herself of all but her under-shift though Caspar thought the air cool now that evening closed around them. But clearly May found it hot. He continued to worry that she was on her feet, feeling certain that women lay down to give birth, and he was beginning to wonder why she kept on pacing like that.

"May, don't you think you might be stopping it with all that moving about? Aren't you supposed to lie down?" he asked.

She flashed him a long cold look, opened her mouth as if to speak but shut it again as though she had neither time nor energy left for explanations and returned to her pacing. Caspar noted she was beginning to mutter prayers to the Great Mother. He assumed that the rhythmical chanting helped the whole process. Time seemed to move very slowly, evening creeping with infinitesimal slowness into dark. Her movements had changed and with increasing regularity she stopped her pacing and slapped her hand against the wall as if trying to relieve herself of pain.

The night grew cold and eventually May lay down, her gentle moans and prayers becoming cries of suffering. "Mother!" she screamed, her fists clenching as she arched her back at the severity of the spasm.

It was Caspar who began to pace now, stopping to soothe her hand every few minutes, but she just pushed him angrily away. Grunting with effort, she was beginning to strain hard every minute or so but what worried Caspar most was, not the look of pain on her face, but her white look of fear. He knelt down beside her, fretting helplessly. "May, May what should I do?"

"Aghh!" she screamed and groaned, arching her back and wrenching her body backwards, her hands punching at the stone of the cave floor as if fighting to escape the pain.

"What should I do?" he repeated.

"Help!" she cried again, her eyes black with pain.

"I don't know what to do May, what should I do?"

"Help! Get help!" she gasped before her words were swept away by a new wave of pain and her throat let out a bestial scream.

"But where?" he asked.

May didn't reply but was slapping the ground with her palm, shouting, "No! No! Great Mother, help me!"

Caspar paced and paced. He couldn't leave her. Where could he get help? And what of the bears?

"Help!" May sobbed. "Spar, get help."

"But I've got to stay with you; there are bears outside. They might attack!"

"Spar, get help! I don't care about the bears; they'll make no odds to me soon. I'll die anyway. There must be someone, somewhere. The baby's not coming; something's wrong!"

"Can't I help? Tell me what you would do."

"I don't know!" she gasped. "Keridwen would do it." She groaned deeply. "I-I— only there when it was easy – oh, Spar, get help! Help me! Agh!" She gasped. "Spar, it's killing me."

Caspar turned from the cave and, taking a torch to light his way, fled out into the night that was surprisingly clear and bright, the full moon huge on the horizon, a crimson red that somehow Caspar feared was not a good portend for May. The landscape was sharply defined; the great teeth of the mountains like vast pointed tombstones raking at the sky. But where would he get help? They had seen the occasional signs of people, like that severed hand and the fire, but they had seen no dwellings or indications as to where anyone might be living. And if he found anyone, who was to say they would help?

Scrambling up a crag that overlooked the ridge, he surveyed the moonlit world below. On the far side of the ridge a tumbling river danced in the silvery light. Bears flitted between the trees but there was no fire, nothing to show that people slept out there in the dark. But, somehow, he knew they were there. An inner sense inherited from his mother, no doubt, gave him that creeping feeling that there were people close by. Besides, the people who had inhabited the cave must have gone somewhere. And if there were people there was surely an old woman amongst them who would know how to help May.

He held the flaming brand high, knowing that small though he was, the light would be visible for miles. As a mountain dweller himself, he knew better than most that any sound in that still clear night would travel from peak to peak and his voice would ring out over the land like a cry from an eagle.

He took in a deep breath, threw back his head and yelled, "Help! Hear me! Help! Over here!"

The echo wailed back and forth between the ridges and, as it died, he strained to hear a reply. After his shriek, the night was ominously quiet before the grunts from the bears returned. He raised his arm and wafted the torch back and forth, sending sparks out in the air, and then he swung it in a big circle that would surely attract attention. "Help!" he shouted again. "Help!"

A cry for help would surely be understood in any language, he reasoned. He yelled once more and then, at last, he heard the cool sweet notes of a horn, the sound piping through the mountains and thrown back and forth by the ridges so that it was impossible to immediately locate from where it had originated. He swung his arm more slowly this time as his concentration focused on the horn then, finally, he saw a small flicker of light close to the west, moving fast as if borne by a horse.

Caspar ran and slithered and leapt down the mountainside to greet them and staggered to a halt, his lantern aloft, as they clattered near. Four men approached, riding bareback, naked legs dangling down round the ponies' knees. Caspar focused on their spears that, even in the moonlight, he could see were crudely fashioned from wood and not metal. The faces of the men where strangely luminous, painted with chalk that reflected the light of the moon. Skull-like, Caspar thought. The four spears were levelled at his chest.

He had no time to be afraid. "Help, help! My woman's in difficulties; she's having a baby."

Spears rattled in his face and he saw that he was not making himself in the least understood.

"No, no!" He stood back and raised his hands in a peaceful gesture. "My wife . . ." He drew the curves of a woman in the air beside him. The skull-white faces watched him curiously. He then drew his arms out in front of his belly, describing the arc of a pregnant stomach. The men nodded, clearly understanding that. Caspar then folded his arms and rocked them back and forth as if holding a baby. The men copied and laughed.

"You must help," Caspar said, wondering how to explain that May was in difficulty. He lay on the floor, again miming with his hands a swollen belly, and moaned and groaned.

The men instantly stopped laughing and muttered anxiously amongst themselves. They made gestures at Caspar to wait and fled back into the night. It seemed like an age before they returned and he was vastly relieved to see that they had brought with them an elderly woman. She was stooped at the shoulders and, when she dismounted, she struggled with the weight of a bag in one hand while she lent on a stick held in her other. A hard ball capped the end of the stick that rattled as she tapped it on the ground.

"Quick, quick! Hurry!" he urged.

They had no trouble finding May for the screams that filled the valley. The old woman, surprisingly nimble for her apparent age, was helped by the men up the slope. She threw aside her cloak the minute she looked into the cave. May was tearing at her under-shift and biting her clenched fists, sobbing and wailing. Caspar was horrified that he had been forced to leave her in such a condition for so long.

Now that she had flung aside her cloak, Caspar could see that the old woman was dressed only in a short animal skin that hung from one bony shoulder. She rattled her stick at the men and pushed them from the cave.

Caspar was also ushered out with the others who gathered close about the fire and sat down, mumbling pleasantly to each other and eyeing him. One patted him kindly on the back and he smiled back as best he could but there was little they could do to alleviate his distress as he listened to May screaming on and on. He took from his pocket the chip of bone that Morrigwen had given him. It was all that he had of the high priestesses and if anyone could help May at a time like this it was them. He fingered it, thinking of the wolves that it represented and, looked up into the face of the moon, praying that the Great Mother would save his May.

One of the men prodded him sharply in the side and grunted a few words, gesturing urgently that he should go into the cave. He could barely think for May's screams. Her arms clawed out at the old woman, begging her to help. The woman tugged Caspar round to May's head and put his hands on May's wrists, pressing firmly. A look of insistence in her eyes told Caspar he must hold on.

She then hurried to May's feet. Caspar had no wish to look as the woman worked her arms under May's skirts and began to tug. May was pulled away from his grip and the woman looked up and shouted angrily and he knew he was failing her by not gripping tight enough and pulling May hard back towards him. There was an urgency in the woman's voice that said if they did not do this and do it quickly, May would die.

May's big round hazel eyes looked up at Caspar. "Stop! Stop! No! You're killing me! Mother! Stop, Spar! Stop it!" She was sobbing like a tortured prisoner. "Stop it! You're tearing me apart! No!"

Caspar gritted his teeth against her pain. "Hold on, May. Keep fighting. I love you!" he shouted back at her, his voice cracking with emotion.

Her deep wailing cries became a sharper yell and she closed her eyes in concentration. The old woman's voice became more excited, urging, encouraging May while Caspar strained to hold her fast as the stranger dragged at the baby within. Then at last came one long scream and May was puce in the face with effort. Finally came a yell of triumph. A tiny squashed wrinkled creature covered in white slime and blood was cradled in the woman's arms. May looked at it for a second, her face expressionless with exhaustion, before she slumped back to the floor.

Caspar stared at the tiny creature in disbelief and then at the great thick purple vessel protruding from the baby's stomach. The woman bit the cord and tied it with a strip of leather. She then began probing the baby's mouth with her finger. It wasn't breathing! Why wasn't it breathing?

Caspar was desperate. "Do something!" he yelled at the woman, who was rubbing the baby's chest and back.

Then it shrieked and gurgled and the little legs kicked. Caspar's heart pounded in his stomach with a nervousness the like he had never known.

"May, it's alive! May, it's fine," he gasped. "Oh May!"

He was squeezing her tight but she was not responding. The woman muttered orders to the men and they rushed about building up the fire and bringing up water from the river. She swaddled the baby and, without any ado, placed it in Caspar's arms while she went to tend May.

Caspar didn't know what was happening. He didn't know if May were all right or not since all his attention was focused on the tiny little girl mewing in his hands. Two blue-black eyes blinked widely at him and his heart jumped with elation. Carefully, he slid his arm beneath her to cradle her and moved cautiously to be closer to the warmth of the fire, all the while looking fixedly into her face. Though aware that all were busy around him, he paid them no heed; at this moment he had the most important job in the world.

After many minutes, he heard May groan and finally he looked up. She blinked her eyes open but was unable to raise herself.

Caspar said quietly to her, "May, well done. It's a beautiful girl and she seems fine. I've counted her fingers and toes."

May nodded in weak acknowledgement and protested mildly when the woman pushed her up and propped her with rolled blankets and furs. Then the old woman carefully took the baby from Caspar and put her to May's bosom and held her there for her. In alarm, Caspar saw that May was too exhausted even to cradle the baby. He held his breath until the little child, after some work by the old woman to position it comfortably, sucked noisily. A collective sigh rippled around the cave. The baby sucked lustily and all could see it was strong.

Caspar had no sleep that night. While May lay there by the fire without moving, he was given the child to hold. Every time it cried, the old woman would take it from him to put it to May's breast, who was so listless that she seemed barely to notice.

He thought that by morning, once May had had some sleep, she would be better. The old woman kept her warm and tried to feed her broth from a small spoon but May would not respond. Dizzy with lack of sleep, Caspar paced the room, his arms aching from stiffly holding the child. Late in the day ,May began to shiver and cried with pain when the old woman put the baby to her breast but the old woman persisted, her face set hard against the mother's pain.

Caspar realized almost at once that the woman believed May was dying and every day that the baby fed from May, was a day longer that it would survive. Caspar watched over her, choked with fearful emotions and uncertain as what to say.

"The baby is strong," he reassured her but she didn't seem to hear.

He sat back, cradling the child, telling himself he had to be strong for the child's sake, but the thought of going on alone without May was unbearable. His only comfort was that Trog stayed close by his side, wagging his tail in great excitement as he sniffed at the baby.

The old woman and the four men remained and after three days the old woman was still persisting in taking the baby from his arms and putting it to May's breast. As May grew weaker so did the child and he feared her milk was lessening. Desperately, he prayed that she would somehow be well again. Though he did know that women died in childbirth, he couldn't believe that it would happen to May – not here, not now, not after everything they had been through.

The men came and went with supplies. Caspar took great pains to nod thankfully at them and to his amazement found that he had learnt one or two of their words, which aided their communication. Once he had stopped focusing on the alien clicks and grunts in their language, he realised that the rest of the words were not so different from the old tongue of the Caballan. Vaguely, he wondered that the people from this continent of Beyond Tethys, as he learned they called themselves, had not drifted across the great ocean from his own world.

On the seventh day, when May had not stirred at all for several hours, one of the men returned, bringing with him a young woman who had a baby strapped to her back. She sat down in the cave near the fire, took a hunk of dripping deer meat that was offered and began to suckle her baby, a fairly large child. Shortly the baby was asleep and, cradling it between her legs, she reached out her hands towards Caspar, inviting him to give her May's child who was listless and sleepy.

It was defeat; Caspar knew it. To let her feed May's

baby was to admit that May would not live and so he clung tight to the child and only relinquished her when the old woman gently pulled his fingers away. She handed the baby to the experienced mother who adeptly put it to her breast. She drank hungrily and Caspar could see that they were doing the right thing for the child. If May died, he would have to leave it here with the women who could look after it.

The reality of it dawned. No longer feeling the need to be strong for the baby's sake, he dropped his head into his hands and blinked back tears. Eventually, he crawled over to May and took her limp hand, kissed it and held it fast against his cheek. He looked across her at the suckling mother who was cradling *his* baby, as he had come to think of her, and took this to mean that May was dying. He couldn't bear it. Scooping her up in his arms, he hugged her tight.

Trog, who all this while had watched over May, now took up a new stance, suspiciously eyeing the cavewoman who held May's child.

"Oh May, I love you! Don't leave me. May, please! I need you!" Caspar begged her, looking down at her face, her bedraggled hair clinging to her damp skin.

Her eyes didn't open but her lips smiled and she murmured, "I love you too."

"May! May!" he wailed happily. "You're talking again."

The old woman hastily pushed him aside and had a cup of water raised to May's lips.

"My baby?" May asked. "My baby, where is it? Where?" Her voice was panicked and Caspar rushed to the nursing mother and tenderly took the small child so that he could hand it to May who sighed deeply as it fed from her. "My baby . . ." She closed her eyes and lay on her side so that she could feed it without having to hold it in her arms.

"I thought you were going to die." His voice was shaking with emotion.

"So did I. The pain! I had no idea the pain could be that bad."

"No. After."

"After?" May asked.

"You've been feverish for a week."

"A week!" May was amazed and then for the first time looked up at the strange faces around her. She drew her legs up to herself in retreat and protectively covered the baby with her arm. They smiled and offered her a round of solid-looking black bread and a horn of water. She drank thirstily but only nibbled at the bread.

The fur-clad people stayed another three days, nursing May until she was up and walking and able to look after the baby. Now that Caspar's overwhelming concern for May was past, he slumped with exhaustion and the nagging pain in his head returned. Then, on the morning of the eleventh day, Caspar woke to find that they had gone. May was already awake and apparently untroubled by their departure. Gazing into her child's eyes, she sang a soft lullaby.

"What shall you call her?" he asked.

May beamed at her child and kissed its tiny, wrinkled forehead. "Isolde, after my grandmother."

Caspar looked around at the empty cave and felt intensely vulnerable without the people that had, for no reason other than generosity, befriended them. He knew that, if it hadn't been for them, neither May nor the baby would have survived.

"We must repay them," he said.

"How can we possible repay what they have done for us?" May asked, still crooning over her baby.

Caspar looked out from the cave and saw the trail of

ponies winding away north along the valley bottom. "We must do something," he insisted, noting their direction and deciding they must prepare to follow them. Besides, they couldn't stay here alone. Perhaps many generations of humans had dwelt here in the caves and perhaps they had been safe from the bears but he could not be sure and he had a little baby to protect. They couldn't risk staying there any longer.

May took strips of the bedding that the people had left behind for them and fashioned a sling and straps to wrap her child to her body so that she could carry Isolde more easily. As they moved out, Caspar was aware of the many eyes that were on them and noted the dark shadows moving at the foot of the cliffs where the bears still lurked. Again, he wondered that they had not attacked and, not wanting to alarm May, he didn't point them out. Clearly, she was not going to notice them herself; she was oblivious to anything except the baby.

"Look, Spar! She loves the sling. Look!"

Caspar had to admit that he found it hard to tell what the baby liked or did not like. It was either feeding, sleeping or crying as far as he could see. But he was relieved that, right now, it appeared to be sleeping, lulled asleep by its mother's stride. The noise of a baby could attract all manner of predators.

Disturbed by the grunts from bears and the peeling cries of a vulture eagle gliding on a massive wingspan, the fingers of feathers tipping air to direct its leisurely glide, they followed the small, neat pony track north through the winding valleys. The blue mountains dipped and levelled into undulating lowlands, unbroken by hedges, field walls or tilled earth but deep with wild flowers that spangled the open country between humped mounds of leafy copses. The happy sound of babbling water filled the air, mixing with the grunts and snuffles of large herds of deer and wild asses that grazed contentedly on the rich grass. About a league ahead, a coil of smoke climbed into the still air from beyond one of the many copses.

"A good fat kill," Caspar spoke his thoughts out loud. "That would surely be a worthy present for them." He was certain that they would be pleased with such a gift.

"Spar, what was that?" May asked in alarm.

Grunts and the sound of large animals charging through the dense undergrowth of a copse to their left was followed by a squeal and then silence. A few minutes later those curious grunts sounded all over the valley and Caspar had the horrible awareness that there were at least a dozen bears moving from copse to copse towards the kill. He had never known bears behave in such a way.

"Why haven't they attacked?" May asked. "I mean why haven't they attacked *us*? They seem to be killing plenty of other creatures."

"Perhaps they don't attack men," Caspar suggested but knew this to be wrong as they approached the village. Only the peaks of the thatched roofs were visible for the high hurdles around the settlement and a ring of outward-leaning stakes much like archers might hammer into the ground to protect them from charging cavalry.

Caspar looked about and noted with satisfaction that, though the deer had fled, a herd of wild asses still grazed some distance from the bear-infested copse. They lifted their heads, certainly aware of him, but made no move to flee and, clearly, they thought him no threat at this distance. Soon they were all head down in the grass, busily grazing. At a hundred yards, Caspar had no trouble bringing down an ass; his bow would pierce armour at that distance. The rest of the herd fled, leaving his kill lying stone dead on the ground, the shaft of his arrow jutting from its neck.

With May close at his heels, he hurried to it, gutting knife ready and, once he had restrained Trog and placated him with a pile of steaming offal, he had the carcass gutted even before the vulture eagles had gathered in the skies above. He tied the ass's hindlegs together with his belt and dragged the beast towards the village. It was a great labour but the grass was lush and slippery with dew so, despite the animal's weight, it dragged relatively easily.

"Hello!" he shouted in their tongue, though he could not reproduce the click that came at the end of the word. "Hello!" he repeated, addressing the lashed logs that formed a gate.

One of those wooden spears with a flint head was hurled with utmost accuracy to land at his feet.

Caspar leapt back, raising his hands in a gesture of peace, and then pointed at the carcass. "We come bearing a gift," he explained, hoping he had the words right.

The gate opened a crack and they were waved inside. Dragging the ass, Caspar was met by the old woman who looked at the carcass and clapped her hands in delight. Several young men hurried forward to relieve Caspar of his burden and they were cordially led to a fire and bade to sit.

"We just wanted to say thank you," Caspar tried to explain but clearly his accent was barely intelligible and they stared at him blankly. He made feeble attempts to communicate with his hands. Some concepts were easy without speech but the notion of offering a gift was clearly a difficult one. Caspar pointed to the ass, moved his fingers to his mouth to indicate eating and the pointed to the individuals about him. They clapped in delight and he was pleased that even if they could never fully repay these people, he and May could at least show their gratitude.

They were led beyond the inner ring of hurdles to a huddle of mud and wattle huts that appeared crushed beneath the weight of their thatch hats. Caspar blinked and, in an instant, took in the scene before him. With mouths open, he and May shrank back in horror. It was beyond thinking that they had slept with these people, shared food and the same living quarters with them for so many days.

Dominating the centre of the village and sculpted with remarkable skill was a huge wooden carving of a standing bear. A flat slab of rock lay at its feet on which the still body of a naked girl, her long black hair fanned out about her white face. Her bloodied chest was an open empty pit; her heart gone.

Shaking with horror, May clasped her baby tightly to her bosom. "To think that the old woman probably brought that girl into the world," she gasped.

Caspar put his arm protectively about her shoulder. "No, I don't think so. See, they all have fair hair in this tribe and that girl is very much darker." He was, however, keeping a polite smile prudently pinned to his face, and was mindful that his hand was on his bow.

"You don't suppose they hunt down strangers and sacrifice them to the bears, do you?" May asked, clearly not fully believing the evidence before her eyes.

"I'm afraid I do," he replied, thinking that he preferred their chances with the bears than he did with human beings that made sacrifices to appease them.

He started to back off, pulling May with him. The villagers looked at them curiously but paid them little heed. Caspar turned and walked casually back, continuing to nod his thanks as he went and trying his best to look as unruffled as possible. They were nearly at the gates and he was beginning to think that no one would trouble them, when four bare-breasted men stepped forward to block their way.

He smiled at the burly men with reddish brown skin clad only in skin loincloths and swatches of bearskin slung over one shoulder. "We mean no trouble, friends," he grunted in their tongue, wishing as always that he had more of his father's or uncle's presence. But he did not and the men showed no fear of him. As casually as possible, he asked to pass but they remained firmly planted as Caspar became aware of a rattle and tap behind him.

"Spar," a voice croaked and then gabbled words he was not quick enough to guess at.

Caspar turned. A grimace of disgust stiffened his lips as he beheld the old woman and thought that her hands that had brought their most precious little girl into the world may also have ripped the heart from the woman on the altar slab. She was smiling and some of his tension eased. Now that he was facing her, she spoke a little slower and he was able to gather from her words and gestures that she was pleased with his gift and concerned about their welfare.

She patted May's child and then turned, clucking and clicking at one of the younger men. He rushed away only to return shortly after, pulling along two scraggy ponies. They had no saddles and only rough rope halters that had made sores on their noses and cheeks. The old woman handed Caspar the reins and closed his fingers on them. She nodded and smiled and Casper understood that she meant the ponies to be a return gift. "We must look after you; the Great Bear wills it," she said inexplicably.

He took them gratefully, wondering why this woman, clearly the matriarchal leader of this savage tribe, chose to befriend them. Still, he wasn't prepared to wait and find out but hurried to help May up onto one of the ponies. Leading the animal at a smart but seemingly unhurried pace, he marched out of the village. With the hairs on his neck prickly, he smartly paced due east.

The old woman ran after him in some distress, shaking her head and pointing west, gesticulating wildly as if begging him to turn away from his chosen path. Caspar wondered at it but smiled and pushed her hand gently off the pony's halter. This was surely a good omen; a place feared by people was a safe place to take Necrönd. Waving his farewells, he strode off, aware of the woman watching his back.

Once clear of the outer ring of stakes, he increased the pace until they had crossed the lowland area. Before them, shapely tapered mountains with wide feet and narrow peaks climbed out of a plain. Long-legged deer and bison grazed in a brown patchwork of shadows cast by the strangely shaped peaks but soon the grass gave way to ash, the landscape black and forbidding. The division between grass and ash was harsh and Caspar guessed that a huge fire had swept through the land. Prudently, he filled their water containers in preparation for traversing the terrain ahead.

"Surely, we won't have to go much further," May sighed. "Look at this land; no one could live here."

Caspar nodded. To keep heading east, as he had first divined with Morrigwen's body, was surely the best. He trudged on, grateful for the ponies, one to carry the packs and the other May and Isolde.

As the day wore on there was still no sign of a break in the black landscape and they spent two cold nights without fires, hoping that they would find water soon. Their supplies were running low. Just before they stopped for the night on the third evening, Caspar at last made out the lumpy shapes of mountains in the far distance and he hoped that they marked the end of the cinderland as they had named this blackened landscape. Exhausted, Caspar helped May from the saddle and, immediately, Isolde began to cry. She seemed only happy when they were moving.

"Is there something wrong? Surely, she shouldn't cry like that?" Caspar fretted.

"Most babies cry in the evening," May snapped back, evidently her temper frayed by the distressing noise.

Caspar couldn't believe that something so little could yell so loudly. Not only did the din make them both bad-tempered but it also added to the constant ache in his head. The next day they climbed into foothills where the cinder gave way to scrubby grass and sandy rocks. The foothills tilted up towards an escarpment and, from here, they looked out over a range of sandstone mountains with lakes glistening from their shoulders and rivers threaded along their broad valley floors.

Dust was swept up into their faces by the wind blowing off the sandy terrain and Caspar squinted at the mountains that rose up to form strange shapes against the skyline. To Caspar's imagination, one appeared as a giant hunched over his belongings, another as an anvil, and another a toppled tower. This at least looked like a hostile enough landscape to abandon the Egg.

In the middle distance, midst the sandy peaks, a silvery black lake caught the sun. Over it sloped a peak resembling a crouched dog, its nose pointing into the wind.

"That one," Caspar said. "We'll make camp here tonight and then make for that in the morning." He was weary and keen to be rid of the Egg so that, at last, he might have peace at nights and that his head would heal. The sore made him tired and sick and he needed to be free of his burden.

May shook her head and looked up from her gurgling baby who awoke the moment they halted. "No, not the peak. The lake. We'll throw it into the lake," she said decisively. "You're only thinking of a mountain because that's where you found it. A lake would be better."

Caspar smiled. "Anything to please you, May."

Still protectively cradling her baby against her, she reached out one hand and gripped his arm. "I have everything, Spar. I have Isolde and I have you all to myself."

He moved to kiss her but, just at that moment, the baby began to cry.

CHAPTER TEN

Pip stood valiantly over Brid as a ring of steaming horses trampled close. Drawing into a tight noose around them, their jostling flanks closed and left no room for escape. The huntsmen whooped in triumph, whips cracking the air to keep their dogs at bay.

Five of them fell on Pip. He struggled and bit and punched but could not stop one of the noblemen snatching hold of Brid's collar and breaking her grip on Renaud. In one hand, the sturdy nobleman lifted her off her feet. Though she struggled and kicked like a snared rabbit, she was small and light and the man had little trouble throwing her over the front of his saddle. The pommel dug into her stomach, knocking the breath from her lungs.

She bit at his thigh but made little impact through the thick leather of his breeches so, instead, she bit his horse. It squealed and bucked and she bit harder only to be rewarded by the man cuffing her across the back of the head. Sick with the pain, her head thumped against the horse's shoulder. She cut her cheek with her tooth and tasted blood.

Pip's bellow of protest drowned her cries. "Ruddy bastards!" he squealed as the men struggled to restrain him. "Everywhere we go in this wretched land you Ceolothians set on us."

"Father, did you hear that?" the younger noble exclaimed in Ceolothian. "These grave-robbing sprites are Belbidian."

Brid giddily wondered how anyone could possibly think that Pip could possibly be a sprite.

The hunt forgotten, their captors set about exhuming Renaud. After overcoming their shock of finding him alive, they laid him over the back of a horse, his cries of terror chilling the most steadfast hearts. Hardwin received similar treatment and, with dogs stirring around the horses' hooves, the Ceolothians wove their way through the forest to a track.

Still head down, the leaf-mould blurring as they cantered along, Brid quickly felt sick with the movement. Eventually they slowed, the ground rising steeply, the roots of the trees breaking through the surface, clawing at the forest floor to grip fast to the earth. The horses heaved and grunted, twisting back and forth to find a footing as they laboured their way up the climb. Hanging upside down, the blood throbbing in her ears, Brid watched the ground, noting that the trees thinned and cropped grass grew over the occasional root. Finally, the ground flattened and she felt a sudden rush of air about her.

She strained to raise her head. They were on a smooth-topped hill that rose steeply to command far reaching views over the forested plain. A dark river curved in and out of the trees that grew thickly along its banks. Brid twisted but still couldn't see ahead for the horse's sweated neck in the way. Then the nobleman wrenched her upright and she found herself looking up at a sheer grey wall, the spearhead of a narrow turret stabbing up above the arch of a portcullis.

The barbican was adorned with a brightly painted crest. The stone carving of a shield bore the emblem of a ram and a goat, their great horns locked in combat. It struck

Brid, immediately, that the dagger in Turquin's chest carried the same device. Though still in Trows Forest, they had very nearly reached the Goat Country and she presumed that this castle was a forest outpost belonging to someone of great importance from that territory. The mouth of the castle yawed open and heavy dark-faced dogs lumbered out to greet them.

The horses' hooves rang out over smooth cobbles, the sound suddenly loud after the muffled plod over the forest turf. The clatter echoed within the hollow square at the centre of the castle. Soon came the scurry of feet, as servants rushed to take the snorting horses that were overeager to get to their mangers. Brid noted that the servants addressed the older noble as Baron Kulfrid and his son as Sir Irwald.

The brutish Baron Kulfrid gripped Brid firmly while two of the larger servants snared Pip, who was staring at one of the Ceolothians as if he knew him. Brid followed his line of sight and spied a very tall man watching them from across the courtyard. As their eyes met, he flinched and hastened away.

Assessing their surroundings, she looked about her and caught the Baron's son starring at her. She smiled to herself, thinking that therein lay their escape. As befitted a young lady, she blinked at him with tears sparkling in her green eyes and, in her best Ceolothian, begged him for help.

He held her gaze, his eyes whispering of a gentler soul within that warlike body, and stared deep into her bright eyes.

"Please," she begged again but he turned away to seek direction from his more surly looking father, who still gripped her savagely.

Baron Kulfrid lifted her high so that all the assembled

servants and nobles could see the object of his fury. "A sprite in my land!" he roared in his own tongue . "And what do we do with such sub-human spawn? We take our pleasure in ridding it from our lands!" He ripped at her clothing, tearing open her tunic. "Beneath all this mud is it flesh or wood?" He grunted in satisfaction at the sight of her soft pale skin and the full curves of her female body.

Brid whipped her head round and at last succeeded in viciously biting his thumb.

"In the dungeons with all of them!" he snarled. "A day in there will tame the beast's spirit so that she knows to give pleasure and not pain."

Brid did not flinch or struggle as they were led deep below the castle keep. She had decided what she must do. Her overriding task was to find the others that must still be buried and get home with Cymbeline and Renaud so that she might free Keridwen – and Branwolf, of course. She gritted her teeth, furious that she had escaped the wizards only to fall into the hands of some rogue Ceolothian baron.

Still, she could not allow herself to be daunted nor to crave the luxury of self-pity. Morrigwen had taught her that she must look for every opportunity to turn bad into good and, after all, she was not without power. Her powers as a high priestess may have gone but, clearly, her powers as a woman were as keen as ever.

She enjoyed being beautiful, not because of the admiration that it brought her, nor the power, but simply because of the sense of nature balanced so perfectly within her.

They were tossed into a cold high-ceilinged cell, the walls etched with the marks of earlier prisoners. Hardwin doubled up and retched. The Ceolothian baron and his son, who had insisted on seeing to it personally that they were locked in, glared at him in horror.

"The two men look like they have the trembling sickness. But the boy and the girl? What if they are some unnatural grave robbers or some devilish wood-sprites birthed from the ground? Shouldn't we get the priest to say prayers over them?" Sir Irwald asked anxiously in Ceolothian.

"Pah! The priests might order them burnt and I'll not have that. Whatever else they are, they're Belbidian, and that makes them spies. I'll know their purpose before the week is out!" Baron Kulfrid grunted.

His son looked more concerned. He opened his mouth as if he were about to speak but shut it again as if preferring to keep his thoughts to himself. Brid gave him a sideways glance and, when he caught her eye, he gave her a nervous smile. He jerked his head up in alarm, however, as Hardwin leant against the wall and slid to the stone floor, flecks of white saliva speckling his lips.

"What's wrong with him?" Pip asked in horror as Brid tried to calm the Pisceran but he only shrieked the more at her approach.

She shrugged and retreated. "I don't know. You and I awoke slowly and together, realizing that what we suffered was only a dream. But we dragged Hardwin out when he was asleep and he seems to still be under the spell."

"He's gone mad, hasn't he?" Pip said.

Brid nodded sadly as Hardwin gibbered fearfully. "I'm sorry, father," he wept between ravings, his desperate struggles making him look as if he were in water and fighting for the surface. "I'm sorry I'm such a disappointment to you."

His ravings infected Renaud, who did not scream but stared down at his feet, shaking with terror. Brid was sorry for the prince and the young Pisceran nobleman, but her thoughts were focusing elsewhere. Fear welled within her. Her throat tight, she was finding it difficult to breathe. Hal was still within the earth.

"Brid, what to do we do?" Pip asked.

She wished he would stop looking to her for answers; she had none.

"Can't you pray or something?" Pip hissed at her when she didn't reply. "The Great Mother will listen to you."

She looked at him, trying to put an enigmatic smile on her face. If only people understood that prayer was not like that. The Great Mother was not there to provide them with every whim. She gave them life yet they had the ingratitude to think that they could ask for more. It was absurd! "No, Pip, prayer isn't like that at all. It's more a sort of deep honest conversation that you have with yourself, trying to train your inner strengths and focus your mind on what you truly want so that you learn how best to handle life. Prayer is a means to avoid self-delusion."

"You mean there is no point praying?"

Brid grunted in frustration. "Of course, there is! First and foremost, to give thanks and to put us in mind that we do not own this land but are privileged to live and tread the Mother's earth and share Her bounty. We pray to put us in mind that we are small and insignificant."

This part Brid herself had difficulties with though she struggled every day to remind herself of the fact. She knew she was but one, a small cog in the wheel of human fortune, but still she was One of the Three. She had accepted that her attributes and powers were to be the service of others in the glory of the Great Mother and not so others might worship her; but sometimes it was hard not to enjoy a little adoration.

She was fearful of Spar for that very reason. He made her sin every moment they were together; he taught her vanity. He worshipped her. Hal did not. Hal lusted for her. Hal laughed at her. Hal sparred with her. Hal tried to better and outwit her and she enjoyed the challenge. She loved him for it as an equal and as a woman. He was brave and daring. So too was Spar – but never with her.

Yet she loved Spar, admired him and, guiltily in her heart, knew that she wished Hal were in many ways more like him. Yet to change Hal would be to lessen him and, in the end, he too would worship her. Her thoughts embraced him. Worried sick about Hal, she watched Renaud and Hardwin gibbering and feared that, if she were ever able to retrieve Hal, that he too would be lost to the same madness of terror.

"That man!" Pip suddenly blurted out, breaking her thoughts.

"What man?" Brid asked.

"The one in the courtyard. I remember now where I had seen him before. That tall thin soldier, he was part of the escort party."

"He couldn't have been," Brid objected. "They were all killed."

"Except for those that were in on the ambush," Pip reminded her. "He must have been one of Tupwell's men who aided the ambushers and abducted Cymbeline."

Renaud shrieked at the sound of Tupwell's name, throwing Brid's thoughts away from the tall soldier. Frowning at the prince, she wondered what ailed him now. Clearly, he and Hardwin suffered new, more terrifying fears to the ones they had witnessed before. It seemed Hardwin was frightened of water, something that would shame his father. Since the Baron of Piscera fished his wealth from the stormy seas off the west coast of Belbidia this was undoubtedly a big problem to them both. But it was harder to guess at Renaud's nightmare. Snakes or fire? Certainly, it was something at his feet. That was it! A fear of heights. He was thinking that at any moment he might fall. She had to do what she could to help him.

"Renaud," she called softly.

He lifted his head momentarily, as if some small part of his mind sensed her presence, but then he stared back down at his feet, his knees giving. Pip, ever eager to help those with influence, placed his hand reassuringly on Renaud's shoulder.

The prince shrieked. "No! Don't push me! Get away from me!"

There seemed nothing they could do to help and Brid sat in the corner, hoping that the answer would come to her. Pip, however, would not give up and turned back to Hardwin.

"You're a stupid man; you're not drowning. It's all in your head. Just wake up!" The lad shook Hardwin but, when the nobleman would not even look at him but clung to the wall, screaming all the more, he sprang at Renaud again. "Sir, you must believe me. There's no drop."

"Get away from me!" Renaud shrieked in panic.

Hardwin's screaming suddenly stopped. Brid started and rushed to him where he sat slumped against the wall, his head sagging forward onto his chest. He wasn't breathing! His lips were blue and deepening to purple before her eyes. She had failed him. She slapped his face to jolt him back to his senses. How could she have allowed Pip to interfere? He had merely intensified the nightmare to a level that Hardwin could no longer endure.

After loosening his clothing, she opened his mouth and, pressing her lips to his, breathed into his lungs, forcing his chest to rise. But he made no response. His face was blue-grey within the minute and his hand was cold and limp in hers. She looked down at him in horror. He was dead! He had died of fright, believing that he was drowning.

"You idiot!" she snapped at the youth.

"It wasn't my fault," he choked defensively.

"Wasn't it?" she said, knowing she was being unkind. "You made him panic."

"I was trying to help!"

"Well, don't try anymore."

Pip scowled and leant against the wall at the far end of the cell by the door. Brid relented. It wasn't his fault but hers for not taking charge of the situation. She shouldn't have expected a young boy like Pip to do the right thing and she should have foreseen the consequences. Sadly, she looked down at Hardwin, stroking back his hair from his chubby face.

"Poor man. He tried so hard, you know. He was a good solid Belbidian—" She stopped short. The guards beyond the door were shrieking.

"They think you've killed him!" Pip exclaimed. "They think you've just sucked away his life. Well, that's done it! They're sure to think you're some evil sprite now. Have you burnt, I should think." He said it callously but Brid knew there was real fear for her in his voice

The men's cries brought Baron Kulfrid. After ordering his men to remove Hardwin's body, he shoved Renaud to the floor, who squealed and clung to the cracks in the stone as if he were clinging to a cliff face. Then he rounded on Brid.

"A witch! A witch, a murderess and a spy!!" he said in Belbidian, pointing at her, his accent extremely well practised and Brid would almost not have believed the words could come from a Ceolothian. "Clearly a spy. Belbidians have no call to be lurking deep in my forests and Belbidians have little cause to learn Ceolothian. It's a well-known fact that, beyond a few scholars, Belbidians never speak a tongue other than their own. The only reason you might would be to spy on us."

He grabbed Pip by the collar and threw him aside before picking Brid up in one hand and shoving her back against the wall. He looked deep into her eyes. "Spies!" he repeated.

Her mind whirred. Why would he assume they were spies? And why were his eyes fearful. Was it that he feared they had discovered his incriminating dagger?

"Help! Help!" Renaud screamed, clinging to the floor. "Don't hurl me off, I beg of you. Put me back in the ground with the others so I can't fall!"

Baron Kulfrid's grip on Brid eased as he stared at Renaud "The others. This witch and her accomplice must have buried more of them. Find them! I'll know what these spies are up to. This sham of madness and paganism is but a front to make me fear them and so turn them loose. Find the others! Scour the forest," he snarled at his men.

Locked in their cold cell, only a square of light on the beaten earth floor, Brid and Pip listened miserably to the sound of Renaud's maddened sobbing. Somewhere far off in the castle his cries disturbed the ears of dogs who yelped and howled in angry chorus at the intrusion. The jangle of distressed howls accentuated her own torment. They would find Hal and he would arrive a lost soul like Renaud, his mind savaged.

"Renaud, please," she begged. "Please hear me. There's nothing to be afraid of."

He made no response and she wondered briefly if he might hear a song. So often a screaming child that could not listen to the voice of reason might be distracted by a song and so become calm enough to eventually listen to sense. Her voice, she knew, like her face was disarmingly beautiful. A song that his mother might have sung . . . she thought, trying to think of a lullaby.

> *"Sing, ho, for the rain to fatten the grain,*
> *And hey, for the sun and the harvest.*
> *Sleep, child, sleep, while the men still reap,*
> *For the moon is bright, the wolves—"*

The mention of wolves brought a shriek of horror from Renaud. It seemed his nightmare had spiralled to new depths of fear.

"Oh no! Wolves! Wolves everywhere! Help me! Someone help me!"

"That's not wolves; it's dogs," Pip said with some irritation. "Just dogs."

Brid hadn't thought much of it but, yes, the castle did seem to be rattling with dogs. On their arrival she had seen in addition to the many deer-hounds, heavy black-faced dogs that she thought, by their build, were probably used to bait bear.

"Pip," she said, snuggling up to him against the cold, "what are we going to do?"

He wrapped his arms around her. "Don't worry, Brid, I won't let anything happen to you. You're a woodswoman like my sister May and I'd never let harm come to any girl from the Chase hamlets," he said jovially, evidently trying to hide his embarrassment over the nightmare she had witnessed.

She clung to him, feeling small, helpless and vaguely ridiculous that she was drawing strength from a mere boy. All that night they slept fitfully and listened in dread for the returning search party but it wasn't until dawn that they came. Renaud was still clinging to the floor, his fingers white with the strain.

"I can't hold on anymore! There are wolves down there, hooded wolves. I told you, Rewik, it would all come to no good in the end if you kept taxing the people. Now see what they have done to me! Brother, listen to me. I said they were good men as fine as any other Belbidian but you've let the realm be split. Help me, Rewik: don't let them throw me from the walls to the wolves below."

"He thinks he's at Torra Alta," Pip sighed wishfully. "If only I could dream such a wonderful dream."

The alarm horn sounded and the courtyard above was filled with the sound of clattering hooves and stamping feet. Brid's heart throbbed in her throat; surely Hal was near: to her it was as if there was a magical hum trembling through the castle that made the very stonework throb, the air speaking loudly of the runesword's presence.

"Dear Mother," she said, pressing her hand to the stone floor, "thank you for this *sight*." She missed it. She had felt it seeping out of her at the time of Morrigwen's death. That greater knowledge of how the world worked was lost to her and she grieved for it. But neither she nor Keridwen had said anything. Separately, they had instinctively understood that the people must never suspect that their powers were snuffed out, and so they had shrouded their intense vulnerability in a cloak of aplomb.

She listened intently for any sound that might be Hal, Ceowulf, Cymbeline or Abelard but none came. The Ceolothians were shouting about a mighty sword. "Oh Mother," she breathed in dismay, "they have the runesword but not Hal!"

And what of Hal? Terrified for him, her turbulent emotions deep within her soul writhing in agony, she dropped to her knees and prayed for his safety. He must still be suffering the torment of terrible nightmares. The fleeting image stabbed through her head of Hal battling to the last, one arm, already half-severed, dangling uselessly at his side as he looked straight into the point of a sword borne by an armoured knight. The image was shattered by shouts close by.

Hot on the hooves of the first party came the thunder of galloping horses, clarions blaring loudly. With a hollow boom of hooves, they charged across the drawbridge into the courtyard, shouting wildly, and Brid had to concentrate hard to understand them.

Pip was frowning. "War?"

She nodded. "They're summoning Baron Kulfrid to arms."

"Against Belbidia?"

Brid nodded.

They were left seemingly forgotten while the castle hubbub intensified. Brid sat in the corner of the cell, winding a finger in and out of a hole in the leather of her boot. Boots never lasted long in the mountains and she had walked far in the past months. What was she to do? She needed Hal. She no longer knew how to make decisions alone. Her judgement was not what it had been. As the Maiden she had vision, a greater understanding of events than others and so knew she was always the one best fitted to make choices; but now she had no more prescience than Pip. And she was very glad of him!

She wondered if Prince Renaud at all appreciated how much he owed to the woodcutter's son who, despite the prince's ravings, did all he could to make the man comfortable and laboured to talk him out of his delirium. Brid realized that, again, she had neglected to make her best effort to help him and she felt shabby and weak. She was nothing, nobody. All her life she had preened herself as having a superior presence of mind; but she had none of it. It was all just a sham.

The only good thing in their circumstances was that Baron Kulfrid seemed too preoccupied to remember them. In fact, the whole castle was too busy for them and, for an entire day, no one brought them any food. Hunger bit deep. Pip rattled the door and shouted angrily, using every Ceolothian curse word at his disposal. Brid spent the time trying to nurse the prince from his fears.

Then at last came food. To Brid's surprise, Renaud stooped to snatch up his plate.

"Raven's eggs!" he cried, looking at the plain bread. Clearly, he still thought himself up on the cliff so his mind had rationalized the situation. Naturally, there could not be a plate of bread on the cliffs and so he had seen it as something more plausible. Brid was glad that at least the man ate.

"They're packing up and getting ready to leave," Pip announced, his ear to the door as always.

"They don't know what to do about us," Brid concluded, "otherwise they would have done it already. They don't want to kill us in case we can tell them something and . . ." She faltered, pondering the situation.

"They've not tried very hard to make us talk," Pip pointed out.

"Exactly what I was thinking. They're afraid to come near us because of the trembling sickness, as they call it." Brid nodded towards Renaud. "Ragwort," she said slowly. "Of course! It does this to cattle. It's just conceivable . . ." she left her thoughts unsaid. If ragwort caused very much the same symptoms as this fear induced by the wizards, it might also cure them. The tiniest amount might strengthen them against it and so enable them to overcome this terror. Still there was no ragwort to be had here. She needed help; they needed to get home and she could think of only one way: Sir Irwald.

Hugging her knees close, she spoke out loud as if Hal were with her. "I do love you, Hal, truly I do and I'm doing this for you. I've got to get you home. You must know deep in your heart that I love you beyond all else, beyond myself." With tears rolling down her cheeks, she said, "Forgive me but I'm doing this for you."

"Doing what?" Pip asked suspiciously.

"I've got to get us home," Brid said. "We've got to get out of here and we have to find the others. Irwald will help us. I must win his trust."

"And how do you intend to do that?" Pip asked scathingly.

"Oh, the usual way," she retorted flippantly.

Pip grabbed her arm and jerked her stiffly back. "You can't do this, Brid."

"You don't own me, though you might wish it," she said cruelly, hoping to shock him into releasing her.

He did, turning away from her in hurt and embarrassment. She moved to the door and rattled it, her big eyes filled with tears and her voice sweet as she called out to the guard. She hated the Ceolothian language but could speak it well enough. It was not so different from Belbidian, being a matter of the tone and the order of the words that told it apart but that was what she found hard. It lacked passion and emotion. In Ceolothian a man would either run or walk; he would not race or saunter. They saw such little use for the detailed words. Their word for lovemaking was entirely lacking in passion and procreation was the closest translation she could think for it. Their stiff morals, surprising in such a belligerent people, would not allow even the pleasures of lust. Still, she did not see that as an obstacle. She might have lost much of her esoteric prowess but there was no doubt in her mind that her womanly guiles were just as keen as ever.

The guard was her first victim.

She smiled at him. "Sir, please, sir," she called gently, her voice a whisper.

"Don't," Pip snapped her back by one arm. "Just stop that." He dragged her back from the door and she tripped over Renaud.

The prince looked up at her. "A hawk, a most beautiful hawk. I've never seen one with green eyes before."

Brid was losing her patience. "Pip," she hissed, "unhand me."

"I will not! I will not let you do this."

"Pip, what does it matter? We must get home and I've got to save Hal. Think of this in perspective. For all that we must achieve, it is a very small sacrifice."

"Hal will kill me if I allow this to happen. This is worse than my nightmare," Pip wailed in despair.

"He'll never wake up to kill you if I don't," Brid reasoned. "Now let go of me. You have no choice in this. Can you think of a better plan? You know I can do this, Pip. You saw the way Irwald looked at me."

He nodded reluctantly.

She jabbed his chest with a finger. "Now stand aside. There's work to be done." Stiffly she returned to the door. This was undignified enough as it was without Pip having to make it harder by watching her.

"Guard," she called out softly in Ceolothian.

The man looked at her edgily. She smiled, batting her long curving eyelashes. He flushed just a little and, already, so early in the battle, she knew victory would be hers.

"I can't take it any more in here!" Her face crumpling, she burst into pathetic sobs. "I'll tell your master whatever he needs to know." Brid noted the triumphant smile that lit up the man's face. "Not the Baron though," she added hastily. "I cannot speak with him; he scares me so and is surely too busy with these preparations of war." She watched the guard think this through and waited to see it occur to him that he, too, had no desire to interrupt the baron at this time. "Take Sir Irwald a message that I will tell all. It will go well with you if you bring him this news, will it not?"

The guard nodded and scurried away. Brid judged she would not have to wait too long for the baron's son to appear.

"Why him? Why Irwald?" Pip asked.

"It's obvious, isn't it?" she said, not bothering to explain what was in her head. He had that haunted look of an underdog. He was surely more easily manipulated than the father who was too busy preparing for war, messengers tearing in and out of the castle as often as the clock turned the hour. Besides, he had kind eyes – for a Ceolothian, that was. "Now, I shall need your help."

Waiting until she could hear the tap of footsteps approaching down the corridor, she turned back to Pip. "I'm sorry about this but you'll have to take the blame. There's no one else fit for the job." She laughed. "Though you're still a bit young, of course." Pressing her back against the wall, she unbuttoned her jacket and ripped open her shirt to reveal the pink curves of the top of her breasts. "Grab me!" she instructed.

"But, Brid, I can't!"

"Well, it's not as if you haven't dreamt of it, is it? Come on, for all our sakes." She grabbed his hand and yanked it to her bosom. "Now put some heat into it. Make an effort to kiss me."

He did but, in her opinion, rather feebly. Still, she could do a good job screaming. The noise was made more dramatic by Renaud who added his own terrified moans to the charade.

"Here, lad, just get your filthy hands off her!" the guard shouted and at last Pip made a good show of grabbing her tight by the waist and pulling her to him, his kisses hot on her neck as he pinned her hands back and pressed his thigh between her legs.

Brid was a little alarmed at his strength and by the sense that he knew what he was doing. In her opinion, Pip was far too young for this, yet he already had a demanding touch. The guard pulled him off, sent him rolling to the ground and kicked him hard in the groin.

Brid swallowed her concern and focused on what she must do. The door was open; Irwald was looking directly at her in concern. Now was her chance.

She ran, flinging herself into his arms. "Mercy!" she begged, her big green eyes blinking tears. "You cannot leave me in there with these men any longer."

She could see his eyes were unable to stay on her face but slid up and down her body, circling her semi-naked breasts.

"She needs a safer place," he declared to the onlooking guards. "Come, wench, my quarters will do fine. You'll be quite safe there. I'll see to it that the women have you properly cared for."

They did indeed, washing her in lavender water and placing her by the fire so her long hair would dry. Brid had expected the man to stay and watch but he did not. She brooded over her plan, knowing that if she were to gain this man's favour, she must lie with him and yet not too eagerly; she must keep him interested. A baron's son would have the pick of any number of beautiful women, she reasoned. She was fair, she knew that, but not so striking as to turn a son against his father.

The servants left her locked in Sir Irwald's chambers. What she did notice immediately about his rooms was the number of jewels set into the furniture. Everywhere she looked there were jewels. Even his dog lying by the fire wore a collar studied with rubies. The dog sniffed at her with interest and she stroked it affectionately. It wagged its tail and returned to the business of basking in the heat of the embers. To the right of the fire was a small door, notable for the three locks at top, middle and bottom. She rattled the handle but it was firmly locked. The dog growled at her, warning her to leave it.

Irwald returned later than she expected, unwashed and smelling of ale, just as she had imagined he might. He was a Ceolothian, after all, not a Belbidian who would have paid her more respect.

CHAPTER ELEVEN

Something was on his back. Caspar twisted to get at it, spinning round like a dog chasing its tail, but it remained elusive. The thing, whatever it was, cackled and drummed at his head. He couldn't be rid of it and ran, pounding his brow against a rock. But now the creature had its long black skeletal fingers over his eyes and was worming them inwards towards his brain.

Blindly, he felt a cauldron's hot rim beneath his fingers, and heard the thrum of its rapid boil. In his madness, he plunged his head into the foaming brew. Raw heat scalded him, sizzling his skin and boiling his brain yet he could still think. It was only then that he knew he must be dreaming.

Waking in the black of night, drenched in sweat, he put his hand to his scalp. It was bleeding. He dabbed at it with a cloth and allowed May, who was awake with the child, to make a poultice of mud and water to seal over the wound.

"We must be rid of Necrönd!" he told her, shuddering. "I can stand no more of it." He glanced over his shoulder, again having that very uncomfortable feeling of being watched.

It was before dawn that they moved out, striking for the dog-shaped mountain that they had seen the previous day in the distance. The mountain air was cool and they were eager to be travelling in order to get warm.

May fussed over her child. "Do you think the damp air is bad for her?"

"I'm sure she's fine. She seems able to cry loudly enough when she wants to."

"She feels warm," May agreed, after checking for the third time.

She gazed wistfully at Isolde as the ponies' hooves crunched on the crumbling, sandy rock that covered the ground. Only scraggy stems of withered grass and weeds grew in the cracks between the rocks and there was no sign of tree nor flower though the air was thick with the pollen from dandelion clocks blown up from the west on the stiff breeze.

"I think we're being followed," he said.

"Mm?" May responded, evidently not hearing his words.

"I said, I think we're being followed," he repeated. "I've felt it ever since we left the boat. Haven't you noticed?" He wondered why he asked. Of course, she hadn't noticed; May barely looked up from her child.

The young mother glanced at Trog, who was contentedly waddling alongside, looking much leaner and fitter since they left home. "Trog doesn't seem worried. Do you, boy?" The dog looked up at her and wagged his tail. "You've not been worried since . . ." She choked on her words and coughed to steady herself. "I haven't thought he's been following us since Runa gave her life to save me and drove *him* off." She drew in a sharp breath that caught in her throat, sniffed and squeezed her baby tight. "You know, Spar," she said with forced brightness, "I'm sure that once we've freed ourselves of our burden and get beyond this devastated cinderland, we'll find a haven of soft hills and green valleys where we can live happily ever after and have many children of our own."

Caspar was not so cheered by that hope as he might

be. He had nearly lost her once in childbirth; he didn't want to risk her life again. Still, he was glad to see her happy and, somehow, despite their burden and the hardships of their travel, and despite giving up everything and everybody else in his life, he felt less lonely and more fulfilled than he had ever done before.

"We can build a hut," May enthused.

"I've never built a hut," Caspar told her.

"If you put your mind to it, I'm sure you could build a very worthy hut for us."

Caspar smiled. May's praise of him did not let him forget that he had no experience of such things and he wasn't going to fall into the trap of thinking it must be easy simply because so many woodsmen could do it. The art of warfare came naturally to him because he had trained for it all his life but he knew little of husbandry and shack-building.

When they were less than an hour from the foot of the dog-shaped peak, the sandy rocks at last were footed in tufts of coarse grass.

"We shall settle in an oak wood. I would feel at home in the wood," May said dreamily.

"With plenty of deer grazing and berries to pick and a stream with trout in," Caspar enthused.

"And Trog will grow fat and play with the baby," May continued.

"Shh!" Caspar suddenly interrupted. "There *is* something following; I'm sure." He turned and stared back at a fold in the landscape behind him that smothered the view. He had heard just the faintest rustle over the crisp ground, which he could easily have put down to a rodent or the wind disturbing the dry brush but he had a hunter's awareness that all was not how it should be.

Screwing his eyes up to scan the shadows around the

many boulders and valleys, he sought the stalker but was quickly distracted form his task by the baby waking. It's face reddened and screwed up into a tight ball before a horrible shriek erupted from its wide mouth. Isolde cried for the next hour, which did nothing to relieve Caspar's frustration at being unable to solve the mystery of what had disturbed him. May turned Isolde this way and that and continually offered it her breast but to no avail.

"Try one of her toys." Caspar dangled a small horn cup attacked to a piece of string in front of her. All their pots and pans were no longer utensils but had become toys, as were buckles, straps and shawls. In fact, almost everything in his and May's life now centred on keeping the child content. Still it screamed and May looked at Caspar and shrugged. Then, at last, they both laughed.

"How can she make such an horrendous racket?" he complained loudly.

The child stopped screaming as abruptly as she had started and he peered over May's arm to see her suddenly asleep again.

"How could she sleep after making all that din?"

"I don't know," May agreed, looking rather flustered and irritable but vastly relieved that Isolde was no longer screaming. "Just don't breathe on her like that. You might wake her up again."

"I can't help it," Caspar admitted. "She looks quite divine – when she's asleep."

At last, they reached the foot of the long, low dog-shaped ridge and looked down into a silvery lake. Caspar grunted in disappointment. It was no safe resting place for Necrönd. The lake was quite shallow and they were able to see to the bottom where large skeletons of ox and deer lay littered amongst dark green boulders.

"They must have been fleeing the fire that swept through this land," he surmised.

"If we're going to throw it into a lake, it has to be a deep one." May peered into the waters in disappointment and then raised her head, searching the landscape that stretched before them. Caspar followed her hopeful gaze. Now that they had set on the idea of tossing it into a lake, neither wanted to come away from it.

They dragged themselves through the mountains, the sound of the rocks disturbed by the ponies' hooves loud in the quiet, and began a slow climb towards a wind-harrowed pass. Vegetation was sparse and they had seen no signs of life, only endless broken rocks. Then they made the top of the pass and both halted and stared in amazement at the extraordinarily dramatic landscape before them.

"It's like glass!" May exclaimed.

"Or diamond," Caspar expanded. "I've never seen anything like it."

From where they stood, the wind tugging at their hair and stealing their breath, their gaze was fixed on a white and glistening spire of rock that climbed above a surrounding ring of black boulders.

"It's like a circle of black-robed wizards bowing at a white-robed priestess at their centre," May murmured. "And look! Lakes! This is surely a magical place. One of those lakes must be the right place for us to choose."

Caspar nodded, staring in silent wonder at an entire network of silver-black lakes lying at the foot of the singular, crystalline rock glistening in the sunlight. He noted the paler hue to the earth and, for the first time in days, he saw a dark swathe of trees smothering the land a little way to the south, and raised a weary smile; this pass marked the end of the cinderland.

His gaze was quickly drawn back to the gleaming peak of crystal that seemed to peer down at the ribbons and pools that collected water running off its base. Each lake was as dark as the next; deep and inaccessible.

There was no life here, Caspar was certain. They hadn't even seen a bird flying overhead. If there were no eagles or buzzards then there were no animals crawling in the crevices below. Such jagged crags at home would have been the chosen domain for nesting eagles yet none harried the skies here.

"We shall wait until dark just to be certain and then throw it in," May said, making the decision for Caspar.

"Mm," Caspar nodded. He was so eager to be rid of the Egg yet some small part of him feared he was shirking his responsibility. The Great Mother had entrusted him with Necrönd; was he breaching that trust?

They made camp in the shelter of a few rocks and wrapped themselves tight within their bearskins, grateful even for Trog's hot breath in their faces. It was cold high on the mountainside and the wind moaned through the teeth of the peaks. May worried incessantly about the baby. Caspar was not unduly concerned. Though her nose was a little pink, she looked fit and well. Then it began to drizzle.

Somehow, he had not expected it to rain. Soon it grew dark and the blue-black of the star-filled sky became patchy with rolling clouds. The rain was cold as it landed on his nose, which was all that jutted out from underneath the hood of his bearskin cloak.

"Which lake?" he asked, not wanting to carry the responsibility of the decision.

"The one with the reflection of the moon, of course," May answered as if it were obvious.

Caspar wondered why he hadn't thought of that. Of

course, as with all great decisions, it was better to listen to the advice of the gods than hear any other counsel. The moon that had been full at the time of the child's birth had waned and was now waxing again, its white light casting silver flecks in all the lakes; but from where they camped the fat crescent of its reflection lazed in an oval pool near the centre of the cluster. He noted the lake but decided to wait until the dead of the night to perform his task. He slipped into a light doze and woke several hours later.

"Ready?" he asked May.

She shook her head. "I think I should stay here. It's too dark, wet and windy to go stumbling about with a baby. You'll find the whole task quicker and easier without me."

"Yes," Caspar conceded. "But I don't want to leave you."

"Trog will stay with me." She smiled reassuringly, the moon lighting her features and threading through her hair.

Isolde, her face white in the light, lifted her hand and grasped Caspar's outstretched finger with a grip worthy of an archer. Caspar was deeply moved and smiled warmly at her for a quiet moment before nodding at May, certain that she was right yet still uneasy at leaving her alone.

He checked that the ponies were secure and gave them each a cup of grain to see that May would not have to trouble herself with them. Then he told Trog to "stay and guard" before tenderly kissing May's forehead and setting out purposefully.

He stopped before he had gone four paces, feeling that this was all wrong. "I don't want to leave you," he repeated.

"I'll be fine here. Isolde will get cold and I'll only slow you down."

Caspar had to agree. The skin on his face was tightening

against the sharp wind and he conceded, for a second time, that May was right and should stay put.

"I love you, May," he called back.

"I love you too. Now hurry," she urged him.

Once he started to move at pace, Caspar's resolution grew. He skipped down the mountainside, keeping his balance by always moving, and soon the spot where he had left May became just another of those strange, hunched shapes on the night skyline. He hurried on towards the chosen pool with his hands tight around the silver casket, telling himself that the moment was coming. He focused his concentration, gathering up all his thoughts on the task.

After what seemed like an age stumbling down the slope from the pass, he threaded his way between two of the black craggy boulders that stood sentry around the crystal spire that sparkled in the moonlight. After picking his way through the boggy earth at the foot of the scree slopes, he waded through icy cold shallows. At last, he stood on the brink of a lake. Everything looked different from down here and he was slightly confused as to which lake they had selected. He studied the dark pools until he recognized the oval one nearest the centre of the cluster and made purposeful strides towards it.

In the gloomy night, it proved quite impossible to judge distances and he stumbled and splashed uncertainly on the uneven terrain. He was heavily aware of the Egg and its loud presence singing out its song across the landscape, its song of magic and binding, blaring and haughty. It still thought it wrong that he was intending to abandon so powerful a talisman without any ceremony and paused to think if there were any grave words he might say.

A waft of air ruffled his neck and he spun round to look up into the blackness. He saw nothing but felt a whoosh and a beat of air, not so very loud but disturbing enough air to make him know that something very large had flown overhead.

He assumed it to be one of the ancient beasts of power drawn to the Egg and hoped that it was still only in spirit form. But he knew there were other ancient creatures of the Great Mother that still walked the earth, like the wyverns in the deserts of Glain, the stonewights living so deep beneath the mountains, and the knockermen and kraken. The Egg spoke to these creatures, drawing them to its power. He was suddenly acutely aware that in this remote land there was every possibility that many such creatures might breed and dwell there.

Again, the starry sky darkened and the air was buffeted by the single beat of a great wing. A black shape thrust past over the lakes and away into the mountains, soaring effortlessly and with remarkable pace. All thought of abandoning Necrönd was gone from Caspar's mind. May was up there alone. He began to run, his legs churning up the wet ground.

Climbing back up the slope was slow. What had taken but a short while to descend seemed to take forever to scale. The night was already softening to a grey dawn that created harsh shadows in this stark black and white world but at least hastened his progress. He scrambled on, horrified at how far away he was from May. He could see nothing now, no sign of any danger, but what he had seen at the lake shore had been enough. He had to get back to her fast.

Then it came again, swooping down onto the mountainside just below the pass where he had left May. The ponies screamed, their terrified cries drowned out by a shriek from the air. It was like the piercing cry of an eagle only far louder. And it was not alone.

Caspar shielded his eyes against the glare from the dawn sky to see more of the creatures gliding down to join it. Each had the head and wings of an eagle and the body of a lion. Their wings were green, the colour of fresh bracken, and stretched perhaps three times as wide as an eagle's. Their lion's bodies were golden red. He blinked as the early morning sun caught their backs and they flashed in brilliant contrast to the black of the world below. No wonder there were no eagles here; they all hid from these terrible predators. Three of them flapped at the ponies. The poor creatures had broken their tethers and were dashing like wild rabbits back and forth in the narrow pass.

"May!" Caspar yelled, running faster than he had ever run in his life, terrified that he couldn't get to her in time.

The griffins dived, swooped and swerved, mocking the ponies. Then one of the great creatures stooped out of the sky, twisted and raked out with its lion's claws, snatching one of the ponies up into the sky. It kicked and screamed as the griffin thumped the air with its wings and climbed higher. Caspar loosed an arrow but missed as the creature dodged and swooped with incredible speed. Another darted straight at him in retaliation. As it dived out of the air, he loosed another arrow, horrified at how quickly the griffin manoeuvred to evade it.

He was so concentrated on the one screeching above him that he didn't see when the third swooped around to his back. He was only saved because it couldn't resist shrieking out its horrible cry of attack. He dropped to the ground as it skimmed over, managing only to strike his shoulder. He rolled upright, bow ready, only to see two griffins hovering over the point where he had left May.

His arrow struck one at the base of its long neck. It squealed, and landed beside May's crouched form, the huge, curved beak ripping at the wound to its lionlike body, tearing its own flesh, blood gushing everywhere. In its frenzy, Caspar saw it roll into May, before its struggles gradually lessened and it lay there, gasping shallow breaths. The two other griffins swooped at him. He loosed arrow after arrow but they moved with lightning speed and he had loosed four arrows before he sent one of them spiralling down onto the rocks below. A fourth creature sprang up from behind the brow of the hill. He steadied his breathing, focused on the gold of its feathers at its breast, anticipating which way it would dodge and, at last, made his mark with his first aim.

The creature fell from the sky, its piercing death-shriek trembling the rocks around. The remaining griffin touched down onto the earth for the barest second before climbing back into the sky and gliding towards the peak of the glass-like pinnacle. Caspar ran towards May, his heart in his mouth, his muscles like lead as dread dragged at his soul. The last griffin had something small in its grip and he hoped beyond hope that it was just a piece of rag torn from May's clothing. Trog was galloping after it, yelping.

Gasping for breath, he reached May, who was frantically trying to claw her way out from beneath the great beast that had rolled and collapsed onto her. Her face was screwed up into an expression of unutterable torture.

"My baby! No! Oh no!" she was sobbing hysterically. He pulled her free and she pushed him aside and pointed up towards the glassy spire of rock. "My baby! My baby! It's got my baby!"

In the distance, Caspar could see the lazy beats of the griffin's wings taking it effortlessly across the lakes to the high spire of crystal rock beyond. Above the clear rock, the dark shapes of more griffins circled in the air

May's shrieks and sobs softened to a quiet note of cold fear. "My baby . . ."

Caspar expected her to lie on the ground and beat the rocks with her bare fists but she did not. Her face was set cold-hard and she simply began to march at a driven pace. In her cracked boots and with her skirts in tatters, she looked like a vagabond but within her slight ragged figure Caspar sensed the will of a goddess.

He trotted after her, sick to his stomach, unbelieving that this terrible thing had happened: that Isolde was surely dead.

He tried to reason with May. "There's no use. She will have died swiftly and painlessly. You must stop. This is madness. They will kill you too."

"I heard her cry. She was alive. And I will get to her."

"She may have been alive for a moment but these are like eagles, they will—" He couldn't say it. How could he tell a mother that they would take her baby to their nest where they would tear it limb from limb and feed it to their fledglings?

"You can't spare me," May said coldly. "I know they will eat her. But some creatures like their food to be alive and kicking. They didn't kill the horse. They took that alive and perhaps they will be busy with it for a while before they turn on my baby. I don't know." Her words were coldly numb as she slipped and slithered at a perilous pace down the rocky mountainside. "But while I have just one chance to save her, I shall. She's my baby. I know now how easy it was for my mother. Her life was nothing to her in comparison to Pip's and mine. Nothing."

Gripped by grief, Caspar grimly kept his eyes on that spire of crystal rising above the lakes and charged after her. He had none of May's hope. It was going to take many minutes to traverse the watery terrain that the griffins had covered in seconds. They moved at pace, jogging and marching, May wasting no energy on speech and breathing painfully hard. Caspar knew that none could have equalled her strength of mind.

Dizzy with exhaustion, they at last stood panting at the base of the glassy peak. The floor around was littered with crushed skeletons of all manner of beasts and high up they could see the spread of a huge green wingspan as a griffin hovered above its nest. They approached the foot of the climb, keeping low to the ground and working their way over broken glassy boulders fallen from the pinnacle. Close up they could see that the strange rock formation, formed perhaps by the immense heat from the earth altering the state of the sandy rocks and thrusting them up above the plain, was full of crevices and fractures, that caught and twisted the dancing light. They climbed the lower slopes coated with a layer of fine crystals that shifted beneath their feet. Then they leapt and scrambled from one ledge to the next until they were faced with the smooth glassy sides of the towering crystalline rock.

Caspar reached up for a handhold but his grip merely slipped on the glassy surface. Trog scrabbled frantically at the frosted wall of stone before him and when Caspar heard the high-pitched piping of the griffin's young high above them, he gave up his attempts to climb, certain that their approach was wrong. "We can't do this. It's too smooth and slippery. And Isolde is already dead," he said with certainty. "Listen to them."

May shook her head. "The Great Mother would not let that happen to her. She is too beautiful, too precious. She cannot be dead."

"You must be rational." He calmly drew her close. "This

rock is a fortress and we cannot storm it like this. We need a plan."

"Hal would know," May blurted. "Hal, Hal," she repeated as if his name would somehow give her strength.

The young Torra Altan put his hand on her shoulder, his mind racing to think of a plan. May was right; they needed Hal. What would Hal have done? Hal wouldn't have let this happen in the first place, he told himself. He had to do something but could think of only one course of action. He reached for the Egg and tenderly drew it out.

May saw his moment of hesitation. "You can't. You said—"

"I know. If it goes wrong, it would mean oblivion. I was stuck in the depths of the oceans of the Otherworld and I could have been there forever."

May snatched the Egg off him before he could stop her. "You can't. I can: I don't care. Anything to save my child." She closed her eyes, her focus so intense that, within seconds, a brown slothful dragon appeared at her feet, a great festering wound at its chest from which jutted the shaft of a rusted barb. The beast stank. May had conjured it so quickly that Caspar was knocked back by the blast of air as it took solid form.

Blinking in amazement, he sprang forward to reach May's side but was knocked to his knees by the dragon's elbow as it lumbered forward and lowered its snout so that May could scramble up its warty hide and cling to the spines on its back. Lazily, the dragon took to the air.

Caspar strained his neck back and blinked into the sky as the griffins launched into the air, while Trog leapt up and down, yelping furiously. Like the dog, Caspar was left helpless on the ground to watch the battle above. The dragon belched a sheet of blue flame that consumed two griffins. The air was thick with their outraged cries and the great beasts crashed out of the sky, drilling deep into the soft ground on impact, their charred limbs breaking away.

May was like a banshee up there in the air. "My baby! Give me my baby!" she shrieked.

The dragon blasted left and right at the creatures but it was already beginning to fade, the effort of belching out so much fire draining its strength. It twisted in the air to avoid the raking claws of the griffins and swooped towards the nest at the very top of the pinnacle. May dived from its back and out of sight into the eerie. Then he saw her holding a bundle and scrambling amongst voracious chicks that pecked and screamed. The dragon caught her upstretched arm and glided down to land heavily some distance from him on the sparkling slopes of the crystal rock amongst the ledges and clefts above the broken scree.

She shrieked and rolled over, disappearing from Caspar's view, the griffins falling out of the sky, mobbing and diving at her, but still keeping a wary distance from the ghostly dragon that was all but faded now.

Caspar loosed five arrows and brought down three of the beasts. He didn't know what he was going to do when the dragon had gone completely but then the air was split by a clarion blast, the terrible notes of a song screaming out of the sky. What beast May had conjured Caspar could not imagine. Then, from a tiny dot that grew and grew out of the atmosphere, burst a winged horse, floating in the air above him. On its back was a golden-haired hunter dressed in green robes. Loosing a stream of golden arrows, the hunter drove back two more griffins, the ghostly horse swooping and diving to avoid their lashing claws.

"Talorcan!" Caspar hailed him in relief and apprehension. Talorcan! The verderer whom he had killed with his own arrow!

Already, Caspar was scrambling over sharp boulders and flinging himself from one ledge to the next towards May while Talorcan's ghost drew the griffins off as he chased and danced on the winged horse. The Torra Altan leapt between broken spikes of glassy rock, slithering and cutting himself on the treacherous terrain. As he climbed out of a crack in the rocks and squeezed out between two boulders, he at last saw her running along a ledge that was separated from him by a narrow but deep ravine ten foot across.

"May!!" he shouted.

"Spar!" she cried and, clutching the baby, ran along the ledge until she stood opposite him. Whereas he was protected by high boulders, she stood exposed on a broad ledge.

Though he could hear a griffin screeching above them, his eyes were fixed on her. Reaching out his hand, he implored her to jump. She looked down hesitantly at the jagged spikes of crystal forty foot below.

The air was buffeted by the swoop of a griffin above that mobbed them despite Talorcan's fierce defence. His image was becoming hazy and unreliable and Caspar guessed that May's abilities to control the Egg were failing.

"Come on, May; come on, jump!" he willed her.

She had to make a leap of ten feet from the ledge to where he stood. She glanced at him, then the drop, then up as two griffins swooped for her. She looked hard at Caspar, her face desperate, determined, and their eyes locked, held fast by an invisible thread of will.

"Spar, promise me you will look after her," May begged and to his horror, she threw the baby.

Still clutching his gaze, she raised her hands above her head in total surrender to the beasts to distract them from her child. Caspar's eyes focused only on the bundle that was tossed to him. May too followed the trajectory of the baby with her eyes for that long second as the bundle spun through the air, a little arm unwrapping, flapping and twisting.

He had it! The soft bundle curved into his body and his arms folded around Isolde as a thud and a cry rang out from the far side of the cleft.

The griffin had swooped.

With both arms clasped around the baby, there was nothing he could do. The griffin caught May by the neck and swung her upwards. He heard the splintering crack of her spine as she was snatched awkwardly into the air and then watched as the limp body slipped from the griffin's claws. It cartwheeled, the tattered clothes fanning out, and it seemed an age before she violently hit rock and crashed from one spear of crystal to the next, tumbling into the cleft beneath him and then down into darkness and out of sight. The sound of tinkling rock went on and on down and down and then came silence.

Caspar was too stunned to think. "May!" he choked out, cringing down to protect the baby. Tucking her into his jacket, he held one arm across her as he peered into the crevice, looking for a way down. Only dimly aware that the griffins were still swarming about the winged horse, his thought were dizzy, struggling with the horror of the situation. May was dead!

The griffins swooped about their crystal spire, squawking and tumbling in mid-air, as if waiting for him to emerge at a place where they could pick him clean off the rock. But then one gave out a scream of excitement and they all turned away in pursuit of other quarry. He stretched his neck up to peer between points of rock and saw, distorted through the crystal, a blur of dust streaking away from the foot of the pinnacle. The stampeding herd wheeled away from a pass by a griffin and he saw them more clearly. He glimpsed the spikes of their horns. Unlike the unicorns of the plains that were like fine horses, these were small goatlike beings and would make a good meal for the griffins. He assumed that May must have summoned them just as she was attacked.

He looked down into the dark of the chasm but decided to climb down the way he had come and then skirt round the foot of the glass mountain to reach the mouth of the ravine and May's body. He had to get to her. She had the Egg! He could not let it fall into the clutches of the griffins. He worked his way out of the crevice, scrambling and slipping as he let himself down awkwardly onto the sandstone base footing the spire where the crystal melded into less remarkable bedrock. The griffins, now a streak of red and green in the distance, still sped after the unicorns.

"May," Caspar cried, as he crawled into a low arch that marked the mouth of the ravine. Trog was ahead of him and was whimpering pathetically, his head tilted to one side as he looked up.

May was dangling just four feet above the base of the ravine, her head hooked up on the rocks at a ghastly angle. He ran to her body and turned it over, pulling back at the sight of her blue face. Death had been fast but horribly painful. His shoulders shuddering with sobs, he put Isolde on the floor for a moment and dragged May's body from the rocks and held her to his chest. But her head flopped away and the horrible sense of holding nothing but soulless flesh overwhelmed him. Too choked to scream out his grief, he focused on the one thing he must do and that was to survive for the sake of the child. Isolde was screaming on the ground, arms and legs flailing, but she was alive and well.

The Egg! If he had the Egg, he could do something. He searched May's clothing and then, suddenly, all reverence for her body was gone as he frenziedly ripped open her bodice. Where was it? The Egg was gone!

In panic he turned to the squirming baby and unwrapped the shawl. The silver casket was tucked into its clothing. Isolde had it! With relief, he left it where it was, safe for the moment in the clutches of an innocent. Tears streaming down his cheeks, he reached around May's neck and took her rune scrip and, for remembrance's sake, cut a lock from her hair. Finally, he unstrapped the baby's sling from around her torn shoulders. Throwing back his head he gave out a howl of anguish before laying her quietly onto the gritty ground.

But he had no time to bury her; in the distance he saw the cloud of griffins swoop and dive and then form a writhing knot about the squealing unicorns. He didn't know how long the griffins would take to shred the flesh from the unicorns' bodies but he wasn't going to wait around to watch.

Trees!! He had seen them from the top of the pass. He must reach the trees! It was his only hope. Eagles didn't hunt in thick woods and he prayed that nor would these beasts with their huge wingspans. It would take him perhaps twenty minutes to cover the two miles but the griffins would surely feast on the unicorns and forget him.

Scooping up the baby, he began to run, Trog fast on his heels. There was no time to lose; the griffins were momentarily preoccupied and this was the only chance he had to cross the open ground. Every ounce of energy went into his efforts to sprint and, for a moment, the horror of May's death was pinned to the back of his mind.

He pounded the soft ground, skirting the lakes, splashing through the shallows and was out into the open plain beyond the circle of boulders. The child hampered his ability to run, and each breath stabbed into his lungs that wheezed like bellows, his pulse pounding in his ears. He hoped he was holding Isolde securely enough to prevent her from being shaken but he had to run.

Then came the noise like a storm of arrows splitting the air. The ghostly unicorns had not satisfied the griffins for long. He feared he couldn't make it, his stamina all but spent, his legs beginning to shake with the effort. Trog was stumbling far behind him but he had to keep on. All he could do was focus on the trees that were a bare half mile away now, willing his legs to keep going, fear and loyalty to May driving him forward.

But something else fed his strength. Someone was running with him. Though he could see nothing, he sensed their will urging him on. He caught a flash of gold and saw a hazy outline of broken light that became a stronger, denser light and finally a flickering figure. Talorcan's spirit was tugging at him, lending him the mighty speed of a verderer so that he felt as though he flew across the remaining distance to the trees.

As Caspar dived for cover, the verderer turned, raised his short golden bow and fired at the screeching griffins, driving them back and giving Trog enough time to come panting in and collapse beside him. Talorcan loosed a last arrow that brought one griffin tumbling out of the sky and the rest swerved in alarm and rose high into the air, circling like monstrous vultures.

The flickering spirit shouldered his bow and silently turned to Caspar whose exhausted legs were quivering.

He raised his hand in salute to the verderer but Talorcan seemed barely to notice him. Smiling, the spirit reached out a hand and then tenderly touched his daughter's brow. She kicked her legs vigorously in delight.

Caspar looked at the verderer in disbelief, eyeing the great wound on his chest where his arrow had pieced his body and ended his life.

"Look after her." Talorcan's voice was like a sighing breeze. "Protect my child. This much you owe."

Caspar nodded and remembered that the first thing he must do was to save Isolde from the onerous burden of possessing Necrönd. He reached into the baby's clothing to lift out the Egg. The child shrieked in fury, screwing up her face into a tight red ball and howling. As Caspar took back the Egg, Talorcan vanished.

He stuffed the casket beneath his shirt and sat back on his haunches, looking at his two companions in despair.

He had run so fast for so long, every ounce of thought and energy gone into protecting Isolde, that there had been no time for him to suffer the grief of May's death. Now it all came rushing to him in a flood of sorrow. May was dead. He slumped into the leaf-mould and sobbed, shrieking out his anguish into the earth.

"Great Mother, how could you do this to me? May! You've taken my May."

He beat the earth with his fists until no more tears would come and, at last, he was aware of another crying as he had done, shrieking with anguish and rage . . . and hunger. Hunger! His own troubles and worries were swept aside by the urgent needs of the child. But he couldn't feed her!

She was bawling. What was he to do? Isolde's tiny body would last a very short time without food. But water at any rate would help! He took his gourd from his back

and tried trickling water into her mouth but she sputtered and choked.

"You've got to drink," Caspar said fiercely in his fear for
the child and wondered what to do next.

He dipped his finger in the water and offered it to the
baby. With great relief, he saw that Isolde sucked hungrily
and that gave him a further idea. He tore a strip from
his cotton shirt and soaked it. The baby seemed able to
suck well off that and drank noisily while he repeatedly
drenched the cloth many times over. But it was only
minutes before she was crying again. The noise made it
hard for him to think. In panic, he realized that she needed
a woman's care but it would take him at least three days
to get back to the village. He didn't know if the child
would make it. Milk, babies needed milk. But where?

It was spring. Surely, there would be a deer with a
fawn somewhere in the forest. The hind would have milk.
He shouldered his bow, strapped the baby to his front,
much as May had done, and was relieved to find that, so
long as he was moving, Isolde stopped crying.

Before he found any sign of deer, he halted in dismay
at the size of a bear print that was made by a creature
at least one and a half times the size of a Torra Altan
brown bear. He stepped round it and took a different
path. Trog sniffed at the print, put his tail between his
legs and scampered after Caspar, who was beginning to
stumble with exhaustion. He felt fuzzy and tired and
every few minutes found himself sniffing and choking
back tears. Though worrying over the baby helped to push
from his mind the full horror of May's death, the shock
of it was only just beginning to hit him.

At last, he saw a herd of deer and noted three with
nursing fawns. He raised his bow and then lowered it. A
dead deer would not produce milk.

"Great Mother, forgive me," he murmured, wrapping the baby securely and making a nest for her at the base of a tree. The thought of all the old tales of wolves nursing babies left out in the woods came to him and he wished such a thing could be true. Since wolves had a very strong instinct to nurture and always helped each other to bring up their young, he knew many as thought a wolf would rear a human. He needed such a wolf now but what he had was a nursing deer and he would have to disable it first, milk it and then kill it.

But first he needed rope. He looked about him and stumbled through the undergrowth until he found nettles. With his shirt sleeves pulled down over his palms, he grasped handfuls, ripped them up and shredded away the leaves. Hastily he plaited the stems and knotted them together until he had a decent length of stiff but remarkably strong twine.

He chose the one with the eldest fawn. He knew he was committing a crime to kill a nursing mother but the fawn looked perhaps just old enough to survive while his baby, as he immediately thought of Isolde, was not. He aimed for the hind's hock and brought the animal down to its knees. The rest of the herd fled and Caspar ran in with rope to bind the hind's legs, struggling to hobble it. He wasn't a cattleman though he had seen Bullback and his sons tackle bullocks like this and had seen that it took extreme physical effort. The animal kicked and writhed, catching him on his chin and the back of the head. He cared little what terror he caused it, only that he had its back legs tied to one tree and the front legs to another so that he could move in to milk it. He got no more than a cupful of milk, the animal's terror and his inexperience spoiling the flow.

When he had taken all he could, he took his knife

257

and hastily slit the beast's throat, ending its misery. Now his mind focused on feeding the baby. Again, he used his shirt to absorb the milk so that the baby could suck at it and he smiled with deep satisfaction, seeing that he had done the right thing. The child drank and then rolled its eyes and fell asleep. He made a little nest for her in his bearskin and turned back to the deer. He didn't bother to gut it but simply cut out hunks of meat from the rump while allowing Trog to carve his own meal. Being a dog, he went straight for the offal that, clearly, he relished above all else, plunging his head deep into the deer's bloody belly cavity.

Caspar found a quiet pool where a clear stream spread through a glade and lit a fire on its banks so that he could cook the meat. He ate hungrily and then painstakingly masticated up small quantities of the venison to feed to Isolde. She seemed to swallow a little, for which he was heartily thankful. Picking up the child to cuddle it, he was acutely aware of how the helpless little creature made him feel utterly inadequate. Isolde was fed but he needed rest before he could make the journey back to the village. Aching from head to toe and wincing with bruises, he nestled down next to the tiny girl.

He slept long beside the pool, his dreams ravaged by the image of May being swept up in the griffin's claws. He awoke, crying, and looked down into the stream, sorrowfully watching his reflection until the child woke. He was stiff from cuddling the baby all night to keep her warm and safe, and his cheeks were damp with tears where he had wept for May during his sleep.

Come morning he had no time for tears. Though his heart was heavy with sadness, he had things to do. Clumsily, he changed Isolde into fresh rags, wondering how May had performed this task without complaint. He couldn't get the rags to stay in place and, after much swearing and struggling, wrapped a huge amount of cloth about Isolde's loins that he hoped would be adequate. The chore of washing the clothes at least occupied him and distracted him from the pain of his grief.

At moments, he thought May was right there, watching and encouraging him.

"I won't let you down," he spoke into the pool, imagining that he could see her reflection alongside his. "I love you, May. I always loved you right from the beginning. And I'm sorry I gave you so much pain. I miss you."

After that, he stalked a nursing hind in the same manner as he had the previous day and soon had more milk for Isolde. Now he was nearly ready to make the journey back across the barren cinderland. First, he would have to keep to the forest to avoid the griffins on their glassy throne before heading back into the cinderland and picking up his trail again. He hugged Isolde and rocked her back and forth, the misery in his heart too profound for tears. Trog nudged his shoulder and nipped his ear affectionately, which hurt. Caspar winced but smiled weakly at the dog.

"I can keep the baby alive for a short while but not for long," he confessed to the dog. "She will need good milk otherwise she'll get sick and I promised May I'd look after her."

Isolde was gripping his finger fiercely and looking up with those large slate blue eyes that seemed now to be lightening in colour. He had heard that baby's eyes were always black-blue at birth and slowly turned to their rightful colour after a few weeks.

"I won't fail you," he told the child.

Isolde gripped his finger tightly and kicked her legs. He smiled and she began to yell. Caspar gave her more masticated food and some water that at least did something to make the crying a little less noisy but she was not fully placated until he had her strapped to his front. With a parcel of meat wrapped in hide and a heavy gourd of water strapped to his back, he set off.

With the glass mountain many miles behind him, it was near morning of the third day that he noticed how Isolde was growing weaker, clearly unable to digest the venison properly. Her crying, that had been loud and insistent, was now more of a whimper. He felt the tears at his cheeks and ran on faster, leaving Trog way behind. Late that evening, he made the village, just as the men were driving a herd of black goats into their enclosure. When he staggered to a halt, the baby barely stirred. He thrust open the wicker hurdles of the gates and shouted for help.

The skin-clad people came rushing out of their huts, shouting excitedly.

Covered in cuts and bruises, his clothes torn, his eyes red from lack of sleep and weeping, he stumbled forward suddenly aware of his own weakness. "I need help! The baby," he gasped. "Where's the old woman? Help! In the name of the Mother, help."

The old woman came hurrying towards him, her approach announced by the rattle of her dried sack of bones that hung from the top of her staff. She took one look at Caspar, snapped her fingers and barked orders. Within seconds, he was being led into her hut and the baby pressed into the arms of a nursing mother who sat cross-legged on the floor and crooned over Isolde. She rocked back and forth with the baby at her breast and shook her head. Trog sat at her feet, whimpering.

Caspar looked down at the floor but didn't know what

to think – couldn't think for his anguish. The old woman patted his shoulder, but he walked out of the hut and sat at the foot of the altar that was stained red with the blood of centuries. Staring up at the face of the carved bear, he wondered why these people chose to live in such a land that could take May and now his baby.

"Great Mother, I know this is a temple to a bear and not to you but there is no other at hand." He took his knife and, as he had watched Brid do when she was in desperate need of the Great Mother's help, he slit his forearm. The skin peeled apart, a dry wound before the blood began to flow. He held his hand up and then let the blood drip onto the cold stone. "Great Mother, hear me. Save the child."

A crowd had gathered around him, humming and chanting, and he guessed they thought he was praying to the great bear god and were joining him in prayer. He reasoned that the Great Mother would understand; the great bear was one of Her creatures, after all.

There was nothing to be done for Isolde but wait and see what the woman's milk would do. Caspar sat on the altar, looking west as the sun set behind the strange-shaped mountains that grew in this land. Throughout the night he continued to sit and stare, praying.

By morning, though he was utterly exhausted, he began to pace up and down, waiting for news. Once he heard noises from within the hut and went back in to see the girl asleep on her side. Tentatively, he drew close and peeked down; Isolde was asleep and snuggled close to her breast. He smiled. The colour had returned to Isolde's cheeks. Elated beyond all imagining, he went back outside again to give thanks to the Mother and finally collapsed into sleep.

When he awoke, it was late in the day and the nursing

mother had May's baby strapped to her back while she prattled to her own child and ground seeds in a pestle and mortar. Trog lay in the dirt nearby, his lazy eyes just open enough to keep a watch on Isolde.

Caspar sat up and began to consider seriously what he should do about the child. It took him very little time to realize that the baby was safer here and better cared for than if she came with him on his mission to be rid of the Egg. If he died fulfilling his task, well, then she would live in a mud hut and worship bears, but there were certainly worse things. It was only fair to the baby to leave her with a woman and, persuading himself that he would be fulfilling May's wishes to care properly for Isolde, his mind was made up.

He rested one more night, waiting to be certain that Isolde was fully recovered. In the early morning, he went to check on her. She was cuddled in the foster mother's arms, her head buried in the woman's bosom. Caspar felt suddenly jealous. He loved that baby. He had suffered with May at the time of the birth, suffered to keep Isolde alive and now someone else slept alongside her tiny, warm, precious body.

Still, his mind was resolved. He must go. Sighing deeply, he thought that he must give Isolde something so that she might know where she came from and who she was. He reached inside his pocket to see if he had anything that would be meaningful to give her. He decided that the moonstone from the Otherworld, because it was so beautiful with a mysterious soft glow would simply be taken from her by the older children or perhaps even the women, so he replaced it with the leather leash knotted around it back into his pockets and searched deeper.

With surprise he noted that he still had three empty vials of trinoxia in his breast pocket, the glass smeared with the residue of the precious healing liquid but naturally a glass vial was entirely inappropriate. He chose her mother's scrip of runes and the lock of May's hair. But he also wanted to give Isolde something from himself.

The most meaningful thing he had was the rune in his pocket, the rune of the wolf. He knotted a thin strip of leather around it and tied it to the girl's neck before patting her affectionately. His farewells made, he solemnly rose to walk out of the village, aware of all the eyes on him. Whistling for Trog, he abandoned the baby.

CHAPTER TWELVE

Caspar stared at the dark opening beneath the hut's heavy dome of thatch, pursed his lips and, again, gave out a whistle. This time the note was sharper and more insistent and he waited impatiently for the dog's blunt, white snout to appear. He waited in vain.

Trog's disobedience only added to the misery of the moment. He wanted to get away as quickly as possible and not dwell on the reality that he was leaving Isolde behind. How could he leave her? She was so precious to him yet what else was he to do? He couldn't care for her properly. He bit his lip to stop it trembling and then yelled angrily for the dog.

"Trog, here!" he commanded, his voice strained. "Wretched disobedient dog!"

Still Trog would not come out of the hut where his little Isolde was sleeping. With tears in his eyes, he turned to walk away and only then did Trog bolt after him.

"No! Down! Stop!" he ordered in dismay when, instead of following, Trog got hold of his breeches and began tugging him back towards the hut.

Caspar struck him across the nose and the dog let go but, when he made to move forward again, the bulky terrier sprang in front of him and curled up his lip, revealing his long fangs and healthy pink gums. A horrible growl gurgled in his throat.

Never before had Trog growled at Caspar and the youth was shocked and, to his chagrin, even slightly perturbed. The blunt-nosed terrier was ferociously ugly when he growled and Caspar was fully aware of the dog's power. He'd often seen him crunch up huge ox bones that would have kept a deer-hound busy for hours.

He braced himself and marched on. Though Trog growled and bit at his ankle, he didn't actually attack him and, when one of the fur-clad men stirred behind them, the dog raced back to the hut and the baby.

"I'm not abandoning her, Trog," Caspar called after him, feeling compelled to explain himself to the animal. "I can't look after her properly but the woman can." He bit his lips and frowned, wondering at himself for making excuses to a dog. Turning smartly, he hastened away, though the thought of leaving without Trog was terrible. Yet there was nothing he could do to force the animal against his will. He could drag him but if Trog didn't want to come, he would just run back again so Caspar hardened his resolve and kept on walking.

Then his heart sank to his boots as the baby began to scream, long and loud and furiously. It seemed to him that she was crying out for him. He could hear the nursing mother trying to soothe her but to no avail. Caspar kept on, his heart sick to the core, and told himself to focus only on his urgent task of rid himself of Necrönd.

He started to run, trying to flee from that terrible sound, and didn't stop until he was deep in the cinderland. The wind moaned and howled, raking up the dust that lashed against his legs, though he barely noticed, feeling only the weight of his responsibility.

He turned north. He could not go near the griffins nor May's dead body but soon found he was thinking of nothing else but her. Without the baby to care for, there was nothing else to fill his mind. He would head north into the unknown and find some wilderness where he could safely lay the Egg to rest, bury it perhaps or find another lake to hurl it into. But he found the problem hard to focus on, always seeing in his mind's eye the picture of May and her broken body.

Now she was gone and he was alone. He lifted his head and howled into the wind, trying to purge himself of his anguish. He began to run, somehow hoping to outdistance the pain of his loneliness and loss. May was dead all because he had not listened to his mother's advice. He was afraid and alone, carrying the burden of the world at his breast and yet, now, that world felt too remote to be of any importance.

For days, he travelled in the grief-induced stupor, walking until late into the night, sleeping only when he fell down from exhaustion, his dreams harried by the sound of May's voice calling him and the sound of the baby crying.

"Oh, Great Mother, what evil have I done to deserve this? Have I failed you just as I have failed everyone?" he cried into the dawn that stirred him from his dreams.

After perhaps a week, Caspar looked up from his trudging feet, and realised that he had no idea where he was or how he had got there. He had been absorbed in his own misery for too long and he must have traversed the terrain without noting anything other than the square yard of turf in front of each footfall.

"May, I'm sorry," he called into the wilderness, half expecting her to reply.

Sometimes he felt her presence close at hand and at others he was aware only of his own breathing. Now he found himself standing in marshland, pools and swamps lapping around wooded islets. His shoulders drooped at what he saw. Hazel hurdles lashed together with twists of reed were laid flat to form pathways through the swamp and link the higher ground. He cocked his head to listen. Something had disturbed him but he didn't know what and he scanned his surroundings, searching for what had startled him from his misery.

Was there nowhere on earth he could go without always stumbling across the workings of man? He scolded himself for managing to stumble through the cinderland only to come across more inhabited areas. But that was what he was doing, after all, stumbling aimlessly, carrying with him a responsibility that he was not wise enough to bear.

He was still berating himself, lost in a morose-filled fug of self-pity, when, again, he heard that sound that must have first disturbed him. It was clearer now, a warning cry, distinctively human and no doubt produced as a result of his presence. He readied his bow and looked about him, wondering which way to tread. He had no wish to make enemies. Then out of nowhere there appeared before him three short but very broad-shouldered men, perhaps twenty yards distant. They had long beards and wore tattered bearskins. Warily, he eyed their javelins and stone axes. They grunted.

Caspar looked back the way he had come only to see a further four, barring his escape. Two had their javelins raised.

He leapt for the swamp. Plunging up to his waist, he made painfully slow progress through the water, swimming with one arm while holding his other high to keep his bowstring dry. A javelin thumped into the water a little way to his left, sending out a sheet of spray, and then another sliced into the water a little too close for comfort.

He turned and, holding the bow flat above the water, loosed three arrows, bringing down two men. He couldn't see the others now and so struggled on as fast as he could. A javelin skimmed his arm just as he made the safety of a willow, whose long curving branches trailing in the water sheltered him from view. He stood for a moment and heard the rattle and tap of soft-soled boots slapping on wet wood and he deduced that his pursuers were running parallel to him along one of the hazel tracks though he could not see it for the trees.

Struggling through shallow muddy water that was now at least not so deep, he kicked his legs up high to get his feet clear of the water. He was hopeful that he would get away since the men seemed reluctant to leave their paths.

Then he stopped. Standing silently before him was a bear, not any ordinary bear but a vast bear towering up onto its back legs and waving its claws. Dark chocolate-brown in colour, the longer hairs of its back were frosted with silver tips. Calmly, with smooth movements, he raised his bow, ready to loose an arrow if it attacked. Behind him he could hear the rattle and slap of feet drawing closer and guessed that his pursuers had worked their way to another track that led in his direction. He was trapped.

More grunts and the sound of heavy movements came from the trees to either side and three more bears emerged to gather around the one reared up on its back legs before him. Caspar spun round and faced the men at his heels. He saw at once that they had not anticipated the bears. They stood in open-mouthed horror at the sight of the great brown bear that rocked forwards through the water and, like them, Caspar backed off, inching away into the marsh. Then he stopped, aghast.

"Do not flee, Master!" said a soft and welcome voice from behind the bear.

"Ursula," he breathed in disbelief, peering into the

shadows beneath the trees. Three more bears waded forward out of the shadows and riding on the back of one huge silver-backed animal, her legs wrapped around its neck, came a strong, lithe woman. The beast she rode waded into the swamp and swiped at the water, sending up a spray of silvery droplets.

Screams and yells came from the barbarians that had been trying to attack Caspar and they flung themselves chest deep into the water, where they beat the surface with the flat of their hands and moaned a chant of supplication. In strong and commanding tones, Ursula spoke their tongue and, with heads bowed, they snivelled their reply, before clambering out. Dripping with mud, reeds wrapped around their legs, they climbed back onto the pathway and fled.

Ursula advanced. She looked so different. Her sleek black hair, a little longer now, was clasped by a gold circlet, and a great long bearskin replaced her lionskin cloak. Her eyes were bright and compelling and she looked powerful, regal even. Marching in grand escort behind the slave girl, as he had known her, came a dozen men bearing iron weapons and leading three more giant bears. Ursula grunted words of command to the men and Caspar wondered how easily she spoke their tongue. He still had no mastery of their grunts and clicks but at least he had enough command of the language to understand, the gist at least, of what was said.

She halted in front of him and he stared up in amazement at her and then dubiously at the long snout of the bear, which was uncomfortably close to his head. She lowered her hand for him, offering a strong firm grip.

"Would you pay me the honour of riding behind me?" she asked.

He grinned, the action stiff on his grief-worn face, put his hand in hers and swung himself up.

"I'm glad to find you safe, Master," she said softly, her tone concerned.

"I'm not safe. May . . . May. She's . . ."

"I know." Ursula stopped him, saving him the agony of forming the words. "I know; I heard. I was trying to get to you sooner but everything was in such turmoil. I sent word to all the outlying villages, expressing my wish that they offered you every hospitality if you came their way. I sent bears out to look over you, but still I failed you."

"It was not your fault," Caspar assured her dizzily. Was she trying to tell him that the old woman in the village had so quickly come to their aid at her command?

He closed his arms about her waist, grateful of the warmth of human contact. She stiffened at his touch, intensely aware of his embrace, but he was too tired to notice.

One of her men returned, saying he had found the village to where the men had fled.

"Come, Master, you need food and rest. And I must see that this village is brought back peacefully into my realm," she said, smoothing her red tunic embroidered with the same marks that were on her arm.

Ursula's men led the way along the wattle tracks, which gave and sprung under the great weight of the bears. The ways led deep into the swamp, branching out into a maze of paths that finally wound through coppiced hazels and vanished beneath a curtain of drooping willows.

Beyond the trees, a circle of rude mud huts were clustered on a rounded mound of higher ground. Like the village where Caspar had left his baby, this one was also centred around a tall pole carved with the effigy of a bear. Given the nature of the bears that roamed this wild continent, he didn't find it the least surprising that these primitive people worshipped the huge beasts, though he was alarmed at the reception that met Ursula and her bears.

At their approach, the village became a mass of hysterical screams. Women threw themselves to the floor before their huts and six men took a goat from its enclosure and dragged it, squealing, to the pole where they promptly slit its neck.

Ursula groaned at this display. "They are terrified of the bears and seek to satiate them with offerings, human or otherwise. If only they would stop, the bears would avoid the villages; but these free pickings give them a taste for humans and stock and teach them that the villages are an excellent place to feed."

Caspar was barely taking it in. Ursula ordered her men to settle the excitement and soon they were seated by a crackling fire and offered food. Though hungry, Caspar couldn't bring himself to eat and picked at his food listlessly. Ursula studied him.

He smiled wanly. "Your new role suits you better."

"Oh?" she prompted, happily chewing at a bone from the goat that had been roasted over a smoky fire. Everything was a little damp and, evidently, they found it hard to get dry timber.

He shrugged but didn't bother to explain himself. He merely thought how competently she ordered her men around; calm, firm but not harsh and, clearly, she had their respect. But why they had chosen Ursula to guide them he couldn't think. Why or how she was here he didn't even question.

"Eat your food, Master," she commanded.

"I'm not your master."

"You will always be my master," she said in the softest of tones. "Why do you think I came here?"

Caspar looked quizzically at her and managed to take

a bite out of a piece of doughy bread. "I don't know. I left you thinking you'd join with Reyna but presumably you decided that you should return home."

She laughed and Caspar smiled and he was amazed to see how the action lifted his spirits. His smile made her grin all the more and he too smiled more broadly, watching how her large brown eyes sparkled with joy.

"What's so funny?" he asked.

"You are. I didn't know where home was. I was only following you. I was worried about you."

"Me?" Caspar couldn't believe it.

"Yes, you, Master. I owe you everything."

"Nonsense!" Caspar retorted, slightly wary of such a responsibility.

"I followed you and crossed a line of marks in the earth. They ran along a ridge for miles in either direction."

"Marks," Caspar repeated stupidly, recalling them vividly.

"These marks." She tapped her arm, twisting round the bare firm skin to see them clearly. "All I had of me, the real me. You know, I didn't see them at first; I felt them. I was standing on them and I looked down, instantly aware of them. A tingling feeling pricked through me, and I felt . . . You know, it sounds completely ridiculous but I felt like a bear. And then I remembered! I remembered standing there before at precisely that point in the landscape. I remembered the forest and that volcano. I was standing holding someone's hand and they were frightened, horribly frightened. We turned to stop once and look homeward. It's strange, for all those years I had only remembered the hand."

Caspar suddenly felt a powerful affinity with Ursula. Throughout his childhood, he too had had those same strange feelings of half remembering. His mother was taken from him at the age of two and they had not found her again until he was fourteen. Throughout his childhood, he had grown up with a haunting sense of abandonment. He reached out and took Ursula's hand, understanding her feelings of unresolved pain.

She gripped him with surprising fierceness. "I've always been nobody. No name from nowhere. All I've ever had were those marks and then suddenly I find them. And I remember! That was when I left your trail. I'm so sorry!" She hung her head in shame. "I was so excited to see the volcano and those slate mountains that I thought only of myself and left you. You see, you didn't appear to have much need of me; you had May."

Caspar swallowed.

"I know, I'm sorry." Ursula held his hand tight and kept talking, saving Caspar the agony of having to force words through his choked throat. "I walked home. The city is set high into the rocky mountains where bare-sided cliffs rise up out of a dense forest full of bears and I felt I knew the paths in the forest. There was a hush as I walked them; I could feel the bears all around me, breathing steadily, listening to my own breath. I smelt their delight. Slowly, they gathered to me as bears had done all my life but these ones were special. So big and powerful, huge bears, godlike bears, they greeted me as if welcoming me home. And when I finally marched to the citadel carved out of the very stone of the mountains, I marched with a dozen bears at my side."

Caspar was grinning at Ursula's expression of delight. "You should have seen their faces?" he finished for her.

She nodded. "I felt in my bones that something was wrong when I saw the people of that fine city clad only in skins and bearing primitive weapons, the glossy black stones of its mighty buildings crumbling and cracked, lying in heaps on the once polished streets. Only the citadel stood as it once had."

She looked deep into the fire for several minutes before continuing. "They spoke in a peculiar grunting language and I knew it at once as my own. They trembled and threw themselves on the floor, fearing that I had come with my bears to wreak my revenge. And before I knew what was happening, they even grabbed hold of two of the younger men and slit their throats as a sacrifice to me. I could do nothing to save them."

"How horrible!"

Ursula nodded. But she seemed less shocked than a normal woman from the Caballan and Caspar considered that, as a slave, she had seen so many atrocities that she seemed to accept them as part of life.

She continued, "To cut a long story short, they took me to be a leader of sorts and thus," she spread her hands broadly, indicating the spread of the landscape from one horizon to the other, "this is my realm. In all this continent, only the Empress of Oran commands a larger territory."

Impressed, Caspar's eyebrows rose. "Wow!"

"I suddenly found myself with a realm to put in order but I sent men and bears to look out for you but they lost track of you in the land that is nothing but ash and cinder. I'm so sorry."

Caspar acknowledged her sympathy with a brief nod.

"I thought you safe and I found myself suddenly home," she excused herself. "Wouldn't you have done the same?"

"I would," he agreed. "So, what happened?"

"What do you mean?"

"Originally. Why were you cast adrift into the great ocean?"

"It seems there was a succession of bad years. The

volcano that had been dormant for centuries grumbled and belched smoke. Then the wind changed, bringing with it a sickness from the east that harried the bears and ruined the crops. And so, the bears became less of a threat to the people and, as a result, the chosen rulers, the household that was born with a natural gift to control the bears, were considered less vital to their existence."

"Your family?" Caspar asked.

"So it seems," she agreed. "Then came a race from the south-east, savage men that hunted our people. The ones that ruled – my family – were not great war leaders like yours and without their army of bears, could not halt the attacks. Many people died. Naturally rebellion followed and others, who thought they knew better how to save the land from these savages, seized control. My family were cast into the dungeons." Ursula fell silent for a moment, looked to the ground and kicked at a pebble with her sandal.

She sighed and looked deep into the fire as if remembering. "To protect me, my mother persuaded one of the women who brought us food to get me out to safety since I was small enough to be smuggled away in a bundle. And she took me to my nurse who led me across the mountains to the sea and put me on a raft, hoping the currents would take me north to a neighbouring country. Foolish woman, she must have heard so many tales of babies being put in floating cribs to find a better life that she believed it would be true."

"Go on," Caspar prompted when Ursula fell silent, a grim shadow darkening her face.

She laughed sourly at the irony of it. "The same ill-wind that had made the bears sick and brought the barbarians west had also disturbed the great sweep of the ocean currents. For a little while more the winds blew west long enough to carry me across the Tethys Ocean. Somehow, I survived the long journey and was cast up on the beach in Oriaxia. An oysterman fostered me and I learnt to love him as a father only to have my love betrayed. It was he who sold me as a slave to Mamluc."

"And your family?" Caspar asked tentatively.

"They were sacrificed to appease the barbarians," she said flatly.

"I'm sorry."

She shrugged. "In time the winds changed and the bears grew strong and returned in numbers but there was no one to keep them out of the cities. The barbarians, who had taught my people sacrifice, turned and fled from the bears. Naturally the sacrifices did not deter the bears, who rampaged through the land as if in vengeance for the murder of my family. The proud civilization that had lasted for thousands of years collapsed."

Caspar nodded, imagining the chaos.

Ursula ran her fingers through her hair and sighed at her own tale. "In terror of the bears, the people fled to the lake villages and deserts and wildernesses but, because they continued their sacrifices, the bears followed like dogs after a rubbish cart." She shook her head and, for once, Caspar forgot his own troubles as he was caught up in Ursula's tragedy.

Distractedly, she looked round at the men and women who sat at a respectful distance, patiently waiting for her command. "Now my people are fragmented across all these lands and I must show them that these sacrifices must stop."

"How do you control the bears?" Caspar asked.

"I don't know. Nor does anyone else here. I have asked but they say only that my father and his father before and his mother before that all bore the same marks as I do. It appears that my family had a peculiar innate gift that was passed down to one child in each generation who was born with these marks. Come, you must rest and sleep. You look tired."

He was led to a hut and Ursula stood silently, watching him, and he had the impression that she was waiting for him to do or say something. He stood at the threshold and shifted his feet, uncomfortably.

She broke the awkwardness by saying gently, "I'm sorry about May."

With a downcast face, he nodded. "Yes, so am I."

He slept badly, tossing and turning and listening to the grunts of the bears outside, his dreams returning over and over to May lying dead and her child lying lifelessly on the altar slab in the village, the old woman standing over her clutching her tiny heart. The nightmare spun into another dream where the silhouette of a woman stared down at him, watching him. Her hand was inching towards his chest where Necrönd lay nestled.

In the still of night he awoke, sweating, his hand clutched over the silver casket. The scent of Ursula was still thick in the air about him but the dream, he knew now, was a warning that he could not ignore. He heaved on his boots, wrapped himself in his bearskin and slipped out into the dark.

The village was surrounded by a ring of flickering light from the guards' torches and, beyond them, he could see the humped shapes of the bears all heaped around the camp like giant guard dogs. This was a dangerous place for Necrönd. This was a place of warriors and civil war. Ursula was trying to muster a nation; she would have good use for the Egg.

One thing was certain; he couldn't stay here a moment longer, but there was another reason just as pressing as

Necrönd. His palms were sweating and his breathing fast as he wondered what might be happening to Isolde. How could he have left her behind? His grief over May must have clouded his reason. Still shaking from his nightmare, only one thought possessed him; he had to get back to her. The sense of urgency was overwhelming.

With great restraint, he nonchalantly ambled through the village, gazing at the stars and acting like one that could not sleep. He nodded at one of the guards, who nodded back respectfully and then he made his way to the animal enclosure at the back of the village, hoping to find a horse.

His eyes smarting from the ash that the wind whipped up off the cinderland and blew into his face, he at last glimpsed the blue mountains ahead on the horizon. He smoothed the tufted hide of the short-legged pony beneath him, grateful that, though the beast had not looked up to the task, she had carried him at a steady speed across rough terrain.

There had been only four ponies in the animal enclosure, all evidently used for light draught work by the ring of sores about their necks, undoubtedly caused by ill-fitting collars. He had taken the leanest of them. Leaving a fistful of coins in its manger and hoping that Ursula would forgive him for his silent departure, he had stolen out into the marsh.

In his heart he had not wanted to leave Ursula but he knew he could not risk staying with one who wielded such power and influence. It must have been Ursula or her minions all that time that he had sensed dogging his tracks. Had she really been after Necrönd all along? He couldn't believe it. He hurried on through the night and, by morning, the smoke from the village where he had left Isolde was a distinct brown pillar rising out of the plain.

After stringing his bow, he scanned the ground for a herd of wild asses. An hour later he had slain and gutted a beast in readiness to offer to the tribe and, with a little forethought, hacked out its bladder, a section of upper gut and a chip of bone from its lower rib. The bone he split and whittled until he had fashioned a crude needle, which he stowed in his pocket. The rest he bundled together to clean later.

With the ass slumped over the back of the stocky pony, he was soon at the outer ring of stakes that protected the village and his heart leapt at the sight of Trog waiting for him at the gate. The dog bounded forward and Caspar, kneeling to greet him, was bowled over backwards by the force of the stocky terrier thumping into his chest.

"Trog! Ugh! No, don't do that!" The dog licked his face, leaving a warm stickiness over his nose and cheeks. "Oh yuk, Trog! Why do you have to do that?" he asked, hugging the dog tight.

Then Trog abruptly butted him aside to get to the kill. He slapped the dog hard across the nose. "Leave! It's not for you." Trog was infuriatingly disobedient and continued to worry at the ass's hock but Caspar had little thought to care. "Now, come on, where's Isolde?" he demanded.

Tugging at the pony's bridle, he hurried into the village with Trog leading. Children pointed and the men and women turned and stared as he marched up to the hut where he had left Isolde. Flinging aside the hide curtain, he distrustfully ran his eye over the circle of people gathered around May's baby and barged in. Sweeping Isolde up, he cuddled her tight.

"I'm taking her," he said calmly. "Her and a goat, you won't mind."

The villagers were so aghast by his appearance and the determination in his voice that they hardly said a word nor did they complain when he showed them the ass and solemnly took a goat in exchange. He left immediately and, since no one came running after him, he considered them satisfied. He also considered the possibility that they were still obeying Ursula's edict to be hospitable. Knowing that he must get beyond her sphere of influence, he jabbed his heels into the pony and examined Isolde as he rode.

She looked plump and was remarkably clean and warmly wrapped in layers of skins, the rune of the wolf still hanging about her neck. They had even fashioned a tiny little cap to cover her head where a tussle of golden red curls was beginning to grow. He kissed her forehead.

Once the village was far from view, he halted and set about cleaning the bladder and length of gut he had cut from the ass before attempting to milk the goat. Unused to the movement, his thumb and fingers soon ached. The goat, however, was surprisingly tolerant of his fumblings and, though it stamped and nibbled at his shoulder and tugged at his hair, he soon had plenty of milk in his cooking pot. With a thin strip cut from the gut to form a coarse thread, he stitched the bladder and fashioned it until he had formed a teat of sorts. He then filled it with the milk and admired his craft. Though some of the liquid seeped through the holes of his stitching, the teat worked exceedingly well and the child sucked quite happily.

He strapped her to his front, just as May had done, and her tiny hands hooked tightly into his clothing. Smiling, she gave him a deep gurgling giggle. He hugged her tight and she gurgled again. Much cheered, he urged his horse on. The swaying motion of its gait lulled them both to a restful state and, somehow, holding May's baby healed much of his pain.

"I'm sorry, Isolde; I thought I was doing the right thing leaving you with a woman," he said apologetically.

Trog pestered the goat constantly and Caspar was soon thoroughly annoyed with the dog. He eventually picked him up and lashed him to the back of the saddle, though he still wriggled and whined and eyed the goat avariciously.

"Trog, just stop it," Caspar snapped irritably and it dawned on him that it was the persistent moaning cry of the baby, though he had fed her, changed her and tried to jolly her by bouncing her up and down, that was wearing his temper thin. It was just impossible to stop her crying. Just when he thought he could stand it no longer, she suddenly fell asleep. He had a moment to relax and think, despite the goat straining to the end of its tether to butt at Trog, causing the short-legged pony too to kick out in annoyance.

The pony had a broad back and a thick skull but it was strong and Caspar had no qualms that he was overburdening it.

"Now, Isolde," he said, glad to have someone to talk to, "what next?" He often talked to Trog but that wasn't the same as talking to a human even if the baby was asleep and also had no language. When she was awake, however, he was beginning to suspect that she understood much of what he was saying. The way those eyes watched him, those huge baby eyes, so alert so knowing, was most disconcerting. The eye colour was changing. They reminded him curiously of Brid who had such striking green eyes.

May had hazel eyes and he had hoped to see May in her baby, hoped that a part of May's soul would look out through those eyes but the child was entirely herself. She was so warm and cosy against him and he cradled her head, just gazing at her as they trudged. Caspar was no longer considering which direction to travel but let the horse pick its way and so, with no particular purpose, he found they were headed west back towards the coast. After two days they climbed a bare ridge and crossed a line of sigils marked into the ground. So, he was leaving Ursula's realm, he thought with relief though a part of his soul cried out in regret.

"I thought I was doing the right thing but I should never have left you," Caspar told Isolde.

Her head bounced against his chest, her little cheek squishing against him.

"But I can't just leave it anywhere," he continued, speaking out loud his thoughts that continually returned to his burden of the Egg.

After several days, he halted and blinked. There was the sea! Unwittingly he had worked his way back to the western shore and was staring at the great Tethys.

"Oh Isolde, if I can find nowhere safe to leave Necrönd, the only thing I can do is take it home. It was safer there than anywhere else. At least my mother was there to tell me what to do. My mother . . ." he repeated and looked at the child, knowing at once in his heart that he must take this baby to her. Only his mother was worthy enough to look after Isolde. He had to get home.

Sitting on the cliff-top, taking care to protect the child from the wind, he gazed longingly west. Huge waves, driven by the ever-constant west wind, crashed against the cliffs below. There had to be a way.

"Oh Mother, how do I get home?" he asked the winds that pressed into his face. He looked up and down the coast, remembering that Ursula had said how her nurse had cast her into the sea, hoping that she would end up in the coastal villages to the north. Villages on the coast meant boats and, if he had a boat, surely, he could find a way home.

A week later, after skirting several hamlets he at last spied a sizeable village. Taking a deep breath, he rode in, the pony's hooves thudding on the beaten earth, barely audible for the shrieks of herring gulls screaming over offal tossed out by the fishing boats recently returned from the sea.

The villagers appeared better nourished and more sophisticated than the peoples of the mountains and marsh where Ursula held her power. They smiled and nodded and seemed to be a small friendly people, which was a great relief to Caspar, though they were intensely curious. He had little to offer them to gain their friendship yet they welcomed him with open arms and large quantities of food for him and even a fish soup for the baby.

He wondered at this magnanimous gesture but they were equally friendly and courteous towards each other. He soon felt comfortable enough with them to broach his purpose. He wanted a boat. He pointed to a small sailing vessel and reached in his pocket for money – gold. They shrugged at it and seemed unimpressed.

"I need a boat," Caspar said carefully in their tongue. "I need to cross the Tethys." He pointed west across the ocean then at himself and then west again, to emphasise his meaning.

They shook their heads vigorously and one or two rose and mimed, blowing furiously with their cheeks and rolling their hands about to indicate the movements of the sea and the onshore breeze that would prevent him travelling that way. One rushed off and fetched a large piece of wood and he was intrigued to see that it was carved with the name *Sea Queen of Oria*. Evidently it was the name of a ship and he guessed it was an Oriaxian vessel that had broken up.

The villages appeared greatly impressed by their trophy that, after all, had come floating over the vast waters from an unknown continent that they had no way of reaching. Yet tiny parcels of that world came to them, washed across the great ocean on the tides and currents that swept ever eastwards.

They also had several barrels and this was clearly the source of their joy. Caspar looked at one barrel and immediately guessed it was either a beer or a wine barrel that had been washed overboard in some storm.

The village elder slapped the barrel warmly and dipped a long thin ladle into the top and drew out a cupful of a dark golden liquid. He poured it into a wooden goblet and Caspar sipped it tentatively. The brew was sweet with a potent kick that felt as if it ripped off the back of his throat. Still, it was good.

"Oriaxian mead," Caspar declared out loud. "Baron Bullback imports it and thinks it's wonderful," he explained to the villagers who clearly didn't understand who he was talking about but he felt happier talking.

They brought more food, and the children came to play with him and the baby while Trog worked his way up and down the shore, sniffing and snuffling among the rock-pools, looking eagerly for sea snakes. His search bore no trophies, which was a vast relief to Caspar.

"We'll sit here another three days," he told Isolde, "until the moon is full." She was watching him with intense interest. He placed her on the sand but she insisted on eating it and, when he picked her up again, she began to cry in frustration.

"Let me find you something else to play with," he told

her, laying out his bearskin to protect her from the sand. "Here, what about your rune?" he suggested, taking it from her neck.

Though he could still see no way of getting home, Caspar was comforted by the baby and felt strangely less burdened when he watched her playing with the rune and its tie. She sucked at it and twiddled it round and round.

The child played for some time while he attempted to puzzle out how he was going to get home against the force of the wind, but then she became fractious. He had tried all the usual techniques that he and May had developed for keeping her happy. She drank for a short while but then began to cry again, so he tried making her toys. She liked the rune but was clearly in need of variety. He tied strips of cloth and a spoon to a piece of string and dangled that before her but she seemed unimpressed.

"I thought it was rather ingenious," he said, admiring his handiwork.

The child swung her arm about and finally dropped the toy. Before Caspar could pick it up, Trog snatched it up and ran off with it, leaping delightedly and thrashing the string back and forth so that the spoon lashed against his head, evidently making him feel as though he were in a real tussle and so adding to his excitement.

Caspar knew there was no point running after the dog, who would not relinquish the prize until it was thoroughly destroyed, so he turned back to his pack to see what else he might have: some knives that of course were entirely inappropriate, as were his arrows and the empty vials, and the bow too valuable. Then he turned out his inner pocket and found two things; the scrip of runes that he had taken from May's body when she died and the egg-sized moonstone that had come with him from the Otherworld.

The sight of the moonstone made him feel quite ill. He had no liking of anything that reminded him of the Otherworld and he wondered briefly whether it had brought him bad luck. Then he saw how the baby's eyes lit up at the sight of it. Kicking her heels frantically, she stretched out for it. Caspar had never seen her grasp an object in both hands in such away. She laughed and immediately tried to put it into her mouth though fortunately it was too big.

Caspar was pleased to see her so content. He sighed. "You know, I didn't realize how much effort mothers had to put into bringing up their babies. I thought they just lay around contentedly cuddling them."

She jangled the rune scrip and sucked at the moonstone while he sat gazing west, wondering what he should do. Before he knew it, he had the silver casket in his hand and was stroking the cool metal. Hastily he put it away, realising how, already, he was drawn to using it. His scalp itched and he looked warily around him.

Trog growled and the baby gave out a sudden shriek of fear, her little body stiffening, and flinging out her clenched fists. Caspar hastily picked her up, dropping the rune scrip and moonstone to the ground.

"There, there, it was only Trog growling. It was only Trog," he soothed.

He wasn't unduly worried because he had heard her make that same explosive cry before when he had frightened her by sneezing. He hugged her tight but she would only stop crying when he gave her the moonstone to play with.

Quite dizzy with the mead, Caspar lay in the warm sand, soothed by the baby's contented cooings yet all the while listening out across the ocean, wondering whether the wind ever lulled. But he wasn't permitted to lie still for long.

"No, Trog, no! Drop it! That's Isolde's," he scolded as Trog teased the moonstone from Isolde's grip and leapt up with it in his mouth and fled, leaping about delightedly and enjoying the sport. The dog splashed into the waves, tossing the moonstone up into the air and catching it again.

Then he stopped and stiffened before, tail between his legs, he fled back onto the beach.

CHAPTER THIRTEEN

Her hair was loose, spread out in a fan over the plump pillow, the firelight from the hearth making the hair seem redder than it was. The sheets were cool. Smooth and silky, they caressed Brid's naked body, though she found they smelt distastefully of Sir Irwald. Dispelling the disgust from her mind, she lay back, forcing her dark lips into a seductive pout, and waited for the nobleman's approach.

He stopped in mid stride. "Well, now!" he said, staring.

She blinked up at him, her eyes wide and vulnerable. About his shoulders hung a cloak of wolf-skin, Yellow Mountain wolf-skin, and his hands sparkled with jewelled rings, the stones deep red with flashes of yellow bursting out from within them. Cringing within, she eased back the sheets to reveal the upper curve of her breast, the nipples jutting through the sheets but not exposed.

He couldn't take his eyes from her. His hand slowly stretched out towards her but paused as if savouring the moment of anticipation.

"In those hunting leathers and covered in mud, I could see you were fair but I had no idea . . ." He was lost for words.

Brid's torcs glistened about her arms, a circlet on her head. All the trappings of her office that had been hidden beneath her clothes now adorned her naked body.

The Ceolothian nobleman knelt at her feet. "They expect me, dear lady, to take my pleasure with you but I cannot."

Cannot? Brid was surprised but made no comment. There might be many reasons for his behaviour; a physical problem, a fear of women, a love of men perhaps; she did not know.

Briefly, she wondered that she might have lost some of her beauty but decided such self-doubt was folly. She was more beautiful now than she had ever been. She was lithe and strong, her breasts heavy but jutting, and her stomach softly rounded, but these were not her greatest assets. She knew that men were most attracted to the intense deep green of her eyes. And yet this man, though she lay naked in his bed, would not touch her.

"I'm cold," she said softly. "Come, warm me." Her tone was inviting; her eyes dark with passion, though her mind reviled against him and her heart grieved for the wolves that had died to make his cloak.

His face twisted. "I told you, I cannot," he hissed savagely and lunged at her.

To her dismay and bewilderment, he dragged her from the bed towards the locked door at the back of his chamber. While she kicked and struggled, he fumbled to open each of the three locks, a different shiny key used for each. The wood around the keyholes was light in colour and clearly freshly worked. Whatever lay behind the door was a recent secret.

Gripping her wrist, Irwald bowed beneath the door lintel and stepped forward, dragging her in and closing the door behind them. Goose pimples bumping every inch of her body, Brid was even aware of the soft tinkling noise of her necklace that seemed rudely loud in the dim light of the hushed interior. Shutters covered the windows and heavy drapes lined the panelled room, muffling all sound from the outside world. Only a few candles cast any light. Sweet herbs and, to her trained nose, the unmistakable scent of embalming oils perfumed the air but could not disguise the smell of death.

Irwald swung her forward to stand beside him, his hand trembling as he gripped her wrist. Hardwin's body lay at the far end of the room on a low wooden table. His entrails were drawn out and the flesh of his chest had been stripped away, revealing the bony curve of his ribs. Something gold glinted within the cavity of his chest. Three old and very ugly women sat on stools about the table.

The floor was covered in wolfskin and behind the broad low table, seven wolf heads looked down from impaling spikes. A man crouched in the corner, holding a mangy, liver-coloured dog on a chain. Several fingers were missing on his right hand and horrible scars covered his face. Man and dog appeared to be guarding five young boys that were chained to the wall, their faces white with misery.

Irwald snapped his fingers at the man with the dog, who limped to a cupboard, delved inside and came turned with a stoppered horn flask in his maimed hands. The three women leapt up and grabbed Brid, one yanking back her head back by her hair and another holding her nose to force her to open her mouth. Bitter liquid trickled down her throat. Someone wrapped a wolfskin about her naked body.

Blurrily, Brid stared at the scars to the man's face and chest and slowly it dawned on her that this was the Ovissian, Fingers, the trapper that had kidnapped Pip and Brock and mistreated them so brutally. Trog had all but killed him and, after the ambush when Cymbeline had been taken, they had presumed him dead and given him no more thought. Hazily, it occurred to her that he, like the tall thin soldier, must also have been in Tupwell's employ. But she found it impossible to concentrate longer on that thought.

She was drugged! The world staggered and swayed about her. Not even the cold fear that rippled through the dark chamber could bring her to her senses. Her head swimming, she gaped around her. Though the objects of sacrifice and augury were sinister in their own right, they were not enough to make her feel this chilled. Something horribly macabre, a cold a sense of evil pervaded the stagnant air yet she was certain it was not caused by any of the people before her.

As the images about her swirled and blurred, she feebly murmured, "Life. I am alive and I worship the glory of life."

Irwald bowed towards the altar. "I bring a great offering!"

Brid could barely see but she could still sense the presence. It was not the cold evil of a diseased god that she felt; no, what Irwald worshipped was human in spirit. She sensed loneliness, self-pity and self-loathing but also power and ambition. Now she understood why he would not take her. He was too terrified of the dreadful power lingering in this chambers that had a better use for her.

The sword! Hal's sword! Brid's head thumped to the ground, her vision swimming into blackness. Just for a second, she had glimpsed it in Irwald's grasp.

Dangling upside down, her head thick with blood that throbbed in her ears, Brid dreamily gazed on the unreal scene before her. A scream had prized her eyes open from her drugged slumber.

"We need bodies," Irwald thumped the altar slab. "He needs them."

"Give him the breath of life. Feed him Önd!" the three women chanted.

"'Tis an unholy business!" Fingers snarled, fumbling to unlock the nearest boy who was too drugged to struggle.

"You'll be next if you don't shut it," Irwald snarled. "Just like your greedy friend, Ryder. Now do as you are bid. He must have a life. The energy of the last breath given out on death is stored," he pointed at Hardwin's chest, "and it gives him strength."

Giddily, Brid wondered at his meaning.

The boy's head was yanked back, stretching his throat. The slit that the women made across his neck was small, the bleeding controlled. As he squirmed and struggled, dying horribly slowly, they held him over Hardwin's chest as if to send his dying breath into the body, though Brid could not fathom why. She barely cared though she tried to make herself. All she could think was that her head swam and lights danced before her eyes. The swirling patterns raced faster and faster until, giddily, she was sucked back into a quiet world of dreamless sleep.

Once or twice over a period of unfathomable time, Brid tried to force her eyelids open but they were like the huge grid of a portcullis with no winding system to raise them. She sniffed. The air smelt different. She had been a student of the natural ways of the earth long enough to know instinctively that time had passed, lots of time had passed. She had the horrible notion that the season had changed. There were people close by. She could feel their warmth and smell their fear.

Her heavy eyes dragged her back down and thought came to her only in incoherent snatches. Then the screams from yet another victim of Irwald's knife pricked her eyelids open. A deathly cold hung all about her. She blinked, her vision clear at last.

Two sets of legs stretched out on the ground beside her own; an expensive pair of boots and a plainer more ragged pair that she recognized as Pip's. Her mind at last sharp, she assessed what had been happening in this threshold to hell. The ones chained alongside her were not the same ones that had been in this chamber when she had first been dragged in. Their life had been taken to give strength to a soul in the Otherworld.

Her gaze darted towards a strip of bright metal. The great runesword lay bloodied on the low wooden table and the room still reverberated with its hungry song of death. The sword! She hadn't dreamt it! Horror chilled her heart.

"Her next!" the Ceolothian nobleman spoke with cere-mony.

Where was Hal? Where was he? And why was she no longer drugged? Was it to give her strength so that the energy of her death was greater? So, her time had come. She was to be the next victim. Someone threw a bucket of iced water over her. She gasped in shock.

The man she had recognized as Fingers jerked her upright but her legs would not support her, stabs of pain running up from her bloodless feet, her muscles weak and unaccustomed to the strain of holding herself up. She knelt and tried to resist as she was dragged to the low table that served as an altar.

She stared into the now rotted and stinking body of Hardwin; the exposed ribs looked as if they had been singed by a great heat. A circle of gold light sprang up at her and she blinked, uncertain of what she had seen. Her eyes adjusted and she almost forgot her own plight as she focused on a small chalice, buried within the emptied cavity of Hardwin's chest.

It was a golden chalice, a hand's span across the brim,

its sides decorated with long lines of runes. Though she had never seen it, she recognised it at once from Morrigwen's vivid descriptions.

The Chalice of Önd! It had the ability to store and concentrate Önd; the breath of life that was the essence of being and the essence of elemental magic. Brid's mind reeled; she had understood the ancient priestesses had used the chalice to transfer power from a source of concentrated Önd to a simple object. Water would have been poured into the chalice and stirred by the powerful artefact, so allowing the water to absorb a little of the Önd. The next object placed into the chalice would then take on some of the power.

But here the pot was dry, punctured at the base and placed in a dead body. Someone with great skill and leaning, equal or beyond her own, had devised a new use for its properties. These thoughts raced through her mind in an instant and she had the answer. The dying breath, the very energy of life of a living person was being channelled and transferred through the chalice and through death to a soul on the other side where it was being inspired to strengthen his spirit with life.

But if the victims were sacrificed with the great rune-sword, the power of the spell would be hugely intensified. Any two great artefacts of power used in conjunction would create a greater magic beyond the simple combination of the two. She guessed that the sacrificed spirit moving to the Otherworld, rushing through the channels of life would now open up a doorway, allowing the spirit on the Otherworld to rush back on the ghostly wind and slip across the divide. Someone with the knowledge to direct such a sophisticated spell had to possess profound knowledge of the mystical arts.

Fingers yanked her back by her hair and ripped away the soft wolfskin that covered her body. Her head was thrust down over Hardwin, the stench choking, her breath echoing in the bowl of the chalice. A pinprick of light shone within. Brid focused on that as they swept up her hair from her neck, the metal of the sword resting cold against the pale flesh of her back. Her face was jammed hard down into the chalice ready to catch her dying breath

"I feel no fear," she told herself though she trembled. "I am a servant of the Great Mother. She will not forsake me. I am a servant of the Great Mother; she will protect me," Brid muttered but at the last her pray altered. "Hal, dear sweet, Hal," she whispered.

Irwald began a long dour chant and Brid felt her mind being sucked deep into the well of the chalice that seemed to fall away into an ever-deepening pit, the pinprick of light, shining up at her from the unfathomable bottom growing brighter.

The light swelled. Her eyes compelled towards it, she looked into the hole and saw a gaping maw ringed by huge yellow wolf's teeth, the tongue quivering with the anticipation of swallowing her breath. The tip of the great sword pricked below her shoulder blade, testing for the right place to plunge between her ribs and through to her heart.

Then the wolf was gone. A woman with dark red hair was yelling her name, drawing the focus of the chalice. Something scratched at the taught skin of her neck. Brid screamed, an agonized but short yell that failed into a gurgle and gasp, blood filling her throat. Then came pain, gripping and cramping her chest; it was all so quick, her life fading so fast.

*

"Brid, no, no!" Pip shouted, crashing against the chains that held him.

It was the end, the end of hope. She was life; she was beauty; she was everything. He worshipped her with every inch of his body. "Brid, no, please no," he wailed, watching in disbelief and horror the blade plunge down through Brid's back and out between the twin mounds of her naked breast.

Bathed in her own scream of anguish and despair, the horror of what had happened crammed her brain. "Hal!" she cried. "Hal, my love . . ."

She was still in the channels between worlds, her hair caught in the winds of magic swirling and tossing about her; he could still bring her back. She couldn't believe that this was the end – the end of everything. The end of her; the end of all hope for the Trinity.

Her dying scream rang about her, mirrored by other pitiful cries that cluttered the ether; the fearful, terrible cries of those taken before they were ready mingled with the more peaceful resigned sighs of those stricken by age and disease. Then something swept towards her, moving horribly fast. Shrieking like a demon, it was nearly upon her and she anticipated that, again, she would see the fiendish jaws of the wolf; but she did not. In the fleeting instant that the spirit passed her, she saw only two bright blue eyes and with it came the sudden sense of someone wishing her hope and strength.

Don't fail! Don't give in; you can do it.

Do what? Tumbling through the blackness, she could make no sense of what was happening, her only relief that the terrible pain to her chest was gone. She jolted to a sudden stop. The blackness all around had turned into a choking smoke, the stench of scorched fat acrid in the air. Pain returned with a blinding vengeance, a more penetrating, more overwhelming and unbearable pain, deep within her belly.

She screamed, her voice deep and bestial, her agony that of a woman straining to birth a child stuck within her womb, the pain so terrible that she thought her body would be torn in two.

People were shouting at her . . . A wolf was howling . . . Others were screaming with the pain of torture . . . On and on went the pain. All was pain.

"Please, please no! No more! Stop! Stop the pain! I can't take any more," she sobbed.

To her amazement it did indeed stop.

"You are ready to move on? Ready to give up your claim on life?" a smooth male voice asked.

"What?" Brid stammered, her voice not her own. She blinked her eyes open and saw she was lying in a vast chamber so smoky that she could not even see the ceiling though great chains dangled from above, supporting beams from which human bodies were suspended by their arms, their charred feet roasting in a fire. Little men with golden hair and yellow-green eyes moved with purpose between the bodies, carrying pokers, branding irons, and all manner of other torture instruments. She could hear the creak and groan of ropes on pulleys and the agonized screams of someone on a rack.

She was in the dungeons under the castle of Abalone! She was being tortured for refusing to move onto her next life. She shrieked in horror and grief at everything that she had lost. She was not ready for death. People depended on her; she had too much love to give. And Hal . . .

One of the verderers looked down into her eyes and frowned. "You've spent all this time resisting me and now, suddenly you beg for us to stop? You agree to move on at last?"

Brid wasn't quite sure. "The High Circle! I must see the High Circle. My death is a mistake. I must get back. They need me!"

"We have told you, old woman, that you had long enough in life, to complete your tasks. One hundred and fifteen years is considerably more than most. If you failed in that length of time, it's unlikely that you would ever succeed." His tone was mocking but fringed with boredom.

"But no, I—" Brid was flummoxed, her mind in turmoil. "I must see the High Circle. I must get back. Tell them it's an evil magic that has brought me here. A creature, some monstrous wolf, snatched my breath to gain life and steal its way back to Earth."

"Old woman, why this story?"

Still, they called her old woman. Did she look old now that she was dead? In despair she wailed out for Hal, her soul bereft of him. "Hal, Hal, my love," she cried, hoping that somehow her voice would reach to him. But it wasn't her voice.

Again, the raw pain cut into her. She curled up around a sharpened hook that was within her slit belly, the pain terrible as they dragged out her intestines and twisted them into knots. She howled with the horror of it.

"A trial! I must have a fair trial! This is wrong! I cannot die now!" She refused to give up on her life. They had killed her wrongfully and she would fight forever not to move on. She couldn't leave Hal. Surely, he would come to her rescue. She had to get back. She fought on, the pain remote, less intense as her will grew.

They dragged her from the cold stone slab and wrenched her upright. Two beings of Rye Errish were looking at her disconcertedly. One was a verderer of high rank and the other she recognized as an ealdorman of the High Circle. The viscous-looking staff of blackthorn in his grip made him easily recognizable as Straif.

He strode forward and pressed his dark face close up against hers. "You will not get in our way, woman. Tartarsus and I shall see that." He grinned artfully. "He is going to see to it that Duir and Nuin never overrule me again and I will have no one spoiling that!"

He stepped aside and it was then that she saw it, the monstrous face of the wolf. He had no eyes. They were nothing but a pulverised mass of tissue, little specks of white gelatinous goo clinging to two spikes embedded into his eye sockets. Clearly, he was aware of her, perhaps could smell her. He howled in maniacally, "Morrigwen! Oh Morrigwen, my pain is worth it to hear your distress."

Brid slumped, faint with the notion. Was it Morrigwen's spirit that had rushed past her through the ether? If she were dead, Morrigwen lived.

Pip's scream stopped in his mouth.

Irwald stood above her bloody body. "Master, we have summoned you here." He pulled the sword from her back and the bleeding stopped. Brid rose.

Pip wanted to tear the Ceolothian noble apart. Brid was dead; her body possessed. "Necromancer!" he screamed.

The body plunged its hands into the decaying carcass on the table, wrestling to pull out a small golden chalice. Then it turned on Irwald. "Free them," it commanded in Brid's soft lilt. "I have no use for them."

With one hand gripping the chalice to her bosom, she closed on the Ceolothian nobleman and grasped the cord of his throat, squeezing with all her might until he choked and gasped. She pushed him away and turned back to the altar as if she had finished with him. Her hand hovered above a knife. Suddenly she snatched it up and spun round, swinging her hand up at his throat to slit his throat. "You devil, you killed her! You killed my Brid!"

Pip blinked at Irwald as he gaped and then fell to the floor.

The creature possessing Brid's body then swung on the Ovissian trapper who was cowering back against the wall. "Get these poor boys out of here," she snarled, her hand raised to strike him.

He fumbled with keys while Brid's walking body turned savagely on the three old women already fleeing the room. She let them go and, pulling the wolfskin up tight around her body, flung open the shutters letting the bright sunlight cleanse the room of its dark evil. Then she clutched the hilt of the runesword in both hands and dragged it from the table. The point clattered to the floor.

"How does Hal carry it?" she muttered in frustration.

Pip ran to help her and, reluctantly, she allowed him to take the sword. "Guard it well!" she snapped.

"You can't just let that evil man go!" Pip yelped, waggling his free arm in the direction that Fingers had fled.

"Silence, boy!" Brid's voice roared with terrible authority. "He is of little account now that Irwald is dead. We must concentrate on our task. If Brid cannot prevail, Keridwen's strength will fail. Fail . . ." she repeated in a lost faraway voice. "Even while in the Otherworld, her stretched threads of life still bond us together." She paused momentarily. "But she is young and not always wise; I must get her back. Hal . . ." She looked around at her as if not fully comprehending her surroundings before fixing on him. "Where are we?"

"The castle," he said. "You remember! The wizards took us. Ceowulf, Abelard, Hal and Cymbeline are still asleep somewhere; we couldn't find them and we couldn't wake Renaud either."

She jerked her head at the thin man that was twitching with fear, a spike of saliva trailing from his mouth. "Ah, Renaud," she said, nodding as if mentally noting his condition.

"But, Brid, what happened to you?" Pip asked.

"Oh nothing! Now be quiet while we get out of here. I haven't got time for any of your troublesome ways." She looked at her hands for a second before pulling the boy from his chains. "Now get Renaud up," she commanded. "We must find the others and get Cymbeline to Farona."

Pip was not comfortable. "Brid, I don't understand what's happened to you?"

The woman patted his head as if he were a child still learning to walk. "Now don't bother me, child, at a time like this. Just do as I say." She turned and gripped Renaud's white hand. "Now, Renaud, we can't leave without you. Just stop this gibbering, you silly man."

He nodded at her contritely and hurried after her as she led them through the seemingly deserted castle, following her nose to the stables. Outside the keep, three of the boys who had been imprisoned in the darkened room were screaming hysterically about demons. Brid waited until the two grooms in the stables left to see what the commotion was before acting. The screaming caused a diversion; only a few old retainers and women-servants were left to trouble them. Pip doubted that, with the servants bereft of Irwald's command, they would meet any opposition.

Hastily, he saddled and bridled two quiet-looking beasts, while Brid kept watch. A moment later, Renaud riding behind Brid, they were galloping out the castle gates and on towards the forest.

Pip's face knotted into a frown of concern. There was an acid energy to Brid that he had never before recognized in her. Nor had she had that effect on Renaud before. Something was different about her. She was changed, more confident; he feared her like he had never feared her before.

"I— I can't go. I can't. It's a terrible place. There are beasts and goblins everywhere. We shall be lost in the forest," Renaud trembled and clung tightly to Brid.

Brid patted his hands that were fiercely gripped about her waist. "There is always comfort to be found," she said softly once they had dropped down into the trees. "Even for the city-pampered nobleman, the forest is very much the safest place to be. Naturally! It is filled with tree magic and it will protect us. You never have to be afraid with me."

Renaud seemed persuaded by this though Pip suspected it was more something in Brid's demeanour that calmed him than the reason in her words. He trotted after, thinking that, somehow, she seemed wiser.

"Pip, don't dawdle," she chided. "Pip: such a silly name! Merrymoon told me that your mother wished a different name for you but your father refused, saying that a simple name was best for simple folk."

"Piperol," Pip supplied but not really meaning to say it. "Sir Piperol would have sounded fine! I can never be Sir Pip."

"Quite so!" Brid laughed very much amused, which was something he had not expected from her recent behaviour.

"Hal, we must find Hal. Otherwise, she is lost," Brid muttered.

"What?" Pip did not know what she was talking about.

"He brought her back before; he can do it again. Now

hurry, Pip," she snapped. "Keep that horse moving; this is important."

"I know it's important," he said defensively but at the same time he was almost uneasy. What if the nobleman had sensed his dreams towards his beloved Brid? Pip looked at the woman now, studying her lithe body and glorious hair but, somehow, he was not attracted to her as he had been before. He couldn't explain it. Perhaps fear had dampened his ardour.

"Here!" he said. "We crossed this stream. I remember. And then, I think, we came down this track by that oak tree."

"You did or you didn't?" Brid asked stiffly. "Weren't you paying attention?"

"Weren't you?" he retorted.

"No, of course not. Don't be silly. I've had far too many things to contend with."

Pip shrugged his shoulders and, as best he could, led them through the forest. He was born a woodsman and understood the trees, recognizing little features that someone from the cities or the mountains or the farmlands might not have done: a toadstool here, a stump fallen and shaped like the two antlers of a stag, the footprints of a small fawn lost from its mother. There were clues everywhere that marked differences in a world that was to others so similar, rank upon rank of oak and ash and beach intermingled with such regularity.

"Old willow," Brid kept muttering but Pip did not understand her. Clearly, she had been unnerved by her ordeal. She dropped the reins and flung her arms up in an expression of vigorous joy towards the sky. "I never thought I would do this again," she whispered and then shouted to the heavens. "The joy! Life without pain!"

Lowering her arms, she looked down at the prince's

clenched hands at her waist. "Life without fear, Renaud," she added. "You need only believe. Stop thinking and start feeling. Feel the life around you. Understand it. Know it. Do not be afraid for we are all part of it." She rode up close to an ash and pressed her hand against the gnarled bark of the tree whose graceful leaves were tickled by a gentle breeze. "Feel the Önd!"

"Here!" Pip said after they had travelled a little further. "This is the glade. Be careful. The wizards might appear at any moment."

Morrigwen waved a dismissive hand at him and sniffed the air. "Silly child, didn't she smell it?"

Pip wondered who *she* might be, but didn't dare to ask. "Smell what?"

"Wizards. There's a chemical smell about them. Alchemists' potions. They're always tinkering with potions to try and make unnatural reactions and it creates horrible smells. Look at the withering on this leaf." She plucked a blackened leaf from an oak. "It's been touched by them."

Pip stared towards the belching cauldron that was already making him feel giddy and disorientated. Brid followed his gaze and snapped her fingers at him. "Quickly, cover your mouth and nose and tether the horses beyond the clearing. Then help me stop this smoke."

Pip was slow to react, his senses already dulled, but Brid was already scooping armfuls of wet moss. Taking a deep breath, she ran into the middle of the glade and threw the moss into the cauldron. Then she used a stick to rake out the embers and quell the fire. He rubbed his eyes and shook his head, trying to keep his mind clear. Already Brid was studying the ground and snapped her fingers in triumph. "See there! You can see their scorched trail. They must be at the edge of the glade otherwise the Ceolothians would never have found the sword."

Now that his head no longer pained him, Pip too could see the tell-tale marks of blackened and shrivelled leaves and his eye soon fell on four low mounds at the edge of the glade. If only he and Brid had originally thought to quell the smoke, they would all have escaped the wizards and never have been captured by the Ceolothian baron. Now it was only a matter of minutes before they had unearthed the four sleeping bodies. They were cold and blue from lying in their shallow graves.

Pip tried not to look at them. Horrible fear twisted their faces and they twitched like dogs in their sleep. Cymbeline was crying, her cheeks furrowed with cuts where she had clawed at her face in distress. Ceowulf grunted, Pip imagined with the effort of battle, and Hal . . . Hal was caked in dried blood!

"His arm!" Pip wailed in despair.

Brid stood over him and dropped to her knees to examine the sleeping man. Hastily, she striped off the clothing, searching for the source of the bleeding but the skin was already healed. Gently she raised his arm to see a long-knotted scar, the shoulder joint yellow and black with old bruising.

"I repeatedly dreamed my face was smashed to a pulp but I awoke without injury," Pip said thoughtfully. "Why then—"

"To make his dream that much more real they must have dragged him from the earth and made his drugged body act out his nightmare somehow," Brid suggested.

She sat back and stared. "It's a horrible injury but it appears to have healed well enough on its own but I've no doubt it will still hurt." She felt over the shoulder. "The bones knotted as if it's been broken but that must have been weeks ago because it's knitted hard now. We must wake them. We have lost much time, far too much time," she said ruefully. "Anything might have happened to Keridwen. Anything might have happened to Spar. How could we have let this happen? Now, Pip, gather fresh wood and get a fire going. There's much to be done."

Brid stared at the bodies about her for a long minute without moving. "Meddling wizards playing with the mind; it is evil work. Evil indeed. Now, Pip, where's that fire? Renaud, you just sit here and stop whimpering. Whimpering doesn't help anyone." She looked down at the four sleeping bodies and shook her head. "I can't believe I left you all so unprepared to face the dangers of life. Now, Abelard, fair man," she was patting his hand, "you understand true fear. Do not worry any more. There now! All will be over soon. Pip!" she called. "Hurry now! I need you to bring me oak to give us protection from our enemies and holly for strength in fight. Let us burn those together with hazel to give us strength of mind. There's so much that can be done to ease their awakening."

They built a large bonfire and, together, she and Pip dragged the catatonic bodies close to the flames. She smiled at Pip. "You're almost as good a helper as sweet Merrymoon." She sighed regretfully.

"I always thought you didn't like May."

Brid scowled. "Of course, I like Merrymoon. So attentive. She loved stories so." She pointed at Ceowulf and then looked at Pip. "Ceowulf?" she asked.

"Of course, it's Ceowulf!"

Brid smiled. "I never imagined he looked so fine. Well now! The very fine Ceowulf. A great man. A noble man though a sad one. Look at the sadness in his face. I never imagined that was there. How much I was missing." She stroked Ceowulf's cheek. "I knew a man like him once. Ah those years, the years lost. Such a long time past."

"Brid, do you know what you are doing? Brid—"

"Pip," she interrupted him. Find me ragwort?" she ordered imperiously.

"It's poisonous," he said suspiciously. "You can't give them ragwort. Brid, something's happened to you and you don't know what you're doing."

"Ragwort, Pip, and don't question me. I am a woman blessed by the Great Mother. I have Her knowledge within my soul. They used to call it staggerwort as it makes cattle stagger fearfully fear and it will serve me well now. Fetch it to me! Or would you see your friends here die of terror?"

"It might take a while to find," he warned.

"Well, hurry then and stop wasting time."

It was well over half an hour before Pip found any of the ragged-leafed, yellow-flowered herb. Hastily, he weaved his way back through the woods, worrying about what might have gone wrong in his absence. This was more frightening than his dreams!

Panting, he dipped under leafy branches and was back in the glade. Brid had laid out the cationic bodies to form a cross, their heads at the centre, and was drawing a circle about them in the earth.

"Renaud, sing! It'll make you feel better," she commanded.

"The wizards! Won't they come back?" he gibbered.

"Now, child, stop fusing. Not for a long while. They will be in utter confusion after the disturbances in the channels of magic and I will have time. I have the chalice now!" She patted the gold cup in her grip lovingly. "I should have looked for it but I was not worried because Hal had the sword."

Pip decided that she truly was demented. The chalice was no more than a hand's span across but was of a bright metal, the designs on it intricate and full of detail. Trees with towering canopies grew above squirming souls trapped in their roots. The tortured faces of starving men screamed for their freedom, hands worming up through the soil, all seeking the sky. Bands of runes circled the rim of the chalice.

Brid fingered them, her nimble fingers stroking and feathering the design as if she were blind and feeling for their meaning. "I was so foolish to think that if I had the sword safe, that the Chalice of Önd would be no danger to us but I was wrong, truly wrong." She sighed regretfully. "I see so much more now. Oh Pip, you are still too young to know what it is like to be wrong. You cannot truly be wrong until you have responsibility. Only when your decisions affect others do you have the chance to do harm. Before that all is but an accident or mischief, no more than a pup chewing his master's favourite boots."

She swung her arms about her. "All this is my fault. You know, Pip, I was the only one that could have stopped it all happening. I should have known better. I should have seen it coming but I didn't. I didn't love enough where I should have done and all of this is the result." A tear pricked at the corner of her eye and she hastily brushed it away. "Still self-pity is a foolish and arrogant emotion; you'd think I'd know better," she sniffed. "Now make an infusion from that ragwort."

"But I—"

"I'm sorry, child, I forgot you know so little. I was thinking that you might have learnt from your poor sister."

"Learnt what?" Pip was indignant. "I'm hardly going to go round trying to learn from girls, am I?" He patted his sword. "I've learned far more than her."

"All battle craft, I have no doubt. All the ways of taking lives. Yet your sister learned how to give life. I wonder which one of you knew the more?"

Pip scowled. "Here's your ragwort. You do it yourself."

Brid sniffed at it and felt it over and Pip had the distinct impression that she was behaving much like someone who was blind though, clearly, she had the ability to see. She kept looking at things and smiling. Most peculiarly of all she seemed overly concerned with Ceowulf and paid no more heed to Hal than she did the others. Still, Pip knew that there was nothing he could do to hurry her in her work and so leaned back against a tree and watched the young woman pace about the four bodies.

Renaud shortly got up to follow her. "But I feel alone without you," he whimpered when she told him to sit. "It's like . . . Well, you see, my mother was never strong. She had many children between my elder brother and me and none survived. She ailed with every birth and, though I lived, she was drained by me. I was always afraid of losing her. I think if she had been stronger, I wouldn't have been afraid all my life."

Pip listened to the man and the honesty of his outpourings, wondering how Hal could ever have thought Renaud capable of plotting to overthrow his brother. Yet, he considered, there was truth that weak men were dangerous, yearning power to make up for their own inadequacies. Pip understood that and shamefully admitted to himself that he was weak because he was nobody and wanted to be someone. He didn't like being the orphan of a common woodcutter; he didn't truly belong anywhere. Branwolf had taken him into his household but that just alienated him from his own kind in the barony.

They were noblemen. People respected them. They had a place, a position in life that nobody questioned. He had no right to anything that wasn't given to him, oh so kindly. He was indebted, forced to be forever grateful.

"Pip, come here and do something useful," Brid snapped,

breaking off from her chanting. She had been pacing withershins around the sleeping bodies for over half an hour with no change in their state and he could see she was frustrated. "Meddling with minds. They had no right. Now this man," she flicked her hand at Renaud, "is troubling me and throwing my concentration. Sit with him. Reassure him. Tell him, all will be well."

"What difference will that make?" Pip asked surlily though glad of the opportunity to sit alone with Renaud for a while. Even in this state, the prince might note him and the comfort he offered. Prince's favours were not easily won.

Feeling rather foolish at first, he began to talk about himself and the things he enjoyed. "I like archery," he said, showing Renaud his bow. "I'm not very good at it of course. I started too late in life to ever be as good as Master Hal or Master Spar. They played with bows when other babies played with rattles. I played with an axe. Nearly took my finger off several times but it means I know how to handle one when I have to. Used to drive my mother mad." His voice softened. "She died at the hands of a Vaalakan axeman."

"Pip!" Brid snapped. "Joyous things. Talk only of joyous things."

"My mother was happy!" he growled angrily. "More wonderful and more beautiful than any high priestess ever!"

To his surprise Brid smiled kindly. "Of course, she was Pip. Elaine was the fairest of all but right now you need to help Renaud."

He nodded, satisfied with her answer, and turned back to the trembling prince. "Cook's cakes!" he exclaimed, trying desperately to think of something heart-warming. "Her honey cakes are the best in all the Caballan, you know. When all this is over, we shall go to Torra Alta and she shall bake you cakes."

"I wouldn't be able to make the climb," the prince admitted. "I'm afraid, afraid of everything."

"We have the best horses too. They're stabled at the foot of the Tor," Pip said, struggling for something else diverting to say.

"I always used to say that I didn't like horses because it took so long to get the smell of them out of my clothes but the truth is I'm afraid of them too," Renaud wailed.

"You wouldn't be if you allowed Master Spar to teach you how to handle them. He could teach anyone. He taught even my sister and she was never keen on horses. And he taught me to use a bow." Pip kept on chatting idly and realized that his greatest excitement came when he explained how thrilling it was to lay out the archery targets and place them just right so that he pleased the Baron.

All the while he kept one eye on Brid, hoping she wasn't listening too keenly. She had mixed her potion, drawn circles of runes and was beginning to chant, calling out Keridwen's name and her own, invoking the Great Mother and calling on Her power. She placed the Chalice of Önd in the centre of her circle so that the heads of the sleeping bodies all touched it. Then she poured her infusion of ragwort over the pot, trickling some of the deep green potion into their mouths.

"A little of what ails, just the tiniest amount, can help them fight the illness. With prayer and a little luck, they should come out of this stupor on their own," she muttered.

She sat for a quarter of an hour while Pip finally ran out of stories and just watched. Renaud gaped in horror at the four bodies. Hal, Ceowulf, Abelard and Cymbeline were trembling in their sleep and occasionally cried out in anguish.

Hal screamed out for Brid; Pip looked at her angrily. "Can't you comfort him? Can't you say you're here and safe? It might reach his subconscious."

"No, Pip. It wouldn't make any difference," she said aloofly. "All we can do is wait to see if the ragwort will work."

She sat another quarter of an hour, Pip biting back his criticism of her plan until he could keep quiet no more. "Brid, this is stupid. It's not working. The wizards will surely come soon."

To his surprise she agreed. "You're right, there isn't enough power in my spell." She looked in disgust at her hands as if they had failed her and Pip thought he even saw tears welling up in her eyes. She sniffed hastily and, with a voice trembling with passion, cried out, "Great Mother, what would you have of me? I cannot fail them."

CHAPTER FOURTEEN

"Great Mother!" Caspar breathed, his eyes wide with awe as he stared out to sea.

The children all about him were fleeing the beach and running for the safety of the village but he was too amazed to move. Rooted in the sand, he stared as three huge white humps and a barbed tail broke the surface of the water at most a mile out to sea. Only moments later they reappeared in the shallows, demonstrating the terrible speed at which the monster had sped beneath the waves.

Yapping wildly, Trog ran to Caspar's side, alarming him into action. Hastily, he wrapped Isolde tightly into her sling, allowing him both hands free for his bow, which he gripped determinedly; he had recognized at once that distinctive barbed tail.

"Trog," he hissed very gently, "give me the moonstone."

The dog allowed him to prize the softly glowing stone from his mouth. Sticky with spittle, he held it up, his hand trembling. The moonstone! He had an answer. The old dragon from the roots of Torra Alta had obsessively coveted the moonstone. Now in his hand he held a similar orb. He wiped Trog's slime off the leather leash knotted around it. The dragon could swim; the dragon wanted the moonstone; would it take them home for it, tow a ship back across the oceans for him?

313

Holding the smooth stone high, he shouted. "Hey! Last great beast of Torra Alta, I hold a moonstone. Take me home, take me back across the waters, and the moonstone is yours forever."

He stepped back a pace. The barbed tail thrashed the water and then the spiked crest of a neck broke the surface followed by a snout that snorted out two jets of steam. The dragon was even bigger than he remembered. Rearing above the waves, its great white head was now covered in barnacles with seaweed growing like mock hair caught on its spines.

He stood stiff with fear. The great worm was swimming towards them. Then its legs must have touched the seabed as it reached the shelving shallows because the beach shuddered beneath Caspar's feet.

"It's coming up the beach!" people were yelling.

With the ground trembling beneath him, Caspar slowly retreated though he still held up the moonstone by its string. "Take me home and the moonstone is yours."

The dragon drew back its neck, ready to strike. A jet of water burst from its mouth, splattering the bare skin of his upheld hand. It stung like the acid of a jellyfish sting and, in seconds, red weals sprang up where the liquid from the dragon's belly burnt into his skin.

"Don't be such a fool! Get back off the beach!" someone yelled from the village.

The dragon waded up through the shadows, its tail thrashing back and forth, sending out great sheets of water high into the air. Its legs, withered and frail beneath its rounded body, sagged and it slumped its chest onto the beach. Like a vast walrus, it was too heavy for its legs and lay there, thrashing its tail and bellowing, its front legs scrabbling at the sand but apparently unable to bear the weight.

Men sprinted down the beach to drag Caspar back. They had billhooks and spears that they flung at the dragon who slithered back into the water and, unharmed, porpoised up and down the length of the beach some distance from shore. "Come on, get back before it spits again."

"You're a madman, a wicked madman," a woman was scolding him.

Caspar's eyes glazed. He was expecting a tirade of abuse about summoning monsters from the deep but instead she was concerned only about the baby.

"You should know better than to leave a babe on the beach. Look at her! She's covered in sand. You've even let her eat it!"

"I didn't let her," Caspar stammered. "You try stopping a baby from eating sand."

"Well, you don't take babies onto the beach!" The woman seemed unduly cross. She was tall with a reddish hue to her skin that Caspar saw was common to all the people here; he had discovered that they painted themselves with fat and red ochre in order to protect their complexions from the sea spray and fierce sun. "A baby should be kept safe and sheltered. Just what kind of a father are you?"

"I am not her father."

"Oh?" The woman sounded even more suspicious. Her eyes slitted and Caspar had the absurd impression that she suspected him of stealing her.

"I'm her guardian. Her mother died and she entrusted the baby to me."

"Some kind of trust! On the beach with a baby in this sort of blazing weather!"

"I've got to get home." Caspar wafted his hands vaguely

in the direction of the ocean to the west and the woman laughed as if he were mad.

"You wish to go against the tides and the waves and the winds? Ha!"

Caspar cradled Isolde's head against his chest and rocked back and forth from one foot to the other to soothe her as she was beginning to croon softly. "I have to!"

The woman spoke loudly to all around. "This boy wants to get home and he's looking at the waves and waiting for the wind to change."

"The ocean wind always blows from the west, always," another explained more kindly though the rest found Caspar's idea of watching the waters and waiting for the wind to turn absurdly amusing.

"I must get home!" he said in anguish.

The woman turned and pointed north. "They say that's the way home."

Caspar looked back at her blankly. "Indeed?"

"You need to get North to Negraferre where you can take a ship bound for the Empress of Oran. There'll be many a trader heading north out of there soon, catching the hot desert winds that'll soon blow up along the coast from the south at this time of year."

"But I live to the west!" Caspar protested.

"My dear boy," the woman said patiently. "Don't ask me the ins and outs of it; just believe me. I've lived here fifty-five years and only once during the year of disease and raids did the wind ever blow from the east. Soon on the horizon the traders will appear, riding the fierce coastal winds that precede the late summer storms and they will go north to the Empress. We've heard tales that she has found a passage to the west. She's your only hope out of here."

*

316

Caspar picked up the road out of the village and kicked on his shaggy little pony that insisted on a jolting trot. The goat bleated mournfully at its heels while Trog trotted alongside, sniffing the moist, salty air that drifted in cold over the land. They kept up a remarkable pace but Caspar had to stop frequently to feed the baby. The teat he had fashioned from the ass's bladder had begun to leak excessively around his stitching but fortunately Isolde was now capable of sipping from a small horn cup that he fashioned for her.

She was also becoming less content to just sleep in the sling. Caspar sung to her and provided as many playthings as he could but the only thing that kept her happy for any length of time was the silver casket about his neck. Isolde and the small casket holding Necrönd had both rested against his chest, side by side, all the while he travelled and the baby appeared to have claimed it as her own personal toy, giggling at her distorted reflection in the polished metal. He tried several times to remove it from her but she screamed so much that he had to relent.

After five days he was exhausted. The baby had picked up a cold and was particularly fractious. Crying and needing to be cuddled, she had kept him awake most of that night. Eventually, he gave up on sleep and set out while the air was still damp with the night fog. The sun was up and he hadn't been travelling long before he noticed two things: first, the horizon to the south-west was dark with anvil-topped thunderheads mounting over the sea and, second, people were joining the road that, up until then, had been almost deserted.

The first group he overtook were scurrying along herding sheep and small cattle with white spots. Then he caught up carts laden with crates of fowl, hogs and grain, and a little further on more carts laden with barrels.

A lone woman, waifishly thin, her head down in her hood, hurried to the side of the road to let pass a group of three young riders. Dressed impressively in full armour made from a notably black metal, they talked loudly and excitedly of how they would be the talk of the Empress's army.

The road became increasingly busy as the port came into view. Negraferre was marked by a jam of ships sheltering in a bay, terraces of cream and terracotta houses ranked on the slopes leading down to the shore. Inland from the port, huge chimneys the size of church towers, disgorging a reddish-brown smoke, sat at the foot of pale purple mountains whose wintry peaks were lost in clouds. More farmers, driving their herds to market, joined bands of men who were talking mostly about different methods of smelting and beating iron and the best thickness for armour for knights and foot soldiers. Caspar had never seen so many smiths in one day.

There was also a notable number of young men, all talking excitedly of the thrill of joining up for the new war. Caspar was intrigued that, though their horses were unremarkable, their footwear shoddy and their leggings of sacking or old leather, they all boasted the fine black armour that he had first seen that morning on the road.

Most people nodded politely, a friendly race in all, he considered as they hurried together, north along the road. Then another small band of young men dressed in a simple uniform of green leggings and green tunics joined from a side road and fell in just beside him. Over their green uniform they wore strips of armour strapped to their thighs and shins, and breast-plates beaten from the black metal. A fine smooth-haired creamy grey hound trotted obediently alongside a young soldier near the middle of the troop, his armour notably more elaborate than his companions with fluted breastplate as well as shoulder guards and fine gauntlets.

Presently Caspar became aware that the soldiers were muttering and laughing and glancing in his direction. Trog snarled.

He told himself to ignore them. What did it matter to him that a few youths mocked him? He had far more pressing things to worry about but, yet, he couldn't put them from his mind and tried to urge the shaggy little pony to a faster gait.

The goat dragged at its leash and bleated pathetically while the pony's head bobbed all the faster. Caspar's breath came in wobbly bursts as it was shaken from him by the rapid trot. He slowed for fear of harming Isolde.

The young soldiers drew alongside again and one or two snorted in their efforts to stifle their laughter. He kept his head down, reassuring himself that it really didn't matter what these young men thought. He slowed and pulled to one side to let them pass, noting their tall horses that he himself held in no high regard, thinking their legs too straight and so prone to lameness.

He would not be riled by them, he told himself. Hal might but Hal always was too concerned about what others thought. All that mattered to him was getting home. He grinned to himself, thinking of the irony that, since he held Necrönd, he was possibly the most powerful man on earth. Yet these youths chose to laugh at him. They totted by and Caspar relaxed. Then he saw that Trog was missing.

The dog would never have left him with so many strangers about. They had stolen him! Caspar was furious. Trog was his only companion apart from the little child. He, Hal and Brid had long ago rescued Trog from cruel men who fought dogs for money, and the thick-set terrier had quickly become part of the Torra Altan household.

"Hey!" he shouted at their receding backs. "How dare you?" Part of his mind told him to hold back to avoid any confrontation even if it meant losing the dog. The baby was all that mattered and he shouldn't put her at any risk. The woman at the beach was right; he was irresponsible. Nevertheless, he loved Trog and the dog was his responsibility; he couldn't stop himself. "Give me my dog back!" he shouted. "How dare you take him?"

"Are you accusing us of stealing! You little warmonger! You impish brat!" The man at the front of the party turned and pushed his way through the troop.

"Yes, I am," Caspar said directly, feeling no need to hide his emotions. "Give me back my dog!"

It was only then that Caspar saw his mistake. Trog was at the fore of the party and was hardly being held against his will. In fact, the young soldier with the fine armour had leapt from his horse and was trying to beat him off from the bitch. With a cream grey coat, blue eyes and rippling muscles all down her perfect pelt, she was wagging her tail furiously at Trog. They were running round and round in tight circles, sniffing one another.

"And this is your dog, I suppose," the young soldier called out stiffly whilst trying to separate the dogs.

Caspar relaxed and laughed amiably. "Yes, it is. I'm sorry—"

"Well, get him away from her!" the thin-faced youth growled. "If he touches my bitch . . ."

"A prize bitch I see," Caspar said gently. "Trog! Here!" he commanded and gave out a piercing whistle.

The dog laid his ears flat, his blunt-nosed face forming that expression that meant he clearly would not hear his master.

"You call me a thief and now you fail to call your dog off!" the soldier shouted angrily, the pulse visible at his temple beneath his short-cropped hair.

Trog was getting more excited. The bitch was clearly in season and Caspar knew that at any moment he wouldn't stand a chance of getting him back. And with a baby strapped to his chest, he couldn't possibly wade in there and drag them apart.

A whip cracked and Trog yipped in surprise at it caught his flank, a strip of red bright against his white coat. The terrier leapt to the attack; the soldier's horse reared and Caspar feared that the man would be thrown on his back. Several travellers had stopped to watch. He had to do something. But what could he do other than shout pathetically at the dog?

Someone tugged at his arm. Caspar looked down to see the thin woman he had passed earlier, her cloak now thrown back revealing a young face. Her hair seemed too fair for her dark complexion and she had lazy eyes but, her hair was brushed and her simple woollen clothes were at least repaired, though she had no footwear.

"You need help, sir. Let me!" She held up her hand for the Isolde who was crying, her hands grasped around the silver casket that she had taken as her favourite toy. Caspar considered his dilemma for only a moment. He needed to get the dog back before there was an all-out fight. He lifted the baby from the sling, her hands still tightly grasped about the casket and he had no time to wrestle it off her. Knowing that he would only be a moment and that it would keep her happy, he looped the chain around her neck. The woman would only presume it really was a toy since no one would leave anything valuable in the hands of a child. Dismounting, he handed Isolde over to the woman and went after the dog.

He was too late. Trog had already violated the bitch; her owner was furious. The same whip that had been used on Trog, now lashed out at Caspar. The leather tippet caught his wrist. It bit hard.

He had the wherewithal not to show any pain. "If you want to fight, let's fight, but do not strike me again with that whip," he challenged.

"Fight you? A boy half my size! Ha!"

Caspar looked the youth up and down and decided that, despite the fancy armour, he was most definitely not outmatched. Though lean and with an intelligent look to his narrow-set eyes, the youth was soft-limbed and moved with none of the relaxed power of a fighter. He had a wide mouth, the line of the jaw soft, which led Caspar to believe he lacked grit. Still, he reflected, he shouldn't be getting into a fight. Deciding on a more prudent approach, he offered, "I'll pay for your dog."

"You have no idea how valuable she is and now she'll have puppies from that gargoyle of a cur!" The man was furious. Dropping his whip, he advanced on Caspar, fists raised. "Money can't help. She was only a gift for the one who reigns over all these lands from the domain of the bear people to the very far north! I was only going to take her to the Empress of Oran herself! I can't give her a bitch in pup now, can I? Especially not when she's going to produce vile mongrels. She's a war dog!"

"A wardog," Caspar repeated. "There's no doubt." She was a large dog and looked fast enough to keep up with the cavalry and strong enough to do a great deal of damage.

"She was my passport into the Empress's private service. She was my proof that I could breed her fine wardogs but now she'll produce pig-ugly pugs. She's a quarter wolf and that takes a lot of skill." He scowled at Trog furiously and then at Caspar. "You've ruined me."

Wild with fury, the youth crouched, ready to leap at him. Caspar slung aside his bearskin cloak and stood there in his tired hunting leathers that were worn through at the knee. Already he had cut the arms of his jacket off at the elbow and the white of his shirt was now a dingy grey from the dust of the cinderland.

"Dogs will be dogs and you might find the puppies more to your liking than you think," he said amiably.

"From that pig-ugly mongrel!"

The other soldiers were becoming impatient. "Come on, Pennard, you can't let him get away with this."

The youth's eyes flitted to his comrades then fixed Caspar before he flew at him in an unbelievable snarling rage, fists flailing. Caspar stood his ground and dodged the charge with ease, now very certain that he could beat this man Pennard without the least trouble. The youth ran at him again, this time managing to place a glancing blow to Caspar's side that caused the Torra Altan no pain but allowed him to thump the dog-breeder hard on the back of the neck and send him stumbling to the ground.

"Enough!" Caspar declared. "I have no wish to hurt you, only to be left in peace."

But Pennard was already back on his feet, his face plastered in grit from the road. He wiped the back of his hand across his mouth and charged again. The Torra Altan hit him hard in the jaw and the youth crumpled. What Caspar didn't expect after that was a clout on the back of his head that brought him to his knees, his head swimming.

323

Pennard who lay in the dirt raged furiously, "Leave him be! He was mine!"

"I'm sorry, Pennard!" a disgruntled voice said from behind. "But you were taking a beating."

"And a fair one. I fought him fairly and you have dishonoured me."

Caspar wasn't listening. It seemed that the young soldiers would be fighting amongst themselves any moment but that was no longer his concern.

"The girl!" he croaked.

No one paid him any heed. "Where did she go?" he shouted frenziedly. "Where's the girl? She's stolen my baby!"

Instantly the troop of young soldiers fell silent and looked around urgently from one to another.

"No!" Caspar yelled, his voice lifting high to the heavens, his panic and his sense of loss intense. "My baby! Find her!"

"Steady there!" The owner of the bitch put his hand on his arm. "We'll find her for you, don't you worry. Spread out, men!" There was a sinister grimness to his voice that Caspar did not find reassuring.

He knew he could not organize a search himself and, weak to his stomach with fear, he let the soldiers take command. His mouth was dry, his fingertips white and all he could do was spin round and around, looking for her.

"If she's not in the port we'll never find her," one of the men whispered too loudly, only adding to Caspar's dread.

The soldiers rode out in all directions, shouting and calling, but came back shortly, saying they had seen nothing. Caspar's legs were growing weak.

"She'll have gone into the port," someone assured him. "The authorities will find her as soon as we get there."

"Someone lend him a proper horse," Pennard ordered.

Caspar leapt onto the horse and charged with the others, his throat in his mouth. In his mind's eye, he could picture the little child screaming desperately for him.

Tears blurred his eyes as he galloped and he beat the horse to a faster and faster pace, his cloak flying out behind him. Once he got to the town of cream houses beneath their bright tiled roofs, he began again to shout for his baby. His eyes flitting around him, he tried to think. The house fronts stared back at him, the unglazed windows fitted with wooden shutters. The streets were smooth, laid with huge paving slabs, the horse's hooves loud and alarming. A few townspeople, wearing mostly long black robes, appeared at his shout, pressing themselves back into doorways as he approached.

He shouted out in their tongue. "My baby! A girl's stolen my baby! Thin with brown hair." He tried to give a reasonable description of the thief but it was not that easy.

The soldiers from the road raced into the streets behind and the youth with the bitch nodded ahead. "We'll get to the square on the quay front."

The fish market was empty, the fishermen having all sold their wares, and only one or two crabs still crawled about in the bottom of crates. Pennard leapt up onto the auctioneer's box and shouted out into the crowd that a girl had stolen a baby. Soon there was uproar and everyone was searching.

He took Caspar's arm. "There's nothing else to be done now but wait," he said, before repeating the description of the woman to another half dozen sincere-looking townsmen.

Caspar's hands were shaking with terror. "What— what has she done with my baby!" he asked hoarsely. "I shall die if she's harmed. She is life to me."

He had never felt such emotion. No horror could be worse than losing Isolde. It meant nothing that she wasn't his own flesh and blood. He had cared for her all these weeks and she would smile at him and kick her legs in delight and reach up and cling to his auburn hair that was now quite long about his shoulders.

"Come, you'd best have a drink with me," Pennard said. "The townsfolk will find her, don't you worry."

"I've got to keep looking," he insisted.

A soldier returned the shaggy pony and the goat to Caspar and soon after Trog appeared in the middle of the square, howling. Caspar ran to him. The dog was sniffing about everywhere but apparently was unable to pick up a scent. Caspar was not surprised; the only things that Trog had ever been good at sniffing out were cakes, sausages and sea snakes.

"My baby!" Caspar wailed. "Where is she?" He felt utterly desperate. All sorts of unspeakable images flashed through his head as to what had happened to her. He prayed she had not been taken back to the villages where sacrifice was a part of their natural order. Perhaps she had been taken into slave labour or maybe she was just with a lunatic woman that wouldn't know to feed her or keep her warm or would leave her on the ground for the stray dogs to pick up. His knees sagged and for a moment he had to sit.

"Look, don't worry, we'll find her," the young man assured him.

An old woman joined him. "That's it, you sit there. It's no good you running wildly about the place. We need you sat here for when we've found her and, since you don't know this city, you'll be not much help looking. Now lad, you won't do us any good getting into a state. Someone bring some sea grass tea. Now get in out of the winds. It'll be warm in the *Armourers' Rest*."

Caspar couldn't. He stood by the inn, waiting, watching, listening as the townsfolk searched Negraferre and officials came and went. People divided into groups to search the various quarters of the town and the vessels moored along the quay. Caspar was amazed by the speed and thoroughness of the operation and by everybody's willingness to help. They came back at intervals to pat him on the back and smile sympathetically.

The elderly woman never left his side. "Nobody steals a baby around here and gets away with it. Don't you worry, we'll have her back. Here, get your cloak on. No use getting yourself all cold and ill. Won't do her no good when we find her now, will it?"

"No, I guess not," Caspar said stupidly without really knowing what he was saying. He certainly hadn't noticed the raw wind blowing off the sea. Trog sat at his feet, tail between his legs and ears laid back.

"Don't worry," the woman was saying. "The thief will look out for your little girl. I'm sure it's not . . ." she faltered, her voice troubled and then she said more brightly, "No doubt it's just a distraught girl that's lost her own babe and is desperate to replace her. No doubt she'll look after her better than her own mother might."

Caspar cringed at this but knew the old woman was only trying to be kindly. "Her mother's dead," he said.

"Oh! I'm sorry," the woman replied softly.

Despite his fretting, Caspar had the wherewithal to note that all the men of the entire port appeared to have dropped everything to find Isolde. He was touched though he saw in their eyes a deep fear that slowly made him realize that more was awry than a simple kidnapping.

"I'm sure it's nothing more than a silly maid that's lost her own baby. I'm sure! We had one like that last year." The old woman patted Caspar's hand. "We found it after just a few hours. The baby was fine."

Trembling, Caspar tried to take a sip of the steaming brew that the woman pressed into his hands but found his throat was too tight to swallow. He spat the liquid out. He couldn't believe he had been such an idiot. How could he have entrusted the baby to a perfect stranger? How could he have been so naïve to think the stranger trustworthy simply because she was a woman?

"Oh May, forgive me," he groaned. "Forgive me."

By dusk, he noted a change in the expressions of the townsfolk. Their earnest, determined faces tightened into expressions of fear. Only then did he finally remember that, since Isolde was missing, so too was Necrönd. Strangely, he barely cared; his worry was all for the baby.

He was beyond tears when the youth, Pennard, returned, his bitch hard at his heels, bristles up as if understanding the atmosphere of dread that now crept like a shadow though the dank streets of the town. Pennard stood grimly at his side. To make matters worse, a sea fog was rolling in from the brooding ocean, its vastness unseen behind the grey-green cloud that hugged the waters, and was now lumbering inland to clamp its wet hand over the shore.

"It's started again," the old woman breathed as she looked at the returning faces.

A man was walking down the street towards them bearing a bundle, a small bundle wrapped in dirty blankets that Caspar instantly recognized. He could see from the man's heavy expression that something was fearfully wrong.

He ran. Slipping on the cobbles, he raced towards the man until he was just a few feet away then he faltered and took one pace back, unable to finally look. She must be dead. He read the faces of all those about and knew she must be dead but still he had to see for certain.

The man stopped and looked Caspar straight in the eye, his face solemn. "I'm sorry," he choked. "It's started again."

Still refraining from stepping closer, Caspar craned to see into the folds of the blankets, his imagination already picturing the blue lips and glazed eyes. "But—" he stammered, thinking he would faint. Pennard was by his side and Caspar leant on him, stifling a scream of alarm. "What have they done to her?" Then he laughed in relief. "But that's not her."

"It's her blankets?" the man asked.

Caspar nodded, staring in revulsion at the greenish brown creature that lay swaddled in Isolde's clothes. He looked in horror at the men about him and realized only now that all the women and children had fled to the safety of their homes hours ago.

"It's happening again!" the old man wailed.

Caspar stood, staring at the creature. "What is it?" He managed to force the question out from his tight throat.

"They're from the mountains," someone explained. "It's a changeling from the mountains. They live inland in a deep canyon, amongst the great ash trees. It used to happen before; a baby is snatched and soon one of their own appears in its place. They're ogres!"

Caspar looked at the creature doubtfully. It didn't look nearly big enough to be the offspring of an ogre. A yellow

puss was weeping from one eye and it was so painfully
thin that he could barely look at it.

"We must go right away to these canyons and find her.
I must have her back."

The townsmen shook their heads. "You can't! The ogres
are terrible."

The old man pressed the sick baby into Caspar's arms.
He wanted to drop it but numbly closed his arms around
it and looked at the poor little creature. Something made
his heart soften towards it.

"It's not your fault," he croaked, his mind racing to
formulate a plan. He must keep the baby well. Somehow,
he thought there had to be some justice in the world
and if he kept this child well then, whatever these creatures were, surely they would keep Isolde well. "Great
Mother," he prayed. "Dear Mother, keep my baby safe."

The townsmen were fearfully drawing away back to
their homes; windows were shuttered, doors were bolted.
Lanterns appeared in large numbers to light the streets.
A heavy sense of fear hung about the town. Soon only
Pennard remained.

"This is my fault," he said. "If I hadn't been so angry
about the dog, this wouldn't have happened."

"No." Caspar shook his head. "No, it's my fault. How
could I have been so stupid? He looked down at the sick
baby in his arms. "Poor little thing," he said without
thinking, his mind focused on how he was going to get
his baby back. There was always hope. Always, he told
himself. His mother had been trapped for twelve years
and, if it took him twelve years to get his baby back, then
so be it but he would succeed.

"Do you know where this canyon is?" he asked the
youth who stood limply by and was beginning to shake.

Caspar was surprised since he had been so calm and collected up until then.

"Yes," he said quietly, a note of horror ringing in his voice. "Yes, I do." A faraway look dulled his eyes.

"You will lead me there," Caspar insisted.

He shook his head. "No, I will not."

"Why not?" Caspar demanded, his voice strained with tension. "I have to get my baby back. Do you understand? I have to."

"You can't," Pennard said flatly. "I'm sorry. There's nothing any of us can do. Nothing!"

The child in Caspar's arms was beginning to stir and, with almost automatic response, he looked to his goat. With thumbs now well-used to the action, he milked her and then poured the milk into the horn cup he had shaped for Isolde. The creature sipped a little but then dropped back into a snuffling sleep. But wait! Caspar suddenly remembered the trinoxia. He felt through all his pockets and finally found what he was looking for.

Reyna had given him three vials for his horse and he had emptied them. He had simply slipped the vials into his pocket and forgotten about them but, although they were empty, he could still see they were speared with a sticky residue. Perhaps there would be just enough. Even the tiniest drop would surely help.

He filled each vile with milk and shook it and then nudged the baby awake. With more frustration than patience, he managed to dribble half of the concoction into her mouth before she was asleep. He saved the rest for later and turned back to the youth.

"You will at least tell me where this canyon is," Caspar demanded, not having the time nor the energy to argue.

If Pennard were too much of coward to offer his help, he was hardly going to be of any use.

"I don't think I should. You'll only get yourself killed."

"Nevertheless," Caspar said with threat, "you will tell me. I have lost my baby, who means all the world to me. I won't rest until I've got her back."

"They'll kill you like . . ." Pennard's words faded away for a second. He coughed and said more stiffly, "They'll kill you like they killed my father."

Realizing that to succeed he had to know more, Caspar said, "You had better tell me about it. Come, we'll find a quiet room to keep this baby warm."

The innkeeper at the *Armourers' Rest* held his door closed against them. "You can't bring that thing in here. Best to do what we always do with them and leave it by the spring at the edge of town. The wolves will have seen to it by the morning."

"We need to get out of the town," Caspar said to Pennard, "away from all this fear so I can think." The need to act restored his strength of mind. He must eat and he must sleep, he told himself, so that he would be strong enough to do all that he must to rescue Isolde. "Can you get me some food?" he asked, handing Pennard a fistful of coins.

The soft-mouthed youth looked at him in surprise. "Where did a vagabond like you get such money?" he asked suspiciously.

Caspar didn't bother going into any explanation and the youth didn't seem to expect any and no doubt had already drawn his own conclusions. He ran off and returned with supplies in a sack.

"Thanks," Caspar grunted and turned his shaggy pony to head out of town to look for shelter, the goat bleating along behind. He was surprised when the youth and his impeccably well-trained bitch tagged along behind, but he made no comment.

On the streets leading out of Negraferre, they passed a great many smithies, and armourers and, in the woods beyond, they came across large numbers of charcoal burners with their little round domes of smouldering logs. Then further off, a good two miles downwind of the port, he saw the tall brick furnaces, red-brown smoke pumping from the chimneys. He was glad that he was upwind of them and noted the brown stain on the landscape beyond. The roar from the flames within was loud even at this distance.

Caspar hadn't seen the like before. "What are they?" he asked.

"Iron smelters," the youth replied.

Caspar nodded, remembering the large numbers of smithies they'd passed.

"We make the finest armour in all the world," he boasted. "The black armour of Negraferre."

"But it doesn't look like iron."

"Well, it is but they add Negraferre to it," Pennard explained. "The port was renamed for the metal when they discovered rich seams of it. The process is a very delicate one and only our smiths have the knowledge. The mineral is mined on the foothills of the purple mountains," he wafted his hand inland, "and then brought to the smelters where it's added to the iron and heated to just the right temperature. The smiths make the most fabulous armour from it – tougher than diamond."

"But it's black," Caspar complained. "A knight should have shining armour."

He then remembered that Ceowulf's sword, reputedly of great age was also black, and wondered that it hadn't found itself to the Caballan from this distant shore. A thick blanket of brown smoke wafted inland, borne on the westerly winds that blew stiffly from the sea, the slanting trees bearing testament to wild winter storms that must sweep over this flat land footing the purple mountains. The smell was surprisingly sweet though it made Caspar's eyes smart and he was glad when they hurried through it, the winds lifting away the smoke.

"We'll need shelter," Caspar said presently, looking about him for a tree with a thick enough canopy to shield them from the wind and the rain.

Pennard looked vaguely horrified by the idea of sleeping rough. Caspar paid him little heed; nor did he pay any thought to Trog, who appeared ecstatic to have Pennard's bitch along for company. The dogs pressed close to one another, flanks bumping and looking rather ridiculous, the long lean hunting hound so elegantly lopping alongside the squat terrier who panted painfully.

"That copse," Caspar suggested.

The oaks on the perimeter provided dense cover and piles of fallen leaves would keep them warm through the night. He gave the baby the last of the milk from the trinoxia vials and a small amount of fresh milk from the goat, though it drank very little. It was shivering and the other eye was now beginning to ooze yellow pus. Peeling back the swaddling cloths, he saw that it was a girl and with horror, he noted dark boils under her arms. His heart raced as he feared plague and, for a moment, he wondered that they shouldn't just abandon her there and then.

But then what chance would he have of retrieving Isolde? He paused for only a moment longer before setting a pot to boil. He took his knife and washed it in the boiling water before using it to lance each boil so that the pus might weep out and so take the poisons out of her body.

Once that was done, he sat back against a tree and, cradling the sickly baby, begged Pennard to tell him his tale so that he might learn everything possible to help him retrieve Isolde. Hal had always told him that he was not good at thinking under pressure and he was inclined to agree, but Isolde depended on him and him alone; he had to think.

Pennard watched Caspar settling amongst the leaves and copied him. "I lived in Negraferre then. It was after a particularly cold winter when the winds had savaged the coast for over three months. The Empress was again at war, as she is now, and we were glad of it as it made for good money and Father was well paid for his work, which he shipped north to Oran. My mother had given birth to her first daughter that year. I was her eldest and she had three more boys after me; she had longed for a girl. At the end of the winter the baby was just beginning to crawl."

"Like my baby," Caspar interrupted softly. The youth nodded.

"It hadn't happened in years. And then one day Ma woke late, worried that she hadn't been disturbed earlier by Priddy. Then I remember the most terrible cry. I was twelve at the time but sometimes, when I close my eyes, I still hear the echo of that cry in my head. We all leapt from our beds to see what the matter was and there was Ma staring into Priddy's cot, screaming. Of course, my baby sister, wrapped in the shawl that my mother had just knitted and embroidered with her name, was gone and one of these greenish brown creatures was in her cot instead. We searched the town, my father puce with rage, but found nothing. So, we returned home and all stared in horror at the sickly thing. Pa said he would take it to the woods at the edge of the town but it was dead within the hour. So thin and cold. And the yellow oozing eyes!" His lips curled and his nose wrinkled as he looked at the changeling in Caspar's arms.

"Ugh! I don't know how you could touch it!" he exclaimed. "Anyway, as you can imagine, Ma was hysterical and demanded that Pa went after my sister. He took me with him, for I was old enough, and we rode out for the canyon."

Pennard stared at his boots and picked at his laces. "My uncle came with my older cousins so there were five of us in all but only myself and one of my cousins got away. When we reached the ash trees my father wouldn't let me go any further. He told me to stand watch at the edge of the trees and left my cousin to guard me, fearing that I would disobey."

Pennard sighed. "We heard terrible shrieks and my cousin charged after them. He didn't come back for two hours and was barely able to speak." He shook his head and coughed to clear his choked throat. "The town elders sent out a further party of men but they went barely a hundred yards into the woods before one went missing so they returned with nothing but stories of huge men and arrows that were shot straight from tree trunks."

"I'm sorry," Caspar said gently, wondering what these men had really seen. One thing he knew for certain; ash trees didn't loose arrows.

Pennard nodded. "That was seven years ago. My father never came back and my mother went quite mad with grief – not so much over losing Pa, I might say, but with losing her baby girl. She just couldn't get over it and sent us all to grow up with her sister, who lived some dozen miles south of Negraferre."

"I'm sorry," Caspar repeated, not knowing what else to say.

The youth drew a deep breath. "So, you see, I can tell you where the canyon is but you can't go there."

"I must and I will." Caspar was too sick with fear for his baby to have any concerns about the dangers. "I'll take the changeling with me. They won't attack if they know I have their baby."

"Don't be so sure. They obviously didn't want it otherwise they wouldn't have taken yours and left that one to die with you." Pennard turned away, disgruntled, and whistled for his bitch, who came with Trog still sniffing at her tail.

The narrow-faced youth went to his bag and, to Caspar's amazement, solemnly brought out a grooming brush. The dog lay down and practically purred as her master groomed her vigorously. "Gives her a sleek coat," he panted. "But it's hot work." Presently he stood up to unbuckle his breastplate and leg-guards and Caspar noted he was remarkably thin underneath.

"Do you always wear such armour?" he asked, glad to talk to keep his mind from sinking into the black sea of dread that underlay all his thoughts. "Isn't it heavy?"

"Only a little but you get used to it. Besides the Empress won't take any notice of anyone without it. You're no one without a good suit of armour."

Caspar shrugged. "You'd get on well with my uncle."

"So, you see, I thought I could make good money with my dogs and now look what you've done to the bitch. It makes a mockery of me."

"It does rather, doesn't it?" Caspar agreed without apology. He had noted that Pennard's expression towards Trog was changing to one of admiration.

"Good spirit," the youth said, nodding at Trog, "though a bit too wilful. But nothing that a bit of training wouldn't put right."

"Ha!" Caspar laughed at this optimism. "Training! Nothing will alter him. The dog thinks he's part human and has as many airs and graces as a clerk to a king," he said, absent-mindedly, stroking the changeling's head.

"Ugh!" Pennard grimaced.

"It needs comfort, poor little thing?" Caspar was vaguely horrified by Pennard's reaction. "It's just a baby."

"No, it isn't. It's one of the monsters from the mountains."

"She's so cold," Caspar said with concern. Hugging her tight, he fed her and then slid her under his clothes next to his skin. All the while he prayed that someone was caring for his helpless Isolde with as much compassion.

At last, he closed his eyes, determined to sleep but his troubled mind just tossed and turned. Why hadn't he noticed that there was something strange about the woman that had followed him and taken his baby? Swallowing against choking sobs, he relived over and over again the moment that he had handed her over to the woman. *May, I've let you down,* he thought miserably. Kicking himself out of his depression, he forced himself to think but he still needed answers before he could form a plan.

He nudged Pennard awake, "Why do they steal the babies?" he demanded.

Pennard groaned in protest at this sudden awakening. "What?" He brushed his hair back off his face and rubbed at his temples. "I don't know. To sell on as slaves? There's a lot of that sort of trade on the north coast. As sacrifices? There's a lot of that to the south and in the interior. Or just to strengthen their bloodlines? Who knows? They're evidently a sickly people. No one knows; we can only guess."

"Hmm . . ." Caspar grunted and examined the baby again. "What should I do?" he murmured to himself and pondered it through again. "But they don't steal them; they exchange them," he blurted out loud.

"It's no exchange. They take a healthy baby and put in its place one that is dying. They are always dead, usually within hours but always within the day – if anyone can stomach to nurse them."

Caspar saw no problem in that. He washed the mucus from the baby's eyes, and the pus from the boils that were now very much smaller. He kept her warm and tried feeding her goat's milk at every opportunity. In his heart he was certain that he must keep the baby alive. How else would they be able to enter the canyon and remain unharmed?

He slept for a while but was awoken abruptly in the early hours. The changeling was retching. Caspar did what he could, feeding her more goat's milk to replace the fluids and keeping her warm. He cleansed her skin with the milk to remove the pus and changed her blankets that were wet with sweat. Trog sniffed at the dirty ones with enthusiasm. By morning Caspar was exhausted with changing her, washing her clothes and setting them to dry by the fire, but the baby was still alive. He thought her to be very small for the baby of some monstrous people. And the young woman had been no monster either.

"Come on, let's get moving," he said grimly, strapping the baby to his front.

"She's alive!" Pennard exclaimed.

Caspar nodded. They set out at a smart pace and after a while he broke into conversation. "So, your uncle was an expert on dogs?" he asked, burying his fingers into the moulting coat of his shaggy pony.

"No, he knew nothing about dogs, nothing at all. He knew only about armour, just like everyone else in these parts. He made me work in his smithy from dawn till dusk. I could make a mail-shirt in half the time he could, you know. His sight wasn't too good and he always complained that his fingers pained him. He had no sons and wanted me to take over his business."

"That sounds pretty reasonable to me," Caspar said, "and quite normal. Why would you object?"

"He wasn't my father. He didn't care about me. He just wanted me to have the business so that he could retire and live off my earnings. Think of it, shut in the smithy all those hours in the blistering sweaty heat. Anyway, he drank the profits. The harder I worked, the more he drank, saying if he were to be lumbered with me, the least I could do was to earn my way. But he simply used me. The only thing he ever allowed me was my dogs."

Pennard slapped his breast, his nails ringing on the metal. "Had me working on this suit of armour for months. It was for one of the Empress's own generals and I never got to go outside for three months during that time. It's a fine piece of work, don't you think? Worth a ransom for the detailing alone." His fingers worked over the lines of the fluted metal.

Caspar said nothing.

"Well, in the end," Pennard admitted without prompting, "I just took it as payment for all those years' hard labour and set out with my best dog to prove to the Empress how well I can train them. Think what she could do with animals like this. They could carry messages deep into the battlefield, moving swiftly from post to post. Fine they are."

"Yes," Caspar said distractedly. "Have you ever seen a battlefield?"

"No," Pennard replied.

Caspar hated to tell him that his beloved dogs would

not last long. The enemy would know of their strategic advantage and pick them off without a moment's thought. He looked at the youth's long narrow face beneath his short hair, his eyes a little close-set but intelligent-looking and his long fingers clearly nimble.

The ground was slowly rising and the air cooled a little as they worked their way up into the foothills of the mountains where vast fields of purple heather brought swathes of colour. A little higher up, green bands of forest shrouded the terrain before again giving way to the purple heather that clung to the steeper slopes and gave the mountains their distinctive hue. A sickly-sweet smell hung in the air. He recognized it at once as the smell from the smelters and noted, too, that the tips of the leaves were a little frizzled and brown at the edges as if touched by an early frost. He wondered at first that there weren't more furnaces up here, however unlikely that might seem but then deduced that the smoke belched form the furnaces at Negraferre was blown inland by the ever-constant westerlies and eventually drifted down here.

The trees gave way to a tract of short grass. Dark rocks pushed up through the soil and more purple heathers scrambled over their backs. Beyond the heath was more forest but this time Caspar could see only ash trees, the sparse grass at their feet a sickly yellow, tired flowers sagging in the glades. Overhead trails of brown cloud drifted west where they anchored on the shoulders of purple mountains jutting up above the trees. The sky above the slopes was streaked with distant rain.

They moved into the open and he took the opportunity to check on the changeling who was, at the least, no worse and he dared to believe that her breathing was a little more restful. The goat dropped its head to munch delightedly at the grass where harebells grew in profusion though many were wilted. Caspar studied the sudden change from oak to ash trees and decided they must be nearly at the ogres' canyon.

Turning to Pennard, he was impressed and surprised to see that, though the youth was clearly nervous, constantly checking his armour, his eyes flitting around him, he had a new-found firm set to his jaw and made no mention of turning back.

"I'll find my way now," Caspar told him. "No need for us both to put ourselves in danger. Thank you for your service. Good luck with your dog."

Pennard hesitated. "Listen, I'm no coward."

"You told me I was a fool."

"You are but a very brave one. I'm going to show you that I'm no less afraid. Besides, I may find my sister. My father rode bravely into that wood and, now I am a man, I'll do no less." He rapped his armoured chest and gave Caspar that wide-mouthed smile. "I make the finest armour in the land, I'll have you know. The very finest."

"I'm sure you do," Caspar said, pressing his mount to step on through the harebells. Curiously, he thought that he could almost hear them chime. His skin prickled; they were being watched, he was sure. He had seen nothing specific but the trees twitched here and there, and the birds were silent as if watching the activity. He pushed his cloak back so that the baby in the sling was clearly visible, and in a loud voice he cried out, "I come in peace. I bring back your baby."

Harsh birdsong rippled through the ash forest, the startled cries of squawking partridges mixed with the cackle of magpies. Though the notes of the cries sounded precisely as they should they seemed to call and answer to one another, which was entirely unnatural. Gritting his teeth, he kept on. The leaves of the trees rustled, whispering of their intrusion, and he was unnerved by the way the shadows of the softly swaying branches didn't quite seem to match the movements of the trees themselves.

"You baby is well," he cried out and reined in rapidly.

Five arrow-shafts without barbs or quills arced out of the trees and landed directly before his pony's hooves. The changeling began to scream.

CHAPTER FIFTEEN

"Oh Hal, I fear I'm letting you down," Pip murmured miserably over the nobleman's twitching body.

He glanced sideways at Brid, wondering whether he should countermand her; she seemed deranged, tearing at her hair in frustration as she sought to find a spell that would free their friends from the unnatural sleep. How much longer could he just sit and wait for her to fail?

Should he try to take control of the situation? Ought he ignore Brid and seek out the other horses to carry Hal and the rest home? Just because Sorcerer and Secret's bodies lay half-eaten did not mean that the others were dead. Again, he suggested as much to Brid.

"If we move them, they might lose their minds altogether and I cannot risk that," the priestess objected. "And I need Hal! She will not live without him."

Who this *she* was Pip had no idea and Brid merely swept aside his questions as she stood over and calmly studied Hal as expressions of fear and pain flickered across his drawn face. Something inside Pip snapped. He'd sat there for nearly an hour and Brid had achieved nothing. He grabbed her to jerk her round to get her to listen to him but was astonished by the force with which she threw him off.

"Get away from me, you idiot boy," she snarled.

Pip looked from Hal to Brid and shrank back. He was failing Hal, the person he admired above all – save for Baron Branwolf, himself, of course. "You're nothing but a girl from the woods," he sneered.

"Ha!" she laughed. "You know nothing of me! Nothing!" Stiffly she turned her back on him and teased open the cord of her rune scrip. Stirring the bones with her hands, she looked at the runes curiously, uncertainty even. "Hmm . . ." She fingered them as if they were unfamiliar. "So many missing yet."

As if suddenly decided, she pushed up her sleeve, took a sickle-shaped blade from her belt and sliced deep into her forearm, letting the blood pool in the crook of her elbow. Dipping one finger in the blood, she daubed the foreheads of the four sleeping bodies with the rune of the Mother. Satisfied with her work, she rocked back onto her haunches, beginning to chant.

"I am One yet Three is in me. I have gathered them to me. Mother, Great Mother be manifest in me. I need your power!"

Renaud ran to Pip and curled into his arms. "The ground shakes. I felt it shake."

Pip had thought it his imagination, but perhaps the trees around him really had rocked, appearing to bow inwards in supplication to Brid. For a moment, there was a blue glow about her, a glow of power, but it had faded and she flung down her sickle in fury. "Great Mother, she is still in the Otherworld; she has not yet passed on to Annwyn. Her spirit is still with us. We are yet Three. Give me your power. I must find Hal's mind for him. Only he can return her to us. We need her!" She was sobbing now, doubled up like an animal retching, her head bent over as she cried at the ground.

Then she stiffened into silence. After a long intense

moment when she seemed to be listening, she pushed back her long hair that had worked its way loose and was now a ragged mass of muddy tangles where she had swished it back and forth in the earth. She gripped the soil in her hands and leapt to her feet, letting the earth dribble through her hooked fingers as they slowly relaxed. She clawed at the sky as if snatching thoughts from the air and drawing them to her. "But I have it now. Of course! I have the one last sacrifice." She stroked her lithe body, her fingers running over her breasts and curving into her tight waist, a sly glint in her eye.

Pip shuddered.

Brid's deep red lips raised into a half smile. "But I am Brid, I am the Maiden," she said as if the idea were strangely new to her. "I have much to give in search of power. I will not fail the Great Mother and she will not fail me."

"Brid, you are not well," Pip said softly, fearing the wild look that had appeared in her eyes.

She lifted her arms, the blood dribbling down her arm in a snaking spiral. "Mother, hear me!" She threw herself down to the ground and twisted sinuously upon the wet surface. Somehow, the more dishevelled and muddy she became, the more Pip desired her strong and deliciously feminine body. "I am the Maiden; I can offer the great magic of the first conjuring." The wild look was suddenly gone. "Indeed! And I will use it wisely!"

She looked around her. "But who to choose? Hal, Ceowulf and Abelard all brave and glorious." She turned and considered Renaud. "And a prince though I fear he has not the spirit for the task." Her eyes swept over Pip without a moment's pause and finally returned to Hal. "She won't forgive me," she said to the young man. "Awake perhaps you would join with passion enough, but not asleep. I have only one opportunity. Oh, forgive me, child, this will pain you but I must."

She glanced about her at the forest, her eyes slitted as if seeking something in the shadows. "Yes, there is the scent of kobolds. She did well to summon them. Their concern will have brought him close." She snapped her fingers. "Pip, the willow tree. Leave the sword by Hal and follow me!"

Pip had guessed at her intention. And now she had chosen him! And why not? He was certainly brimming with youthful energy. He trotted after her, his mouth dry with anticipation. Uncertainly, he halted beside the willow and waited as the young woman addressed the tree.

"Saille of the Earth, Old Woman Willow. We await the night and the moon when the magic in the willow is at its strongest."

Fretfully, Pip looked to the wizards' cauldron, fearing that the wraiths might return at any moment though Brid told him he worried unnecessarily. Silently, they stood there, just waiting for the sun to go down. After a while Pip found his enthusiasm waning and, leaving Brid to her vigil, went and sat on a log, chewing at a twig to pass the time.

The darkness crept up on Pip and he was almost surprised when at last, it was fully night and the moon climbed above the trees. Brid stirred. Pip glanced up at the waxing moon. It was not quite full but it seemed brighter and larger than he had ever seen it before. Brid began to sing, her voice deep and strong in the quiet of the forest.

Pip sat back and blinked, his mouth moving in astonishment. The twig slid from his lips.

"You summon me!" a creaking female voice spoke from the dark beneath the willow tree. "It has been a long

347

time. I didn't expect to find you so well. And so young! Your magic has grown strong, much stronger than I could possibly have imagined."

"It is not yet strong enough. I need more. I have but one chance and I will do all I can with this power, this one sacrifice."

A bent figure stepped out from the shade beneath the tree and shuffled forward. Pip recognized at once the strange old woman who had been at Hobs Slack when the kobolds were attacked with fire.

She nodded, pushing back the sagging folds of her hood from her head so that the light of the moon washed over her face. She paced around the spilt willow. "I'm glad that you have not forgotten me. Too long it has been since the Trinity chose one of our kind. Too often they have been driven by their own passions."

She sucked in a deep breath and Pip thought she would howl but it was more of a deep moan that turned into a bellow, the wind soughing through her like the sound of a gathering gale whistling and moaning through the boughs of an ancient tree. Then came the unmistakable, answering bellow of a stag, deep and hollow.

Brid threw up her arms. "Let the dance of life begin!"

The old woman stripped young whiplike shoots from the base of the willow and laid them end to end on the ground to form a circle around Brid, who placed the golden chalice at her feet. Slowly, the old woman paced around and around the perimeter of the circle.

"Let there be born of this magic great life! Let there be life!"

She paced on and on, thumping the boughs of other trees at the edge of the glade as she passed. Then out of the dark came others like herself, old and treelike. Pip rubbed at his eyes, his mind dizzy from watching the pacing. The trees themselves seemed to join the dance, their great boughs swaying to the rhythm of the old, crooked and wizened, men and women their arms long and flowing in mimicry of the trees about them.

"Life, great life!" they chanted. "We are of the Earth, trees of the Earth and we will life." They continued their dance that went round and around the glade, calling all to their purpose.

Pip shrank back in wonder as animals came out of the forest; badgers, hogs, foxes and rabbits all caught up in the great dance of life. Brid snapped her fingers at him as she swirled around. "And you too, Pip. Dance! Why else are you here?"

Then came light-footed deer and, some distance behind, moving with majestic power, a great white stag. Bellowing, his huge antlered head, tilting and swaying at any that crossed his path, he strutted towards the circle. As he crossed the line formed by the willow wands, Pip gasped. It was no longer a stag standing there but a man, a tall man with a longbow in his hand, handsome, indeed, but in an earthy way. A peasant like himself, he was dressed in hunting leathers and a green tunic, his ragged hair long to his shoulders.

"Welcome, Harle!" Brid greeted him.

They too began to circle each other, the tall man flinging aside his bow and ripping off his shirt so that he was naked from the waist up. Well-muscled, his skin dark, he moved with grace and energy, snarling at any animal that came too close, sniffing at the odour of lust that hung heavily within the circle the trees. Harle took Brid's sickle from her hand and slit open the garments that wrapped her body, pulling them away so that she stood naked in the moonlight.

There was to be no modesty. The watchers chanted

louder and louder, faster and faster, urging the couple on. Harle kicked off his trousers and stood naked and large before her. With a bestial moan, he grabbed her savagely and threw her, face-down to the ground. Like a lion possessing a lioness, he fell on her, bit into her neck and pulled her to him.

Pip could not see. His own body was hot with the excitement of the moment, the rhythmic pulse of the chant bringing all to the rhythm of lovemaking, their own lusts adding to the heat of the atmosphere, charging it with the combined energies. He must see! Ducking beneath the arms of the strange people about him, he pushed through the circling dancers.

Brid gave out a yelp of pain. "Great Mother," she squealed, "I offer the magic of the first union. Free their minds from the wizards. Release them from the prison of their sleep. Free them! Free them! Free them!" she yelled as Harle covered her, his grunts deep and satisfied.

Pip stared, too amazed and too caught up in the throbbing atmosphere to feel any revulsion at what he now saw. It was neither man nor stag but something between the two; a white crest of fur frosted human shoulders and the great antlers of a stag sprouted from its head. The beast grunted as his body moved with Brid's, taking her like an animal, his neck upstretched, pulling her back and thrusting into her in rapid time to the dancers' pounding feet.

"Free them!" Brid yelled again. "Free them!"

Harle's hips beat faster and, with a deep bellow, he pulled her tight to him. The ancient beings of the forest beat the earth with wooden staves. "The magic! The magic! The magic!" they cried. "Bring life!"

A terrible cry burst through their chants.

Pip did not know what had hit him as he was flung

aside. Squeals of terror rang through the forest as the animals scattered. All fled save those central to the circle.

Hal was on his feet, holding the runesword high before him. Every inch of his body trembling with rage, he roared at the coupled pair.

The half bestial form of Harle pulled away from Brid and lowered his antlers against the enraged man before him.

"You won't touch him," Brid said coldly to Hal.

"How could you do this? You were my love, my only love. You denied me this a thousand times, and then you give yourself to a beast. Vile woman!" he shrieked, his jaw trembling with anguish.

"It was all I could do to bring you from your sleep," Brid spoke calmly, showing none of the torment of a tortured love. Coolly, she stood by her actions and made no apology for them. "Hal, stand back. You do not understand."

"I understand this well enough, this rut of passion."

With one eye on Hal, Brid stooped to pick up the chalice. "Harle, go!" she commanded with terrible authority.

"I cannot leave you to this man," he grunted. "He will kill you."

"I am already dead," she replied coldly. "Now go!"

Harle turned to run and, as he crossed out of the circle, Pip saw that it was a white stag that bounded away into the forest.

Still naked, her body white in the moonlight, Brid stood before Hal and said gently, "It was the only way. I had to use the magic. I am sorry for your torment but you must understand and forgive. It was not her fault."

Hal blinked, seemingly unable to listen. Pip, too, was deeply shocked by all that had happened but he knew someone had to act quickly. Ceowulf and Abelard were already on their feet, though they swayed unsteadily.

"Steady, Hal, steady," the big knight soothed. "Stand back now. Don't let's be hasty."

Brid made no move. "I had no choice," she said gently, her eyes fixed on the point of the runesword that Hal held at her. There was no fear in her eyes, only anticipation.

"No!" Pip yelled and leapt into the circle, grappling for Hal's sword-arm to hold him back. "Something happened to her. She was not herself. You can't blame her. She did it for you." Hal swung the blade up and thumped him hard across the temple with the pommel but Pip desperately clung on. "Hal, please!"

Another jab with the butt of the sword to Pip's jaw knocked him to the ground but the boy would not give up. He slipped and fell at Hal's feet, the great runesword slicing into the flesh of his upper arm and he clutched the wound in agony.

"Get out of my way, boy," Hal growled. "She was my love. Mine! Only mine!"

"Hal, no, she did it to save you. She needed the greater magic."

"And this saves me? This betrayal? I would rather die. She was mine!"

Pip could not bear to watch and curled up around his injured arm, listening in fearful terror as Hal cuffed Brid's head with the hilt of the sword, beating her harder and harder until she was on the floor. Though both Ceowulf and Abelard tried to drag him off, they were still sick from their ordeal and did not rise from where he threw them down. "Mine!" he shrieked, kicking her though she made no move to defend herself but kept the chalice always before her as she lay on the floor.

"Say something, witch," he howled.

Her fingers tight on the golden chalice that she held

before her body like a shield, she would not reply but kept on staring up at him as if willing him on in his madness. Goaded to a frenzy, he drew up the sword and plunged it downwards towards her breast.

"No, no!" Pip screamed. "Not Brid!"

"Die!" Hal yelled as the blade struck, the scream of its death knell loud as it clashed against the chalice, piercing clean through its centre and on into soft flesh beyond. He drove his weight hard behind the blade, forcing the steel through her body into the ground beneath as she fell back. Only when the guard of the hilt pressed against the golden rim of the chalice and would go no further did he let go.

Sitting back on his heels, tears streamed down his face. "Why Brid, why? Brid my love, why did you do this to us?"

She writhed and kicked, bloody saliva bubbling up into her mouth and dribbling from her nose. She gasped and choked, trying to speak. "Hal, forgive . . . Try to understand it wasn't . . ." She said no more. Her jaw sagged open and her eyes clouded to become dull and milky, the spark of life gone.

He flung himself to the ground and sobbed, beating the earth in rage and torment.

"She was my love, my life," Hal choked and pressed Brid's still warm hand to his lips. "Oh Mother, Great Mother what have I done? What madness is this?" Hal despaired. "How could she? Such a vile, unnatural act, an orgy of lust." He hated her and yet he loved her more than life itself – and now he had destroyed her. Deep in the back of his mind, he knew that no one would ever forgive him. He had destroyed One of the Three and put an end to the Old Faith but he cared only of his personal loss. It was as if someone had plunged a billhook down his throat and was trying to yank out his innards. His soul was screaming with the agony of his loss.

He sat, cradling himself in his distress, unable to think. Something hit him across the temple and he reeled sideways. Then he was punched in the back. The instinct of a highly trained fighting man took over his body and he rolled over and sprang up at his assailant. Abelard ran at him again with the fury of a wounded boar and punched him repeatedly in the stomach. Hal had little will to hit back yet he reacted instinctively and punched the archer straight in the jaw.

Abelard staggered back, dipped onto one knee but came at him again. In the corner of his eye, Hal could see others moving in to separate them. Ceowulf grabbed Abelard about the waist while Pip dragged at the archer's arms until they had prized him off. Hal knew he could have beaten the man to a pulp but he didn't have the energy or the will. Abelard's cursing accusations were right and he hated the man for it.

"Stop it!" Ceowulf shrieked, the urgency in his voice so sharp that both snapped their heads round to stare at the big knight who was hunched over Brid, a shaking hand cupping her cheek. He was staring at her breast for a full minute, a sense of urgency, of disbelief, of hope caught in the tautness of his still body.

"Abelard, hold him back," Ceowulf ordered, indicating Hal with a jerk of his head.

But there was no need. Hal took himself away of his own accord and stood at the edge of the circle, his face dark with self-loathing.

"Hal," the words whispered from Brid's lips. "Tell him I love him." She groaned. "The pain of it, the terrible pain of it. Morrigwen suffers this and more . . ."

"She lives!" Pip yelled in joyous amazement.

Brid lifted her head, gasped in agony and gaped in disbelieving horror at the sword speared through her chest.

Cold looks stabbed from Ceowulf's eyes as he glanced round at Hal. "Get wood! Build up a fire. The girl is stronger than all of us and she lives yet."

Shocked, disorientated and gradually becoming aware of strange pains in his arms and shoulders, Hal hastened about the task of dragging logs near to Ceowulf; but he could not face Brid. He watched, trembling, as others tended the one he loved most in all the world. She was life to him and yet she had betrayed him. He did know what to think. Much of him wanted her to die. Yet he loved her more than himself and wanted her to live. Unable to bear any more, he turned and fled into the forest, trailing ivies lashing his face and holly raking his back as he ran.

At last, he reached a glade at the banks of a quiet river where swaying forest flowers, like a fairy pageant, made a bright moonlit scene in the forest floor. He plunged his face into the water, hoping that the sudden cold would clear his head. The emotional turmoil of his nightmare hadn't yet left him. The sense of panic still lingered, as did the pain from his wounds, but his nightmares were nothing; he had awoken to a worse dream; the beast upon her was real!

He felt sick to his stomach, the image so deeply imbedded within his mind's eye that he didn't think he could ever see anything else. In his rage, he was barely aware that he had done anything wrong though, somewhere deep in his soul, the pain of his guilt swelled. At last, he lay face down into the earth and sobbed, the image of his sword plunged deep into Brid's breast bright in his mind's eye. "Brid, my Brid," he moaned.

It was some while before he could think clearly and,

when he opened his eyes, it was to see an old woman crouched beside him, brushing back his hair.

"Youth suffers terribly over things that really do not matter. She is a priestess; she belongs to the Great Mother. I know this is hard for you to understand but all this will be as nothing in the end."

Unconsciously cradling his left arm, Hal blinked at the old woman and recognized her as Pip had done. He shrank back from her in disgust. "Your son has defiled her."

"Hardly. It was but a magical rite not an act of love. And necessary, Hal, to heal you. But it was not Brid." She nodded at his arm. "Does it hurt? Let me look; I am a skilled healer."

Hal nodded, barely caring. "What do you mean, it wasn't Brid? Whether she was acting the part of a priestess or not, it was still Brid. Ow!" he complained as she probed his arm.

"It is an old wound; the bones are already knitted but the pain is because they are set a little awry. There is little you can do except chew willow bark to ease the discomfort."

"I prefer the pain," he growled. "It reminds me of what I have done."

"But it wasn't Brid. No, Hal, it was Morrigwen."

"Ha! No one could mistake Brid for Morrigwen and, besides, the old Crone is long since dead."

"I know Morrigwen when I see her, no matter whom she looks like. That was Morrigwen," Harle's mother insisted.

"So, where's Brid?"

"Oh, she's Brid now. It was Morrigwen with Harle. You plunged your sword into Morrigwen, which brought back Brid. The runesword of the Great Mother pierced the

Chalice of Önd, an act of great symbolism, and it opened a pathway between worlds. Morrigwen is gone and Brid returned."

Hal did not fully understand. He had killed Morrigwen who was already dead while now Brid lay with his sword speared through her, though she lived.

"Come, Hal," Harle's mother coaxed him from his thoughts. "I have done what I can for her. She needs you."

Limply, like a scolded puppy, he followed the old woman back through the forest to the point where the group was huddled around a fire, Cymbeline sitting apart from the others and wringing her hands in distress. Harle's mother had managed to extract the sword from Brid's breast. Ceowulf held her in his arms and Abelard marched up and down like an expectant father. When he saw Hal, he growled in his throat with a savagery so deep that Hal was almost afraid. The world about the edges of his vision was black. Even Brid, who had always been light to him, now seemed a dark purple. She was no longer his Brid.

He didn't understand it but, even if it had been Morrigwen's will that had performed the vile act with Harle, she had still used Brid's body. Now she lay in Ceowulf's arms.

He came close. "How is she?" he croaked through his tears. "Will she live or have I killed her?" His misery was so deep that he was utterly candid about his crime.

"I don't know," Ceowulf admitted. "I have seen many wounds and this should have killed her; yet she still lives."

"Hush," the old woman said. "There is far more to this than a simple wound. There is magic in all of this. I do not believe that the Great Mother would have allowed one of her own tools to be used against a high priestess unless there was need. The wound may not be all that it seems because it wasn't Brid that Hal killed; it was Morrigwen."

Pip was shaking his head vigorously. "That's ridiculous! Morrigwen died months ago . . . but then there was something." He shuddered, remembering. "Hal, there was something very odd about Brid," he began, his hand still pressed to a bandage wrapping his arm and hastily tried to explain what had happened in the dark room off Irwald's chambers.

"Just hush now," Harle's mother begged. "Hush!" She soothed the girl's brow. "Hal, she needs your comfort. Hold her hand."

Sick to his stomach, Hal reached out and forced himself to grasp her hand. Now the energy of rage had left him, the movement sent sharp pains up his arm. He could see she was stirring slightly, her body tensed against the deep pain.

"Just soothe her and keep her warm," Harle's mother advised. "I have done all I can."

Hal was about to protest and beg her to do more but, when he looked round for her, she was gone. The great old willow at the far end of the glade was swaying back and forth, more than the light breeze warranted.

Ceowulf eased Brid's body into Hal's lap and the young Torra Altan sat cross-legged as if nursing an infant, his cloak wrapped about him and his love. The tears fell from his cheeks onto her face.

"Oh Brid," he murmured. "I love you beyond all else and yet I can never look at you in the same way again."

Abelard growled quietly. "Someone should keep him away from her. He has no right to be near her. Think what he did to her."

"Steady, Abelard," Ceowulf's calmly advised. "Remember Morrigwen arranged it like that. For all we know, she was relying on Hal's jealous rage to force him to wield the runesword against her. Clearly, she knew that, when he struck through the chalice, he would bring Brid back – and he did. Hal did no wrong. He restored her life; he did not take it."

"Oh, practically maybe. But he *sought* to destroy her. All because of his petty jealousy," Abelard snarled.

"Petty? Well, I'm not too sure how I'd react if I found Cybillia with another man."

"But it was a religious rite," Abelard objected. "He could hardly be jealous of that."

"Oh, come on, Abelard!" Pip said indignantly. "You can hardly think that!"

Hal was relieved to hear that his friends were standing up for him even if he could not forgive himself. But Abelard was right. Whether it was Brid or Morrigwen, the fact remained that he had sought to destroy Brid and that made him vile. Utterly ashamed, he saw no way to redeem himself.

Guilt sapped his strength and overwhelmed his fury. As the energy of his rage ebbed, he slumped weakly and finally lay down on the earth and curled up beside his love. For a while, he was vaguely aware of Pip's cries of excitement that he had found Hardwin's and Renaud's horses but then he must have dozed because suddenly he was waking. Brid was groaning and crying out for help. The others were awake and came hurrying to her side.

"Hal," she groaned. "Hal, get me home. Get me to Keridwen. Get me home." She mumbled incoherently for a while and then blurted, "I must tell her how the old crone suffers . . . suffers . . ."

"Oh mercy!" Abelard exclaimed. "Morrigwen must be in the dungeons of Abalone." His face whitened. "We must do as Brid says."

"Sir!" Pip saluted Hal. "I have found mine, Hardwin's and Renaud's horses. Secret and Sorcerer are dead and the others have disappeared into the forest. You can have mine; she's well-natured enough so that you can ride carrying Brid. I'll take care of the princess," he added with a hopeful smile.

"No, Pip. Abelard is right; I cannot be entrusted with Brid. I have failed her."

Abelard nodded in satisfaction but then turned to Ceowulf. "Nor should I carry her. I'm not horseman enough; it should be you."

"I agree!" Ceowulf conceded. "But, Pip, don't you get it into your head that you're looking after the princess. She's far too valuable!"

With a heavy heart, Hal picked up his sword and immediately felt sick. Though the weapon still charged him with energy, he could no longer bear to have it in his possession. He had turned it on Brid and had heard its triumphant song as it gloried in its last blood-letting. Gritting his teeth on his pain, he made to sheath it but, as he slid it into its fleece-lined scabbard, he noted a nick in its keen edge near the tip. He gave it little thought, intent only on handing the weapon over to Ceowulf for safe-keeping.

With the Chalice of Önd strapped to his saddle pack, and chewing at willow bark to ease his pain, Hal rode with Cymbeline up behind him. Ceowulf rode with Brid in his arms, her head slumped against his chest. They travelled for four days like that, in which time Pip repeatedly retold his extraordinary story of his imprisonment in Baron Kulfrid's castle and of the mad son, Irwald and his macabre sacrifices.

Hal puzzled over this story though he found it hard to think clearly as Brid's moans became deeper and louder and she began to kick and writhe against her pain. She struggled so much that Ceowulf had trouble holding her and so, at the edge of the forest, they stopped early for the night and banked their fire high to keep them warm.

"She's coming round, Hal," Ceowulf beckoned him.

"Hal," she groaned. He crept close. "Hal." She reached out her hand for him. "Hal, the pain . . . you can't imagine. The pain!" she gasped. "Lend me some of your strength. I was in the Otherworld. What happened? Hal, why won't you hold me? What's happened? What's wrong with me?"

Hal retreated and stood in the deep shadows that nibbled at the ring of bright light thrown out from the fire. He felt dark. He felt that he belonged only to the furtive shadows. For a while he could not think but merely experienced the hideousness of his jealousy and guilt but, at last, sensible reasoning returned and he went to his saddle and sought out the chalice. He took it to Brid who looked at it in amazement.

"The Chalice of Önd!" she croaked. "But look at it! It's been ruined! But that's impossible; it's made of metal as strong as the great runesword itself. Nothing can destroy it." Her breath was laboured after the effort of speech.

"No, only the runesword. Abelard, you must tell her everything," Hal said with quiet resignation.

"Gladly!" the man replied with venom.

"No, Hal, don't leave me," Brid implored.

"I must," Hal told her. "When you hear what there is to hear you will not want me near."

He returned to the shadows, unable to hear for himself what she would say. Without seeing anything other than the vile image of Brid with Harle he glared at the sword until suddenly his eyes focused and he saw, with horror that its sharp edge was chipped. But for once he didn't trouble himself to hone it. Too wrapped up in his misery, he could not free his mind from returning to his love coupled with a beast. He even welcomed the dull ache in his shoulder and arm though he had a horrible fear that, if he didn't keep touching his arm, it would suddenly disappear.

The hideousness of his nightmare where Ceowulf had amputated the limb came flooding back to him.

As Brid gave out a moan of anguish, he looked away, drawn by a movement in the corner of his eye. Cymbeline, who had kept herself so very quiet all the while, was looking at him thoughtfully, her head cocked to one side. He smiled at her and she smiled back. Beautiful and attentive, she seemed to crave his company. Though she was certainly fascinating, he knew he didn't love her, but that meant she couldn't hurt him. With her, he would never suffer the soul-tormenting anguish of soured love. She could never induce this jealousy, this gut-wrenching jealousy that had forced him to such a heinous crime.

Welcomed by his smile, Cymbeline drew close.

"The Great Mother will never forgive me," Hal told her, glad to have someone listen to his confession.

"You should not be so hard on yourself," the princess sympathized. "Think what she did. No Ceolothian man would have tolerated the sight of his woman doing such a vile thing."

Hal nodded grimly. Cymbeline seemed more beautiful to him now than ever before. Her voice soft and she had taken pains to brush her hair though there was nothing she could do about the mud that caked her dress.

She smiled at him. "It's you that's been wronged. You don't really believe all this hocus-pocus about her soul being swapped with another?" She laughed lightly.

"Well, I do," Hal argued though a frown grew on his face; he had to admit that it sounded very bizarre.

Cymbeline soothed his shoulders as he lay back. "She's just a peasant girl. What more would you expect from her?" She pressed close, her breath very, very sweet.

The others were preparing the horses and making ready to ride on. Hal led Cymbeline to his mount. "I just want to know why she had to choose Harle. Surely, she could have used me in her magical rite?"

"Magical rite indeed! It was vile bestiality! I saw every bit of it."

Hal found some ease in having the soft warmth of Cymbeline's body pressed close against his back as they hurried through the forest, west towards the coast.

"I hate travelling by boat!" Cymbeline groaned loudly. "Why can't we go overland through Vaalaka?"

"I'm sorry but it'll be quicker by sea to get to Farona," Ceowulf explained. "Besides, we can't risk going near Torra Alta. Remember King Rewik has handed it over to the Ovissians and it was Tupwell who had you abducted in the first place. No, we must keep our heads low until we reach Farona. Who knows that there won't be some other ambush laid on for you?"

"Absolutely we can't go through Torra Alta," Pip exclaimed, his reins in one hand to allow him to rest his injured arm. "I told you all that Baron Kulfrid had Ovissians in his employ; firstly, the tall soldier whom I saw secretly meeting Ryder and Fingers and, secondly, Fingers himself!" The boy's eyes were black with excitement. "Fingers, the one that captured Brock and me. He was there!"

"Was he one of the men I handed over to Tupwell's care?" Hal asked, for once suppressing his misery. At last, some small piece of the puzzle fell together in the back of his mind. "Of course! I couldn't understand why Tupwell knew so much about the lay of the land when we were travelling through Ceolothia and he actually told me that he had cousins there. Godafrid and Kulfrid must be related." He groaned. "And to think I just gave Tupwell back his man."

"It wasn't your fault," Ceowulf reassured him. "None of us knew at the time what Tupwell was planning."

"Mmm," Hal muttered uncertainly. "But something still doesn't add up. Granted that they're cousins but why would Kulfrid join with Tupwell against his own King?"

"Tupwell paid him well?" Pip suggested. "Kulfrid's castle was sparkling with sunburst rubies."

Hal frowned and pondered a while. It still didn't add up. He could understand that Tupwell had coveted Torra Alta for the wealth of sunburst rubies he had found in its mountains. He could see how he had planned to ambush Princess Cymbeline and put the blame on the Torra Altans so that the great castle was given into his father's guardianship. But he didn't understand Kulfrid's motives for helping.

"Tupwell might have offered Kulfrid and Irwald mountains of sunburst rubies in payment," he voiced his thoughts, "but King Dagonet would undoubtedly have given more for the information that would lead to rescuing his daughter and catching her abductors. Kulfrid must have had a stronger reason for turning against his own king."

Cymbeline's grip tightened around Hal's waist.

CHAPTER SIXTEEN

Trog stood beneath the pony's forelegs, growling and snapping at the arrow shafts stuck in the ground at their feet, the points buried deep in the soft soil.

"I warned you that the very trees would attack," Pennard wailed.

"Oh, don't be absurd!" Caspar snapped edgily.

Looking up from the short shafts of the arrows, he hastily scanned the forest shadows for any sign of their attackers but was unable to see anything out of place amongst the low skirts of the ancient ash trees that drooped around sturdy trunks. He was beginning to understand why the men of Negraferre thought that the very trees were capable of attack.

The sick child was yelling so loudly that he found it difficult to think but at least her hearty cries announced to her people that she was alive and coming home to them. Presuming that her yells would prevent further attack, he urged his pony forward on a tight rein. The forest was once again alive with the cackles of marauding magpies.

The two dogs whimpered and yapped at shadows and even the goat tugged at the leash that tethered it to Caspar's mount. Pennard looked from the jittery animals to the trees. "I told you it was the trees!" he croaked.

"It's not the trees!" Caspar snarled impatiently at him

though he had not found the slightest evidence to the contrary. The canyon could not be too far ahead and, rather than worry about things that he had no control over, he concentrated instead on preventing his pony from stumbling on the increasingly rock-strewn path.

Pennard's bitch whimpered, adding to the noise of the baby's crying. Caspar cradled the child close and she was soothed a little. Still, his muscles ached with nervous tension by the time the forest thinned. Blinking, they stumbled out into the light and, before them, the ground dropped away. The noise of cackling magpies lulled for a moment and the forest was unnaturally hushed as if invisible eyes were watching them intensely as they stood on the brink of the canyon and looked down on the haven below.

The thread of a silver river wound along the canyon bottom, cutting through meadows and spreading trees. But for the sickly yellow tinge to the grass, Caspar could not imagine a more idyllic place. The Tor at Torra Alta jutted up from the floor of a deep canyon such as this and the world below him reminded him of home.

"A quiet paradise," he breathed, looking for a way down. A gully cutting down by his feet was stepped with ledges of rock, an easy descent on foot and passable only for a skilled horseman. He made for it.

Pennard hung back. "I knew we shouldn't have come."

Caspar ignored him and called out into the canyon below, "I'm returning your baby!"

He held the swaddled creature up so that she was clearly visible. She gave out a howl at this and he hastily cuddled her close. Swallowing hard, he pressed the pony forward to the edge. The pony jerked back its head, hesitating. Caspar kicked on more firmly.

"You'll be fine," he said with reassuring confidence. The

terrain was no steeper than that of his homeland and he was totally untroubled by the drop. He looked round to see that Pennard had dismounted and abandoned his horse, clearly preferring to tackle the descent on foot.

"Bravery is one thing," the youth muttered, "but stupidity quite another. I'm not going to be thrown clean off the edge of the cliff."

"I have your baby," Caspar continued to call out at intervals.

Hearing the soft tinkle of rocks and the scurrying of feet, he was now acutely aware of others around him though he could still see no one. The air smelt sweet and he twitched his nose. Lavender and rosemary, he thought concentrating on the awkward descent and leaning back to take the weight off the pony's forehand. All the while, he could hear soft noises close by but still could see nothing until, at last, they alighted on the canyon floor.

He reined in sharply. More than a dozen figures suddenly stood in a half-circle before him. They appeared to have simply materialized out of the air. Caspar blinked at them in astonishment and thought it prudent to dismount.

"Oh!" Pennard exclaimed more in wondering admiration than fear. "Oh, my!" Then his eyes narrowed. "I can't believe these people murdered my father!"

Ignoring his comments, one of the figures stepped lithely forward and Caspar couldn't help but stare at her luscious figure. She was stunningly beautiful. Her hair, a silver mass of ringlets loose to her shoulders, was kept back from her face by a circlet of silver above her brow. She had wide-set eyes, strangely peaked ears and was unusually thin though there was no weakness about her. Her eyes were silvery and, to Caspar, she seemed to move like honeysuckle swaying in a light breeze. In fact, the air around her was filled with the scent of wild flowers. She was more beautiful than anything he had ever seen.

He looked from her to the others and saw that he and Pennard were confronted by a dozen females dressed alike in green leggings and bodices that were cinched very tightly about their tiny waists. Their leggings stopped above their slender calves and all went barefoot on tiny feet. They had pale skin with a slight silvery tinge to it and long curling silvery hair. Without exception, they were fascinatingly beautiful in the most enticing way. Involuntarily, Caspar licked his dry lips and found himself staring at the bulge of the woman's bosom pushed up above her tight bodice, before he remembered himself.

His movements deliberately careful, he unwrapped the baby from the sling and offered her to the woman but she raised her hands as if to ward him off, wary of his intent.

"Why do you come? To poison us? You bring the black metal to our valley," she accused, twitching her simple bow at Pennard.

Since he was very much an expert in the field of archery, Caspar had already noted the lightness of the bows and the shortness of the rustic arrows and concluded that the women must have got very close to them indeed before loosing their arrows.

"No, we come only to return your child and to find mine," he assured her and then hissed at Pennard. "For pity's sake take your armour off; it's obviously a threat to them."

"Take it off? You must be mad. It's probably the only thing keeping me alive," he objected. "You forget these people are murderers and stealers of children!"

"Strip it off!" the woman ordered, her voice melodious, almost teasing, yet at the same time heavy with threat.

Twelve bows were now levelled at Pennard's head and he threw up his hands in defeat and sulkily obeyed. "Fetch the mother!" she ordered a slender woman to her right.

"Yes, Izella," she responded in the silkiest of voices before turning to skip away through the grass like a leaf wafted by the breeze.

Caspar stood, fidgeting awkwardly while they waited. "You see, Pennard, they weren't trees or ogres but extraordinarily beautiful women."

"We're not women; we are the hunters of Ash," the beautiful female before him said stiffly but Caspar was no longer listening.

"Who said there weren't ogres?" Pennard murmured.

The slender woman returned accompanied by one smaller female figure and two dozen huge creatures. They approached at a frightening speed and quickly formed an outer ring beyond the hunters of Ash. Caspar stared up at the huge brutish men that towered over him. All stood to at least seven foot and had girths and bull-like muscles twitching on their necks to match. Like the hunters, their hair was silvery and their skin very fair, almost frosted. Bare breasted, their muscles flexing in readiness, they were terrifying figures in all ways except that their eyes looked dull and, now that they were standing, they swayed a little on their large unshod feet as if all their energy was already spent.

Pennard was breathing heavily beside him though Caspar kept himself steadily under control and showed no signs of alarm. He feared only for Isolde. He focused intently on the small woman accompanied by the ring of giants. She wore a dress that was tight fitting about her bust, waist and hips and then spread out into flowing, swirling skirts. He could not tell whether the garment was green or silver because it changed colour as she moved. Tiny bells were stitched along the length of the sleeves, which sang out the softest melody when she moved her arms. Judging by the taught look of distress on her face, he knew immediately who she was.

"I have your baby," he said, stretching out his arms to offer her the child.

"My baby?" she repeated in disbelief, huge tears rolling from her large eyes. "Mine?" She tottered forward and peered at the bundle that Caspar offered to her. The men bristled close about her, seemingly reluctant to let her get too near. She reached out a slender, trembling hand and then, in a sudden rush, snatched the child, clutched it to her and sobbed in overwhelming relief, "She lives!"

"And mine? Where's mine!" Caspar's composure cracked and the aggression was plain in his voice. The silvery-skinned giants pressed close and growled at him in threat.

The woman didn't seem to hear. "You brought back my baby. She lives," she gasped, tears streaming down her proud cheeks.

Izella stroked the woman's shoulder, "I am glad for you, Mirandel," she murmured though there was a hint of bitterness in her voice.

Caspar nodded, acutely aware of the woman's great love for her child. "Yes, yes, she lives."

Mirandel fell forward onto him and hugged him in fervent gratitude. "Thank you! You brought her back. My baby!"

Caspar was trembling. "And mine?"

"Yours?"

"My baby." He looked at her intently, his throat choked with emotion.

"But you are a man."

"What of it? I need my baby. Is she well?" His voice was strained.

370

"Of course she is well." Mirandel did not look up from her own child. "She's playing happily in the garden."

"Take me to her!" Caspar demanded. "Hurry!"

The giants paid no attention to this imperative from Caspar and, in fact, some of them wandered off aimlessly while others lay down in the grass and began to coo to themselves like contented infants. Only one followed the women as they made their way along the riverbank.

Graceful ash trees dotted the meadows whose grass was split half into sun and half into hard shadow by the cliffs above. The narrow river bucked and dived in its rage at being confined but was clearly not the beast that had gouged this rift in the landscape. Thick green ivies dangled from the rock-face and ferns that stroked the falling sunlight gripped the walls. Flowers brushed against Caspar's thighs as he waded through yellow and gold blooms that crumbled as he touched them; but he took none of it in at all. He could hear a baby crying and he knew that sound as well as the sound of his own breathing.

Trog barked insistently and ran ahead.

They rounded a copse that had blocked their view ahead, Caspar marching stiffly in his urgency. Without breaking his stride, he took in the layout of the strange village. A level meadow, the grass cropped short, was broken by curious high mounds of earth that looked for all the world like giant molehills. As they drew closer, he saw that the earth was firm and shaped like a vast periwinkle shell, spiralling grooves decorating the structures that stood to at least twice Caspar's height. There were twenty in total forming a circle, little puffs of smoke winding out of three of them. At their centre was the most enormous ash tree that he had ever seen.

On entering the ring of earth mounds, he saw that each had an arched door of solid wood facing the great ash tree. Each door had a knocker that might be found on any house in Farona and looked quite strange in this mysterious canyon. He took in very little else; he could hear Isolde.

He spun round to see a small, grassed garden hedged by lavender tucked between two of the earth-mounds. His eyes clouded with tears. There she was! Gurgling with laughter, his little girl was crawling towards an elder child in a green dress, who was probably seven or eight years old. Her movements were remarkably quiet and graceful for one so young and her laughter bright as she dotingly played with the baby. They were rolling about a carved wooden ball.

For a moment he just stood and stared to gather himself, not wanting to alarm Isolde with an outburst of emotion. The older child looked up at their approach and Caspar knew instantly that this was Pennard's sister. She had those same narrow-set brooding eyes and a wide smile that on him was slightly weak but on her was devastatingly charming. She sat back, head on one side, and studied Caspar precociously as he stooped beside her young playmate.

The young girl finally looked at Pennard. Her smile dropped and a faraway expression came over her as if she were trying to remember something that could never be remembered.

Mirandel, the beautiful mother of the sickly baby gripped Caspar's shoulder, the rows of tiny bells stitched into her sleeves tinkled like ice water running over polished rocks. "Thank you for my baby. Please stay and feast with us," she asked, smiling radiantly through her tears. "We shall feast! Never before have the people that make the brown cloud returned one of our babies."

Caspar was aware of a hundred people scampering

around, most like the beautiful but fey Mirandel a few like the hunter, Izella, and others like Pennard's sister and the young woman who had taken Isolde from him, clearly of human blood but who had developed many of the fey characteristics. They moved with such ease, sometimes tinkling with the bells that were pinned to their clothes and other times, when they wanted, moving with such smoothness that the bells were silent. He stared about him in wonder. These people were beautiful, so gracefully blending with the trees and swaying and merging with the shadowy patterns that they could barely be seen. The people of Ash they called themselves.

Jubilant with the return of the child, they broke into song, one picking up a refrain and the others lifting it to a grand chorus. The song was alive and fantastically beautiful but Caspar barely noticed; he focused only on Isolde. She sat up and looked around her at the singing. Her eye fell on Caspar. To his gratification, she gave out a shriek of pleasure at seeing him and began to shake the wooden ball in her hand.

"Hush, Isolde, my sweet. Hush! All is well," he said as calmly as possible. He had never before seen that wooden ball but he knew what it contained. He had no doubt that Necrönd was within it. His neck prickled and his pulse quickened.

In all the fear and excitement over the last few days, he had noticed that his mind had been less troubled by the talisman. Now that he saw it again, the weight of its responsibility bore down on his soul. He could feel the air thick with the hungry presence of creatures. Everywhere he turned, he fancied he could see ghostly shadows pressing to get closer. He wondered whether these strange silvery people could see them or not. Certainly, they paid them no heed.

The little baby rolled the ball again and Caspar's heart swam in his throat, fearing that at any moment the Egg might break. He knew it was well-cushioned within the silver casket but it was not a toy. She rattled it again, a great smile beaming from her happy face.

Caspar approached as if stalking a wild horse. "Steady there, steady now."

He crept forward so as not to alarm the baby and, to his relief she did not fling the ball as he feared but eased it to the ground, holding up her arms to him in anticipation of being lifted up. His heart flooded with love and he caught her up in his arms, stooping down seconds later to scoop up the wooden ball. Pennard's sister rose and cocked her head on one side, looking at the ball with curiosity as if realizing from Caspar's behaviour that there was more to it than she had thought.

Pennard frowned at the girl in the green dress and for a long moment, the two stared silently into each other's eyes.

"Priddy? My sister, Priddy? You are surely Priddy; you look so like our mother," he stammered, staring at the piece of blanket that one of the toys was wrapped in. Tired threads of embroidery were loosely clinging to the dirty rag and Caspar guessed it was the same blanket that Priddy's mother had so lovingly embroidered with her name.

Her faraway expression twisted into one of contempt. She spat. "You are no kin of mine, murderer."

"I've never harmed anything in my life," he protested. "Whereas these people murdered Father!"

"Ha! All your kind are murderers. Six other babies fell ill today and soon they will all be dead because of you and your kind."

Caspar was amazed by this outburst and tugged at

Pennard's arm, willing him to keep calm though he fully understood the youth's simmering hatred towards these people. "You're more than out-numbered," he reminded him.

"Come now, Priddy," Mirandel said to Pennard's sister. "Come, my love, things might be better now. They brought her back whole. She is well. She still snuffles but the boils are gone. Never have I seen one survive once the boils develop but, praise the trees, she lives!"

Much excited gossiping hummed amongst the people and Caspar found himself the centre of attention while Pennard and his sister were pushed to the edge.

Mirandel gripped Caspar's arm. "You are not from the coast, I can tell. Your skin is fair and your eyes blue. If I'd known we would not have taken your baby."

"You should never take anyone's baby," Caspar said softly.

"We take a like for a like. We love our human babies dearly and we bring them up as our own but nothing compensates fully for the loss of one's own flesh and blood. I can never thank you enough for saving my baby."

"Indeed," he acknowledged her distractedly, still too intent on fussing over Isolde to note much else.

Mirandel snapped her fingers at the women about her. "Come on, come on, hurry. We have a guest that deserves our finest hospitality."

Pennard muttered and grumbled disgustedly at this invitation.

It dawned on Caspar that, while there were more women rushing to and fro than he could count, he could only see seven of the large males that now slumped down, as if exhausted, and stared vacantly into the fire. Several women rushed to give the giants steaming goblets of a bitter-smelling brew while the rest darted to and fro, bringing out simple chairs and tables from what Caspar could only guess were their underground homes. They set the furniture in a wide circle about a pit filled with glowing embers. Slabs of meat were thrown over a grill; bowls filled with yellow petals were passed amongst the people of ash and ample goblets of wine were filled.

Caspar was cheered by the fire. Despite the warmth of this continent, he felt chilled by the gloomy skies.

Following his example, Mirandel glanced up at the sky and then looked at Caspar. "We are still well in ourselves, perhaps a little tired, but our children are ill – poisoned by the people of the coast."

"That's absurd. We do nothing to harm you. Nothing!" Pennard protested. "But you murdered my father and you steal our babies!"

"You kill ours!" Mirandel returned with venom. "Many are born twisted and weak; few survive. You are the brown cloud-makers that bring the disease on us." She turned on Caspar and her expression softened. "But you are the miracle-worker; you will cure us."

Caspar pressed his hand to his chest and rose nervously. "What me? I did nothing."

"My baby was dying yet you brought her back alive."

"I did nothing," he stammered, though he was certain that it must have been the trinoxia that had cured the infant. But how could he tell these desperate mothers that he had cured one baby but had no way to cure their own dying infants?

"Oh, you did. You saved her. You must have done something," she insisted.

"I did nothing but feed her and keep her warm," Caspar protested.

Several sobbing women appeared bearing babies whose eyes wept sickly yellow pus. The women pleaded with big tearful eyes but Caspar could only stare back at them helplessly.

"Why are they dying?" he asked Mirandel.

Rather than replying, she held out her hand in dismay as the first drops of rain fell from the sky. Caspar was amazed at how quickly the people gathered up their belongings and fled into their homes.

"Well, don't just stand there," Izella chastised him. "Get that baby inside!"

While one of the huntresses led the ponies and his goat away to the shelter beneath a low, spreading ash, Caspar ran, covering Isolde's head with his hand. He followed the people of Ash into the stuffy gloom of one of the underground shelters and watched as the mothers hastily rubbed thick green oils into their children's skin. It finally occurred to him that their unhealthy hue was caused more by this grease than by their ailments.

The brightness in the woman's face fell as she looked at Caspar. "I thought you, who clearly have such power, might save them."

His heart in his throat, Caspar was aware of Pennard's sudden focus on him. "What power?" he asked.

"Nothing," Caspar retorted hurriedly. "Nothing at all."

"Oh, it is everywhere about you. Everywhere!" the woman said knowingly. "And you know you can heal our babies."

"But I cannot."

"But you can. You healed one to get your own child back; do you now refuse to heal more?"

Caspar racked his brain. What could he say? "Perhaps it would help if I understood why the babies were dying in the first place."

"The rain!"

"What do you mean, the rain?" he asked, puzzled.

377

The beautiful woman sighed. "The coastal people, that make themselves rich fashioning armour for the Empress, burn something poisonous in their furnaces that are built, you will note, inland and downwind of the town. The plumes of vapour sweep inland over us and gather on the mountains. The rain falls on us and fills our river or seeps into the ground to rise in springs within our canyon. The water is poisonous to us."

"There is a simple answer to that," Caspar began.

"Move?" she interrupted. "Oh no. Though as adults we are strong, our babies are not so hardy as those of your kind. Our bodies are easily poisoned and this canyon is but one of the few places where we can live. We need more water and purer water than you do and we need the leaves of the ash tree and the petals from the Tethys orchid to keep our bodies healthy just as you need wheat or meat. There are very few places on this earth where both grow in the same place but our fair canyon is one of them."

Gloomily, he watched the rain as Mirandel continued to explain, "It's that black mineral Negraferre they burn that causes the problem. They triple their output of it every time the Empress starts a new war. She was quiet for a time and we recovered but, again, they have fired up the smelters. The town gets wealthy and we get sick."

"Surely the rain fills the same river that feeds them?" Caspar asked.

"Oh true, but human babies are very much more robust and drink less water. The effect, however, is cumulative. Maybe now they are fine but the girls that have drunk it all these years will eventually give birth to weaker babies. Soon they will be born frail and susceptible to disease and no doubt, they will blame it on us, being upriver of them. Then they will come with their black steel spears and see us all destroyed."

"They will not destroy us," one of the huge men pushed himself up and staggered forward, his eyelids heavy with sleep. "I shall see to it!" His eyes brightened as and his voice filled with energy, fired by the thought of battle, Caspar guessed.

"Has he had his tea?" one of the women asked anxiously. "See to it that he gets some more."

Caspar frowned at this strange behaviour. The women were evidently keen that the warrior didn't excite himself, and hastily they pressed a steaming brew into his hands. Grunting, he sipped at it and was soon dozing, his back against the wall and mumbling peacefully to himself.

"You can help us," Mirandel told Caspar firmly. "You could persuade them that they don't need to make this steel. It is for a war far to the north that has raged for thirty years, on and off. And it will rage for another whatever armour they have. They are rich now; that is all the difference. Rich but at what cost? You will stop them."

"I cannot," Caspar said hoarsely. He was truly sorry for these people but he was only one man and he was becoming increasing eager to get Isolde far away from this polluted atmosphere. "No city gives up its source of wealth for the sake of some strange, secretive tribe living many miles from them."

"Oh, but you can," Mirandel said. "You have the power." Her voice was cold and Caspar clutched Isolde tight to his chest.

Pennard drew closer. "What power?" he hissed insistently.

Caspar was intensely wary of the youth as they huddled down into the dark of the underground caverns. There was a loud thump, the shockwave buffeting the tunnel air, as the outer door was closed. Someone lit a firebrand

and he cringed at the sights before him. Faces of women leapt out from the dark, feeble, mewing babies cradled in their arms.

"See what we suffer," Mirandel told him and led them deeper.

More faces, twisted and ugly this time, sprang out from the walls but, after starting back and blinking in alarm, Caspar saw that they weren't real. The tunnels passed through clay and the faces were moulded into the earth walls. The underground corridor opened into a broad chamber that was luxuriously adorned in a manner that had not been reflected in their mode of living on the surface.

Their simple stools and honest fare had made him think they were a rustic woodland people but, evidently, he had misjudged them. Glorious tapestries of vibrant colours, the like of which he had only seen in King Rewik's own chambers, covered the lower half of the walls. He admired scenes of forests, canyons and tranquil lakes where delicate houses nestled beneath ash trees draped with strings of lanterns. The women were busy at looms and spinning-wheels, merrily creating the yarns and vibrant fabrics of their tapestries.

What Caspar noted above all, however, were the vast bows hung on the walls, alongside giant swords. He wondered at the strength needed to wield them.

Set apart from the chatting women was a tight huddle of five crones all bearing ornately carved staves. Caspar took the staves to be a mark of office and assumed the old women were the people's respected elders. The huntress, Izella, who had first confronted him, was stooped over the crones, muttering and pointing in his direction. He bowed in acknowledgement of their stares and withdrew with dignity.

Above them, the circular dome of the ceiling was formed by the underside of the vast root system of the ash tree he had seen on the surface. Its great tap root formed a central pillar, the other roots spreading out and down over the walls almost like blood vessels of the earth, the large veins and arteries dividing into small vessels and capillaries.

Three fires were set in clay pits guarded by a low wicker fence to keep the crawling female babies away from the fire. Shrieking savagely, the enormous male babies were contained in pens and they were clawing at each other in an earnest bid to escape. A weave of rushes was laid over the beaten earth floor and benches, made from stakes hammered into the ground and topped by thick slabs of sawn branches, were draped in all manner of skins, fox, deer, badger and horse. Caspar was ushered to one of these padded benches and relaxed onto it.

He took the opportunity to cradle Isolde and feed her some goat's milk he had ready in a stoppered gourd for her. He was delighted that now she would eat much of his own food so long as he chewed it well first – though that was a surprisingly long and difficult task. He kept her happy by giving her his belt and letting her play with the buckle that she fiddled with endlessly, laughing with her peculiarly deep giggle. While she was busy, and under cover of her blankets, he surreptitiously examined the wooden ball she had been playing with in the garden and discovered that, with one twist, it came apart into two halves to reveal the silver casket beneath. As if she had known what he was doing, Isolde squealed and pointed at him, trying to clamber up his leg to grab what she considered to be her toy. Caspar feared she was becoming overly possessive of the silver casket and he hastily pushed it within his clothing, though it pained him to deny her.

Soon Priddy drew close and, with a quiet smile, offered to play with Isolde. Gladly Caspar let her though he was anxious that she didn't go more than a yard from him. He nodded in gratitude as the five elders shuffled over to offer him a goblet of wine. It was fresh and clear, exuding the rich scent of honeysuckle. He sipped it tentatively, suspicious of their intent. He had seen that the men of Ash were clearly sedated by their women and he didn't want to suffer the same fate.

One of the elders smiled but it was without warmth. "You may as well drink it and enjoy yourself. I wouldn't be such a fool as to make your stay uncomfortable but I warn you that you will not be leaving here until you have helped us."

"And just what do you expect me to do?" Caspar asked.

"Wield your power."

"I have no power."

The warrior who had stirred earlier growled. "He lies!" he slurred over his cup. "You women have had your say and it is now time for some action." He tried to push himself up but thumped heavily back down onto a bench, groaning and holding his head.

Izella twitched her nose and pursed her lips at the warrior. Now that he was no longer terrified for Isolde, Caspar's eyes wandered more leisurely over her exquisite female form. Her silvery-blonde hair caught at the ends in coloured twine, she was elegant and strong, but also intensely feminine. She had long lean legs, was lusciously curvaceous and possessed the tiniest waist he had ever seen, which Caspar guessed he could close his hands around. But it was the way she moved that made her so fascinating. His eyes began to ache with staring at her hips that gently swayed as she advanced towards him.

She moved with power and ease. He adored the way these females moved, like panthers in the shadows.

Though she was slight and the warrior nearly twice her size, their expression and liquid silvery eyes were so uncommonly similar that Caspar had little doubt that they had shared a womb.

"I agree with Izen," Izella said stiffly. "You should stand aside and allow the warriors to do their work and force this man to help us."

"Izella, this has nothing to do with you. You do not make the decisions here," an elder scolded her.

"Well, if you will not let the warriors fight, you should at least allow the hunters to do something. All you do is talk! You should make him wield his power."

She was, Caspar guessed, no older than twenty. Her lithe body looked younger still but there was a wariness to her eyes that comes only with a few years beyond the excitement of childhood.

"Your power, youth, where did you steal it from?" she demanded. "Can you wield it?"

"I did not steal it. The power is in my guardianship; but I cannot wield it," Caspar blurted.

There seemed no point in hiding the fact that he had Necrönd. He was merely puzzled that they made no attempt to wrest it from him. The others gathered in the chamber seemed to tire of listening and settled down, picking up their looms, or threading gossamer threads into tapestries.

"Come and sit," Mirandel tugged at the huntress's bare arm. "He has been kind to us."

"You might have had your baby returned, Mirandel, but I lost mine!" Izella said with acidity. "We shall make him use it."

"You will do as she says," the brother demanded, towering over Caspar.

"I cannot," he said flatly. "The power is too strong for me."

"Oh, I see. A man with power but not the wisdom to use it," Izella sneered.

Caspar ignored the taunt. "It's too dangerous. The beasts on the other side are stirred up against me. Can't you feel their presence?"

"Indeed," Izella said. "The moment you found your daughter again, the shadows came out from the rocks. Shadows haunt you."

Caspar shuddered. "Why don't you deal with your problems yourself. Why not send your warriors?" he asked.

The people of Ash all gasped as if this was an appalling idea and even the ring of human changelings that sat nearest the fires broke off from their quiet chatter.

"The warriors must never fight!" Mirandel addressed Caspar.

"What's the point of having warriors then?" Caspar began to argue but was silenced as the elders of Ash pressed menacingly close.

"You will not leave until you have helped us so I suggest you think about that quietly in there," one gesticulated towards a side chamber and then clicked her fingers at Izen.

Lumbering to his feet, the giant heaved Caspar up and, pinning his arms to his sides, carried him into a small circular room that had a heavy wooden door sealing it from the communal chamber. They relieved him of his knives and arrows and locked him in but, thankfully, allowed him to keep Isolde. There was a bed, a cot for the child and food and water.

They kept him in there for three days and two nights, when he slept fitfully, Necrönd strapped to his chest so that none could steal it from him. Then on the third night, they sent Izella to him. It was clear what she offered the moment she appeared in the doorway, bathed in candlelight.

He stirred uncertainly and sat up, feeling overly self-conscious. "But you are a hunter," he said.

"Oh yes." Her voice was silky. "And you are my prey." She stroked his hair and pushed him back onto the bed. Sitting astride his loins, she began loosening her cinched bodice. Her breasts were large, much larger than he had imagined when they had been bound by her firm garment. He wriggled back, pushing her away.

"No," he objected. "You are beautiful but you can't make me."

He had to admit that he was tempted but, with Isolde close by in her fur-lined cot, he felt uncomfortable, feeling that it would be a betrayal of her mother to enjoy another woman so soon. Somewhere in the back of his head, he heard Hal's voice laughing at him for being such a sentimental fool. Izella was fascinatingly beautiful and he had no doubt that he was turning down the offer of a lifetime. He was enjoying her demanding approach but he had responsibilities to the child, May's memory and to Necrönd and so he shrank from her.

In disgust, she rose from the bed and pushed him back down. Caspar was quite startled by her strength. "You've made a fool of me!" she exclaimed.

"How?" Caspar asked in surprise, trying to regather some of his own dignity. He retreated to the end of his bed and dragged his breeches up to cover his lower half.

"They will laugh at me and say I am not a true woman of Ash. And to think I volunteered! The others thought you too distastefully weak."

"Weak!" Caspar snorted though he had to admit that in stature he did not compare well with their menfolk.

To his amazement, Izella began to cry. Tentatively, he put his arms around her. "Dear lady, even if you did seduce me, I would not wield the power for you."

"Ha!" she laughed. "There speaks the voice of one that has not lain with a woman of Ash. I am told that, to a human, a kiss from one of us is beyond all bliss and that you would do anything for more."

"Dear lady, I have seen many things and none as bewitchingly beautiful as you but still it would still make no difference for, even if I tried, I would fail. The thing is now stronger than me." He stood up uncomfortably and watched her as she swung her slender legs over the side of the bed and looked forlornly at the ground. Hastily, he wrapped her cloak about her in his embarrassment. He had no fear that he might weaken. She was too beautiful, too terrifying and made him feel inadequate.

"You know, I am truly sorry for you, the people of Ash, but I cannot help you. You must use your own resources."

She looked long at him and then his bow that they had let him keep, though they had removed his arrows. Her nose wrinkled in disdain. "A very crude weapon. You are a strange man. There is an air about you that speaks of knowledge and command and yet you dress like a peasant and appear so self-apologetic." She lifted his bow, strung it with ease and stroked the arc of the wood.

"Holly. Whoever uses holly for a bow?" she asked.

"Strength in combat," Caspar told her. "It isn't a hunting bow but a war bow."

"You?" she said. "You are not a warrior?"

Caspar was affronted. "I can assure you that I would not be daunted to draw one of your warriors bows."

She laughed at him as if he had no idea of the absurdity of his boast. "The string would slice your fingers off."

"Well, I doubt that but I would out-shoot any one of your warriors with my own bow."

She smiled at him knowingly. "That's a fine boast! It would be mildly entertaining to see you try." She left with a haughty swagger.

Caspar sat and waited but was left alone for many hours, wondering what he should do to get out of here before his next visitor entered. It was Pennard. Scowling over every inch of his face, he was clearly enraged.

"That was my sister, my sister I tell you, and she says that our people should die. Those murders have destroyed her mind. If you're the great wizard that they claim, you should do something to get us out of here! And where, peasant, did you steal this great power?"

"I did not steal it," Caspar said coldly.

"You're not telling me that a ragamuffin like you has claim to such powers."

"Why is it that, when a man just wants to be left alone, everyone thinks they can just come in here and shout at me?" Caspar asked angrily. "Now, leave me be."

"Can't. They've taken the dogs out and shoved me in here with you. They told me I'll never get home unless I've persuaded you to help them. Can't you just use your magic whatever-it-is they think you have, and get us out of here?" he asked sourly. "I came here because I had noble notions of rescuing my sister and avenging my father's death. Ha!" he said bitterly. "Now I'm locked up by a bunch of women and my dog no longer listens to me. I should have just stuck to my plan. Now, to make it worse, I'm going to miss my passage. The winds will turn again in another week or so and then I'll have to go back to my uncle." He scowled for a moment at his hands and then, as if dismissing his brooding thoughts, asked more curiously, "But tell me, where did you steal this power from?"

"I didn't steal it! How many times do I have to tell everyone?" Caspar growled.

"But a vagabond like you . . ."

"I'm not a vagabond," Caspar said wearily.

"Have it your own way." Pennard shrugged. "I'm not so far off a vagabond myself save I'm trying to build myself a respectable career – a career you've pretty much ruined, I might add, with your damned cur. Now get us out of here."

Caspar did his best to ignore Pennard, who finally retreated to sulk in one corner, but still was not left in peace. Izella returned but, to his relief, he saw she brought her brother and Priddy with her this time.

"A meal and wine," Izella offered. "The wine is very, very good. Grapes grow well in our valley."

Too tired to refuse, Caspar happily took the food and ate and drank in silence while the twins watched him and Priddy tended to the baby. Soon his head was heavy with sleep.

"What . . . What have you done to . . . er . . . I . . . er?" he mumbled groggily, as his legs began to fold under him.

Instantly, Izen was at his side. His strong arm hooked supportively beneath Caspar's armpit, he lowered him onto the bed. Soon, he slipped into a deep sleep where every sense was leaden and laboured. He could see and hear but he had no ability to move. Two faces were peering over him and, giddily, he knew that the twins were watching him intently.

"Come, it's time. He's asleep so get it off him," Izella hissed.

Caspar tried to scream out in protest but no sound escaped his lips. The horror of what they were about to do filled his mind with a terrible pain.

"Are you sure?" Izen asked, clearly not so confident as his sister about the scheme.

"Of course I'm sure," his sister snapped. "We have the opportunity to do something to save us all; we must act. A couple of monsters conjured at our command could pound them to pieces. Ogres perhaps?"

No! Caspar screamed in his head, the terror of oblivion like a red-hot dagger within him.

"Don't touch him!" Pennard's voice spat out of the dark. "You leave him alone."

Izen turned menacingly. "Stand off!"

There was a scream of rage as Pennard charged, pummelling his fists against Izen's chest; but the great man of Ash swatted him aside with one flick of his massive fist. Pennard crumpled to the ground.

"Take it quickly," Izella hissed at her brother. "Quick! Before the others get here."

Izen ripped open Caspar's tunic but then faltered. "But the elders warned against it."

"Ha! Weak old fools. I told you not to drink their tea. Age has made them fearful. But I'm not going to lose any more babies. The men of Negraferre will pay for taking my baby." She was sobbing almost fitfully. "Get out of my way. Let me do it, Izen."

She didn't bother cutting the straps that secured the silver casket to Caspar but simply flipped open the clasp and reached inside. "Three ogres!" she cried.

Caspar instantly felt their presence before a terrible blackness crammed his head.

Pennard's voice quaked, "What in mercy's name is that?"

"Mistress, what do you want of us?" a deep voice asked.

"The furnaces outside Negraferre, destroy them!" Izella shrieked and the vast presence of the three ghostly ogres was gone, vanished through the very stuff of the earth.

Battling against his pain, Caspar heard a terrifying growl as something huge within him began to form. He thought he would be split open. He gagged and choked, unable to breathe as something hairy forced its way up his throat, cracked open his jaw and wormed out of his body. The pain was excruciating and he could only moan, his dislocated jaw dangling onto his chin, his mouth full of blood.

"What have you done?" a voice cried from without the chamber. "What terrible things have happened here?"

The horrible scent of death was thick in the air and Caspar knew at once that the wolfman roamed the earth once more.

Suddenly, there was silence all around. He lay still amid the agony of what felt like a thousand swords mincing up his eyes and stabbing into the soft tissue behind.

"Warriors!" the shout came from the elders above. "Warriors, awake!"

The chamber emptied of all but the soft sounds coming from Priddy who was nursing the baby. Pennard had seized his opportunity to flee his captors. Izella and Izen were also gone and, in his miserable pain, Caspar moaned, listening to the busy humming of the elders beyond the open door. The ground shook above and there were screams and cries and, in time, silence. He didn't know how long he lay there but, at last, soft-soled shoes came padding back to him.

"We must take him down to the old woman," Izella panted as though she had been running hard.

"No living man has ever seen her. She hides from them now," the elders objected.

"I have done something I should not," Izella said honestly. "All is ill and I must put it right. Only the old woman can help us. I can feel the pain within his head. He will die unless we help him."

"Go then!" an elder spoke with calm insistence. "Take him to the old woman. We can't let him die; it seems he has the power to save us."

Caspar presumed it was Izen who scooped him up and carried him out of the chamber and along an echoing passage. Through his pain, he vaguely sensed that they travelled downwards, winding deeper and deeper into the cool of the earth. Finally, he heard the gentle sound of water running into a pool. He was lowered to the ground, cruelly aware of the earth pressing against his cheek and the fearful pounding in his head.

"What have you done?" an ancient voice demanded as he swooned into blackness.

CHAPTER SEVENTEEN

Still confused with pain, Caspar looked about him at the low chamber hollowed out of the earth, rugs made from the skins of badger, deer and fox warm underfoot. An old woman was staring into a still pool that lazed in the centre of the chamber and beyond her was a huge hairy figure slumped in a large, ornately carved, high-backed chair. Caspar laughed nervously, thinking for a second that the bulky figure was a bear.

His jaw throbbed but he was relieved to find he could ease it open and shut. Someone had worked it back into place, he thought with relief. Isolde's snuffles and little cries came from just behind him accompanied by the sound of Priddy making soothing noises. Isolde was safe! He murmured a prayer of gratitude to the Great Mother for his baby's well-being. His immediate fears allayed, he returned to trying to make sense of his circumstances.

What he had thought to be a bear, he now saw was a huge man wearing a bearskin, much like his own, only the long hairs were tipped with black. He looked at Caspar, his small, dark eyes sunken and cloudy, and made a weak attempt at a growl. Like the warriors of Ash, he was very large.

"My son, Arthnau," the old woman said with a slight tilt of her head towards the figure in the high-backed chair.

Caspar grunted in acknowledgement and twisted to look back at the old woman, who was tall herself but more slender than the man, her hair light and curling right down to her waist, which seemed odd in one so old. Her skin was wrinkling and a greyish brown that gave the slight appearance of bark and he recognized in her something familiar, something that he had seen before in Harle's mother. But whereas Harle's mother was strong, this woman looked frail and stooped with worry and constantly cast her grey eyes towards Arthnau, who never once stirred from his chair.

Caspar glanced around him at the hollowed-out chamber within the earth, which, he presumed, was directly below the communal chamber he had been in earlier since a tap root also plunged through its centre only here it was thinner and its whiskery end coiled into the pool puddling the floor. The old woman lowered her hand into the water, thoughtfully swishing it back and forth.

She forced a smile to her wan face. "Now, son of Keridwen, what brings you to such foolishness? We must see you home." She eyed the silver casket at his chest. "Something terrible has happened. Terrible!" She swished the water. "Here at the roots of the sacred ash that is embedded so deep into the Great Mother, I learn much about the world. The ash, you see—"

"Is the tree that links all parts of the cosmos, its roots deep in the earth and its branches spreading high into the sky. By studying the tree, we form an understanding of how all things are linked, that our deeds, however insignificant, are a part of a greater, endless chain of happenings," Caspar interrupted.

She smiled. "Wiser, perhaps than I thought. Nevertheless, though your head might be stuffed with knowledge, you sorely lack sense." The smile faded. "My people suffer. They are of a delicate balance of pure elements and the poisonous brown smoke from the smelters destroys them. The filth from the furnaces has also poisoned the waters, which seep down to me from all corners of the world, telling me of things from afar. But now the roots are brown and my *sight* is gone." She sighed. "And my son is dying. I shall surely die too if I lose him."

"Old Woman Ash, we thought this man could use his powers to help us," Izella said, stepping forward alongside her brother.

"Ours is not his destiny. This is our own problem," Old Woman Ash snapped, rubbing at her eyes that clearly pained her. She glowered at Izella. "How could any of you have been so foolish as to try and wield such a power?"

No one answered her as they were interrupted by the sound of rapid feet lightly tapping the firm earth of the tunnels. Panting heavily, three huntresses burst into the chamber. "Old Woman Ash, we chased after him through the forests but the youth from Negraferre had too much of a start on us and got clean away."

"He will lead them to us," the old woman croaked. "The men from Negraferre will attack and there is little I can do about it."

"You must fight," Caspar said. "And I will stand with you."

"But you are one of them!" Izen exclaimed in surprise.

"What they do is wrong," he said simply. "My mother is a high priestess of the Great Mother and she would see it as her duty to protect the ways of Nature. What these people do with their furnaces is sacrilege." He fixed her fiercely in the eye. "But I do not want to see them slaughtered; only repelled."

"We shall be glad of your help, son of Keridwen. Our

knowledge of warfare is lost and your guidance would be welcomed."

Caspar checked the smile that sprang to his flattered face. "It is my duty to help," he said as solemnly as possible.

Old Woman Ash smiled weakly at him and continued, "They will attack now that Izella has sent the ogres on them; that in itself will be enough to provoke them into overcoming their superstitious fear of us. Moreover, Priddy's brother will tell all and they will come boldly to destroy all trace of us. Am I not right, Caspar? Tell me if that is not the way of man."

He nodded. "They are men; they wouldn't come to save a child but they will to save their livelihoods."

Old Woman Ash continued, "They are thousands and we but a bare hundred; they will come out from the smelters and out from the town and we have no way to stop them."

"I can stop them – but not with Necrönd." Caspar sighed, knowing it was the right thing to do. These were an ancient people of the Great Mother and he could not let them be destroyed.

"How?" Izen demanded sceptically.

Caspar coughed and prodded gently at his jaw. He had enough knowledge in his head to form a solid tactical plan of defence but he hadn't yet pieced one together. Besides, they would need more than that; they needed to put a stop to any future threat. The thought that the people of the coast would savage the women and children cowering in their homes was too terrible. "First," he said, thinking out loud, "we must maintain as much of your fearsome reputation as possible."

The elders nodded eagerly at this.

"The hunters must hide in the trees and strike at the flanks of the attackers. Believe me, it's a most disturbing experience! It will alarm and thin their ranks but, I'm certain that when they come, they will sweep through in large numbers. You may kill many but you won't be able to stop them all and they will find your homes and . . ." He did not need to say more.

"We're listening," Old Woman Ash assured him.

Caspar rubbed at his jaw. "You must arm the warriors and defend the earthworks."

Izella immediately found fault with his plan.

"Even our warriors can do little against an army of men from Negraferre, especially if they are joined by the men from the mines or the soldiers on their way to Oran. We are few and they so many and the hunters' arrows are useless against their armour," she pointed out.

"Yes, but you made Pennard leave his armour at the foot of the canyon wall. He will have fled in too much of a hurry to have searched for it. We can melt it down and tip the arrows with it."

Izella shook her head. "No, it's no use. We can't touch that black metal; it burns our skin."

"Oh!" Caspar said lamely, trying to think. "But at least you can pick out the unarmoured men in their number."

"Do you know what you are doing?" Old Woman Ash asked sceptically, undermining his confidence.

He nodded firmly though his heart misgave him. "I am the son of a warlord. For a thousand years, my line has held a frontier castle pinning back vast armies with but a few. And all done with the bow."

Izen smiled at him and grunted his approval. There was an unnerving glint brightening his eyes and he had lost his lumbering gait.

Caspar weakly grinned back at him, swallowing his own doubts, and girded himself up to give orders. "Izella, send one of your people to find that armour. I might still have a use for it." He raised his hands to stay her objections. "Get them to use a stick to drag it back with and then they won't have to touch the metal. Then send three of your hunters to spy on Negraferre with orders to report back to me the moment they see the men moving out to attack."

Izella nodded and was quickly gone.

Caspar turned to the elders that were gathered behind him. "See to it that you wake your warriors and set them, with the women's help, to cut thick posts. Have them sharpen the posts at both ends. We shall have to build some defences as best we can. Izen," he commanded the huge man at his shoulder, "I want to have a look at your weapons."

One of the elders insisted on accompanying them up to the communal chamber, the old woman muttering nervously. Eyes wide, Caspar stared at the thickness and length of the bows, which he was certain he could not draw, and the weighty swords, the latter sorely rusted. "Do you know how to use these weapons?" he asked Izen.

"No, of courses not," the elder snapped, interrupting.

"We do. We practise regularly," Izen glowered down at her.

Caspar frowned at this, wondering what to think.

"It's not practise; it is no more than a ceremony. I strongly advise against this," the elder said, waggling her staff at Caspar. "The hunters and the young mothers have not been told what it was like but we, the elders, know."

"Would you have us all slaughtered?" Izen growled, ripping one of the vast swords from the wall and wielding it as if it were no more than a stick.

Caspar watched Izen's eyes taking on a frightening gleam as he stroked the blade back and forth.

"Now, I can use it as it was intended," he grunted.

"They are normally forbidden to us; only in the dark of the new moon when the Gods cannot see us do we take them from the walls."

"And the bows?"

He nodded and grinned. "Weekly. Any less and we would lose the skill entirely." He led him to a back chamber, which was stacked with wicker baskets filled with sharpened wooden shafts of perhaps four foot in length and at least five times as thick as his own arrows. Caspar had no doubt that, propelled by the great bows, such missiles with or without steel barbs could pierce armour and cause considerable damage to flesh.

"How good are you?" he asked, gathering up a half dozen arrows.

Izen grinned slyly. "Good enough. We can all hit the target."

"It is not a target!" the elder was indignant. "It is a mark to be aimed at only as part of a religious ceremony to remind us of the horrors of warfare. The men are forbidden to wield weapons. We cannot allow them to fight!"

Caspar raised his eyebrows. "Then you will die," he said calmly though inside he was screaming with frustration. "Why can't they fight? Why is it forbidden?"

She rubbed at her eyes, that were clouded by a yellow film, and led him back to the communal chamber where the magnificent tapestries hung on the beaten earth walls. "See how we used to live," she said, pointing at a tapestry that showed a glittering village lit by lanterns, nestled beneath magnificent ash trees.

"We are the people of Ash," she continued. "Once we were as numerous as the trees. Our ways are not as yours. We birth many girl children and few boys and each boy grows to be big, strong and lustful, too much man for just one wife. But such power carries with it greed and rage. They fought like the stags; they yearned for battle, loved it, and so long before your own people spread thickly over this world, the wars began.

"One warrior decided that he would have more than his allotted three wives. He stole his brother's wife who then murdered him and took back his wife and more. At first, they fought simply for more wives, just like the stag, and then they fought for land. So, it progressed until all were killing each other and they joined into bands, needful of larger areas of land to support their families."

She paused and, sensing that she had more to tell, Caspar nodded at her to go on.

"Soon, they fought because they knew no other way, joining in great armies for the glory of it. Two leaders grew up, one in the north and one in the south, and they desired each other's lands. For a hundred years they fought until none could remember anything but war and the ruin it brought on us. In their madness, they destroyed each other's crops and then came famine and death; thousands, hundreds of thousands perished all because of their lust for war. Though we women rose up and cried out against them, there was nothing we could do until finally their numbers were so depleted that they themselves saw the awfulness of their own aggression and surrendered their weapons.

"By then we were but fragmented bands around the world and the men have never borne arms again and are plied hourly with a calming brew to quell their nature. The warrior's mind, however, is still savage. Infants are not safe around them."

Aghast, Caspar stared at Izen. "Well!" he said inadequately. "Now that I know, let's see how useful you are with these arrows. What is your range?"

Izen's silvery complexion darkened as he looked at the bow with obsessive fascination and felt the point on the arrow. A glint twinkled in his eye as he turned to Caspar. "Two hundred paces, two hundred *warrior* paces. There's not one amongst us who will miss." He grinned proudly.

"Indeed!" Caspar was a little sceptical.

"Come, I shall show you!" Izen led him up into the daylight and along the river to a long, wide-spaced avenue of ash trees. "See there?"

Caspar noted a flat stone, the grass around neatly trodden down and kept short by the grazing animals. Beyond it, at what Caspar estimated to be four hundred yards, a hog strung by its rear trotters dangled from the boughs of a large ash tree.

"We replace the carcass every week," Izen explained.

"And you can all hit that?" Caspar was impressed.

Izen nodded. "Without exception. Even with the effect of the brew."

"Show me," Caspar said, handing him one of the hefty arrows.

Izen moved to the stone and, without appearing to take any effort to aim, he drew the great bow, the silvery skin of his chest and arms bulging, the cords on his neck taut, as he tensed and loosed the arrow. The execution was fluid and skilful but lacking in thought. With child-like delight, the great warrior watched his arrow tear through the carcass. A glazed look was in his eye that spoke of intense pleasure. Oblivious to all else, he strode all the way to his pierced target, drew the sword and, with one swipe, cleaved straight through the hog's body. Caspar shuddered at the warrior's power and glee with which he wielded his weapon.

"Great!" Caspar praised him when the warrior returned.

"Now take another ten paces back and hit what's left of the carcass."

"But why?"

"I want to test your skill and range."

"Range?" Izen asked.

"Just do it?" Caspar said as patiently as possible.

The warrior obeyed and, with the same movement, raised his bow and loosed his arrow. It fell short by twenty paces. Caspar looked at him in disbelief and paced forward to the smooth stone from where Izen had loosed his first arrow.

"Let me get this straight. You always stand on this spot and fire at that target and only that target?"

Izen nodded. "And we never miss."

"I should think not," Caspar said quietly and turned to Izella. "Tell me that your hunters can hit a moving target."

She nodded. "But at no great range. We are a stealthy people and can get in very close."

"What is your range?" he asked.

She shrugged. "Well, I could hit that tree." She nodded to one not twenty paces off. "And possibly the one just beyond."

Caspar swallowed. This was not going to be easy. His ancestors had always seen to it that the men of Torra Alta practised at every range and at moving targets. He did not know how long it would take the men of Negraferre to form their attack but he guessed that he had at least the rest of the day and one night but probably no more than that in which to prepare.

"I need you to take out as many of the enemy's key men as possible. Can you get in close enough to do that?"

She nodded. "We can; your kind finds us very hard to see when we choose it. But you said our arrows won't pierce their armour."

"I hope we have Pennard's armour," he reminded her. "It will make a great many barbs."

"I've already told you we cannot touch their metal; it is poisonous to us," the woman reminded him. "We might manage to loose the arrows without touching the barbs but we couldn't work the metal. The fumes from the melted armour would be lethal."

Caspar nodded. He had thought on the problem and come up with a simple solution. "True, but not to the human children in your number."

In all directions from the earthworks, he had the men pace out their precise two hundred paces – a good distance – and had them draw a ring.

"Good. Now we have work to do," he told them authoritatively. "We must stop them at exactly this point. If we can halt them here and instil panic in the first instance, let us pray that the rest will flee and that will be an end to the bloodshed. Stakes!" he ordered. "Drive them into the ground facing out at exactly the point we have marked." Once the first was in place, he nodded at Izen. "Now, hit that stake."

With the same casual indifference, the warrior drew his bow and Caspar was heartily relieved when the arrow found its mark. He reached up to slap the solid wall of Izen's back. "Well done," he said cheerfully before shouting orders for the rest of the staves to be driven in. He turned to Izella. "Can your women camouflage them? I want the men of Negraferre to charge straight onto them."

Izella nodded and called her hunters to do their work.

Within minutes he had everyone busily setting about tasks to make a stronghold. They cut stakes from the young trees in the surrounding woods and cleared a circular break around the earthworks. Toiling throughout the night, they drove the sharpened staves into the ground, angling them outward against attack and draping them with twigs and greenery to soften their outline. Caspar stood back to examine their handiwork and was very impressed; the women of ash had a certain understanding of trees that gave them an amazing ability to camouflage even the hard line and regular formation of the stakes. A tower was raised near the great ash tree at the centre of the earthworks.

Amazed at how fast and furiously the warriors of Ash worked now that they were no longer obliged to drink their soothing teas, Caspar set about his own task. Sitting at a smouldering fire someway downwind from the earth shelters and assisted by the older human children, he dipped the points of wooden arrows into the smelted metal from Pennard's armour. The girls considered themselves to be people of Ash and not one of them raised any doubts about making weapons that would be used against their true kinsfolk. Caspar examined a finished quarrel. The barb was now of the very same stuff as the armour from the men of Negraferre and so would surely pierce it.

By morning they were exhausted but were ready to meet the attack. The children and their mothers were all deep down into the lower earth chambers with Old Woman Ash and Izella and her hunters had slipped out into the trees, ready to do what they could to terrify and thin the enemy numbers.

Izella came back with the good news from her scouts that the men of the port were still gathering and had not yet reached the edge of the mountains. But they also had bad news that the miners from the foothills were hurrying to join their number. Caspar considered that he had a couple of hours yet until he must have the warriors in position.

Now there was just one affair of his own that he must attend to in the depths of the earthworks. Curling around and around the interlocked tunnels into the cool gloom that was lit only with small braziers flickering against the beaten earth walls, he hurried to find Isolde who was still in Priddy's doting care. He swept the baby up into his arms and cuddled her close, telling her how much he loved her. Then with Priddy on his heels, he took her down to the other women in the domed chamber at the roots of the ash.

He approached Old Woman Ash, who was fussing over her son. The great man was groaning, trying to force himself to his feet to join the warriors, but was evidently too sick to stand.

"Old Woman Ash, you must look after my baby," he begged.

"Gladly! I shall," she promised gravely. "Come, Priddy, keep her warm by my fire."

"Trog! Guard!" Caspar ordered. The dog whipped the beaten earth with his tail and pressed up close against Isolde, who affectionately yanked his ear. Trog appeared to enjoy this ill treatment.

Caspar hurried back above ground to take up his central post in the wooden tower and he found that Izella had not yet returned to the woods but was waiting for him.

"I just wanted to thank you now in case . . ."

Caspar smiled warmly but then he replaced the grave expression of command onto his features. "Once you have loosed your arrows, I want you to stay in the safety of the trees. Leave the warriors to the close combat; the women will only get in the way."

She acknowledged him with a brief nod and, with her teeth already gritted, she slipped away over the defences.

Now there was nothing to do but wait. A turgid silence

thickened the air. The hectic preparations of the last night were done and now came the wait. The air was tense, too tense. He could feel the angst boiling within the warriors. This was not their way to stand and wait and he suddenly had huge misgivings about his plan. They would be unable to do it; they would loose all their arrows too soon, he was certain. Somehow, he must stem the flood of their bloodlust and maintain discipline.

The first screams of pain and terror came ringing out from the woods and Caspar knew that Izella had started her attack. He looked around him at the ring of mighty warriors. Izen was twitching at his bow, his lower lip sucked in and white where he bit it. Caspar's mind wrestled to decide what he should do as he feared that the warriors would break out from the defences, eager to assist the hunters. What would his father do? Of course, the Torra Altan men were meticulously drilled and it was unthinkable that any might defy the Baron, whereas these were people of a more independent nature. He ground his teeth, wondering. What would they have done at home? What gave Torra Alta that fearful presence so that none would dare attack?

All knew of the undoubted bravery of the Torra Altan men, of course. All knew they would stand to the very last. All feared their courage. It was the courage born of discipline. It was the courage of knowing that they stood shoulder to shoulder and none would break from the line; and they knew of that courage because they sang of it with one voice. That was it! The song! The war song of his people passed down through the centuries.

"Izen," he asked, "do your people have no songs of war?"

"Oh, we have many songs. It was the only joy not forbidden us."

"Sing then!" he ordered.

Their great voices muffled the yells and squeals from the woods that continued for several minutes. Caspar ordered silence as the screams died away and only the sounds of men and beasts marching through the trees came to his ears. He braced himself, ready to see what force would break out from the trees, when Izella suddenly appeared at his shoulder. She was followed by the rest of the hunters, who were breathless as if they had been running fast.

"I told you to hide out in the trees!" Caspar despaired.

"We couldn't when we might still do something here," Izella told him stiffly. "We have knives!"

"Women shouldn't fight," Caspar grumbled but saw it was too late to argue now. "Tell me everything. How many are there? How successful were you?"

"There's about eight hundred in total in the woods down river of us. Smiths, townsfolk, men from the smelters and many more from the mines, all led by a troop of black-suited soldiers." She grinned. "A small troop of soldiers now."

"You have done well," he told her. "Now, I need you out of the way so the warriors can fight. Get down into the shelters."

She shook her head. "I told you we still have knives and must do what we can."

Caspar saw he had lost this battle and shrugged in resignation. "As you wish."

The huge warriors closed a tight circle around the hunters and the earthworks. Caspar was proud. These were magnificent people, strong and passionate, and he felt honoured to be chosen as their leader. "Sing!" he cried again. "Sing!"

Their voices were trembling with power and he had no doubt that even the most fearsome of men would be daunted by the sound. Within his own head he thought only of the simple chant of his people. "Torra Alta! Torra Alta!"

"Steady!" he warned as he stared south along the canyon and saw the first glint of sun on metal. "Save the arrows until they are close in and at the stakes." Caspar's gaze skimmed the approaching men. They marched in a snaking line with little formation but he had anticipated that since few were trained troops. Izella had said they were mainly miners and smiths, he reassured himself. They were craftsmen not warriors, used to forging weapons not wielding them; they would easily be driven back once the last of their black-armoured vanguard was destroyed.

The excitement screamed through him. Never had he imagined this. He knew what to do; how to steady the men, how to lead them; he felt no fear. At last, I am a man, he said to himself and imagined his father's proud grin as he reported the tale of his great triumph. Hal had never led men in a major battle. Of course, they had fought in several skirmishes with up to half a dozen men and Hal had always fought with great skill and bravery but he had never proved himself as a war leader. Now all Ash's people were relying on his ability. They knew nothing of tactical warfare and he knew everything.

"We can hold them back," Caspar shouted loudly, his confidence swelling as he glimpsed the sparkle in Izen's eyes. Ever since the warrior had been allowed to wield his sword, his expression had changed. There was blood-lust there, a fearful underlying simmer of anger; the will to live, to survive, to conquer. Caspar did not consider it a horrible dark emotion but a great strength. Of course, it was a strength! Every man in Torra Alta needed that quality, needed to know that, when he had to kill, it was right.

The wind gusted up the valley from the south, bringing with it the sound of clanking armour and steel. Silence fell over Ash's people. Caspar felt the tension.

For a moment, his mind filled with doubt as he saw, in detail now, the huge picks and axes born by the miners. He glanced at the slight feminine bodies of the hunters of Ash and imagined them shattered and shredded by the fearsome weapons. They would all die; the soldiers, smiths and miners enraged by the attack of the ogres would cut them to pieces, every last one of them. He gritted his teeth, forcing the fears from his mind.

The miners and smiths spread out. Though not fighting men, they would be strong and well-used to wielding their hammers, axes and picks. Before them rode a band of mounted soldiers, several clad in full armour, the black metal drinking up the light. Caspar's eyes ran up and down the line. These were the ones that the warriors of Ash must bring down with their javelin-like arrows.

They had only seconds now before the mercenaries would reach the stakes and his stomach knotted and squirmed. He feared that the warriors of Ash would charge out and break their line of defence. Strong and brave they might be but, if they spread out, the men of Negraferre would swarm past them to attack Izella's hunters before pouring down into the chambers below.

Courage came from unity, he fiercely told himself and began in his clear bright voice to sing his favourite ballad about heroes and warriors. Naturally, he sang it in his own tongue because that filled his heart with mettle and, in his mind, he heard the song as if his ancestors had sung it, their voices ringing out from within his soul. The warriors of Ash followed his lead and roared out their war-song just as the men of Negraferre turned their steady advance into a wild charge.

The ground trembled with the furious pounding of heavy hooves as the line of mercenaries broke into a thunderous charge, horses snorting, men hollering. From that moment, it was as if he were outside himself, observing from afar, his mind detached and cool, his fear swept away. This was a task he was born to and he would do it well.

"Stand firm, men!" he cried, leaping up into the centre of the wooden tower from where he might best be heard. "Stand fast! No one looses a single arrow until I command it."

He had his own bow ready. Fifty paces before the horses reached the stakes, he knew he could kill any of the armoured knights. He had time to bring down two or three but that would set a fateful example. If the warriors followed his lead every one of their arrows would be spent before a single man was brought down.

He held his breath and waited, wondering when the horsemen would see the stakes but he needn't have worried; the hunters had done their job well. The front line of horses charged straight onto the points that were driven deeper into their breasts by those crashing into them from behind.

The warriors' arrows darkened the sky.

Caspar could not hear the screams. He knew the air was thick with the horrible cries of the dying but all was distant, remote to him as if he were watching a boardgame in some country inn. The townsfolk charged behind, clambering over the fallen.

At first none broke through. The warriors of Ash were deadly accurate and their huge arrows impaled flesh and bone, splitting skulls, tearing through breastplate and ribs with such force as to throw the men from their horses. Other mounts were cut from under the knights, barely an arrow wasted.

But the force of numbers tipped the scales in favour of the attackers. Wave after wave of townsfolk drove over the bodies of the fallen and the warriors could not loose arrows quickly enough to stop them all. At first only a handful broke through and they did no more than throw themselves to the ground to avoid the hail of arrows.

Then the arrows were spent and the townsfolk surged forward. With cool deliberation, Caspar brought down the leading half-dozen men but he was one archer alone and the force of numbers was against him.

"Izella, please!" Caspar cried. "Get your hunters below and out of the way!"

She paid him no heed as at first only a dozen men reached the ring of warriors, who had no trouble cutting them to pieces with their mighty swords. But soon more and more men were clambering over the bodies of the fallen. His arrows spent, Caspar was forced to drop his trusted bow and reach for his own sword as he leaped down from his tower. Smaller than the warriors of Ash, he was an instant target but he was well trained and the townsfolk, though full of vengeful courage, were not fighting men.

The attackers came on, still shrieking and wildly thrashing their weapons, only to stagger back in a line as one of the warriors ran out at them, a terrible cry bellowing from his throat.

"No, no! Stand fast!" Caspar yelled. "Hold the line."

No one heard his cry. Once one of the giant warriors broke out from their circle, the rest went berserk, charging forward and slashing savagely. It would have been an easy victory, the power of the warriors hacking through the slighter bodies of the men. They had done so well. They had fired on his command, held his line but now the circle was broken.

Already a dozen smiths and miners were amongst the women, slashing cruelly. Caspar shoved women aside in his efforts to get to the marauding men, stabbing one man in the back, then plunging his sword deep into the shoulder blade of another.

"Look out!" one of the hunters shrieked just as Caspar plunged his sword deep into a man's chest.

His sword stuck. He put his boot onto the man's ribcage, heaving upwards and raising his sword only just in time to shield himself from the blow of an axe that drove him to his knees. He rolled over to regain his position, leapt forward and, with trained speed, pierced his attacker through the throat. More men were amongst the howling hunters who had defied Caspar's orders and remained above ground. He could hear the splinter of wood as men with axes hacked at the wooden doorways, sealing the earthworks.

Exhausted, he battled on, man to man; unaware now of how the battle fared about him. He could hear nothing for his own breaths and the grunts and cries of his opponents. Three men set on him at once and he was aware of Izella beside him, dagger in hand.

"Stand back! Give me room!" he snarled.

"You're exhausted!" she shouted back.

It was true; Caspar's muscles trembled with the effort of combat but he couldn't think with this woman beside him. Though he growled at her to leave, she remained and there was nothing he could do about it. The first miner attacked and he threw him off with a sideways slash of his sword. The second was on him. He was about to swing his sword in a great arc to slice through his neck when he caught sight of Izella in the corner of his eye and feared that the through-stoke would hit her. He struck feebly, his sword deflecting off hard armour, and left himself vulnerable to attack from a third man.

He was certain that the man would strike at his undefended side but no axe cleaved into his flesh. Quite suddenly the miners were shouting fearfully to one another and within seconds they had laid down their weapons and fled. The townsfolk and smiths hotly followed.

Caspar staggered and dropped to his knees, resting his chin on the hilt of his sword, amazed by the sight. The warriors of Ash, deep in the field of battle, hacked remorselessly at their fleeing foe.

He did not need to wonder why the men had fled so suddenly. A strange cry, a high-pitched animal scream, trembled up through the ground beneath his feet. The miners had recognized the sound at once. Thin green figures were worming up through the earth and snuffling towards them over the grass. Knockermen!

Caspar's hand went to his breast. The cold power of Necrönd was against him. They smelt him; they were coming for him, but that was not his fear. The knockermen were emerging from the shell-like mounds of the earthworks. Naturally, the miners had fled at the very first sound, their panic infecting the soldiers and smiths. Miners had always feared these underground creatures that they claimed caused shafts to collapse and ate lost or trapped men, though very few people who did not work underground believed their tales. Caspar had met knockermen before and he was equally afraid – but not for himself.

"Isolde!" he cried, his voice hoarse.

Izella was at his heels as he ran for the first entrance, thirty of Ash's hunters out pacing him as they too raced to protect their kin. He half-slipped, half-fell into the dark of the tunnels and charged with them, coiling down to the roots. When they reached the lower chamber where they had left the women and children with Old Woman Ash, Caspar was horrified to see the heaps of knockermen clambering through the infants. The male children, some no more than babies, were already fighting, their teeth sunk deep into the knockermen.

Caspar's eyes searched the dark. Isolde, where was she? He couldn't see her! But he could hear Trog's savage growls and, inexplicably, he could see Pennard standing over Priddy! The youth was standing his ground, slashing at the knockermen like a man possessed, his sword cutting easily through the creatures' thin flesh.

Praying that Priddy still had Isolde, Caspar cut his way towards her. While Trog tore up three of the slimy green creatures around her, Caspar at last reached Priddy, who was doubled over, protecting Isolde with her body. He stood side by side with Pennard, standing over the girls, slashing and cutting and stabbing until he thought he could fight no longer.

It was perhaps only ten minutes before the first of Ash's men reached the chamber but by then Caspar was already beginning to stumble and his strokes were becoming laboured; he didn't know how much longer he could hold the knockermen off before he was overwhelmed. However, the moment one of the big warriors appeared, the chamber emptied.

The warrior was joined by another and the two giant men roared and bellowed, charging about the room looking for something more to kill. Five more warriors crashed into the room and they became frenzied. One of them lashed out at a crying child, kicking the small thing and sending it flying across the room. Each was like a raging bull and the women and children around shrank back from them in terror. At last, the bloodlust abated.

The knockermen were gone; the men of Negraferre fled. A strange silence filled the atmosphere. Then a child began to sob and an injured elder groaned; the battle was over.

"My baby!" Caspar begged of Priddy.

She handed Isolde to him with a smile. He clutched her tight, telling her all was well, though she seemed completely unperturbed by the carnage around her and, grinning, she reached up to pinch his chin with her warm little fingers.

He bit back his tears. "I was so afraid for you," he said, hugging her to him.

Caspar held out his hand to Pennard. "Thank you from the bottom of my heart. I don't know why you're here but thank you."

"I came to save Priddy," he said simply.

Caspar nodded though he didn't understand. "But she wouldn't need saving from the men of Negraferre."

"I would never have gone to warn Negraferre of Izella's intention to destroy the furnaces if I had thought it would put Priddy in danger," he explained himself. "But when I got there, I was too late; the ogres had already pulled down the furnaces and slaughtered many of the people of the outlying hamlets; the townsfolk were outraged and ready for revenge. I begged them to watch out for the human children living in the canyon. But, when I explained that Priddy thought me a murderer, they said they would destroy all of them human or not. They wouldn't listen when I said that in time they could be brought back to our ways. They said they must be bewitched and therefore must be destroyed. So, I marched with them, hoping to break into the tunnels and get to Priddy to protect her from her own people."

"I can't say how grateful I am," Caspar repeated and

then spent a good minute looking Isolde over before slipping her into the sling.

Only then did he look up at the scene around him. Someone had rekindled the braziers. Women hurried to and fro, collecting infants and scooping up the male children, who were now fighting amongst themselves. These they dropped back into their pens. Dazed, Caspar walked through them, trying to find an exit to the surface. He stopped as Old Woman Ash, supported by Mirandel, shuffled towards him.

She held out her hand. "Thank you, my boy. That was well done; we owe you much."

Leaning against Mirandel for support, she led him to the surface just as the gloomy silence was broken by a strange cry. The single cry was taken up by others and became a chant. Caspar saw that the warriors of Ash were dancing and whooping in a circle.

Old Woman Ash looked sadly at Caspar. "These, my people, are out of place now in this world. Once the world was a savage place; once bears and dragons and griffins rampaged across all the earth and then we were glad of our fearless men. But the world is tamer now and there is no place for my warriors." She watched them lovingly but sadly as they continued their dance.

"But it is good to see them dance once more," she continued. "They were born to fight and then sing of their victories. The rage of battle is in their nature and it is sad to keep them subdued as we do." She sighed and Caspar felt her sorrow.

"Is it?" Mirandel sniffed. "They have killed five of the children."

"But they also saved the rest and, if it wasn't for their blind fury, we should all be dead," Caspar said as kindly as he could.

"A man! You speak like a man! You wouldn't be saying that if it were your child that was killed!" she retorted.

"Come build the fires and rejoice! The smelting will cease and we shall be freed from this illness," one of the women offered.

Old Woman Ash sighed. "My people have suffered. They cannot be healed; not now. Perhaps those freshly born will live but the poisons are already in the bloodstream of the rest of us."

"Trinoxia!" Caspar blurted. "I didn't tell you before but I gave Mirandel's baby a powerful medicine called trinoxia," he explained. "But I didn't want to get your hopes up because it was my very last drop rinsed out of empty vials. And I cannot get any more. The people of the coast say there is no way for me to get home."

"You must get more for us," the old woman said simply.

"I cannot," Caspar said forcefully. "I know only of one person who can make it and she lives across the western ocean – and I cannot get home."

"Of course, you can get home," Old Woman Ash laughed.

"But the winds blow always west and—"

"You must go north over the top of the world," she interrupted him excitedly but then her voice dropped. "But you are too frail to survive such a journey."

"Frail! I'm not frail!" Caspar insisted but then watched in dismay as the woman's eyes dropped down to the child.

"She is very young for such an extreme journey."

CHAPTER EIGHTEEN

Brid's world was concentrated in the writhing pit of agony of her chest. In the dark of her pain, she reached another dimension where, she could see all about her shining, beautiful women with glossy hair that shimmered like starlight. Their lithe bodies, naked bar the cobweb gowns that caught the light and twisted it into rainbows, danced about them. Ondines of the Earth; she knew them at once and tried to acknowledge them but the pain was too great.

"We are with you, Brid," one murmured, drawing close to help her. "We need you; the world needs you. Have faith, have faith in yourself. You will survive the pain."

"Keridwen," Brid pleaded. "I need her. I need her terribly."

While the others danced, several Ondines sat about her and cradled her body, holding up her head to give her greater comfort. "Hush, little one, hush. You represent the Great Mother for all of us. Feel Her power."

"I cannot. I feel only pain," she admitted. But worse than the physical pain was the knowledge, that Hal had tried to kill her. For many days she languished in their midst, accepting thankfully the slight relief they gave her body and tortured mind.

Only brief moments of lucidity came to her. Then the Ondines faded until she sensed their presence only in the flickering broken light of their gowns, which split into many colours like sunlight caught in the beaded dew of a spider's web. Ceowulf was holding her across the front of his saddle and she gasped in agony while she looked up into the large brown eyes that looked sorrowfully down on her.

Unable to find the strength to speak, she wallowed in self-pity. Hal had tried to kill her and she could think of nothing else though she knew there were so many things of vital importance beyond herself that needed her attention. She was a high priestess and yet she thought only of her own misery.

She could sense Hal's breathing close by and longed for his comforting touch but couldn't bring herself to cry out to him even if she had the strength. He had tried to kill her. Oh, Spar she thought, if only I had fallen for you instead. Caspar had sensitivity; Caspar had imagination; Caspar had vibrancy for life. Yet, she felt no passionate love for him. He didn't have the same glamour, the dramatic self-assured masculinity that Hal exuded.

Hal was with Cymbeline; she knew it. She could hear the princess's light laughter and knew that only Hal's seductive powers could induce that. Couldn't he understand that it had not been her, that it had been Morrigwen who had chosen Harle? Morrigwen had clearly no doubts that Hal's rage would drive him to murder. Brid had thought he had grown beyond such all-consuming loss of control but now knew that he had not.

He and his brother Branwolf were so alike! They were born of an unbroken line of warlords that had held a remote outpost for a thousand years, the sons of men who had taken it from the dragons. Of course, Hal was savage, boldly wildly savage, but he was the stuff of a survivor, a conqueror, a man of glory. Whatever lay in their future, she still loved him – and would always love him even if she could never again look into his eyes with trust.

Her thoughts were shattered by the return of the blinding pain within her breast. She turned and twisted, fighting to be free of it, the words of her fellows about her distant and muffled.

"Look at her! You must believe me; I do not wish her harm. The sword is chipped and she will not heal if part remains inside." Hal's voice was filled with anguish.

"Y' think there's a splinter of it within her?" Abelard asked fearfully.

"Lie still; try not to move. You must be still," Ceowulf told her.

Brid faded back into her quiet world of pain. The Ondines, clearly unseen by the others, came out from the woods to soothe her. "Sweet Brid, have faith. The Great Mother is with you." They twined their bodies about her keeping her warm, but she could barely breathe for the pain as the movement of each breath stabbed through her.

A soft drizzle dampened the scrubby landscape of the Goat Country as they halted to make camp. Hal stood over Brid, acutely aware of how the others blamed him for her suffering; he could feel their accusing glare on his back. He spun round on them, the rage that he had trapped and contained so well for so many years bursting out now like a wounded bull broken from its pen.

"How dare you criticize me! You have no idea what I've been through. What would you have done if it were your wife there with that thing, that monster? Your wife whom you loved beyond all else."

"Oh aye, loved her enough to kill her! Happen, that's deep love," Abelard sneered.

Hal flew at him, his mouth a wide scream that rattled the air around him. He punched, almost enjoying the pain in his knuckles as they jarred against solid bone.

Abelard's knotted fists punched back, his body lent strength by the anger. "How dare y'? Y' don't love her one ounce as much as I do," the archer snarled.

Hal tried to reach his knife but Abelard was quicker, knocking it from his hand. "Y' high and mighty lords, y' think y' know more about fighting than the common garrison soldier. Y' with your great weapons that's worth naught to a pair of grubby fists."

Hal was almost inclined to agree as the man hit him in quick succession hard to the temple, stomach and chin. His mouth flooded with blood and he was dizzy with the shock.

Abelard grunted, "And don't think I'm afraid to hurt y' just 'cos y'r arm's still ailing. I suffered four hundred years of torture to protect the Trinity and then to have an imbecile like y' try and kill her . . . ! She might die yet." Abelard slammed his fist into Hal's left arm.

"Hey! Hey! Stop it! Stop now!" Ceowulf shouted, dragging the archer off and flinging him to the ground. "Both of you stop it. She's trying to speak."

"Brid, my love," Hal whispered involuntarily, the words escaping before he had a chance to stem them.

Her eyes were unfocused but she kept on mumbling and appeared to be talking to people about her though she did not react to anything he, Abelard or Ceowulf said.

"She's lost her mind." He felt sick to his stomach and withdrew, horrified by what he had done to her. Cymbeline was watching, waiting for him and he stepped back to her side. Behind him Brid began to rave.

"They are coming! Hurry!" she shouted then her voice

dropped to almost nothing. "Morrigwen, give me strength to return home."

Ceowulf looked at the others uncertainly. "What is she talking about?"

Hal was listening but didn't reply. The world seemed to be moving slowly about him as he noted every tiny movement, detail and sound. The ears on his horse twitched. Pip's mare stamped a foot, the sound strangely loud. The horses were listening to something. Brid had given a warning, he was certain, and he had never known her to be wrong.

"Goats!" she blurted and returned to her mumblings.

"Goats," Pip laughed. "It's nothing; she's only dreaming. Poor Brid!"

"Hush," Hal hissed as he stared beyond the lumpy boulders that rose above the wind-scoured heath. He had seen a shape.

The landscape was bleak, treeless. Heather in the purple of autumn clad the rocky ground, the only green in the crisp reeds growing in the hollows. He stared harder; yes, there was no mistake; a huge billy-goat. Brid surely could not have seen it yet she had known it was there.

It was at least the size of a horse with the most amazing curling horns, its neck thick as a tree-trunk and rippling with muscles to support the weight of its heavy head.

Feeling the strong desire to be alone, he left the camp and set off towards high ground to get a better view. After perhaps ten minutes he had climbed a small knoll and glared into the russet and purple landscape. The terrain was folded, hillocks and humps hiding boggy hollows. Beyond, rose pyramid-shaped peaks widely spaced on a level plain. He found the landscape curious, looking as if some giant had sliced off the summits from a range of mountains and replanted them here in the lowlands. He listened and, as the wind swung round into his face, he heard from their flanks the booming crash of great fighting rams peeling out from the peaks over the landscape.

But surely, the goats were no threat? Puzzling over Brid's warning he reminded himself that Ceolothian goats were remarkably big, with huge coiling horns that made them attractive to trophy hunters. Of course! Goats might not be a problem but goats meant hunters and that was a different matter.

He squinted into the landscape, scouring the foot of the nearest peak, searching for any movement. He had it now; a creeping dark shape amongst the heather! Once he had spotted that first hint of movement, it was easier to see the others.

At first, he was satisfied that the men were only hunters after the rams until he saw they were whooping and flapping their arms, herding the goats before them straight towards the camp. The goats were hidden from the camp by the terrain and they could not see the danger.

"Get Brid up on a horse!" he yelled wildly to Ceowulf but his voice was drowned in the thunder of hooves and the terrifying clatter of massive horns as the goats knocked against one another.

"No!" Hal yelled. "Get Brid clear!" With terrible fear in his heart, he ran down the slope, stumbled and rolled awkwardly onto his bruised arm. As he scrambled up the men were already on him.

They hauled their lean horses to a halt and looked down at him. Then all three snapped their heads up and stared beyond him as something of far greater importance caught their attention. Without a word, they turned and trotted away as if they had completed their allotted task and were no longer required.

Hal gave them no more thought. Relief flooded his veins;

Ceowulf was mounted, daggers of sunlight flashing off his polished armour. The goats had swerved away from the camp and, bleating wildly, were scattering back to the peaks.

Then a movement beyond his friend caught Hal's eye; he had been wrong. Riders were attacking from the rear. The stampede of goats had been a ploy to distract and split them. Breaking into a sprint, he shouted out in warning, "Look out behind you!"

Hal was still running when they finally heard the threat and turned to face it. Pip called out a brave challenge while Ceowulf was positioning his horse to defend the camp. Hal kept running, cursing himself for leaving Brid. He came too late. Already the riders had broached the hill and were nearly upon them. But they weren't riders. Hal knew them only from books: centaurs; half man, half horse. Shrieking savagely, the beasts were charging in to attack the huddled group.

"Hal, your sword," Ceowulf shouted, lobbing the weapon to him over the heads of the others, who ducked lest it fell short of its mark.

Sprinting beyond Brid and Cymbeline, Hal leapt into the air to grasp the hilt and, with the throb of battle humming in his ears, he sprang into action. Ceowulf veered out to the left and Pip to the right to allow room to swing their weapons.

An arrow whistled past his ear and speared the human breast of the first centaur that was roaring towards him. It stumbled to its knees and skidded on, thumping into him and knocking him down. He pushed himself upright off its flank, and still silently thanking Abelard for bringing another one down before it came too close, he raised his sword and slashed upwards into the hide of the next centaur. His blade cleaved upwards through the tough equine breast and on into the human belly.

Cymbeline's squeal of terror warned Hal of the threat to his rear. With a grunt of effort, he swung the heavy runesword, slicing clean off the forelegs of the centaur that reared before him. With blood spraying out, soaking his face and shoulders, he turned and ran to reach Brid.

A great sleek black centaur thundered directly towards her, the human body brandishing a club. Pip loosed an arrow and hit the creature in the shoulder. But the arrow didn't stop it and the next arrow only grazed its flank as it reared over Brid. Then, before Hal could reach her, Abelard flung himself over her quiet body.

The centaur crashed down. Hal heard the sickening sound of splintering bone and a truncated yell. He slashed at the centaur that again reared up over Brid and felt the runesword jar as it bit into the bone of the beast's shoulder. Its human half screamed and raised its weapon against him. The club grazed his forearm and, swinging away, he brought his sword round in a full circle that swept on through all four of the beast's equine legs.

The centaur squealed, its hindquarters giving way, but it still had strength in its human body and as it fell, it smashed the club down on Hal. The raised hand with which he tried to defend himself was slammed back awkwardly against his shoulder, but for the moment he felt no pain.

The ground shuddered as the beast crashed to the floor. Without moving from where he stood, Hal thrust the tip of his blade into the human breast of the centaur, a grimace of effort hardening his dark features. Tails high, the few remaining centaurs fled with the speed of Oriaxian purebreds.

Reality hit him hard. Brid! His limbs were trembling.

Ceowulf was already peeling back Abelard's cloak. "Oh Mercy," the weary knight murmured.

"Brid, Brid! Is she alive? Brid!" Hal moaned and stepped forward, his sword dropping from his hand, both arms hanging limply at his sides.

Ceowulf gently lifted Abelard from Brid. The archer's head swung freely, the back of his skull stove in where it had been smashed by the centaur's hoof. But the expression on the face was serene, content. Ceowulf's face was grim as he gently placed him on the ground and closed the archer's eyes.

Hal could do nothing but watch as the Caldean knelt over Brid, his brow knitted with tension. A sickening pain was swimming out from Hal's left hand. The urgency of battle had kept him from noticing it before, but now, the throb was so great that he felt confused and dizzy. He began to sway on his feet.

"It's all right," Ceowulf was telling him. "Abelard saved her."

The meaning of the Caldean knight's words washed over him and his trembling limbs began to shake. Ceowulf was looking at him with concern and someone else was supporting him about the waist. He was aware of little but the cold within his body for several hours after that. Sometimes he thought he was back entombed in the earth and reliving that moment when Ceowulf was about to hack off his arm to save him from gangrene.

"No, don't do it. I'd rather die," he moaned deliriously.

Someone, he thought it was Ceowulf, made him drink something. Poppy juice, he realized afterwards as he swam into a painless oblivion. It was days before he came round and, when he did, it was from a dream of Spar wandering midst a strange company of giants and nymphs with a baby cradled in his arms. Then a deeply sorrowful lament swept Caspar away, blowing him high into a storm-tossed cloud. Only the mournful song remained.

He shook himself from his ridiculous dream and blinked his eyes open. He couldn't see but he could smell something unpleasant. It was dark and it was a moment before he could focus on the blacker shapes in the night. His nerves jangled with an overwhelming sense of loss. A terrible pain stabbed up his left forearm.

Someone was singing, the voice beautiful, deep and melodious and now he realised it was the voice from his dream. Ceowulf was sitting cross-legged by the fire, singing into the flames a song of loss for Abelard.

Hal tried to sit up.

"Steady there, lad. Lie easy; there is no rush." The knight hurried to his side.

"Where's Brid?" Hal demanded.

"She still sleeps," Ceowulf hastily reassured him as Hal began to move but the pain in his left arm was so fierce that he slumped back. He was aware now that the evil stench about him was rising from his hand but he couldn't bring himself to look at it.

"Did I dream it or was Abelard killed?" he asked, choking on his words.

"He's dead," Ceowulf said heavily.

"I'm sorry," Hal mumbled. "He was a great man."

Ceowulf nodded and said hoarsely. "The finest."

"We owe him everything," Hal croaked, wondering what might have been if Abelard had been any less noble. "And all he ever knew of me was that I am a jealous, small-minded man, a danger to my friends and loved ones."

Ceowulf grunted. "Brid would be dead if it weren't for him."

Hal lay back in silence, thinking only that he was sorry that he had not won the man's friendship and wondering if Abelard's soul would ever know how grateful he was for his selfless act. His mind trudged through the gloom until, at last, the pain from his injury stung him from his misery.

He needed to occupy his mind, "Where are we? Is there anything I can do?" He could smell a fresh salty breeze that took away the smell from his hand and the air was damp about him.

"Nothing. Just lie still and rest. I've sent Pip to find a boat. We're on the west coast of Ceolothia on the peninsula of the Three Sisters."

"What! But I must have been out for days." Hal tried to roll onto his side to push himself up but the pain racked his whole body and he sagged back again.

"I wouldn't do that if I were you," Ceowulf gently advised. "I don't want you dropping back into the fever and, besides, it's good to hear your voice again, friend." He smiled. "I was getting lonely." He paused before saying more seriously, "Hal, there's a decision we must make. I've bathed your—"

Hal knew by Ceowulf's tone what he was going to say. Though he had not looked at his left hand he knew from the pain and the smell that all was not well. "No! I need my hand! You just mend it for me!" he exclaimed harshly, the terror of his nightmare under the wizards' spell rushing back to him. Groaning, he lay back and asked groggily, "Brid? Has she stirred at all?"

"No," the knight replied solemnly.

Hal nodded. "We must get her home." He looked down at his body and glared at the large bandage around his left hand. Already, an unhealthy yellowish ooze was seeping up to stain the fresh bandage. He raised his eyes to Ceowulf. "Tell me the worst."

"The centaur shattered the bones of your wrist; the shards of bone broke the skin. You've been running a fever and the area around the break is badly infected. The poison from your wrist is killing you. If Brid were able to help perhaps it would be different but already too much time has passed. I must—"

"No! I've told you, no! You leave my hand there. We'll get back to Keridwen soon enough. She'll see to the fever and put me back together good as new!"

He stared up into the heavens, his throat tightening in grief as he thought of Abelard. "I wish I could have proved to you that I am not a weak man," he murmured. Craning his head, he looked for Brid and made out her low shape wrapped warmly by the fire alongside the seated figure of Cymbeline whose golden hair was bright in the firelight. The princess discarded her plate of food and moodily rose to walk a little distance from the camp as if she wanted to be alone with her thoughts. Hal concentrated on Brid.

"Brid," he called out in hope, but still she would not stir. He jerked his head away. Though he longed so much just to touch her, he could not bear to look at her. The image of her with that half beast flooded his head. He cared that she was safe but for now, he could not face her. Groaning, he closed his eyes, aware that the ache in his arm had spread through his whole shoulder.

"Do you want more poppy juice?" Ceowulf asked, looking up from his hands. He was sitting cross-legged by the fire and was fumbling with something in his lap. "It'll stop you thinking clearly but it will ease the pain. Nothing else will really do that for you."

"I want to think for a bit," Hal said stiffly, trying to blot from his mind the fear that he would lose his hand and the horror of the image that would not leave his head. "What's in your hand?"

"Rubies," Ceowulf replied blithely. "Rubies and a ring."

Hal grunted in surprise. He didn't have much energy for talk.

"I went after the men who stampeded the goats."

"Did you find out what they hoped to . . ."

Ceowulf shook his head. "I killed them all. I could not help myself but I see that was foolish now."

"But understandable," Hal interrupted.

The knight shrugged. "I searched the bodies. I had a feeling something was wrong. It troubled me that anyone would want to attack us with no provocation like that." He tossed the ring up in the air and caught it again. "One at least was an Ovissian, it would seem." He studied the ring. "A ram wrestling a serpent. An Ovissian ring on his finger and his pockets full of sunburst rubies."

"Show me the ring," Hal demanded.

Ceowulf placed it into his right hand.

"It's not Baron Godafrid's crest but close enough to be a relative of his. They must fear our return, fear that when we bring the princess back, they will lose Torra Alta and all the wealth that is to be had in our mountains. The minute we get home, the Ovissians will be discredited."

"But how did they know we were there?" Ceowulf asked.

"The Ceolothian baron, Godafrid's cousin that Pip keeps telling us about," Hal suggested.

Ceowulf nodded and dropped the rubies back in his pocket and moved off to stand guard through the night. The pain swam back to Hal and he groaned through the long hours before morning, aware of the sense of Abelard still strong about them. Hal grew weary and the pain in his hand more acute. But worse was the pain of thinking about Brid, the horrible thought that he could never again look on her with passionate longing and yet was still captured by her love. And worse, she would never love him now, not when he had tried to kill her.

429

"Oh, Great Mother," he cried, "what should I do?" But there was no answer. All that was beautiful was now spoilt. "Ceowulf," he croaked. The knight was right away by his side, his broad shoulders blotting out the morning sun. "Ceowulf, I've changed my mind; I do need more of that poppy juice." He was quite happy not to live with his thought just yet.

As Ceowulf measured out a dose, Pip came running, over the rise. "You've already given the princess her breakfast, haven't you? Oh, Ceowulf, you said you wouldn't. You've ruined everything."

"What do you mean?" the knight asked half-laughing. "If you're determined to become her puppy dog there are still plenty of other chances to wait on her."

"I just want her to notice me, that's all."

"Oh, I see," Ceowulf mocked. "You want to be the Queen's Champion just so that I will be forced to bow at your feet."

"Quite so!" Pip laughed back.

Ceowulf's tone became suddenly serious. "Don't waste your time, lad. Rewik wouldn't allow a Torra Altan so important a position. Now tell me what news."

"Good news," Pip beamed. "There's a ship to Gorta on the morrow. A spice trader. You'll need to perfect your Ophidian accent a bit since, it seems, they're none too keen on Belbidians at the moment," he explained with a cheerful shrug. "They say it's a good wind that's blowing and that it'll be a fast passage home."

CHAPTER NINETEEN

The rain dripping from his nose, Caspar huddled down into his thick bearskin, and patted Isolde at his chest. She was contentedly asleep, oblivious to the storms blowing in off the Tethys Ocean that swept sheets of rain inland. Head low and mane and tail thrashed by the stinging wind, his horse laboured through the mud that sucked at its fetlocks, and he thumped his heels into its sides to keep the beast trudging forward.

He glanced back at the rest of the company. After leaving the purple mountains and hastening away from Negraferre, Izella had stealthily acquired mounts and an extra horse to carry the food and large quantities of water. It seemed she had little trouble moving amongst men without them ever knowing she was there. Pennard and Priddy, having less horsemanship than himself, fared badly in the heavy mud but Izen, marching on his own strong legs, was untroubled by the going. Trog bumbled alongside Pennard's sleek, long-legged hound but Izella was nowhere to be seen at present.

To give Caspar all the help she could, Old Woman Ash had instructed that Priddy, since she had bonded well with the child, as well as Izen and Izella should accompany him. Pennard had offered to join them as far as the Empress and Caspar was glad; he hadn't realized how much he had missed the companionship of another youth.

He was also particularly glad of Priddy's help with Isolde and he flashed her a bright smile. Rain dripping from her fringe, she just stared flatly back.

Caspar shrugged, thinking that he shouldn't have expected more. Though she was clearly Pennard's sister in looks, there was something very inhuman about her; even her captivating singing voice was not entirely human. But she adored Isolde and Caspar was relieved to share some of the responsibilities of child rearing with her. Though she was no more than eight, the women of Ash had allowed her many responsibilities and Caspar would have guessed by her behaviour that she was nearer thirteen.

She was delightfully pretty though thin and wary, her eyes overly large in that wide-mouthed face. She kept her own company most of the time but her eyes were often on her brother. Clearly, she was intrigued by her older sibling but also bore a look of deep resentment towards him and, as the days wore on, Caspar became more suspicious of her behaviour.

The rain was easing as they rode into the shelter of a beech wood where hogs snuffled noisily. Here, they chose to rest and Priddy eagerly set about feeding the baby.

"May I hold her now?" he asked after Priddy had fed and cleaned Isolde.

Reluctantly, she handed Isolde to him. Day after day, he and Priddy played out the same scenario until the fourth day. This time when he asked for the child, she looked him straight in the eye and said, "No!"

"What do you mean, no?" He laughed nervously.

"She's not your baby. She is one of Ash's people, not yours."

"Izen!" Caspar called to the warrior whose great strength gave huge comfort to the whole party. "Izen, explain to Priddy that Isolde is mine."

"Oh, all right," Priddy said begrudgingly and handed him the child who squealed with delight and hugged Caspar affectionately. His heart melted. They rode on and, cuddling Isolde, he searched the broken terrain ahead for Izella. Where was she? The woman kept disappearing and was more elusive than a wren.

"Izen, where's Izella?" he asked.

The warrior smiled congenially at him. "How would I know?"

"Don't make the mistake of thinking him stupid," Priddy told Caspar haughtily. "They are strong and aggressive but it doesn't make them stupid."

Izen looked at them both and grinned and Caspar found it hard to believe that this was the same aggressive creature he had seen ripping men limb from limb. He shuddered but couldn't help smiling as the big warrior picked a dark purple flower and sniffed at it. They had come fifty leagues north along the coast and, each day they had travelled, the brighter Izen had become.

"The air!" he exclaimed. "The air is fresh. I feel strong."

Izella suddenly appeared only a few yards in front of Caspar and he started. Judging by her expression, he guessed that she didn't seem to share the same sudden lightness of heart as her brother. "Our babies are ailing; Arthnau is desperately sick and, if he dies, Old Woman Willow will surely die too. We must hurry," she complained.

At last, the road led them back towards the coast. Beneath them the sea was black, tipped with white crests where the fresh wind skated across the surface. A headland broke the dark water and they could see the yellow sand above the light grey of the shallows. A scatter of islands crowded around the shore to the east and Caspar counted thirty ships tossing in the swell and noted that, as with the ships moored off Negraferre, they were remarkably broad across the beam. Huge white mountains floated to the north beyond. He frowned at these, not knowing what they were and thinking it wasn't cold enough for an island to be so smothered in snow, though there was a new crispness to the air.

He looked at Pennard. "So how do we find audience with this Empress?" Caspar had hoped to come up with a plan before they reached this point but he had not. There seemed no reason why the Empress would see them so he had to rely on Pennard's scheme.

"I had it all planned. I was going to take a ship straight to Oran from Negraferre but now we can ride to Ardenan at the end of the peninsula and take a ferry across the strait. Even in pup, I believe my dog speaks for herself and when the Empress hears word of her, she will want to see me. I shall ask if she would be interested in a kennel master."

Caspar doubted that Pennard's plan would work. The boy was an innocent with high ideals but no understanding of the real world.

The next day they reached a hill overlooking Ardenan and rested for a filling midday meal. While the humans dined on bread and fish-paste, readily available in this part of the world, Izen and Izella drank astonishing amounts of water and nibbled at the petals of the Tethys orchid. They had gathered armfuls of the flower before they left to sustain them on the journey.

After their meal, they made their way down into the town, the stone houses heavily shuttered against a fierce wind blowing off the sea. The people were small but friendly and the port was very busy, the roads in and out crammed with carts.

"The thing about war," Pennard said knowledgeably, "is that it makes for trade."

Caspar, for once, agreed with the youth.

With Izen and Izella heavily cloaked to disguise their strange faces, they approached the nearest ship moored against one of the deep-water piers, rolls of rope fending the wooden vessel from the stone jetty that was slippery with seaweed.

"To Oran?" Pennard asked.

"Where else?" The sailor nodded and Caspar sought within his pockets for his last few coins. He had set out with plenty of money and was horrified at how quickly it had vanished. Soon they were on board and settled in their quarters, which were nothing more than an area on deck with a canvas sheet above. Caspar was relieved though a little surprised that no one queried Izen and Izella's strange looks.

Every man aboard ship wore the black mail made along the coast and Caspar wondered how long it would take before word spread that the supply from Negraferre was ended.

But a darker pit of self-doubt twisted in Caspar's stomach. Should he really be taking Necrönd into the nest of the Empress, to a person who thirsted only for power? Yet, he had to do it. He had to get home and, if she were the only one who knew the way, that was what he must do.

The canvas awning provided little shelter and Caspar's face was blue and raw with cold by the time they had crossed the channel. Floes of ice knocked against the ship as they went and it was only then that he learnt that those snowy islands were vast chunks of ice broken from an icecap somewhere to the north.

After the grandeur of the Empress's fleet, he was disappointed when they reached her abode. He had expected a great castle but instead he saw only a long low, turfed mound that resembled a large barrow with low wooden doors set into its leeward end. Dressed in heavy bearskins, sentries stood guard, the muffled clank as they moved evidence of their armour beneath.

"The Empress, we desire an audience," Pennard blurted.

The guards looked at him and laughed and then scanned the others. Their eyes lingered on Izen and Izella but it was clearly Caspar who interested them most. Their eyes fell on him and a slow look of excitement flickered across their faces.

The most senior guard saluted. "Sir, we have been expecting you." He clicked his fingers at the other guards.

The double doors of the grassed mound swung open and a wall of heat burst over them and embraced them as they entered the building. Once within, they looked around at the interior of a dark timbered hall, shields hanging on the part-exposed wattle of the walls, bearskins covering the simple wooden furniture and trellis tables set in rows on the beaten earth floor. Looking up at the beams and struts of the roof, Caspar saw that the hall had been clad entirely in thick turf to provide the protection and insulation needed against the winds. This was not at all what Caspar had expected as the home of a great empress.

The woman herself was even more of a surprise. An old woman, wearing rustic clothes and with a bitter set to her down-turned mouth, was sitting on a wooden throne set on an elevated platform. She was observing them and he noted at once that she had an old scar on the left-hand side of her face that cut beneath her cheekbone, accentuating the contours of her weather worn face. In attendance were three even older women who stood at her side, their faces hideously scarred.

The Empress looked straight at Caspar. "So, you have come," she said in a commanding voice.

"I— Your royal . . ." he began, wondering how best to address this aged despot. She wore a plain wool tunic, her dark hair in two plaits with a silver circlet about her brow. Her hands were wrinkled and discoloured by age but they fiercely gripped a short dagger that rested in her lap.

"Bring food, drink," she ordered impatiently to the women beside her, who passed her orders on. "Come, my lord," she whispered. "We must make you and your friends comfortable. Baths? Fresh clothes?" she asked.

Despite the harsh lines around her mouth, Caspar considered that she was still beautiful and, though apparently well into her fifties, her body looked strong and firm. Beneath her rough tunic, she wore similar garments to her soldiers, being dressed in trousers, belts and boots.

"You and I must talk," she said invitingly. "I shall see that your servants are well attended to."

"Servants?" Pennard picked up on the remark. "No, no, my lady, I come in my own right. I have a fine dog."

"What do I want with a dog?"

"A war dog," he said brightly.

She looked at him with disdain and then laughed raucously, her courtiers following her example. "Dogs! What do I want with dogs when . . . ?" Her eyes fell avariciously on Caspar. Her scorn turned to a gentle and alluring smile and she swept forward. "So, this is the face of a warlord," she said. "You are not what I expected. A little young; a little small . . ." she shrugged. "No matter. Come, we shall dine."

Caspar was bewildered by her remarks as he was seated opposite the Empress in the hall that was rapidly filling with soldiers. But he was grateful of the food that consisted of fatty meat – good quality beef, he thought – ale and bread. What he did not like was the way the three hideously mutilated women in attendance at him stared with such clear horror.

"What are they looking at?" Caspar quietly asked his companions.

"Him," Priddy replied, nodding at his back.

"Him?"

"Your shadow," the girl said simply.

"What are you talking about?" Caspar demanded, disturbed by the girl's clarity of mind. He felt weak and his only desire was to get Isolde and Necrönd home to his mother.

"So, you need my army, warlord?" the Empress asked, waggling a part-chewed bone at him. She bowed her head towards the three mutilated women beside her. "They dreamed you would come and now you are here."

Caspar was about to ask her what she meant but she waved him down. "No, no, friend! I forget myself. Eat! Drink! You must feast first before we discuss our plans."

The noise in the hall grew as the Empress's men became rowdy with ale and Caspar, now fully replete, began to wonder how this strange woman could help him.

Izen on his left was growing impatient. "Spar, stop wasting time on this feasting. There's no time to be wasted," he hissed, his voice too low for the Empress to hear above the revelling.

"We must do this the right way. She is an Empress," Caspar warned though he was anxious that he did not overexcite the warrior of Ash.

Izella, on the far side of the warrior put her hand on Izen's arm. "My brother, be eased."

"Now, Spar, why don't you ask for passage? That's what we've come here for. We can pay." Izella insisted, putting her hand to her breast where she kept the purse the elders had given her.

"No," he said. "She is powerful; we must do things at the right and proper time. Now we must behave as befits guests. Only when the feasting is over is it proper to talk business." He smiled across at the woman, as he was acutely aware of her stare.

She rose and the hall immediately fell silent, such was her commanding presence. "Come, my lord, join me."

The Empress moved to a curtain that hung behind her throne and slipped behind it. Caspar handed Isolde to Priddy and followed the woman into a secluded chamber lined with furs, three couches set close to a crackling fire. The Empress sat stiffly on one of the fur-covered couches and nodded for Caspar to sit beside him. "Come, we shall talk in private," she murmured hoarsely.

Private didn't quite mean private. The three disfigured women followed. They were tall and strong but their mutilated faces made them disturbing to look at. All had their ears and the tips of their noses sliced off. Caspar found the situation awkward and looked anxiously at the dagger in her hands that she still toyed with.

"They came out of the west – barbarians," the Empress said in a low tone, staring at the dagger. "Driven by the winds across the great Tethys. It was thirty years ago now and we were no more than a nation of simple farmers."

Wondering what the Empress was talking about, Caspar looked more closely at the dagger. Vaalakan? Or Salisian perhaps.

"They killed my husband and butchered my son." She fell silent for a moment, the pain of her grief still strong, undimmed by the years. "This is the very dagger that killed them. I pulled it from my son's chest. He was only three but as brave as a wild ox. They raped me and left me for dead. For the rest of that year, they ravaged our lands until there was nothing left. And then they were gone. I gathered my people and raised an army, joining with those of the other lands that had been savaged. I needed men. We conquered kingdom after kingdom, principality after principality until I had an empire of men at my command."

She lowered her voice and admitted. "Cruel but necessary. I needed anything that would give me the edge and then, when I thought my army strong enough, we set after them. We heard the barbarians now looted the lands to the north and, just when we should have had them pinned against the ice caps, they vanished into the northern mists. Though we searched, we could not find them and were forced to retreat by the winter storms. Then last spring, one of my men returned, saying he had found a way that would lead us across the top of the world. Here was a way to reach the land to the west across the Tethys."

The Empress caught Caspar's stare that was flitting between the faces of the three crones. "They did that to them. These three women are from the very north of my great empire, the last people to be savaged by the barbarians from the west. Terrified by their power, they mutilated them."

"What power?" Caspar asked.

"Vision, foresight, call it what you wish. They see more than most. They saw you coming. They told me weeks ago that a great warlord was coming to lead my army."

Caspar laughed nervously. "I can lead no army. I merely came to see if I could beg passage through to the west. I have to get home and I learnt that you knew the way."

"Indeed, I do. But why should I help if you will not help me? After all, you did destroy my supplies of armour!"

She sidled closer to Caspar's couch and draped herself beside him. He had the horrible sensation that she was trying to seduce him. She was indeed beautiful, her body strong, but she was old enough to be his grandmother. And with those three strange women watching, his skin crept in revulsion.

She looked at him in disappointment. "One of my younger women perhaps," she suggested. "A great warlord such as yourself must have need of many women."

Caspar pushed her away, wondering what he must do. "All this army, this wealth, this empire of yours is only for revenge?"

She nodded her head. "Revenge! Of course, revenge. They took my son and my husband. I will see them suffer as I have suffered; it is all I live for." There was a terrible rage within her and Caspar shrank from it.

"I have no powers," he assured her.

"He lies," the woman with her eyes put out said matter-of-factly. "He throbs with power. It is all about him."

"You lie," the Empress repeated. "You will help me, of course. The ship builders of the north, the swordsmiths from the south, the sword masters of the west, all have aided me in my quest and now I have the most terrifying army that any person on earth has ever possessed. But, I hear, you have the ogres and I cannot get my army to the west without them; they are the last key. I must have them to get across the top of the world. The horses and mules die; they are not hardy enough. I need your ogres."

Caspar frowned. "I command no ogres."

"He lies. His shadow leads them. They destroyed the furnaces at Negraferre."

"My shadow?" Caspar asked uncertainly.

"Never mind," the Empress said. "I shall see that we talk more in the morning. You are tired." She snapped her fingers. "Bring the women. Let him have his selection."

A score of women paraded past him. Though dressed in delicate clothing, their hair smelling sweet as if freshly washed in lavender water, he found none appealing. He only wanted May back; he only wanted what he had never had; to lie in her embrace and feel her warm flesh on his.

"No, no, send them away," he begged. Though he was being treated like a king, he had no doubt that they were prisoners of this woman so obsessed with revenge. He asked to return to his friends but found that, when he joined them, they looked at him with distrust.

"What has she said?" Pennard asked. "Why have you been so long?"

"She can't get across to the west without help. She believes that I have the power to summon ogres that will help her draw her army across the ice."

"But you could!" Izella objected. "They came when . . ."

Caspar shook his head. "No, the power is way beyond me." He felt horribly uncomfortable and kept looking at his shadow, wondering what it was that these strange women saw in it. His head hurt so much that he could barely think and he longed to find a way home.

"They cannot get across what?" Priddy asked without taking her eyes from the baby still cradled in her arms.

Caspar lifted the child from her and Trog pressed close, wagging his tail. Isolde was now able to crawl and could stand up as long as she had something to grip hold of and Caspar found it quite comical the way she clung to Trog's back. The dog clearly adored her. "The top of the world. Apparently, the way to the west lies beyond ice-locked mountains."

"We have to do it." Izen looked at them all, his eyes suddenly darkening. "We need this trinoxia. I might be half the size of an ogre but the bear rages within me and

I am just as strong. I could go back for the rest of the warriors."

Caspar scratched his head. "I think, Izen, it would be well if we did not take the Empress across the top of the world. I set out to protect the world, not to bring a terrible war and destruction to the west. But what do we do?" he asked.

Pennard looked at him almost in disappointment. "I thought you were a great leader. A great leader does not ask."

Caspar sniffed. "I never said anything of the sort. But for your information, dog-breeder, all great men know how to listen."

"Humph," Pennard snorted. "Great leader!"

"What's it to you?"

"Nothing." Pennard shrugged. He then grinned. "It's just that great men usually pay better than vagabonds and sometimes more than an empress."

"Indeed!" Caspar laughed and turned his mind back to puzzling over their problem. This Empress was dangerous indeed and he could not risk leading her to his own continent. The combination of the Empress and Necrönd; the idea was unthinkable! Yet, they needed her ships and navigators to find the way.

"What if we go along with her to the point that she can go no further?" Izella suggested. "You will say that you'll summon the ogres when they are needed. That way she'll take us in her ships and show us the way but we shall go one alone. If ogres could get her whole army across then surely Izen could get just the few of us through. We shall simply leave her behind."

"You're all fools, the lot of you," Pennard interrupted. "It's obvious. We steal her best boat and go alone. We need to escape her now, not in some unknown frozen land beset with dangers."

Caspar laughed. "Steal a ship big enough to take us into the ice floe! Don't be absurd."

Izella, however, was not laughing but said thoughtfully, "I shall find out if it's possible. Sailors are more lonesome for female company than most." She slipped away, unseen, into the shadows.

Anxiously awaiting her return beside the heat of the great fire that blazed within the hall, Caspar eventually asked the question that was highest in his mind, "How will she find out?"

Izen laughed. "Men find the women of Ash irresistible. In fact, you are, as far as I am aware, the only one that has never succumbed when invited. They will tell her anything."

Some hours later, she returned, grinning. "Sailors! There's nothing like the hot blood of a lonesome sailor." She looked at Caspar and lifted one slender brow. "You don't know what you're missing. You must be a zealot to refuse me."

Caspar decided that Hal would have thought him an idiot. She was incredibly seductive, there was no doubt, but he felt an intense loyalty to May whom, he knew in his heart, he had never treated rightly. He would never get over that; she had died before he could make it up to her.

"Aren't you listening at all?" Priddy, as ever, was the one to point things out to him.

Never before had Caspar felt that he had so little impressed someone. She was a very aloof young girl with a well of inner reserve that he could only guess at. She also had a strange way of melting into the background until he could no longer see her and that made him uncomfortable. Trog was snuffling up to her and he wondered very briefly whether he wasn't bringing her home to Keridwen and Brid to be the new Maiden. There was that strangeness and strength about her after all. She looked back at him with that inscrutable expression that he found so disconcerting and a part of him hoped he was wrong.

"You're not listening," Izella repeated Priddy's words indignantly. "Now, my sailor is waiting for me – a red-haired pirate all the way from the north shore of the lands to our east. He and his crew are keen to escape the Empress's service. Seemingly, he has little love for her and is no more than a slave valued for his seamanship. He has only a handful of men and he assures me that I can rely on them. They are all slaves and all eager to escape the tyranny of the Empress."

"And I said you couldn't steal a ship. When do we sail?" Caspar asked enthusiastically.

"As soon as we can get to the ship."

"And how do we get out of here?" Caspar couldn't believe she had been so successful.

"Simple!" Izella smiled. "Priddy, Izen and I can walk past the guards without them ever noticing if we wish."

"Well, what about me and Pennard? Caspar asked.

"I'll distract them. Just stick as close as you can to Izen. He'll look after you while I see to the guards." Izella seemed to have everything planned.

"I must see to my goat and the horse," Caspar told the guard at the door. "And we need a little fresh air before we can sleep."

The guard looked towards the Empress who nodded and twitched her head at him, telling the guard to follow. Laughing and talking loudly, the company strode to the animal enclosure where they spent a little time milking the goat and then stood around one of the great bonfires that spat sparks high into the night air.

The dogs followed Priddy, who cradled Isolde. One minute they were sniffing around her heels and the next they were walking alone, sniffing at thin air. Even the goat, which Caspar had surreptitiously helped break out from the enclosure, trotted along behind, raising a few smiles and laughs from the Empress's men but no one troubled themselves with her. Caspar thought he saw Priddy as she crossed through a shaft of moonlight but it might only have been a drift of smoke from one of the beach fires. She was so silent and moved with such stillness that she simply vanished.

Izen explained, "The human eye, in fact the eye of any animal, is trained to catch movement and once you are wearing the right clothes and learn to move in the right way the eye is deceived."

Pennard snorted in disbelief. "Magic. You use magic. We have always known that."

"And what, Pennard, is magic?" Izen asked as his sister suddenly took form by a guard at the edge of the encampment, who rather than showing surprise smiled welcomingly at her approach.

"Well, I— I—" he stammered. Then he looked at Caspar and grinned. "That, fellow friend, is magic." Virtually salivating at the mouth, he watched Izella sidle up to the guard, her soft hands soothing his chest.

"Quick now!" Izen urged, shoving Caspar under his cloak. "I'll be back for you, Pennard."

Caspar had the curious sensation that he was floating; Izen was powerful but so fluid as he carried him. Unfortunately, however, it smelt strongly beneath his cloak. Caspar had no idea where he was until Izen slipped him out from under his coat and put him down onto wooden planking. He found himself in pitch-blackness, the smell of tarpaulin all about him, and deduced he was under some canvas shelter. Boards beneath his feet were stirring and he knew at once that he was aboard one of the Empress's ships that was wallowing in the shallow water.

He felt around him and found something to sit on. He could see nothing but he could hear Trog's snuffles and the occasional gurgle from his baby and he was happy that all was going well. It was several minutes before Izen returned with Pennard and then a longer time passed before he heard Izella.

"Quick now, away," they heard her voice order and then felt the ship stir beneath them.

Caspar gripped the bench and pressed up close to Priddy. "My baby," he demanded, wanting to be certain that she was well.

Priddy reluctantly handed her over. "You are not fit to care for her."

"I love her; she's my baby," Caspar hissed, biting back on his temper.

"Well, I love her too," Priddy snorted.

"Then perhaps you should be friends," Izen interrupted.

The warrior was remarkably tranquil and Caspar found it hard to believe that this same creature had hacked, cleaved and shredded men limb from limb with such ferocity.

"I wouldn't be friends with a man, not for anything," Priddy said indignantly. "All they have ever done is try to destroy my people."

Pennard looked at her with hurt. "Our mother grieved so much for your loss that she never cared about me but now I'm beginning to wish I'd never found you."

"You are not my brother. I am a daughter of Ash. I serve her and she needs our help."

"Isolde is human too," Caspar pointed out.

"Oh no. She, too, is a daughter of Ash."

Caspar looked to Izen for help and the big warrior looked kindly at Priddy. "She is still very young. I didn't realize that she didn't understand that she was human."

"I am not human," Priddy raged. "Vile creatures destroying the freshness of the air, making my mother sick with their furnaces only so that they can kill even more."

Pennard groaned and Izella patted her soothingly. "It's not in their hearts to be wicked, Priddy. It is merely their lack of understanding, their ignorance that makes them so."

Caspar was no longer listening. He was feeling horribly sick and his only focus was on getting out from underneath that canvas. Trog, too, was lying on the deck, moaning as the sea tossed and thrashed them.

Izella soothed his brow. "It is indeed more unpleasant than I might have thought."

Caspar tried to fill his mind with pleasant thoughts, of anything that would drive away the all-consuming sickness but his discomfort was only added to by the constant throb in his head growing more intense.

"Great leaders," Pennard teased, "don't get seasick."

Caspar groaned and crawled out into the salty air. The men of the crew seemed quite at ease, pulling on ropes and fastening halyards. One gave Caspar a ship's biscuit.

"It often helps just to eat a little," he said.

But Caspar crawled back under the canvas and lay there all night, clinging to the deck. Nothing made him feel any better until they had rounded the headland and the waves no longer buffeted them broadside.

By morning, the winds had eased and, though still fresh, they didn't toss the boat about quite so vigorously. Caspar was also eased by Izella's gentle touch, stroking the back of his neck. It took his mind off everything.

"Never before have I been refused by a man," she said in that soft voice of hers. "In fact, I've never heard of any woman of Ash being refused. Did you want to change your mind?"

Caspar shuddered with the thrill of her touch. "No," he said, wondering why he said it. May was dead; he couldn't possibly be expected to remain faithful to her ghost and he felt a hot passion for this creature that was so overwhelming it drove out all sensible thought. However, he found that strangely emasculating. She had too much power over him and he wanted to retain some of his dignity and mystique.

One of the crew was shouting from atop the mast where he was letting out furls in the sail. "Ships to the south!"

"She's after us!" another of the slave-crew cried.

Caspar and his companions crawled out from under the canvas to greet the sharpness of the day. The wind was brisk but running behind them now, which gave the boat less of a roll. Caspar staggered to find the ship's master, a red-haired man, who looked grim and was hectically shouting orders. The young Torra Altan looked ahead and saw that they were steering a tight course to a headland.

"Won't there be rocks?" he asked.

"Oh aye, there will but I want the fastest course. I for one am not going to be taken alive by the Empress. Do you know what she does to deserters?"

Caspar didn't but he could imagine.

"Once we make the ice-floe, we can slip out of sight more easily," the man said calmly though his knotted brow spoke loudly of his trepidation.

Caspar hung over the bow for the next two hours, occasionally raising his head to see if the great plain of white ice to the north had grown any closer. There was nothing he could do to help the progress of the ship as they weaved through the icebergs and so he spent his time in deep thought, watching the armour-clad bow slicing through the waves.

"I thought you said this was their best ship," he said to Izella as she joined him.

"I did indeed."

"Well, how come the Empress is gaining on us?" he complained.

She pouted, turned sharp on her heel and moved to attract the attention of the ship's master. She returned just a short while later looking anxious. "Apparently, he never said it was the fastest just the best, by which he meant it was best able to cut through the ice floes and was the sturdiest in rough conditions. Apparently, that means it's far from the fastest."

Caspar looked doubtfully at the four ships in their wake. "Will we make the ice-floes before they catch us?"

Izella shrugged.

Caspar bit his lip and watched.

The ship's master, a large man with thick skin that was a purplish hue from the stiff briny breeze, came and stood at his shoulder. "We have time now. You get some rest, lad. We might need you in the morning. They won't catch us until then and we might yet make the ice floes first. But if we don't, you'd best be ready with your bow. That great big, strange fellow there says you're very handy with the weapon."

Caspar nodded. It felt better knowing that he might be able to do something to help them. He took himself to bed under the canvas and strangely found it easier to sleep now what he knew he had a task to do.

He was awoken soon after dawn and quickly handed

the baby to Priddy who took her with that earnest expression of one devoted. Though Caspar did not particularly like Priddy, he was glad of her now as he knew that, if anything happened to him, she would do everything she could to look after his baby.

The Empress's ships were gaining fast. "What's happening?" he asked.

The ship's master pointed ahead to flat sheets of ice that formed a broken pattern over the dark waters. They were perhaps a mile distant.

"We'll make them at just about the same time as they catch us, so be ready," he said calmly.

Caspar nodded and took his post alongside Izen, Izella and those of the crew not needed to handle the ship. They stood at the stern, braced and ready.

"The master's just trying to raise our spirits," Izen said flatly. "We can see, plain as day, that we won't make it."

"It's there again!" Priddy pointed with her free arm out to sea, her other arm around Isolde who sat on her hip, pointing in mimicry.

"What is?" Caspar asked.

"Oh, you've been asleep!" she said scathingly. "I've seen something move in the water twice now."

Caspar braced himself. The Empress's ships were closing one from either side, landing planks raised and ready to crash onto their deck. With frustration, he noted that he had no good target as the decks were well shielded by a high bulwark. Izella nudged him. "Be sure to stand back from Izen."

Caspar looked towards the warrior, whose expression was glazed as the bloodlust flooded his body, preparing him for fight. And fight they would have to. There were no more than ten of them to defend themselves from four ships' companies.

Caspar could hear the shouts now. "Traitors! Deserters!"

"Priddy, hide!" he ordered urgently, focusing acutely on the nearest ship that was cutting in at an angle from his right. A hand moved to adjust a rope and he loosed his arrow. With satisfaction, he heard the yell of pain as his arrow speared the palm. Then he turned to the ship on his left and saw he had a good view of the man on the helm, a perfect target. He focused on him and was on the point of loosing his arrow when the first ship rammed them.

A great screech of timber rent the air as the ship lurched, sending them rolling to the ground. Hoots and yells rang through the air. Men hollered as they leapt aboard. Caspar staggered up and fired in fast succession but there were too many. He found himself being flung to the ground as Izen thumped him aside in his blind rage to attack the enemy.

Men were screaming with the lust of battle. Axes split timber, the decks reeled and it was hard to focus and get a grip but Caspar knew he must. He raised his arm, loosed one last arrow before he was forced to reach for his dagger and stab at the flesh of a man that fell on him. The face was pressed close up against his as he thrust, using all his strength to drive the dagger as he twisted his blade, weaving it in through the layers of the man's clothing, seeking a seam to pierce. Finally, he had it and, with a grunt of rage, stabbed his blade into the man's gut.

He spun round as great screams of horror filled the air. Men were in the water. One of the ships was on end, sinking fast, and another was rearing up above the waves. He saw the glint of a barbed tail above the waves. Sheets of water washed over the deck. Caspar stared stupidly for a moment but then came to his senses as he saw that Izen had seized the opportunity to throw the Empress's men overboard while the crew were uncoupling the ships, slashing through the lines that lashed them together.

They were free and, with great prepossession, the ship's master was steering straight for the ice floe. Within minutes, the sharp bow was cutting through the ice, the sound like tearing metal.

Caspar stared in horror at the sight behind him. The men in the water thrashed feebly and he knew that they would survive only the barest of minutes. Another ship was turned onto its beam and reared up into the water, driven by the monster. Then he saw it and gasped. "The dragon!"

."That's not a dragon." Izella was next to him while Izen was already dancing and whooping his victory chant.

"Oh, it is," Caspar said quietly. He had seen the white of its snout rising over the water, the bulging lumps of its blind eyes, the armoured crest along its back and the great teeth.

"Dragons are green; they fly not swim."

"It's a dragon," Caspar assured her. "It's my dragon," he added, wondering whether the ice floe would protect them from it. He saw it dive down into the water. Then the last ship rose up and came crashing down, a huge spray of water fanning out from its hull.

The screams were terrible mingled with the screech of tearing wood. Silence followed so swiftly. Then the monstrous albino head powered up above the waters and sang out a great roar, the sound full of despair.

"Doesn't this ship go any faster?" Caspar demanded.

He had his bow ready but was grateful when Izen stood beside him. The white monster heaved itself onto the ice, its withered wings still evident where once a magnificent spread of flesh and muscle would have borne it into the air.

"Dragon!" Izen roared. "I have no fear of you. Come, meet your death."

"Izen!" Izella begged. "It's far bigger than the griffins of our continent."

The warrior of Ash ignored her. As the dragon gave out a great thunderous bellow, he returned the scream.

"Izen, stop, stop!" Caspar begged, suddenly knowing why the dragon pursued them. "I have it!" he cried out in Belbidian. Reaching in his pocket for the moonstone, he held it aloft and it glowed brightly in the dull light of the far north, like a miniature star caught in his hand.

"A slice of magic!" Pennard gasped.

Caspar looked at it, anticipating a shock of blinding energy that would allow his mind to travel through the channels of energy but instead he felt only a dull ache and a heaviness to his brain. The sense of the air thickening to a solid mass around him was overwhelmingly oppressive. For the briefest moment, he caught a glimpse of Perren's stony face. Of course! Perren had been tampering with the channels of magic when the moonstone was formed; it was Perren's image trapped within it.

He stared into the orb for a long moment, caught up in the nightmare of its magic, the sounds all around suddenly distant and faded. Then the shriek of the dragon pierced the moment.

CHAPTER TWENTY

Hal awoke with the echo of a scream from his dreams ringing in his ears. Dread swept through him and he dared not look down at his body. With his eyes screwed closed, he lay back on his pillow and concentrated on the smell of the sea and the sound of flapping sails and snapping rigging intermingled with the cry of seagulls that filled the air, anything to distract him from the truth.

But he could not delay forever and would soon have to face his fear. Lying in a cot that rocked to the swell of the sea, he clenched his jaw, trying to summon the strength of mind.

Finally, he forced himself to raise his left arm. He looked at it for a long minute, his mouth clenched tight, before yelling, "Ceowulf, I'll kill you! I'll bloody kill you! Ceowulf, you butcher!"

The knight appeared as a big black silhouette in the doorway of the cabin. Hal tried to spring at him in rage but his legs were weak and he took two paces before stumbling and collapsing into a heap on the rough, boarded floor.

"How could you? I told you not to. My hand!"

"I'm sorry, friend, but I had to. The putrid flesh was eating up your arm. Better to lose the hand rather than your life."

"But my hand!" Hal wailed. "I'll kill you."

Ceowulf smiled weakly at him, helped him back into the cot and left him to calm down on his own. After some while, Hal reflected that the pain had eased and the fever was gone and that it was better to be alive.

Ceowulf seemed to avoid him after that and it was mainly Cymbeline who came to tend him during the voyage. He had thought her mind half lost to fear over these last months but now there was a keen edge to her behaviour.

"How are you?" she asked, pressing a cool palm across his brow and feeling for his fever.

"Not so bad," he grinned. "And better for seeing you." It pleased him that Cymbeline found him no less attractive now that he had lost his hand. He was reconciled to the fact now, having satisfied himself that there were some things he didn't need two hands for. He eyed Cymbeline's curvaceous figure, glad that he was feeling very much stronger.

She brought him cool ale and thin slices of bread with Nattardan cheese that they had acquired just before setting sail – a sure sign that they were nearing civilization.

"When we reach Gorta, you and I could take another ship." She smiled and he smiled back, wondering how he had managed to forget her strong beauty. "You don't seem so taken with your lady anymore," she remarked. "And I remember, you had a certain fascination for me before," she added coquettishly, smoothing her dress over her knees.

"And you rather enjoyed that?" he teased, trying to ignore his strong sense of guilt produced by Brid's presence so close at hand. He loved Brid to the bottom of his heart but could he really spend his life with her now?

He ground his teeth, the jealousy eating him up from within, and squeezed his eyes up tight, trying to fight from his mind the image of Harle's grimace of pleasure as he mounted her. He blinked them open to see Cymbeline's creamy white face, brightened with just a hint of rouge, smiling sweetly at him. She never let her appearance drop for one moment despite her lack of retainers.

She crossed the cabin and closed the door. "We shall reach Gorta by morning. You and I don't have to go to Belbidia. Ophidia is lovely, I'm told. You don't want to leave me with Rewik, do you?"

He smiled at her. "I have a war to stop."

"Renaud will stop it. He'll know what has happened and my father will know my writing and my seal," she said persuasively, pushing close to plump his pillow.

Her hair was freshly washed in lavender water and her breath was sweet. She remained close and, helping him to sit, offered to massage his shoulder to ease some of the cramping pains caused by the bruising.

Her fingers gently kneaded his broad shoulders and her cheek brushed the back of his neck. "Hal, we've got just one night before Gorta. I have money of my own. We don't have to go on to Belbidia," she repeated.

He smiled weakly. The only thing that was worse than the pain in his maimed limb was the raw stabbing pain to his heart every time he thought of Brid. Perhaps, just perhaps if he lay with Cymbeline and felt the hot flesh of another female against him, it might lessen his jealous rage. If he wronged Brid in that way perhaps, it would bring back some equality into their relationship.

Cymbeline's gown was cut low. He stared at her bosom that was somewhat larger than Brid's and rose and fell level with his eyes as she leant over him to gently anoint his shoulder. Yes, it would feel better, he told himself and then, looking up, gave the princess a half smile, his eyes glinting wickedly in that way he had learnt that women found so irresistible. Everyone branded him as a philanderer though, in truth, apart from his trips to the knight's school in Caldea, he had kept himself to himself – a particularly hard task since Brid refused to lie with him.

And she had refused him often with protests that, oh no, she was the Maiden; it was her duty to remain a virgin until the moment she took on the office of the Mother. He had thought that would happen with Morrigwen's death but no, she said it would only happen when the new Maiden was found. But after all that, she had given herself to Harle! Moreover, she had told him that it was to save him. Save him! It had ruined him!

"Hal?" Cymbeline said softly.

"Yeah?"

She didn't reply but looked into his eyes.

Hal sensed he was on safe ground. "Are you trying to seduce me?" he teased.

"Oh yes, Hal, I am!" Her answer was beautifully wicked. She slid her dress from her shoulder, revealing the silk shift underneath. She disrobed with such ease and pressed herself to him with such confidence, and obvious knowledge of how to please that Hal had the uncomfortable sense that she had done this many times before. But a princess, a bride for a king? It was impossible. Revelling in the sight of her fulsome figure, he could not quite dispel the vague sense of unease.

Rebuking himself, he concentrated harder. Indeed, she was very beautiful. The Ceolothian women were strong, goddess-like in their stature, and she was no exception. Moreover, she was a princess, a young, glorious princess promising him sensual pleasure and wealth. For the moment, all thoughts of duty and responsibility were lost. Cymbeline was right; Renaud would sort everything out.

The princess pushed herself forward, her lips brushing against his neck. "Take me with you."

Hal slowly moved his one hand forward and stroked around her firm slender waist. He felt her shudder and then, trembling, she grasped his hand and slid it up towards her breasts that were large and soft and heavy. Hal could only think that they were not like Brid's. He was attracted to Cymbeline, naturally – any man would be – but he couldn't stop the image flashing through his mind of how he had plunged his sword into Brid.

He wanted to be rid of the image and get even with Brid by savagely possessing Cymbeline but, instead, it felt as if she possessed him. Roughly, he pushed her off. "Leave me be!" he growled, suddenly ashamed.

"But Hal," she sobbed, "you can't let me go to Rewik."

"I can and I'll make sure you get there," he said harshly. "My brother needs you." He pushed her aside and, cradling his arm, stepped out into the crisp air of morning, watching for Gorta's coastline.

She followed him, staring forlornly at his back but he would not acknowledge her.

Pip gave him a dark look and hastened to the princess's side, offering to fetch her breakfast and a cloak to guard against the cold. She flicked him aside as if he were a troublesome fly.

When, finally, they moored at Gorta and disembarked, Hal faced up to Ceowulf and gave him an open and apologetic smile. "Ceowulf, I wronged you. I'm sorry."

The big knight slapped him on the back. "I can't say I blame you," he said, hastily brushing aside the awkward situation. "Come, let's see if we can get news of home and a ship to take us there. We heard rumours of war as we left Ceolothia."

The Gortan port was thick with gossip of a Ceolothian

armada at anchor off the western coast of Belbidia; but they could learn little more other than that the country was still open to trade. Hal ruefully thought that even if the entire country was ravaged by war, the Belbidian merchants would still find a means to trade.

It took them little time to find a small vessel with a cargo of oysters that was headed for Belbidia and the winds were favourable. Hal stared westward most of the voyage. There was no exact moment when he was certain he had seen land; there was just a general awareness that out of the grey haze came the harder shades of land. The dun outline became green hills rolling down to a misty sea and soon the ship was cutting through choppy waters and heading for the deep estuary that snaked inland towards the heartland of Belbidia.

Hal hung over the bow. Home! Belbidia, he thought, his mind lifting with joy. Running his fingers through his long black hair, he thought to make himself more presentable.

After working his way back to the pilothouse, he took his razor and shaved the stubble from his chin – a more difficult task than he might have imagined with only one hand. Then he looked in on Brid, whom they had placed in the hold below. Ceowulf stood up from his place of vigil and beckoned him closer. Hal looked down on her sadly. So small, so beautiful, so perfectly formed, nestled like a sleeping child in rugs of bearskins. Still, she slept, kept drugged by Ceowulf's poppy juice to numb her pain. Hal sat awkwardly beside her, not knowing how to live with his emotions.

"Oh Brid, my love," he murmured, tears welling into his eyes. He looked at her now, remembering how it been during that summer they had first shared in Torra Alta. That was when he had first been certain that she loved him and not Spar. Brid was too wise, too aware for his inexperienced nephew, and Brid had clearly been fascinated by his own more daring manner. He stroked her hair back from her elfin face. "Oh, my sweet true love," he murmured, not allowing himself to think but just wallowing in her close presence.

Then she blinked, her face puckering into a frown. "Where . . . ? What . . . ?" She stirred restlessly.

Hastily, Hal stumbled onto his feet. "Ceowulf," he grunted anxiously, "she's waking."

"You should nurse her yourself," the knight said gently. He was crumbling some oat biscuits into a bowl of warmed milk.

"Hal, Hal!" Brid whimpered, crying out deliriously.

"Hush." Ceowulf said, putting his thick arms about her. "Hush, sweet lady, Hal is here. Now you must eat." He trickled some of the gruel into the corner of her mouth.

Hal could not bear to be near her as pain twisted her face. He had caused that pain and there was nothing he could do to undo it. It brought the entire vile episode flooding back to him; he felt used and wronged and guilty, and scuttled away to look blankly over the gunwale.

The shoreline was now suddenly close. Quertos' major eastern port of Appledore was now bright on the shoreline, white houses jostling for position on the quay-front, others pressing down from higher on the hillside behind. He growled at the big Ceolothian traders that lay at anchor in deep water, surprised that no Belbidian vessel paid them any heed. He presumed this must be at King Rewik's orders and concluded that Rewik was still negotiating with King Dagonet. Then he looked at the shore and frowned. Smoke was rising from the town though he could hear no alarm bells clanging.

He stood tall, straining to see more detail. It was a large

fire. He had been to Appledore before and surely, the fire came from the square.

His heart plummeted. They had been abroad well over a year. Much might have happened. Perhaps to appease King Dagonet, Rewik had returned to the ways of the New Faith and begun the burnings again?

Renaud was beside him. "Smoke! The devil is rising from the ground."

Hal looked at him sadly but could offer him no comfort. The experiences with the wizards had savaged his mind. He edged away towards Cymbeline. She was radiant, not a flaw on her powdered white face, her hands gloved, her dress stiff and crisp, rustling as she moved.

"Hal," she put a hand on his. She was trembling slightly. "We should have taken another ship to Ophidia, you and I. Think of it! I have money of my own. We would be rich, you and I!"

Hal smiled at her weakly. "Oh Cymbeline, if only I could. But you would not want me for long. Too soon you would discover me bitter and cruel."

He could say no more because already Ceowulf was hastening to stand between the couple. Cymbeline withdrew, evidently displeased that her association with Hal was so actively discouraged by the knight.

"You shouldn't be on your feet," Ceowulf said blandly to Hal. "You still need to rest."

"I'm strong enough," Hal growled.

"Indeed, my friend. But not strong enough of mind, it seems, to see the truth of the situation. You must not blame Brid."

Hal's defences crumbled. "I don't but, Ceowulf, I tried to kill her! You know I love her more than life; she is the world to me, yet now, just to look at her, makes me ill."

Ceowulf placed his hand on Hal's shoulder. "Do you

love Torra Alta just as much though her tower was crumbled and her battlements were shattered by the Vaalakans? Remember you love Brid for her soul and her soul is without blemish. Besides it was Morrigwen that used her body not Brid."

"I know," Hal admitted. "You keep telling me that, but her body is mine! And now it has been violated."

"That's a lot of self-conceited, weak-minded foolishness," Ceowulf grunted. "You're just making yourself miserable for no good reason."

"How would you like it if it had been Cybillia? You don't understand," Hal retorted but immediately regretted his words as he read the expression of hurt on his friend's face.

"Don't I? You forget what the Vaalakans did to her," the knight said coldly.

Rebuked, Hal muttered his apologies but still could not make himself feel better about what had passed.

"You don't know how lucky you are to have her love," Ceowulf chided him.

They fell silent as they drew into the port. Ceowulf ran to the bow and strained forward. The ship bumped alongside the quay and Ceowulf leapt for the shore. Self-consciously cradling his stump, Hal leapt after him, hurrying inland to find officials to help them while Pip stayed to guard the Princess, Renaud and Brid.

The harbour was deserted and further into the town everyone was hurrying towards the square. Following in their wake, Hal staggered in his stride at the sight before him. Bonfires were built high. In the centre of each fire stood a stake and on each stake hung a body.

But they were bears! The people were burning bears as if they were witches! He knew at once they were Torra Altan brown bears. He looked in horror about the square where their withered and charred heads were impaled, rows of claws, dangling like buntings, strung between the gaily painted houses.

"Oh Mother, oh Great Mother, mercy!" Hal had no explanation as to why the Torra Altan brown bears were here or being murdered but he understood at once the implications. The Torra Altan brown bear was not a plentiful species like deer. They did not have the ability to reproduce at any great rate to replenish their numbers and here were hundreds of them dead and slaughtered, the people about triumphant as if burning an enemy.

True, Torra Altans wore bearskins but, they killed only the weak and those beyond the age of reproduction and each skin would last three maybe four generations. The more worn and tattered, the better loved the garment. Torra Altans were mountain people; their lot had always been to pit themselves against the elements and they abhorred wastage and extravagance. Hal looked about in rage to see whom he might blame, his hand already on his hilt.

Ceowulf steadied his arm. "We need to go directly to the King. No good getting entangled with skirmishes when we have a war to fight."

Hal nodded, conceding to the knight's argument. He looked around for someone of importance and saw that, with the town gathered for the spectacle, that wasn't going to be hard. Soldiers in Quertan livery stoked up the fires and one in an ivory and black tunic with shoulder brocades was doing a lot of shouting and seemed to be in charge.

Covering his mouth and nose against the sickening stench from the fires, Hal approached him. "The shire's reeve," he demanded. "I've just landed and have news of great import for the King. I must speak to the reeve; we need an escort to provide swift passage to Farona."

The man frowned at him uncertainly. "And who might you be?"

Hal hastily assessed his surroundings and some instinct warned him against declaring his identity. There were priests everywhere, exorcising what they saw as the devil in these bears. The man was eyeing his bearskin suspiciously.

"You know there's a law that all these beasts must be burnt and that don't permit you to kill them yourself and skin 'em," he threatened. "They have the pagan devil in them, these bears, seeing how they come from the traitor's barony."

Hal's fist and chest muscles stiffened; no doubt, the pulse in his neck was throbbing furiously but he managed to keep his expression calmly enigmatic. He didn't know what was going on but he didn't like the sound of it.

Ceowulf caught his eye and jerked his head in the direction of the edge of town. Hal struggled through the crowd to follow him. The crowd parted for Ceowulf in his red and white checked surcoat but not so for Hal who fingered his torn hauberk and decided he looked no more than a yeoman.

Finally, he caught him up in a quiet street at the edge of Appledore. "I don't think we'll get much help from the authorities here," the knight advised.

Hal nodded and they spent some while exploring the countryside at the edge of the port until they found a forge on the main road to Farona. Both immediately spotted the cart round the back and the nodding head of a long-eared carthorse quietly grazing in a nearby meadow, the grass worn thin by over-grazing.

Ceowulf chinked his purse. "Let's see if the blacksmith will give us a ride into Farona."

The blacksmith was unwilling. "Them Ceolothians are all over the capital. They just marched through Quertos and they say they're camped all over the wheat fields of the mid-shires."

"We just want the cart," Hal said, annoyed that the man kept staring at his stump.

"You can't have it; I need it," he grunted back.

His wife bustled in and whispered loudly in his ear and the man nodded in accordance. "Matt!" he yelled. "Here, Matt, I've an errand for you."

A young lad of fourteen or thereabouts appeared smartly at the front of the forge. "You're to take these fine gentlemen to Farona. Get the old nag harnessed."

"But, Pa, the reeve said that all able-bodied youths were to enlist for bear patrol."

His father nodded. "Aye lad, but if you ain't here, he won't be able to make you. Your ma thinks you're a mite too young to be eaten by a bear. And I agree with her for once. Now get along." The smith held his hand out for Ceowulf's money. "This way I get my horse back and keep my lad out of trouble – for a while at least." He never looked at the coins but hastily thrust them into a pouch at his belt as if they might simply disappear if he didn't get them pocketed fast enough.

Within an hour, Hal and Ceowulf were back on the quayside, helping the others into the cart. Ceowulf carried Brid, who was asleep wrapped in her bearskin, and laid her on the flat bed of the cart. Hal wanted so much to kiss that innocent face but could not bring himself to do so. With difficulty, he swung himself up onto the bench at the front of the cart to sit beside Ceowulf and the blacksmith's boy, Matt. The horse pulled well and they were soon out of the port and inland on a dusty road that was remarkably free of other travellers.

"It's the war!" Matt explained.

Hal nodded, prompting the boy to say more. "We have been far from civilization and only heard rumours."

"Torra Alta fell. Pa said right from the first that a barony of sheep farmers would never hold the castle and he was right. The Ceolothian army barely paused in its march south."

"And the Ceolothian traders in the port?" Hal asked, swallowing his dismay at the news.

Matt nodded. "Oh aye, they brought more troops soon after that. They landed at three ports along the coast but we could do nothing about it. My brother was called up to help the bear patrol. He lost his arm. Is that what happened to you?"

Hal shook his head.

Matt continued. "They say the Ceolothians have control of the capital and could claim what's left of Belbidia within weeks but Dagonet has merely forced King Rewik to disband his army. Pa says King Dagonet's still waiting for King Rewik to return his daughter."

Hal nodded thoughtfully and shifted on the bench to ease the discomfort of the jolting ride. The road cut straight through the Faronan plain and he surveyed the vast open fields. A ragged forest of weeds grew where once yellow seas of wheat had rippled in the breeze for as far as the eye could see.

Within three days, they reached the outskirts of Farona and Hal looked in horror at the forest of tents surrounding the capital. The Ceolothian army was vast and hung like a noose about Rewik's capital. To the north and west, Ceolothian flags fluttered above the pitched canvas and even within the city itself he could see the bear standard of Ceolothia dancing in the Belbidian breeze. Ceolothian guards manned the city gates and, as Ceowulf steered the cart straight for the south gate, soldiers rode out at their approach.

"Friends," Hal spoke loudly in Ceolothian. "I bring news for King Dagonet."

The soldiers were uneasy but allowed them past and followed as they rolled on through the broken gates. The city was a shambles; debris littered the streets, mangy dogs slunk up and down the steaming gutters and Ceolothian soldiers stood on every corner. The faces of the Faronans peering out of their doors were dark, sour and haunted by fear. They halted in a wide square near the palace that was dominated by a red and white striped tent. Judging by the way Ceolothian troops streamed to and from its entrance, like worker bees buzzing to and from the hive, Hal concluded that the tent was where he should find King Dagonet.

As the cart rolled to a halt, a hush settled over the square. Then came a murmur as Hal took Renaud's hand and helped him down. The Faronans recognized him at once and the Ceolothians understood their excitement. Then it was the Ceolothians' turn to gasp. Cymbeline lifted her head and boldly stood tall so that all might see her.

Hal found the knot of adrenaline tight in his stomach. He took a deep breath. "I have the princess. King Dagonet's daughter is free!" he cried. "Friends! Ceolothians! Take me to your king. Summon King Rewik," he shouted to the Belbidians. "Hal of Torra Alta has returned. I bring with me Princess Cymbeline."

Clarions blasted all around him. Troops were scurrying in all directions. He stood waiting and watching until the excited clamour steadied before him and Rewik appeared on the southern arch that led into the lesser chambers of his palace. King Dagonet emerged from his grand tent just as Ceowulf lifted Princess Cymbeline down from the cart.

There must have been two thousand men in that square, Belbidian and Ceolothian alike, and they all fell silent. Hal was weak with relief. He was home; all this suffering would soon be over.

He offered his hand to help the princess forward but she pushed him away disdainfully.

"I can manage," she said and began to walk stiffly towards her father. She approached with dignity but the Ceolothian king did not possess the same self-control. A big man, the movement ungainly, he ran towards her.

"Cymbeline, is that you? Is that really you? It can't be you. My own daughter, my greatest love!" he blabbered in Ceolothian.

She smiled almost patronisingly and Hal shuddered at her control over her emotions. Looking towards Rewik, he took Renaud by the hand and marched on his own sovereign.

"Rewik," Hal said curtly without regard for rank, "I have rescued your brother and bride from the clutches of the Ovissians."

Rewik's mouth was opening and closing. He looked stupidly at Renaud. "Brother, what madness is this? Is that girl Cymbeline?"

"Yes, it's Cymbeline. Of course it's Cymbeline," Renaud replied dismissively. "Aren't the roses fine this time of year? You've let them overgrow a little."

"Renaud, what are you blathering about?" Rewik looked uncertainly at his brother, his heart visibly pounding, his breath quick and sharp.

"I was wrong," Hal said slowly, finding it hard to talk civilly to this man who had imprisoned him and still held his brother. "I was very wrong. It wasn't Renaud masterminding the scheme to kidnap Cymbeline. It was the Ovissian, Tupwell."

"Tupwell! Godafrid's son!" Rewik stammered. "But I've given Branwolf's lands to Godafrid."

"And Branwolf?" Hal said slowly. It was the only thought on his mind.

"Yes, yes Branwolf. I shall see to him at once," Rewik said vaguely, his eyes seeking Dagonet who was fervently clutching Cymbeline's hand.

The Ceolothian King caught his gaze and came striding over to Rewik. "Son," he embraced him, "my daughter is safe; all is forgiven."

Hal smiled briefly at this, still not yet ready to celebrate. He barged between them. "Rewik! My brother! Where is my brother?"

The King smiled apologetically. "Indeed! Men see to it that Baron Branwolf is made aware of the happy situation so that he might refresh himself and prepare for the feasting."

Without thought for rank, Hal took Rewik by the shoulder and jerked him round. "You'll take me to see Branwolf yourself and right away."

Rewik nodded quietly. "As you wish."

Hal's stomach knotted as the King led down into the bowels of Farona. He would never forget what Rewik had done to him and he felt weak at the thought. They descended below the main dungeon and then along an unlit tunnel. It was cool so deep below ground, the stones of the floor so ancient that a depression several inches deep was worn into the rock by the passage of feet. It smelt dank. A small low door banded with steel blocked the way ahead.

"Gaoler, the keys!" Rewik ordered.

Once the heavy door swung silently outward, Hal pushed past Rewik and stared into the grim dark. Two figures lay huddled together on the floor. One, a man, coughed repeatedly, his long hair and beard hiding his features. A thin woman cradled his head in her lap, her bare arms blistered and red with sceptic weals. She didn't look up when they approached but kept on gazing down at the man.

"Hush, Hal, don't wake him too suddenly," she said.

Hal didn't wonder that Keridwen knew it was him. He nodded, his eyes willing Branwolf strength.

"He was tired and only just fell asleep. He'll be pleased to see you." She soothed her husband's brow until he began to stir and then looked up and smiled at Hal. "I heard the fanfares. It is good to see you again, Hal." Her eyes briefly lingered on the stump of his left arm but she made no comment. "Hal, where is she?"

He stooped to put his good arm around his brother's waist, who was now blinking and staring at him. "Who?"

"Brid." Keridwen's voice trembled.

Hal shook his head. "She ails; an injury," he croaked.

"Stretchers for my dear cousin Branwolf," the King was shouting vigorously along the passageway. "Stretchers! Medics!"

"We need no medics," Keridwen said coldly.

Somehow, though her face was covered in sores and the sockets around her eyes were black, she had the strength to walk. Branwolf did not and soldiers eased him onto a stretcher. He was hot to the touch and delirious with fever. He was also half-starved, and Hal growled as he saw the marks of recent beatings on him. Trembling with anger and suddenly no longer able to keep up the pretence of tolerance towards Rewik, his hand went to the hilt of his sword.

Keridwen caught his arm, her movements still quick. Bright eyes still smiled out of that grubby and bruised face. "Haven't you already done enough with that sword? He is not worth it. He was just misinformed and was in

471

his own way trying to do the best for his country." She walked with dignity behind the procession as Branwolf was led up into the light, Hal grinding his teeth beside her.

"My chambers are yours," Rewik offered.

Keridwen shook her head. "When we first arrived, I saw at the back of the palace near the fruit trees a splendid grove of oak, ash and willow; we will be happy there. The air is warm. It is early autumn, I see." She smiled, blinking, her voice tired and slow, but she still had the stubborn courage to walk unassisted. Hal did not know how she managed it. Her feet were bare and the skin of her heels cut and shredded where it had been flailed. It made him forget the pain in his stump.

Keridwen had Branwolf laid down in the shade and gave him fresh water to drink. "All is well, Branwolf," she said in a silken whisper. "Hal is home with Cymbeline; it's over." She then rose and spoke directly to the sergeant-at-arms. "You will fetch me fresh sage and bloodwort," she commanded. "The herbs will work well in his sleep." She then turned to Hal. "Where is Brid?"

He pointed. Ceowulf was striding solemnly across the lawn with the limp body of Brid in his arms, her hair swishing back and forth against his thigh as he walked. Reverently, he laid the wounded woman at Keridwen's bare feet.

Keridwen flung herself down beside the younger priestess and cradled her head against her bosom. After a brief moment, she looked up darkly at Hal. "Explain."

"I can't," he replied stiffly.

Glumly, he looked down at Brid's body and then retreated, stepping back into the gathering crowd, numbly listening to the orders being shouted in both Ceolothian and Belbidian. The two kings were marching, arm in arm, about the tree-lined square to reinforce the message that all was now well between them. Hal joined their procession.

Cymbeline was present and fidgeting unhappily, awaiting the right moment to interrupt the two kings. "Father," she spoke in Ceolothian, her voice lowered, her face distressed.

Hal heard nothing more, though he saw Dagonet's shoulders droop, his hands fall loose in shock. "Turquin! Turquin!" he cried forlornly, punching his fist into the laden apple tree beside him. His knuckles came away bleeding. After a minute or so of this, King Dagonet retreated and sat gazing stupidly at the knife that had been pulled from his son's body. Trembling, he kept his arm tight about his daughter. "But this is Kulfrid's emblem."

Hal had too many of his own problems to care.

Messengers were rushing in and out all that day though Hal hardly noticed as he brooded over Brid. His greatest relief was that her face had lost that contorted look of pain now that she was under Keridwen's care, though she showed no signs of recovery. She rolled and tossed and occasionally twisted over and vomited.

"Oh Brid!" Hal whimpered in despair and, unable to witness her pain any longer, he turned to his brother who at least looked better after a wash and a shave.

"How is he?" Hal asked as Keridwen stroked the Baron's brow.

"Hal? Hal, is that you?" the Baron blinked his eyes open and raised his arm weakly to grip his brother's hand.

Hal squeezed Branwolf's fingers, reassuring him of his love but could think of nothing to say.

"He's a strong man but he's endured too much," Keridwen said quietly. "They starved us and poisoned him with drugs to try and make us tell him where Cymbeline was hidden."

"You are strong, Keridwen," Hal said. "Strong when all the rest of us are weak. I tried to kill her . . ."

"Yes," Keridwen said gently, without judging him. "But there is something you should know."

He looked at her, the tone of her voice making him certain that he did not want to hear what she had to say.

CHAPTER TWENTY-ONE

Brid rolled over, retched and curled up again around the pain, trying to suppress it; but it was too strong for her. Arching her back away from it, her fists tight, she writhed and screamed. It was as if a jagged blade was within her breast, stabbing and shredding at her heart. Sobbing into her fists, she prayed for mercy and release from the torment.

At last, the blessed sleep swept over her as the poppy juice drew her back into the dark world of nightmares. Sneering faces leered and they reached out to claw at her. "You are the last of your kind, the very last priestess and soon you, too, shall die."

Her own screams shook her from her sleep. Was there no end to her agony? At times she could hear and see blurrily and at others, she was lost to the stretched and shifting world of pain. The divide between the real world and dream-filled sleep was slight. Once she thought she saw Hal but she was unsure; Hal would have given her comfort but the dark face that had stared down at her had recoiled in disgust.

"Hal," she moaned. "Hal, help me," she muttered and fell back into the blankness of her stupor.

She had no idea how much more time had passed but when she next awoke, she knew something was different. It was still too much effort to open her eyes but the pain was not so sharp and had become more of an all-enveloping throb. The sickness swelled up again and she felt clammy and green but it was better than the pain. Something had eased. Wake up, she willed herself. Open your eyes. Open them! But she could not.

"Is she dead?" someone asked.

No, no, she wanted to scream. *I live*.

"Brid, Brid my sweet," a familiar, dulcet voice breathed warmly onto her face.

Keridwen! It was Keridwen! The relief flooded through Brid. She wanted to cry but could not even do that. Someone stroked her brow though her senses were still so dull that the touch felt as if she was being brushed with cloud.

"We must stop the poppy juice," Keridwen said dolefully. "She will not live if she has any more; she needs strength to fight this wound. And even then . . ." Keridwen paused before continuing in a voice laden with sadness. "The Trinity is broken and without the united powers of the Three, I do not have the skill to heal her."

The emptiness came again, its darkness intensifying into a black swirling world where monsters lurked behind vast trees even blacker than the huge stirring void beyond. Then, from that unattached gloom, there came singing, beautiful and lulling, calling her to peace.

A glistening point of light appeared in the middle of her dark world. It grew and stretched out to become a path of mercury drawing her through the black of the forest, a way out, a way home. Happiness lay beyond. Wolves howled around her. She knew she was in the ether of the spirit world but had no strength of will to do more than observe.

Hazily, she saw beautiful golden-haired people singing and laughing. They had a creamy white horse waiting for her.

"Come, Brid, come. You have done more than could be expected of anyone. Take the horse; ride through Rye Errish. Pass quickly along the paths and we shall guide you to the Great Mother and the bliss of oneness. Hurry, Brid! She is awaiting you!" they coaxed.

Her mind began sliding down that path. After all. was there anything to live for? Hal hated her. The Trinity was lost. She felt weak and giddy.

"Child, your suffering had purpose!" a gentle voice called out of the darkness. "I am sorry, truly, but you will understand my reasons."

"Morrigwen?" Brid knew the voice even though she had never before heard it without the croaking, unsteadiness of old age.

Morrigwen's voice was firm yet kind. "You suffer; that is the lot of a high priestess. It is a burden but also a privilege. Ours is a position of sacrifice, not ease. Our lives are dedicated to the Mother. You suffer for Her. Embrace the pain."

"I am weak. I am but one," Brid protested.

"My sweet, I taught you to be strong," Morrigwen chided her gently.

"He does not love me."

"Self pity! You have no right to self pity." Suddenly the shimmering bright pathway of light welcoming Brid on to the afterlife was blocked. Morrigwen took her hands. Brid would not have recognized her. She was strong and upright, her hands straight and firm and her eyes bright. "Go home, Brid, and fight; they need you. We all suffer but if we survive, we shall be stronger so that none will ever vanquish us. Get up and fight. I did not raise you to give in just because of a little pain." Morrigwen squeezed her hands, willing her strength. "Old Willow Woman will not let you die. You must tell Keridwen to get you to Old Woman Willow."

"I haven't got the strength . . ."

Morrigwen drew her up and embraced her heartily. "Get home, Brid. We depend on you."

"Willow. Old Woman Willow," Brid mumbled in her stupor.

CHAPTER TWENTY-TWO

"She will live? You can help her?" Hal demanded urgently.

"I don't know." Keridwen admitted honestly. "I am but one and can no longer call on the power of the Trinity. I've done all that I can yet she is slipping away from us. All I can do now is pray for her." She paused and looked intently at Hal. "And I pray for the life of her child."

"Child?" Hal felt the colour drain from his face. "A child?" He was rising unsteadily to his feet; the world distant around him.

A child, just to be certain that he could never forget what had happened. A child, so that he might constantly be reminded of the foul episode. He had to be alone. Walking to the walls, he looked out over the golden plains of Farona, north towards Torra Alta, and swore that, just as soon as the Ceolothian army withdrew, he would leave them all forever. He drew a deep breath, trying to gather some inner sense of self-worth and, turning, stood eye to eye with Ceowulf.

His face was grim. "Forgive her, Hal. She is your world. Do you not see that there are no new beginnings for you? Your soul is tied to Brid's; you are hers and she is yours."

"She's a priestess; she can never be my wife. She is already married to her duties," Hal said with disgust.

"Don't let your jealousy ruin something so full of beauty," the big knight advised.

Hal shook his head but couldn't grasp his friend's words. He wanted to. He wanted to be rid of this foul feeling in his stomach that twisted him up and strangled his love of life but he could not. He thumped his temple with the heel of his hand but that made no difference. He looked at his feet and kicked at the dusty grass in rage.

"Hush!" Keridwen said urgently. "She's saying something."

Hal knelt by Brid and listened intently. "But it's nothing. Just something about the willows." He nodded at the drooping trees around them.

Keridwen shook her head. "No, no! She means Old Woman Willow! Of course!" Slowly she pushed herself up and gesturing for them to stay by Brid, she left them and hurried towards the trees.

Hal looked at her as if she were mad.

Ceowulf studied him for a long moment, "Well, I've got some news to take your mind off things until you decide to grow up and stop ruining your life," he said calmly.

Hal scowled at him. "What?"

"Tudwal, Cymbeline's brother! He's alive."

"Oh hoorah, and what of it?" Hal knew there was more to come but did not feel like playing guessing games with Ceowulf. The last he had seen of the Ceolothian prince was when the Ovissian, Tupwell, had dragged him off the wizard's island in Ceolothia. Evidently, he had escaped the Ovissian's clutches.

"He's at Torra Alta."

"What do you mean?" Hal demanded, stiffening.

"He holds Torra Alta. Half of Dagonet's army are

apparently living very happily off your boar and deer and horses."

"What!" Rage burst up from Hal's stomach then he calmed himself. "Dagonet will call him off."

Ceowulf nodded. "He's sent word though it will be some days before the messenger arrives."

"And?" Hal prompted, seeing that his friend had more to tell him.

"Dagonet has trouble at home. He's already sending his troops back. Apparently, there's some woman thinks she is the rightful heir to Ceolothia. She has a huge following too."

"What? A queen in the Caballan? Don't be ridiculous, Ceowulf." Hal snorted.

"No, come and listen. They're in uproar."

Hal was glad of the distraction, which at least took his mind from his own problems, but he still thought it some sort of joke. The story was absurd. Apparently, some woman was claiming to be the direct descendent of the long-dead King Dardonus and his rightful wife, who had been supplanted by Dagonet's ancestor. She was claiming Ceolothia in the name of her son and, moreover, she had an army with which to press her claim. The slaves from the mines of Kalanazir had risen up and the people of Castaguard were behind her. She was, they said, already marching on the capital, Casta-brice.

"It seems the Ceolothians are having a rather bad time of it," Hal said flippantly.

Dagonet was racked by grief over the death of his heir and for three days only his daughter was allowed near him. His generals took control of the army and marshalled them in steady streams toward the western ports. The relief that sighed out from Farona at their exodus was almost tangible; within four days much had changed.

But there had been little change in Brid's condition. Though Keridwen had summoned Harle's mother and together they had administered every herb and spell known to them, Brid was still lost in a stupor of pain.

Old Woman Willow wept at her bedside. "I did all I could for her and prayed you could save her, Keridwen."

The high priestess looked from the old woman to Hal and shook her head sadly. "Without the Trinity, my powers are too weak to save her; I'm sorry . . ."

Hal turned and strode stiffly away, not wanting the priestess to see his face as he swallowed hard on his emotions. Nor could he stay beside Brid's sickbed any longer; he could not bear the terrible sight of her failing body. His heart heavy with grief and guilt, he made his way to Dagonet's grand tent.

Cymbeline kept tight to her father, who now, like his daughter, wore black in mourning for Turquin. Although King Dagonet had trouble at home, he was not prepared to leave until he had tied up all his affairs in Belbidia. It seemed he greatly valued his alliance with King Rewik and was uneasy about leaving until he had Tudwal with him. Messengers were returning from the north and, knowing they came from Torra Alta, Hal hurried out to greet them for his brother.

The man flung himself from his horse and knelt before King Dagonet. "Your Highness, your son will not withdraw."

"But I have sent my seal. Tudwal must retreat," Dagonet said, aghast.

"No, sire! He has taken the fortress as his stronghold and claims he will send an army to march on

Farona." The messenger was breathless, his voice high with excitement.

"This is nonsense!" Dagonet's voice cut through all other conversation. Hal was relieved to see that Dagonet was eager to avoid war. "Now I have my daughter back, I have no wish to fight with my trading partner. Tell my boy to withdraw. Someone give me a parchment. On the morrow we shall ride north to see to this misunderstanding ourselves."

Hal returned to Branwolf to give him the news and found that he was sitting propped up now, King Rewik close at hand still trying to offer him the help of his best physicians.

"Get me a horse, Hal," the Baron croaked. "A horse! They have my castle and my son." He twisted towards his sovereign. "Rewik!" he bellowed, the effort bringing on a coughing fit, spots of blood spitting into his cupped hand. Keridwen pressed a glass to his lips and they waited in respectful silence until he was able to speak again. "Rewik, you fool, you gave my land to the Ovissians."

King Rewik nodded his head uncertainly. "Cousin, I confess, I have wronged you. But I have not harmed your son. Long ago I demanded that he was sent to me but the Ovissians swore he was not within the castle when they took control of the barony."

"Impossible! I left Torra Alta in his hands. He would never forsake his duty," Branwolf spluttered. "Never!" He was sitting up now, the need for action, the need for someone to provide command and authority forcing him to his feet, his legs trembling with the effort of simply standing. "If anyone dares say my son would shirk his responsibilities, I'll run him through."

"Perhaps he had a higher duty," Keridwen tentatively suggested.

"There is no higher duty," Branwolf growled.

"Of course there is," Keridwen snapped. "Necrönd! He is its guardian. He must have known that the Ovissians were coming and fled with the Egg to prevent it falling into their hands. It is indeed a higher duty."

Branwolf growled in dissatisfaction. "Well, where is the boy now?"

No one could answer him.

Another messenger arrived later that day just as they were preparing to head north. He was holding one hand awkwardly as if it were injured and his face was white. He stumbled towards Rewik but fell to his hands and knees before he could speak.

Several soldiers rushed forward to help him up. His eyes rolled and his mouth moved to speak though no words came. His hand, they could now see, was ragged, the flesh torn, the bones of his fingers poking through gnawed skin, pieces of jagged, bloody sinew and flesh dangling in tatters from his palm. Keridwen pushed her way through the soldiers and poured a draught of one of her medicines down his throat. He spluttered and choked.

Gripping his forearm, she examined the mess of his hands; bites of flesh were missing from his forearm. He blinked at her. "Trolls and hobgoblins!" he gasped. "The northern baronies are crawling with them."

"Ceowulf, your sword," Keridwen said. Her potion had begun to work and the man slumped forward into her arms.

Hal winced as he heard the swift slash of the sword crunching through bone and clutched at his own stump. Numbly, he listened to Keridwen's demands for fire for cauterising and cat-gut for stitching as she worked on the man's injuries.

Over the sickening sounds of the amputation, Hal queried, "Trolls and hobgoblins?"

"Necrönd," Keridwen said coldly, the word ringing like a note from a clarion through the crowd.

Hal looked her in the eye, his own pain forgotten. "And where's Spar?"

CHAPTER TWENTY-THREE

The ship groaned and creaked at the immense pressure around its thickly armoured hull as the metalled prow sliced into the ice-sheet. Caspar gripped the gunwale to steady himself. His eyes were fixed behind him at the huge white shape porpoising through the ice-choked waters in their wake.

"I have it! I have the moonstone!" Caspar yelled, knowing how the dragon had once sought a similar moonstone, though trapped within that orb had been an image of Keridwen. For twelve long years the dragon had guarded the moonstone and when Caspar had taken it, the monster had dragged its great body all across Vaalaka and Belbidia to try to retrieve its treasure.

The dragon roared, its forelegs scrabbling for the edge of the ice. Its weight spilt the frozen sheet and the ship surged forward into the ice flow while the beast plummeted out of sight. Then it heaved itself up again. Lumbering forward like a great walrus, it pursued them, slithering forward on its smooth belly. The dragon's years in the sea had fattened it and it moved slowly, its massive body too heavy for its withered legs.

Caspar hurled the moonstone, which thudded onto the ice, a blue glow throbbing out from the orb. The dragon crooned over it and put a great claw out, hooking the moonstone to it. For a moment, it nuzzled it with its snout, a deep purr rumbling from its throat, its head cocked in an expression of great pleasure. Then it gave out a roar of intense anguish as it discovered it was not the orb that contained the precious image of Caspar's mother and snapped at it with its dagger-long teeth.

The beast dragged its great bulk towards them. Caspar loosed one arrow then another but they clattered useless from the dragon's back and onto the bone-hard ice. For a moment, he thought they were saved as the ice split and gave way beneath the dragon that was swallowed by the sea. Save for the howling wind whisking up the frost that rolled and skimmed over the ice, all was enveloped by a turgid silence. Still open-mouthed with shock, they watched anxiously as a shadow moved rapidly towards them under the thin layer of the ice. All stared in silent horror, knowing what would happen.

"Hold fast! Hold tight to whatever you can!" Caspar yelled, grabbing Priddy who still held Isolde.

Timbers shrieked and the boat lurched up and seemed to float in mid-air before crashing down again. The dragon's great snout came up by the side of the deck, teeth snapping as it turned furiously on Caspar, the orb still dangling by its leather thong from the beast's mouth. It sucked in a deep breath, filling the bladder at its throat. Caspar flung himself down over Priddy, who was protecting Isolde, covering them both with his body as the steaming gastric juices of the dragon splattered out over the deck, narrowly missing them.

A bestial roar burst from Izen's throat as he charged the dragon, hurling two of his great arrows as if they were javelins. Both glanced harmlessly off the monster's snout. Enraged, the warrior rushed on, one remaining javelin in his grasp.

"Izen, no!" his sister cried. "No!"

The great warrior kept running, his scream of bloodlust all enveloping as the ship lurched and creaked with the weight of the dragon's claws on the gunwale. The dragon spat, covering Izen in a dark green slime, the acid bubbling on his skin. But the warrior's legs powered him on and he flung himself straight into the dragon's claws.

The creature raked and twisted its head awkwardly to get at him while Izen stabbed upwards. One arm was bitten clean off but that did not stop the great warrior of Ash pressing home his assault, jabbing the arrow with his remaining arm, seeking the soft spot at the monster's throat. Deftly, the dragon kept his head tucked down, his claws snatching out until it caught Izen about his chest. The dragon's claw closed. Crushing and squeezing Izen's ribcage, it lifted its head, roaring out in triumph and the warrior made one last heroic effort, driving his arrow up through the unarmoured flesh at its throat. He slipped from the dragon's grasp as it thrashed its head from side to side to be rid of the spear. Its struggles slowly weakened and, choking and spluttering, it crashed to the ice. A grunt of victory squeezed from Izen's gasping throat.

The ship was listing heavily and Izella leapt the few feet from the deck to her brother's side upon the ice. Caspar looked on stunned. People were shouting all about him. The dragon was slipping slowly back into the water and with a sudden rush, the carcass was gone. The very last of the great dragons of Torra Alta, he thought with a twinge of regret. Izen was still alive though blood was pumping from the huge open wound that had once been his shoulder.

One of the crew was tugging at Caspar's sleeve. "The ship's going down; she'll not last the hour."

Grabbing Priddy, who had Isolde firmly strapped to

her chest, he pushed her into her brother's arms. "Get them onto the ice," Caspar ordered and Pennard nodded grimly at him.

At last, he was able to think. "Throw everything you can overboard; food, clothing, wood, everything of value to our survival," he shouted.

They moved whatever they could and at last threw over the sledge that Izen was meant to pull before scrambling over the side themselves. With the hard ice beneath their feet, they watched as the ship sank very slowly, inch by inch. Caspar felt the despair overwhelm them. They were stranded on the ice thousands of leagues from comfort and safety.

He had several layers of clothing and his cloak but that was not enough against the desperate cold. Without Izen, they would never make the journey and Izen was dying.

The crew built a great fire from the timbers of the ship that they had managed to salvage before she went down and did what they could to make themselves comfortable, ready for the evening. Throughout the night, the warrior raged and screamed and fought to get to his feet but, with each hour, he grew weaker. There was nothing any of them could do and at last, he lay still.

The wind, that had been blowing steadily, stilled and Izella began to sing a haunting melody that rippled out into the chill night air. All those assembled prayed to their own gods that the great warrior who had saved them might now find peace. Strange ghostly lights danced on the horizon, adding sorrow and mysticism to her song. Priddy, too, picked up the lament and the two of them, like nightingales, filled the empty air.

Cuddling the baby to him, Caspar kept close to the raging heat of the fire and mourned for the warrior. The man had died nobly and saved them all when none other could do it. How would they cope without him? The thought rumbled around his head until finally he slept.

A grey dawn came very slowly to the world. As usual, his head throbbed with a sickening pain and his dreams had been ravaged by dark shadows stealing towards him, the echo of an evil chuckle still ringing through his mind. As he shook his head and rubbed gently at his temples to numb the ache, the horror of their predicament flooded back to him. He kept his head down over Isolde and sniffed back the tears, mourning for Izen but also for them all.

The return of the stinging wind that carried with it a light snow shook him from his self-pity and he stood stiffly, the bones in his legs aching with cold. At once, he was aware that Trog and Pennard's bitch had noted something out of the ordinary. He investigated and not more than fifty yards from their camp, he found wolf-prints and prayed they were made by tundra wolves and not hooded wolves drawn to him by Necrönd. Hurrying back to the others, he decided not to burden them further with his news.

Pennard was talking to the ship's master. "Do you think we can make it?" he asked the red-haired man, who had been barking orders at his crew since sun-up.

The man shrugged. "If you must go on, the way lies up there over the mountains on the horizon. The men of the snow villages are on the other side. It don't look so far but the Empress's best men barely made it back to tell of it."

"And you?" Pennard asked.

"I've been that way before and I've no wish to try again." The man nodded east. "I'll take my men back home by skirting over the top of the Empress's lands. My intention was to sail round once I had dropped you off but, now,

I'm just going to do it on foot. I don't know how far it is to the nearest settlement but at least the Empress will never find us in those mountains." He nodded east to a range of white peaks that scratched at a grey, snow-laden cloud.

"Listen to you!" Caspar grunted. "You're mad the both of you." He fell back to cradling the child. "How could I have let this happen to you, Isolde, my sweet?" He felt sick and was angry at the enthusiasm and foolish bravery of his companions.

"We have to do it," Izella declared. "I must get this trinoxia. I will not let Arthnau and Old Woman Ash die. I will not let my brother's death be in vain."

While the crew salvaged ropes and timbers from the pieces of the shattered ship that had landed on the ice to make his own sledges, Pennard began packing the sledge that Izen had been going to tow. "See, it skates easily over the ice," he enthused. "We need only get ourselves across that one range to the north. It's not like we're trying to get a whole army and all its armour and war engines across."

"You fools!" Caspar snapped. "You have no idea of the task. Those are mountains!" He nodded northward. "Don't you see? Here we're on the flat and we have a great fire but we're still freezing. Those are mountains!"

"So! We can climb mountains," Pennard said brightly. "What are you afraid of?"

Caspar hardly thought the question worthy of a retort. "You come from a warm clime where a coastal wind keeps away the ice of winter. Clearly, you have never been up into high mountains. We will be exhausted by the cold; we shall be unable to climb through the drifts and when there are no drifts there will be ice blasted smooth by the wind. The snow will drag at us like quicksand; the wind will tear away are faces; our fingers will go black with frostbite. Exhaustion, apathy and confusion will follow and then death. We shall perish."

A hush fell over the camp.

"But we must try!" Izella exclaimed

Caspar smiled faintly. He himself was always one to believe in trying. He knew they would try, of course. He stared north. They had to try because none of them would simply lie down where they were to die though he knew with all certainty that they didn't stand a chance – whether they went north or east. Still, it was within the human spirit to keep going – and evidently the same doggedness ran through the veins of the people of Ash.

He looked at Pennard. "Do you still want to come with me or try your chances with the crew? You could always go that way. And Priddy too."

"I'm not leaving Izella," Priddy protested.

Pennard looked from the sailors to his sister to Caspar. "I'm not leaving my sister. Besides," he said brightly. "There's nothing much for me on this continent and, if you're supposed to be this great warlord, I might find me a better post with you than I ever would have done with the Empress."

Caspar laughed, Pennard's mercenary attitude raising his spirits. "I'll give you a post, Pennard. A man with your skills would do well in my country."

"You want wardogs?"

"Of course not, but a good armourer is always welcomed."

Pennard scowled light-heartedly at this and Caspar admired him for his spirit in the face of the gruelling adversity. He milked the goat, fed the baby then looked at everyone. "Now we must eat well and drink as much hot water as you can before we go. Conserve heat. Keep your hats and gloves on and don't start eating the snow if you are thirsty; it'll lower your body heat. We'll track single file, the strongest of us taking it in turns to beat a track."

"I knew you wouldn't give up," Izella said warmly.

Caspar could not return her smile. Already she was blue with cold. Her body thin and delicate, he guessed she would be the first to perish.

"We'll load the sledges with whatever food we can," he said, setting about the task. "Come, Trog!" He whistled. "Get away from the water. We don't want you getting wet or that'll be the end of you."

The ship's master and his crew left first and Caspar raised a hand in farewell, wondering which party would perish first. He brushed the thought from his mind and turned back to the dogs.

Trog's hair was thick as it stood on end to keep him warm. The animal seemed to have little worries about the cold and was playing with Pennard's bitch, the two of them running around in circles, steam belching from their mouths. They were playing with something. Caspar whistled again but the dogs paid no heed until the party was moving off, one behind the other, all hands on a rope to tow their sledge and supply of food.

Still tossing their plaything between them, the dogs came running and, as he saw it was the moonstone, Caspar held out a closed hand to Trog as if he had a titbit to offer. The dog was suitably fooled and dropped the prize in his mouth to snuffle at his glove. The youth snatched up the orb in triumph and deftly pocketed it. Trog cocked his head on one side and whined, just to tell him he had been unfair, before bounding after Pennard's bitch.

"Not too fast," Caspar warned Pennard, who was first to lead.

"You're determined to be as feeble as possible. You've already condemned this as impossible," he snapped back. "You just lack the spine to give it your all."

Caspar held his tongue. Squabbling would just waste energy. If anyone could make it out of the party, it would be himself. He knew about the cold, was used to the snow and steep terrain, and all he could hope was that the heat from his own body would keep the baby warm. His bearskin was warm and windproof, and he prayed he could do it though logic told him he would not.

Even before they had reached the foothills, his doubts were increased when Priddy began to cry and stumble. As they climbed, trudging back and forth to find a way, the wind picked up. The dogs' tails were clamped beneath them and they loped alongside mournfully. Occasionally they glanced up, sniffing the air and Caspar followed their gaze, fearing that the hungry wolves were waiting to pick them off as they fell, one by one. He still wanted to hope they were only tundra wolves but his head was cramped with pain that warned him that the wolfman's spirit was close.

His cheeks stung and his muscles ached with the cold. Even his eyeballs smarted and he had long since lost the feeling in his feet. He had wrapped his boots in cloth but still the cold came up through the ice. Pennard was slowing rapidly, his breathing laboured, and he looked round anxiously to help his sister.

"She must ride on the sledge," he insisted.

Caspar agreed. He didn't have the heart to leave any of them behind while he still had the strength to help and, moreover, there was still the possibility that this child might be the One.

Izella was stumbling and starting to drag on the rope but when they reached yet another valley deep with snowdrifts, Pennard's bravado crumbled. He stopped every five paces and shook his head in despair. At last, he slumped down into the snow. "I must rest," he breathed, the drifting snow rapidly building up round him.

Caspar shook his head. "Get up or you'll die right there."

Leaving Pennard to struggle up alone, he trudged on, heaving at the sledge but, when it sunk into yet another drift in the lea of a ridge, he turned to Priddy. "You'll have to walk. I can't pull you alone. You've just got to get to the top here, where the snow will be firm, then you can ride again." He knew that the wind at the summit of this rise would have polished the snow to a firm crust that would be slippery but easier going than the deep soft drifts that swallowed their legs at each stride.

"Priddy!" he snapped when she didn't move.

Clearly, she didn't have the strength to answer. She was blue with cold. Her eyes flickered open, looked at him blurrily then closed again. It was happening already. Fearfully, he peeked down inside his layers of clothing at Isolde and rejoiced to see the steady rise and fall of her breathing. He was glad that, so long as he could keep going, his body heat would keep her warm.

Looking around, he noted that the goat was no longer with them; he hadn't even noticed when it collapsed, he thought shamefully. Trog was limping on but was alone. Caspar looked back to see the hump of Pennard's bitch lying in the snow. Pennard crawled up onto all fours and then staggered to his feet. "I'm sorry, Spar, that I doubted you. I thought you nothing but a foolish vagabond. I thought you unworthy of power." His glazed eyes darkened as if a thought had suddenly occurred to him. "Wield it! Get us out of here. We are all going to die. Summon the ogres."

"I cannot," Caspar choked. He felt the presence of the dark beast all around him and could hear the faint chuckle that haunted his dreams, night in night out. He feared that the minute he put this hand on the Egg, the dark spirit would be on him.

Caspar looked at Pennard frankly. "It would be better to die than go to the hell that Necrönd opens up for us."

Pennard lunged at him but Caspar still had the strength to hand him off and deftly reached for his knife. "Stand back!" he hissed, the cold air stabbing at his lungs as he breathed more deeply. He shoved Pennard back into the snow and could see the youth would struggle to rise again.

He had to look after his baby. With that thought alone in his head, he began to trudge on but soon he was slowing and could hear the dark breath of the shadow behind him, breathing in his ear.

"You shall die, all that is precious to you lost," the voice snickered and somewhere, far in the distance, Caspar heard the lamenting howl of wolves.

"Touch Necrönd and your pain will be over. Touch it; give me back life and I shall see the baby lives. You won't make it; I'll take her to safety for you."

"As flesh, you won't make it any better than I," Caspar reasoned, terrified of this half-human voice.

"Of course, I will. I am barely a man now; I'm a wolf. I will make it."

Caspar was tempted. He cared little about himself but he cared about his baby. "You'll save her?"

A cloaked shadow loomed out of the swirling snow. "The baby will live if you give me Necrönd."

Caspar began reaching in his coat but, as he did, his hand touched on the moonstone and he hesitated. He knew he was confused by the life-sapping cold and struggled to work through the problem. He could not trust the wolfman who had stalked him for so long. The spirit would steal his baby and kill it. But he was dying and this was his one last chance to save Isolde. He looked into the moonstone and immediately sensed the spirit's fear. The shadow was retreating. Hope lurched into Caspar's soul; he looked deeper into the softly glowing orb.

"Perren, Perren help!" he cried.

There came no answer. He felt for a moment the heaviness, the turgidity of the stone, and then the orb began to darken and shudder, becoming heavier and heavier in his hand until he could barely hold it. Surely, it was heavy with the weight of the stonewight, he thought. Then from its heart burst out a shower of sparks, which erupted into flames that slowly took solid form and cooled. He could see horses!

Caspar would have cheered if he had the energy. Dazzled by the sudden appearance of bright golden animals all about him, he stared stupidly. The wolfman was gone, the wolves fled but Caspar was convinced he must be dead or at least dying. Horses were everywhere. They stirred, parted and there he was.

"Talorcan!" Caspar gasped.

Talorcan moved towards him, bright light shining all about him, and held out his hand to pull Caspar out from the drift of snow.

"Spar, I am not angry with you. I owe you everything. You carry my soul."

Someone else stood by Talorcan. The tears pricked at Caspar's eyes. He could see her but only faintly, as broken dots of light.

"May, my love . . ." He reached out his hand for her.

Talorcan barred his way but there was understanding

in his eyes. "Come, we must get you home. We have little time; they are right behind us."

Caspar understood what Talorcan meant. The hunt was after them, the verderers of the Otherworld would soon be on Talorcan and May to drag them back to the dungeons of Abalone.

Caspar found a horse beside him. "The others!" he said. "We must go back for the others."

"What? There's no time."

"I won't go without them," Caspar insisted.

Talorcan conceded, racing away with two of the golden animals.

Caspar raised his hand to stroke the soft warm muzzle of the horse Talorcan had left him. The beast was bright gold, a horse from the Otherworld, and he could not fully believe it was real, fearing that the fatigue and cold had finally conquered his body and, that near death, he was seeing things.

Half reassured, he felt its steamy hot breath and struggled to mount the fine creature. His joints stiff with cold, he heaved himself up and cradled Isolde close to his chest. He could hear sobbing beside him and looked to see the ghostly outline of May. She looked tired, her arm hung limply and there were stains of blood on the same cloak she had been wearing when she died.

"Rest, May," Caspar said. "Do not torture yourself."

May didn't seem to hear him clearly. "My baby. She reached out her hand. "I must see her. I miss her so."

May came so close Caspar could feel the coldness of her dead spirit pass into him beyond the coldness of the air about them. She put her hand over the bearskin that was tightly wrapped around Caspar's body, protecting the baby. He felt the girl kick and stir in her sling.

"Keep her safe," May begged.

"She is everything to me," Caspar reassured her. "She is all I have left of you, May, my love."

May waved his words aside. "All is honesty in Rye Errish. You never loved me, not truly. You wanted to but you didn't love me like Talorcan does, wholly and truly. I am his now and forever so do not feel guilty anymore, Spar. You do not have to save yourself for the sake of my memory."

"But, May, I do love you."

She nodded. "That may be, but not to the bottom of your heart. But you will cherish Isolde and love her with all your being."

Caspar nodded.

"Talorcan was waiting for me on the other side. He was suffering pitifully, his new-found soul dying without me. He is a part of me; he shares my soul. Do you understand that? He loves me more than he loves himself. But we both must wait until you have Isolde home to Keridwen. My child must live."

The ghost stepped back, tears still streaming down those cheeks as the fleet horses came galloping up through the deep drifts of snow almost as if they skimmed the ground. Talorcan threw Trog up to Caspar but there were no buckles or straps on the simple saddle and so he had to lay the dog sideways across the horse's withers in front of him.

Exhausted, the others clung to the great mounts, too tired, too near death to care about the strangeness of the situation. Pennard clutched his sister's limp body before him and Izella rode alone, clinging on tightly. Caspar was amazed by her strength.

They climbed up high into the cruel cold but the heat from the horses' backs warmed them. Caspar was so grateful for this help that he didn't question how Talorcan had achieved it. The verderer was racing along beside him like a shadowy vapour that sometimes had form and at others was no more than sparkling dust in the driving snow. Ahead lay two peaks, both cones of white with plumes of wind-tossed snow rising like mare's tails from their peaks. Between lay what Caspar hoped to be the pass.

Soon the dark of evening engulfed them, the violet light making the white world glow a magical purple. They plunged and leapt through the deep fields of snow and approached the pass. Here the wind seemed to blow from both sides at once and the snow had formed a hard wind-packed crust that the horse's hooves barely cut into. In places, sheets of blue ice coated the rocks with only a light dusting of snow tumbling over it, driven by the raw wind. They reached the top of the pass and halted in the shelter of a wind-blown cornice.

Talorcan's hollow voice breathed beside him. "You'll make it from here. We must leave you; they are nearly on us."

Swirling lights sparkled and danced between the two twin peaks at the top of the world. Caspar felt the magic of the Great Mother tremble through him and knew that they stood at a point of great power. His horse reared and shrieked, undoubtedly sensing the trembling energy about them.

Pennard and Priddy clung to their horse with terrified expressions but Izella, as Caspar should have expected, sat tall and confidently on the beast though her fine face was still grey blue with the cold.

"Head straight and keep going. You'll find a village of snow." Talorcan pointed through the driving snow though Caspar could see nothing.

Talorcan was beginning to struggle. Hands were grappling for him. Disembodied arms hovered in the atmosphere within the dancing lights. Spear points jabbed at his sides and then a sweet yet powerful voice that Caspar recognized as Nuin's, rang out from afar.

"Talorcan, my keys! Give me back my keys."

Other voices were shouting. "Get the woman too. They will be punished for this. Get those horses back. No one sneaks through Nuin's Door and gets away with it."

"Get my baby safely home!" May cried and her voice turned into a shriek of pain.

Hands snatched at her, dragging her back. For a moment, she clawed at Caspar but her insubstantial flesh slipped through his fingers as he tried to hold her.

"Farewell," he cried, as her ghostly body became sparkles of dust. The spangled air swirled, shimmered and condensed to form one bright point of light that imploded on itself and was gone. Caspar stood staring at the empty air for a long second.

"May!" he choked.

Izella's hand was on his. "Come. Let's head for the village."

The moment Talorcan was gone, Caspar heard the haunting howl of a wolf and then another. The wolfman was back!

Spurring his steed into a fierce gallop that was yet graceful and smooth, he imagined they were flying. The pace was so fast that even the hooded wolves were left far behind, caught in snowdrifts up to their chests that the golden horses of the Otherworld were able to leap over. The steeds were magnificent, the glow from their coats throwing off enough light to banish the night around them. They galloped on with the bright halo about them, the tears from Caspar's smarting eyes whisked away by the rush of air in his face.

The wind was dying down, allowing the streaks of

drifting snow to settle back to the ground, and up on the golden horse, Caspar could see clear to the horizon where white ogres of mountains were hunched either side of a white plain. He thought he could make out a circular shadow in the landscape that he hoped marked the site of the settlement. He looked back and the twin peaks at the top of the world were gone from sight and only the dancing lilac lights were still visible.

Pennard was looking at his horse in disbelief. "How?" he asked as they slowed their pace through the dark, strangely glowing world of the tundra towards the circular shadow that was so clearly manmade in this icy wilderness unmistakably manmade. "Where did they come from?

Caspar managed to raise a grin on his cold-chapped face and looked ahead to the sheet of flat ice and the ring-shaped shadow that was now discernible as a circular wall of snow. "They come from the Otherworld."

"But how? They're not ghosts," Pennard argued.

"Through Nuin's door." Caspar understood now. He had begged Perren for help and the stonewight must have found Talorcan who had more knowledge than any other of the ways of the Otherworld. Talorcan must have led the horses through secret ways to Nuin's Door, one of the ways between the worlds, to reach them.

They halted uncertainly in front of the circular wall of packed snow.

"Hello," Caspar called brightly in the tongue of the far continent, not knowing what else he could say.

Deep growls, evidently human but in mimicry of some kind of bear, roared out from the enclosure. The prospect of safety had boosted Caspar's strength and lifted his spirit but one look at Izella told him she was still in desperate trouble. He cantered around the enclosure but saw no way in apart from a small hole in the compacted snow that was just big enough to wriggle through but he felt that might not be the safest form of approach.

"Help! We need help! Warmth, food and shelter!" he shouted.

The growls persisted so he cried out his plea in Belbidian but still there was no response. Then he did his best to beg in the tongues he knew of all the other countries of his own continent, and even the western continent where the diamond seas were reputed to sparkle so brightly that they would blind a man if he stared at the waters for too long. He had a few words of Waerlogian, five in fact, but one of those was friend.

At last, the growls eased and someone anxiously repeated the word back to him. The tip of a knife appeared through the smooth wall of the snow and began slicing out a square window. A little red face squinted at them and Caspar jumped down from his horse, wincing at the pain in his feet. He gripped his knees and stood up.

"Friend!" he repeated in Waerlogian.

The face smiled and said friend back.

"I'm sorry," Caspar returned to his native Belbidian, "that's the only Waerlogian I know."

The squinting, red-cheeked face looked troubled and grunted some words, which to Caspar's ears sounded vaguely questioning. He looked at the man and then vigorously rubbed himself, shuddering and stamping his feet to explain that he was cold, and pointed at Izella, who was now hunched over her horse and looked as if she would tumble any moment.

The little face nodded and withdrew. The long blade again appeared until a doorway had been cut into the compacted wall of snow. Caspar blinked, his eyes stinging from the glare off the sparkling snow. Within the wall there was no form of shelter, only a pack of dogs, and he feared they would not find the help they needed so desperately. He dragged his and Izella's horse into the enclosure and caught her as she slid from its back.

"Spar!" she gasped.

"Don't worry, you're safe now," he reassured her. "I'll look after you now."

Her eyes smiled at him though her face was too weak and grim with cold to look anything but bleak. Grunting away though evidently quite happy, the short man from this frozen world took her arm and led her towards the centre of the enclosure. There appeared from a hole in the ground four others, dressed as he was in the most massive layers of animal skin from a beast with extraordinarily long shaggy hair. Encumbered by their clothing, they waddled with a strange, wide-legged gait to the wall, slipped outside to rebuild it with freshly cut blocks of snow and then wriggled in through the narrow tunnel.

The horses were glad of the shelter that broke the wind but Caspar had no water or food to offer them and hoped he could redress that later. At that moment, they weren't his first concern; Izella and Priddy needed help.

Lying close by the hole at the centre of the enclosure were twenty or so dogs curled up in the sun, their thick tails like a cushion beneath them to insulate them from the snow. One or two growled at the horses but most were interested in Trog who managed to beat his tail feebly but was too exhausted from the cold to react more.

They stumbled towards the opening that was nothing more than a hole in the ground with a wooden ladder leading straight down, the ladder apparently made from driftwood, judging by its bleached colour. Before Caspar could begin to help Izella down, half a dozen young men came scrambling up the ladder, gave him and his companions a momentarily glance before looking at the horses and gasping and exclaiming. Caspar had no doubt that they had never seen horses, let alone golden ones. One or two tentatively put their hands out to touch the beasts.

"Just don't eat them," Caspar warned in Belbidian.

Though the men looked at him blankly, he hoped they understood his proprietorial attitude towards the animals. Below it was warm! Beautifully warm. Soon he was shivering violently as his body made great efforts to restore his circulation.

The room was simply a hollowed-out dome under the snow, and he was astonished when he realized how thick the snow must be since the chamber was twenty foot high at least. It's like a badger set or like the earthworks of Ash's people, he thought, seeing how tunnels led off, presumably to more private family chambers. A small fire was burning beneath the centre of the dome and Caspar wondered how it hadn't burned its way down and melted all the flooring of the chamber. Then he saw that the firepit was lined with some kind of clay. They were not burning wood, which clearly would be a very precious resource this far north, but apparently some kind of oil. Caspar guessed it was the fat from some beast.

He was invited to sit on a rug near the fire and he unwrapped Isolde from within his cloak. She looked cold and sleepy and Caspar was deeply worried. Faces stared at him. The men waved their arms about in gestures of helplessness and they were pushed aside by a short but enormously fat old woman who crooned and spluttered over the baby and gave Caspar a little pot full of some foul-smelling, reddish grey mash. She put her hand to her mouth, indicating that it was to eat and, sniffing at it suspiciously, Caspar presumed it was masticated meat.

Scooping out a little with his finger, he offered it to Isolde but she would not touch it.

Frowning, the old woman tutted and, when Caspar looked up to her for help, she led him to a woman who was sitting cross-legged a little way back from the fire, suckling a largish baby who was happily naked in the warmth of the dwelling. The old woman muttered something and the mother eased her own child from her breast, set it down in a fur-lined cradle and took Isolde from Caspar. She responded eagerly to the offer of warm milk and a warm body to lie against. With huge relief, Caspar smiled his thanks and the woman nodded in acknowledgement.

Now that Isolde was being cared for, his only thought was to get warm and fed. Though he found he could drink the warm water he was offered, his stomach was still too tight with the cold to eat and one mouthful made him feel sick. He put the fatty meat aside and, with shivering hands, took more sips of water. His extremities began to throb as the heat returned to them though he still could not feel his nose.

Izella was moaning with pain. Caspar was glad; it meant she was warming up. The women of the snow village were looking after Priddy and Izella, purring and gossiping over their slender bodies as they eased off their outer garments and provided them with light skin tunics, which were all that was needed to wear inside the snow shelter. The men stared, open-mouthed, eyes agog.

That night and the next day passed like a dream, all the while the noise of the wind moaning and whistling as it teased and tugged at the snow chimney above. Caspar fretted about the horses exposed in the raw wind but when he made neighing sounds and pointed upwards, the man pressed him down reassuringly and acted out a scene for him. He concluded that they had built some form of snow shelter and fed them but with what he could not imagine.

He relaxed and finally his appetite returned and he managed to chew his way through great slabs of meat they toasted over the fire. They were each offered huge steaks that Caspar judged were enough to feed half a dozen men. He was unable to converse with these people but slowly overcame the problem by drawing pictures in the soot-coated walls and pointing at the pictures they painted onto the inside of skins and had hung on the walls.

"A whale!" he exclaimed. "It's whale meat." He could not understand how in the middle of this tundra they ate whale. After they had showed him several crude paintings, he understood that they were hunters of the wild yak and the great white bear whose skins they sold to the whalers in exchange for the food and fat from the whale. Caspar pointed to the strange picture that showed the men in their curiously high-prowed boats harpooning the whales.

"Please can you take me to them," he said, his voice shaking with emotion. These were pictures of ships and he needed a ship to take him home.

The men nodded at him and he wondered if they understood. Insistently, he pointed again to the picture of the ship and then moved his fingers to indicate that he wanted to ride to the ships. The men looked at him as if he were mad and, shuddering, they rubbed at themselves and howled like the wind. For the moment, Caspar was too tired to argue. He sat back and smiled, tears pricking at his eyes. A few days ago, he was certain they would die. He thought that his sweet baby would have frozen to death on the top of the world but she was alive and happy, gurgling away delightedly with Priddy. There was hope.

For the first time in days, his attention was drawn back to Izella. She had eaten and her strangely silvery skin was now bright and her eyes sparkled in the reflection of the flickering firelight. He wondered, not for the first time, how he had ever managed to refuse her initial offer. The men from the snow village had noted her at once and, now that she was well, one or two of the younger men were edging eagerly closer. Caspar moved to her side and put a proprietorial hand on hers.

She smiled at him and laughed. "I told you that the men of your kind find me irresistible."

He grinned sheepishly.

Slowly the people of the snow village withdrew to the covered benches that formed a circle along the perimeter of the chamber and began a moaning song, the women whimpering and howling though in a most tuneful manner. Gradually, it dawned on Caspar that they were singing the song of the wind.

It lulled him to sleep. For another thirteen days and nights they stayed down in the chamber and daily Caspar begged to be taken to the ships though every time he was met with the same response. The short fat men of the tundra chattered their teeth and howled like the wind. In frustration, he spent the time idly playing with Isolde or teaching his companions the rudiments of Belbidian, which they were very quick to pick up, their own language not being too dissimilar. On the fourteenth day he woke up and was instantly aware that something was very different.

The dreadful howl that moaned above the chimney was silent. The men of the north were already awake, gathering their belongings, and Caspar and his companions were bundled into bulky skins. Even Trog, whom they laughed at for his thin coat, was wrapped in skins and his feet bandaged to protect his tender paws. They emerged into a crisp bright world to find their horses while the men from the snow village whistled up their dogs that had stayed all that time on the surface. The dogs yapped excitedly as they were harnessed to sledges and Caspar wondered how they withstood the cold.

With his baby tucked inside his clothing in her own fur pocket, he wondered at the speed with which the dogs towed their masters over the wind-moulded snow while he and his companions followed on their gleaming horses. By evening, they could see the startling blue green of the sea in what, up until then, had been a pure white world.

Soon they were above a great natural harbour and he could see five ships bobbing in the water. Like the whalers pictured in the snow village, they had remarkably high prows and the sterns were equally pointed; one of them would take them home. Tears pricked at Caspar's eyes that were permanently squinting against the glare of the sun reflecting off the diamond-bright snow.

"Isolde," he murmured, "we're going home."

CHAPTER TWENTY-FOUR

Tudwal's messenger grunted at the great oak doors to Bullback's manor that King Rewik had commandeered for its proximity to the barony of Torra Alta.

"I am sent to return your messages," the emissary said in his flat Ceolothian accent, the muscles of his thick arms bulging as he held out a heavy sack.

Hal's heart thumped in his throat. One of Rewik's men opened the sack and gave out a scream, dropping it with a heavy thud to the floor and retreating in horror.

Hal stepped quickly forward and, with only one hand, fumbled to open it. He swallowed hard. "Take it away and have the contents buried and blessed by the appropriate religious officer," he ordered, handing the sack to another soldier standing by.

"What's in it?" King Rewik demanded, rising from the table within Bullback's main hall where the noblemen were gathered.

"You don't wish to know," Hal assured him.

"I am the King and I will know."

"Heads," he grunted. "The messengers'." They had been mostly younger than himself; war was war but this was outrage.

The King blinked but his hawklike face remained firm. He nodded at Hal. "Carry on, good man."

Hal saluted smartly and, after finally succeeding in

510

excluding Pip from the room – the youth had becoming annoyingly forthcoming when serious debates solidified the noblemen into a tight knot – he turned back to his brother. Branwolf was sitting nearest to the fire but was shivering despite the warmth of the flames and the bear-skin cloak wrapped about his broad shoulders. But at least his voice was strong now, dominating the discussion of the disturbing reports brought in by Bullback's sons and of the vile beast they had dragged into the manor courtyard. They soon fell silent as, across the room, King Dagonet of Ceolothia rose from the table to speak to one of his own messengers who came panting in.

Hal did not have to strain his ears to hear Dagonet roar at the man who brought news of the situation in Ceolothia.

"Queen Reyna!" King Dagonet burst out incredulously. "But no one has heard of such a woman. I have no bandits even in the mountains of Kalanazir that go by such a name."

"She claims to be the direct descendent of King Dardonus and his lawful wife and, already, she and her slaves have secured Castaguard," the messenger exclaimed.

Hal cared little for Ceolothia's problems. All he needed from Dagonet was troops to help take back Torra Alta from Tudwal, but most of his men had, long since, set sail for Ceolothia to quell the uprising of slaves in his kingdom. Only his personal bodyguard of a hundred men remained.

Hal's attention was caught by Bullback. Deeply troubled, the Ovissian baron was pacing up and down while Ceowulf was arranging transport for the women to take them south away from the danger. The moment they had arrived in Jotunn, Cybillia, who had been staying with her family while her husband was away, had proudly shown him his son. From that moment, Ceowulf was no longer quite the same man as he had been before. Uncharacteristically nervous, he snapped and snarled impatiently, demanding that Cybillia hurry and join Princess Cymbeline, whom Dagonet had ordered to return immediately south out of harm's way. The Princess was ready to leave.

Cybillia, however, was not so easily ordered around. "But, my lord, I haven't seen you in over a year and now you're sending me away," she complained, a large pout puckering her pink lips.

The knight boomed, "You, my girl, are leaving at once for Caldea with my son." He pulled her close and kissed her fervently. "Wife, do as you're bid for once."

Finally, she conceded that for the safety of their son, she would leave. Once Cybillia was on her way, Ceowulf was very much more at ease and able to participate in the war councils.

Baron Bullback now joined them around the table. "Tudwal's and Godafrid's combined armies would repel an all out assault; Torra Alta is too easy to defend. But if we could get just a few inside the castle to release your men, Branwolf, and retake the castle from within, we would have more of a chance."

Branwolf grunted in accord.

"Indeed, but how do we get our men inside?" Rewik demanded.

The Baron shrugged his bony shoulders beneath the bearskin. "You can't."

"The Ovissians are not your archers," the King reminded him.

"No, but there are wolves snivelling around the roots of the Tor. And if we got past them, which is conceivable – though with heavy losses – we would never get past the trolls and certainly not the hobgoblins," Branwolf said flatly. "The canyon is crawling with them and you all saw the size of the creature Bullback's sons dragged in. They're eating up everything they can lay their filthy hands on, sniffing out even the barned animals in the dead of night and have no trouble killing unarmed men."

There was a general nodding of heads and Hal grimaced as he remembered the lean, sinewy body of the hobgoblin. It had matched him in height, its pointed teeth cramming its lipless mouth, its belt stuffed with knives. Judging by the number of cattle that had been slaughtered, skinned and gutted in the fields, carcasses half eaten, the flesh stripped and carried away, there were a great many of these creatures roaming the land.

"We can do it." Hal moved closer to the table, drew up a stool and reached for a tankard of ale. He took a long draft, wiped the froth from his mouth and, reaching across his brother, tapped the map. "Here's Torra Alta." Pointing out the canyon, he traced his finger north beyond the castle to draw their attention to a narrow gorge in the western wall of the rift valley, an insignificant feature in the scale of the grand landscape. "Whitehart's River crashes out of the Yellow Mountains and cuts deep into the rock here. A ravine. Halfway along the ravine is a narrow crack in the rock that leads to an ancient lime quarry."

Branwolf nodded. "You're right, Hal. If we can draw them into it, a few of us might safely get within the castle walls and release my men from the dungeons." He smiled at the thought but then looked dubiously at his half-brother. "But there is one monumental flaw." Branwolf was able to walk now though he still spat blood and doubled up, coughing, as soon as he exerted himself.

"Two score men," Hal continued as if he hadn't heard

Branwolf's last comment. "We can pin them into the old quarry with that. The mouth is very narrow."

"A lure," Keridwen said to clarify the situation. Hal had barely seen her in the days since Harle's mother had mysteriously stepped out from the willow grove. The two women had constantly been at Brid's side, Keridwen's eyes were black-rimmed with exhaustion, and her hands were beginning to shake. There was a tautness about her face that told Hal what he least wanted to know; Brid was no better and clearly even Harle's mother had found no way to save her. This knowledge only increased his resolve.

"Yes, a lure," Hal said with forced brightness. "These creatures are ravenous. If we fill the quarry with beasts, we can draw these wolves and hobgoblins off and with a few chosen men trap them in the ravine."

Branwolf was now equally enthusiastic. "Yes, it would work; open the way up for the rest to retake the castle."

"What are you talking about?" Keridwen's voice cut in. "It's utter folly."

"This is a war council," the Baron's previous strength was returning to him, "not a place for women and their sentimental ways."

Keridwen ignored this remark. "I agree we must get inside the castle but not one of these men posted to hold the wolves and hobgoblins in the quarry will live – not one. Once the hobgoblins have finished with the animals, they would turn on the men. It would just be a matter of how long they could hold out, how much time they could buy for the others to get inside."

Branwolf nodded. "That is right, my lady. That is why I shall lead it."

Hal shook his head. "No, Branwolf, you are not strong enough. If we are to break into the castle and free our own men, we'll need as much time as possible and that's why I shall lead the party to draw the hobgoblins to the quarry." He looked around at those gathered about the table. "We cannot order any man to make this step. It has to be his own choice."

"I know some of my men will volunteer," Bullback offered. "We have lost vast numbers of cattle to these hobgoblins and wolves and we shall lose everything if we do not throw them out. The wolves were bad enough but the vicious, stealthy hobgoblins . . ."

"I shall stand." Bullback's middle son, Thane, stood up. He was tall like his father, full-bellied already, and his face was remarkably aged for one not yet into his middle years. "They took my wife and baby. They took everything from me. I shall stand and fight. I shall be one of the few."

"I am with you," his brother, Oxwin, pledged.

"We need but two score," Hal said. "The mouth of the quarry is a narrow gorge. If we lure them in, we can pin them into it."

Branwolf patted him on the back. "You are right, Hal, you shall lead but I will stand with you."

"No," Hal objected bluntly. "You shall not. You must lead the men into Torra Alta."

"No! You are going nowhere, Branwolf," Keridwen assured him. "No one doubts your bravery but you are simply not strong enough."

"Who then will lead the men through the secret tunnels to release the prisoners? There is none other who can do it," the Baron pointed out.

"But there is," Hal said quietly "Pip can do it."

"Pip!" Branwolf laughed. "He is just a boy, just a common boy."

"And a true Torra Altan to the heart," Hal reminded him.

Branwolf groaned. "Mmm . . . I'll talk with him first before I decide." He paused to cough and spit before resting his hand on Hal's shoulder, leaning heavily. "Two score?" he asked.

Hal nodded.

The Baron nodded calmly but then suddenly exploded. "No! Hal, no, I cannot let you do this!" His voice trembled. "Not one of you shall get out alive, not one."

"There are always casualties in war and we are warriors." Hal held his head stiffly. "I am not afraid."

"Well, you should be. Isn't losing your hand enough? You are my brother. I told our father on his deathbed when you were not yet a year old that I would look after you. Do you suppose this is looking after you?" Branwolf put a cloth to his mouth and wiped the red spittle from his lips.

"My lord, I have nothing left to live for. I cannot live with what I have done to Brid. All else in my life has failed but I can still fight. I can stand fast; I have the runesword that I can wield in one hand. And if I have that, there is always hope."

"There will be no hope," Ceowulf grunted. "If it is to work at all and you held out even half the day, the moment you turned to run, they would be on your heels and tear you limb from limb. You cannot do this."

They argued deep into the night. Hal knew he did not want to die but he had a duty and he would not let Tudwal use Torra Alta to launch his attack into Belbidia. Worrying for Branwolf and for Caspar, who was still unaccountably missing, he finally retired to bed and slept poorly. He was woken early by news of an attack on a Jotunn village. Babies had been ripped from their mother's arms and eaten by a band of hobgoblins. To make matters worse another of Tudwal's men was already standing on the threshold to the manor with a heavy sack.

Wanting to spare the others the horror of what he knew it contained, Hal took it. Tudwal's messenger said grimly, "Another head will appear every hour until you surrender to Prince Tudwal."

But it was not these horrors that so disturbed the noblemen.

Still believing that Tudwal was either held against his will or had not received any message that he, King Dagonet of Ceolothia wished for peace, he sent messenger after messenger. Now no more would go; all that had returned of the previous messengers were their heads. When the first man stood up to the Ceolothian king, he drew his dagger and plunged it into the messenger's heart.

"No one defies me. No one!"

Except Tudwal, Hal thought to himself and, with an eyebrow raised, he turned back to his heated debate with his brother. Desperate to think of a plan that would better his idea of luring the hobgoblins into the old lime quarry, they were locked in argument. Hal was acutely aware that all the while they argued people were dying.

He was also puzzled by news brought to King Rewik by a messenger that a number of unusually high-prowed ships had landed in the barony of Piscera on Belbidia's western coast.

The news from the distant barony was soon forgotten when word came of the death of one of Bullback's sons. The broad-chested baron was driven to rage. "I will go alone, if need be!" he bellowed and reached for the huge sword that hung in his hall. "Who is with me, men? We have talked too long and come up with no other plan than Hal's. My people are dying; they are my responsibility. I will not let it go on. Those breaking into the castle have a chance if the hobgoblins and trolls are lured away. That is what must be done and I shall be the first to stand and fight at the mouth of this quarry."

Helena, his wife, who had refused to leave her home, began to sob. "No, my husband, no."

"I thought you no longer loved me," he said with surprising tenderness.

"Of course I love you." She blushed.

"Well, why in all these years have you given me such a hard time?" he asked gently, folding her within his amply fleshed arms.

She shrugged. "It is my nature, and you would not have me change. But I beg of you, let only men without attachment go."

He looked at her gravely. "My sweet love, I am an old man; my sons ready to take my place, every one of them fit enough to handle my affairs. It is right I should go."

"No!" Dagonet insisted. "Tudwal will withdraw! I have commanded—" his voice trailed off. A man, bleeding from a cut to his head and his clothes bloody and torn from fighting, stood at the threshold to the room. "I know you!" the Ceolothian King accused in a tight, hoarse voice.

The man nodded. "I was leading the Princess's escort. The hobgoblins spared me only so I might bring you the news. Princess Cymbeline and Lady Cybillia have been taken."

"My daughter!" Dagonet wailed. "Not again!"

Hal was little concerned about Dagonet's distress. He was looking for Ceowulf. The knight was trembling and clutched the back of a chair for support. Never had he seen his friend's face so ashen.

His eyes wide and black, Ceowulf caught Hal's glance and, stiffening, marched over to him. "Hal, they have my wife and my son – my son for pity's sake! Next, it will be his tiny head and Cybillia's in a sack. You are my friend and I do not wish to lose you, but you must draw these devils up into the quarry so that I can break into Torra Alta and save my wife and son."

There was a resounding crack that snapped up everyone's attention. Baron Bullback hacked his great sword down on a table and split the wood in two. "First my son and now this. They have my daughter," he raged. "I would die a thousand deaths to save her."

Ceowulf was grim. "We must prepare." He was shaking with emotion.

"Now listen," Hal said gravely now that none forbade his plan. "Only a small force can penetrate Torra Alta."

Branwolf nodded.

Hal would not disclose the position of the entrance as no Torra Altan would ever speak aloud the one weakness in their castle defences. "Ceowulf, you will be guided by Pip. He knows the entrance and the correct passages that lead to the dungeons. First, liberate the Torra Altans. Then go straight for Godafrid, Tupwell and Tudwal."

"I'll have my son alive," Dagonet growled. "He has stolen Cymbeline from me and he shall answer to me for it."

"I must find my volunteers," Hal said quietly and strode from Bullback's stuffy halls.

The Belbidian troops, men from the fields of Nattarda, Jotunn and the lower villages of Torra Alta as well as a mere handful of Dagonet's men were encamped in the fields about Bullback's manor. Weary and untrained, they had kept up a constant watch to drive back the floods of hobgoblins that repeatedly struck at night.

Hal quickly had them assembled and, standing on a dry-stone wall, prepared to address them. "Our numbers are few and are being cut daily. Now Princess Cymbeline and Bullback's own daughter have been taken hostage.

Tupwell and Tudwal demand that the kingdom be handed over to them. We shall, every one of us, be slaughtered if they are not stopped. I have a plan to break their stranglehold." He did not shout; his voice, calm but deep and commanding carried easily out over the subdued crowd.

He could not tell them how it was to be achieved only that to follow him would be the greatest sacrifice they could ever undertake. "Those who stand with me shall almost certainly not return," he said calmly. "But if we die, it shall be with the knowledge that we gave our lives to save others. Our lands, our women, our children are being taken from us. We will not let this happen. We shall stand and be counted and, through the annals of time, those who stood and gave their lives shall be remembered. Who shall stand with me?"

A huge cheer rang out from the troops and it was some while before Hal could speak again.

"You are all good men, but the number that go will be few." He spoke loudly into the stillness. "Those willing should present themselves to me in the forecourt in one hour. Spend the time wisely. Talk to your friends and think. Do not come to me in haste. If we must fall in accomplishing this task let it be as free men and by our own choice. I salute you all and know that I am proud to be amongst you." He saluted, climbed from the wall and made his way back towards the manor. A silence the like of which Hal had never known spread throughout the fields behind him.

Near seventy men had presented themselves long before the hour was out. His heart sank. He didn't want to have to choose. Worse, Pip was there.

He called the lad over. "No, you cannot come." he said firmly.

Pip looked at him resentfully. "My father gave his life for the Baron. I shall do no less."

"Pip, I know how brave you are." Hal gripped his shoulder. "But you have already been allotted to another post."

The boy scowled. "I suppose, I'm to run errands at the rear and keep out of everyone's way."

Hal smiled though sadness filled his heart as he thought that he would miss this youth. "No, Pip, the Baron needs you to lead Ceowulf with a select party into the castle. There's no one else."

"Lead Ceowulf! Lead the men!" the youth grinned from ear to ear.

Hal slapped him on the back. "I'm proud of you, lad."

Pip grinned even more broadly. "You know what, Master Hal, I'm proud of you too," he said cheekily.

Hal could feel the tears pricking at his eyes. "Well, Pip, you'd best get on. Report to the Baron and he'll explain everything."

Hal surveyed the volunteers. The seventy were now nearer a hundred and still growing and he wondered how he would select his forty men. He waited the allotted hour and then, with no need to call for silence since an unnatural hush hung over them, he addressed the throng.

"Which of you has children?" he bluntly demanded and thirty put their hands up. He smiled. "Thank you. You are brave men, but we shall not be needing you."

They looked mostly relieved and shuffled off, only one or two casting back over their shoulders. Hal needed men that would stand, who at the last moment wouldn't suddenly remember that they had a greater purpose to live than to die for. There were to be no regrets.

He spoke to the rest one at a time and dismissed any that seemed weak or ill. Still another half dozen, he learned, did have children but had still wanted to fight but he quickly persuaded them to step down except one.

"Listen, Master Hal, I never thought I'd be dying to save Torra Alta let alone my country but I ain't really you see." He pulled up his shirt to show Hal a large ugly growth stretching the skin of his belly. "This great lump's doubled in size in just a month. I'm dying anyway."

Hal nodded. "Can you still use a sword?"

"Oh, I've lost little of my strength as yet. Been scything wheat all my life. I'm sure I can scythe through a few skinny goblins." He grinned, his teeth yellow.

By late afternoon, Hal had his forty men. "We leave on the morrow," he said. "In the meanwhile, I want you to make your farewells, tie up your affairs and we shall reconvene here at supper time." He dismissed them and marched through the main camp where he stopped a passing soldier. "Find me a minstrel," he demanded.

"A minstrel, sir?"

Hal nodded. "Yes, a minstrel. Or as close as you can get to one."

He returned to Bullback's hall to see how the battle preparations were going. His brother smiled though there was deep sorrow in his gaunt face and Hal found it hard to look at Branwolf without the tears flooding up into his eyes. The balladeer arrived smartly and Branwolf quizzically looked the whimsical-looking man up and down.

"What do you want a minstrel for?"

Hal grinned. "I want to hear my name sung as a hero before I die. I want to feel the glory. No fun otherwise," he joked and, beckoning to the balladeer, held out a parchment to him, "here's a list of names. You have an essential part in this battle," he told the thin little man.

"With these names make a good song and sing it well. They are the names of brave men all."

After finding a blacksmith to make him an evil-looking hook to fit his stump, he spent the next few hours simply moving amongst his volunteers, nodding here and nodding there, before returning to his brother who was still in conversation with Pip. Hal did not find it the right moment to say farewell to Branwolf and so instead, he shook Pip's hand.

"Good luck, Master Hal," the lad said sincerely and then added. "You're a fine man. The finest!"

"And don't I know it!" Hal quipped.

He took Ceowulf by the arm.

"Thanks," Ceowulf said. "My son is in there." He nodded north towards Torra Alta.

Hal nodded. "Just make sure you get him out. It's been a privilege to know you, friend."

Ceowulf nodded back. "Likewise, and an honour."

Hal shook the hand of everyone he knew even the King's, though that was difficult after the brutality he had suffered by his command. He hugged Branwolf and then Keridwen and at last drew a steadying breath. There was one more farewell to make.

She was groaning in her sleep, her legs hunched up around her pain. Her hands were rigid and her eyes staring, a frown tight on her forehead though she was not awake. Hal sat beside her, gazing at her for several long minutes. "Brid, I love you," he said. "I love you to the bottom of my heart and with all my soul but I cannot forgive you and I cannot forgive myself."

He tried to hold her hand but it was ridged with pain. The truth of his feelings burst beyond his pride and he pressed his face into her neck. "Oh Brid, how have I done this to you?" Suddenly it no longer mattered about Harle.

He broke down into sobs and only stopped when he was aware that someone was standing at his shoulder. A light hand gripped his shoulder.

"Hal, I'm sorry, so sorry. I do not have the power to heal her: I need the magic of the Trinity."

Hal hastily wiped his eyes. If Brid was dying it was only right that he too went to an early grave.

"You do not blame me?" he asked Keridwen, feeling so young in her presence.

"I do not blame you. None loved her more than you." She kissed his forehead and smiled. "I came to tell you that, of course, I shall adorn you and your men with the runes of war."

Hal gave her a lopsided grin. "Thank you. I shall be a braver man for them."

"Not even runes would make you braver, Hal. There is none braver than you – and never was, and I doubt there ever shall be again."

Hal smiled and gripped her small hand. "Keridwen, there is just one thing you must do for me."

She nodded.

"Spar. When you find him, tell him I love him."

Keridwen smiled sadly back. "I shall, of course, but there is no need. He knows you love him just as you know he loves you."

When Hal thought of his nephew, who had been his constant childhood companion, he felt the tears pricking at his eyes again. If there was someone whom he wished to bid farewell to more than any other, it was Caspar. Then he swallowed his regret. No, he was glad Caspar was not there. Caspar would not have let him go alone; he would have gone with him to his death. His stomach tightened and he thought for a moment whether he shouldn't write a letter to the youth but decided there was nothing he could say that would come near describing the intensity of his emotions. Instead, he took his ring and handed it to Keridwen.

"Give him this." He looked sorrowfully at Brid lying in quiet pain. "I have no need to give her anything because I am hers; I shall wait for her on the other side. I cannot go on without her."

He crouched to kiss her and then rose to meet his men. The forty volunteers sat around a fire, apart from the main camp. They drank sparingly from a shared pitcher of ale and ate of the finest quality Jotunn beef, baked breads and vine-fruit from Caldea. At first, Hal thought he had little stomach for food but then, when he saw the men's bright faces, he himself fixed a courageous smile onto his lips and found that soon it came naturally, for though they would die once their trap was set, they would die bold men.

"Balladeer, sing!" he commanded.

He sipped the ale that was honey-sweet but with a touch of sour to give it guts but then he sipped the water and thought just how much better that tasted. Gazing about him, he saw how beautiful the fire was and how spectacular the stars were above as they came one by one to life out of a lilac sky.

The song went on, verse after rousing verse, praising each man, and Hal was delighted with the balladeer and his delivery. The men sang the chorus as one and soon they all were familiar with their companions.

One raised his tankard and spoke. "I've been a thief, a wretched thief all my life and now, at last, I get the chance to do something for the common good. It feels fine to be praised."

All were asked how best their pleasure might be fulfilled that night. Of their own accord, women were lining up, eager to lie with a warrior in the hope of conceiving a son with some of his father's heart. But none of the men would have it for fear of breaking their sense of brotherhood created in their common bond. Instead, they anointed themselves in oils and put on their finest clothes ready for the morning. Hal whetted his sword and honed the blade and, when it was perfect, he slept.

He awoke early to a pink dawn and awaited Keridwen's promised arrival.

A small dark figure with the sun behind her, she stood in her white robes of office. The sun touched her head, outlining her silhouette in glinting red. She stepped closer and turned around so that the sun fell on her creamy face, her hair a magnificent flame. From her mouth came the sweetest notes as she chanted her words of magic and, in a sudden violent movement, she raised her sacrificial knife and slashed her forearm, the cut shallow though it bled freely. Her dark blood brightened to scarlet as it trickled down her arm and over her hand, dripping from her fingers.

Solemnly, she let the drops fill a small flat bowl and then daubed each of the men's cheeks and forehead with Tiw's rune: ↑, the rune of war.

The volunteers linked hands to form a circle and Keridwen gave her final blessing. Hal felt the magic of that circle as their wills and hearts were joined in one purpose.

Collecting the last of their belongings, they were finally ready. Hal turned once to look back at the manor and his brother, who stood now a distant figure, arm raised in farewell. Keridwen had already returned to the manor and was in tight conversation with a short figure that held a lean horse that pranced on the end of its rope. Hal raised his arm in final salute and at the head of his men rode west into the mountains.

Over the next few miles, they commandeered two hundred head of goats, horses and cattle, to be sure of providing for the hobgoblins' taste, then driving the live-stock before them, they picked their way through the deep shade of the valleys, working slowly round to the north for three days to Whitehart's River. Once they reached the river, they followed its course east towards the canyon, the valley sides steepening into a rocky ravine.

At last, late on that third day, they came to the old quarry. A crack in the hard rock of the northern wall of the ravine had been blasted out and formed a narrow mouth to the quarry. Through the gap was a huge bowl-shaped hollow cradled on all sides by jagged mountains. Under the light of the moon, they herded the livestock through the narrow mouth and then penned them within.

Near dawn, they slaughtered two dozen beasts and withdrew, waiting for sunrise, which would bring with it the vultures, their great circles in the sky summoning the hobgoblins and the trolls. Hal signalled to his men to retreat to a safe vantage point high above the ravine from where they could see along the course of Whitehart's River to the point where it disgorged itself into the wider canyon.

In the cool before dawn, they shivered in their cloaks and waited. Then as sunlight flooded the canyon, they watched the hobgoblins scurry like ants from the main canyon, running barefoot to the feast. Hal was disappointed that only a dozen trolls lumbered up the ravine but at least his plan had worked well to draw off the vile hobgob-lins. His eyes ached from counting the swarming rabble of long-limbed creatures but he made a rough estimate that at least a thousand had been drawn into the trap. That was good! They had done well!

Within an hour, the bleats of the animals had ceased and only a few hobgoblins still hurried to the ravine. Hal decided now was the time to move; they needed to get into position before the feast was over.

Silently, they approached the quarry mouth. Five men abreast, they marched along the river towards the hideous sound of the hobgoblins' baneful squabbling. Standing firm, they blocked the quarry mouth and waited for the contented sounds of eating to turn to grunts and squabbles, as the hobgoblins fought over the last scraps, and then he knew they would come. Drawing a deep breath, he focused only on his men, his weapons and the task at hand.

He looked magnificent. The morning sun shone in his raven black hair, his face freshly shaved, his body oiled. Five javelins were stuck into the ground beside him, ready to hurl. His sword was in its sheath on his back and on his belt were five throwing knives and a dagger. His padded hauberk was especially oiled, his boots polished and his dark eyes glinted with excitement. He swung his sword-arm, flexing his muscles, and looked down the line of men; their faces were composed, and they were ready.

Drawing in even lungfuls of the crisp Torra Altan air, he listened, waiting to catch that first sound of the enemy leaving the quarry. He wasn't afraid. He was strangely elated, the adrenaline in his twitching body making him tingle.

They had given Pip and Ceowulf a chance by drawing off the hobgoblins but it took time to claim a castle from within, time to breach the earthworks and find their way in. He and his volunteers must hold these creatures here for as long as was humanly possible. He had fought in many skirmishes and prepared for battle all his life; he had been hurt many times; but it wasn't that which daunted him now. It was awareness of the exertion that was needed, the physical exhaustion from wielding his sword time and time again that played on his mind. Would he have the stamina for the huge muscular effort required for the lengthy combat that awaited him?

He grinned at the men beside him. Bullback's sons, Thane and Oxwin stood, legs astride, and looked as solid as bulls. They were brave but he could feel their tension like bands of steel in the air, tightening around them.

One of Bullback's men behind grunted, "Listen!"

Hal could hear nothing but he could feel the ground begin to tremble. A rock was dislodged from the cliffs above him and tinkled down, disturbing the scree that rolled, crunched and came to rest just feet from them. The sun glinted on metal at the mouth of the quarry; one flash at first followed by many as if twinkling stars were caught in the shadows.

Raising his horn to his lips, he blasted out his arrogant challenge then grinned at the men beside and behind him.

"The day is ours; this is our moment of glory!"

CHAPTER TWENTY-FIVE

The horn of Vaal-Peor, a promontory of western Vaalaka, was a line of grey to the port side of the whaler. Caspar, who had at last found his sea-legs, spent a short while gazing wistfully at the joyous sight of land and then turned back to the more diverting task that had preoccupied him for most of the voyage. The other men aboard ship were also watching her.

Mysteriously pretty and disarmingly graceful, Izella laughed with the men, gliding about the ship, telling tales and singing songs in that wondrous voice of hers. The men loved to watch and listen. She lifted their hearts and dispelled their fears and discomforts.

The way she played with Isolde made Caspar laugh, too, it had been a long time since he had allowed himself the luxury and it felt good. She sat with Priddy and the baby and they rolled on the floor, giggling for no apparent reason. Her carefree gaiety was infectious and he adored her. They had been at sea for several weeks, and during that time, he found himself thinking about Izella more and more.

Finally, she invited him to his bed and this time he did not refuse; May had paid her farewells, and he felt free to accept. He revelled in the pleasure, the indescribable, purely physical delight of lying with a woman of Ash. But already that intense joy had turned sour. Clearly, the act had no emotional meaning to Izella and, though he had glowed with satisfaction, she had asked for more and more of him and he had found her too demanding. Where he wanted love, she sought diversion.

He shrugged. Though it had galled at the time, he didn't care anymore. Tomorrow they would see Belbidia; he could barely sleep for the excitement. But, when they did land on the west coast of Ovissia and his feet touched the soil, his joy at returning to his homeland was swept away by a sense of dread. Caspar looked around him at the quiet cove where they had landed, the small village about the harbour was entirely deserted, doors and shutters banging in the wind.

He took the baby from Priddy, who would merge into the shadows too easily and he was terrified of losing his child. Isolde was no longer so easily contented as she had been aboard the rocking motion of the ship and he struggled to wrap her up tight against the breeze and place her in the sling at his chest.

"What's wrong?" Izella asked, her cool hand on his.

He brushed it off uncomfortably and stroked the top of his head. His head ached. Dizzily, he longed for escape from the chronic physical discomfort.

"Wolves, I should think."

"We have fine horses. Surely none, not even the hooded wolves you told us about can catch us," she said brightly, her breath sweet in his face. He stepped back now, wary of her close physical presence. She laughed at him. "Your kind take themselves too seriously. Live to the full; enjoy life! Smell the air; it is sweet, the warmth of the sun so glorious." She held out her hand as if catching the sun's rays, her face aglow. "And there is hope; we are in your land where we shall find the precious trinoxia."

Caspar scratched at his sore scalp. "I have to take Isolde

home and see Necrönd into safe hands before we can go in search of Reyna and the trinoxia."

"What!" Izella's face was serious and taut, her charm evaporating. "Old Woman Ash does not have time for this. What are we waiting for? We must hurry!" She was mounted quickly and impatient for the others to follow.

With Isolde safely in her sling, he mounted and, calling for the dog to follow, set off into the wolds above the village. He put Izella from his thoughts. He needed his mind clear; there were too many things out of place. It wasn't just the deserted fishing village or the overwhelming silence of the wolds; there was something else.

The golden horses tugged and shrieked, fresh from their weeks tethered aboard ship and Caspar was glad of their speed. Weak with the dull ache that throbbed within him, he led the way home along the southern edge of the Yellow Mountains. He had wrapped the silver casket containing Necrönd in lays of fur but it felt so vulnerable at his chest, nestled alongside the baby, who constantly played with the chain. They rode along deserted roads. Gone was the industrial fever of this wealthy land and, in its stead, a nervous wariness seeped out of the wolds.

"It's not how you described it at all," complained Priddy.

When they stopped to feed Isolde, Izella picked a bunch of speedwell. "Like your eyes," she said, "such a bright blue."

"I'm immune to your charms," he told her.

"No man is immune to us. We are irresistible."

Caspar laughed at her boldness. "It's true, Izella, you help me forget some of my pain and I thought I would love you but lust isn't love."

"You are too much of a romantic."

"Is that a fault?" Caspar asked injured.

"Of course! You get hurt too easily and do not know how to enjoy yourself."

"Love," he said with a sigh, thinking of those last moments with May, "is the most enduring aphrodisiac."

She spluttered into laughter as if that were the quaintest of ideas and then suddenly her apparent gaiety sombred. "Come, Spar, I suffer more than you. My kind are dying, the Lady Ash is dying. If I do not quickly find this trinoxia you have told me about, no more will the quiet footsteps of the people of Ash tiptoe across the earth. Let's hurry, but remember nothing is ever so serious that you must deny yourself what joys the Great Mother freely gives us."

The horses of Rye Errish galloped with such breathtaking speed that soon they had traversed the breadth of Ovissia and were nearing the mouth of the canyon that was Caspar's home. They had passed three deserted farmsteads on the southern slopes of the Torra Altan mountains and he was becoming increasingly uneasy. As they reached the next farm, a barn door was banging in the wind and he left the road to investigate. The fences were down and there was no sign of life.

"Look!" Izella cried and he hurried to her side.

Strange long thin footprints pocked the farm tracks.

"What are they?" he asked.

"Hobgoblins!" Izella exclaimed at once. "Blackthorn's people. Vile vagabonds, sewer-dwellers! What evil has drawn them out of their dank caves?"

They hurried on, to the wooded mouth of the canyon. His heart in his throat, Caspar rounded a cascade of boulders tumbled from the bare cliffs of the Yellow Mountains, knowing that in the next second he would see his beloved home, the castle of Torra Alta perched high above the canyon floor. Bow drawn, he edged his horse forward into the half-light. He gasped in horror.

Where the Dragon Standard of Torra Alta should have fluttered above the towers, the black head of the Ovissian Ram danced in the breeze.

He stared open-mouthed for a full minute, before suddenly realising that they were in danger and, half expecting an ambush of hobgoblins or wolves to leap out from the trees ahead, he searched for a place to retreat. The last thing in all the world he was expecting was to find was his own horse.

Firecracker had trotted out from the trees not fifty paces from where they had halted. He snorted excitedly at the golden mares, pawed at the ground and tossed his head. A little man with sandy hair, big eyes, a long thin face and a jittery disposition stood beside the snorting stallion. He put his hands on his hips and said, "Well, *you've* been a long time getting here, I must say."

"H-how? But Fern—" Caspar stammered.

The woodwose flicked his hand at Caspar as if to say he had no time to waste with questions and explanations. "I couldn't do as you bid me and take Firecracker to Torra Alta. I got as close as I could and had to wait until now to find any of your kin here in Jotunn. Your mother said you were coming home and I smelt you on the wind." Fern's nose wrinkled in disgust. "You have been near him, the vile wolfman."

"Mother, Father . . . are they safe?" Caspar demanded.

Fern shrugged. "They're at Bullback's manor."

"But what are they doing there while Godafrid's flag is over Torra Alta?" Caspar demanded, dismayed and flummoxed by the whole situation.

"Ovissians, hobgoblins and wolves!" Fern said as if that was meant to explain everything. "But they failed to claim the castle and Hal . . ."

"What of Hal?" Caspar felt the surge of panic turn his skin white and his mouth dry.

"He led a party north to the quarry at Whitehart's River to draw off the hobgoblins. The idea was to buy Ceowulf enough time to enter the castle but he has failed and now Hal and his men are being slaughtered in vain. Branwolf's men can't get through to him because—"

Caspar didn't wait to hear more. The quarry at Whitehart's River! Normally it would take two days at least from here over the mountains but, on one of Talorcan's horses, he could do it within the hour.

Hastily, he unbuckled the sling and handed his baby to Priddy. "Keep her safe! Fern, take them to my mother!" he yelled over his shoulder as he galloped like the wind, barely able to breathe for the pace. Hunched up over the horse's withers, his mind melted with the steed's as they leapt rocks and ravines. "Faster! Faster!" he urged, stabbing his heels into the mare's ribs.

The black circle of vultures in the sky told him that he neared the scene of the battle. A horrible stench of rotten guts wafted to him on the wind and the air was thick with deep booming cries more like that of a heron than any animal he knew. His blood ran cold in his veins and his head pounded as if a thousand tiny men picked at the stem of his brain with axes. His muscles were cramped with dread and he could barely think; his only wisp of joy was that the air trembled with a metallic peal, a sound so great and awesome that he knew Hal lived. It was the victory note of the runesword, its song of triumph loud in the air.

He galloped to the top of the gorge cut by Whitehart's River and looked down. For a long moment, he could not work out what he was looking at. The narrow gorge at the mouth of the old lime quarry was alive with a stirring mass of creatures. He stared harder to see what they were. Long-limbed, greenish-brown creatures, hobgoblins he decided, clambered over the bodies of their fallen kin to attack a tiny knot of men who held the narrow mouth of the quarry.

Caspar could get to their backs and, without thinking what he would do other than stand and fight and die alongside Hal, he spurred the horse to the edge of the ravine, flung himself from the saddle and slipped and slithered down a gully to get to his uncle's side.

Shrieking out the Torra Altan battle cry, he loosed his arrows, until his quiver of forty was empty and forty horrible wails of death pierced the barking cries of the hobgoblins.

Hal, stripped to the waist, his torso covered in sweat and blood, hacked with enormous effort, at the waves of creatures that pressed relentlessly forward. Caspar stumbled through the severed limbs and slipped in black entrails until he was at his uncle's side, his short sword drawn and already wet with the blood of goblin.

Five others still stood with Hal. Caspar had recognized at once two of Bullback's sons, Thane and Oxwin. Large men, well-armoured and well-trained, it was inevitable that they would outlast the common soldiers whose fallen bodies littered the stony ground. Several had been dragged off by the hobgoblins that, like vultures, buried their heads in the men's stomachs and feasted on the offal. Sweat poured from the few left standing and one, whom he did not know, was constantly being knocked to his knees though he kept on fighting.

Caspar was aware of all of this and noted immediately that Hal's left hand was gone, replaced by a hook, as he hacked and slashed, his bones jarring as his sword cut through the goblins' sinews and cracked against their steel-hard bones. Hal flashed him a look from the corner of his eye but clearly had no energy for speech as he swung the great runesword at an attacking hobgoblin and sliced up the length of its belly. The creature fell against him and Hal shouldered it aside just in time to defend himself against another. "Necrönd!" Hal yelled at him. "Wield it!"

"I can't!" Caspar grunted back, now shoulder to shoulder with his uncle, the two of them protecting one another, the music of their art so free and harmonious that the enemy momentarily stepped back. Though Hal wielded the runesword, he was exhausted; Caspar for the first time in his life had more strength than Hal. Willpower alone kept him on his feet.

"Is the castle ours?" Hal gasped.

"No!" Caspar replied and wished he hadn't as Hal paused in his efforts and a hobgoblin got underneath his guard to nick his thigh with his dagger before Caspar cut the creature down the length of its knobbly backbone.

"Then we die here for nothing? Wield Necrönd, Spar and get us out of here!" Hal gasped.

"I can't," Caspar repeated.

A squeal of pain came from the fifth man as he was finally overwhelmed and only Hal, Thane, Oxwin and one other remained beside Caspar. He stabbed again as a hobgoblin leapt at him from above, the force of the blow driving him to his knees.

"Use it or we die here!" Hal yelled, staggering and touching down with his stump but fighting his way up again.

Caspar was thumped backwards by the sheer force of another goblin ramming into his stomach. The wind was knocked from him as his back crunched against rock, though he thrust his arm upwards and forced his blade into the creature's lungs. Black blood spumed from its screaming mouth and, for a moment, Caspar was blinded.

He had the strangest notion, however, that the rock stirred behind him. His sword still buried deep in the hobgoblin, he reached for the knife at this belt and stabbed wildly until his eyes cleared. He fought on, facing wave after wave until he thought he could no longer lift his arm. Hal had been fighting for many hours more and he knew he must keep going. In numb exhaustion the thought played at the back of his mind that the rock at the mouth of the quarry had somehow moulded to help him. A stonewight perhaps?

If there were stonewights here, surely, they would help him. He racked his brain, trying to remember the words that Perren had used to awaken the old ones that slept as rocks in hollow mountains of Kalanazir.

"Stonewights, hear me in the name of the Mother," he bellowed. "I am guardian of Necrönd and friend to your kind; stir from your slumber and help me do Her will!"

Nothing happened.

"Earthquake!" he shouted in desperation, lunging at a hobgoblin and kicking it away with his bloodied boot.

Still nothing happened and then at last he remembered it; the ancient name that Perren had uttered.

"Virlithos!" he yelled.

The ground trembled and Caspar found himself tumbling onto hard rock. A hobgoblin fell on top of him, biting his leg, its pointed teeth clamped around his shinbone. The air rich with cries, he stabbed his dagger into the base of the goblin's skull and staggered. Stones were falling from the steep sides of the quarry then, with a mighty rumble and crash, huge sections of rock sheered from the man-cut walls and came crashing down. Dust and debris filled his mouth, nose and eyes.

The ground stilled and the hobgoblins' cries became strangely muffled and remote. As the dust settled, he stared ahead. Rather than facing a savage sea of screaming creatures, he and the few remaining men stared at a wall of rock.

The quarry was gone from view. Only seven hobgoblins stood with them, who shrieked fearfully when three pairs of massive fists came out of the rock beside them and lifted them off their feet. Two were merely pummelled to the ground while the rest were swallowed into the rock and then spat out again in bloody pieces.

Hal and the three other men that had fought alongside him slumped to the ground, uncaring as to what had saved them, only knowing that the sudden silence meant their fight was done. It was until after several minutes of simply staring up at the bright sky that Caspar at last focused on the ring of five stonewights looking down on him, blotting out all view of the ravine and the quarry.

"You spoke the ancient words of our people. Where did you learn them? Who are you?" a stonewight's great voice rumbled.

Caspar trembled. He had forgotten how fearsome and *huge* the adult stonewights were. Glistening granite eyes glowered at him.

"I— I—," he stammered.

"How dare you, feeble creature, awaken me from my sleep! Answer me, trespasser!"

"I am Caspar, son of Baron Branwolf of Torra Alta," he managed to splutter.

The world was darkening now as the monstrous stony beings crowded close. Collapsed in exhaustion, Hal was lying on his back, exhausted, staring up with a vaguely puzzled look on his face.

"Spar, what have you done now?" he gasped.

The stonewight reared up, towering over them, and bellowed like a bear. "Vile thief! Desecrater! It is you that has stolen my home and axed my father's resting place."

Caspar protested loudly. "What? We've done nothing—"

"You've hacked great chunks of our home away and you say you've done nothing!" The stonewight's great voice trembled the air. One lifted Oxwin from his feet and began to squeeze him until his eyes bulged.

"Leave him, it's not his fault! He's not a Torra Altan and we would never have opened up the quarry if we'd known it was your home." Caspar didn't know what else he could say as he was lifted from his feet and held in a massive, iron-hard fist.

The stonewights leant over them and, in swaying strides, took them to the wall of the ravine. The rocks stirred and a black cave opened up. Caspar was aware of little else other than the echo of slow footsteps as they entered the hollow hillside within the mountain. There was no light at all and the dark sharpened Caspar's senses. Intensely aware of Hal's breathing and the panted gasps of the other men, he could smell them too; smell their sweat and their fear. But he could not smell the stonewights, only feel their rough hard skin crushed close around his body.

The echo from the footsteps was taking longer to reach them and Caspar was certain that they had entered a larger cavern within the rocks. There was a foul stench of rotten animals and a curious singing, deep and full of mysterious notes that were tuneless but remarkably soothing in tone. He guessed that some of the older stonewights were attempting to lull their young to sleep. The sound of trickling water whispered all about him.

"No, a story! Another story!" a gravelly voice protested.

"You do not need a story now," the stonewight that

gripped Caspar by the waist boomed. "I have men! These are the very creatures that have hacked away our home to make the Big Hole!"

There was a general gasp and many shouted for blood.

Caspar swallowed hard, trying to keep his control above his rising fear. "You do not want our blood for we have the finest stories ever to be heard. I have been over the top of the world!" he proclaimed grandly.

"Indeed!" The fierce grip around his waist lessened and Caspar was set down though, whether on rock or the knee of a stonewight, he couldn't tell. After a moment, tiny yellow specks of light appeared, giving out a faint amber glow and, as Caspar blinked, trying to see, he decided they were glowing stones.

"Amber eyes!" the stonewight said and Caspar guessed they were like the sunburst rubies only these were purely yellow. In the dim, light he saw around him the faces, craggy and round, of thousands of stonewights stretching away in all directions to fill the huge chamber. A nest of smaller ones like Perren, were huddled together at the centre, some lying down and some being encouraged to do so by their fathers. Between the stonewights, the floor of the great chamber was riddled with a network of rivulets that wove in and around the stonewights' feet.

"More amber eyes so we might see what we are eating!" one demanded.

"No," Caspar shouted. "Hear my story first!"

"Yes! Yes!" the younger stonewights enthused.

"We must. A story! A story!" one or two of the little stonewights leapt up from where they were being encouraged to sleep and clamoured so loudly that the older stonewights yielded.

"This had better be good!" Hal growled at Caspar. "It's so like you to make an even worse hash of things. Until you thought to rescue me, at least I was going to die a hero rather than just becoming some creature's supper."

"Don't worry," Caspar said under his breath. "I know these creatures. Once upon a time," he began loudly; "there lived a young stonewight called Perren."

"Oh!"

"Ah!" gasped the young stonewights appreciatively.

"His father was called Ham, son of Tecton, son of Heel, son of Bollon, son of Lias, son of Colossus, son of Rollright . . ." And so, Caspar continued. He had a good memory and Perren had told him so many stories. He remembered well that, whenever the stonewight spoke of himself, he started with his forefathers, reciting back seven generations.

"That's not a story," Hal hissed at him.

"Hush, I know what I'm doing," Caspar whispered before telling the stonewights how many teeth Perren had and that he claimed to have six hundred and twenty-three hairs in each eyebrow.

"Well begun!" one of the older stonewights cheered him and Hal gave him a lopsided smile.

"From his cave where the darkest and largest sunburst rubies grow in all the world, he took me under and over the eastern range of these very Yellow Mountains. We crossed forty-five valleys and waded through twenty-six streams on our way to the great water."

"Ah, the Great Water," another of the huge stonewights sighed.

Caspar did not know how long he could make his story last but knew that every moment he kept them enthralled, the longer they would stay alive.

"But Perren stayed too long in the hot desert sun . . ." Caspar began what he thought to be the interesting part of his tale.

"No wait. You have not told us of the sand and where it came from and how the wind lifted it and swept it up into mounds," a stonewight objected.

Caspar tried to describe the sand but could not satiate the stonewights' curiosity about how many grains there were or how deep it was or what it was like to be without water and therefore bereft of the knowledge of the world. The stonewights became restless and annoyed.

"We do not want stories from him. He has destroyed our home, stolen our rocks. Moreover," the largest of the stonewights growled, "he has come to subjugate us." The great creature swished his hand through the pool that they had diverted into shallow channel that flowed in loops and canals around the floor of the chamber.

Caspar's trembling hand went to the silver casket at his neck and he looked the creatures that crowded in on him.

"Leave him alone or you die!" Hal bellowed, sword drawn though he swayed on his feet with the effort of holding it.

The stonewight swatted Hal aside before he could summon the strength to react and, now, he lay gasping on the floor, face down in the water. Caspar had only enough time to pull his head up and drag him clear before he found himself pinched in a stonewight's grip.

"We've heard this one's tale. Let's put him in the larder and we'll make a feast of him and the others once we've tired of their stories."

Grateful only that they had not already killed him, Caspar found himself in sudden darkness, no sounds reaching him through the solid rock about him other than a steady drip, drip of water like a pulse in the extremities of a vast body. With neither light nor sound about him, he quickly began to feel disoriented and only knew that time passed because he was growing cold and his muscles were stiffening after the exertion of battle. "Hal!" he shouted frantically, praying that his uncle could hear him. "Just keep telling stories."

He heard nothing in reply, only the steady drip, drip of the water. He sat quietly, trying to listen until eventually he could hear only his own pulse, thunderous in his ears, and his rasped breathing. Panic, overtook him and he crawled about the damp cell within the rock, fingering his way round and searching for an exit. He found a splinter of something that was either wood or bone and began to chip away at the rock without success. He reached for his knife and worked that into a tiny fissure but it was hopeless.

Unable to help himself, he lost control, began to scream and shriek, thumping the rocks about him with his fists until his voice was hoarse and his knuckles wet with blood. Still nothing happened and the cold realization that he would die here swept over him.

Exhausted, he sat back and again tried to listen for any sounds of movement. Still, he could hear nothing apart from a steady drip, drip of water. He hung his head but then . . . No, wait! There was something else, a pounding hum in his ears. He didn't know if it was ringing in his own head or something outside him only that it was getting louder. Every fibre in his body was tense with anticipation; he could feel a great power all about him, welling out from his breast, the energy contained and concentrated within the stone cell, unable to escape.

It was then that he realized that his fingers were on the silver casket and that he had been toying with the idea of wielding the Egg. He snatched his hand away, fearful that, already, his weakened mind had caused harm. Swallowing hard, he sat back and, fists tight with tension, he listened. Still, he could hear nothing more than a drip, drip, drip of water.

He rubbed at his crooked nose and opened his mouth, feeling for the rocks with his tongue so that he might catch some of that dripping water and so quench his thirst. He banged his nose as he caught it against a protruding rock and pinched it to relieve the pain. He sniffed, and then sniffed again. He could smell something, a powerful stale smell.

With his heart pounding, he strained to listen and at last, he heard it, a soft padding noise. His heart was in his throat. Something was snuffling closer, seeking him, sniffing him out. The hairs on the back of his neck stood on end.

Pressing himself back against the cell wall, he trembled in alarm, his ears echoing with the sound of manic laughter. Something soft brushed against him and the air was pungent with the foul stench of rotting flesh. In the utter blackness, Caspar cradled himself in his own arms, hugging his knees tight to his chest and praying to the Great Mother for mercy.

"It's just you and I now," a voice thick with saliva growled at him, out of the blackness.

Caspar yelped as something bit him on the toe. He lashed out but could feel nothing.

The laughter rang out again. "I have you now!"

Caspar yelped again as this time something bit him hard on the thigh, sharp teeth sinking deep into the flesh. He lashed out with his knife, cutting the air of the chamber, but there was nothing there. If only he could see. But the moonstone! Of course! Why hadn't he thought of it before? He foraged in his pockets and plucked it out. The soft glow filled the tight cell but he could see only the limy walls polished by rivulets winding down them, seeking out the cracks to work their way deep down to the roots of the mountains.

The glow brought him comfort and he realized for the first time how much the ancient moonstone that had once held his mother's image must have meant to the blind dragon beneath Torra Alta. He cradled the glowing orb against his chest and, for a long while, was filled with a sense of great relief; the light must have repelled his attacker. Near exhaustion, he slumped down on the smooth floor and gazed into the moonstone's glossy white surface that stirred like scudding clouds on a stormy day. The clouds darkened and billowed like gathering thunderheads as he stared closer.

"Help me!" he murmured to the stone. "Someone hear me! Please!"

The stone darkened to granite and grew heavier. "Perren!" he called. "Help me. You must still be there. Help me!"

Nothing happened. Caspar closed his eyes and gritted his teeth against his fear and the overwhelming throbbing in his head. He clutched his knees to him and rocked back and forth, fighting to find his last vestige of courage. Then out of the dark, something snapped at his neck making him squeal with the shock of it. He twisted round to fight it off and his fingers briefly brushed against soft fur; the chamber rang with laughter.

"I shall have my revenge," a bestial voice snarled.

"Who are you? What do you want with me?" Caspar curled his legs up to him and hugged himself tight, certain that he knew the voice despite its guttural growl.

"I want you to suffer as you have made me suffer!" came the snarled reply. "I shall nibble away at your flesh and then, when your hands are no more than bone, I shall rip Necrönd from you!"

"No! Never! The Great Mother will never allow it."

"The Great Mother! She has no power over me! I have bought power with your father's wealth. Think what a joy it was for me to take from the mighty Baron. The verderers tiptoe about me now and even Straif listens to my word and Old Man Blackthorn has pledged him the help of his people. I have power, little nephew, beyond your dreams!"

"Gwion!" Caspar gasped, at last recognizing the voice wrapped within the lupine growls. What should he say to appease this tormented soul? "Gwion, be at peace; I had no wish to hurt you. You were my uncle, my flesh and blood. Morrigwen—"

"Morrigwen!" the bodiless voice howled. "Morrigwen! She only ever loved my sister. She never loved me!" His wail turned to a scream and then a snarl of rage. Human hands were at Caspar's throat, ripping at his clothing while a savage mouth with sharply curving fangs tore at his face.

He had no breath to scream. The wolfman's mouth was around his windpipe. All he could do was thump at him with the moonstone in his hand though he was rapidly weakening and his vision was swimming into red. He struggled and kicked but knew that, too quickly, he was losing consciousness. At last, his fingers loosened around the moonstone and it began to slip from his fingers. He was letting go of life. He sensed the triumph in Gwion's body as the wolf stiffened.

The moonstone dropped. Caspar heard it tinkle to the floor, the soft glow of its light gone from his vision. The world was black, silent and still. Numbness conquered him and apathy swaddled his body; he knew it was over.

A mighty roaring filled his ears, like the sound of rushing water. His head spun and he felt horribly sick

– but that meant he was alive. Pain was good; sickness was good. He lived! Curled up in a tight ball, he cringed from the roaring noise until he realized it was his own breath suddenly rasping through his body.

He could move! Gwion's wolflike body was no longer bearing down on him. His hand went to his throat and he felt the dampness of blood and ragged skin. He pulled his fingers away not daring to explore his injuries further. With the moonstone gone, all was dark. Grunts, squeals and crashes now reached his ears. A wolf howled long and high, the noise abruptly silenced by the sound of a stone club cracking down on its skull. Then there came quiet, the fearful silence of the dark.

Caspar fingered the hem of his shirt, ripped at it and took the length of material to bandage his neck as best he could. He felt unbearably cold, the sense of death all around him. Too weak to respond, he merely cringed as a cold hand closed around his wrist. He could see nothing as he was dragged upright in the low chamber, his head pushed down by a heavy hand to stop him cracking his skull on the roof.

"Quickly! Quickly! This way!" a deep rumbling voice coaxed him. Rocks tumbled and crashed and then Caspar saw the faintest chink of light cascading down through the dust and the faintest outline of two huge grey legs and a squat round body.

"Perren! You came at last!" he exclaimed but already the ghostly image was failing. A hand was raised to wave him farewell and a hollow voice begged, "Get Necrönd back to your mother before it's too late for us all."

Left in the silence, Caspar stared up at the chimney that had appeared in the twisted rocks around him. With trembling fingers, he began the slow hard crawl up, painstakingly working his fingers into the rock to find a foothold.

His mind was a storm of emotions. Though exhausted and in pain, he knew his wounds were surely only superficial and the wolf must have missed the larger blood vessels of the neck; otherwise, he would have been dead almost immediately. Instead, he was alive and the weight of his burden was even more onerous than before.

"I must get home," he told himself out loud. He hated to leave Hal and yet there was nothing he could do on his own to get him out. He prayed that his uncle knew he would never abandon him and that he would be back with help as soon as he could. His fingernails ripped down to the quick, he struggled up out of the hole in the earth and rolled over onto his back, thankful of the warmth of the sun on his face.

His horse! Where was the horse? Staggering and stumbling, he clawed his way to the top of the rise to survey the scene. The quarry was silent, the stench of crushed and half-eaten hobgoblins thick in the air. Not even the vultures and the ravens would pick at their festering bodies. Caspar looked around him and at last saw a flash of gold that could only be the sun glinting off the sleek back of one of Talorcan's horses.

It took him as long to reach the horse, which whickered softly at his approach, as it did for him to gallop across the Yellow Mountains and tear across the wooded plain for Bullback's manor. Barely seeing what was around him, he swept through the fields and skidded to a halt outside the closed gates of the manor. Ranks of tents were closely packed around the ruins of the ancient castle and pressed up to the walls of the manor, but it was not the sight of the gathered army that halted him. Fern was running towards him, sprinting across the fields from the nearby woods, Priddy and Izella hurrying after him.

"What are you doing here? I told you to take Isolde straight to my mother," Caspar complained.

"I know, but I couldn't face bringing them the news that you had disappeared again when they need you so much. I see you haven't got Hal," Fern pointed out painfully.

Caspar shook his head. Anxiously, he reached down to take his baby from Priddy's arms and cuddled and kissed Isolde before sliding her into her sling. With Fern, Priddy, Pennard and Izella at his heels, Trog barking and running on ahead, he approached the closed gates.

"Halt! Halt in the name of the King!" A voice called out from the gloom, and a tired-looking soldier thrust a pike at Caspar's blowing horse, while his eyes slid towards Izella and fixed on her.

Caspar turned his horse. "Stand back or you'll never take another breath."

"I've orders. I—"

"Just stand aside and take me to Baron Bullback," Caspar snarled. His thoughts were only on one thing. Hal needed help.

The sentry on duty trotted breathlessly through the fields of tents and the heaps of soldiers sleeping uncomfortably alongside smouldering fires. The men were exhausted, many groaning. Women moved amongst them with bandages and pitchers of water. There was a grim look of the vanquished about them. Caspar's heart pumped sickeningly in his stomach.

"What has happened here?" Izella asked.

"A battle," Caspar said with surety, his big eyes flickering back and forth at the scene about him. A man was in his tent screaming horribly, another his skin half shredded and bubbling with scorched blisters, lay on a stretcher while women sobbed around him helplessly. Other charred bodies lay in heaps, awaiting burial.

"They're dying," Izella said sorrowfully.

Caspar could hardly take it all in. His head throbbed with pain. Desperate to know what had happened to his family, he galloped ahead to the Manor, scattering aside men who shielded themselves, quaking in fear from the golden streak that swept through them.

A defeated army! Caspar knew at once that these were not the men of Torra Alta. They were not born fighting men but labourers brought in from the fields to have swords stuffed into their hands. They cringed and screamed, shouting of demons, devils and dragons. Caspar battered his fist against the Manor door, the soldiers too aghast by his arrival to bar the way.

He knew his mother was within; somehow, he had developed a sense that told him when she was close. But there had been a terrible battle and he feared for his father. Servants ushered him in and, without thought for Izella, Priddy or Pennard who trotted in his wake, he barged into the central hall, which was noisy with anxious argument.

Standing still for a moment, he took in the scene, searching urgently for his father but there was no sign of him. His eyes flitted over the men in the room, instantly recognizing Pip standing beside Ceowulf, who appeared to be trying to calm Bullback and a fat man in heavy purple robes. Caspar blinked; but surely, that was King Dagonet of Ceolothia! He couldn't believe it. Then his eyes fixed on the red hair of a woman that had her back to him. She turned slowly and stood, staring across the room at him. She held out her hands.

Slowly the rest of the room fell silent; they looked at Keridwen and then followed her gaze. The silence made the baby at Caspar's chest burst out with raucous cries. Suddenly Caspar was overwhelmed; all were moving at him, yelling and asking where he had been. Isolde was clinging to his chest in fright.

"Silence!" Keridwen commanded "Make room for my son!"

With the baby screaming into the silenced throng, Caspar crossed to her and grasped her hands.

She looked deep into his eyes, her chest rising and falling with emotion. "Spar, you are safe!"

Pip was at Caspar' s elbow and looking at him quizzically. "What the hell is that fearful noise?"

Caspar stood back to lift the red-faced and yelling child from her sling but, already, Keridwen was pulling Isolde from him.

"She is a very fair child," she said simply, her eyes sparkling with excitement, the power of her presence suddenly overwhelming the room.

CHAPTER TWENTY-SIX

"Brid, fight the pain. You are strong enough. Great Mother, give her strength." Keridwen's voice was strained and fearful.

"Keridwen, Keridwen! Help me!" Brid shrieked certain that she could take no more.

A baby was screaming, echoing her cry of suffering.

Caspar's enraged voice was shrill with panic. "What are you doing to her?"

Her eyes, big and black with the terror of the pain, blinked open and stared up at Keridwen who clutched her hand. "My sweet child, you will live. We are Three again."

Brid could not take the words in. Someone had their hand in her stomach, plunged in up to their wrist in her belly. It came out glistening with blood, a sparkle of gold in their pinched thumb and finger. Brid didn't have the strength to look up and see who it was but she knew it was Old Woman Willow. She had plucked out the shard of blade that had broken off within her.

"There is nothing more powerful than my own willow bark to ease pain," the old woman assured everyone.

Brid had the strangest sensation that she was in a tree being rocked back and forth; perhaps she was, she wasn't sure, but it was soothing and she felt safe, at last, undisturbed by the dark forests of the Otherworld. The pain was gone and she felt weak yet at the same time extraordinarily alert.

"Poor child, you must be strong; you have my grandson within you. You have to be strong for his sake," the old willow woman crooned.

"You are strong," Keridwen's voice was in her ear, powerful, reassuring and elated. "We are Three again. Spar has come home with the baby."

Power thrilled through Brid's body. "We are Three!" she echoed. "I am the Mother! The magic returns!" Her eyes sprang open and with a clear head she stared about her and fixed on a pretty little child with extraordinary holly-green eyes.

"Hello, Runa," she greeted her.

"Mama," the baby babbled and stretched out her arms towards her.

Caspar stood by, blinking stupidly and trying to pull Trog away from Brid to stop the over-excited terrier licking her face.

"No, no, that's my baby," Caspar started to explain but no one was paying the slightest attention to him. "But I haven't got time for this. Where's Branwolf? I need him urgently."

"Hush, Spar. He insisted on talking to the men out in the camp. We'll send a messenger to tell him you're here. He'll only be a moment," his mother calmly reassured him. "Your baby, you said?"

"Well, not mine, but May and Talorcan's."

"May's?" Brid asked weakly, her gaze suddenly fixing on him.

"It would take too long to explain," Caspar told her, not knowing where to begin. "The baby's name is Isolde."

Keridwen laughed softly. "Of course, it isn't, Spar. She's Runa."

"May might have loved the wolfling but she wouldn't name her child after an animal," Caspar protested.

554

"No, I mean that *is* Runa," the high priestess continued. "Morrigwen was right; she was the wolfling that would lead us all to the new Maiden."

"What are you talking about?" Caspar demanded. Already he felt that his baby was being taken from him.

"You return with Trog but without Runa," Keridwen continued. "The two were inseparable. I conclude, therefore, that the wolfing is dead."

Caspar nodded, gravely. "I'm sorry, I failed . . ."

"When did she die?" Keridwen cut through his apologies, her voice edgy with excitement.

"The wolfman attacked," he said. "He attacked May. She was heavily pregnant and couldn't move and Runa flung herself into the wolfman's jaws to save May. Trog was inconsolable until—"

"Until the baby was born," Keridwen finished.

"Just look at those strange eyes," Brid continued.

"Of course, they are strange," Caspar interrupted, his voice taught with frustration at waiting for Branwolf to appear. "Her father's eyes were like amber that had caught a lost sunbeam."

"You're quite blind," Brid interrupted. "Those aren't Talorcan's eyes. Those are Runa's. They're a deep green."

Caspar laughed nervously. "You mean Runa and Isolde . . . ?"

"Yes." Keridwen nodded, the gleam in her eye brightening. "The moment you walked through the door, I felt her presence."

"And she is the new Maiden?" Caspar couldn't believe it. He hadn't considered her simply because he had never thought of her as an orphan. He had always thought of her as his own. "But she's just a baby!" He didn't want any of this for Isolde. He wanted his baby to be free of responsibilities and unburdened by the same troubles that weighed down Brid and Keridwen. "You can't do this to her."

"We're not doing anything; she simply is," Brid said calmly, though her eyes were bright with excitement. Her strength growing rapidly, she raised her hand to Caspar's head and pulled him gently towards him. Welcoming her embrace, he hugged her back as she kissed his cheek. "Spar, you did it! You found her!" Exhausted, Brid slumped back onto her pillow.

Caspar did not quite feel the same sense of elation. He felt bereft; they had taken away his baby. But he didn't have time to worry about that anymore. Where was his father? He needed men to get Hal out.

He went into the camp and at last, he saw a gaunt old man limping hurriedly towards him. Caspar stood and stared as the old man staggered to a halt and began to splutter and cough, spitting blood into his hand, before stiffening up to meet Caspar's gaze.

"Father!" the youth cried out in alarm, horrified at how his father had aged. His hair was grey, his temples sunken, his skin ashen. He looked so thin.

Branwolf clutched Caspar's outstretched hands. "Spar, my boy!" he said breathlessly and grinned, his teeth gritted against a further racking cough. His eyes searched his son's face, and his grip tightened. "You are home and we are all saved now. Torra Alta is saved. You have Necrönd. You must have Necrönd? Tell me you have it and that it is not in the hands of the enemy." Branwolf's face was tight with anxiety.

Caspar nodded. "Yes, Father, I have it but—"

Branwolf slapped him on the back. "Tell me all when we're inside."

"But, Father, but what has happened to you?" Caspar demanded, bracing himself as Branwolf leant on him.

Baron Branwolf raised his hand to silence him. "Hush, Spar, do not disgrace me. Praise the Mother, you are well and home. Spar, my boy!" With trembling hands, he embraced his only child.

Caspar fell into his arms and clung tight to the man, whom he considered to be the centre of all strength but was horrified to feel how thin his father had become and to hear his rasped breathing. They hugged for a moment and then pulled apart.

The baron leaning heavily on Caspar's shoulder, he stumbled back into the main hall of Bullback's manor. "Someone bring my boy ale. Spar is home!"

Once inside Caspar helped his father to a chair close to the warmth of the hearth. "Father, I have heavy news. Hal . . ."

"I know." Branwolf's shaking hands clutched his. "Someone had to go. We thought if we could pin the hobgoblins back into the quarry, we would be able to enter the castle unobserved but we didn't know of the three great dragons within the walls until it was too late. They were at first no more than ghostly shadows but soon were fully formed and the fire that they belched was real enough. Hal has given his life for nothing."

"No, Father. You do not know it all! Hal survived. There were stonewights! I called up the stonewights. They shook the earth; the quarry sides collapsed and buried the hobgoblins."

"So where is he?" Branwolf demanded clutching Caspar's shoulder and staring deep into his eyes as if he would find Hal there.

Caspar shook his head. "The stonewights took him into the depths of their caverns and I couldn't get him out."

"I do not understand Spar; does he live or not?"

A shriek filled the room. Brid had clawed her way out

of her sick bed and, doubled up, was working her way from one chair to the next to reach Caspar.

"Brid, no! You must not exert yourself," Keridwen pleaded with her, trying to pull her gently back to her bed.

"Hal!" Brid wailed in wild desperation. "Hal! Where is he?" With enormous strength, Brid staggered to Caspar and clung to his jacket. "Where's Hal?" she begged.

"Under the Yellow Mountains, trapped by stonewights," Caspar said simply, holding out his arms to support her.

"Get him out!" Brid shrieked. "Wield Necrönd!" She shoved him away and beat at his chest.

"I cannot," Caspar said calmly, stepping back as all turned on him.

Branwolf was on his feet. "You must! I order you. Wield it. Rescue Hal and save Torra Alta. Our people are dying within the castle even as we speak."

"I cannot," Caspar repeated, his mind reeling as he tried to find the courage to stand up against all those he most loved and respected.

"Wield it!" King Dagonet roared from the doorway. "They have my daughter. You have it in your power to give me back my daughter."

Ceowulf stepped into the room. "Spar, you must," he said calmly. "They have Cybillia and my son."

"It will mean the end for all of us," Caspar said quietly. "If I wield it, Gwion will take my soul and with it control of Necrönd."

"Gwion?" Keridwen asked slowly, her arm about Brid to support her.

Caspar nodded; it was all clear to him now. "He tore the hair from my head," he fingered the spot, "Do you understand? He stole a part of me and kept it in the Otherworld. And through his knowledge of the arts manipulated my dreams to shape my actions. When I wield Necrönd, he feeds on its strength and twists its magic to his own will."

"Now listen, Spar," Branwolf said with deliberate patience. "You are tired and have obviously suffered but the important thing is that you still have Necrönd. You can rescue Hal and drive these dragons away. Send them back to the Otherworld. Think of Hal, think of the men."

Caspar shook his head. "I am not a coward. I would do anything to save them but you must understand." He pressed his hands to his head, desperately searching for the words that would convince them. "The channels of magic have become distorted. I used it once and it dragged me to the Otherworld and I was nearly trapped there."

He looked at their faces and knew they could never comprehend his meaning. The thought was already forming in his head that there was only one way left to him to rid himself of Gwion.

"Give it to me! If there is a chance that Hal lives, I will get him out," Brid demanded, her voice razor sharp.

Pressing her back, he was about to protest yet again when a vast shadow momentarily darkened the room. He only realized how noisy the thousands of men encamped in the fields about the building had been when a sudden silence fell over them. Everyone pressed against the windows and stared out. Caspar could barely breathe as all stood still and listened. The roar, like that from an open furnace, shook the air, quickly followed by howls of pain and shrieks of terror.

He stared in horror. A jet of flame burst from a shiny green dragon and scythed through a line of tents that exploded in tongues of green and yellow flames. Then something fell from the sky and landed on the stone flags of the manor courtyard with a heavy thud, the contents spilling out and rolling across the courtyard.

Caspar's mouth fell open at the sight of the severed heads and he dug the nails of his fingers into his palms. His father stood at his side; his skin drained of colour.

Branwolf cleared his throat and, with venom, turned on his son. "You can do something about this. You are Lord of Necrönd; wield it. How many more of your countrymen must die before you see what you must do?"

Keridwen rushed from the manor out into the ravaged camp to give what help she might, leaving Brid on her couch, breathing heavily. She was weak and clutched at her stomach but still had the strength to glare icily at Caspar.

"You can still save him. Get him out of there," she hissed at him.

"I cannot; I have told you. Brid, I'm sorry. You know I love Hal just as you do—"

"No one loves Hal as I do!" she raged. "Spar, save him!" She coughed and spluttered and the tears ran down her cheeks. "I cannot live without him, Spar."

Caspar clutched her hand, his thoughts hardening with grim resolve. "I cannot do what you all ask but I will get him back for you." His hands hooked like claws, he hugged her to him, knowing there was only one way. It would take an army of men to dig Hal out from the stonewights' cavern. They had an army but it was pinned down by the shrieking dragons. And all that would stop if he could get to Gwion. He could not destroy Gwion in this world but he could in the next. He must go alone.

His mind was made up. He knew but one way to get there. He had no time to say farewell to anyone except Isolde and there was but one duty he had left in this life that he had to fulfil and that was to pass on his guardianship. He knew he would find her with Priddy and hurried straight towards the solar that was off the main chamber.

Isolde was playing with a wooden doll and a peg dog and was laughing at them excitedly. She had the rune of the wolf that Morrigwen had charged him with and was using the chip of bone as a hammer against the wooden toys, enjoying the noise it created.

Caspar lifted her into his arms and went to the window. There were excited shouts outside, exclaiming that the ships that had landed on the west coast had disgorged an army that was nearly on them. Caspar put Isolde back down on the floor; he had no time to waste. Gwion must be sending more creatures to trap them from the rear. From within his shirt, he took the silver casket and placed it amongst her toys and kissed her.

"Isolde, you are life to me as you were to your mother." He looked at Priddy. "Tell her how I loved her. Tell her how her mother loved her. And tell Keridwen that Isolde is the guardian of Necrönd; she will understand."

If Isolde were to be inaugurated as the new Maiden, there was none wiser than her in her innocence to be its guardian. He couldn't give it to Brid because she would wield it and he couldn't give it to his mother because she would stop him from doing what he must do. Isolde was the only one left.

Priddy, too young to question what he was saying, nodded in understanding. "Oh yes, Spar, I will."

"I have to help my father now," he said, trying to keep his voice steady.

Free of his burden, he now wondered how best to complete his task. He would take his horse and head into the woods where he would find courage. And if he didn't find enough courage, he was certain that it wouldn't be long before the wolves and the hobgoblins reached him.

With that in mind, he purposefully left his bow and short sword behind and took just his knife.

With the camp still astir after the impact of the dragon, he fled across the fields at the back of the manor, unobserved. He glanced back and, to his horror, saw a white shape bounding through the long grass after him. He wheeled Firecracker at the edge of the trees and waited until Trog was close, the animal panting hard. "Home!" he ordered sternly. "Stay with Isolde."

Trog wagged his tail at the command and, remarkably, obeyed, turning and waddling back the way he had come. Caspar spurred his heels into his horse's sides and soon he was dodging branches, his head pressed down close against the sweated crest of Firecracker's neck. The stallion shrieked and started once or twice and Caspar heard the grunts of a large animal. Soon he was in the depths of the forest and began looking for a suitable place to complete his task.

He laughed at himself. It didn't really matter where but, somehow, he wanted it to be at a significant place to mark, for him, what was to be a momentous act. An oak! He had spied a single oak in the midst of a circle of beech. Oddly, he felt that May had been there before him. But she wouldn't be waiting for him on the other side. No one would be waiting. He would have to fight his way through the verderers to get to Gwion and he would drag him to the afterlife, drag him through the forests of Rye Errish to the commoners, to the dark creatures that roved that world, where he might be devoured until his soul was no more. It was the only way.

He dismounted, stripped Firecracker of his tack and, smacking the horse across the rump, sent the animal off into the forest. Alone now, he was acutely aware of the loudness of his breath that he must silence and the thump of his pulse that he must still.

The horn handle of the knife was worn smooth and nestled comfortably in his grip. "How?" he asked out loud, gripping the blade fiercely, staring up through the leaves of the oak into the blue of the sky. He didn't want to die; but Hal had put his duty first and led his men to the quarry, believing that there would be no escape, and he could do no less.

He had the courage; now it was simply a matter of practicalities. The throat, he decided, would surely be the quickest.

He loosened his collar and brushed his thick auburn hair back in readiness.

CHAPTER TWENTY-SEVEN

A familiar bark jerked Caspar's hand from its purpose. The knife was sharp and had still managed to slice into the soft skin of his neck, the shallow cut releasing a tiny red bead from the end of the inch long cut. The bark was followed by the creaking and snapping of twigs and branches, made by the passage of a large beast through the undergrowth.

"Oh, Trog, no!" Caspar said in despair as a white snout poked from between the bracken. The heavy-set dog came leaping towards him, its thick red tongue lolling out of the side of his mouth as he panted excitedly. Caspar couldn't help showing his affection for the faithful animal and, kneeling, grappled with Trog in the way he knew the dog liked. "Good boy, Trog! Good dog. But you should go home to look after Isolde. Now, go home! Go—"

He stopped suddenly and both turned their heads and looked up at the huge silver-backed bear that came swaying into the glade. On its back was a woman, her straight black hair swept off her face and her long lean legs buried in the fur around the bear's neck.

The woman eyed the knife in his hand. "It seems, I have got to you only just in time, Master," Ursula's soft tones caressed his ears. "I came as quickly as I could; you were very hard to follow!"

"Ursula! Oh no!" His hand sunk from his neck in

dismay. "But Ursula, no. I must do this. They are dying. I must stop Gwion."

She dropped from the bear's back and landed lightly on her feet. "Master, I will not let you!"

"Master, you call me. Well, I command you to leave me to my task!" Caspar roared with as much authority as he could muster.

"I have crawled over the top of the world for you," Ursula said sternly. "And I'm not giving up on you now. I call you Master, not because I am your slave, but because you are master of my heart."

Caspar could think of nothing to say beyond, "Oh!"

Ursula stretched out her arms towards him, the silver torcs against her reddish-brown skin like black pools of water in the shade of the forest. Her brown eyes holding his determinedly. "Put down the knife. If you take your life, I shall use that very knife to take my own."

"No, Ursula. I must do this. Too many will suffer if I don't!"

A fierce look filled the woman's eyes and she snatched her knife from her belt and pressed it against her wrist until a thread of blood darkened the edge of the blade. "You gave me back my life but it is nothing without you. I love you and I won't live without you."

"Ursula . . ." Caspar breathed helplessly, the grip on his knife easing.

"Come with me now," she begged him. "I have brought with me an army of bears and a troop of men to direct them. They are well-used to the griffins of my continent. Together, we can fight your enemy."

"We can?" Hope flooded Caspar's heart and, wondrously, he took Ursula's hand. His heart thrilled at her touch and he wondered that he had never realized before how fine she was, perhaps not as beautiful as Brid nor as gentle as May, nor as sensual as Izella, but to him she was more perfect than any of them.

For perhaps a minute, they looked into each other's eyes and then, not so much with passion but more with the relief of welcoming home an old friend, they embraced. Caspar buried his face into the crook of her neck, breathing in the warm sweet scent of her body. She smelt of sweat and lavender and he thought his heart would burst with joy. Nothing had ever felt so natural, so complete before. He would have stayed like that for hours if she had not pushed him away. With a nod of her head, she commanded the bear to kneel onto its forelegs and scrambled up onto its neck.

Caspar leapt up behind her. "I love you," he said without thinking and wondered that the words he had taken so long to say to May came so easily now.

The bear was surprisingly fleet and they were soon within sight of the manor, and Caspar looked joyously at the huge number of humped brown shapes now surrounding the tents. There were hundreds of bears, more than he had ever seen in his life.

Branwolf welcomed them at the gate and walked with Caspar to the main buildings. "We must prepare quickly," the Baron spoke his thoughts aloud. "The bears have changed everything. This girl, Ursula, is a find indeed. Why did you not tell us of her?"

Caspar shrugged.

"It is of no matter. She put fear into our hearts when we saw her approach but she quickly explained everything to us."

Caspar nodded in numb relief and glanced over Branwolf's shoulder to his mother. "Spar!" her face was white and drawn as if she had sensed his purpose but she could say no more for the Baron's booming voice.

"With the bears to aid us we can at last gain entry to the castle. Once we are through and can release the men, the archers of Torra Alta will bring down the dragons just as their forefathers did. If there's enough of us, we can do it. Only then can we consider Hal."

Caspar heard it first; a low rumbling that rattled the hinges of the manor's heavy oak door. Immediately he knew it for what it was and, leaving his father, he hastened into the manor.

He ran to the solar where he had left Isolde, his mother's instinct already forcing her to follow. Priddy must have fallen asleep because she was now stirring and rising from the bed. Isolde was sitting, shrieking in delight.

"You idiot, Spar," Brid hissed acerbically, pushing past Keridwen into the room. "How could you have given it to her?"

Keridwen's face was white and Caspar's blood ran cold, his eyes fixed on Isolde as if his gaze alone would hold her still. Somehow, she had managed to open the clasp on the silver casket and now she held the Egg in her two chubby fists. The strong smell of animal filled the room.

Trog was growling, his spine stiff with bristles. The baby was looking into the air and pointing excitedly at the great face of a lion placed on the body of a horse with vast red wings. She was cooing and laughing.

"Now just put that down," Caspar said calmly. "There's a good girl."

The little child shrieked again, raised Necrönd up above her head and laughed delightedly as Caspar crept towards her, hands extended. "Isolde, my sweet," he cooed so softly, "give it to me."

He watched with horror, every moment seeming to last forever as Isolde, her grip tenuous, waved her hands above her head. He stepped closer and Isolde threw the Egg towards the corner of the room. The little baby clapped delightedly as it landed heavily amongst her other playthings. The ominously audible crack as it landed was plain to all those in the room. In the silence that followed Caspar leapt across the room and looked down. Necrönd had fallen onto the chip of bone marked with the rune of the wolf that Morrigwen had given him. Necrönd had cracked open along the jagged black flaw that marred its marbled surface.

As the fields outside the window grew dark and low billowing black clouds filled the sky, Caspar looked down stupefied for the moment. Somehow hoping to remedy the damage, her reached down for Necrönd. Stunned by the awfulness of what had happened he stared, wondering how such a thick shell of gold could have broken so easily. But it had landed on the rune of the wolf that Morrigwen had given to him and he, in turn, had given to Isolde. The runic magic . . .

But before his hand reached the broken orb a dim shadow of a dragon shot out of the fault and passed through him. The shadow was followed by another and then another, quickening in its wake, until a continuous stream of sparkling vapour burst from the crack. A twisting storm filled the chamber, buffeting Caspar to the floor. His one thought to protect Isolde, he crawled to her and curled into a ball around her. All about him, things crumbled and crashed to the floor. Plates and glasses were smashed into tiny shards that scattered through the dust of tumbling rubble. Men were screaming and the massed primeval howl of thousands of monsters shook the air.

His hands clasped over Isolde's ears to protect her from the brain-splitting noise, coughing and spluttering out the dust that filled the chamber. How long it went on he could not say but at last the fearful maddening noise that overwhelmed the atmosphere, ringing on and on, began to fade until it was no more than a distant, droning roar.

Caspar got to his feet and stared at the disarray about him. The clamour rumbled into quiet save for small objects still tinkling to the debris-strewn floor. The windows were smashed, and through the open door, he could see that the far wall of the Manor was reduced to rubble. Together they left the room, picking their way through broken chairs and tables everywhere. A unicorn and a centaur lay dead by the hearth of the great hall and Ceowulf had his sword drawn, dripping with blood. Baron Branwolf pushed slumped against a table. His sword drawn but unbloodied, he looked around for his wife. She was by the hole in the wall with Brid and Priddy, all unharmed.

Ursula clung to Caspar as he moved towards the gaping hole in the wall and looked out on a different world. The creatures released from Necrönd had torn through the camp, leaving a muddied swathe of trampled tents and broken bodies. The sky was dark with winged beasts flying out in all directions towards the horizons, spreading out like ripples across a dark pool, to find a place in the world.

"The creatures banished by the First Druid are free," Keridwen murmured in shock. "All released."

Caspar picked his way through broken chairs, helping one or two of Bullback's household to their feet.

"What— what have we done?" he stammered in disbelief and terror. "They are everywhere; the beasts have returned to prowl the earth once more."

Keridwen was suddenly laughing as if enlightened. "Don't you see? Can't you understand? This was meant to happen. She did it on instinct. They had a right to freedom, a right to be part of the cycle. They are part of the Mother as much as you or I."

"Are you mad, woman?" Branwolf growled at his wife. "Look! Look what they have done!"

"Don't you see? Isolde followed her own innocent sense of justice. She has undone the wrong committed by the First Druid. Önd is given by the Mother; the marriage of death and life that the Druid created within Necrönd was always against Her nature. The world is once more as She planned it!" the priestess exclaimed, plucking up the rune of the wolf. "Morrigwen gave this to Caspar, effectively declaring him the guardian of the savage side of nature. Unwittingly, he transferred that guardianship to Isolde when he gave her the rune and she has done the only right thing; given those savage beasts their freedom. We have no right to control them."

Branwolf scowled at her and picked his way through the debris of the courtyard to meet several sergeants and officers who had assembled there. "Get help to the injured and then get those that are able ready. We will march in the morning."

Caspar had followed him and when the soldiers left, he met his father's glare.

"How could you have been such an idiot? Dragons, Spar! The world is now heaving with them. There will be no man left alive by the end of the year."

"Nonsense," Keridwen interrupted; she had not finished with her husband. "They won't bother with us; they'll be too busy fighting the griffins."

"Eating our horses more like."

"Oh yes, they will eat a few – and kill a few people too – but they are a part of the natural order and only now do I see how wrong it was to entrap and subjugate them. In the end they will be no more of a trouble to us than the Yellow Mountain wolf who, after all, helps keep the deer numbers under control otherwise we'd have no forests left and then no boar and then—"

"Enough! Men are dying!" Branwolf was red with anger.

"You shall see that I am right," Keridwen argued stiffly, unafraid to stand up to him. "Brid, don't you agree?" Keridwen spun round. "Brid!"

All were quiet as they stared about them. "She was here with us as we came out of the building," Caspar said. He couldn't put into words his dread that she might have been dragged off by one of the monsters.

Fern was trembling by the threshold to the manor, looking for Caspar. "She went in there." He wafted his hand vaguely towards the stables. "Didn't any of you see?"

Caspar shook his head.

"The stables," the woodwose said distractedly while staring up in panic at the sky. "Shouldn't we get into the cover of the trees? Dragons, you know . . ."

Caspar couldn't think what Brid would be doing in the stables but, judging by Keridwen's reaction, his mother had guessed. She ran ahead of the others and soon was back, shaking her head. "We can only pray. None of us will be able to catch her; she's taken the golden horses of Rye Errish."

"But why?" Caspar asked. "Why would she suddenly leave now when the Egg is broken, when we all need her so badly."

"And she needs Hal," Keridwen said simply. "She is not just a priestess but also a woman."

"We march at dawn," Branwolf reminded them. He bowed towards Ursula. "My lady, I trust we still have your support."

She looked at Branwolf and then at her son. "With all my heart."

Caspar could not sleep. Though Isolde was safely cuddled up with Priddy, under Keridwen's watchful eye, and Ursula was warm against his naked body, the cries of the camp were loud as they defended themselves from the rogue wolves and the savage creatures that lurked beyond the sentries and fires of the camp. Ursula's bears guarded them well.

When it was near dawn, he rose to find that his mother was also restless and was pacing up and down the large hall.

"Spar, I need to go after Brid," Keridwen said to Caspar urgently.

Caspar nodded and went to fetch Ursula. "We must find Brid. I need the protection of your bears."

Ursula wasted no time and, wrapped up against the night, she chose her favourite bear and two others, while Caspar hastily packed a small bag of provisions. Soon they were mounted on the one animal and riding north towards the canyon. Dawn broke and, in the shadow of the trees, he looked at the strange world that yet was his home. What should have been quiet was alive with grunts and snuffles and snarls, though no beast came close to the great bears.

With his arms closed tight about Ursula, he had no need to speak to her, so acutely aware was he of her warm, comfortable presence. He kissed the back of her neck, felt her shudder and then, squeezing her tight, watched the way ahead.

Caspar blinked. He had seen a flash of gold. A griffin tore through the sky after it. More griffins mocked it but the streak of gold was moving so fast through the valley that the winged creatures couldn't keep up with it. The great bears roared and the griffins rose to a greater height and circled warily. Caspar raised his horn to his lips and piped out the notes to muster.

Moments later, two golden horses were galloping towards them, and skidded to a halt before the bears. Two dark olive eyes stared out from beneath Hal's long dark fringe. His face was dark with stubble, his cheekbones gaunt. He looked Caspar up and down in quiet surprise, warily studying the great bears and nodding politely at Ursula.

"I hope you brought some supplies, Spar. Brid forgot," he said with a grin. "I'm starving."

Caspar patted the satchel slung over his shoulder and brought out a loaf of bread, salted meat and crumbling biscuits. "Hal, you're safe!" he exclaimed with overwhelming joy.

His uncle acknowledged this sentiment with a quiet nod. "I thought I'd lost you too!" Gratefully, he accepted the offering but nibbled only tentatively.

A griffin stooped out of the sky and they all ducked but the bear to Ursula's right reared up and one lash from its great claw sent it shrieking away.

Impressed by the bear's fearsome power, Caspar urged them to hurry. "Come, we must get to the mouth of the canyon and join the rest who march on Torra Alta. You can tell us how you escaped on the way."

"Well, I didn't need rescuing," Hal said indignantly.

"Of course you did," Brid said tartly. Her skin was still a little off-colour and she sweated slightly but her eyes shone brightly. "You would never have got past all these creatures without my help and the horse you're sitting on."

Hal sniffed. "I have my sword; I would have made it!"

"How did you get away from the stonewights?" Caspar asked hastily, sensing the tension between Hal and Brid and hoping to prevent an argument.

Hal turned solemn. "Weak from exhaustion, Oxwin

and Thane died all too soon and their bodies were tossed to the younger stonewights," he said simply.

"I don't suppose we need tell Bullback how they died," Caspar said quietly.

Hal nodded. "No, it would not be a kindness. I didn't know what had happened to you when they dragged you off but I heard you shouting that I must keep telling them stories. But they don't like stories at all; they like facts. They like to learn about the world above; I kept them going for three days on the various methods of making armour. They even fed me to keep me talking. After that I told them about battle plans and tactics and described troop deployment from as many battles as I know. Which is quite a few."

Caspar grinned. "Of course!" No one knew about battles better than Hal who had studied them so avidly as a boy. Caspar had been hungry for tales of people and how they lived but Hal was only ever interested in the tactics. His head was stuffed with facts.

"I didn't know I knew so much but, as I talked, I wondered why these creatures were so curious about a world that was not their own. After all, we are never interested in anything that we can't relate to. And I slowly realized that the world above must once have been their world and that they had once looked out at the stars and the sea and that was why they were now so hungry for news from above. Then it occurred to me; they live in their burial chambers, waiting to die. The world is no longer a safe place for them and they are trapped below, living in their graves. So, when I sensed they were growing tired of my facts about warfare, I told them what I guessed to be their own story of how these great creatures once danced across the earth and formed huge circles."

Caspar laughed delightedly at his uncle's cleverness.

"And of course, after we spent so much time looking for the stone circle that held the clue to where we should find Necrönd all those years ago, you knew many facts about the layout of the circles and the number of stones."

"I know a lot more about it now," Hal said wearily. "Once I had started on the tale, they began to talk in great detail and with huge enthusiasm and finally explaining that they had been down in the dark so long that the sun had become too harsh for them. They were so involved in their telling that I was able to get some sleep at last. But then I was awoken by a great commotion; the stonewights were running hurriedly and shouting that something momentous had happened above ground."

"The release of the creatures of legend?" Caspar asked.

Hal nodded. "They had forgotten all about me. This event they had to see for themselves and gasped and howled as the great storm of monsters swept overhead. Of course, I didn't know what had happened but just crawled out into the sunlight after them and, when none stopped me, I slunk away. And I would have made it back too. On my own."

"Oh, don't be so silly," Caspar snorted.

"I've got to stop," Brid gasped. "Just for a moment." She slithered from her horse and doubled over retching. "Ugh! That hurts," she moaned, clutching her stomach.

"Brid, what's the matter?" Caspar asked, leaping down to help her. "I thought you were better."

"Leave her be," Hal growled, dismounting and shouldering his nephew aside. "She'll never be better. She's pregnant – pregnant with Harle's child."

Still there was tenderness to his movements as he put his arms around her shoulders and helped her upright. "But your wound is better, Brid?" he asked in concern. "I thought I'd killed you."

"I'm better," she smiled. "The only thing that would kill me was if you stopped loving me."

"Of course I love you; it wouldn't hurt so much if I didn't. Here, have some water. It might help you feel less sick."

"I'll have one of those biscuits," she smiled, gripping his hand.

Caspar looked up; it was still dark in the trees but the sky above was clear and already bright with the morning sun. His father would already be underway towards the castle. "Branwolf needs us. The day is begun. We must hurry," he said urgently.

Hal tenderly helped Brid back onto her horse. "I suppose I did need your help," he conceded as they hurried west towards the southern mouth of the canyon.

"Mother, have mercy on us," Brid gasped as they broke into the canyon.

"Ursula, take Brid back to Bullback's Manor," Caspar ordered. "You two should not be here."

"Don't be ridiculous. You will need help with my bears and I'm not losing you again," Ursula said stubbornly.

Hal looked at Brid. "You're not strong enough yet."

"And you think you are? I am One of the Three. I have never run from anything in my life."

All stared north at the towers of Torra Alta that stood proudly on its pinnacle of rock thrusting, lancelike, up from the canyon floor. A dark green dragon, its armour of scales glinting in the sun, perched on the north tower. Its wings were spread, casting a dark shadow over the entire castle, its neck stretched up and, from its snout, puffed a black, billowing cloud of smoke. The smoke swirled and twisted but wasn't swept aside by the wind, which fluttered the Ovissian standard, but condensed and formed a giant face. Caspar made out the hollow eye sockets and the great snout and recognized the icy laugh that filled the canyon. "Mine! Mine! All mine at last!"

"Gwion!" Hal exclaimed in horror.

Caspar's heart thumped in his throat. He felt sick. The bears might protect them from the freed creatures of Necrönd but what could be done against a ghost? They raced to join the column of Belbidians and Dagonet's personal bodyguard that was flanked by Ursula's huge bears and her men. The grunting beasts roared at her in welcome and she gave back a strange ululating cry as they raced to the fore where Branwolf, in his studded-hauberk and mounted on a high-stepping destrier, led the column.

He called a halt at their approach and held out his arms in welcome. "My boys, you are here! Come, ride one either side of me as we march to reclaim our home. Balladeer, sing! Sing loud! We are warriors brave but a song still cheers our hearts!"

Caspar noted at once that his mother was in the second rank behind Branwolf and protested loudly. "But, Mother, you should have stayed at Bullback's. And you have Isolde! What are you doing? Take her back!"

"We are surrounded by bears; this is the safest place for her."

Brid shook her head at Caspar and stooped over Isolde to kiss her. "Do you still not understand, Spar? She is the new Maiden. She is life to us all. She is One of the Three. We three march with you. The glory of the Goddess is with us!"

Caspar kept a length behind, riding beside Dagonet. The Ceolothian king's flabby cheeks wobbled as they trotted.

"What's the plan?" Hal asked, eating as he rode, his horse bumping flanks with Branwolf's.

"While the bears keep the hobgoblins, and dragons at bay we shall station our attack at the east wall. Once through the outer defences, a handful of us will go in through the water gate."

Caspar nodded at this. Branwolf had ordered the secret gate built as a last means of escape from the castle after the Vaalakan siege but they were not happy to disclose its whereabouts to any that were not Torra Altans.

The youth lifted his head at the three shiny green dragons that had previously circled the castle. They were perched on the battlements, lashing out at any other dragon daring to approach. The hobgoblins seemed to have replenished their depleted ranks and stood in dark rings around the edge of the Tor.

Keridwen followed his gaze and, with cutting perception, read his thoughts. "They will be receiving payment of some kind. Dragons are greedy creatures. Gwion must have something that they want."

"Treasure," Hal said. "The old dragon Caspar and I found at the root of the Tor had a nest of treasure."

"I can be more specific," Branwolf said thoughtfully. "He has sunburst rubies. That was what all those Ovissian trappers were doing in my mountains – getting sunburst rubies for Gwion."

"Old Man Blackthorn's people!" Brid exclaimed. "The hobgoblins. Straif has something to do with this."

Hal looked at her in puzzlement and then pressed ahead with Branwolf. "So, we go in through the water gate. Then what?" Hal asked.

"We must release the men and get to the weaponry. Once they have their bows, we can do something about the dragons. Then we'll get the bears in up the road with King Rewik, Bullback and Dagonet's men and the castle will be ours."

"How do we get past the guards in the dungeons without them raising the alarm and trapping us?" Caspar asked.

"Izella has volunteered," Branwolf said with a smile and for a moment he looked ten years younger. "What a creature!"

"Father!" Caspar chided.

"Son, your mother might be the most beautiful woman on earth but I'm still a man." He coughed and dropped forward onto his horse's mane, his hand pressed to his chest.

"Who is Izella?" Hal asked and Branwolf nodded behind him. Hal flashed the woman of Ash one of his winning smiles.

Caspar glanced over his shoulder to check that Ursula was out of earshot. "She smells of roses and she feels like warm silk. And it's like being in a warm river and eating buttered toast at the same time or running faster than the wind or climbing to the highest peak." Caspar stumbled for some way to describe the indescribable. "It's like watching the moon over a silvery lake or seeing a hawk stoop out of the sky; but she doesn't make you feel safe or loved."

"Indeed, Spar!" Hal laughed at him. "You are the strangest fellow alive."

Rewik was not amused. "You talk like drunks round a tavern table. Don't you realize how serious this all is?"

"Of course we do," Branwolf retorted. "But we're born of a long line of warriors and we know that, when you stare straight into the cold face of death, you must know what it is you live for, what you are fighting for, and so know what is worth dying for."

"I would die for my daughter and she's in there, held by that demon and your wayward Ovissian countrymen, who must have deceived my son into maintaining his stance," Dagonet snarled.

"We'll get her out," Branwolf said calmly.

Dagonet was not so easily pacified. "I would give my entire kingdom for my daughter. Anything."

Snarls and yaps came from the perimeter of the column. Mounted and foot soldiers alike instinctively ducked as griffins screeched out of the air and swooped overhead. Caspar was not surprised at how easily the bears drove them off. Ursula's bears were vast, twice the size of a Torra Altan bear, and their great long arms and vicious claws had a tremendous power and reach. Three griffins were already dead, pulled out of the sky and torn to pieces with tooth and claw. Ursula's song was shrill and clear, commanding and encouraging them.

Caspar was awed by the sight of her and braced himself for the moment when their roles diverged and he would have to bid her farewell. They had reached the outer defence walls, no more than a ring of raised mounds topped by pointed stakes, but it was here they would make their stand, drawing the hobgoblins to them while the small party slipped further around to the east. The intention was to break through the outer earthworks and make for the base of the sheer cliff beneath the east wall of the castle, where the cliff was undercut by the bubbling wash of the Silversalmon.

Ursula kissed Caspar lovingly and squeezed his hand but said nothing. Her eyes, however, had said it all and Caspar swallowed hard, hoping that it wouldn't be long before he would be back with her again.

While Hal pulled Brid close and kissed her hand in farewell, Keridwen cast a loving, anxious eye at Branwolf. "I'm coming with you."

Branwolf shook his head but she raised a hand to quiet

him. "We have spent too much of our lives apart, husband. I would be with you now. Remember what we agreed?"

Branwolf nodded and gave her a faint smile.

Keridwen turned to Brid. "Take Isolde and stay close by Ursula."

As the bears roared their challenge at the castle and the hobgoblins swarmed in attack, the select few slipped away from the area of combat. Creeping around the outer defences, Branwolf and his wife, Hal, Caspar, Ceowulf, Izella and the irrepressible Pip slunk down towards the river. Keeping to the shadows beneath the overhanging bank, they crept forward to the bend in the river at the foot of the Tor.

"Sir," Pip offered. "I'm a good swimmer. Allow me the honour of checking that the way is clear."

Branwolf nodded. "Good lad."

Pip slipped into the river and soon all that could be seen of him was a trail of bubbles rising from the air trapped in his clothing. He was soon back.

"All clear though it's very dark."

"We'll find the torches. They'll be on the other side," Branwolf said. "Right, Spar, bring up the rear with me. Let's have Pip, Hal and Ceowulf through first and then the women," Branwolf ordered.

They slipped into the water in quick succession, Caspar following up last without allowing himself to think that he was diving into black water. Fortunately, the water gate, as they called it, was only two yards below the surface and he was soon through, kicking upwards and breaking the surface of the water on the other side. It was indeed dark. He could hear all the others about him, feeling their way until Ceowulf exclaimed. "I have one!"

"Good man," Branwolf grunted and stifled his coughing.

Someone struck a flint and after a few moments, all

wet and cold, they huddled together in the low chamber. On first sight, there was no apparent way out but, above their heads, was a crack in the rock, somewhat like a chimney flue. Caspar knew that at its top the channel twisted and turned before cutting upwards again. It was a difficult climb and certainly would not allow a large body of men quick access to the castle. They had to hope that the exit had remained a secret; if it were discovered, it would be an easy matter for the Ovissians to pick them off one by one as they crawled out.

They began the slow climb, Ceowulf struggling a little simply because of his size and he was continually wriggling his shoulders to work his way upwards. With only one hand, Hal managed by using the hook he had strapped to his stump. Small and light, Caspar found the going easy but was acutely aware that his uncle was weakened by his recent traumas and was breathing heavily. However, his father was worse, the exertion forcing him to splutter and cough fitfully. Once through the initial climb, they reached the old dragon tunnels that honeycombed the rock of the Tor beneath the castle.

"I'll go ahead with Izella," Caspar offered. "It'll be quicker."

Branwolf nodded. "We'll be right behind you." He leant against the tunnel walls and Keridwen offered him a draught from a vial.

"Drink it, Branwolf," she chided. "The bloodwort will make you stronger."

"Mm," he grunted sceptically.

Izella trod lightly behind Caspar and, in the gloom, he was barely aware of her presence. At last, they reached a tight, near vertical tunnel notched with steps. It was newly blasted and gave access straight to the kitchens without the need to climb up through the wellroom that would most probably be full of men. Caspar stopped and looked deep into Izella's mercurial eyes.

"This is where you leave me. The quicker you can free the men, the quicker I can send word to Reyna that I shall buy as much trinoxia as she can make to heal Old Woman Ash and your people," he said, trying to encourage her. "Now, it's only a matter . . ." His voice, already a whisper, trailed away.

They had climbed high enough to hear the noise of the castle above, shouts from soldiers, moans from the dungeons and that horrible shriek like a giant hawk that Caspar knew came from the dragons. He pulled Izella close and put his mouth to her ear.

"This leads into the kitchens through a trap door over the salt cupboard beside the hearth. You need to go out through the kitchens across the courtyard, down the well of steps on the other side and you'll reach the dungeons. Can you do it?"

Izella nodded. "Of course. No one will see me and I can slip the keys off the guards as easily as you can string your bow."

"Here's my ring," Caspar said. "Show it to the Captain. You'll know him at once; tall and thin with a hooked nose. He'll know my ring and will organize the men. Once they're out and creating enough disturbance, the rest of us will join you."

She nodded and Caspar inched open the trap door into the warmth of Cook's salt cupboard alongside the fire at the back of her kitchen. Once she had gone, he pulled it to and slipped back down a little way into the tunnels to wait for the others. They still hadn't made the upper man-cut tunnels and Caspar hurried down into the larger, tunnels that a more than a thousand years ago had been worn smooth by the dragons.

Alarmed to see that the others' torches were not yet casting their swerving lights towards him, he hurried down, his footsteps slapping on the stone. They couldn't have got lost, surely not.

His fingers clenched tight around his torch as it sputtered in a breath of wind that came from a side tunnel. He stopped dead in his tracks. How could the wind possibly be stirring down here?

He turned to face it and felt the warm moist air on his skin and the breeze lift his heavy auburn hair up off his cheeks and neck. In contrast, the hair at the back of his neck prickled where he had felt a cold breath. He spun round but could see nothing though he had the sense that whatever it was had circled behind him.

"I have you, I have you all now!" a voice shrieked from the darkness. "You shall all die in terror, one by one."

Caspar shrank back. "Gwion, we mean you no harm."

"Ha! How can you say that, you treacherous brat, you who killed me?"

"But Gwion, you attacked me! I wouldn't have harmed you if you hadn't tried to kill me."

Caspar glanced over his shoulder and saw, at last, the light coming, Branwolf's panted breaths loud in the echoing tunnel.

"Get back!" Caspar yelled. "It's Gwion."

"Run, Spar!" his mother shrieked and he could see her now, sprinting towards him.

"No! Get away," Caspar warned fearfully, his short sword drawn as he stepped slowly back from the black shape of a wolf reared up on its back legs. It stalked him, a yellow glow burning out from each eye socket.

"I have you!" it snorted.

Behind the bestial form of Gwion, a flash of yellow filled the tunnel, tongues of flame, like curving petals of scarlet roses lapped the sides, forced in and forward by the tight walls of the tunnel. Caspar glimpsed the dark outline of a vast snout and the raking claws of a dragon but he focused on the wolfman, who was black against the orange glow. Caspar stood his ground.

"You wretched fool, do you think your sword can harm me now?" Gwion's laugh rattled back and forth in the tunnel. "I am dead already."

A hand on Caspar's shoulder drew him back. "Stand aside, Spar; this is not your fight," Branwolf commanded.

"Of course, it's his fight, oh mighty brother," Gwion sneered. "He killed me! He prevented me from having ultimate power over everything in this world and the next and I shall have my revenge."

Caspar was aware of Ceowulf at his left shoulder, his arm raised to aim his javelin at the dragon's throat but, while the beast held off, the knight kept himself steady. Caspar was at once aware that this dragon was red with a long snout and three pairs of upturned fangs lining its drooling mouth and was not one of the three that held the castle at Gwion's command. The ancient dragons released from the Egg were returning to the Tor. He noted the wolfman glance once over his shoulder at it but Gwion appeared so enraged by Caspar's presence to concern himself with this rogue beast. With all the power and speed of a wolf, he leapt and Caspar felt the cold bite of death on his leg.

Keridwen was screaming. "Brother, brother, leave him be. Take me instead; he might have killed you but it is me that you have always hated."

Gwion roared with such violence that the deathly smell of his breath choked Caspar's throat. The wolfman sunk low on his haunches, ready to spring. Caspar tried to rise to block Gwion's path to his mother but was flung aside by his father who burst forward and, with head down like a charging bull, rammed into Gwion, his force taking them both back into the flames of the dragon behind.

"No," Caspar shrieked and ran forward, his face covered by his sleeves to protect him from the heat.

The dragon drew back his neck and breathed in, sucking back the flames and, for a moment, Caspar saw his father wrestling with Gwion, pinning him to the hard stone of the tunnel. Then the jet of flame spurted from the flaring nostrils.

CHAPTER TWENTY-EIGHT

"Father! No!" Caspar yelled. "No!"

He tried to go after Branwolf but was held back by Ceowulf. Instead, it was Pip who ran forward only to be forced back by the intense heat of the flames that filled the tunnel.

Caspar staggered and swayed. Gripping Ceowulf's shoulder, he turned to his mother, who stood, watching silently. "Why didn't you stop him?" he yelled in his distress.

"He was dying. Now he has gone to finish what you tried to do. It is only right." She swallowed hard and there was a dullness to her eyes that Caspar had never seen before. She leant against Hal, her hand raised to shield her face from the fierce heat and stared in desolation at the two foetus-like forms at the white heart of the flames.

"Father!" Caspar screamed again into the flames and sank to his knees in despair.

"Get you bow ready, Spar," Keridwen urged him firmly, her jaw set firm.

Though shaking with shock, Caspar still had the wherewithal to do what he was trained to do and fight.

"Wait until the flames die back," Ceowulf shouted. "The dragon can't see us anymore than we can see him but we must take him quickly before he spits more fire."

Caspar nodded, took aim and waited. The flames evaporated; he loosed arrow after arrow, taking out the eyes first, while Hal hurled his throwing knives. Ceowulf lunged forward and jabbed his javelin upwards, purple blood jetting from the dragon's throat and splattering the knight's face, neck and shoulders. He leapt backwards just in time to avoid being crushed by the dragon as it toppled and crashed to the ground.

All stood back, watching and waiting. Caspar wiped at his eyes, seeing before him the blistered and blackened remains of his father.

Stiff with grief, Keridwen stepped forward and stood over the blackened skeleton. "Great Mother, look over his soul and draw him quickly to your bosom."

There was no sign of another body.

Caspar looked to his mother and reached out a shaking hand for her comfort. "Where is Gwion?" he managed to ask, his throat tight against sobs.

"Back in the Otherworld, locked in combat with Branwolf's spirit." She hugged her son close.

Gently, he pushed her away and knelt over his father's remains, the tears welling up and dripping from his nose. Without fear of his father's dead body, he reached in and plucked out a ring of gold; the ring forged a thousand years ago for the first Baron of Torra Altan and handed down through each generation from father to son in an unbroken line.

He was about to hand it to his mother but she would not take it and instead closed his fingers about the ring. "Spar, it is yours. The wheel of time has rolled on and you are Baron of Torra Alta now."

Caspar gulped. He wasn't ready for this; nor did he want it. He only wanted his father back. But there was no time for grief now; there were Torra Altan men above whose lives still depended on them and he knew his father would want him to fight on. Pip was already pulling hard at the mighty leg of the dragon, trying to move it so that they might squeeze by.

"Out of my way," Hal roared, his grief twisting into hard savagery. He raised his sword and smote at the dragon's legs, carving up the carcass so that they could get past. Caspar dragged away the legs, uncaring that, although he loosely wore the ring of the Barons of Torra Alta around his middle finger, it was Hal who automatically took charge.

They squeezed past, snagging their cloaks on the sharp points of the dragon's shiny scales, and at last were in the tunnel beyond. Caspar halted. He had heard something else over the muffled hum of battle above.

The others had heard it too and stopped to listen. A slow thump, thump of something vastly heavy lumbering forward echoed from a tunnel to their left but, racing before that, was the slap of human feet.

"Cymbeline!" a deep male voice cried and then shouted something in Ceolothian.

"But we're lost," the princess's voice wailed. "Lost! And the dragons!"

"Over here! This way!" Hal shouted. "Cymbeline, it's Hal. Quick! Over here!" He paused at the mouth of the next tunnel, every fibre in his body tensed as he heard that lazy, slop, slop of vast legs following the panicked patter of human feet.

Cymbeline's white face sprung at them out of the dark. Somehow, she had escaped into the dungeons. Caspar stood and stared as another face appeared at her shoulder. Tudwal was standing behind her, knife raised.

Caspar focused on the knife and his mouth dropped open.

"But that's—" he started. He would never forget that

magic blade if he lived a thousand years. He had taken it from a verderer in the Otherworld and Mamluc had taken it from him – Mamluc, the slave trader who had used Ursula to steal Torra Altan bears; Mamluc, the slave trader who had said he would give it to his master.

"Just get out of my way," the young prince threatened as the thumping grew louder behind him. "This knife will cut right through the lot of you if I will it."

"Look out! Look out behind you!" Ceowulf yelled.

The Ceolothian prince glanced over his shoulder at the dragon whose snout lunged into the tight recess, a claw snapping out and snagging Cymbeline's dress. She howled in terror and Tudwal spun round and hurled the knife. It spun through the air and stuck right up to the hilt in the animal's thick skull, slicing through its heavy armouring of scales as if they were no more than gold leaf. The dragon fell dead.

"Cymbeline, Cymbeline!" Tudwal cried in confusion.

She nodded feebly at him and, in the moment's hush, there was again that steady rasp of scales along the wall followed by the loud thrash of a dragon's tail against rock, the sound distorted by its echo. Then from three more tunnels they heard that same heavy thump as more dragons approached. There was no time to retrieve the verderer's knife.

"This way, quickly!" Keridwen urged.

"No, I'd rather die in the dragon's flames," Tudwal snarled.

"And Cymbeline too? Do you want to see her shrivelled and charred into ashes?" Hal growled, raising his sword to Tudwal's throat.

"No," the prince said uneasily, his shoulders drooping in defeat. "No!" he repeated more fervently and grabbed Cymbeline's hand to speed her.

Ceolothian and Belbidian alike raced for their only means of escape; the tight chimney that was too narrow for the dragon to snake its head in after them. Caspar reached the salt box first and burst out into the empty kitchens. Hal came next, and then the women followed by Pip and Tudwal and lastly Ceowulf, both of these great men squeezing out with enormous difficulty.

Hal held his sword at Cymbeline's throat and growled at Tudwal. "Get outside and order your men to lay down their arms, otherwise she loses her ears."

Caspar was about to exclaim that he couldn't do that but then swallowed his words as he watched Tudwal's face whiten. The Ceolothian raised his hands in surrender and marched before them, out into the courtyard.

In a loud voice, he bellowed for Godafrid, Tupwell and Kulfrid. "Call off the men. Stop the fighting!" he shouted several times to be heard above the shrieks and screams of the dying.

There was little need; already the Captain had the Torra Altan men deployed to the walls. Half were focused on the Ovissians and rebel Ceolothians within the court-yard and the other half had their great war bows raised to the skies and the hovering dragons. At Tudwal's command, the few rebels that still battled on let their weapons drop.

"Look out!" Hal yelled as a red dragon swooped over-head, and the arrows deflected off its pale scaly belly came clattering down onto the cobbles of the courtyard. He groaned something about the poor quality of marksman-ship in the young men of Torra Alta.

Caspar raised his bow and loosed one arrow and then another, twice piercing the creature beneath the throat. It screamed and twisted in the air, its wings folding. Then it crashed onto the newly built north tower, tearing off the top turret as it fell, crushing men beneath stone and its own mighty bulk.

Caspar's eyes flicked around the castle and at last spotted the Captain. Tall and lean, he stood above the barbican, his sword bloodied and Ovissians heaped at his feet. Still steeped in the rage of battle, he roared out the Torra Altan war cry, defying any more to come.

None came. All had heard Baron Godafrid's order and were now cowering in the central courtyard or making their way there. Pale-faced and hungry, Torra Altans pressed them on all sides, sharp with the lust for revenge after their long imprisonment.

But the dragons released by Necrönd were not yet defeated. Another swooped up from below the battlements and skimmed over the walls, the bladder at its throat bloated, before disgorging its belly of fire. Shrieking and screaming, men rolled on the floor, others rushing to them to beat out the flames. High on the battlements, the archers sent a cloud of arrows into the sky to drive it off but no sooner was it gone than a flock of red-winged griffins swarmed to attack.

"Open the portcullis," Hal cried. "Let the bears in."

Caspar wished he had thought of that as Ursula's ululating cry wailed into the castle. He could barely see as the bears clambered up onto the battlements and bellowed furiously at the griffins, keeping them from harrowing the men. The Belbidians turned all their attention and arrows to the airborne beasts but Caspar's aim was suddenly poor. He could not see for the tears that sullied his vision. They had won, but his father was dead.

All this was his, this ruin, this heap of smoking rubble, yet he was not the one taking command.

"Magnificent, isn't he?" someone murmured at his side as at last the fighting subsided.

He blinked and saw Brid beside him, cradling Isolde in her arms.

Caspar nodded. "Yes, he is; he's just like his brother."

"The King!" someone shouted. "King Rewik is in our presence!"

A hush smothered the castle and all eyes were turned inwards as Rewik ordered a table to be dragged from the kitchens so that he might stand up high above the men. It seemed he had no wish to speak from the back of his horse.

"I return this castle to the Baron of Torra Alta. Come forth, Baron Branwolf, and receive my appreciation and gratitude; the whole country is indebted to you and your house."

Keridwen nudged Caspar and her choked voice commanded. "Go, my son, and claim what is yours."

Caspar tottered forward and all but stumbled on the gore-covered cobbles. It was Ursula who caught his arm and prevented him from falling. She gave him a smiling nod of reassurance. She believed in him but he knew, too well, that even her confidence in him was not enough.

He looked down at his feet, biting back the sobs that crammed his throat and then up at his sovereign lord. "My father, Branwolf has . . ." He clenched his fist to try and gain control of his grief and proudly tossed back his head, knowing suddenly how his father would have wanted him to behave. "Branwolf fell in the battle," he announced, his voice somehow steady and confident. "I am Baron of Torra Alta now."

He felt small and foolish and stared heavenward, blinking back the tears at the murmur of shock and sorrow that ran through the men. He was aware of their critical gaze and the cold silence with which they greeted him.

Then a great bellowing cry came from the beyond the close-packed men. "Hail, Lord Caspar, Baron of Torra Alta! Hail!"

Through a blur of tears, Caspar looked across at his uncle and met his sad but grinning face with his own smile and raised his hand, acknowledging the support.

"Hail, Lord Caspar," Ceowulf echoed, his arms tight around his wife and his son. Then the voices of the Captain and the sergeants were drowned out by a cheer from the men.

Rewik raised his hand for silence and Caspar gratefully made his way to Hal's side.

The King drew a deep breath and then turned on Godafrid. "We accuse you, Godafrid and your son, Tupwell, of treachery and treason. What say you?"

The Ovissian Baron hung his head shamefully and held out his hands. "Sire, I am dumfounded—"

"Oh, shut up, you old fool," Tupwell sneered sourly and then arrogantly stood up to his king. "It was nothing to do with my father. He couldn't organize a sheep-market successfully. It was all Prince Tudwal's doing. He approached me through my cousin, Baron Kulfrid, who owns the Goat County in Ceolothia." He thrust his finger accusingly at his relative. "Prince Tudwal was offering me the prize of Torra Alta if I helped him to gain the Belbidian throne. I considered the barony worthless and was not so interested at first until he revealed the great wealth of sunburst rubies within the Yellow Mountains."

"The bears! It was you, then, who trapped all the bears," Ursula exclaimed in outrage.

"What's a few bears? We merely took them from the Yellow Mountains and had them cast ashore in Quertos to stir up the other baronies against Torra Alta. The barbaric Torra Altans—"

He broke off as a stir ran through the crowd and men spread aside to allow the violent passage of King Dagonet to his daughter. At his back were harassed-looking messengers eager to impart important news to him, though he shoved them behind him and ran to Cymbeline, holding out his hand to embrace her.

She flung herself into his arms, sobbing wildly. Dagonet raised his hands in greeting to his son. "I knew you would call off your men once you received word of my command to relinquish the castle," he began but his tone lost confidence as he studied his son's sour expression. "But you didn't, did you? You disobeyed me, boy! Why?" he asked, not in anger but in hurt.

All stared, waiting for an explanation but Tudwal said nothing.

"Dagonet, my friend," Rewik said into the silence. "We have learnt that your son, Tudwal, even more than the Ovissians and your subject Kulfrid, is the cause of all this treachery. He organized Cymbeline's abduction in order to throw the blame at the already unpopular Torra Altans. His aim, as we all now know, was to use the barony and its castle to gain control of my kingdom."

Caspar was impressed with King Rewik's summing up of the situation.

Dagonet shook his head and laughed nervously. "That is not so. He was captured along with Cymbeline. You are mistaken. The accusation is absurd." He glowered at his son. "Tell me it's absurd."

Tudwal stood and glared back darkly but said nothing. He was surrounded by Ovissians who all pointed accusingly at him.

"But why? Why?" Dagonet asked in disbelieving horror. His eyes were wild and his normally deep voice rose in pitch. "Because you would marry my sweet sister to

the King of Belbidia and I could not let that happen."
He was shaking his fists at his father. "If I had Belbidia,
if I were king, I could have her for my own and none
would stop me."

"What? What vileness is this?" Dagonet roared, protectively clutching his daughter to him. "I would have stopped
you, Turquin would . . ." Dagonet faltered and took a step
closer. "And Turquin? You didn't! You were in collabora-
tion with Baron Kulfrid and it was Kulfrid's knife . . .
You couldn't have! You had him killed!"

"It was Kulfrid's knife, true. He discovered my contract
with Kulfrid's cousins. But it was my own hand that
thrust it into his belly," Tudwal snarled. "With him out
of the way I would have had Ceolothia too."

Dagonet sank to his knees, gasping with shock. The
men all around looked from one to another of the great
noblemen whose lives were stripped of the disguise of
pleasantries to reveal the ugliness of their bare emotions.

"I don't believe it. But how did you ever think of this
evil?"

Tudwal laughed. "In truth, I didn't. I had for some time
dreamt of simply running away with Cymbeline. I would
have done so to if it wasn't for the apparition of the
priest. Many times, he came to me and each time he was
less like a man and more like a wolf and each time I was
more persuaded by his scheme. He said he would help
me keep Cymbeline and even give me a kingdom if I
provided him with enough sunburst rubies. I explained
that our own mines were mined-out but he said that the
Yellow Mountains of Torra Alta were footed with rich
seams of sunburst rubies."

"The rubies," Brid murmured and turned to Keridwen
whose eyes were equally bright with enlightenment.

"Of course," Keridwen exclaimed. "A snatch of the sun,

the same sun that looks down on both this world and the Otherworld. Of course! He did not just want rubies to bribe the dragons. The rubies were to buy him power with the verderers of Rye Errish."

Keridwen and Brid, who still held Isolde, slipped away into the crowd but few eyes followed them. All watched Dagonet turn to his daughter.

"My poor sweet girl," he said softly. "I am sorry that you had to hear of your brother's vile intentions towards you. What would you have me do to punish him?"

Cymbeline was sobbing.

"Poor, sweet innocent," Dagonet cradled her to him.

Hal looked as if he were about to laugh out loud at the absurd notion of her innocence but Ceowulf caught his arm. "It would be a cruel thing to tell him. He is an old man and she is his only daughter."

"Innocent!" Hal laughed scornfully but kept his voice low. In the light of Tudwal's revelations, he read Cymbeline's past behaviour quite differently. He remembered how she had shrieked in despair when she had been separated from him in the wizards' island. He remembered her overwhelming grief when she thought it had been Tudwal murdered and not Turquin. He remembered, too, the practised ease with which she had tried to seduce him. "Dagonet must surely guess she is not."

"He may choose to guess otherwise," the knight said kindly. "It is seven hundred years since the Ceolothian royal house was shamed by the act of incest and it seems that the desire has not quite been bred out of them. But whatever I think of Cymbeline and the suffering she has put us all to, there is little need to hurt Dagonet; he suffers enough as it is."

Hal nodded, watching how the weighty king hugged his child and how she clung to him.

Caspar barely took all this in. He felt sick, only now beginning to accept that his father was truly dead. The empty emotion in the pit of his belly felt as though it would devour him from within. He withdrew from the raucous shouts of the outraged men only to find himself brushing shoulders with someone he hadn't seen. "Izella!" he said in surprise.

"My Lord Caspar," she smiled sweetly, "I am sorry for your loss but I must speak with you. I have done you a service and I must ask for my payment. The trinoxia! Old Woman Ash suffers and I must get it to her."

"Indeed, the trinoxia. I shall see that you have it," Caspar assured her and nodded at King Dagonet. "He is at present at war with the woman who makes it."

Dagonet was shouting. "My eldest son is slaughtered, my youngest mad, my middle son an evil traitor, whom I shall see banished from this continent. Why then is my army fighting to defend my country from the rebel Reyna and her slaves? Why? Let her have it, I say!"

He drew a deep breath and then sighed, his eyes flitting between Cymbeline and Tudwal, his expression pensive and quizzical, as if he too was slowly coming to the same conclusion as Hal. "A scribe," he demanded. "I will not send men to their deaths to save Ceolothia for madmen and traitors. I have only my daughter to succeed me now and a woman cannot rule so great a realm. All Ceolothia is too much for one woman. Send word to the rebel Reyna in Castaguard that the eastern baronies of Ceolothia are hers. I shall keep the west for my beloved daughter. Let us pray she is satisfied; I have had my fill of bloodshed."

Dagonet then turned to Caspar and Hal. "I have wronged you deeply. And you have suffered." He nodded at Hal's left arm. "Moreover, you have returned my precious Cymbeline to me. Let me make what amends I can and reward you for my daughter's safe return. Name your price. I can give you the Goat Country or Trows Forest. The Marshes perhaps. What part of my lands will you have?"

Caspar thought on it and shuddered; he had no love of Ceolothia's cold wet climate. He particularly remembered the persistent drizzle. He took Ursula's hand in his and said, "I have all that I need in my hands now and want for nothing more."

"Hal?" Dagonet prompted him. "You brought my girl home. Rubies, the town of Skuas Ria. Name it!"

Hal laughed. "No, I want none of Ceolothia. I have no time to oversee a distant manor or lands. But I would have you procure for me the finest suit of armour to be had in all the Caballan."

"A suit of armour? Is that all?" King Dagonet asked in surprise.

"Is that all!" Hal echoed. "Of course! The skies are now filled with dragons. Someone must see to them."

Caspar turned and, seeking his mother, looked past Pennard, who was eagerly pushing himself forward to offer his services. At last, he saw Keridwen huddled with Brid and Isolde around the sunburst ruby embedded in the Torra Altan heartstone, a circle of rune-carved rock set in the cobbles at the centre of the courtyard.

"Come," she said quietly, her hands shaking with the grief of losing her husband. "There is something we must see."

"What?" the youth asked.

"Branwolf," she replied.

"But how?"

"Hush!" his mother scolded and beckoned him to kneel beside her at the heartstone.

"Look!" Brid gasped. "Look!"

Just as the setting sun touched on the great gem and

599

shards of gold and scarlet light flashed out into the smouldering ruin of the castle, the three priestess joined hands in a circle about the heartstone. Isolde, giggling happily at the spectacle, released her hand from Brid's grip and reached out to touch the gemstone. Others gathered around the tight knot of priestesses.

Rewik gasped and shrank back. "What evil magic is this?" he cried out in alarm.

"There is no magic," Keridwen said solemnly, tears clouding her eyes. "The baby's father was a verderer of the Otherworld. Though he attained a soul, he is made of the stuff of the sun, which looks down on both this world and the Otherworld. Since Talorcan was of the sun so, in part, is Isolde and she sees through the sunburst of the ruby into his world."

Caspar knelt down by his mother and blinked at the image reflected in Isolde's eyes.

"Father!" he murmured.

Keridwen gripped Caspar's shoulder tightly.

CHAPTER TWENTY-NINE

Raging hot liquid poured into his body but Branwolf could not scream; the heat had torn away his throat. The pain was all consuming, the acid fire of the dragon blistering his insides. But he had to save them, save his dear wife, save his son and free them from this demon, Gwion. He could do it; he was certain he could do it so long as he held on.

Then the pain was gone and the pungent stench of dragon's gut evaporated. His scorched and shrivelled hands were still about Gwion's throat as they were suddenly wrestling on a floor covered by soft wolfskin, the sound of a fire crackling nearby replacing the roar from the dragon's maw. Fiercely strong hands were dragging him off and his fingers were snapped from their grip.

"Great Master, what shall be done with him," the golden-eyed man, whose strong grip restrained Branwolf, asked Gwion.

"Let him suffer in the dungeons of Abalone!" Gwion snorted. "Let him know the atrocities that I shall inflict on his household. And when the last of his line has been removed from the cycle of life, feed him to the Commoners in the midst of the forest. Then his soul and all those of his dear ones shall be gone to oblivion and only my memory of them will remain."

"Gwion, you fool," Branwolf hissed at him. "Happiness awaits you if only you let go—"

"Let go of this? When soon I will have ultimate power? I have brought them rubies across the divide. The magic of the sun trapped within the stones increases the power of the verderers' voices; soon they will be stronger than the High Circle. I have altered the balance of the power in the cosmos. I am as a god!" Gwion shrieked. "Take him away!"

Branwolf bellowed like a bull in protest. He could not fail. He was their last chance. Someone had to stop Gwion's evil and he would do it.

Kicking and screaming, he was hauled down a dark corridor. The more he fought and kicked, the stronger the verderers' piercing song screamed in his ears and rang around his head. He was swaddled in the magic bonds of their song and soon was dragged across the corridor past rows of cells to the foul stench of a dark hall. Men were spitted over fires, their fat dripping and sizzling as if they were sides of roasting boar. Strange sounds worried the hall; the creak and click of a rack, the groans of ropes as they stretched some poor soul, dragging arms and legs from their sockets.

Surely, in all this number, there must be Torra Altans here, he thought, knowing regretfully that a great many had been slaughtered over the last few years. His instinct was to shout out the great war-cry of his fathers, to howl out the name of Torra Alta so that any others of that banner would muster to him but something altered his mind. These tortured people were no longer Torra Altan, or Ovissian, Belbidian or Ceolothian even; they were of one nation; they were of the Great Mother.

He was descended from a long line of warlords who held a frontier castle and knew that his ancestors had only been so successful because they didn't struggle as individuals but worked together, united under one leadership. Perhaps if he mustered all these poor suffering souls under Her name, he could do something against the crippling song of the verderers.

He threw back his head and sucked in a deep breath. "Men, hear me! Join with me. Unite in the name of the Great Mother."

His deep clear call cut through the screams and there was a lull in the shrieks of agony but not for long. Soon, they returned, each individual too impassioned by their own plight and needs to heed him.

The verderers were laughing at him. "You are in Rye Errish now. Only those with the power of song can rule here. You might once have been a mighty man but you are no one here," the nearest sneered.

"Oh, but he is someone," a huge voice rumbled behind him.

Branwolf looked in alarm at the giant stony-grey creature that grumbled low in its throat, the sound like rocks grinding together. Verderers were chiselling into the back of his heavy head with hammers and drivers.

The creature rumbled on. "He is one of us, one of the many that would be happy to pass onto the bliss of Annwyn if you verderers had not fallen under the powers of Gwion."

"What manner of creature are you?" Branwolf asked.

"A stonewight, of course. My name is Perren and I had the pleasure of knowing your son."

The verderers worked hard around the stonewight, singing shrilly though occasionally he lightly swatted them aside when their concentration dropped.

But Branwolf didn't trouble himself with the strange being. "She must be here," Branwolf spoke his thoughts out loud.

"Who?" Perren asked.

"Morrigwen," he answered. "If I could find her, she would tell me what to do."

Souls were dragged to and from the torture chambers. Branwolf saw them only as a blur as his world swam and he found himself tied to a board. A verderer drove white-hot irons into his stomach. He screamed and writhed, trying all the while to focus on what he must do. This madman, Gwion, had control of their souls and he had to stop him. He twisted this way and that, gritting his teeth against his screams and fighting all the while for an image of his wife so that he might escape his mind and find peace. He had read that men survived torture by freeing their minds from their bodies but he could not achieve it. The pain spread out from his belly and screamed through every nerve. He bellowed on and on for what felt like hours and then, quite suddenly, it stopped.

A yellow-eyed verderer was smiling down at him. "Feel the pain. All will be pain until you let go of your last life!"

Branwolf thought he would give anything to stop the pain, anything *but* the suffering of his son. For Caspar's sake, he must succeed. If he did not destroy Gwion, Gwion would destroy his son. He smiled back at the verderer. "You cannot break me," he challenged.

The verderer twisted his poker in the flames. "You are not an evil man; I can see it in your eyes. The evil ones are hard to break because of the madness that controls their minds and steals their pain. I can break you."

Branwolf's eyes flicked towards the white tip of the glowing poker and he prayed the verderer was wrong. The golden-eyed man raised the sizzling iron over his exposed belly but then paused as another verderer appeared at his side and murmured in his ear. The torturer swung the tip of the white hot-poker until it came to rest just an inch from Branwolf's right eye and he could feel the heat from it dry his eyeball. The creature grinned at him. "It's to be your eyes."

Branwolf thrashed his head from side to side, trying to avoid the poker and it was then that he saw her. He must have given out a strange shriek that disturbed the verderer because he momentarily withdrew to follow the Baron's gaze.

Though she was no more than ten foot from him, he would not have recognized her for she was taller and more upright, her hair red rather than a yellowed grey but there was a proud aura about her that made her unmistakable. "Morrigwen," he whispered. "Morrigwen," he cried with all his might as she was dragged away.

The verderer regained his concentration and returned to his task. Strong hands gripped Branwolf's head and fixed it still while the sizzling poker was thrust into his eye. Savage pain consumed his every thought.

As his eyeball boiled, his tongue swelled and he screamed and screamed, fighting to be rid of a pain that he could never have imagined.

"Courage, man," Perren's voice bellowed out but reached Branwolf's ears as only the echo of a whisper as the white-hot poker gouged into his eyes. "Saille will come to mend your wounds."

At last, they plucked the poker from his maimed eye socket and he was dragged away by his feet, his head banging on the greasy stone flags; exhausted and drained, his mind was nothing but pain.

"Saille!" the name stuck in his mouth and, gasping like a landed fish, he lay in his miserable cell alone.

So, this was the pain Gwion suffered; no wonder he

was mad with it. At last, a hand touched his forehead and he knew at once it was neither a human hand nor the fierce grip of a verderer. He had never before imagined a hand could be so gentle, so full of womanly succour.

"Saille," he gasped. "Saille, is that you? You must help us."

The beautiful woman with sleek golden hair that fell to her waist soothed his brow. "The law allows me to take away your pain only that you might be tortured again. It is a respite only. I can also take away the wounds of your death if you will move on to Annwyn."

As Saille gave him a cooling draught that so quickly eased the searing pain to his eye, he began to think more easily. What should he say to this fabulous creature? He could not go on to Annwyn; he could not give up on Caspar and, besides, he would never reach the bliss of oneness with the Great Mother. The verderers under Gwion's influence would see that he was fed to the commoners and his soul destroyed. He knew there was no point bartering with the verderers; he had nothing to offer them, and so his only hope was to plead with the ealdorman of the High Circle that his son had explained ruled this land.

"I must speak with the High Circle," he said with control.

"Of course, but only if you wish to be released from the torture chambers so that you may move on to Annwyn," Saille explained.

He nodded eagerly. "I do. And there is another that wishes to move on as well. Morrigwen—"

"You mock me. She will not relinquish her grip on her last life. I have spoken with the old Crone many times; none is more stubborn."

Branwolf considered that to be true. "I have news that

will change her mind," he said. "She and I will move on, as is your will, but only on the one condition."

"Condition! You are in no position to bargain with me!" Her hand touched his eye and he could see clearly, and sat back to study her with both eyes. Glittering hair and golden eyes looked at him with such sweet sympathy as she swayed very slightly on her feet. A vast pair of translucent wings was folded at her back.

Branwolf ignored her assertion. "We shall freely move on if the High Circle summons Gwion, a man already half wolf, so that we might talk with him – just once."

Saille gracefully raised her hand to silence him. "We know of him. The verderers listen to him." She shook her head. "No, it is not permitted for you rebels to band together."

"We can persuade him to move on," Branwolf said cajolingly. "He is gaining power in this world."

"You think we don't know that? But you might be one of his minions bringing him more power."

"Ha!" Branwolf laughed. "He has ruined me and my family. He will continue to torture my son if I cannot lessen his grip on his last life. I want only so that my descendants might live in peace."

A taller, stronger woman with curling golden hair floated to stand behind Saille. Then a solid-looking man with crinkling skin joined them and following a little way behind was a shorter dark-skinned ealdorman with a staff barbed with long black thorns.

"Nuin, Duir," Saille greeted them in turn. "And Straif. This man wants audience with us all so that he might beg to move on."

"Yes, yes," Nuin dismissed her with an impatient flick of her wrist. "I heard it all. Oh, noble words, Branwolf, so noble!" She smiled. "I didn't think the verderers would break you so soon. But, of course, we cannot permit you to converse freely with other souls of your choosing. Your life is finished. You cannot resolve your unfinished business here; you must simply move on."

"Your torture will be tripled until you do," Straif threatened excitedly and Nuin looked at the small ealdorman sideways. Straif continued, "You should be taken straight to the commoners and eaten. And what is it that you want to say to Gwion?"

Nuin stiffened and Duir glared down at Straif and growled low in his throat, "Straif, having his soul destroyed by the commoners is a little excessive and why are you so interested in this soul, Gwion?"

"Send for the old woman!" Nuin exclaimed imperiously. She sniffed at Straif. "I am unhappy with your interest here and so I am curious to get to the bottom of this. See that Tartarsus is persuaded to bring his so-called prisoner to our judgement chamber, Straif. We can have you excluded from the High Circle and replaced by one of our choosing, if you are accused and found guilty of treachery against the ealdormen."

"He'll be there right away," Straif hurriedly assured them. "I have no interest in the matter whatsoever."

Branwolf marched behind Nuin, working through his mind any plan he might have to destroy his brother-in-law. If they went through the forest together, perhaps he could drag him aside from the columns and see him fed to the commoners. He wondered that if he didn't hack out his heart here that he would be gone forever. There had to be a way.

Nuin led him to the fabulous inner chamber of the High Circle and took her place as one of the thirteen ealdormen hovering in the air on their gossamer wings around a marble table whose plinth was supported by a single pillar, twelve foot high. Branwolf felt unclean in all the brilliant glory of Rye Errish.

His fingertips brushed over the hilt of his dagger as he looked about him at the glistening marble and sparkling, mirrored walls but then a verderer's song at his back cramped his muscles and forbade all movement. His arm was locked rigid one inch from the hilt of his dagger and, though the raging blood within him throbbed and swelled his blood-vessels, trying to force life back into his muscles, he could not break free from the bond. A strange hum filled the halls from the buzzing wings of the ealdormen. His mind raced. Surely, there was a way that he could put an end to Gwion. His eyes fell on the blue steel blades of the verderers and wondered that one of those might not help him.

"Bring in the other prisoners," Straif commanded.

Morrigwen marched in boldly, escorted by four verderers but Gwion hobbled painfully on the arm of the chief verderer, Tartarsus who wore a string of sunburst rubies about his neck and appeared to float through the air, borne up by the magic of his song. Tartarsus started and his eyes fixed up at Straif in accusation but then he hastily lowered them and fixed a bland smile on his face as his eyes scanned all thirteen of the High Circle.

Branwolf had noted at once that Tartarsus had clearly been expecting to meet with only Straif, but he didn't care. His eyes were fixed on the creature beside him. He sucked in his breath in shock; Gwion was shaggy all over, his mouth and jaw grown long and twisted and his lips were parted by the fangs of a wolf.

Morrigwen staggered to a halt alongside Branwolf.

"We must get to Gwion. We must destroy him," the Baron hissed to her.

"I know what he has done but I cannot destroy him,"

she answered. "He is my son in all but blood. I held him as a little baby in my arms. Whatever madness possesses him is my own fault for my lack of motherly love towards him. I am sorry for you, Branwolf; I love you, Keridwen and your boy dearly but my task is all but done. Keridwen and Brid have found the new Maiden; I feel it in my bones. All they must do is have her ordained so that the Trinity is once more complete. Then I am released."

"Morrigwen, no, you must help us!" Branwolf cried but there was defeat in his voice.

Gwion snapped his head round at the sound and growled at Morrigwen.

"Unbind me!" she snapped at the verderers. "Let me go to my son."

He snarled and snivelled. "I shall tear off your head if you come near me, you old hag."

"Let the old woman free," Nuin ordered the verderers. "Let us see what this is all about."

Morrigwen stepped quietly forward and held out her hand as if approaching a frightened animal.

Though he was restrained in no way, Gwion made no move to harm her but surprisingly stepped back in retreat until he was pressed up against one of the arched mirrors that lined the circular chamber. "Foul witch, deceiver!"

"Gwion, my boy," she said softly, taking another step towards him so that she might touch his hand. He flinched away but kept staring at her.

"You loved only Keridwen," he accused.

"I did not. I loved you both equally. You would play on my lap together, draw pictures in the dirt, and sing beautifully. Keridwen would cuddle you but she longed always for her real mother. You were old enough to pay your farewells to your mother on her deathbed and seemed able to let her go more easily but your younger sister needed her so much at that very tender age. She never loved me as you did. But Keridwen was destined to be the One of the Three and I had to give her much of my time because of her training; but that did not mean I gave her more of my love."

"You do not love me!" Gwion accused, though with deep pain in his grating voice.

"Gwion, my son, I love you."

"After all I have done, after all I have tried to do to Keridwen and her son?"

"Hold me." Morrigwen stepped boldly towards him, the little woman finally picking up his hand and dragging it to her.

He faltered towards her and then, sobbing, fell against her chest and clung tightly to her.

She stroked the back of his head. "Sweet boy." She kissed him. "You are my son. Here in the afterlife on the way to the Great Mother there is nothing that I would not forgive you."

He snivelled and wept and Branwolf felt the bonds fall away from him. His hand was on his dagger but he saw there was no need anymore.

"You never wanted power, Gwion," Morrigwen continued. "You wanted only love and you have it. And when we reach the Great Mother, you will be overwhelmed by it and fall into its bliss."

"I don't want Her love," Gwion snivelled. "I want only yours."

Morrigwen drew him close. "Sweet boy," she kissed the hideous tufts of hair sprouting from his neck, "tell me, " she said after a moment of hugging him and rocking him back and forth in her arms, "why was it that in death you wished to be reborn as a wolf? Did you seek to be stronger and more savage?"

He did not reply for a moment. "No, Ma," he said after some considered thought, his voice now soft and innocent. "No, the wolves of the Chase were of large families and they always showed such a deep love for one another. I wanted to be reborn into the pack of wolves so that I might be surrounded by a family that loved me."

She nodded at him. "So be it. They have found the one that is to be the Maiden; I go now to meet the Great Mother. Will you come with me?"

He clutched hold of her hand and nodded with tears streaming down his face. Tartarsus gave out a great cry of anguish, his song trembling the air and flashes of yellow bursting out from the jewels at his neck. But his melody was matched by Nuin. Her voice sweet and quiet, she sucked in his song, twisted the sounds and quelled his magic.

Great doors were thrown open and sunlight flooded the chamber The three souls were led out to where the brilliant sun of Rye Errish anointed their heads. Without troubling himself to think too much, Branwolf joined a column ready to be guided by the verderers to one of the gateways to Annwyn.

"I hope that we meet again in another life," Morrigwen saluted him, "for I would surely recognize the nobility of your soul."

He saluted her smartly in return and halted to hear her speak to her son.

"Come, Gwion, ride with me. They have promised me a horse that will race through the forest and take me speedily to the gateway. To the Mother!" she cried. "To the Great Mother!"

Then she, Gwion and the fleet-footed escort of the thirteen ealdormen rode off through the forest of Rye Errish.

Keridwen's hand shook as she held Caspar. His mouth was dry and he could not speak as he stared into the yellow world mirrored in Isolde's eyes. The image was drawing away from Branwolf now as he began a steady march through the forest.

"His pain is over," Keridwen gasped with relief. "Farewell, my love. I might never know you in another life but I shall always love you."

The image glided above one of the paths following Morrigwen and Gwion's dazzling escort on their way to the gateway. They skimmed over many thousands of souls marching in columns and, for a second, Isolde's gaze stooped down and stared closely at a couple walking hand in hand. They looked up and reached out as if aware of her presence.

"May and Talorcan!" Brid breathed. "They have found happiness!"

Caspar jerked forward and called out, "May, I looked after her. I have brought her home. She is safe."

"She cannot hear you but she knows," Keridwen assured him. "A mother always knows."

Then ahead they saw the soft light of a dawn, a pearly gold swelling on the horizon. Their gaze sailed over a misty lake, Morrigwen's horse floating over the waves, and to a circle of yew trees. Gwion and Morrigwen stepped into the circle and, in a sudden blaze of scorching light, were gone.

Feeling utterly drained by the harrowing experience but overwhelming relieved that his father's suffering was over, Caspar slumped back and could do nothing but look around him at the chaos. Already Hal was in conversation with the Captain.

"Give him time," Hal said quietly. "He's just lost his father. Let's sort this mess out for him and get these

Ovissians marshalled up and sent back to the wolds where they belong. We need a comfortable place organized for the sick and another for the women and I suppose we ought to find quarters for the royalty, otherwise they will complain forever that we Torra Altans have no courtly manners."

"I have had time enough," Caspar said quietly, coming over to him. "Strangely, I feel stronger than I have done in years. My head no longer hurts." He rubbed at his scalp and found that the scab was healed. "But my tasks are not yet done. I still have an obligation to fulfil to Izella. I must see her safely to Reyna to get the trinoxia she so sorely needs and then back across the Tethys."

Hal grinned. "Oh, to travel, to see the world; the glory, the honour!" His smile fell flat and he tugged Caspar to the battlements and pointed at the ruined towers, the smoking heaps of rubble, the wounded men and at the great scaly beast that lay dying on the canyon floor. "Do you not think you have a greater obligation to fulfil here? Your men need you."

Caspar took the baronial ring from his finger and pressed it into Hal's hand. "You can do it better than I. Let's not pretend that we haven't always known that. Will you look after Torra Alta for me?"

His uncle clutched the ring and then swung his arm around his nephew and hugged him tight. "As if it were my own!" he said with a broad grin.

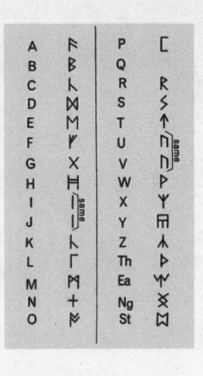